Praise for FEED MY DEAR DOGS

National Bestseller

"*Feed My Dear Dogs* is a wonderfully written story of familial love, of change, loss and the ties that bind. . . . One is regretful when this extraordinary novel comes to a close. It is one which lingers in the mind."
—*The London Free Press*

"*Feed My Dear Dogs* is big, bold, brave, brilliant and very, very funny—a formidable literary achievement that from the get-go puts readers inside the magical hyper-realistic world of the Weiss family as perceived by Jem, a highly sensitive narrator who knows how to use more than a deerstalker hat to ward off dread and disquiet." —*Books in Canada*

"Jem is a literary gem." —*Georgia Straight*

"The Weiss clan remains an engaging, individuated family—an art-loving, art-making, frequently funny and sporadically endangered crew. . . . Richler is an antic riffer in the finest jazz tradition and, at book's end, she blows this long solo about Jesus Christ, Ernest Shackleton, her sister Harriet and herself that is a room rocker."
—*The Globe and Mail*

"A book shot through with love." —*Quill & Quire*

"*Feed My Dear Dogs* tackles a surprisingly difficult subject: how to write about a childhood that is idyllically stable and loving. Richler does so with warmth and some brilliant left-field humour."
—Jonathan Coe, *The Guardian*

"The gap between inside and outside—of the body, of the mind and of the family—is what powers this dramatic and intense novel. The voice that struggles to describe it, and the ventriloquism used in the attempt, are what give *Feed My Dear Dogs* its considerable emotional strength and rawness. Novels of family life are commonplace; although usually marked by their integrity and directness, they frequently lack the force to travel from the particular to the universal. Emma Richler's impressive and ambitious recapturing of youth brings us a family that is unlikely to resemble our own, but that is presented to us by a voice that seems immediately familiar." —*Times Literary Supplement*

"Jem's voice is a great accomplishment: confiding, ingenuous, with a convincing thirst for answers and approval. . . . A profoundly moving elegy for lost youth that bristles with intelligence, verve and wit."
—*Scotland on Sunday*

Also by Emma Richler

Sister Crazy

EMMA RICHLER

Feed My Dear Dogs

VINTAGE CANADA

VINTAGE CANADA EDITION, 2006

Copyright © 2005 Emma Richler

Published in Canada by Vintage Canada, a division of Random House of Canada Limited, Toronto, in 2006. Originally published in hardcover in Canada by Alfred A. Knopf Canada, a division of Random House of Canada Limited, Toronto, in 2005, and simultaneously in Great Britain by Fourth Estate, a division of HarperCollinsPublishers, London. Distributed by Random House of Canada Limited, Toronto.

Vintage Canada and colophon are registered trademarks of Random House of Canada Limited.

www.randomhouse.ca

Library and Archives Canada Cataloguing in Publication

Richler, Emma, 1961–
Feed my dear dogs / Emma Richler.

ISBN-13: 978-0-676-97672-4
ISBN-10: 0-676-97672-7

I. Title.

PS8585.I3673F44 2006   C813'.6   C2005-905087-X

Typeset by Palimpsest Book Production Limited, Polmont, Stirlingshire

Printed and bound in the United States of America

2 4 6 8 9 7 5 3 1

For Daniel,
Noah,
Martha &
Jacob,
and for my mother, my muse,
and in memory of my father,
with love.

Every Space that a Man views around his
dwelling place,
Standing on his own roof, or in his garden on a
mount,
such Space is his Universe.
And on the verge the Sun rises and sets,
the Starry Heavens reach no further;
And if he moves his dwelling-place, his heavens
also move
Wher'er he goes.

WILLIAM BLAKE

Tamar Rahmani,
    for many things

ONE

Jude always said a kid is supposed to get acclimatised to the great world and society and so on, and just as soon as he can bash around on his own two pins, but the feeling of dread and disquiet I experienced on leaving home in my earliest days was justified for me again and again on journeys out, beginning with the time Zachariah Levinthal bashed me on the head for no clear-cut reason with the wooden mallet he had borrowed from his mother's kitchen. It did not hurt much, as I was wearing my Sherlock Holmes deerstalker hat with both ear flaps tied up neatly in a bow on top, providing extra protection from onslaught, but I must say it struck me that Zach, who was nearly a whole year and a half older than me, same age as my brother Jude in fact, Zach was the one in need of a few pointers regarding recommended behaviour in the great world and society at large. Never mind. The way I saw it, he was just testing out his enthusiasm for tools and surfaces, and, possibly, exploring a passing fancy for a future in architecture or construction work, and in my household, enthusiasms were encouraged, which is why I regularly went to and fro with a handful of 54mm World War I and World War II soldiers in my pocket for recreation purposes, with no one to stop me, although I am a girl and expected, in some circles, to have more seemly pursuits. You have to allow for enthusiasms, you never know where they may lead, so I knew to keep my composure the day Zach hit me on the head with a meat pulveriser. No. Tenderiser. So there you are, that is what I mean, it depends on how you look at things, how bashing away at a piece of beefsteak with a wooden hammer can induce a quality of tenderness in meat is just as surprising, perhaps, as my

1

not protesting the risk of brain damage I incurred at the age of eight or so, instead, forgiving Zach on account of his enthusiasms and general spirit of endeavour.

I think all stories are like this, about looking out for a way to be in life without messing up in the end, a way to be that feels like home, and if you bear this in mind, it's easy to see some situations as OK which might strike you otherwise as downright odd, and that story about Francis of Assisi and the crow is just one example of many. At the latter end of his life, Francis befriends a crow who is fiercely devoted, sitting right next to Francis at mealtimes, and traipsing after him on visits to the sick and leprous, and following his coffin when he died, whereupon the crow lost heart and simply fell apart, refusing to eat and so on, until he died also. Now, if you nip along the street or go about the shopping with a crow at your heels, you are not likely to make friends in a hurry, because it is odd behaviour, and not recommended. Unless you are a saint, in which case it is OK. So that's one thing. The other OK-not-OK thing in this story is how that crow did not choose to make life easy and fall in love with his or her own kind, another crow with whom that bird might have a bright future and bring up little crows and so on. No. For the crow, Francis was home, that's all there is to it, it is OK.

This is also how it goes for *le petit prince* in the book of that name by M. Antoine de Saint-Exupéry, a story about a small boy in a single suit of fine princely haberdashery, living on an asteroid with a volcano, a baobab tree and a rose, and having nothing much to do but watch the sunset. In the scheme of things, it is not so odd that he falls in love with the rose, and leaves his tiny planet in a fit of lovesickness, taking advantage of a migration of wild birds for his journey, hanging on to them, as it shows in the water-colour, by way of special reins. The prince finally lands on Earth wherein he has a shady encounter with a snake who has murder in mind, albeit concealed in a promise to this small lovestruck and visionary boy, a promise of return, a single ticket home by way of the eternal worlds.

Upon landing, the prince asks, Where did I fall, what planet is this?

I remember everything.

Everything and nothing is strange. It depends how you look at it.

Zach, now, is something in law, Jude says, although I keep forgetting the details, because all I can think is how Zach found a place where everything ought to come out right, and where even hammers crash down upon suitable surfaces for the tenderising of felony and injustice, and I hope he is happy, I hope so, though I don't know, as I do not go in for telephones and letters these days, not now I have fallen out with society and the great world, but still I have enthusiasms, ones I pursue in low-lit rooms, with my handful of soldiers here, entering my world in unlikely ways, it might seem, to strangers.

October 1935. Joseph Goebbels issues a decree forbidding the inscription of names of fallen Jewish soldiers on war memorials, men who fell for the sake of younger men who are now getting busy scratching out offensive Jewish names from tablets of stone with what you might call corrupt and frenzied enthusiasm.

Me, I turn away and weep.

Where did I fall, what planet is this?

I hear it, I see it, and I was not there, it's a vision. I remember everything.

Under the influence of gravity, stars in orbit in an elliptical galaxy such as ours are always falling, always falling without colliding, and the greater the mass, the greater the attraction, and the faster a thing falls, the faster it moves in orbit, so the Moon, for one, is always falling towards Earth, but never hits it, and I like to think William Blake, b.1757, d.1827, would appreciate this, as he was very interested in fallen man, and for William, memory is merely part of time, an aspect of the fall, and the visionary worlds are the true regions of reminiscence, a realm wherein every man is uncrowned king for eternity and there is no need for memorials because, so he wrote, Man the Imagination liveth for Ever.

I hate to say it, but William sounds like a man talking himself out of reality and hard knocks and brushes with dark times, a place where, for him, memory and vision meet in the most colourful manner, though not without violence, no, and the glorious thing is what he knew, from maybe the age of eight or so when he had his first visions, that as long as he was bound by time, and striding across London in an impecunious state and an ailing body, in a world that largely considered him crazy, he was OK, he had found it, the means of escape, a kind of resurrection in the eternal worlds,

3

this was his country. William dies singing and when he is gone, a close friend reaches out and brushes William's eyes closed, a drop of a curtain, a small gesture of infinite grace in one touch of the fingertips. To keep the vision in, that's what he says. Blake was always falling, never colliding, it's a trick of gravity. Everyone has a home.

—What country, friend, is this? William Shakespeare, b.1564, d.1616! Do I have an obsession with numbers? Ben says I do. Said. Ages ago.

   —What do you think?
   —I asked you first!
   —Mmm.
   —Holmes: I get down in the dumps at times, and don't open my mouth for days on end. Just let me alone, and I'll soon be right! *A Study in Scarlet*, 1887!
   —I don't think that is what you want, for me to leave you. And if I leave, you won't have to talk to me about your bandages today.
   —A tiny accident! I am always falling.

I tell you a brief story about Eadweard Muybridge, b.1830, d.1904, and his obsession with speed and motion, and most of all, with photography, how he set up a row of cameras in a great field, cameras with tripwires attached so the galloping horse in his experiment would race by and take self-portraits in rapid succession, enabling Eadweard to capture this one moment he craved, the picture of a horse with all four feet off the ground, a moment passing too quickly for the naked eye, and proof that a horse at speed is so close to flight, achieving lift-off ever so briefly, in joyous defiance of gravity. What I cannot tell you yet, and I think you know, is how my tiny accident is also an experiment in speed and motion and photography, in my mind's eye, how for a moment, in a desire for return, I find a means of escape, rising, not quite falling, a dangerous trick of gravity, I know it, I said I was sorry three times.

   I do tell you, though, about a postcard I received from my mother, a card postmarked in another country, depicting two cherubim either side of a woman holding a chalice with an egg aloft, they are heavenly escorts. Triptych. The three figures are all white, statuary, and the cherubs are saucy and graceful, and the woman is draped in elegant folds with an expression on her face of surprise and fatigue, as if she has just packed off all the kids to school and now it is time, finally, Breakfast! Except that the title of this painting by Raphael is *Faith*, and in Christian art, of course, the egg is symbolic of Resurrection. It depends how you look at it.

From the very day my little sister Harriet and I thrashed out this business of fallen man on our way home from the convent one afternoon in extreme youth, clearing up a small matter of catechism arising from morning assembly we are forced to attend as civilians, not Catholics, just for the headcount so to speak, a morning I saw Harriet twist around on her class bench to gaze at me wide-eyed in a mix of alarm and mirth it is not always easy to tell apart, from that very day, she took to these two words, fallen man, with great glee, and particular delight. She has an ear for sayings and will not let go of them, so any time now that she sees Gus tip over, a regular occurrence around our place as Gus is a baby still and only recently up on his feet and moving around under his own steam, Harriet will say it, in grave and knowing tones.

'Fallen man,' she pronounces, soon giving in to the wheezy snuffly sounds of Harriet laughing.

On the day we first discussed it, she was not so breezy.

'I don't get the snake part.'

'Forget the snake, Harriet, it's a symbol, OK? It's not important.'

'Is important. She said, snake, snake, snake. Sister Lucy did.'

'We are not Catholics. It doesn't count, so don't worry.'

'Is it in the Bible?'

'Yeh. Look, um, try Mum, OK? I'm not sure I get it either.'

I remember it, this morning, the sudden picture I had in my head, of soldiers flying out of trenches into gunfire, falling men, and of people ambling along all casual and keeling over, hurling themselves to the ground, they can't help it, and there were cartoon images too, of people falling down wells, or off clifftops, or through holes in a frozen lake, hovering in mid-air for a full horror moment of realisation, unless, of course, the character is a hero, in which case he will be saved by a skinny branch on the way down, or land softly in a passing boat, and this is what is so depressing about the snake part in Sister Lucy's story, and what I do not want Harriet to know, that somehow, due to the events in the Garden, according to nuns, not even an all-out hero can count on a passing boat, which accounts for that story from Mum's childhood, about the very nice boy at her school who fell down a lift shaft by mistake. In my opinion, telling the fallen man story first thing in the morning at assembly is dodgy behaviour on the part of nuns, kicking off everyone's day with this terrible news, and giving kids like my sister a doomy outlook on life when they are barely seven years old and have yet to face the facts. Furthermore, I am now deeply worried about lifts, especially as I forget, each time I step into one, to check first off that it is there. I give myself a very hard time about it so I will not step through the doors unawares again, but it is hopeless. I have been lucky so far, but I am only nine and have a long way to go. It is very weird, if you are not a forgetful type, to carry on forgetting the same bitty thing every time. Bloody.

'So why is everyone falling, then?' says Harriet, kind of cross.

'Fallen.'

'It's silly.'

'Right. So let's drop it.'

'BARKIS is willin',' says Harriet in a growly voice, using her new favourite saying from *David Copperfield*, a book by Mr Charles Dickens Mum is reading to us at present, which is great, because she does all the voices in a very realistic manner, the posh ones going, my dear, my dear, all the time, and the rough ones, such as Barkis. Harriet is very keen on Barkis. It is possible he reminds her of our dad, who is also a man of few words with a growly voice that is not scary once you get to know him.

'Harriet Weiss!' my sister adds. 'Where are your shoes, put on your shoes! BARKIS is willin'.'

'Did you say that to nuns today? Barkis is willin'?'

'Tired of shoes.'

'Harriet. Don't say the Barkis thing to them, they won't understand. They'll think you're being rude. Save it for home, OK? And try to keep your shoes on at school. Please.'

'Why?'

'It's rules, Harriet. They have to have rules.'

'Why?'

'Because they need to keep control of things. Like in wartime, in the army. You know.'

'Is this the army?'

'No. Forget that. I mean – they don't want us to run wild, that's all.'

'Like golliwogs,' Harriet says, her lower lip all trembly.

Oh-oh. It's a Golliwog Day. I look at my sister who is only 3ft 4$^{2}/_{8}$in high since last measured, with her fluffy fair hair mashed down flat, that is, for top accuracy, my little sister with big blue eyes and, I happen to know, one or two tiny soft woollen chicks with plastic feet and beads for eyes in her pocket, I look at her and I wonder how it is nuns can foretell trouble, and suppose she will run wild, as if chaos begins with Harriet taking off her shoes in a classroom, like the first step on the way to the Fall of the Roman Empire and barbarian invasions and so on. Nuns are not very hopeful regarding Humanity.

'Harriet. Remember what Mum said on that subject?'

'Golliwogs are made up.'

'Yup. And what else?'

'Rude. It's a rude word. It starts wars.'

'Yes. No. That's prejudice. Prejudice starts wars. Got that?'

'Think so.' Harriet is not happy, I can tell, because she does a little soft-shoe shuffle and then grins at me, meaning she is trying to forget something bad.

My sister is going through a golliwog phase and it will soon be over, I hope, but I do see her problem. We are five kids in the Weiss family with me bang in the middle and Ben the eldest, and very tallest, and the only one with a taste for jam and other stuff from jars, of the sweet kind, i.e. not peanut butter, aside from Mum who eats honey, though not on toast like a regular person, but mixed into plain yogurt. She has special ways, but that is another matter. OK. When Harriet first saw it, the golliwog leaping around on the label of a strawberry jam jar, she was downright spooked and refused henceforth to sit at the same table with golliwog jam upon it. Preparations had to be made. Everyone needs protection from something.

After my dad finished up laughing and teasing and leaping around with mussed hair, there was a discussion, beginning with Mum explaining about prejudice and African slavery and made-up words, and even my dad getting serious and telling us about yellow turbans on Jews in ancient times leading to yellow badges in later times and cartoons of pigs, until I had a sudden confused and stupid feeling going back to the golliwog, because I had no idea a golliwog was meant to be a person at all. I thought it was a grizzly bear. What an eejit, as Jude would say. The golliwog is deepest black with shaggy spiky hair and wild eyes and I always thought the artist drew stripy colourful clothing on it so it would be less scary for people like Harriet, the way stuffed bears in shops have little bow ties and other accoutrements so that a kid will think it is not an animal, it is a person, and therefore very friendly. No one is thinking straight. A plastic baby doll is a person, and just about the most gruesome thing a kid will ever clap eyes on, and no amount of stripy clothing can take away the spook element from a golliwog. Harriet's fear of golliwogs has made me see the light on a few subjects of pressing importance, and I am now quite interested in prejudice, whereas Harriet has taken to slavery, and is now very inquisitive regarding slaves and slavery BC and AD, which is fine with me, as it means she is likely to find rescue in her big thing for slaves any time she is rattled by golliwogs, on a day when a golliwog is a monster chasing her straight off a label of a jam jar.

We do not buy this jam any more, but there was worse horror to come for Harriet the time she crossed paths with Mary Reade in the playground, Mary and her golliwog doll tucked under one arm, a sight so bad, my sister was a jibbering wreck and I was called for to restore sanity and peace. Harriet held my hand and would not let go, like she was right inside a nightmare and needed my company until she could remember that a made-up thing is a made-up thing and ought not to have lasting spook power, it does not exist. On that day, I tried to distract her courtesy of intellectual matters, raising fond issues of war and prejudice and slavery and so on, and today, I am wondering whether she has had another brush with Mary's golliwog.

'Anything else you want to tell me, Harriet?'

'We are all God's creatures.'

'What? Was that Mean Nun? Did she give you the creatures speech?'

'Yes. Mean Nun.'

Mean Nun is the only bad nun around the place and I am beginning to think she is a little bit crazy. Any time there is some kind of slip-up committed by a girl, spillage in the mess, lateness, shoddy penmanship, missing items of kit, scuffy shoes, or anything, Mean Nun lifts her gaze skyward and does the creatures speech. We are all God's creatures, she says, not sounding too happy about it, and then she runs through a list of beasts of the field, usually selecting the less fetching type of animal such as aardvark and hippo, and then she numbers up the categories, colours, religions and countries, rich and poor, one-armed, blind, and those various nations of the wider world in need of missionary work. It's a sorry list, if you ask me, and quite depressing, so one time, I just had to correct her, the urge came upon me to remind her that Jewish is not like Indian and African, it is not really a country-type situation, not really, and Mean Nun was not at all pleased with this news, probably because I did not ask special permission to pipe up, which is definitely against the rules and a very bad move on my part. Mean Nun hates me now and I am anxious she will declare war on Harriet also, although I doubt it, as my sister has a fine temperament and is very pleasant company compared to me, so everyone likes her even if they do not understand her all the time. If you have an unusual personality and a fine temperament to go with it, you will be OK in the world, I can see that.

'Tell me what happened.'

'Mary had her – I said, it's a slave! It's rude, it starts wars! We are ALL God's creatures.'

'I see. Look, Harriet. You are right about the golliwog thing but you can't just do the headlines, like in a telegram, you have to fill in the gaps a bit, or people will get it all wrong. Do what Mum does, right? Slavery is a sad thing, golliwog is a stupid word, prejudice . . . rah-rah, etc. At home, no worries, we get you, but outside, you have to explain more. OK?'

'Tired.'

'I know it. Come on, let's go.'

'Creatures,' my sister says in a mournful voice.

'Creature sounds like monster, but it doesn't mean monster. Got that? It's just a word for all things, you know, everything breathing.'

'Is Daddy one?'

'Yup. Definitely. Feeling better now?'

'Yes, my dear. I am going to sing.'

Great. If Harriet is plain happy, or has had a fright and is on the road to recovery, she sings. She skips ahead of me now, and sings that song Gus listens to over and over on his kid-sized private record player he got for his birthday, a small red player with a crank and a tiny speaker he sits huddled up against, hearing out this song with an expression of concentration and dreaminess, because it is a tune regarding flowers, and Gus is keen on flowers and is likely reminiscing, I believe, about trips around the garden in Mum's arms, with Mum dipping him into flower beds, saying, Breathe, Gus, breathe in! which goes to show how even a three-year-old can look back on life, and even a three-year-old can have specialist subjects and a specialist vocabulary. Gus knows the names of flowers and he speaks them. Peony, clematis, lavender. Rose.

'Lavender's blue, dilly-dilly, lavender's blue!' sings my sister, suddenly stopping in her tracks and turning to frown at me. 'What's dilly-dilly?'

'Um. Name of a person, I think. The one the person who is singing about lavender, is singing to. Yeh. It's a person.'

'A creature.'

'Yup. Dilly.'

'No,' goes Harriet, correcting me. 'Dilly-Dilly.'

'It's just Dilly. It's a song thing. Poetic. Like if I said, Harriet, Harriet.'

'You never do.'

'Right. But if I did.'

'Why? Why would you?'

'Harriet. Is this the Why game?'

The Why game involves asking a lot of pesky useless questions, largely to blow off steam and get some attention, and it is a game to play when you are tired from kid-type pressures and want to hang up your gloves for a while and take a rest, which is the case with my sister who is clapped out just now due to catechism and rules and golliwogs. The Why game is best played on a grown-up who will rattle easily and fall apart where a kid will not, a kid knows the ropes. Usually I can handle it just fine, except I am not in the mood today, which is what I tell Harriet.

'I am not really in the mood.'

'Why?'

'HARRIET!'

'OK, my dear. Amen. BARKIS is willin'.'

I hardly ever play this game myself because there are two chief grown-ups in my house and I do not want them to crack up and fall apart, and I know also they will not play it according to the rules. They are too smart. Here is my dad.

'Dad, why are you reading that newspaper? Why are there three newspapers on the floor, why? Why do you always lie down on

10

the sofa to read them? Why can't you read sitting up? Why are your eyes brown when every single other Weiss has blue ones? Why?'

My dad ruffles some pages and pays me no attention at all. 'Jem, have you done your homework?' he says.

'Why should I do my homework? What is homework? Why?' I am losing heart and getting flustered. This is not working at all.

'Jem. Go and get me a tomato. A big, firm red one. Ripe. A tomato and a knife on a plate.'

'OK, Dad.' End of game. And remember, Jem. Do not cut up the tomato, he likes to do it himself. Don't ask why.

The other chief grown-up in my house not to play the Why game with is Mum. Here are a few things to know about her first off. 1) She is very beautiful and was a mannequin. This word had me very confused at first because I know mannequins are plastic life-sized dolls who stand in shop windows and have pointy fingers and zombie looks. Mum is just being shy and using a poor word in place of the posh one. Model. Mum was a model, and quite famous. OK. 2) She is pretty weird in a spooky but friendly way. 3) She is of unknown origins. I have a few theories about these unknown origins, however, they are only in the development stages and still require all-out investigation. I am on the case. Mum explained to me once, how she was a foundling, definitely a new word to my ears, and a pretty one, it seems to me, for something it is not very good to be. When Mum said, I was a foundling!, she said it in a voice that gave me a suspicious feeling, because it was sad and lively at the same time, like when you fall down and cut your body someplace and need to communicate the blood situation you are in without freaking anyone out, or being sissy. OK. I knew it was not the time to ask a lot of questions, this is what you learn if you listen hard to people and watch them carefully, that you have to pick the right time for questions. My first one would have been, What is a foundling exactly? But it was not the time to ask that question, so I just said, Oh, in a momentous way, the way you speak in the cinema when someone passes you a liquorice toffee and you do not want to disturb anyone in the audience but you want to say thank you for the liquorice toffee.

Here is one thing I am pretty sure of. When you are a foundling, your ideas about countries are more free and loose than most people's, and you do not suppose, for instance, that your country is the best just because you were born in it, meaning a foundling can grow up being always on the lookout for a better place, the top place, and in some cases, maybe even the sky is no limit. I believe Mum is such a case. I definitely have my suspicions and she is aware of my suspicions and tries to throw me off the scent. Here is an example. I am sitting at the kitchen table messing with homework and my *Tintin* book is right nearby, a reward for when I finish up my homework. The *Tintin* book is *Objectif Lune*, called *Destination Moon* in English. Mum is cooking.

'As soon as there is a passenger ship to the Moon, Jem, I will be at the head of the queue for tickets! How divine!'

This idea of being first in the queue has me worried, my insides feeling all hot and empty at the same time, like when I arrive at school and realise I have left something very important at home, such as homework and money for tuck. Oh no. Does she want to leave us? Would she rather be up there where the Moon is? I hope the passenger ships do not start up any time soon and I am going to have to look in my dad's newspapers for news. Which part of the paper will that be in? I will ask Ben, who is well up on weird stuff most people are not yet apprised of. Right now, though, I try to forget this worry about passenger ships.

'Maybe I'd like to go too,' I say. 'And, Mum? Tintin went on the Moon way before the Apollo, Apollo, what number?'

'Apollo 11,' Mum says, no thinking required, no pausing and eyes lifted skywards in reflection or anything.

'Right! 11, and they landed in, um . . .'

'1969, the 20th of July. They stepped out at 9.56 p.m.,' she says in a gentle voice, chopping things with a big knife and stirring up stuff.

'Yes? Well, Tintin was there in 1953. So there.'

Here's how it goes playing the Why game with Mum.

We are going to Zetland's in town and this is a favourite bakery of the Weiss family's. OK.

'Mum?' I say. 'Where are we going?'

'Well now, that's quite a philosophical question. I'll have to think about it. Is that all right with you?'

End of game.

We ride a bus and if I lean forward too far as I gaze at things out of the window, Mum lays her hand on the metal bar of the seats in front of me, she wraps her long fingers right around the spot where if the bus stops suddenly, I would go crashing into it and smash my chin or bite my lip and get into a casualty situation, the way a lot of kids do if someone like Mum is not looking out for them. Mum has long arms so she can do this without making a big thing of it, lifting her arm slowly and resting her hand there like it is nothing to do with you, and this way you do not end up feeling pathetic and helpless. Also, she never says, Be careful! or, Don't do that! or, Lean back! or anything because I think she wants us to be free and move around and gaze at things in a spirit of investigation, so that even if you do something kind of crazy like test out the sharpness of a knife by running your finger over the edge, she won't yell at you which can be downright spooky for a kid, no, she will open up a discussion about that knife and pretty soon you find something a little less crazy to do, as well as having a few new thoughts on that particular experiment, and how to go about it if you feel the urge again, to test the sharpness of knives. Mum is a very cool person, and has special ways.

I am pretty keen to get to Zetland's and Jude is going to be happy when we bring binoculars home, it is a favourite comestible of Jude's and mine. A stranger might not be able to tell Jude is happy, watching him open up a paper bag with Zetland's written across it and containing binoculars, a stranger thinks you ought to crease up in a big smile and say how happy you are, etc., but you do not, not always, not if you are Jude who will go 'hmmm' in a slow and quiet manner, and raise one, maybe two eyebrows, and push out his lower lip, that is to say, he is happy about the binoculars, even though he may not want one straight off. When you know a really fine thing is around, such as a binocular in a bag, you don't need it straight off, sometimes it is better saving it for later, and just knowing it is there.

A binocular is a roll with a crunchy crust in two parts and a crease in the middle but connected, therefore resembling binoculars. They do not call them that at the shop. They look confused if you say, Whoa! binoculars, and point to the big wicker basket they are heaped in, they won't know what you mean, although it is pretty easy to work out. Never mind. There is a lady there who never smiles and is a bit scary. I decide she is Mrs Zetland because she seems in command, the way a teacher does, or an officer in a war film. She wears a white ribbon around her head like a bandage, and most of her hair is on top, sort of growing up out of the bandage, so her hair reminds me of candyfloss on a stick at the fair except hers is grey not pink. I look at her and I kind of want to get the scissors out and do some trimming. Topiary work.

Mrs Zetland is OK and does not scare me any more ever since Mum sent Jude and me in once, on our own, to pay the bill and collect some rolls, whereupon Mrs Zetland slipped us each a lemon tart. Jude and I have been in a few times now. Two lemon tarts, every time, slipped to us like she is a World War II spy and we are two other spies on the same side. I don't like lemon tarts much or any kind of tarts and just about two bites is all I need to be sure of this, and then I pass it on to Jude who likes a lot more stuff than I do, adventurous is what Mum calls him. I would never tell Mrs Zetland though, or she might be hurt, and I think she has a thing for Jude and me, something probably Mum knew all along, which is why she sent us on the solo mission with no fear in the first place.

After the bus ride, we walk. Mum is a great type to go out walking with. Here is why. Sometimes you will see a little kid out walking with a grown-up and you can tell right away he is having a hard time. He is reaching up high to squeeze his hand into the big grown-up hand and he is getting a bad shoulder ache, plus he is stumbling along with loose crazy legs like a drunk, just trying to keep the pace, and carry the flag, and not let anyone down. He is sending a few frantic looks upwards at the grown-up as if to say, Whoa, can't you see what's going on here? I'm in trouble. And each time he sends that frantic look skywards, he nearly trips himself up and sometimes there is no choice but to tip right over in a messy sprawl in an effort to put the brakes on the grown-up, which is when you might see the little kid dangling like a stuffed animal, his limbs making no contact with earth at all, just swinging there pointy-toed and skimming the surface in a desperate and foolish manner. This can happen when the grown-up is mad about something, I believe, which is why he is barrelling along at high speed with scanty regard for the kid, and nothing can stop him. Or else he does not know that a regular pace for a long-legged person is racing speed for a kid. You have to explain some things to grown-ups you would not think necessary. It's disappointing, but those are the facts.

My dad walks slow. He does a lot of thinking when he walks, requiring a slow pace, which is perfect for our Gus, who is new at being upright and walking to and fro in the earth, but it is too slow for me at times, so I find myself drifting ahead of my dad, I can't help it, and I do this until I get a wrenching feeling in my wrist and have to pause and hang back a little, and go at my dad's pace, looking all around, and staring at the pavement, and doing some deep thinking. You can learn a lot from the different walks of people, the speed they move along at, and the way they hold your hand, and all of this is interesting and surprising if you are crazy about a person and want to fit in with their pace and way of doing things when you are together and out for a stroll, instead of struggling and trying to do everything your own way which is already familiar and not very educational or surprising at all.

When I walk with my dad, I do not say, 'Dad, do you mind holding my hand the way Mum does? You are mashing all my fingers and my thumb is trapped and it feels bad.' No, I don't. I don't even wiggle my fingers to restore the blood flow, or just so I can recall how they are separate digits and not one single clump of fingers like that crazy feeling I get if I have to wear mittens for school regulations, a feeling of being impaired and suffering from leprosy or something, only having a thumb available for active duty. I try to steer clear of mittens in life, and when my dad holds my hand, I get a mitten feeling and it is pretty terrible, but the thing is, I don't mind, because it is cool to be with him, and to see how he is so different from Mum, and everything on our walk is different, and newish, even if I have walked the same ground with her, and this is what I mean by not struggling against a person you are crazy about. I get busy thinking about my dad, and wondering what he is thinking, and other matters. Will there be an ice-cream cone at the end of this walk, or a packet of crisps? He doesn't talk much at all. Has he forgotten I'm here? No. He gives me a big hand squeeze, a torture-type squeeze, and I yell out, and this creases him up with mirth. He knows I'm here, yes.

Mum walks at kid pace, no matter which kid she is out with, and she does it without making you feel bad, like she has to make this big adjustment just for you. No. She acts as if this is the very pace she had her heart set on when she decided to go out strolling with you. Why, thanks, Mum! Also, I notice things I would not normally pay a lot of attention to. Let's say there is woodland roundabout, I will notice what stage the buds and leaves are at, what type of tree it is, and whether or not it is healthy and so on.

If there is birdlife, I will think about the birds hanging out in the trees, and muse on bird varieties and the ins and outs of general bird activity. In town, now, on our way to Zetland's, walking past buildings I have seen many times before, Mum has me noticing nice gates and windows, carvings and decorations, angels and lions and mythic things, and I wonder how I missed them every time. I wonder if topography changes according to the person walking about in it, like in the theatre, especially in ballet, with scenery shifting in the blink of an eye almost, I love that, how you are in a whole new place suddenly, according to good swans or bad swans. When the nice swans are out, the scenery is pretty cheery. When the bad swans dance in, quick sticks there are big waves and stormy lighting and the music is noisy and makes my heart pound. In my opinion, they go a bit overboard in ballet, as if they cannot trust the audience to tell the difference between good and bad behaviour in a swan, which is why they dress them in two colours for extra emphasis, and the two colours, of course, are black (bad) and white (good). Heavens to Betsy. If one swan with stary eyes is casting evil spells and committing felonies right there in the spotlights, a person will not require all those big hints in scenery and costume to be sure that swan is on the wrong track and in sore need of reform. Never mind.

I look up, I look down, I hold her hand. We walk, my Clarks Commandos just breezing alongside Mum's fine and marvellous shoes. I do not know many people yet, but I do not expect to see finer or more marvellous shoes looking so natural on a human being, as if they were made just for her, one pair with little scales on it like a snake but not scary, and another pair of dusty-pink suede with a fine bow, and all of them long and narrow with heels of various heights and widths and pointy fronts, like sailing boats. We sail along.

Hands. I think if you are an artist and want to go all out for Art, then you have to practise eyes and hands a lot. Eyes need to be seeing things and hands need to look as though they can feel. I take note of eyes in old paintings on gallery outings and most of them have a zombie look, which is quite disturbing, so I cannot concentrate on the rest of the painting. Statue eyes are the worst. All the details are nicely carved out, the lids and eyeball separate and everything, with sometimes even a tiny bump where the pupil and iris go, but it is still plain naked white stone, and worse than a blind person staring at you and making you feel terrible for having vision and not being able to help the blind person in the vision department. In the *Tintin* books, M. Hergé draws two black dots for Tintin. These are his eyes, and they are always seeing, which goes to show how an artist does not need a lot of detail to make a thing real. At times, hands are painted in so much detail, limbs and clothing are a bit boring, as if the artist knocked himself out doing the hand part and kind of gave up after that. Other times, hands resemble stumps of wood with little bits of kindling for fingers.

I don't like to see tons of paintings all at once, because I get them all mixed up, and that can be depressing, but here is my favourite so far. This is the name of the painting. *The Annunciation*, by Fra Filippo Lippi, b.1406?, d.1469. I am quite interested in dates, partly since the nuns told me how in olden times people had very short lives, and it made me a bit anxious, so I like to do some calculations of my own. B.1406? I don't understand why they are not sure of Filippo's birth year, did his parents forget to write it down? Mr and Mrs Lippi were so happy when Filippo came along, they just forget, and friends ask, how old is he now, when was he born? And the Lippis scratch their heads and look at each other in a merry distracted fashion and say, We don't know! About 1406? Or maybe Filippo was a foundling. Of unknown origins. It's possible. They knew when he died though, someone wrote that down all right.

In the painting, the Angel Gabriel is giving the big news to Mary about the Immaculate Conception that is coming up for her. She is reading a book before calling it a night, and you can see her bedroom with the blanket neatly folded back at one corner like in a hotel. I have been to two hotels and I am most impressed by this foldy thing they do, some stranger worrying about you last thing at night, and just not wanting you to tussle with sheets and blankets at this difficult time in the day when you are all worn out from life. I do it to my own bed now and then, and pretend someone else did it. OK. Mary is listening to Gabriel and she is quite pleased about the news, even though she will not be able to get much reading done for a while, which was the only bad thing for Mum regarding the five babyhoods in our house, the loss of reading time, but she is catching up now that we are not so pathetic and helpless.

In the painting, Gabriel's right hand is doing something strange. His first and second fingers are in that two-finger position signifying, I happen to know from nuns who are well up on this sort of information, the dual nature of Christ, human and divine. For nuns, these are the facts. Gabriel's third and fourth fingers are furled backwards, holding on to his red cloak, and I tried to do this myself, pointing with two fingers and gripping my jumper at the same time, and what I got was an almighty pain in the hand, meaning an angel maybe develops special muscles in his hands the way piano players do. Special-purposes muscles. Most of all, I want to touch Gabriel's hand, I want it to touch me. I do not care if it is unrealistic.

It's autumn and Mum wears kid gloves, this is the kind she always wears. She wears kid gloves and has a kid on the end of her hand. Kid gloves are very soft and thin and made out of baby goats, a piece of news I aim to keep from my little sister as she has a very big thing for fauna, especially the lamb species to whom goats are closely related, and she does not need to be reminded that Mum's gloves are made from goats who never had the chance to be grown-up goats and lead a full life, b.Monday, d.Friday, over and out, goodbye.

I can sense Mum right through the gloves, the gentleness, the slender bones, the little changes in pressure she applies for fun, she knows I'm here. I imagine the blood flowing in her fingers, and the little pulses pulsing until I cannot tell the difference any more between the feelings in her hand and the feelings in mine, like we are only one hand now, and suddenly I am in panic stations about it, I start flipping my thumb wildly from inside her palm, to the back of her hand, and as we get closer and closer to Zetland's, I have a superstition moment, involving having to count to eighteen before we reach the door and Mum lets go of my hand, or else. Or else there will be no binoculars left. Or else there will be only one, and all seven Weisses will have to share it out, tearing off seven miserable pieces and saying prayers over them, and eating very, very slowly with a poignant cheery expression on our faces, signifying courage in the face of asperity as in nice poor families in books by Dickens. It will be terrible.

One, two, three . . . don't let go . . . eighteen!

'Here we are,' says Mum, releasing my hand and maybe wondering why I am close to fainting and in need of stretcher-bearers.

Mrs Zetland smiles an all-out smile at Mum, because Mum is the kind of person people smile at, no matter what, even if it is not their big thing in life, to show signs of merriment for no obvious reason, and I clip my thumbs into my jeans pockets, and waltz up real casual to the binocular basket in the front of the shop, worrying that even though I made it to eighteen, I had called upon disaster anyway, because I am a fallen type, and must stay on my toes and never count on soft landings in passing ships.

The basket is brimfull of binoculars, and they strike me as the most rare and miraculous binoculars of all time, because fate did not mess with me, and also because of this new thing, how if I imagine a bad thing happening, I have a lot of grief, as if that bad thing has already happened, it is news. Mostly I do this late at night when I cannot sleep, I picture it, all the ghastly outcomes, beginning with small things, such as no more binoculars and always ending up with the same doomy thing, Mum going missing, which is a ridiculous fear to have and plain silly, but I saw it in my head, so now I worry, and I feel responsible, so I will have to watch out, like in that poem Mum reads to Gus from Christopher Robin.

> James James
> Morrison Morrison
> Weatherby George Dupree
> Took great
> Care of his Mother,
> Though he was only three.
> James James
> Said to his Mother,
> 'Mother,' he said, said he;
> 'You must never go down to the end of the town,
>   if you don't go down with me.'

There is a tip-off in this poem, when the mother goes missing, that James may be imagining things. Here it is. James bashes off on his tricycle at breakneck speed and petitions the King. Nothing wrong with that. But the King's name is JOHN. I looked this up. The right king at the time of Christopher Robin was George VI. Good work, Jem.

King John
Put up a notice,
'LOST or STOLEN or STRAYED!
JAMES JAMES
MORRISON'S MOTHER,
SEEMS TO HAVE BEEN MISLAID.'

James may be imagining things, but he worries, and you can't take the worry out of the boy, even with bare facts. Your mother is right here, around the corner, coming soon. James James has a problem with fear and worry, and he is only three.

I check out the basket, which is brimfull.

'Whoa!' I say. 'Binoculars.'

There are questions I want to ask my mother today, but never will, not even in fun, in the spirit of the Why game, say, because these questions would worry her, and worrying is bad for her, alarming as I now find strong light and some frequencies, and society at large. The great world. Everyone needs protection from something.

Worry. This is an interesting word and it derives from the Old English *wyrgan*, a hunting term meaning to kill by strangulation, and *worrier*, for so long, meant someone tormenting something or someone else, most typically an object of desire, and not until modern times has *worrying* become a word for a self-inflicted torment, that passion all one's own. I worry.

Whither thou goest, I will go.

Come back.

Still no passenger ships, but I do not rule it out, I do not rule out the Moon. Or thereabouts.

When the small lovestruck boy with the fluffy blond head and single suit of fine clothes, finally touches down to Earth, in an African desert, he meets a snake, a funny old creature, he observes politely, slender as a finger, flicking through the sand, he reflects, a chain, colour of the Moon.

—*Bonne nuit*, he says.

—*Bonne nuit*.

—Where did I fall? What planet is this?

This prince is homesick.

—I can take you farther than any ship.

—Will it hurt much?

The prince has a single vision of a rose and he closes his eyes, I am sure of it, to keep the vision in, and just as he falls, ever so briefly, both feet lift off the ground.

Navigation is an art. The DFC is an award for distinction in flying. Well done, little prince.

Whoa, the Moon.

On 20 July 1969, Apollo 11 approaches the Moon by way of its shadowy side, lit only by earthshine, and seeming blue-grey to Neil Armstrong whose heart rate rises to 156 beats a minute. He has a vision of a great sphere, a perfect round evoking Earth, something he takes as a sign of welcome, and the blackness of the sky is so intense, the surface so inviting, it recalls Earth again, a night scene illuminated for the cameras.

The Apollo lands in the Sea of Tranquillity and, before stepping out, Buzz Aldrin celebrates Communion with a chalice lent to him by a Presbyterian church. On the Moon, he appreciates one-sixth gravity and the sense of direction it gives him, a feeling of being somewhere, he says, something he will miss once home, where he drinks too much and suffers from bipolar disorder, quite understandable in a person who has flown so high, achieving a flight of true distinction, only to splash down suddenly to hopeless dreams of return.

—See my planet, says the prince. Right above us . . . but so far!

—So what are you doing here?

From here to there. How far? Not very.

Robert Falcon Scott. Wednesday, March 21. Got within 11 miles of depot Monday night; had to lay up all yesterday in severe blizzard. Thursday, March 29. Last entry. For God's sake, look after our people.

From here to there. What do I need? A small suitcase, a fine pair of shoes. A tiny nip of venom, a stroke of a knife. Escape velocity.

Gravity is a universal law of attraction. Escape velocity is the minimum speed required to keep moving away from a planet or star without falling back to the surface or entering a closed orbit around it, and gravitational pull diminishes the farther the surface of a star or planet is from its centre. In the case of a black hole, a star with a concentration of matter so dense it falls in on itself, and with a gravitational field so strong, spacetime, as Karl

Schwarzschild first explained, will curve around it and close it off from the rest of the Universe so nothing can escape it, not even light, trapped in a body whose radius is less than a certain critical number, and where the escape velocity is equal to the speed of light. This is the Schwarzschild radius, a short straight line to the horizon of a black hole through which no signal can pass, named after Karl, astronomer, pioneer in optics, soldier, German Jew, b.1873, d.1916, winner of a posthumous Iron Cross for his pains on the eastern front, a horizon, you might say, he never escaped.

Black hole, dark star, dark matter, over 90 per cent of the Universe is invisible, unknowable. So far. Black hole, foxhole, dugout, trench, dead soldier, unknown soldier, mark him with a cross. Lost, stolen or strayed. Dark matters. I will find her. What do I need?

Begin with an eye.

Galileo will go blind, but in 1609 he points a telescope at the Moon from his garden in Padua, and in the shadows, he finds mountains and seas, writing, 'Its brighter part might very fitly represent the surface of the land and the watery regions darker.'

An eye is a camera and it is 80 per cent water, forming in the dark of the womb into a small sphere with a lens in front, and a screen at the back with 137 million separate seeing elements, and nerve lines leading to the brain where out of a storm of electrical charges, a picture ought to appear, with all the qualities a person expects, of colour and light, contour and transparency, near and far. The eye is subject to tiny flaws and aberrations, everything has to be right, the pressure in the aqueous solution determining the shape of an eye whose lens must be clear as glass, and curved just so, and placed at the correct distance to focus the light on to the retina with its photosensitive cells, able to screen and unscreen, and produce the purple pigment that will allow for seeing in low-lit rooms, call it visual purple.

I trap the light, I remember everything, nothing escapes me, and I see marvellous things, no ticket required, a great picture show, one night only, every night, a spectacular! *Son et lumière*, a starry cast, and I can see clearly, I've got visual purple.

The first time I saw you, Mummy, you wore a red dress. It was red velvet and very slim-fitting, and you smiled at me and reached out with long sensitive fingers, a small gesture of infinite grace. I remember, even though I was only eight days old. I saw you.

TWO

When Gus came home that first time, wrapped up in Harriet's pink baby blanket, I had a thought regarding Mum and unknown origins, and how you might expect a foundling to be a bit edgy about babies of her own, worrying, perhaps, they will go astray like a gang of puppies in a park, to be scooped up later by a dog-catcher, unless they meet a bad end in the sweeping beams of onrushing cars, like sorry spies in wartime.

The dog-catcher delivers them to a dog home, a Salvation Army type place, but for dogs, and now they are puppies of unknown origin, each one hoping for a person to come along and choose him, and take him to a better place, but whatever happens, even if the new owner is one fine person, the dog will always be looking over his dog shoulder for the other puppies and his first home, and wondering what happened and was it his fault, etc., and maybe give in to a lifelong identity crisis, who knows.

Clearly, this dark matter of unknown origins is not a problem for Mum, because instead of looking over her shoulder and acting edgy, she has gone all out for babies, with Gus the latest, and between the day he first came to us up to now, I can only recall a single event which might be understood as an open display of nerves on her part, and that was the day of the Harness Affair, when Mum unwrapped a parcel before our very eyes, unfolding leaf after leaf of white tissue paper to reveal an arrangement of white suede straps resembling reins, reins most typically attached to sledge dogs in Antarctic regions.

'For you, Gus!'

'Mum,' I say. 'Um. He doesn't have a dog. We don't have a dog. Are we getting one?'

'No, no!' she says, laughing now, and tickling me in the neck so I don't feel too much of an eejit. 'It's for holding Gus. In busy roads. Until he is older.'

Well, blow me down. I never knew they made leashes for kids. One time I strapped it on Gus myself and held on patiently, waggling the reins a little in an encouraging manner, waiting for him to go walkabout in the garden.

'Walk on!' I said, which is what coachmen say to coach horses in old films. 'Walk on, Gus!'

And Gus just stands there, in contemplation of the flowers or something, not budging an inch.

'Roses,' he says.

'Right. Roses.'

I am not worried that Gus's vocabulary is limited at present to the names of flowers. He has a long life ahead of him and therefore it is not a cause for anxiety in me. Neither am I all that worried about accidents of the scurrying into traffic kind. This baby is simply not aiming to scoot off anywhere in a reckless manner, I don't think so. He is not the type.

I unstrap the harness and have a go on Harriet. I ought to have foreseen the difficulties ahead. Harriet is very meek and polite as I wrangle with straps and buckles and then her eyes grow large and suddenly she is scampering all over the joint at gallop speed with me flying on behind, missing a step or two, until I realise I just do not have to be doing this, grappling on to my sister in a frenzy of determination like a charioteer in a chariot race, no. I drop the reins and decide to let her be a wild pony in a field all by herself, the harness flapping loose, and me going in for deep breaths on the sidelines. Bloody.

The thing is, Mum never used the harness on Gus. I believe there was just something about it she fell for, the soft white leather, the beautiful silver buckles, the idea of it, I don't know, but I saw it, two years or so into Gus's life, how Mum has her own way with this dark matter of unknown origins, how it is different for everyone maybe, one person ending up a one-man band, taking no chances on spreading out and having a family that might go astray, and another being Mum, fearless, filling a whole house with kids, no leashes required. It works the same in a bad-mood situation, my sister, for instance, turning to song and dance in moments of strife and confusion whereas I imagine even worse calamities, hoping my

bad situation might seem rosy in the fearsome light of my imaginings, and now it's just a habit, I can't stop it, my bad mood
opening a door on a whole roomful of bad-mood ideas, such as
naval disasters and captains going down with ships, and firing
squads, and amputations in wartime, no anaesthetic, and so on,
and then I usually feel a lot worse. Clearly, my method is not a
prize-winning method. I may need to review the situation.

Sometimes my dad helps out. If he happens to come along and
catch me in a pathetic droop over some maths homework I am
messing up, or a drawing of footballers that is an outright disaster
because I have been so busy doing all the muscles in their legs, I
have not noticed, until too late, there is no space left to draw heads
and sky. It's awful. This is when my dad will do a boxing count
in a loud boxing referee voice, and a frantic sports commentator
voice, while raising one arm in the air above me, to bang it down
sharpish on each count, his pointy finger grazing the top of my
drooping head.

'One! Two! Three! . . . IS SHE OUT FOR THE COUNT?
Six! Seven! . . .'

Etc. It is pretty annoying, except that I do perk up before he
reaches the count of ten, braving this task of recovery with show-
off vigour and a spirit of endeavour, whereupon my dad walks off
beaming, because he has sorted me out again, and all it takes is to
yell a boxing count over my head and waltz off to tell Mum the
fine job he did. Jem is OK now. Well done, Dad.

My mother is the top person to seek out in perilous times, at
any station from mystery grumps to head wounds. A head wound
can bring on stark-eyed horror and a sense of being pretty close
to the end of things, like dropping out of an aeroplane on to enemy
territory, and at times like this, she can calm me straight down
while patching me up, until suddenly I am interested in how the
head bleeds (profusely), and I have a new word (profusely) and a
new subject.

To begin. There are groups for blood. I never knew that. Anyway,
the main idea is not to mingle the groups in emergency situations,
when you might be running low on blood and need someone else's
for a top-up. You have to check first off about groups. Whoa! Hold
on! What group are you? If you are too weak, you must hope for
someone to ask on your behalf, so it might be best just to leave a
note in some handy place upon your person, with the name of your

group in neat writing. Or simply make sure never to be alone in a dangerous place, never to be without a member of your family who has the right blood, the same type, that's how it goes, it's a family thing. OK. Next. Blood is made of cells and platelets. Cells come in red and white. In red there is haemoglobin, meaning iron plus globin. What is globin? I don't know. I could not pay attention, too busy wondering about this news there is iron in me, and having visions of blacksmiths in bare chests and leather aprons plunging bits of iron into boiling vats, and then bashing them into horseshoes and weapons, farm implements and household knives, red sparks flying everywhere, like drips of haemoglobin perhaps, so the blacksmith is in a state of wonder also, not about ironworks in him, but about blood in the ironworks. It's possible.

Haemoglobin is responsible for colour and carrying oxygen, and white cells are for fighting off disease and so on, and then there are platelets. Very important. Platelets are for clotting, i.e. to stop all your blood flowing out after injury, the blood going from watery to sticky and hard, reminding me of the coating on toffee apples. It's all very interesting, and pretty soon, listening to Mum, I lose my throw-uppy feeling, waiting out for it keenly, this clotting of platelets, and thinking deeply on the subject of blood flow, and the whole business of ferrying and fighting, and how I am in this O group, Mum says, which will be a breeze to recall in an emergency situation as it is the shape of a mouth calling out after injury, before the clotting part of things, white bandages, some nice toast with Cheddar, and friendly cuffs in the upper arm from immediate family, same as winning a medal. For Valour.

On other days, without a wound to show for it, everything hurts for no good reason, and I want to unzip my body and make a hasty exit, slamming the door on myself, no goodbyes.

'Mum! Everything hurts!'

'Growing pains,' replies my mother who is in the know about such matters.

'Oh.'

My mother is sitting at her dressing table with the lovely bottles on it, some with little tubes poking out and bulbs you squish, as in Ben's chemistry set, except these are covered in velvet with golden tassels and are not dangerous to play with. The table has delicate drawers and one of them contains wide silver bracelets that are great for armlets when Jude and I are Romans. Mum lets us borrow them, no problem, and sometimes we invite Harriet to join in, because the bracelets fit right around her ankles and she is so good at slaves, though we tell her straight off she is a mute slave, otherwise she might mess up the game with inappropriate dialogue. We keep her instructions brief. For instance, we make sure not to tell her she had her tongue cut out in torture, or she will go overboard in terms of emotions and take over the whole game and it will be embarrassing. Harriet is not always appropriate but one day, maybe, she will be famous for acting.

Over the creamy gold wood surface of Mum's table with the design of twigs and leaves carved in it, is a thin sheet of glass, kind of like ice, and there are mirrors at this table, a middle mirror that tips to and fro, and two side ones you can adjust the way my dad does in our car, frowning as he reaches up to twiddle the oblong driver mirror, like someone has done sabotage and moved it on purpose, then he fixes the side mirrors, wing mirrors, he calls them, and plunges out his window, before stretching across the passenger seat to do the other one, huffing and puffing the whole time. They have to be angled just right, so he can see what's coming, and I suppose Mum can do the same, fiddle about with her wing mirrors so she can see who is coming in the room, such as Dad with a glass of wine, or me, today, with growing pains I am not thinking about any more.

The dressing-table mirrors are framed in creamy gold wood also, reminding me of famous paintings in museums, those three-in-one pictures with a middle bit and right and left bits connected by hinges, but here the famous painting is always Mum. Three of her, one in three. Cool.

When Gus came home that first time, it seemed to me things were just right, no more Weisses required. I'm not saying if Mum left us and bashed off to hospital again, coming home with one more Weiss wrapped in the pink blanket, my dad hovering and shoving us gently not so gently out of the way, that it would be not OK with me, no, it's only a feeling. Things are just right. Now we are seven, counting Mum and my dad, not counting birds, i.e. two doves, two budgies and two finches so far, and how we might get a dog when Gus is bigger, but not yet, because at present any dog is bound to be bigger than Gus, which would be spooky for him, so we will hang on until he is round about dog-size, no smaller.

King Arthur must have felt this way too one day, thinking, OK, that's enough knights, no more knights! King Arthur was very welcoming, and anyone brave and fine with good works in mind could come along and be a knight at his Table, and then the other knights would squish up to make room, while, of course, there were a few casualty knights making room for unhappy reasons (demise), but I do not see this accounting for all that many free places. There cannot have been endless space at the Round Table. In Arthur's heyday, perhaps there was standing room also, but a great king ought to keep track of his knights, otherwise things will get slapdash and he might mix up everyone's names, simply too tired to pay attention to each knight as is befitting, due to over-crowding of knights, with some of the more complicated ones, the softy knights, growing offended consequently, kind of hurt and dithery and likely to slip up on the job, I don't know. It could happen so quickly.

I have borrowed Ben's King Arthur book and it is the real thing, written nearly five hundred years ago and it has a French title, which is quite unusual, as the book is in English. I have read a few versions so far but they are not the real thing, the way those Bible storybooks for little kids with a lot of coloured drawings of animals and flowers and smiley types in tunics wandering about the countryside are not the real thing, and a bad mistake in my opinion, inviting high hopes and confusion. How are you going to break it to little kids as they grow up, that the Bible is not about farmyards in warm countries but a story featuring plenty of death and war and leprosy and so on? It won't be easy, and I've seen it, how when the time comes to talk about strife in the Bible, nuns try to nip on by the strife parts and head straight for the miracle parts, because the bare facts have become a problem for them.

Take that twin brother story, the one about the sons of Isaac, Esau and Jacob. The Esau and Jacob story is really not hard to take for little kids, but the nuns make a right mess of it, thinking the only way to make it OK that the younger brother (Jacob) goes in for a passing phase of criminal behaviour is to say that the older brother (Esau) had a terrible personality and was extremely hairy, resembling a beast, making it OK what Jacob did, buying his land for only a few pence and then disguising himself by wearing a hairy jacket so their father would mistake him for Esau and give him a blessing as the firstborn, which is a top important blessing, and ought to have gone to Esau, but Esau is very hairy and not all that smart, making everything OK but very confusing for kids regarding men and beasts, and land deals, and whether or not hairy = bad. What a mess.

Mum cleared this story up for me in no time and here's how I see it. Jacob slipped up due to extreme youth. It's forgivable. He fell into criminal activity because he did not know how to come out with it plain, how he is a leader of men and Esau is not, and maybe Jacob should get the firstborn blessing so he can get on with being a leader of men. Plus, Esau is only interested in hunting, he is not one bit interested in farming and being a leader of men, meaning he and Jacob can shake hands in later life, and bury the hatchet, because Esau is happy with the turn of events, free now to hunt at all hours with no other responsibilities, reminding me of Westerns, where there are two main types of cowboy, the homesteader-farmer type and the hunter-cattleman type, and the homesteader is usually more sensitive, and has a long-term view of matters, whereas the cattleman is always rushing around on horseback and shooting from the hip, as the saying goes. A hunter is prone to rash behaviour, and excitable activities, deep thinking is simply not his bag, and this is how I will break the story to Harriet when the time comes. I cannot leave it to nuns. The Bible ought to be a nun's best subject, a real thing and not a story about farmyards in warm countries, but this is clearly not the case. Oh well.

Ben's King Arthur book is definitely the real thing, and it is very good. It is complicated.

'Jem, you're a bit young,' Ben says, handing over *Le Morte D'Arthur*. He says it gentle, not bossy. 'You're not ready.'

'I'm ready, Ben.'

'Well, remember the glossary at the back, OK?'

'Glossary?'

'See? See what I mean?'

'What? See what?'

Here is why the book is complicated. 1) There are 999 pages in it. In two volumes comprising XXI Books comprising maybe 35 chapters each, though every chapter has a handy headline at the beginning, announcing the main topics and events therein, which is very helpful, without spoiling the suspense as you might suppose. 2) There are odd words here, ones not in the dictionary. If Ben is passing, he will help. Or I can flip to the glossary at the back, which is sometimes no help, as I have to look up the meanings of meanings, there being an example of this straight off, right there in the 'a' list.

Assoil v. to absolve.

I skip down the list. *Ubblye* n. oblation.

Then there are words with two separate meanings, completely different ones. Memorising these is recommended, so you only have the one job of picking the right meaning, and no second job of flipping to the glossary also. Example: *wot* v. to know/to blame. Whoa! It seems to me knowing a person and blaming a person are completely different things. Maybe not.

When you have to look up the meanings of meanings, and memorise at least some, so you can read a few pages in peace without filching in the glossary, and/or getting up for a dictionary every two minutes, things are complicated, but I don't care, I am in a fever to learn this book and reach the parts Ben has already read out to me, such as the part about the Round Table and how it is symbolic, which is how I can sort this problem of too many knights and concentrate instead on symbolism, how King Arthur flung his arms open wide in a welcoming and heartfelt manner that is a bit symbolic, with no stampede of knights or anything, no dangerous overcrowding, a bad scene caused by my dodgy thinking, my concentration on numbers and hard facts instead of symbolism also, and you have to go for both ways of thinking, or else you get mixed up and depressed.

I race ahead to the place Ben marked for me because I like it so much, the Round Table part which is also the Queen of the Waste Lands part, and I remember her especially because of the stupid thought I had at the time to do with nuns, and how they are always threatening me with starvation, pointing at my plate in an accusing fashion, at remains of spam and peas, or smears of rice pudding and rhubarb I am trying to hide under my cutlery, food I am WASTING, a terrible sight for a nun, and all she needs to get going with speeches on starvation in far-off lands, and that is what I saw the day Ben read to me about the Queen of the Waste Lands, a sad and angry nun waving her arms in the night sky, over a field of terrible waste, of spam and peas stretching to the horizon, out of reach of the starving children of India, and it is all my fault. Sorry, Sister.

The Queen of the Waste Lands is a recluse, having fallen on

hard times. She used to have the most riches in the world and now she has Waste Lands, and this is symbolic, I believe, and to do with war and grave human failings, which is what she muses upon in her recluse, recluse being a person AND a place, she muses upon grave human failings and related topics, chiefly the Holy Grail, and who will find it, and will it be found, etc. OK. When she meets Perceval, who has dropped into her recluse for some road directions, he doesn't know she is his auntie, maybe because she has undergone physical change in her new life as a recluse, or because they never met before, I don't know. Never mind. When this matter is cleared up, she asks Perceval has he heard from his mother lately. When heard ye tidings? She asks, which is kind of a trick question, because she knows perfectly well Perceval's mother died from grief, waving goodbye to her son as he bashed off to join the Round Table, but she won't say so, no, she waits for him to say he has had no tidings, except in dreams. I dream of her much in my sleep, he says. And therefore, he adds, I wot not whether she be dead or alive.

Wot v. to know.

Now she tells him. Now he knows.

It's all very interesting, and goes to show two things. First, how when you are a recluse your behaviour may be open to question, a recluse may lose touch with the niceties of behaviour and conversation, that's one thing, and the other is how valour and dreaminess in a knight can go together, how dreams are not sissy or anything, and all the knights are apprised of this. This is why Merlin, or a passing gentlewoman, a complete stranger even, can step up and talk pretty freely on any manner of extravagant issues, such as God and dreams and symbols, etc., boldly interrupting some knightly chat, perhaps, about sports and jousts and war injuries and so on, and no one is embarrassed or annoyed. This is how it is when the Queen of the Waste Lands, who has lost touch with the niceties of regular conversation, addresses her nephew quite suddenly, and out of nowhere, it seems, on several pressing matters regarding the Round Table, such as why it is round / why he is sitting there / why his mother died waving goodbye to him when he left home to sit there / why there is an empty place no one can sit in / and why he has to go on a quest for the Grail which will heal the Lands, so they are not Waste Lands any more, whereupon he is expected to come back and sit in the special empty

place. It's an awful lot to take in in one go, and it's symbolic, so
Perceval listens carefully, though he is a bit young for symbolism
and is no doubt wondering, is his auntie blaming him about his
mother, and how much should he pack for the journey and how
long will he be away, how many days, how many pairs of pants
and hankies should he bring? Perceval is counting, instead of
thinking about symbolism, and he is in a tizzy. He has a lot to
learn, but he listens carefully. It's a start.

'Also Merlin,' begins the Queen of the Waste Lands, 'made
the Round Table in tokening of roundness of the world, for
by the Round Table is the world signified by right, for all the
world, Christian and heathen, repairen unto the Round Table;
and when they are chosen to be of the fellowship of the Round
Table they think them more blessed and more in worship than
if they had gotten half the world . . .'

When Ben first read this part out to me, when he said, ALL the
world, Christian and heathen, I had a second thought to do with
nuns. It was about Mean Nun and the creatures speech, with heathen
meaning dodgy, i.e. Jews and Africans and aardvarks and maimed
types. Since I corrected her on that little matter of countries and
religions, Mean Nun will sometimes say LOST SHEEP OF
ISRAEL instead of Jews, thinking she can fox me with this line
about runaway sheep in Israel when I know full well this is merely
code for Jews, because I checked it out with Jude who is very learned
in many departments, something not many people are aware of,
seeing as Jude is not forthcoming, he is more the silent type. I drew
up a list of his departments of learning so far: history / inventions
/ explorers / Latin / prejudice and wars / mythology / pollution /
football / rugby / brass rubbings / Roman digs / criminals / spies /
trains and locomotion. Oh. And boxing, I forgot boxing.

Anyway, the round business is very interesting and Ben says it
is a holy shape and astronomical also, the table with all the knights
around it akin to the Earth in a firmament of stars, and he says
round is symbolic of wholeness, the way a straight line is not,
because a circle has no beginning and no end, and everyone is equal
around it, all the world, Christian and heathen, etc., and I think
how my dad would hate that, as he needs to sit at the same place
always, at one end, and he would be downright confused at a round
table.

If you sit in my dad's place, he will pull up short and look at you like this is the wildest thing he has ever seen, same as if he went upstairs to bed at night and you are lying in his bed next to Mum, ruffling up a newspaper and saying, What, dear? That's how weird it is for him. No one sits in Dad's seat, not even in extreme circumstances such as illness or temporary loss of mental faculties.

Another reason I thought that's enough knights, no more knights! is that my dad needs about three or four people's worth of space everywhere he goes, though he is a regular-sized man and not very tall. I watch him walk along in our big house, and he will get tangled up in things like books or shoes or one of his kids lying around on the floor, in spite of the fact there is plenty of room for him to step in, reminding me of Westerns again, how a sheriff, or some top important cowboy in a Western, my dad's favourite type of film, walks straight down the middle of a main road if he feels like it, even if there is tons of traffic. When he strolls into a saloon for a wee drink or a spot of steak and beans, and coffee in a tin cup, everyone nearby shuffles over, no problem, no protest. They know he is a top important cowboy and needs all this space. They make room.

The whole journey up the stairs to Mum and Dad's room, my dad keeps batting us away and running his hands through his hair in a ragged manner, nearly ready to fall apart in his effort to protect Mum from us, though he is the one in need of protection and a lie-down in a quiet room, it seems to me, not Mum who is calm and smiling, and once we all make it to the bedroom, she perches on the end of the bed and lays the pink bundle down.

'Say hello to Gustavus,' she says.

Suddenly we are shy and helpless. We don't know whether to move in close in a single huddle like Roman legionaries locked tight with oblong shields overhead in what is called a turtle formation, or to nip in one by one, single file, and Dad is no help, looking cross without meaning to, merely trying to get everything right and protect Mum. It's a hard time for him.

'Shake a leg!' is all he can think to say, one of the two things he might yell at us in the morning when we are messing about with duffel coats and satchels and pieces of toast, not really in the mood for school. The other thing he yells is Make tracks! I hope he does not do so now, as it would be a bit rowdy in the circumstances. You have to be quiet around a baby. Settle down, Dad.

Gustavus. How is it the last of the Weisses has a weird name, a centuries-old name with a strange sound of snowy countries, countries with kings at the helm, a name too big for a baby unless you know he is headed for kingship of a snowy kingdom? Gustavus.

'He can't see you. Not yet,' Mum says. 'You can come closer,' she adds, turning to Gus and reaching a long finger towards him and slowly pulling the pink blanket away from his head so we can get a better view. Gus is definitely bald. 'Hello, Gus!' she says, which is kind of an invitation for us to get going with the greet-ings and stop standing around all shuffly-toed and pathetic.

Ben gives Harriet a little shove, a tiny one so Harriet will keep her cool and not have one of her unusual reactions to very usual things, a small shove, a slightly raised voice, minor events that will send my sister reeling as if she has just been shot by firing squad, or stumbling about in a desperate fashion in the manner of Oliver Twist's mother at the beginning of that black-and-white film. Oliver's mother is pregnant and lost in a storm at night. She has been abandoned or some such thing, and is on the run and has to give birth in a workhouse, the only pit stop on that stormy night, and Oliver is of unknown origins forthwith, because his mother dies from childbirth moments after kissing him gently on his bald head, falling back on her pillows with a sad and painful sigh, whereupon her identity locket is stolen by an old woman who is suffering from poverty and grave human failings, and now Oliver is in for a lot of hard knocks, all because of this sleight of hand, this one small flutter in a darkened room, passing too quickly for pause.

I don't like it, this business of death and childbirth and I am stricken suddenly, even though I can see Mum right here on the edge of the bed, completely alive, with a completely alive baby in her arms and there is simply no cause for grief and anxiety. Stop it, Jem. Everything's OK.

I watch my sister trip forward a step or two, very courteous and everything, leaning forward at the waist, and bending a little at the knees, her hands slipped neatly between them and her fluffy head dipping Gus's way like she is smelling flowers in a flower bed. I just know she is struggling with some instructions I have given her lately in the run-up to Gus's birth, advice regarding unseemly comments and how not to say them, beginning with, Isn't that my pink blanket?

'Hello, Gustavus,' says Harriet in a fine display of seemliness. I feel proud. Here is why.

Walking to school is a much bigger job than it used to be for me since Harriet joined me at the convent in the year 1 BG. Before Gus. The bare fact is Harriet rarely moves in a straight line or at regular and unchanging speed, so the main thing is to keep her in my field of vision. I pretend I am a commando with a pair of binoculars, concentrating hard on a fellow commando. I watch him with my binoculars and I am ready to cover him with gunfire (Thompson sub-machine gun) and nip in close, if need be, in a hand-to-hand combat situation (Colt 45, Fairbairn-Sykes knife). It is the year of the Great Raids in France, 1942. In that same year, Jude says, Hitler ordered the execution of captured commandos, an order some German soldiers refused. Some, not many. I made a note of this. I try to keep an open mind about German soldiers and not give in to prejudice, recalling what Jude said. Some, not many, because for most, orders are orders, even if the chief is crazy, reminding me now of Mean Nun who is in charge of clocks and tidiness and being on time for school and so on, no excuses. No prisoners.

Where is Harriet?

I try not to boss my sister. She needs to stray a little and explore the flora and fauna on her way to places, though she will come across a sad sight now and again, mashed up wildflowers a person has stomped all over by mistake, or a limping bird or some such thing, and this is grievous for my sister though not so grievous as it is if I boss her, calling out, Forward march! or, Move it! Instead, I keep a 1½ oz box of raisins in my pocket and call out, Raisins! if ever she strays too far and, mostly, this reels her in like a fish. Raisins are second best after chocolate, her favourite comestible, which we are not allowed except on special occasions, and definitely not in the morning apart from Christmas Day. Raisins are permissible at all times.

'Harriet! Raisins!'

Harriet scuffles out of the bushes in a shivery sad state like she is a small animal herself, with no mother animal around and no animal homestead or anything. Oh-oh.

'What, Harriet?'

My sister points into the bushes. She just can't look, so I brush through to investigate. Lo! I spy four, maybe five eggs, not the eating in an eggcup kind which come from chickens for that very purpose and with their full knowledge, I believe, but eggs that were on their way to be birds and will now never be birds. The shells are swirly with colour like decorated Easter eggs hidden in the garden, but these are broken, and sprawled across the ground, the guts spilling red, streaks of red like ribbons. It is impossible not to think about blood and baby birds who never got anywhere. It's a battlefield.

I cross my fingers in a wish I can help Harriet recover from this bad scene, and get her to school on time also, I cross two fingers of one hand, not both, or the wish is cancelled out, Jude says. I aim to tell my sister about embryos and I need to get it straight first in my own head, I need to recall the main points, so I stare at the ground for a moment, I look down in thought as opposed to nuns who look up in thought, because they are married to God and look to Him for answers to all questions, except ones to do with sports. Sister Martha, for instance, is keen on sports and she looks me right in the eye when she has a sporting question, largely Manchester United questions due to her big thing for Charlton, Bobby, and Best, George. Sister Martha supports Manchester United although she comes from County Cork. This is because she goes for the man and then the team, and there is nothing unusual about that, not to me anyway.

Nuns look up, and in paintings relating to catechism, all eyes are on the sky, aside from the eyes of criminals and heathens. The sky will take up a lot of space in the painting, and bristle with angel activity and light beams and doves and so on, though in reality, that sky is empty and all the activity is symbolic, and the artist knows this, but he has painted it in, same as he paints trees and buildings and passers-by with their feet on the ground. It depends how you look at it. Maybe I should look up more, maybe there are too many distractions on the ground for clear thinking, or maybe I look down because I am not a Catholic or a nun.

Embryo.

Not long before Gus arrives, I press Ben with a question on the subject of something Mum described to me, how the baby is an embryo and feeds IN THE WOMB, and it is all so wondrous, etc. Yikes. If our new baby is feeding off Mum, in my opinion, she needs to pop a few more snacks to make up the shortfall. My mother does not eat much in regular life, and I certainly do not see her changing her ways now that she has an embryo within. In the weeks before Gus, therefore, I keep pushing my toast her way in the mornings, going, Sorry, I'm not very hungry, sorry, because I know she does not approve of waste, though she is not a bad case like nuns are, nowhere near. I do think she is likely to finish my toast, however, so I pretend I cannot finish the toast, or have a big urge to share, or, for variety, I act like I am in a terrible hurry. I am simply trying to save this woman from starvation, that's all.

'Want a bite, Mum? I'm late!' I say, waving my toast in the air.

'I'm LATE! I'm LATE, for a very important DATE!' she sings, whereupon Harriet leaps out of her chair to do some accompaniment, singing along, and dancing a jig. 'My fuzzy hair and whiskers took me MUCH TOO LONG TO SHAVE!'

Jiminy Cricket.

I take the problem to Ben and he puts me straight on this question of embryos and not being fully formed, and early stages of life, etc., hauling out an encyclopaedia and splaying it open on the floor. *Embryo. Various vertebrate embryos.*

'What's vertebrate?'

'Having backs and spines. For locomotion, right?'

'OK,' I say, reading on. 'The different species are hard to distinguish in the early stages of development; later they develop individual characteristics.'

Above the words are two rows of drawings in a large box with three up-and-down lines, making eight compartments, with the top row for early embryos of a fish, chicken, pig, man and the bottom row for late embryos of a fish, chicken, pig, man, reminding me of Harriet's bedside cabinet with her display of little animals within, little chicks and lambs, each one in a box, no man in any box. I stare at this drawing and feel a bit woozy. All the early embryos LOOK THE SAME. Kind of like fishhooks or seahorses. Yuck. Below, there is a second drawing of a late embryo with lots of pointing arrows and detailed information such as: 'A few weeks before birth this foetus is practically fully formed.' A few weeks. The embryo has a head and squeezed-up eyes, and feet, ears, all the accoutrements. A mouth and a stomach. Hands for wielding cutlery. I close up the book.

'Ben?'

'Yup.'

'Does Mum look OK to you? Thin?'

'She's fine, Jem. She's always thin.'

'Right,' I say, flipping on to my back to stare at the ceiling, like Jude, my brother who does a lot of lying down and staring at ceilings. 'Ben? Is Jude a vertebrate? Ha ha. Joke.'

'Let's go ask him,' he says. 'Ambush time.'

'Weapons?'

'Pillows,' commands Ben.

I salute him and we gather up pillows, and on the way to Jude, I wonder if there is a moment in the womb when the embryo is aware he is fully formed, I wonder do growing pains start then, and is it the same for everyone, every embryo of mankind? I make a note to quiz Mum on these points as she must know the ropes by now. Some day I'll ask her, but not today, I'm not in the mood.

'Raisins?' I ask Harriet who is still quivering from shock and so on.

'No! Explain!'

Whoa. 'Harriet. I'm going to explain, but we have to move along at the same time, OK? Now don't look back, it's a mess, I know it, but listen to this. NO ONE GOT HURT BACK THERE. It's a blood-no pain situation, I mean it. OK, come on, let's make tracks.'

I take my sister's hand and I don't have to stretch for it or anything due to being just about the same size as Harriet. We are different but the same, i.e. if I comb my hair out of a tangly state into a fluffy flying around state and put on a big smile, a stranger might confuse the two of us, though I'd also have to be in motion, Harriet is almost always in motion, usually of the dancing and skipping kind. Harriet is a deep thinker but she does not show the marks so much, or maybe her thoughts come out better than mine, I don't know, but anyway, that is the chief difference between us and pretty plain it is too, so there ought not to be the mix-up there is for some nuns and non-nuns at our school. It's annoying. The mixed-up type will say Harriet-Jem and Jem-Harriet and this is the same type who will say, Girls! to a whole classroom, looking somewhere over our heads, like she simply can't do it any more, pick out the differences between us, and no doubt she goes home and looks at a plate of food and says, Supper! instead of checking out all the different items and taking them in separately for a moment, chicken and broccoli and potatoes, it's just the way she sees it now, everything in groups, a pair of sisters, a gaggle of girls, a plate of food. Things could get worse. Pretty soon, this lady is wandering around in her own street at night, key in hand, not even recognising which house is the right house. Where is her house? Her husband has dark hair and a close beard. One day, all men with dark hair and close beards are her husband. Hello, dear. Hello dear, hello dear. She has a problem with me maybe, and my sister, two girls about the same size with a last name she cannot pronounce. Now she has a problem with all girls bearing last names she cannot pronounce. It's depressing.

Sister Martha always gets it right. Harriet collapses into me in the dining room or in the playground, nestling her head against me because she is a small beast fed up with running around in too much company and if Sister Martha comes our way, she makes no mistake, looking us straight in the eye, saying the right name to the right Weiss. When she is put in charge of a body count, a practice nuns go in for at regular intervals, unfolding that list of names tucked away in each nun pocket, reading them out in a feverish manner like we are prisoners of war just waiting to dash for the wire, Sister Martha is calm, hand on hip, speaking soft, eyeing us one by one, with a kind of amused expression. Harriet, she says. Jem. She always gets it right.

Harriet is not supposed to collapse into me in the dining room. She is supposed to stay at her table with the other little kids and Sister Martha is the only nun who does not freak out about this, the only one who can lead Harriet away, my sister sliding off my bench and slipping her hand into Sister Martha's, quite happy, like she is off to a garden party. If you do not understand Harriet, you will not be her friend and the main thing is not to boss her, which is what I bear in mind the day of the broken eggs with blood spilling out. The carnage.

'It was an accident. Here's what I think happened. Are you listening? The parent birds made many eggs, they had to keep flying off for supplies and they picked the wrong tree. Too wobbly. They were tired and not thinking straight. Big breeze, skinny tree, accident. Nobody was pushed, got that?'

This is hard for my sister. She has a special relationship with animals, I've seen it, animals coming right up to her and taking food from her, from an open window, say, and they don't just pinch the food and bash off, no, they hang out with her a while, and for

Harriet, this is nothing strange, which is the best thing for me about her special relationship with animals, how it is nothing strange to Harriet.

'Now. I need to tell you about the blood part. Ready?'

'Ready.'

'You know when Mum breaks an egg in a bowl, she looks out for a tiny red speck, a blood spot? OK. That speck MIGHT have become bird but it never happened because the egg was taken away before the mother could warm it through all the stages, early embryo, late embryo, bird. See? The blood is left over from then, but it's not a sign of pain or death or anything because it was never alive. That's why it's better to be a mammal, you know about mammals, humans are mammals. Eggs INSIDE, not rolling about on the ground for someone to step on, or going cold in a nest on a busy day for the parents. No. You stay warm through all the right stages and it's convenient for the mother. Wherever she goes, you go, no problem, until it's time, and even then, a baby gets swaddled up in blankets so the temperature shock isn't too bad. So that's it.'

'My dear! Just like the Little Lord Jesus!'

'Harriet! Remember what I told you? We don't talk about that at home, we don't say Little Lord Jesus. Because of Daddy. Remember?'

'Away in a manger,' begins my sister, singing in a dreamy voice, fluttering her lashes.

This is one of the two hit tunes everyone in our convent learns from the very first year. These are the two hits. 1) 'Silent Night'. 2) 'Away in a Manger'. In the first year, or Preparatory as it is called by nuns, or Babies as it is known to girls, tune one or two is played on the wind-up music box on the mantelpiece every single day ten minutes or so before lunch. Dining-room Nun, who is also Babies Nun, cranks it up and says, Now put your heads down, whereupon you fold your arms on top of your desk and rest your head there, sleepy or not. Why these tunes? In song number one, there are the words silent and night. It's a hint. OK. In song number two, there is a line that goes: The Little Lord Jesus lays down his sweet head. Nuns think this is very persuasive to little kids who may be too old to take naps in the middle of the day but are going to want to do like Jesus, no matter what, because Jesus is the best who ever lived. I hate to say it, but frankly, being a baby and sleeping is nothing special, it is not a remarkable Jesus activity in my opinion. As I see it, babies are always dozing off, lolling about in pushchairs or out for the count on blankets spread out in the shade, like just getting here, birth itself, is going to take a lot of recovery time.

Harriet sings all the way to the gates where I get serious with her, assuming a grave expression the way my dad does when he wants to warn me that if I do not read enough I will end up stupid and have to work in a soup kitchen or the shmatte trade. What is a soup kitchen? What is the shmatte trade? Is he talking about slaves? I do not ask, as it is hard to reason with my dad on a day it slips his mind I am not quite eight and have plenty of reading years ahead of me and furthermore, I read all the time, goddammit.

I lay my hands on Harriet's shoulders and swivel her round to face me and she goes all googly-eyed like she has completely lost her balance. I try to stay serious.

'Now. What did I say?'

'Little Lord Jesus, don't say it.'

'Right. And no singing it. Away in a manger.'

'Where is Amanger?'

'It's not a country, Harriet! It's a shed or something.'

'Spider shed!'

Harriet is thinking of the shed in our back garden, the shed of fear for most Weiss kids who are not keen to ferret about in there when Dad says, Bring me a hoe! A rake! Or Mum asks for twine, meaning gardening string. The shed is always dark for a start, especially when it is super bright outside and you are blinded and helpless as you step within, and at a disadvantage, knowing anything you go for, in any part of the shed, you have to grab and scoot away with, slamming the door after you, because there will be some huge spider rushing straight for you on all occasions. Why do they do that? Why can't a spider pause and merely move elsewhere in a seemly manner? Everyone is an enemy to a spider, like for shell-shocked soldiers in World War I, so used to scrambling out of trenches, going over the top, as Jude says, and roaring into the dark, guns blazing, they just don't know how to stay cool any more, even in the face of nurses and doctors and so on. There are enemies everywhere. For Jude, the shed is not a problem, so we all make him go for tools and stuff. He may take some time, which drives Dad wild, Where's my hoe?! Where's my rake?! but this is not a problem for Jude either.

In a minute, Dad, says Jude.

And then we all say it. In a minute Dad, in a minute Dad, in a minute Dad, whereupon Dad turns on the hose and nobody is safe from ablutions except Mum, of course, and Gus, who is too young for torture.

We don't get a lot of gardening done, but it's not a bad time.

'OK then. Don't say the manger or the Little Lord thing. Got that?'

Harriet salutes me and slaps her heels together smartish. This is the only thing she knows about soldiers, the only thing. War is not her subject.

'I'll see you later. Right here, Harriet. At the gates.' I swivel her back around and give her a bitty push in the shoulder area and she flies forward like she has been shot from a cannon as in that famous circus act.

'When Harriet is FREEEE!' she says, running towards the little kids' entrance, and that is how it is for Harriet as she enters the gates in a little uniform she has to wear just so with different rules for different seasons, and special times to work and eat and lay her head down to the sound of tunes chosen by nuns, it's not quite right, like a bird in a cage, not prison and hard labour exactly but not quite right, not until ten to four in the afternoon when she flaps free and meets me at the gates. My sister needs a lot of air and open spaces, that's how it is.

When Harriet's time is up and it is my turn to take my first peep at Gustavus, Gus, I tug at her green jumper twice, meaning, move along, your time is up, it's my go, and as she steps past me, I can tell she has something to say.

'Don't say manger or the Little Lord thing,' she whispers.

I roll my eyes and move in close, and the funny thing is, I think about it, the manger situation and how with Jude and Ben behind me, we are like the three kings, I can't help thinking it. I have been in three Nativity plays so far at my convent, the Nativity being the only play the nuns know how to do, I guess, and my dad is OK with this as long as I have the low-down.

'It's just a story, you know,' he says, all serious, a bit gruff, leaning up against the kitchen counter where Mum is cooking, crowding her a little, it's a habit of his.

'Right, Dad,' I say in a patient but busy voice. I am trying to finish my homework before supper so I can play Action Man with Jude afterwards. Also, my dad tells me this every December, how the Nativity business is just a story, and God can't have sons who are also God, etc., and I know what's coming next.

'Jesus Christ was a Jew. A rabbi. Don't forget that. OK, Jem?'

'A rabbi. Jewish. Not God. Got it,' I reply, and my dad yanks my hair three times, which is his way of saying, I am not mad at you, although I sound mad at you. I know, Dad. No worries, Dad.

I have just about had it with Nativity. The fact is, I don't want to be in any kind of play, it's so embarrassing, but I am especially fed up with Nativity ones because of shepherding, quite a vexing role, though not too bad compared to Drummer Boy.

One year I was tried out as the Drummer Boy. I was fairly keen, due to having no words to speak and due to the military aspect and the bravery of drummer boys in military history but what I do not understand is how he comes into the Nativity story. What is he doing here? Does he think there is a war on? Or is he just wild for parades and processions? Never mind. My one job was to do drum rolls on a tin drum looped around my neck and head up the parade to the Baby Jesus while the girls sing that depressing song about the Little Drummer Boy and his drum, ra ta ta tum, but I lost my job and was switched to Shepherd because I was pathetic at drum rolls. My effort at drum rolls was deeply frustrating and induced palpitations in me, and a feeling close to terror, what with Music Nun glaring at me in that horrible manner. It was a horrible experience all in all and definitely a relief to be shepherding flocks again.

A shepherd has two jobs only. 1) Lurk about a fire at night in a shepherdly fashion, at the end of a long day of herding up lambs and sheep, sitting up with two other shepherds usually, unless there is a girl going spare in which case we might be four. We are careful NOT to act like we are waiting for the Angel Gabriel. Whichever girl shepherd knows how to play a recorder has a recorder stuck in her shepherd costume and she has to WAIT for some other designated girl shepherd to say, Dan! DO play us a tune on your pipe! Then she plucks out the recorder and plays a tune. She must not jump the gun or the girl with the line about the pipe, a Nativity play word for wind instrument, will feel downright silly and not know what to do, to say it or skip it. That girl was me one time, another horrible experience, my ears aching like someone had turned the volume up everywhere, the breathing of the audience, soft, the breathing of Directing Nun in the pit, cross, the flutter of girls in the wings, and the awful noise of Lucy White rustling her garments and hauling out her pipe, playing a tune without being asked first. Last year, though, it came out all right, though I was pretty knocked out from how my heart raced gearing up for my big moment and as soon as I spoke it, Dan! DO play us a tune on your pipe, I had a ferocious desire to lie down in a faint and have ministrations. No, Jem. Remember job number two.

Lo! Here comes the Angel Gabriel.

Gabriel points two fingers at us to signify the dual nature of Christ, even though catechism has not been invented yet and it will make no sense to shepherds, Gabriel waving two fingers in the air like that. Never mind. When Gabriel shows up, shepherds have to act spooked and make ridiculous movements, lunging away from the angel and throwing arms aloft like we are being ambushed by German Waffen SS and have no weapons. This is goofy, let's face it. If I were a shepherd and an angel came my way, I would have no problem with it, but you cannot tell nuns this because they are too excited directing this play and will get confused if they have to make changes, such as maybe having one shepherd NOT in a state of fear and terror. The way they see it, shepherds have to act spooked so the Angel Gabriel can say, Lo! Be not afraid! I am the angel of the Lord! etc. If we do not act as if we were riding the ghost train at the funfair, it just won't work for nuns. We have to show some hysteria and then we cool our jets for the next bit, the tidings bit, so all the attention can be on Gabriel, no distractions. 'I bring you great tidings!' Meaning, news. The news = the Nativity = the birth of Jesus. The Queen of the Waste Lands speaks this word also. When heard ye tidings? I tried it out on my dad once.

'Any good tidings?' I asked from the doorway of the living room. 'In your tidings-paper?'

'Jem, take my dirty plate back to the kitchen, will you?'

'OK, Dad.'

Shepherd job number two. Go to Nativity. This is the topmost important part of the play for nuns and they get fretful trying to organise it. It is the Adoration part wherein we all traipse to the manger to peek at Jesus, all the shepherds, royalty and Drummer Boy, and Mr and Mrs Innkeeper who would not let Mary and Joseph have a room, maybe because Mary and Joseph were too shabby for their inn, and now, of course, since the great tidings and ensuing events, the innkeepers feel pretty bad about this. Thems the breaks. OK. Now we crowd around the Little Lord Jesus and show our great joy and next, it is time to face the audience and hold hands and sing We WISH you a merry Christmas, we WISH you a merry Christmas and a HA-ppy New Year, which is quite a boring song but it is the end of the play, one more Nativity over and out, and after the clapping, we take off costumes and go home and have a big snack and this is the beginning of the Xmas holidays. Yay.

Last year, Directing Nun had a big idea for the Adoration part. She decided the shepherds and kings and Drummer Boy (girl), etc., ought to go on a long march to the Baby Jesus and not merely sweep in from offstage in the usual scrummage, making it so obvious how we are all just waiting to do this, huddled in the wings ready to sweep in all at once and do some adoring. It's not realistic, she said. I don't think realism is a big issue for nuns. I think Directing Nun wanted more of a party scene last year, that's all, like a Trooping of the Colour parade involving a long march, drum rolls and singing and gifts at the end.

Directing Nun decided we must go down the stairs on the offstage side that leads to outdoors, putting on outdoor shoes first, of course, as we are all in olden times bare feet or sandals and also because nuns are very keen on the right shoes in the right places no matter what kind of emergency situation a girl is in. Girls have three types of shoes. 1) Outdoor shoes: dark brown / lace-ups. I choose Clarks Commandos for type 1 due to the word commando. 2) Indoor shoes: dark brown / buckles. Most girls have the kind I have, with buckles and little holes over the toes part like on a cheese grater, and soft soles so as not to scuff up the stone floors or old wooden floors of our convent. In my view, you would need ice skates to scuff up convent floors, but you cannot say this to nuns. 3) Plimsolls. This is a nun word for gym shoes: black canvas / lace-ups or slip-ons. I choose slip-ons for variety and for the funny feel of stretchy elastic in a tongue shape where laces or buckles usually go. I slip them on and off, on and off. These shoes are like gloves for feet.

Playground Nun is an old nun who watches over us in the playground. I don't know what else she does apart from praying and wandering up and down the playground. Sometimes she plays tricks. I am patient with Playground Nun who is maybe not all that well. She seeks me out quite often.

'Jemima Weiss!'

'Yes, Sister!'

'What is plimsoll?'

'Um. Gym shoes, Sister. For gym only.'

'No! It's the waterline on the hull of a cargo ship! A safety mark! Named after Samuel Plimsoll, MP, and his Merchant Shipping Act, 1876!'

'I see. Great. Thank you, Sister. Is that all, Sister?'

'Yes, my girl!'

Playground Nun pushes her glasses from the speaking to girls position (all the way down the nose for close-up inspection purposes) to her wandering the playground position (top of nose for general countryside vision). She pats me on the head, well chuffed with her trick on me. I don't like pats on the head because I am not a dog, but Playground Nun is old and she is a nun and she may not be entirely well and you have to allow for things. Furthermore, she is full of special information that is not all to do with God and I believe she needs to impart it from time to time. She chooses Jem. Fine with me.

Three types of shoes. And then come rules. Shoes rules: Do not wear plimsolls outdoors. Even in sports. Do not wear Clarks Commandos indoors. Do not wear indoor shoes in gym (unless you have forgotten your plimsolls) and definitely not outdoors where they will get ruined and become perplexing, unfit for indoors or out. Nowhere shoes. If you have the wrong shoes, a nun will get flustered and usually call upon Mean Nun to sort out the bad situation of the wrong shoes. Mean Nun has an eye out for crime. She is the only no-good nun around, though I am not wild about Sister Clothilda, Nativity play Directing Nun who is also Music Nun. She makes me sing separately from the other girls, standing on a chair on my own, far off from the other girls standing up on benches and singing happily in one voice on the stage of the assembly hall.

Music Nun sits down below in the nun pit, looking up at girls and glancing my way now and again with a cross and confused expression on her face, like she is not quite sure what the bloody-bloody I am doing on her stage, or why I am causing such a terrible disturbance in the sound department. The waves. She is also confused due to my Jewish side. Not all nuns are the same, not all of them have this problem, and I can easily tell the ones who do, catching them looking at me with a cross face and confusion in their eyes, as they try to fathom it, and simply cannot, how I am alive and not Catholic, and nevertheless quite hearty, by which I mean not downtrodden or obviously impaired in any way. Mean Nun has a very bad case of confusion and she will watch me until she comes up with a crime of some sort and then she makes straight for me.

The day Susannah Bonnington found a maggot in her banger, I was right there and saw it poking its little head up like a periscope in a U-boat, weaving left and right, checking out the scene aloft, and I must say, I never want to see a thing like that again, not ever.

'Sister!' says Susannah, keeping pretty cool in the circumstances. 'There's a maggot in my banger!'

'So there is, my child,' replies Dining-Room Nun who is definitely crazy, 'so there is.'

Sister Catherine is Dining-Room Nun and Babies Nun. Sister Catherine escorts those first year kids all over the joint like she is a bodyguard, and when they are dining, she is happy, as she can do her two jobs at the same time in one same place and she is free to carry on her favourite activity of strolling up and down the alley between dining tables, muttering to herself and twiddling her thumbs in a demented manner, hands clasped before her in woolly gloves she wears in all weathers, woolly gloves with the fingers cut off.

In my opinion, some of her behaviour is open to question. For instance, babies need their own little chairs for dining, due to their small size, and they have to transport the chairs from their classroom to the dining room under the eyes of Sister Catherine, passing by her like a row of ants struggling with crumbs nearly twice their body weight and it is painful to see the little kids stumbling along, crashing the chairs against their little legs and generally making a mess of things, looking sad and worn out but resigned to fate, reminding me of the galley slaves in *Ben-Hur*, men chained together and marching in the hot sun on the way to the Roman galley ship in which they will be chained to oars and fated to row at varying speeds unto the end of days. Babies enter the dining room first and bigger kids queue up with plates after the babies have settled in and been served. They get served because they are deemed too young and wobbly to carry plates of food without tipping everything on to the decks. It seems to me carrying a plate is not such a hard task, but grappling with a chair round about two-thirds your size is definitely a hard task. Possibly, for Dining-Room Nun, an avalanche of spam and peas and gravy on the nice convent floor is more of a problem than bruisy shins and outright exhaustion in a four-year-old, and this is one instance of behaviour in Sister Catherine which is open to question, and another is when she said, So there is, my child to Susannah Bonnington, bashing off straight away to do some more strolling and muttering, and leaving Susannah and me in the lurch, stark-eyed as in a horror scene from a horror film featuring graveyards and screaming.

A few words on horror. So far, I have seen the beginnings of three horror films only, as I am always sent to bed before things get too grim. Here are reasons why. I am too young for horror films and will have bad dreams and get hysterical. Horror films are not much good or educational, and so there are no loopholes regarding bedtime the way there are with good films and/or documentaries. Fine with me. Horror films are frustrating and give me a headache, due to the endless screaming and the lack of daylight, requiring a lot of squinting to make out what the bejesus is going on, usually just endless screaming and silly things such as people going walkabout in graveyards way past their bedtime when everyone knows there are killers and/or wild beasts on the rampage. Why? Why not stay home until it blows over, or go for a saunter in a more populous area where there are bobbies and lamplight and means of transport for hire in case of emergency? Because it is a horror film, that's why. So there is screaming in the dark when characters are getting murdered, screaming in the dark when characters are stumbling across maggoty murder victims in graveyards, and in two out of the three films I have seen the beginnings of so far, there is screaming in the dark from raving maniacs in loony bins and it is no wonder so many people are losing their marbles, what with the high rate of murder and all that strolling about in graveyards, etc.

I would quite like to go in for some screaming in plain daylight right this minute because of the maggot before me, but I do not. I am not a baby. I am seven going on eight and have a fair grasp of language, and decent manners, and screaming and howling is not fashionable behaviour in a person my age who is not in a horror film. I do feel sick though, and ask to be excused. I step out into the courtyard for a deep breath or two, a remedy of Mum's, and extremely useful, according to her, in all walks of life and eventualities of a trying nature. It is something I recommend for characters in horror films.

Oh no. Here comes Mean Nun, flapping my way.

'Weiss!'

Mean Nun has a big thing for calling my name out, ever since I corrected her pronunciation one time, informing her as gently as possible about the V sound in the W, so that now she hits the V sound real hard and lingers over the double SS at the end. It's annoying and it is her revenge on me for correcting her for the second time in my life. What is the problem here? Some grown-ups correct kids about every little thing, blaring hasty hints and instructions before you touch anything or go anywhere, so sure you are going to slip up or do some destruction, and that your mind is merely an empty place with breezes blowing through it, but the moment you correct a grown-up of that type, it's a criminal act, worse than sticking your tongue out and swearing which can usually be chalked up to insanity, whereas correcting is close to a capital offence, i.e. deserving of death. Jude says capital comes from the Latin word for head, and denotes beheading by axe, sword or guillotine and even though there are many kinds of capital punishment that do not involve having your head chopped off necessarily, the word capital still applies for all methods, and I can see why. Let's face it, when a person is killed, his head is no good to him, attached or not attached, but this has me thinking again about graveyards and screaming, so I try to concentrate instead on deep breaths and recovery from the sight of that maggot poking its white head out of Susannah's banger.

'Weiss! Where are we?' demands Mean Nun.

This is a trap. What does she want? The month, the country? Is it a nun-type question, a matter of catechism? Right near me in the courtyard is a statue of the Virgin Mary, Mother of God with the Baby Jesus in her arms. Mary has a dreamy limp look, like Jesus is just a bunch of flowers or something. Maybe Mean Nun does not like me standing so close to the statue, due to my Jewish side. Is that it?

'Well, child? Are we indoors or outdoors?'

'Sort of half-half,' I say, wondering about covered courtyards and what category they are in. I don't want to make a mistake.

'Sister!'

'Sister! Sorry.'

'We are outdoors. What shoes are you wearing?'

Oh. It's a shoe crime. Bloody. 'Indoor shoes, Sister. Thing is, I feel sick and I need deep breaths, I had to rush out here!'

'Outside, we wear outdoor shoes. Inside, indoor shoes. Plimsolls for PE. If you are poorly, see Sister Martha. You are a very rude girl, Weiss.'

I want to tell her that she wears the same type shoes all over the shop, indoors, outdoors, the same hard noisy black nun shoes, and that I am not rude, my mother knows I am not rude, and then I think about something Jude told me, because of my new big thing for knights and chivalry, he said not all knights are good, and Crusader knights were downright dodgy, going in for massacres of Jews, or else selling them into slavery and this is very depressing news for me, how being a knight is not necessarily good, and wearing a big red cross on your knightly tunic, like on an ambulance, is not always a sign of hope and rescue, and therefore, perhaps, seeing a lady flapping your way dressed in nun clothes and wearing a cross around her neck does not always mean you are safe. It's confusing and I want to see Sister Martha now, but I need to do some crying first. Not in front of Mean Nun. Go away, Mean Nun.

At my convent, it is important to wear the right shoes in the right places, no matter what emergency situation you are in, such as on the night of the Nativity the year of the big idea, when Directing Nun sent girls on a long march outdoors in the dark and back indoors, and all the way down the aisle through the audience in an embarrassing procession of kings and shepherds, Drummer Boy (girl) and innkeepers, and up the little wheely front steps, no tripping on garments allowed, up on to the stage to kneel in our specially organised places around the angels and Mary and Joseph and baby, kneeling so as to indicate Adoration and also, so as not to hide the angels and blessed family from plain view because angels and blessed family are more important, they are the stars.

I am looking for my shoebag. Where is my shoebag? Oh-oh. I scramble about in heaps of costumes and stuff and my shepherd hat is slapping at my cheeks and it's dark back here and pretty quiet all of a sudden. Hey. Where is Mrs McCabe? Mrs McCabe is a non-nun teacher and Irish and she wears a great white cardigan with brown leather buttons and bumps in the knitting. Mrs McCabe is quite lively and jovial and prone to short sharp hugs, which is an Irish custom, I believe, as Sister Martha is prone likewise, though a Sister Martha hug is a less hazardous experience than being in the grip of Mrs McCabe who mashes me against her so I can feel all the knitting bumps digging into my temples and eye sockets. I like Mrs McCabe very much, but I make a note never to wear bumpy apparel in my lifetime, in case I am prone to doling out hugs also, and hugs ought to be all good, with no risks involved, no smothering or bruising. I take note. Smooth apparel is better and less hazardous. OK.

Where is Mrs McCabe? On Nativity night, she is supposed to be here, she is always here in the offstage regions, cracking jokes and larking about in a lively Irish manner and all the while doing her important job of snapping on angel wings and haloes and shoving us onstage at the right times, and she is not here, she has already shuffled off outside with the shepherds and kings, etc. They have left me behind. This is a bad feeling. I am hot and I cannot think straight and I wish I were in bed, waking up on a Saturday with nothing to do but play with Jude all day.

There is my shoebag, glowing white with a red F embroidered on it, the bag Mum gave me, hers, and now mine, old, not new, and very nice indeed with the first letter of Mum's name thereupon, better than J for Jem, a gift to me from her, and a fine thing, a bag made especially for shoes, and I never knew there were such things, bags made especially for footwear with fancy embroidered letters standing proudly for the name of shoebag owners upon them. Whoa. I fumble with the drawstring and haul out my shoes but they are the wrong shoes. Indoor, not outdoor, and yikes, I know who is in the cloakroom ready to receive shepherds and kings coming in from the cold and send them down the aisle in the assembly hall, making sure all our bits are on just so. Sister Teresa. Mean Nun. Now I am having a nightmare of epic proportions as Ben would say. Epic, a short sharp word to do with gravity and size.

I slip my bare shepherd feet into shoes and skip out on the buckling action. I'm late, I'm late, for a very important date. I push the door open and clamber down the stairs with my toes curled tight to keep my shoes from flying off. It strikes me I might as well head straight for the wire and wait there for Mum and Dad and not bother with the Adoration seeing as I've spoken my nine words and done the abiding and the fear not part, and anyway, there will be two other shepherds in a whole gang of adorers, that's enough, plus I cannot sing and Music Nun will show me her cross face and Mean Nun is waiting for me and there isn't a king or a shepherd in sight out here. Fuck-hell.

Come on, Jem.

Go to cloakroom doors. Knock softly. Sister Teresa will let you in. These are my orders. I dash like a commando for the double doors and lose an indoor shoe on the way. The grass is wet and I have bad visions of slugs and worms and spiders in the dark wet grass so I run back for my shoe. OK. Now, knock softly. No answer. Knock louder. Nothing. Here come prickly tears, a rush of them, and I don't care any more about orders, I pound the doors like a maniac until I hear Mean Nun calling for me. Where is she? She is poking her head out of some doors further along and waving her arms in a frantic manner. What is she doing over there? Oh no. Wrong doors, Jem. You have been pounding on the assembly-hall doors with audience on the other side wondering what all the racket is and who is causing this big-noise crime. It's me. Jem Weiss.

Mean Nun is speechless, she hates me beyond words. I kick off my shoes and let her grapple me in the shoulders and propel me out of the cloakroom into the assembly hall and I get whiplash in the process so that my shepherd hat slips over my eyes and I have to fix it quick sticks. It's not really a hat, it's a dishcloth with an elastic strip around the forehead to hold it snug and I hate it, it makes my ears hot and the elastic gives me a headache. I would quite like to ditch my shepherd hat but I am already in trouble and going in bareheaded would freak out Directing Nun for whom a dishcloth on the head is the main distinguishing mark for a shepherd who might otherwise get mistaken for a fourth king, some character NOT in the Bible, and thereby her great fame in the Nativity department will be in ruins, ruins.

The worst thing is having to catch up the other shepherds in the procession headed by Drummer Boy and kings. Kings are posh and the boy is symbolic so they are most important, they go first and I note they have just about hit the stage steps, with the lowly shepherds following on, and last of all, the innkeepers who made a bad mistake shutting out Mary and Joseph due to snobbery and prejudice. I need to scoot past Mr and Mrs Innkeeper and join the shepherds, then slow my pace right down to seemly Adoration speed, but both shepherds turn round to gaze at me in pity and accusation, making it plain obvious it was me doing the horrible noise at the doors, and now I can hear my dad's laugh out there in the audience, I picture him in my head, his hair flopping around and his shoulders shaking and then there are chuckles from other people, strangers, so I try to think about Mum and how she might say, Never mind, darling, and stroke some hair from my eyes so that, before too long, the horror scene is over and I feel it is OK to carry on being Jem, to carry on being alive. I work real hard to see her face.

It's always the same. I tell myself, don't blush and a blush stains me hot and fierce, red as a traffic light, an alarm. I tell myself, don't cry and my eyes fill and the world is a haze of sharp sound and coloured light and impending doom, worse than stepping out of the bright sun into the spider shed. My face is wet, I want dry land, somewhere safe to sling my hook and that's when I look up and spot Harriet flouncing around with the rest of the angels. It's her first go as an angel and she is a natural, no directions required, only Mrs McCabe to pin on a halo and a pair of spangly wings and launch her mangerwards. Go on, Harriet. Be an angel. I must say, though, regulation kit for angels is definitely helpful for identification purposes, much more so than in the case of shepherds, because, frankly, the sight of all those babies flapping about the manger with dreamy expressions on their faces brings to mind runaway loonies, and this is Sister Clothilda's fault, she has simply not come up with reasonable guidelines for the behaviour of angels, such as the possibility of even temper and serenity. There is not one single angel out here in command of her senses and my sister is Chief Angel, waltzing about the manger with great swoops of her wings, batting her eyelashes in Adoration whenever she does a flyby, and halfway into one of her circuits of the manger, she looks straight at me and smiles a spooky smile, lips apart and teeth snapped tight and then she does it, she goes cross-eyed. It happens in a flash and in that flash of time I know she is trying to tell me something, my sister who is a whole three years younger than I am, and new to Nativity, but not one bit nervous tonight, knowing what is important and what is not so important, and how this is not worth crying about, being late for the Adoration, it's only a play, Jem, and we'll be home soon, having a snack at the white oak table and gearing up for holidays, with Christmas stockings in mind, and hopes of snow. Thanks, Harriet.

Lucy White is the Virgin Mary this year and, so far in life, she is my best friend in the outside world. I like her brother also, even though he locked me in their attic once and left me there for a while, I have no idea why. Never mind. Lucy's mother comes from India and she is a very gentle lady who serves me biscuits on a blue-and-white stripy plate and tea in a blue-and-white stripy cup and saucer in their dark and polished dining room whenever I come round to play, and she is such a gentle lady, I just cannot tell her tea makes me gag a little and is very low on my list of favourite drinks. One weekend, Mr and Mrs White invite me out for my first Indian meal and I am quite excited in the back of the Whites' car, up until when Lucy's mum asks me whether I like ladies' fingers, a question that throws me into despair and perplexity, especially with Lucy and Paul behaving in a raucous manner, going ha ha ha and poking me in the ribs with pointy fingers while Mrs White explains in a gentle voice, ladies' fingers are a SIDE DISH, information I accept with a wise nod and a slight frown, not understanding at all. Do they have special plates in India? Or is it a biscuit? Mrs White likes to give me biscuits. I have never been to a restaurant without my family and am already quite worried about where to sit and who will order for me and will I say yes to something expensive by mistake, and now all I see are long delicate fingers on a blue-and-white stripy plate, fingers on a side dish with bloody stumps where they once joined happily at the knuckles to form a lady's hand, fingers that danced across piano keys and the fluffy heads of small children. Stop it. I try to think about comestibles with finger in the title and no death. Shortbread fingers, chocolate fingers, fish fingers. Lady fingers. Two pointing fingers, human and divine.

Lucy is pretty good at the Virgin Mary, doing a fine job of pretending she is NOT seven years old going on eight, no, she is the mother of an immaculate conception type baby and she is doing a fine job of pretending that baby is Jesus and NOT a plastic girl doll with a stark-eyed expression and real eyelids that shake loose at irregular intervals, flying open and slamming shut in an alarming manner, suggesting shock and outrage and giving me palpitations and a strange guilty feeling. Lucy is doing a fine job but I avoid looking her way or at the terrible doll, I gaze at the floor of the manger instead, trying to keep my cool and my face hidden, because I am thinking about Harriet's angel act and an unseemly roar of hilarity is rising within. I wonder what would happen if one shepherd suddenly fell apart and had a fit of hysteria bang in front of the Little Lord Jesus, would he get carted off to a place where there are other mad shepherds dressed in white jackets tied up at the back, wandering a field, going in for wild bursts of laughter and maybe muttering in a demented fashion about angels and lost sheep? Or would it seem realistic, and forgivable therefore, this shepherd simply overcome by awe and ceremony, the hard work of bearing witness and so on, the sheer weight of it all, which is kind of how I am on special occasions, my birthday, anyone's birthday in my family, an outing with Mum, a game with Jude, Christmas night, how I am kind of crazed and slap-happy due to festivity, lying awake to linger over the marvels of the day until I have this desire to leap out of bed in a flap of blankets and check on every Weiss, and sit up in their beds and review the day in all its marvels, as if by staying up and talking the day over, I can stop this thing a while, a feeling close to pain and sickness I do not understand.

Now we join hands and face front and swing our arms to and fro in an embarrassing fashion while singing that endless song, wishing everyone a merry Christmas and ha-ppy New Year, etc., a song to which I am to move my lips ONLY on orders from Music Nun, orders I do not require, seeing as she has put me off singing outside my own household for all my days, and I worry now about my shoebag, and where I left it, and will it get mucky, and is Jude out there with Mum and Dad, gazing at me up here in a silly old dressing gown and a dishcloth on my head tied up with elastic, elastic that was not even invented in Bible times, and I decide I am ready to turn my back on Nativity. I am ready, Ben. Next year, I will ask for a note.

Kindly excuse my daughter Jemima from Nativity. She has just about had it with Nativity. Thank you. Sincerely, Mrs Yaakov Weiss.

'Don't say manger or the Little Lord thing,' whispers Harriet as I take her place in the queue for Gus, rolling my eyes at her before composing myself, trying not to think about embryos and how early embryo fish, early chicken, early pig and early person are no great shakes to look at and resemble each other much too closely to boot, seahorses, fish-hooks. I also try to forget about that picture of the human embryo a Few Weeks Before Birth, all tucked up and upside down and feeding off the mother by way of a cord, quite like those nice bendy straws Mum buys, straws with little curlicues at the top end for bending purposes, so you can drink and read at the same time, no little adjustments necessary, no interruptions, and that is exactly what I am trying not to think about, this non-stop feeding business, this emptying of Mum.

Mum looks fine, though, not worn out or empty at all, and Gus is lovely, more like a baby in a painting than a regular baby and regular babies, in my opinion, are often a bit dodgy in close-up, squirmy and cross with squeezed shut eyes and clenched fists, gearing up every few minutes for great displays of the singlemost skill babies are born with, the howling and screaming skill, a sound that fills me with doom and panic, though I note that grown-ups largely find it amusing and delightful, which goes to show there are different rules for babies regarding howling and screaming and other matters. The howling and screaming skill is not generally encouraged in a kid, and in a grown-up, unless they are in horror films, it is definitely not recommended and also quite rare. I look around at school, in shops, in parks and museums and I just never see it, grown-ups howling and screaming. I am on the lookout always. The fact is, once a person can speak in full sentences and listen to reason, he is not supposed to rely on howling and screaming for communication purposes except on special occasions like blood situations, world war or physical calamity in the dwelling place, i.e. damage by collapse, fire, flood or air raid, etc. That is to say, screaming and howling over the age of four or so is not delightful and amusing, it is a call-out for emergency services.

'He can't see you. Not yet,' Mum says.

That's another thing. A baby is born more or less blind but this is not a case for panic and blind person accoutrements, such as white sticks, golden retriever dogs, dark glasses and books with bumpy writing. Braille. No. Everything is OK, and it seems to me a wise plan for a baby to be born blind when every single thing in his field of vision is a new thing to him and too much surprise might tip him over the edge into howling and screaming. Furthermore, a person needs sight for self-defence. He needs to see the enemy approaching. What use is that to Gus when he cannot put up a fight yet, or run away, even? He might as well not see the enemy. It will only be depressing. And a person needs sight for navigation, so as not to bump into things or have crash landings. Gus is not going anywhere at the moment, not solo anyway. We are right here. There are six pairs of eyes looking out for Gustavus until he is ready for sightseeing and ruffling up newspapers and wandering about the Earth.

Gus is very pretty and he is also quite bald with fine blond hairs on his crown like the little feathers on a bird breast. I want to touch him there but I remember Ben telling me how the skull is not fully formed in a baby, having a hole on the top or something, reminding me of Harriet's broken eggs, and I don't like it. Maybe Gus should wear a hat for a while, I don't know.

He makes barely any noise, definitely no howling, just a soft blowy sound like someone riding a bike and getting out of breath, and this is probably due to lung size in Gus and how a tiny scoop of breath for him is same as a deep breath. One puff and that's it. Empty. Start again. It's hard work, I can see that. I can hear it. Every breath for Gus is a deep breath. No. There is no deep for Gus. When you have been alive only a day or so, there is no such thing as deep or far, what with his beginning so close to his end and no spare room for anything but the important parts, his organs and little bones all wrapped up in a fine covering of pale skin with the blue veins showing through, like the first spray of snow in winter, how it makes you see the ground in a whole new way, frozen blades of grass and stones and earth sparkling for my special attention, showing up cold and clear and kind of marvellous and delicate, stopping me still because I don't know where to go any more, I might break something. I don't touch.

'You can come closer.'

Mum hikes Gus up a bit for my viewing pleasure and the pink blanket slides down so I can see his heart bleating right there in his chest in a map of blue and white, and I want to touch it but I don't want to hurt him, worried my light touch in the heart region would feel to him next stop to reaching inside and holding his heart in my very hand. I don't touch. Maybe tomorrow, maybe later.

'Hey, Gus,' I say, real shy, stuffing my hands in my pockets. 'Hey there.'

I glance up at Mum and my dad and I want to say, Well done,

Mum! Good work, Dad! and, That's enough knights! Now we are seven, our number is up, I know it, this is the real start of everything, like we are born on this day Gus came home for the first time. I am born, that's how I feel, and I want to make an announcement or hand out nice certificates, something formal in joined-up writing with a red seal at the bottom and maybe a little red ribbon hanging out. Now these are the names, it will say, of the children of Frances and Yaakov: Ben, Jude, Jem, Harriet and Gus.

These are the names.

What country, friend, is this?
   The Science of Deduction and Analysis.
   Because the speed of light is finite, we can only see as far as the age of our Universe. The earliest light has simply not had time to reach us and when astronomers look at distant galaxies through an instrument such as the Hubble Space Telescope, launched in 1990 beyond the obscuring veil of the Earth's atmosphere, what they are seeing is light as it was when it left that distant galaxy and not as it is today. They call it look-back time, the telescope a kind of time machine, and the astronomer, a sorcerer perhaps, gazing into the past with his tube of long-seeing and his particular passion for gathering light, looking farther and farther into space and into clouds that are the birthplace of stars, a place in the forever then, never now. Now is not visible, only imaginable, deducible, so what, the earliest light is so startling, it is so bright it obscures. It depends how you look at it.
   I remember everything.
   My mother groand! My father wept.
   Into the dangerous world I leapt.
   Before the Hubble, came the Hooker with its 100-inch mirror, the most powerful ground-based telescope in the world, set up in 1918 at the Mount Wilson Observatory in California and built by George Ellery Hale, an astronomer prone to nervous breaks, to howling and screaming maybe, and to headaches and visions and a strange ringing in his ears. The Hooker is the telescope through which Edwin Hubble stared at clouds of light, realising they were galaxies beyond ours, the Universe is expanding, there was a beginning. There he sat night after night in his plus fours and high leather boots and tweedy jacket nipped in at the waist, a pipe in his pocket, giving himself over to the science of deduction and analysis, a realm

demanding such rigours of perception and truthfulness he shrouds the rest of life in fantasy and bold elaboration. Hubble writes a law measuring velocity and distance, stating that the farther away a galaxy is, the faster it flies. Speed increases with distance. He looks back on his past flirtations with amateur boxing and professional soldiery and sees what no one else ever saw. Fantasy increases with distance. He was so fine a boxer, he lies, he is urged to take on the world heavyweight champion Jack Johnson. In the war to end all wars, he is wounded in the right arm by flying shrapnel, despite arriving in France too late for hostilities, the war is over. Edwin, you might say, is an unknown soldier.

It is possible that on some long nights in the observatory, Hubble sees exploding shells in the showers of light that are galaxies rushing away from him in every direction, or Jack Johnson, maybe, dropping to the floor in a knockout punch, Jack at his feet, a man seeing stars. Liar, fabulist. Never mind. It's a tiny flaw in his make-up, whatever keeps a man going on a long night in a dangerous world, fantasy nothing but a deep breath to someone else. It depends how you look at it.

A tiny flaw.

When the Hubble Space Telescope is launched in 1990, all the starmen huddle around the computer terminals for the first images from deep space, but the Hubble does not focus, it has spherical aberration. They believed they had built the most perfect mirror in the world, testing its shape before launch, again and again, by way of little mirrors and lenses and measuring rods $^{1}/_{2}$m long and 1cm wide, but in the end the mirror is too flat, the light reflecting from the edge and from the centre focusing in two different places. How did it happen?

The Science of Deduction and Analysis.

It is discovered that the cap of one measuring rod is chipped, a 2mm fleck of black paint falling away to expose a chink of metal, deflecting light, and so distorting the dimensions of the most perfect mirror in the world by one-fiftieth the width of a human hair.

Watson: You have an extraordinary genius for minutiae.

Holmes: I appreciate their importance.

The science community at NASA falls apart. Hope has become a problem for them. Astronomers are carted off by guards to rehab centres where they lie next to each other in identical beds, suffering from drug and alcohol abuse, from hopelessness, a state of temporary aberration lasting long enough only for the starmen to swing loose a while, and take the time to make a little order out of chaos.

In three years' time they are ready to correct the optics on the Hubble, installing a new camera and fitting a new mirror to match the flaw in reverse, and so cancel it out, a mission entrusted to seven astronauts who will go on five space walks to achieve it, stepping out from their space shuttle named *Endeavour*, just like the ship James Cook captained in 1768 under the auspices of the Royal Society, sailing off to observe the transit of Venus across the Sun and finding time also to locate New Zealand and the east coast of Australia, and come up with fine ideas about diet and sickness and high doses of vitamin C. In three years aboard the *Endeavour*, not one of James's men suffers from scurvy.

Navigation is an art.

1993. The astronauts step out with great resolve and fortitude and the special encouragement of their space commander, a leader of men.

'We are inspired,' he says, before the first walk. 'We are ready! Let's go fix this thing!'

The men fit the new mirror, they install a camera.

'Good work, guys!'

Now the starmen huddle around their screens again, pointing the HST into clouds of gas where new stars are forming, and in an experiment named Hubble Deep Field, they focus the telescope for ten days on the least obscured, the most bland patch of sky they can find, looking for the earliest light from the earliest stars from the beginning of time, and in that seemingly bland patch of sky, they see some four thousand new galaxies, but these galaxies are fully formed, kids, as one astronomer puts it, not babies at all. What is going on here?

The scientists realise they are not looking back far enough, and to probe what they call the Dark Ages and see galaxies taking shape and coming together and changing in time, they will need to build a new telescope with a more perfect mirror, so large it will have to fold away. Will it work? one of the starmen is asked.

'I can't tell you how long it will take or how much it will cost,' he replies, leaping around a model of a folding mirror. 'But it will work. Eventually,' he adds, smiling, because hope is not a problem for him any more.

* * *

Mrs Rosenfeld, my mother has unknown origins. Nobody knows them. But one day, a soldier comes for her and takes her home with him, because it's a dangerous world and everyone needs protection from something.

Be prepared, the soldier learned that, he remembers everything. The night before he chooses you, he lays out his things, he is ready, he will be well turned out, he can see himself in his shoes and they are the right shoes, always the right shoes, no matter what emergency situation he is in. He has ironed his shirt, Sunday best, the cuffs still fine. He has filled the stove for tomorrow. He won't be gone long and when he is back, the soldier will be two not one. It's late, he's not sleepy.

He fills his pipe and steps on to the little balcony. No smoking inside, she doesn't like it, it makes her cough, it makes her tired, she is always tired. No one in the courtyard, no one about but him, and he stares through the archway to the big tree, he loves that tree. It's so big. A pint would be good. No drinking, he doesn't drink any more, not since she left him in the lock-up that night. Wow. She was right though, she is always right, and now it makes him smile, and there is spare money too, he'll need it, for little shoes and things, hair ribbons, you need all kinds of things for a baby.

Things will be different this time, it's a choice he makes, no pretending this time, no pillow under her dress when they go out, the shame of it, except it's all his fault, there is something wrong with him, from the gas, the poison in his lungs, in his body, it must be his fault, how she can't have children, not since the awful first time, her dead son and the dead woman in the next bed and her live son, and the swap the nurse made, pass the parcel. Thomas. They never told anyone, he'd like to tell someone. About Tom. Then Dot, Dot who was a pillow once.

She says she won't come with him tomorrow, so much to do. He misses her, he has known her for ever, she used to be so funny. Things will be different soon, tomorrow, she will be different. Maybe even let him back in. He just wants to smell her again, but he can't say it, he can't find the right words, and something else, something he'll never tell her, how he hates this moment each night, unfolding his camp bed in the kitchen, the ringing in his ears suddenly so loud, a sound like bells, and then always the same thing, this sound of other men unfolding other beds around him, other men not there. He wants it to stop.

Emma Richler

At the Salvation Army Foundling Hospital, they are expecting him, he has an appointment. This morning he is immaculate, he walks a firm line, his step is light, no shuffling, back straight, he is a soldier. Eyes right, eyes left, the nurse following on, take your time. Thank you, Sister. The soldier is looking for someone, he will know her when he sees her. Yes. That one.

She is six months old, fully formed, with large blue eyes, and dimples, and she is smiling at him, he could swear to it, but it's not only that, he can't describe it, a rattle in his guts, not fear, something new, and so he chooses her or she chooses him. No, that's silly. He chooses, he thinks so. Never mind.

'Yes, please. Her, please.'

When he scoops her up, he is worried someone will stop him. You can't have her, stop there. But no one stops him and he holds her in his corded arms, tight not too tight, as he remembers holding a man once, feeling the looseness in the man's neck, limp as a dead pigeon, knowing it was nearly up with him, how he tried not to hurt the other soldier, just hold him a while without hurting him, tight but free, like they are just one body. What was his name? He doesn't remember that. Don't think about that.

Please sign here and here.

He hands the baby to the nurse and this worries him also, he might never see her again, the big blue eyes on him still, the dimples, the dark hair. Silly man. Pull yourself together. The soldier signs for her, there, and there, he does it proud, he makes an X, like a leaning cross, it's all he knows.

Hope is not a problem for him any more.

Science, says Carl Sagan, is what we call our search for rules, and the ideal universe is a place governed by regularities of nature as well as the experimental, somewhere, I guess, between stasis and motion, between knowledge and abandon.

Into the dangerous world I leapt.

Carl writes there are 10^{11} neurons in the brain, circuits in charge of chemical activity, circuits and switches. A neuron has close to a thousand dendrites, these are wires, connections. If one connection corresponds to one piece of information, then the brain can know one hundred trillion things, 10^{14}, not very many things, Sagan says, as one hundred trillion is only 1 per cent of the number of atoms in a grain of salt.

Watson: You have an extraordinary genius for minutiae.
Holmes: I appreciate their importance. Here is my monograph
upon the tracing of footsteps, with some remarks upon the uses of
plaster of Paris as a preserver of impresses!

I want to tell you, Mrs Rosenfeld, about something I read in the
Book of Ruth, something concerning the transfer of shoes, and
redemption, and how this offering of shoes is symbolic, it's a
symbolic act. With this shoe, I redeem you, I redeem her, him, this
house, this debatable land. I am in a fever to tell you about it, I
am not sure why, perhaps because Israel is your country, and it
might be mine. I need to tell you this thing about shoes, Ruth 4:7.

Now this was the manner in former time in Israel concerning
redeeming and concerning changing, for to confirm all things; a
man plucked off his shoe, and gave it to his neighbour; and this
was a testimony in Israel.

I am in a fever to tell you, but when I arrive and lie down, I
think about lying down, how it is a symbolic act, a sign of grief,
as is walking barefoot, I read that also. *Then Job arose, and rent*
his mantle, and shaved his head, and fell down upon the ground.
Job 1:20.

I remember it, how I walked barefoot, to and fro, to and fro,
and how it happened, the thing I did, my experiment in escape
velocity, and how I fell upon the ground, seeing stars. My hair was
cut, not quite shaved and now I am here, because hope is still a
problem for me.

—It's very difficult for you to talk to me today. I wonder what's
going on.

—I am writing a monograph upon the tracing of footsteps!

—Ah. Do you want to tell me about it?

—No! I need to ask something. Did you choose me or was I
assigned to you? Did you choose me? Did you choose me, did you
choose me? I don't see why you can't answer that question.

—No, you don't see.

—What if I die from this? I think I am going to die from this
and no one can stop me, you can't stop me.

—That is true. But you can let me try. I can try not to let it
happen.

Then pluck off your shoe, Mrs Rosenfeld. Pluck off your shoe.

THREE

Holmes: How are you? You have been in Afghanistan, I perceive.
Watson: How on earth did you know that?
Holmes: Never mind. The question now is about haemoglobin.
No doubt you see the significance of this discovery of mine?

If the brain can know one hundred trillion things, can a person ask one hundred trillion questions? That's one. Here's two. Why don't you wear the red dress any more, the one I saw you in when I was born, the one you wear every Christmas until now, red you, falling snow, you've stopped wearing it, I want to know why. Red, white.

Whoa, the Moon.

The Earth has one natural satellite, the Moon, its twin, born around the same time, 4,600 million years ago. The Moon is almost all rock, with an iron-rich core, the haem in haemoglobin. It has no atmosphere, gravity at the surface being too weak, only one-sixth that of the Earth. Early in its lifetime, the Moon was bombarded by asteroids, so its surface is scarred and crenellated and distinguished by plains and seas. Birthmarks. Because tidal forces have slowed the rotation of the Moon, it is locked in orbit around the Earth and shows the same side always, completing one orbit every 27.322 days, at a distance of around 1.3 light seconds, showing this same face always. Are you there? *Whither thou goest, I will go. Where thou diest, will I die.*

A star the same mass as the Sun, at the end of its life, will collapse into a white dwarf, though a white dwarf is not really white at all, ranging in colour from blue to red, depending on the temperature at the surface. A star collapses because nuclear fusion at the heart of it can no longer sustain it, the white dwarf now an ember of itself, a stellar remnant, shedding the last of its heat into space, cooling and fading and compressing until its surface is so close to the centre, the beginning so close to its end, gravity at the surface is 100,000 times that of the Earth and light has to fight an uphill struggle to escape, and because light always travels at the same speed, it shows this loss of energy in increasing wavelengths, the light redshifting. Red, white.

One hundred trillion things.

According to a rabbi writing in fourteenth-century Spain, the Talmud states that the father 'contributes the semen of the white substance' that makes up the bones and sinews in a body, the nails, the brain, the white of the eye. The mother contributes the semen of the red substance that is flesh, hair, blood and the black of the eye. God's contribution is the soul, but it is only on loan. The red and the white stuff dies with you, but the soul is up for grabs, or the Rightful Owner calls it in, no interest. It depends how you look at it.

In alchemy, red and white are the colours of man and bride and they ought to be together, masculine and feminine, in one same person, between two people, in Nature itself, it is the best state of affairs, the union of the opposites as they call it, with far-reaching consequences otherwise, dark times, wastelands, the lot. What a palaver. This was Merlin's subject also, red and white, his Grail, a mission that pressed him so hard in his role as Lightbringer, he simply fell apart, going through a very bad spell of lurking in the forest and acting up, more like a wild animal than a bringer of light, everybody said so. And then his sister rescues him, building him a house in the forest, a house like an observatory, with seventy windows and doors so he can indulge his passions for astronomy and prophecy, closing himself up, as Blake might say, seeing all things thro' narrow chinks of his cavern. His sister does all the cooking and she pours the wine and Merlin teaches her the fine arts of astronomy and prophecy until, he tells her, she is his match.

Merlin does not forget about the Grail, he does not forget about Perceval, a knight who dreams much in his sleep, Merlin appearing to him in many forms, sometimes as a hermit all dressed in white.

*   *   *

'I'll never drink milk again. Never.' That's what I say to Jude.

'Yeh, I know. You'll feel better soon,' says Jude.

'When?'

Jude does not answer me. You don't get a lot of answers from Jude who is nearly my twin, and hardly ever when you expect one. You could ask him a question and get an answer some three days later, when you are riding bikes together or coming back from doing a shopping message for Mum. I am used to it, but some types are spooked by it. Not me.

We are reading comics. Well, his is not really a comic though it has little pictures in rows running across the page in separate boxes just like in regular comics and is the same shape and size as the comics I like most, such as *Victor*, *Valiant* and *Tiger* but these are largely to do with war and sporting prowess and not so full of special knowledge as Jude's, which is called *World of Wonder* and to which he has a subscription, or a prescription as Harriet would say. It's quite special to have a subscription. Jude's comic has 'Weiss' written in the top left-hand corner and he goes to collect it each week at the newsagent. Whoa. I would like a subscription to *Victor*, or to *Commando*, which comes in a very nice book shape and has long stories in it featuring commandos having hard knocks before defeating Nazis who throw their hands in the air and go *Kamerad!* but neither of these comics are all that serious, so I only get them once in a while, for a treat, or else Jude steals one for me, sliding it away with his *World of Wonder*, or just walking out with it under his arm all casual, like he paid for it of course, of course. I've seen him do it and he is very good, but I am not witness to all his thefts any more, being so stark-eyed watching him, that nowadays Jude makes me stand outside. He mainly steals for me and Ben, comics, sweets, that sort of thing.

I am reading a story in Jude's *World of Wonder* about stars, etc. It has pictures of olden times scientists, Sir Isaac Newton and René Descartes, a man with a lot of curly hair like a girl, plus Einstein, and I've definitely heard of him, and also Galileo, a man from the seventeenth century in a big beard and a wee hat resembling a yarmulke, a hat worn by my dad and the boys on Passover, but not by me, due to sex and me being the wrong sex for nice hats. I don't think Galileo was Jewish at all, it is just an Italian-type hat, and quite fashionable in olden times, as I suppose.

'Jude?' I say. 'Light year. What is that?'

Jude is reading the latest *World of Wonder* and he is lying on his back holding his magazine in the air not far from his face, sometimes switching hands to avoid pins and needles, turning pages and breathing in and out without any palaver, no shuffling and rustling or unnecessary movements. Jude never flaps about the way I do, it's nice to watch, how he is, how he moves. Answering my question might disturb his whole set-up, but I ask anyway, he always hears me, he'll remember, and three days later, here we are walking home from the fishmonger.

Mum has rung up Mr Jarvis and Mr Jarvis has all the fish ready for Jude and me. I refuse to carry it, not having a big thing for fish, especially slimy fishies with heads still on and staring-right-at-you eyes, no thanks. We made a pit stop at the newsagent and Jude has stolen a packet of fruit gums, my favourite. Wait outside, he said.

'Light year,' he says, stepping out of the shop. 'The space light can travel in a year. It's distance, not time.'

This is hard. 'Oh. Do I need to know this, is it important?'

Jude frowns as we stroll along and he takes another fruit gum from the roll. He is thinking. The fruit gum is red, my topmost favourite, so he passes it on and eats the next one, which is yellow and also pretty good if you are not in the mood for red. 'Yeh. Important.'

This means I have work to do and will need to go to Ben for more information, Ben who is patient and can do a lot of talking all at once without getting fed up. Suddenly Jude chucks our sweets right over the fence by the pavement we are walking home along.

'Hey, Jude.' Jude does strange things and if you get upset, his forehead bunches up and blue veins show at the temples, like railroad tracks. So I say it quiet. Hey, Jude.

'Too many sweets. Bad for you.'

OK, Jude.

So that is one example of how long it can take to get an answer from my brother, three days in this case and something I do not mind because Jude is great and nearly my twin and it is why I don't really expect him to tell me straight off when I will feel better, what does he mean by soon, and what is a light year, on the day we had the milk race and lay about reading comics, feeling mighty throw-uppy and pathetic.

I am in Ben and Jude's room, I am lying on Ben's bed, which is the top bunk of the bunk beds and Jude is down below on his bunk. He never wanted the top one because of all the movement involved, going up and down the ladder. I am crazy for going up and down the ladder, it's like being an officer in a submarine in World War II. Cool. Jude and I have used the bunk beds for a lot of military situations, as a submarine, a Roman galley in wars against Egyptians, a tent in the desert war against the Afrika Korps and a hut in a Nazi prison camp before we dig our way out. We are happy that Mum and Dad bought the bunk beds and sometimes I even get to sleep in here with Jude if Ben is staying over at a friend's house, though this is upsetting for Harriet, who will ignore me completely the next morning, building a wall of cereal boxes around her place so she won't have to look at me, but spending the whole breakfast time peeking through the cracks and then quickly shutting her eyes and turning her head away if I happen to catch her, signifying her great disgust regarding me, and how I am the most boring and stupid person she has ever known. But I like sleeping with Jude because there is no end to our game and we can do night scenes if we are not too sleepy. It's very realistic.

'Jude, are we taking the bunk beds with us, do you think?'

'Doubt it. Bet not.'

'Too bad,' I say.

'Yeh.'

Things are kind of messed up in our house at the moment, what with items not in the right places and this feeling all the time of nearly being late for school even when it is not a school day, and my dad stomping around the joint with his hair all mussed and breathing hard, sometimes stopping short and scratching his head with both hands and a lost expression. This is because we are leaving this house soon, not only for a new house but a whole new country, my dad's country, and it is his idea so I do not see why he is acting so huffy and puffy. I am not sure I want to go, I don't know what they've got over there, do they have good things, maybe it will be fun, maybe not. When my dad gave us the big news one night before supper, like an annunciation meeting I guess, he said we could come right back home if it doesn't work out over there, but he just has to go now, it's something he has to do due to his roots. Roots. Like my dad is a plant or something. During the tidings, I kept looking at Mum to see what might show up on her face and she said nothing and just smiled and played with Gus, who was trying to pull the mats out from under the cutlery and plates in a spirit of scientific endeavour, I believe. He seems quite interested in the motion of things through the air ever since he can walk about by himself for great lengths of time without falling down drunk like most little kids, falling down and staring at the ground that hit them before going in for some howling and screaming. I kept looking at Mum because I thought I could tell if this were a good or bad thing we were about to do, go to my dad's country, and in a ship, but it was hard to tell, as if Mum were not in the meeting at all, here and not here, and I got a racy scared feeling for a second, like when bike riding and my feet come off the pedals and the pedals spin wild so all I can do is steer away from large impediments such as trees and lamp-posts and other people and hope for the best.

One of the messed-up things around here at the moment is too much milk delivered by the milkman. Maybe he got it wrong or maybe Mum was too busy to put a note out saying how much milk, etc., I don't know, but Jude decided we should have a milk race so as not to waste the milk and that is why we are lying around on bunk beds like sea lions at the zoo on a hot day, not budging much, even when zoo men are pitching slimy fish snacks at them. We lie on our backs like sea lions and keep our arms to the side because any pressure on our stomachs leads to a throw-uppy feeling. We stare at the ceiling and try to forget about milk, which is not easy.

'I wish we could take the bunk beds, do you think they have bunk beds over there, Jude?' No answer. 'Jude? I was talking to Sister Martha – I told you about her – and I must have said something about you, some football thing, and she went, Jude. Patron saint of lost causes! and kind of laughed. In a nice way, not a bad way. But still, what does it mean, how does that work, patron saint, is it the top saint, and what is that, lost causes? And are you named after him? I wish she hadn't said that, it's weird.'

'We're Jewish, we don't have saints.'

'What do we have then?'

'I don't know. Rabbis. No saints. Anyway, I'm named for a book,' says Jude, and I can feel the bunks sway, meaning Jude is rolling over. Meaning Jude is getting better and can take the pressure. Possibly my time for feeling better is coming up too. Coming soon. I hope so.

'What book?'

'You don't know it.'

'I might. I might know it, tell me,' I say, a bit hurt he maybe thinks I am a dummy due to getting less homework than he does and being at a school with lots of nuns and girls where the books are thinner and have a lot more pictures inside them. Illustrations. Sometimes Jude comes right up to my homework stuff splayed out on the oak table or outdoors on the white wrought-iron table near all those statues Mum has of Italian people with not a lot of clothes on and one hip poking out to the side in a relaxed manner, Italian people carrying maybe a flower or a bunch of wheat or some fish or something weird. Where are they going? If I had a fish to haul someplace, I'd do it quick sticks and not in a relaxed manner with hips swaying side to side, or I'd make Jude do it like when we collect them from Jarvis for Mum, when I refuse to carry the bag even. A fish never looks properly dead to me. It's a problem. Jude comes right up to my work and fingers the books, flipping pages and going mmmm and waltzing off with this private decision he has just made about my homework and my mental capacities and how I might be losing my mind because of nuns. He thinks my books are a bit sissy, I can tell. I feel bad when he does that and I would like to go to Jude and Ben's school and peruse heavy tomes with small diagrams in black and white, and wear a blue cap like a cricket cap the way they do, and grey shorts down to the knees and so on, but I cannot because I am a girl, I am Jem.

I also wear school hats, two types. In winter, Harriet and I have navy-blue beret hats and my dad says we look like U-boat officers and when he sees us traipse in from the convent, he salutes and goes Heil Hitler! and wanders off, shaking with mirth. He never gets tired of this joke, not ever. In summer, we have to wear flowy dresses with blue-and-white up-and-down stripes and the skirt part flies all around in the merest breeze unlike the winter tunic which stays neat and close to the legs, making it hard in summer to run with a football, for instance, without stripy material flapping in the air and your undies showing. Bloody. Whenever outdoors, a girl has to wear the summer hat, a creamy white straw hat with a hatband and a metal school badge in front and turn-ups like on a bowler hat except for the gruesome white elastic running under the chin to hold it all in place which gives me a choky feeling if I concentrate too hard on it, suddenly conscious of every single swallow going down my throat so that I start gulping like baby birds do when the mother is feeding them and you see it all happening, the entire voyage down the throat of the little worm bit or whatever and that's when I get throw-uppy and have to sit down for a while for some recovery time, same as today, for different causes, for milk-race causes.

'*Jude the Obscure*,' says Jude.

'Oh yeh,' I say. 'What's obscure again?'

'It's Latin for dark, *obscurus*. Or strange. Difficult, I mean. Hard to see. See?'

'Think so. Anyway, I'll read that book then.'

'No,' says Jude, quite firm.

'Why not?' I roll over, feeling a bit better now, and I hang over the edge to peek at Jude, my hair dangling his way.

'It's bad at the end and you're not ready, I'll tell you when.'

'OK.' I flip on to my back and I think about it, how Jude looks out for me, knowing what is good and bad and when I am ready for things, even if he will not explain it in a lot of words when I want him to, because he has tons of things on his mind at all times. He is busy. 'Jude, will you tell me about lost causes?'

'Later.'

'You might forget. Please. Just a bit.'

Jude rises and ambles over to the big bay window with the piano in front of it that Ben can play, and he sits on the piano bench and stares out the window. Jude won't take lessons in piano, just pausing when Mum asked him if he wanted to and saying no thank you, very politely, and that was it. Harriet and I have piano at the convent. Harriet never studies and I study hard and then we sit with Mum who helps us practise and when it is Harriet's turn, my sister flies all over the keys making some pretty fine sounds though I am pretty sure not one is in the piano homework she is supposed to do. She sits up straight and makes this whole rush of sound, whipping her head from side to side in a dramatic fashion and turning round now and again to grin at Mum. It's all very unusual. When Harriet is keen to stop, never wanting to practise long, she shuts the piano lid and scoots across the piano bench to lean into Mum, resting her head there, like she has just been on some long journey and not everything she saw was good.

I myself have some piano problems and the solution to my piano problems is not in sight. I note that it is possible to overcome human failure in some fields and this is quite cheering, but it is not a rule and I am not foxed by my occasional prowess in those fields where I suffer from human failure. Bike riding for one. I am not all that good. I get by. However, I did a feat for Jude the other day when we were riding with Zach and Jeremy, a feat I have never done before and will not try again by myself, but the other day I did it just like that, no problem, because Jude wanted me to and it was important to him, plus he told his friends I could.

'Jem can do that,' he said meaning push-start the bike with one foot on one pedal, flinging the other leg over while the bike is careening ahead before settling in the saddle, cool as anything. And I did it, I did it for Jude, no crashing, just as I would like to over-come my piano problems for Mum, but I simply cannot match the notes in my book to the keys without taking a lot of time and then poking at the piano with stiff fingers and it's awful, because you are supposed to string the notes together to make a tune, not let a lot of time pass between them and this makes me so edgy I can hardly see any more, I know I'm taking far too long and thinking about that makes me even slower, and the sounds I make are down-right bad and give me a sick heavy feeling. I look Mum's way and she smiles that smile, but we both know it's all up with me, I'm no piano man, nowhere near.

Unlike my mother. I just know it, how she can play this piano though I never see her play this piano, and how she can do it without books, easy, something I am sure of while knowing also not to ask her about, sure of without ever being told, like I heard it in my sleep. There is some stuff you can count on in dreams as real and true, even when you know it is a dream thing, such as eating peanut butter sandwiches with Jude and he says 1942 was the year of the Great Raids, and you wake up thinking I know he said that, but you cannot tell which came first, the sleep time or the real-life time but it doesn't really matter, because it's a true thing and has some bearing on life. Other stuff in dreams is not so reliable. I rule out flying, for instance. If you are flying without an engine or glider wings, there is usually no head-scratching in the morning as to when and where it happened, and in which realm did you do it first, the sleeping one or the waking one. Forget it.

I know she can play, it doesn't matter how I do. And I know not to ask her to play, or why she never touches the keys, not ever, even when she is helping me practise, sitting there at the far edge of the piano with her hands in her lap, sometimes counting out beats for me in a soft voice and when it is very bad, she will reach my way, gently shifting my hand to the right keys, her long fingers covering mine and I can hear the music in her, I swear it, like she is playing, no hands, and all the sounds come out right, beautiful, the kind of tune that makes you down tools and stop breathing because you may never hear it the same again, a sound like everybody you are crazy about calling your name all at once. This is the only good thing about piano practice and why I stick with it for now, all because of Mum and this feeling I get, making me forget my trouble with clefs and joined-up notes and one notes, and pedals I slam like a racing driver, I can't help it, and most gruesome of all, my non-nun piano mistress who stabs me in the hand with a pointy pencil when I make a mistake, going in for fisticuffs when I get slouchy, winding up like a boxer before crashing her fist into my vertebrae and smiling at me in a shifty manner thereafter. Once, when I came through a whole tune no problem, she gave me two sweets, one green, one yellow, boiled sweets in see-through paper, the kind I hate, but never mind, I was so surprised, I stared at them in my palm for a while before saying thanks, still quite depressed by stabbings and thumps and thinking about secret agents captured by Nazis, fingering suicide capsules in their pocket, coloured capsules perhaps, wrapped in see-through paper. This woman definitely comes low on my list of favourite persons in life, and I am very glad Harriet has prowess in piano and a fine posture, and an improving effect on people in general, no doubt bringing out the sweetie handout mood at all times. I don't tell Mum about piano mistress because it will upset her and anyway, pretty soon piano mistress and Jem will be in separate countries, no goodbyes, and Mum has too much on her mind right now, everything is messed up in our house.

Jude is staring out the big bay window. 'Let's go outside,' he says.

'Lost causes, Jude, please!'

'When you work very hard even though you'll never win, you'll never change a thing.'

'What do you mean?'

'Well. Like wars, there will always be wars.'

'Why, why will there?'

'That's how it is, Jem. But you fight anyway, even if it's a lost cause.'

'Why, what's the point, I don't understand.'

'It's good to try, it makes you good – forget it, Jem, ask Mum, it's hard to explain, I'm tired.'

'OK, sorry. We can go outside now. I think I'm better.' I start to climb down the ladder. 'Know what? Dad might be a lost cause in the mess department. We can try to help him be less messy, but it's no good. We can say, Oh Dad, when he drops food between the plate and the pot and make little suggestions like Wait till I get a bit closer with my plate, Dad, or Slow down there! or some such thing, but it's no good, he's a lost cause, right? And Harriet! She –'

'Jem. You have to stop making everything to do with us. We are not the world, the Weiss family is not the world, you have to learn the big things, science, history, all that. And you can't stay in your family for ever, I mean, you don't even know what you want to do.'

'I do!'

'What then?'

'I'll tell you later. I'M TIRED.'

'Yeh-yeh.'

'I have ideas. I might do what Dad does.'

'See? Just because Dad does it. And you can't anyway. Sports writing is not a girl job, I want you to do a girl job.'

'It was just one idea, I have others. I'm only ten, Jude, it'll be OK.'

I get it all wrong with Jude sometimes, nothing I say is right, and I hate it when he is cross with me, why can't he explain properly, what does he mean about the world and our family, what did I do wrong? I have this bad-news feeling now, a locked-in-the-attic feeling and I need to get rid of it fast.

'Let's drink milk!' I say.

'Don't say milk.' Jude hauls on his blue rugby top and I have one too, one that is a bit too small for him and I think to grab it from my room but he might not be in the mood for me to wear the same top as him so I decide to wear something else. We are going outside. We'll play some game. Great.

'Jude? Just one thing. Is it good, do you think, going to Dad's country, changing countries like that?'

'Sure. It will be fine. We have to travel.'

'Why? Why do we?'

'We just do. It's important, travel is important,' he says in a voice meaning this is the end of the talk we are having, it is time to move on.

'MILK,' I say, stepping up to him with a horror film killer look. 'MILK.'

I am running now, Jude chasing, both of us scrambling down the stairs and I forget about other Judes, there is only one, not lost, no saint, not obscure, but my own brother who is only fifteen months older and so nearly my twin, it's scientific, it's historical, it's nothing to do with me.

'Mum! Mummy!' I am kind of cross, and stomping all over the house, where is she?

I ask Lisa who is feeding Gus in the kitchen. Lisa comes from Portugal and she lives with us. She wears a shiny blue dress with buttons down the front like our painting smocks at school, same colour, same arrangement of buttons and pockets, different feel. Convent painting smocks are matte and soft, not slidy and shiny, and they are for ART ONLY. Lisa is sometimes friendly, sometimes not. She is not very friendly if some item has gone missing and you ask her about it. If you ask her if she knows where a thing might be, she grabs the edge of one pocket of her shiny blue dress open and holds it like that until she has finished saying, IS IT IN MY POCKET?!

I like Lisa even though she is grumpy. Also, she needs me. Some days, when she is having a rest in her room, she calls me into her room and we do one of two activities, sometimes both. 1) Photographs. Lisa shows me the same old photos of her family every time, pictures of scowly boys with dark floppy hair standing near big white walls and old men with pipes and dark hats on, black hats with little brims. Then there are ladies in dark dresses and black napkins wrapped around their heads though it is not raining. The focus is not all that great but I don't remark upon it. It would be rude and clearly it is not a problem for Lisa who tells me the names of all the people and I pretend I remember some of the names that go with the people, though this is hard because they all look pretty much the same to me and because Lisa covers each face as she goes, kind of lingering there a while and mumbling soft things in the Portuguese language. 2) Football Pools. I help Lisa choose which football team to bet on for the match on Saturday and I fill out the forms for her. My dad says little kids are not allowed to bet, it is against the law and I am now on the slippery slope and had better watch out, etc. Yeh-yeh. I like to help Lisa out and I know quite a bit about football and I can spell Sheffield Wednesday and Norwich no problem whereas it is not so easy for her without checking every single letter and still getting it wrong. English spelling is a bit weird, I tell her in a comforting manner. And hey, Dad can't spell! I do not want her to get depressed. Lisa comes from Portugal.

Lisa is never grumpy with Gus who is taking his time right now over some squashed-up bananas, eating slowly, with a thoughtful expression, holding his right foot in his left hand and flexing the toes to and fro, a habit of his I believe will stick with him. I can see it. And I see a day when Gus will catch up with me and be at an age when the difference between us doesn't count any more, we are grown-ups, and we sit in a bar and have drinks, wine for me, like Mum, and Scotch for Gus, like Dad, Scotch he will sip with a thoughtful expression, maybe reaching for his foot now and then, he doesn't know why. I do.

'Lisa, have you seen Mum, please?'

'IS SHE IN MY POCKET?!'

Bloody.

Lisa is not coming on the ship with us due to love and sex. Mum says she has a boyfriend here but I can tell Mum is worried about the boyfriend situation. Dad says, He's a *ganef*! *Shiker*, shmuck! This sounds bad. In my opinion, though, Lisa will go back to her old country with scowly dark-haired boys standing against white walls and old ladies with napkins on their heads, that's what I think.

'Mum? Mummy?' I'm calling a lot louder now, reminding myself of Joey in *Shane*, my dad's favourite Western he took us to the cinema to see. A revival, he said, whatever that means. I never saw him so excited. At the end of the story, the boy Joey calls out for Shane, he calls his name many times, Sha-ne! Shane! Come back! Etc. He runs after him a long way, running with his dog, but Shane is not coming back, not ever, he is not coming back even though part of him would like to stay because he has a big feeling for little Joe's family and they have a big feeling for him, but he rides off anyway, maybe thinking like Jude. Travel is important.

When we came home from the cinema, Ben, Jude and I were a bit giddy from going, Sha-ne! Sha-aane! in the same voice as the boy, the whole way home in the car, flopping around in hysterics in the back seat and driving Dad a bit crazy. At supper, any time anyone stood up for a glass of water or something, one of us would call out, Come back! in poignant tones and I believe Dad was a bit disappointed as *Shane* is a favourite film of his, and this was a little traitorous on my behalf because I remember feeling a bit desperate at the end of the film, tears rising up in me when Joey chased after Shane who is not coming back, Shane who is a hero and ought to stick around. I don't tell Jude or Ben, they might think I am a bit sissy, which is strange, as my dad certainly has a big thing for Shane and he is not a sissy. Oh well.

'Mum!' Where is she?

'Jem!' My dad is calling for me from the living room.

'Yes?'

'Come here!'

'I'm busy!' My dad always wants you to get real close when he has a thing to tell you, especially if he is about to send you off on a mission, like he needs you to travel the greatest distance, go a long way for him, even for some little thing he wants. 'I'm looking for Mum, what do you want, Dad?' I try not to sound too cross, it's bad for my dad, he gets rattled.

'Come here,' he says, lowering the mess of newspapers to his knees.

I can hardly stand still. 'What, Dad? What? I have to go now.'

'I am taking your mother out to dinner, I want you to let her be while she gets ready and you can't eat those before dinner.'

He means my packet of crisps I am clutching, chicken curry flavour, not the ones I wanted, but Jude said I couldn't have smoky bacon due to being Jewish and pigs are not allowed for Jews, even half-Jews. I'm not sure about this. I think smoky bacon flavour is just fake bacon, not from real-life pig juice or anything like that and also I think Jude is just being mean but I am too tired to fight him today. Dad sent us across to the shops saying we could have crisps for later which usually means he is taking Mum out to dinner, a time when we all need some kind of treat to make up for her not being around, I guess. Fine with us. Crisps are very nice.

'I know that, I know both those things, can I go now? May I?' Damn and bloody, I'm always getting this wrong. Mum says anyone

CAN go, do you see, Jem? You are perfectly ABLE to go, MAY I is different, it's permission, right, OK. I do not think my dad notices what I say.

'So. Leave Mum alone,' he says, raising his newspapers.

Like I'm about to hurt her, like I would do that.

'Dad? You eat bacon, right? I've seen you.'

'Yup.'

'Isn't there a rule or something?' I ask. 'For um, if you're Jewish?'

'Well, yes. It was about order and purity, I'll explain some other time. Pigs eat everything . . . it's not godly, you understand? But I'm not kosher, this is not a kosher house, we are not Orthodox, don't eat those crisps before dinner.'

'Dad? Are you in a bad mood?'

'Not yet. How about a head rub for your old Dad?'

'No, sorry, I have to do my homework, I'm going now.'

It's scary saying no to my dad, my insides go all fluttery but I don't feel like getting my fingers all greasy in his hair, not today. I don't mind mostly. I like the smell of Dad's head and how his hair sticks up at the end of the head rub and how now and again he goes, Ahhh, that's great, Jem! while I am in the thick of it. Ahhh! he says, making me quite happy and proud when I leave him, even though my fingers are a bit slippery and the tips of them are all tingly and worn out, like I have lost a layer of skin maybe.

I have noticed something about him, how he is more prone to telling a person what not to do instead of what to do, unless it's a mission, such as go get me a tomato and a knife on a plate, etc. He says, Don't bother Mum, Don't eat those crisps yet, Don't read in the dark. And how does he expect me to know all the rules for being Jewish when I go to a convent, a school I think makes him mad at me because of nuns who are possibly contaminating me with nun-ideas and turning me into a kid who is not his all-out daughter, confusing him and giving him a cross look like when he can't find something in the fridge, a thing that is usually right in front of his eyes. It's there, Dad. It's me, Dad.

I think my dad sees nuns and being Catholic, or even Protestant like Mum, as kind of weak, full of fancy clothes and secret things, quiet voices and angel paintings and his religion is big, with tough rules to do with comestibles and other matters, and full of beards and dark clothing and loud praying and calamities in history, in World War II for instance, the Holocaust, a calamity he is very worried about, like it is not all over yet and we must not forget it, we must be prepared for all eventualities, and his religion is maybe better for that, for readiness. Dad is happy I am a girl but I have to be ready also, cowboy-tough. Shane has put away his gun, it is for emergency purposes only and he will only ever need one shot. I don't know what religion Shane is, it's a private matter with him, but he has readiness.

What kind of school will I go to in Dad's country, do they have convents over there? If I go to a convent, will he give me that speech about signs of the cross and spiritualities and not joining in, a speech I know by heart? Of course he will. In the name of the Father, the Son and the Holy Ghost, say the girls in time with one another, looking a bit depressed and all sounding the same, like zombies. Then comes the prayer part, the sad one about daily bread, and I can't help but say it in my own head, just because I have heard it so often and because it puts me in mind of tribulations and of Oliver Twist in his workhouse days, days of bread truly unworthy of the name and in far too meagre allowances for a boy not yet fully formed. Give us this day our daily bread. Please can I have some more? Daily.

After the prayer, the girls speak those same words and sign off once more, like this is code for Hello God, Goodbye God. In the name of the Father, they say, and I say it too, seeing my dad every time, my father with a cross face because I have joined in by mistake when he asked me not to. It's not a catechism thing, it's a Charles Dickens thing, it's really not a problem.

Don't bother Mum.

I don't call her name out, I do not want Dad to hear me, I just nip in close to the door of their bedroom which is nearly but not shut, they never fully close it though that does not mean waltz straight in, it's not polite. I speak through the open part of the door, squishing my face into the space she left.

'Mummy?'

'Just one minute, darling.'

I count. She doesn't mind this, it's a thing we do. I sit with my back to the door, on the long raised step outside, the landing she calls it, like a railway station platform. I sit there with my crisps, my crisps for later. 'One, two, three . . .' Maybe I could go back to the shops and swap for smoky bacon. No. '. . . fifty-eight, fifty-nine, SIXTY. Ready now? Is it OK now, can I – may I come in?'

I think about Oliver for a moment, and how he gets it wrong. Please can I have some more? This is sad too, and maybe no mistake, just something to do with duress and despair, that he simply cannot tell the difference any more, the space between capability and permission. I step into Mum's room.

'He-llo!' she says, like she is all surprised to see me.

She is striding in from the bathroom that connects her room to Gus's and she heads for the dressing table. Her bathroom contains a bidet, a bidet is for women although she lets Gus play with it, watching him peer over the side and faff with the taps, giggling like a wild man when the spray goes in his face. I walk over to my mother and stand next to her.

'I'm going to stand right here and watch, is that OK?'

'You know it is, what's wrong, Jem?'

'Jude said I couldn't have smoky bacon crisps, Dad wouldn't like it because of um, kosher rules.'

'I think Jude was joking, what do you think?'

'Yeh, well. Anyway, that's not it, I heard something bad.'

'What did you hear?'

'Ben's not coming on the ship with us. Why not, I want him to.'

Mum lays down her little eye make-up stick, it's like a conductor's wand for orchestration. Not wand, baton. She turns my way on her little piano-type bench, the one with gold legs and a little cushion with a pattern of pale stripes and wispy leaves, the cushion attached to the legs by way of posh drawing pins with rounded ends coloured gold also. It's the nicest bench I've ever seen. Mum holds her arms out and I lean in there and I want to cry suddenly. I swallow hard the way Harriet does when she is eating something undesirable and wants everyone to know about it and mark the occasion so it will never happen again. Do not ever press a sardine on me again. Thank you.

'Do you remember I told you Ben has special exams to write, O levels, and then he'll join us, he'll come by air?'

'No. Maybe I wasn't listening, maybe I forgot, maybe you just said O levels, I don't know what that is, are you sure you told me?'

'Yes, Jem.'

'Why can't we wait for him?'

'We have to find a house and furniture, all kinds of things, it will be fun, I'll need your help.'

'Everything's changing, it's all different, I hate it – will Ben stay in the house by himself?'

'No,' my mother says. 'He'll stay with Chris, with Chris and his family.'

'Well, do they know he needs nuts and raisins in a bowl when he comes in from school, do they?' I feel right pathetic now, I can't do much about it, and the tears fall, kind of leaping out of my eyes, it's weird. 'Do they have binoculars where we're going? You don't want to go, do you, Mum, I know you don't!'

'Jem. Sometimes we do things we don't want to do because we love someone.' Mum wipes my tears away, her long fingers brushing my cheeks like windscreen wipers on a car.

'Dad, you mean Dad. Because he has to go, right?'

I think of learning to change Gus's nappies, trying to copy Mum, how she raises his ankles with one hand and slides the old nappy out from under him with the other, then swabs the decks with damp tissues and pats him dry and bundles him up neatly again, all the while having a friendly chat and tickling him in the ribs. It's not so smooth an operation with me but that is not the main thing, the main thing is how it does not feel like a poo situation, usually quite grievous and appalling, situations such as walking slap into a mound of poo on the pavement or in a field and having a doomy feeling for hours thereafter. Gus's poo is not a problem for me at all, just as Harriet barf is not nearly so bad as stranger barf and the day she marched up to my table at the convent and spewed a wee pile of swedes at my feet like I was the only person who could handle the barf situation with poise and even temper, that was not a problem for me either. In my opinion, Harriet displayed fine judgement that day. No one should have to eat swedes in their lifetime. I had a conviction swedes are nun food only and do not exist in the great world so I looked them up and I was nearly right. *Brassica napus*: used as a vegetable or as CATTLE FOOD. Hmm. This is possibly a catechism issue with nuns, how we should all eat off the same menu, cows and girls, the whole zoo. We are ALL God's creatures.

The main thing is, not everything that spews forth from a person is lovely and charming, poo, barf, blood, but depending on your feelings for that person, this will or will not be a problem for you, and fine feelings are likely to predispose you to cheery mop-up operations, and willing journeys by sea to uncertain destinations.

81

'Can Ben bring some binoculars when he comes?'

'Maybe,' says my mother, turning back to face the mirrors, 'or maybe we can go out hunting for something you will like as much, something new. We will look until we find it. What do you think of that idea?'

I am not hopeful. A not-binocular, just as good? I don't know.

'OK,' I reply because I don't want to let her down. She needs me, she said so.

Mum loops that cross around herself, the one with the pale stone at the heart of it. It is art, she says, made by an artist, a man from Ireland, and I wonder about him, whether he is prone to cracking jokes and doling out hugs or whether he is too caught up with the forging of silver and the embedding of pale stones for such things. Mum tucks the cross under her clothes because of Dad and Judaism, or else she hangs other stuff about her neck, shimmery silver chains or a wispy scarf so the fine cross is kind of hidden, like seeing a person you know standing under a weeping willow in a slight breeze and the picture keeps breaking up. Kaleidoscopes give me the same feeling, part excited, part depressed. I twist the tube and the pattern comes, marvellous, and just as I get an idea about it, close to recognition, it turns into some new pattern and I have to start all over again, like nothing is clear for long enough, there is nothing you can swear to. Hey, you, standing there, do I know you? Is that a cross I see?

'I love that,' I say, pointing to the cross, trying not to say the word though my dad is downstairs. 'And in the middle, the –'

'Moonstone,' says Mum drawing it out from the tangle of chains, willow. Binocular, moonstone. Memento. Where she's been, where she is headed. Mrs Yaakov Weiss, destination Moon.

'Well, I love it.'

'It's lovely, but you don't really love it, Jem. You love people, not things.' She says this gently, stroking the top of my head and taking the opportunity, as per usual, to untangle some of the mess up there. Like my dad, I do not have a big thing for combs and combing.

Here comes my dad. You can hear him coming a mile off. Is he worried about spooking people, is that why he goes in for all that shoe scuffling and throat clearing? I don't think so. He finds it very funny indeed if you suddenly leap in the air limbs akimbo because someone has just spoken loudly in a quiet room or you are watching a film and there is a gunshot out of nowhere. Ha ha ha, he goes, watching you try to recover your senses. He loves this, people losing their cool. So that's not the reason. He wants to make an announcement, that's all. It's a long hello. When an important cowboy enters a bar, he will pause a moment at the swing doors, stopping short in a slap of heels so everyone has a moment to turn round and get the picture before he bats the doors open, and this is no show-off thing, but a courtesy and a greeting, the only kind he knows, because he is an important cowboy and a man of few words.

Dad is carrying two glasses, white wine for Mum, Scotch for him. It is time for him to slap soapy water under the arms and put on a new shirt and tie it up with a tie. This will take him about three and a half minutes and there will be a lot of commotion.

'Jem,' he says. 'We'll have another boxing lesson soon. Maybe tomorrow.'

I think he has forgotten about telling me not to bother Mum. Anyway, why can't I be in here if I want to?

'Tomorrow? OK.'

My dad pulls on my hair, two tugs, like my hair is a bell pull and he is ringing for servants. It's a show of affection and now I feel guilty about skipping out on his head rub, something I hope he has also forgotten.

'Tomorrow we'll do the rope-a-dope!' says my dad, putting his glass down and shuffling from foot to foot like he is doing a war dance or some such thing. I have no idea what rope-a-dope means, or whether I am supposed to shuffle around also. I don't bother. 'Put up your dukes! Ha ha ha! And don't eat those before dinner,' he adds, prodding my bag of crisps and picking his glass up again.

Bloody. Not again. It is possible Mum asked him to look out for this tonight, the eating of crisps before dinner, because she is always in charge of health matters and that can be a full-time job when there are a lot of kids roaming around like in our house. The thing is, when Dad takes on a task of this kind, of handing out advice or rules, he is a lot bossier, clearly believing a kid will not get the message unless you yell out the advice and make a cross face and repeat it eight or nine times. We are not spooked, but if one of us has a friend around when Dad is marching through the house, poking us in the ribs in passing and yelling out advice, or going Heil Hitler! ha ha ha, the type of friend who is a bit jumpy near my dad, wondering if he is a crazy person or dangerous or something, for a moment I think I should explain to the friend that my dad is not scary, he is funny, that's how he is, he's not mad or anything, and then just as quickly, I feel clapped out and know it is time to get a new friend, because some things are too hard to explain, and I am real choosy about friends now, finding ones who can relax around Dad, which is a lot easier than trying to explain things to people who will never really understand. This may be an unusual way to pick friends, I don't know, but that's how it goes.

I pause on the landing outside Mum and Dad's room. Where are you headed, Jem? I'm not sure. I am not wild about this time of day, it's kind of lonely, too soon for supper, long since school, what's it for, this time of day? I am skipping homework as it is Friday, which is my day off from homework and tomorrow is Saturday, Harriet's favourite. She gets so excited about Saturday, she will rise up quite often in the night to tell me the latest in her departments of special expertise, or fill me in regarding what happened to her on Friday and what she aims to do on Saturday. A lot happens to Harriet, so there is a lot to say and sometimes she will also ask me to sing in my no-good singing voice or else we make beastie shadows on the wall in the light of passing cars. Saturday will never be as great for me as it is for her, but I would never have learned this were it not for Harriet waking me up all night to tell me stuff, waking up and chirping at me like a bird just so she can have that fine moment over and over maybe, of falling asleep with this exciting idea she will be waking up on a Saturday, a feeling like rewrapping your own present late at night at the end of your birthday, and unwrapping it slowly to have the surprise again, or something close, never quite the same, but not too bad and definitely worth a go on a long night.

I take a step or two on the landing and I know what's up. I'm heading for Jude. I think I could find him in a room with no lights, easy. When we walk together, sometimes we veer into each other, not quite crashing, it's more of a gravity thing, I believe. I'm not that well up on gravity yet and I have written the word in my Questions Notebook, the one I am filling up too quick which is why I do tiny writing, in the Brontë manner. I have read two books so far about the Brontës, a family of three sisters, Charlotte, Emily, Anne, and one brother, Branwell, who all did a great deal of tiny writing in small books wherein they made up stories about soldiers. They lived on the moors, rocky, cold, windy, not a very good place when it comes to health matters. There was a lot of dropping dead up there, especially from consumption, anxiety and too much walking in cold weather, and too much drinking at the Black Bull Inn in the case of Branwell, a great worry to his family who sat up waiting for him in darkened rooms, waiting for him to come home, and then waiting for him to stop raving in tussled sheets, raving from too much walking and drinking, etc. Branwell was a bit of a lost cause in all callings in life, and he took it to heart in the end, I guess, and even in his heyday of making a stab at things, when he painted a portrait of Charlotte, Emily and Anne with himself among them, he scratched his own face right out of the painting, which is a sad thing, one of the saddest.

Consumption. I add this word to my Questions Notebook. Consumption does not sound like a doomy disease, it sounds like what a person does to a peanut butter sandwich. I write it in near Gravity, making sure to leave enough space for notes and answers. My notebook is filling up fast. It measures 15 x 10½cm and the pages are sewn to the binding, not stapled. The cover has a painting of an olden times boxer with no gloves on and my dad gave it to me.

'That's Daniel Mendoza,' he said in a proud voice meaning there is more to come, more information regarding Mr Mendoza. 'He was Jewish, a Jewish boxer.'

I knew it. I take a look at Daniel who is putting up his dukes though there is no one else in the painting to box and I feel proud also. Maybe Daniel is practising. He is ready, always ready and he knows all the rules for boxing. He is a gentleman boxer. And maybe Jude is wrong, I can be a sports writer too, it's not only a man job.

Gravity. What did Ben say? Pull, there is pull in gravity and a field where the pulling happens. Gravity is not just about not falling but about forces also, forces in a gravitational field, that's it, and I think there is one between Jude and me, one I aim to fight because Jude is not in the mood for Jem today, I can tell by the smoky bacon crisps joke he played on me, a pushing-away joke, not a Jem-and-Jude-together joke, which is much nicer, close to a friendly cuff on the arm whereas the pushing kind makes my ears ring. Everything is messed up in our house and Jude is edgy, he does not want to be with me. Travel is important.

I move on past Jude and Ben's room quick sticks. Jude is in there reading and thinking, going way past me in terms of world knowledge. I don't care. I move on downstairs and across the kitchen, staring down at the red tiled floor and frowning like I have some great purpose in mind but mainly I do not want to see Lisa, I am not in the mood for Lisa, though I cannot help tossing some info her way before making it out the back door. Lisa is laying fish fingers in rows on a grill and cutting up broccoli for our supper, without separating the treetop part of the broccoli from the stem part. Harriet does not eat treetops and she is going to get depressed. Treetops are for birds, she says. She eats a broccoli top and all she can think about is a mouthful of dear birds and Lisa ought to know that by now. I glance swiftly at Gus who is in his pen, which resembles the sea lion cage at the zoo, a pen with no roof due to tameness of sea lions, and he is playing with his rubber hammer, tapping thoughtfully at the frame of his cage like he is doing repairs or something.

'Mummy was UPSTAIRS,' I tell Lisa. 'She is in her room getting ready!' I say, barging out the back door, not even looking at her as I speak, knowing she knew all along where Mum was and was too bloody to say so, bloody. I am on to Lisa and I am fed up with that pocket business.

I tuck my crisps in the bushes in case of robbers/animals/accidental crushing by passing feet, and I climb up into our tree, Jude's and mine, the tree with twisty limbs and no fruit to bruise that is a great commando lookout, planted not far from the back door and right at the edge of the big garden for full strategic viewing in many directions all at once. A soldier will always find a lookout post, it's the first thing he does, the very first. I can see everything from up here.

Jude and I read up here, lying back on the branches as if they were sofas in the living room. I prefer it with Jude, like crossing the road or riding a bike, I do it with him and I don't think about crashing or calamity. I get the wobblies up here and there is Jude to grab my elbow, calm and firm, and I'm OK, no falling. Alone, it's weird. Climbing the tree, I have to concentrate hard on each step, put your foot there, Jem, now there, hey, is that how we usually do it? Hold tight, do I always hold this tight? Suddenly I am all conscious of handholds and footholds, same as when I wear my summer hat with the strangly elastic and go all conscious of swallowing. And I even forgot to bring reading material. I'll just have to do some more thinking. Fuck-hell. I'm tired out today.

Ben is at Chris's house, he went there straight after our trip to the shops, I don't know if he will come home for dinner, meaning Lisa will seem about three times the size she usually is. Looming. When Ben is around on Mum and Dad nights out, I don't notice Lisa so much, she is just regular-sized, even when hovering in the doorway of the study after supper while Ben and Jude and I watch some not-allowed telly programme, Lisa standing there on the side-lines whimpering, and hauling out a hanky from her pocket to pat her eyes, a hanky being the only thing that's ever actually in her pocket, I guess. Lisa weeps no matter what we are watching, even if it's a horror film or a film with larks, a comedy. Maybe there is no TV in Portugal and for her, all telly programmes are strange and sad.

When Harriet and Gus are stashed safely in their beds, and I sit up close to Ben with Jude lying on the floor, it's a good time and if Lisa shows up to lurk in the doorway, we say, Come on in, Lisa, come in, and she never does. I am busy, she says, I am just leaving, but she always stays a while, patting her eyes with a hanky while Ben and I dig each other in the ribs and get a pain from holding in hysterics. If Ben is not there, but at Chris's house, it's no fun and watching Lisa in the doorway makes me sad and kind of cross and I give up on telly, going for *Tintin* books instead, to read in bed by torchlight so as not to wake Harriet. I hold out hopes for not waking her, but she usually knows if I am reading and will do two things to annoy me. 1) Slowly rise up from under her sheets with one outstretched arm and pointy finger and very straight back and wide-open stary eyes after the manner of Egyptian mummies in a spook film she once saw, the only ten minutes of horror film she has ever seen. This slow rise and pointy-finger act can have a terrible effect on me and Harriet loves that. Here is the second annoying thing she does. Pop right up from pretend sleep and wave her little arms around yelling Boo! Even if I am expecting it, it gets me. If it doesn't get me, I must act scared anyway or Harriet will feel a big failure in the horror department.

Chris is Ben's best friend and I am pretty sure I want to marry him although he doesn't know that, I don't think you can tell a person a thing like that when you are not in your prime, and especially not when you are a girl. It's not a girl job. I am a bit worried because Chris will reach the marrying time way before me due to being a whole five years and one month older plus I am going to another country and I don't know how to keep an eye on things from so far away. I will have to come back, that's all, and show up at his house and maybe he'll take a look at me and I won't be just Ben's little sister any more, and he'll say I am pretty sure I want to marry you and I won't have to say anything at all on my part. I'll just nod sagely or something.

I think it went this way between Mum and Dad when they first clapped eyes on each other. Not many words necessary to get things going, no weighing up of matters, no decision time. When you have a big feeling for someone, nothing can stop you, like in World War I, in the case of a soldier rushing out to save a wounded friend lying out there in no man's land, and the soldier has only this one idea of rescue in mind, nothing can stop him, not fear, not other soldiers flying in the air around him, exploded by shells and whiz-bangs from Big Berthas (Krupp 420mm) and Slim Emmas (Skoda 305mm), from howitzers and mortars, from all the great guns blazing, nothing. When you have a singlemost desire and no time to lose, fear is like an engine not a stop light, switching on at all the right moments, for all pressing engagements in trying times, for grabbing a tool in the spider shed, for marching up to Chris's front door one day in the future, and for Nelson, yes, Nelson in the Cape of Trafalgar, facing the enemy while not in the best of health, missing bodily parts usually thought vital for a leader of men, one hand, one eye, never mind, who needs two? He has a singlemost desire.

Right now would be a good time for a boxing lesson but my dad is busy. He is probably all dressed and shaved, with maybe one little cut on his face like a war wound on an Action Man. A going-out-to-dinner wound. He will be standing around Mum right about now, drinking his drink and going, Ready, dear? Ready, dear? and driving her a little bit crazy. Five minutes, darling. Why don't you check on the children? Yes, right now would be a good time for a boxing lesson. Oh well. Maybe that is what this time of day is for, figuring out when is a good time for things, I don't know.

My dad does not give lessons in a lot of things, or many lessons in any one thing and when he does, they do not last very long, maybe eight minutes or so and then he's knackered and needs a drink or a tomato on a plate because he has had enough of your company, the only person he wants for long is Mum. When he decides to give a lesson in a thing, it's wise to be at the ready and abandon all other activity. Up in the tree, Jude's and mine, I try to think of what else besides boxing I have ever had a lesson in from my dad. Not much. But that is because we need to learn for ourselves plus we go to school five days a week and we have Mum. And Ben. I don't believe my dad knows how much Ben teaches us.

I'm not tired any more. I'm getting stiff up here.

Here's a thing. Dad is a sports writer and he hardly ever plays sports with us. A football rolls up to him on the terrace when he is reading and he ignores it completely, or he says, Oh! the way he does when the telephone rings and ruins his concentration. One time he tossed a cricket ball at Jude but kept aiming at his head for some reason, with Jude stepping away neatly each time and me chasing all over the shop for the ball and trying to explain the rules of bowling to my dad all by myself, because it was just too many words for Jude who could only say, She's right, Dad, she's right, Dad, while Dad shifts impatiently and says, OK OK OK, to my instructions, and then goes right on pelting the ball skyward like Jude is a coconut on a stick, my dad simply unable to do two things at once, listen and bowl. It was pretty terrible all round and I do not recall which one of them walked off first, dropping bat and ball in the middle of the garden for me to stare at, both of them slamming the door on sports.

What exactly does my father do around here besides sports writing and lying on sofas and talking to Mum, sometimes twirling her about the room in an olden times dance step involving twirls and sudden dips that look a bit dangerous? Sometimes he messes about in the kitchen, OK, and mostly on Saturdays. Other times he grapples with our homework mainly to see where we are in terms of world knowledge. NOT VERY FAR, he thinks. Also, he drives Ben and Jude to school, yelling at them in a jovial manner while shaking the car keys in the air. Make tracks! Shake a leg! Did we get you out of bed, Jude? Keeping you awake, are we? Feel like walking to school? Ha ha ha! It's kind of noisy, but my brothers do not mind, carrying on cramming their satchels in a leisurely manner, with pieces of toast clamped in their jaws and Gus peering at them with great attention and a slight frown, and Harriet raising her arms aloft and crying out What larks! We shall have larks!

which is her new favourite expression from another book Mum is reading to us right now by Mr Charles Dickens, *Great Expectations* it is called, and this sounds to me always like the name of a house but it is not, it is the name of a feeling.

Here's another thing. My dad is good at short cuts and he has taught me one or two. 1) How to tidy up your hair when you do not have a big thing for combs and are in a needing-to-be-neat situation. Step out of sight and make your fingers comblike, as in a garden fork, say. Keep your fingers stiff and push them through your hair from the front to the back, going slow to allow for snags. Too fast and you get a pain in the roots. You can use both hands. 2) If you are not in the mood for cutting and cutlery, here is how to have a sandwich snack quick sticks. Spread out what you want on one slice of bread, peanut butter, Cheddar, etc. Now FOLD over the bread. This way there is one less edge things can spill out of and your sandwich is ready fast, and you need a single knife only, a spreading knife. Lastly, use your palm or a napkin for a plate, or eat outside to reduce clean-up operations. 3) In an emergency, here is how to unscuff your shoes. Stand on one leg and polish the toe part on the back of your standing leg. Forget about the heels. It is too hard and people do not pay a lot of attention to heels unless they have very fine eyesight and are watching you walk away and by then, you are gone, so what. Unscuffing works best on trousers, but socks and tights will do also. Another shoe tip from Dad is handy for when you are bashing off to school in a flurry, or from indoors to outdoors when at school. Do not tie your laces too tight. That's it. Now you can slip your feet in and out, no tying and untying necessary, just as if your lace-ups are slip-ons! Be careful NOT to do this in front of Mean Nun who hates you, or she will say, as she did one time, Weiss! Weiss! Untie those laces and tie them up at once! You are a very lazy girl! Mean Nun is a bit crazed when it comes to shoes.

So these are some useful short cuts my dad has taught me, and I certainly hope he will teach me more as we go along because I am only ten going on eleven and cannot take everything in at once and there are things I do not need to know just yet. It changes all the time, the things a person needs to know. A stranger might think a small girl does not need to know how to box, but that is an opinion among others. I have had just one boxing lesson so far and here is how it went.

'Hey, Jem,' my dad says. 'It's time for a boxing lesson. You will need to know how to box where I come from!'

Whoa. What does he mean? I am getting all kinds of strange ideas about this place, this place where in winter it never stops snowing, which is what I explained to Lucy White, how it snows all the time, all-out snow, nothing like the wee sprinkling of frost and fluff we have here.

'In winter,' I said in a proud voice, in the manner of an Antarctic explorer, 'it snows non-stop. That's how it is.'

One proof I have of this ferocious snowing in my dad's country is from *Victor*, my second favourite comic after *Commando*. In *Victor* there is a story about a dog called Black Bob, who is a sheepdog, not the roly-poly hairy kind resembling a sheep himself who traipses about Alpine passes bearing a tiny keg of cognac for types who have fainted in Alpine passes, no, Black Bob is a real sheepdog, the looking after sheep kind. There is a proper name for this kind of dog and Harriet will know it. All I have to do is slide my comic her way one day without asking anything directly, and she will tell me the name of this dog plus related details. It is not important right now.

Black Bob is good-looking and pretty sleek, a word denoting strength and slimness in a dog or horse, and possibly even a human, and seeming to me a handy word to call upon if I get to be a sports writer. I make a note of it in my Mendoza notebook. Black Bob goes to Canada in this story, though I do not know how he got there from Yorkshire where he lives with a handsome shepherd in a flat cap and waistcoat, thick black belt and dashing little white scarf. I do not know how he ended up in Canada having adventures because I missed out on some issues of *Victor* due to Jude taking a little time off from robbery. Never mind. Maybe for Black Bob travel is important, who knows.

In Canada, Black Bob stays with a Mountie, a Canadian type of policeman in a very big hat which must be downright annoying to run with against the wind. It could fall off, the chinstrap grabbing at the Mountie's throat, or it could hold him up like a sail on a boat. It is not an aerodynamic hat. Jude has explained a thing or two to me regarding aerodynamics. This is no hat for a man on active duty. The Mountie and Bob have a big feeling for each other, close to how it was with the shepherd, a man Bob misses a lot. He needs to get back to Yorkshire, but meanwhile he has adventures in Canada largely involving the chasing of criminals in snowstorms, meaning nearly all the boxes in the story are white spaces except for Black Bob and the Mountie peeping through the snow, and skinny lines scraping across the page at a slant to indicate fierce winds, not very hard work for the artist, it seems to me, when the background is all snow.

The Mountie has a problem. He has a problem of snow-blindness, which I am now quite worried about also even though it seems to be a passing sort of blindness, for storms only. There is the Mountie, suddenly snow-blind, trying to chase criminals with his arms outstretched like Harriet doing her Egyptian mummy act and now Bob has to do everything, catch the criminals, take care of the Mountie, all of it. This is no surprise to me because Black Bob is always the main hero in every adventure, having a single-most desire plus the qualities of calm and modesty, making him an even bigger hero. Nothing matters to Bob except that his master is safe and the criminals not safe. In Canada then, it all ends OK, with the Mountie drinking a nice drink, cognac maybe, and his eyes carefully swaddled in a bandage until he can see straight again, and a fire going in the log cabin. There is no box to show him doing all this, feeling his way around the cabin and so on, so Bob must be the one who poured the drink, lit up a fire and wrapped the Mountie's snow-blind eyes. There is no one else. Stories in comics are not always very realistic. Never mind.

It is possible I need to learn boxing because of criminals wandering around with bad intentions in concealing snowstorms, though I doubt it, I think this is just another cowboy lesson from my dad, another sign of his anxiety regarding me and my convent life and the weakening effect it may be having upon me. Don't worry, Dad.

Here is where my first boxing lesson takes place: in the kitchen at the end of my dad's day of sports writing. Here is why. When he gets fed up, and tired of teaching, he can turn around and, lo! there is Mum making dinner, Mum, his all-out favourite relief from everything, sports writing, giving lessons, talking to kids. Here is what else he needs after a lesson. A drink. I notice he already has one poured and waiting, right there on the kitchen table.

My dad stops me as I amble across the room.

'Hey, Jem. It's time for your first boxing lesson. You will need to know how to box where I come from!' Then he goes, Ha ha ha! but I take it pretty seriously, that's how it is with me.

'OK, Dad.'

I put my book on the white oak table, far far from his Scotch glass, so as to allow for spill situations which are quite regular with him. And that is the moment I realise the lesson will not last long and I might as well take a chance on my dad as teacher and not ask too many questions. Spotting the glass and making this time calculation is a sleuthing activity, something you can do about people the more you stick with them and get to know things. It is possible to sleuth strangers also, and it is good practice, though you cannot always be sure where clues lead. *The Adventures of Sherlock Holmes* are very good and they are written by Sir Arthur Conan Doyle, who was first a doctor and then a writer and then a man who died of heart failure. I wonder did he see it coming, with his medical insight, and was that better or worse, to see it coming? Sherlock Holmes is a top unofficial sleuth and sleuthing is his chief preoccupation, whereas Tintin, another unofficial sleuth, also has a dog, and later on he meets a sea captain, and for the companionship of le Capitaine and Milou, I believe, Tintin has gentler manners and a less edgy temperament. OK.

'Right. Now. Take a stance!' says Dad, jumping around in front of me.

I stare at my dad. What is he talking about? He is going to have to do better than this. Teaching is not his big thing, I can see that.

'What do you mean, Dad? Where?' I look around for what he might mean, I look around for a stance.

'Get into position, Jem! Stay loose, drop your shoulder, bend your knees, so you're a moving target, not so easy to hit, get it?'

'Oh. OK.' I bend my knees and hold up my fists just like Daniel Mendoza the Jewish boxer on my Questions Notebook. I feel a bit silly, my knees pointing in opposite directions and my chin in the air.

My dad is laughing at me, he laughs at my stance, ha ha ha! 'Jem, remember Cassius Clay? We saw him on TV, remember?'

'Yup,' I say.

'He dances around the ring! He does the rope-a-dope. Right? Right!'

'Oh, Dad, that's so ridiculous, rope-a-dope, what does it mean?'

'Just do it, Jem! Dance around, stay loose, come on!'

My dad is getting a bit testy. His drink is waiting and my time will be up, cut the questions, Jem. 'OK then!' I say. I dance around.

'Now. Very important. Always, always hold one hand in front of your face. Make a fist and hold it there. To protect your face. Most fights end with head injuries. Use the hand you don't write with. Go on! I'm a southpaw, I hold up my right. Got that?'

'Southpaw?' I can't help it, I have to ask. If he is going to use technical terms, I will need to understand them, that's how it works in teaching.

'Leftie, I'm a leftie!'

'So I'm a northpaw then, am I? Um, whatever's your best hand is what you are? Or, does everyone have a north and south? Is it for sports only? Or what?'

'No no no! It's a word for the left-handed, all right? And only if you are left-handed,' says my dad scraping both hands through his hair and breathing in and out noisily.

'That doesn't seem right, Dad. Are you sure?'

I think about Horatio, Lord Nelson, probably born right-handed and suddenly with no choice in the matter and I wonder if it counts, if he is never really a true southpaw because in his head he is always reaching for things with a hand not there, his right, and always looking to one side for a man he can never have again, a right-hand man.

'Jem! Come on, I'm teaching you, goddammit! Stop standing there like a goof!'

'OK, sorry.'

I hold my left hand up, my southpaw not a southpaw because I am right-handed, making it just a regular paw, I guess, I hold it right there in a fist shape in front of my face. I dance around, doing the rope-a-dope, bloody, I do it all for my dad who is looking happy now.

'Great! Let's go. Try and protect yourself, remember? Now – BOX!'

Then my dad pushes my left hand, which is protecting my face from head injury, right into my face.

'Hey!' I shout. 'You can't do that! Unfair! And that hurt!'

'Ha ha ha! You were holding it too loose! It didn't really hurt, did it?' he says, ruffling my hair. 'I said hold your fist up but don't forget about it, or that'll happen every time. I didn't need to punch you! You knocked yourself out! End of lesson!' he adds, turning away to collect his drink, walking close to Mum and standing next to her with his back against the kitchen counter and his legs crossed at the ankles, reminding me of one of the dark-haired boys in Lisa's photograph, leaning up against sunny white walls, and feeling jaunty. My dad tricked me and he feels jaunty and he has gone right back into boyhood, I think so.

'Not fair, Dad,' I tell him, settling in at the table with my *Tintin* book. I'm not mad though.

'That's right, Jem! Not fair!' he says, real pleased. 'Tough bananas!'

'Thems the breaks?' I ask.

'RIGHT!' he says, sliding an arm around my mother and squeezing her tight.

I'm not mad at my dad, though I have changed my mind about this being a good time for another boxing lesson. I'm not in the mood. And my dad knows I am not going to join the boxing profession, he is just training me in cowboy toughness, he trains us in games and by other methods, by way of documentaries and little speeches. When he mentions the Holocaust for instance, he gets a grave look which is a warning to us, that's all, a reminder to keep on our toes and hold that non-writing hand up in front of the face, don't let it go loose and limp, keep it in a fist shape, just in case.

My dad reminds me of another commander. He reminds me of Julius Caesar in some ways. In his prime, Caesar was a soldier and then he became the first emperor of the Roman Empire whereupon he messed up and lost control of things. Julius had no time out between commanding legionaries and ruling a whole empire and he got that lost feeling when it was just not timely.

When Caesar was a soldier and at his best, his men were devoted, as Mum would say, meaning they would do anything for him, go anywhere, no matter what, no questions asked, no Who started this war? or What are we doing here? or Maybe we should just go home. No doubts. There was fear of the sensible kind but no cowardice in Caesar's army because of trust and devotion on the part of the men, and because Caesar had great expectations. On the eve of a battle, he exaggerates the might of the enemy, that is Caesar's trick, and suddenly his men have twice the might, out of pride and so on, and they smite the enemy in half the time, a breeze for them since they expected to be smitten themselves by an enemy so much greater, Caesar had said, in numbers and in might. It's a good trick.

Smite. This is a little bit like wot, having two meanings to bear in mind, usually very easy to tell apart. Smite is largely an olden times battle term so when Mum says I was smitten! there ought to be no confusion. She does not mean she was assaulted by battleaxe, halberd, poisoned arrow, javelin, sabre, scimitar, crossbow or mace in a field of battle, of course not, she means she had a very nice feeling due to something a person said or did in her presence. I hope she will be smitten by me one day, for something fine I do or say, because she is so happy when she says it, I was smitten! like she is about ready for song and dance.

My dad and Caesar are the same in some ways, not all. Dad may exaggerate the might of the enemy but he is in his prime as ruler, with no lost feelings, quite unlike Caesar who kept looking back in a wistful manner during his days as ruler, days that came upon him too quickly, and spent musing on the good trick he played on his men and on his prowess in commanding soldiers who were smitten by him and his leadership of soldiers. He wants his old job back. He can't have it.

The Caesar method of facing the enemy is not uncommon. My swimming master has the same idea. In his opinion, the enemy here is fear of water, a fear he supposes to be lurking in every girl. This belief is the main influence on his teaching method. It could be worse. My friend Lucy White told me something very interesting one day on the way to swimming lessons and I summon up this thing she said when I am in the middle of a swimming lesson and am suffering horribly from the Caesar method. I am not sure I had fear of water before, but I think it's coming.

It strikes me swimming baths would make a very good setting for a horror film, what with the non-stop scary echoes and shrieks giving me a pain in the ears, and shards of light bouncing off the water and ceiling and walls, hurting my eyes, sharp as needles. Swimming master prances up and down, always laughing and yelling out instructions, no pausing, and I wonder if he is like that at home, yelling and laughing and giving his kids a headache because he thinks maybe if he falls quiet no one will know what to do any more, or how to do it, his family now a gaggle of lost souls wandering the house in a state of perplexity, sometimes stopping in front of him to gaze his way in a pleading manner, just waiting for him to start yelling and laughing instructions.

'HOLD ON!' he shouts. 'LINE UP! KICK! KICK! KICK! PUT SOME LIFE INTO IT!'

This means it is time to swarm against one edge of the pool and hold on to the edge and kick up a storm of water. This is quite a horrible experience. Clearly, life for swimming master = a great deal of frantic activity and noise. Jude lying on his back and staring at the ceiling in deep thought, for instance ≠ life. Now swimming master strolls up and down the deck doing his favourite thing, filling a bathing cap full of water and dashing it over our heads from a great height. Filling and emptying, filling and emptying. Why? He wants us to overcome our fear of water by all-out exposure and heavy attack by water. Soon we will all be cured of water fear.

'WATER IS SAFE AS HOUSES!'

I have a different feeling though, involving a desire never to be in a swimming baths again while I walk this earth.

In the next part of the lesson we have to about face and let go. 'LET GO!'

Off we go into the open, grappling on to a white polystyrene slab and kicking like crazy. The slab is a life raft but this is only an afterthought, the main thought is how it is meant to lead you into real swimming so that before you know it, you simply cast off your slab and there you are, swimming, like in a miracle involving crutches then no-crutches. Yay! There is probably something wrong with me because this never works and I am still very far from the miracle stage. My polystyrene slab flips up in the air in a grotesque manner and bops me on the head on the way down, falling out of reach so I have five or six near-death situations a lesson, with swimming master hauling me out of the water each time, by one arm only, laughing and yelling and nearly wrenching my limb out of its socket.

'TRY AGAIN! THERE'S A GIRL! DON'T GIVE UP!'

Why not? I can't wait to get home. I can't wait for the whistle signifying the end of the lesson and friendly cuffs and slaps on the back from our teacher who is so pleased to be battling fear of water on our behalf. He must be proud of Harriet. I am. Harriet swims like a fish. I see her in all the commotion, floating and flipping around happily, no struggling, just about ready to pass up on the polystyrene, an amphibian perhaps, a duck-billed platypus, I have learned about those, equally happy on land and water, amphibian. My sister swims like a fish.

I do not. I just don't see it, this business of floating and so on, of larking about in water like it is a proper home for a human,

water see-through as air but SAFE AS HOUSES! Maybe the
Caesar method is a problem for me, simple as that. It could be
worse though, it's what I tell myself ever since the day Lucy White
informed me how some kids learn to swim, a day we were waiting
with Harriet at the convent gates, waiting for Mrs White to meet
us and take us to the baths.

Harriet is on a wee wander roundabouts. I keep her in my field
of vision.

'Kids are thrown right into the pool,' says Lucy. 'Or the sea.
And they swim because they must. Otherwise they sink and die.'

'That can't be right,' I say, frowning.

'Oh yes.' Lucy knows.

This would definitely save a lot of time, I think. One lesson.
And Mum would not have to come on a bus and collect us once
a week. Maybe we could even skip out on the single lesson and
learn only when truly necessary, in an emergency situation such as
a sinking ship, or a fall from a Hawker Hurricane shot down over
the ocean in a dogfight whereupon we wait for rescue in the freezing
waters, doing the dog-paddle. You swim or die, it's a mechanism,
coming naturally as breathing, unless you are not a regular person
and are missing this mechanism, in which case you die. It is not
always easy to tell who is regular and who is not which is why we
need lessons, I guess. Just in case.

'Anyway,' says Lucy. 'It's a bit cruel but it happens. In some
cultures.'

Lucy knows about cultures, she is half-Indian. I am half-Jewish,
maybe more than half.

'Please don't tell Harriet, OK? The swim or die thing. Please.'

Harriet is sitting under the conker tree, perched on her towel
with her bathing suit furled up neatly within, elbows on knees and
her little face in her hands and her straw hat hanging by the elastic
around her neck and tipped right back over the shoulders like she
is a Mexican in a Western. My sister clearly is not bothered by
elastic. She doesn't get that strangly feeling. She calls out to me
suddenly.

'A straight line is the shortest distance between two points! Sister
Martha said!'

Though she does have the swim mechanism, my sister is definitely not a regular person.

'Great, Harriet!' I call back.

'Why not?' asks Lucy. 'Why can't I tell her?'

Not can't, I think. Shouldn't. Anyone CAN tell her. Anyone could. 'Just don't,' I say. 'She won't like it. Please.'

'OK – oh! There's Mummy!' says my friend and we pile into the car, Harriet in front where she will chirp away at Mrs White the whole journey. Harriet and Mrs White are friends. I feel glad we are learning to swim in a lessons fashion and not the toss into a pool and hope for the best fashion. I am also glad my dad is not apprised of this last method, as it might fit into his style of teaching. Maybe he does know. Maybe he suggested it to Mum.

'No, darling. I don't think so. No,' she says.

Mum is the only person he obeys at all times, no problem, and that is the third thing I am glad about.

If I lose my grip up here without Jude, if I give in to the force of gravity, I will fall splat on to the stone terrace below, falling in a straight line, unless of course I am thrown off this line by a protruding branch on the way down. I doubt it. I think I will fall in a straight line which is the shortest distance between two points. If this happens, there will be a lot of crying plus a funeral and then maybe no one in the Weiss family will go to my dad's country, the place where he has roots, because the Weiss family will be in shock and travel will not be that important any more.

I may skip dinner. I may just stay up here all night until someone finds me. I may have to scoot down and grab my chicken curry crisps from the bushes in case of starvation and climb back up again. Maybe Mum is saying, 'No, I cannot go out to dinner without saying goodnight to Jem! No! Jem? Jemima? Je-MIII-ma!'

No answer.

Soon comes the search party and men in uniform spraying torchlight all over the back garden and dogs sniffing the air and pulling hard on the leashes so the men lean backwards as they walk, digging their heels into the dark ground, arms at full stretch. The dogs are hunting me, like I am an escaped prisoner of war and have nearly made it to Switzerland and when I am found, there will be bear hugs and everyone will stick by me, everyone will stick together, a little lost for words, thinking deeply, counting lucky stars, it's been such a close shave.

I recall stitches under my chin, six of them, three years ago, and a car ride back from hospital and a big white bandage and everyone speaking soft when I got home and giving me careful looks, kind of shy. Harriet even did me some dance steps, a jig, a celebration, because my six stitches, I suppose, could so easily have been two hundred. Do you need anything? I'll get it! Don't move, stay right there, Jem. It was a close shave. It can happen so quickly. Sometimes people need reminding.

It's really not much of a drop. I'd get a few scrapes, that's all. Or I might mess it up and things will end in maiming and paralysis and being pushed around in a wheelchair whereby there goes my career in sports writing, a roving type of job, though not a girl job according to Jude, who may be wrong for once.

I think about supper and how if I am not there Harriet will be oppressed by broccoli because Lisa will try to make her eat the tops as well as the bottoms and Harriet will not know what to say. If I am there we can do a broccoli exchange, my bottoms for your tops. Without me, it's a problem. Here's another. A picture of Mum with a worried look – Where is Jem, where is Jem? – a picture that gives me a rushing pain in the chest. And one more problem. I have to pee.

Someone's coming. It's Jude.

'When are you coming down?' he says.

Whoa. I watched him all the way since hearing the back door slam, all the way along the path and he never once looked upwards. He just knows I'm here. He knows.

'Why?' I ask, sounding breezy.

'Just wondering,' he says, strolling to the edge of the terrace to gaze deep into the back garden, stuffing his hands in pockets. 'Oh yeh. Forgot to say. Got something for you. Black Cat, two pieces, all yours.'

Black Cat gum is my favourite, liquorice-flavoured. It is very good gum. Jude probably stole it when Ben was paying for the crisps.

'I might come down in a bit. Well, I was coming down anyway, actually.'

'We need to sort our Action Man stuff,' he says. 'For the ship. I've already started.'

I climb down. I pick up a twig and swish it about and don't look at him. I try to sound as bored as Jude. 'I'm free now. I could help.'

'OK, let's go,' he says and we head for the back door.

'Jude, do you think I'm a lost cause? I might be a lost cause in everything, do you think so?' I forget to sound bored. I sound lively.

'Yeh . . . probably. Hey. You left your crisps in the bushes.'

'Oh right, thanks,' I say, dashing back for them. 'Wait for me.' Jude waits. 'Don't eat them before supper,' he says.

OK, Jude.

Hope is not a problem for the starmen any more and pride is not a problem for them either. It is never a problem. They have no time for modesty, which is very time-consuming. Pride is definitely not a problem for many scientists and this is a help to them because there ought to be no distractions in this business of making discoveries which is a full-time job chiefly requiring hope and foresight, and it is why the men at NASA fell apart only very briefly when they discovered a flaw in the most perfect mirror in the world and were able so soon to turn calamity into triumph, instead of slamming the door on NASA and maybe wandering off into forests without shoes.

Edwin Hubble, champion boxer! war hero! publishes a paper with his colleague Milton Humason in 1929 on what he discovers to be an expanding Universe, based on thoughts to do with redshift and distance, and in it he is largely removing the vagueness in previous speculations made by Georges Lemaître two years earlier, but he never mentions Georges, not once, Georges who was an ordained priest before taking up astronomy, a pursuit interrupted by the Great War in which he won *La Croix de Guerre avec palmes*, a great distinction in my opinion, though he may well have preferred something else, a telescope in his name, a theory, rules and laws.

The recession velocity of a distant galaxy, its redshift, is directly proportional to its distance. Hubble's Law. The number representing the rate at which the Universe is expanding = Hubble constant. There is Hubble time and a Hubble radius and a Hubble diagram and there is the HST, the Hubble Space Telescope.

Milton Humason went to summer camp near Mount Wilson in 1904 when he was fourteen years old and he fell in love with the mountain, quitting school shortly thereafter and taking on joe jobs when they were building the dome of the observatory at an altitude of 1,750 metres to house the Hooker telescope designed by George Ellery Hale. Milton begins as donkey driver, hauling equipment up the slopes and then he is janitor, then night assistant, until Harlow Shapley takes note of Milton's great skills of observation and his ability to make photographic plates of faint astronomical objects, and offers him a post in 1920, putting him to work with Edwin Hubble.

Humason is shy about his lack of education but he is a great observer, one of the best ever, even Shapley says so, and Hubble certainly knows it, making him do a new kind of donkey work, Humason the one spending long dark nights in winter which are best for star watching, freezing in an observatory open to the sky and lit by a dim red bulb only, so as not to mar the photographic plates, and unheated because currents of convection can blur the field of vision. Because of the Earth's rotation and the vagaries of the clockwork tracking system, Milton must never let go of the telescope if he wants to hold one same object in his sight across the sky, the telescope becoming an extension of him, in step with him, it is him.

There was quite a lot of fighting in the astronomy community of the 1920s, the heat of argument, say, tending to blur the field of vision. In science, these are called debates. Here are men arguing about the distance to the stars based on the observation of variable stars, measuring absolute magnitude and periods of luminosity, unsure whether the nebulae they see are part of the Milky Way or galaxies out on their own, confused by stellar outbursts of light and power they don't yet know are supernovae, signifying the gravitational collapse of massive stars that can shine briefly, each one, as hot as a hundred billion suns. How can a star so bright be so far away? Or so close?

Wishful thinking can blur the field of vision.

When Milton Humason compares plates he has taken of the Andromeda Nebula, he finds minute specks of light in some plates and not in others, variable stars he believes, variable stars Shapley insists do not exist in the Andromeda and so when Milton brings him his finest photographic plate with the careful ink marks mapping what he has seen, specks of light he has been told are not there, Shapley takes the plate away and wipes it free with a white hanky produced from a pocket, making a little nothing out of something, setting his own limits on the possible, an example perhaps, of how pride is not a problem for him.

I don't see it, it's not there.

* * *

Saturday, and you watch the clock you have placed at the kitchen table. You are going to the cinema, you don't want to be late, you are never late. You love the way time works, how one same stretch of time can take for ever to pass or else slip by in a reverie, you love this, it's lovely. Your books are spread out. Homework. Everything is lined up neatly, the edges of books parallel to the rim of the table or at perfect angles to your right and left, leaving fine triangles of table in each corner. You appreciate geometry, straight lines, hospital corners, perfect folds in white linen, you learned this, you have a Brownie badge in bed-making. You are nearly a Girl Guide, the youngest ever. Most of all though, you appreciate words, you can travel with words as with music and the seasons. Change. You even love this word change, it's a travelling word and travel is important.

The soldier marches around the kitchen, keeping busy, he doesn't want you to know he is watching you, he can't help it, he loves to look at you. Frances. He wants to say I won't let you run late, let me do this thing, watch the clock for you, but he stays quiet, tamping the tobacco down in the pipe he will not smoke inside, no smoking indoors, it gives Emily a headache. My wife, my wife, my old pal. In bed now, always in bed, his fault. He tamps the tobacco down, a sound like ticking, sound of the clock you are watching, it's nearly time. The soldier is on the move, fiddling with the stove, stealing glances, like he is more than your father. Soldier, labourer, husband, father. What else? Nothing. Sometimes it hurts to watch you, what does it mean, forget it. Keep moving.

At times like this, he has a sudden urge to travel, not anywhere special, just to ride a train. A friend tells him a person can ride for whole days across this country and see nothing but fields of snow or corn until coming upon sea again, but mountains first, mountains like the edge of the world to stop you falling straight off, or the wall of a trench perhaps, craggy with things, limbs sometimes, and over the wall, noise, a sea of it. Stop that. It would be a fine thing to ride a train for whole days across this country he was not born in, a place he can fit his old country into twelve times over at least, but he walks instead, he walks for hours, fast, because the outdoors is good for him, for his lungs and everything else that hurts him indoors, a pain that can pass as he strides the city, passing sharply, quickly, a view from a train window.

He doesn't see it though, making that train journey, not as long as you are here. He made choices, he is husband and father and he will not leave. He is not sure how long you will stay, it can all happen so quickly, comings and goings, the sea maybe his enemy, and all the things you know, his enemy too, each badge on your arm one step farther away from him, there is hardly any more room on your arms to show all the things you know, that you have learned so quickly, so easily, and meanwhile he knows one thing only, no one goes hungry in his house. He is not sure if that is an achievement, no one says anything, my wife never says anything.

Watching her is different. How can she be right here and so far away? He misses her. She is right here and he misses her. Watching you is different, special and fearful at the same time, a church feeling, there is a word for this, why does there have to be a word for everything? The soldier taps his pipe out and plugs it again. A church word, Creation, Incarnation, what's that word, damnation, ha! Damnation. Bless my soul! Damn and blast it. No swearing, Bert, she won't have it. Don't swear, Albert. Damnation, bloody hell, Salvation . . . Salvation Army. He chose you, he remembers it, marching in, eyes right, eyes left, not at ease but proud, erect, and halted by you because you looked at him, you really did. Yes, please. That one. Sign here.

You are already beyond him, too much for his arms, though he could carry you if necessary, he has carried men, for heaven's sake, dead weight. He thinks he ought not touch you somehow, it's a feeling, that's all. Don't touch. You sit close some days, you are teaching him to read and you are so beautiful, he could never have made you. Don't touch. Awe. That's the word! As long as you stay, he will try to learn but he knows he will not do as well with words as you hope and this kills him, the way the sight of you does sometimes. He remembers signing for you with an X, a leaning cross, and he worries it is not good enough, it might not count at all and someone will be coming to take you away. Coming soon. He knows also that in history, kings sign with a seal, he has no seal, and he knows that all kings are soldiers but not all soldiers are kings.

'I'll be outside,' he says. 'I'm just stepping out. I'll be right on the balcony.'

He is cross today, have you done something wrong? Is it Mummy? It's so dark in there, she can't take the light, she is in bed, hospital corners. Bed-making. Daddy, I can do it for you, lots of things, stoke the stove. Fire-lighting. Nearly time. You have a new ribbon, red, rose red, and you can tie it in your own hair, cleat, half hitch, sheepshank, bow. Knot-tying. You love the cinema, especially right before the beginning when everything is black except for tiny specks of light, electric candles on the walls, faint like distant stars. You have been to a planetarium, twice! It made your heart race, your blood rush. There is so much to learn.

My brain can know one hundred trillion things.

Charlemagne, King of the Franks and the Lombards became emperor in the year 800 but he was a reluctant emperor. He drank little and studied a lot and was in awe of teachers, showering them with honours, learning Latin and Greek and mathematics and how to trace the course of the stars, though he came so late to learning, it grieved him, he will never catch up. He kept writing tablets under his pillow for practice in times of insomnia, because this is the skill he prized most, the writing skill. He was a light sleeper and had high hopes of acquiring calligraphy but he did not get very far, nowhere near as far as hopes.

Charlemagne was a king and a soldier, a man with a particular devotion to St Peter and Peter, he learned, is not a name at all but a Greek translation of an Aramaic word meaning rock. There is so much to learn.

I read that our Galaxy is not the Universe itself, it is an island of stars amongst maybe fifty billion islands of stars and this news has no bearing on me, no withering effect, as much to me as ink marks I can swipe away with one flick of a hanky, hey presto, my universe still the Universe, a place I wander with a slight swagger, a cowboy entering a saloon and heading for the bar in a straight line which is the shortest distance between two points, and drinking his drink, intent on a world all his own, one with no trespassers and no change, and nothing to prevail against it, a place he knows, and upon this rock, he builds it. Everything.

Noli mi tangere.

What cannot be touched can never be taken away.

FOUR

I am on a mission.

I am going to the convent today and it is not a school day and this is down to a decision I made, though all the thinking on this matter was done by Mum. She has this way of throwing out an idea in a breezy manner which is really a solution to all your deep troubles, and you do not even realise it at the time. I am sitting at the kitchen table with a glum expression clutching a *Tintin* book it is impossible to concentrate on even though it is *The Castafiore Emerald*, a favourite.

'Maybe you should go to school today and say goodbye to Sister Martha,' Mum says, pausing in her activities to gaze out the big kitchen window, like she is talking to herself and not to me at all.

I didn't know a kid could do such a thing, go to school on a not-school day, and the goodbye business definitely did not occur to me. Whoa. I sit up straight, same as when Ben showed me the other day how to unhook the straps on my satchel and carry it around by the handle in a grown-up fashion. I spent a whole four years of my life wondering why the satchel men sewed a handle smack in the middle of my satchel flap, feeling pretty sure they made a mistake due to sitting up too late sewing satchels. I check out everyone else's satchel to see if theirs have a handle plus straps. Mostly they have a handle OR straps, meaning I have a downright strange satchel, a thought I had until recently, when Ben showed me how mine is a two-way satchel: an on the back kind which is fine when you are an Antarctic explorer or Coldstream Guard but a bit babyish when you are a mere person, and a carrying around by one hand kind, the man in a suit with urgent plans kind. Grown-up.

'Now? Today? Shall I go now? I'm going to get my jacket!' I tell Mum, jumping up from the table while she rings Sister Martha to warn her, I guess, that I am on my way, and that is another thing I never knew, that nuns can speak on the telephone just like non-nuns though it must be a bit hard for them with only a little part of the ear poking free of the headdress. Not headdress, Jem. There's a proper word for it. What is the name of the nun hat? What is the name for the sit-up-straight whoa! feeling? Word questions go in the Words section. Write it down later. My Daniel Mendoza book is filling up fast.

Whoa. Sit up straight. Not Awe . . . a longer word. It's the word for when the shepherds have recovered from shock and are listening carefully to Gabriel who has just introduced himself very politely the same way he does with Mary. Fear not! he says, etc. This is so they know he is on the same side as them, and not an enemy and now he can get on with Annunciations. Whereupon they all have a feeling denoted by a long word starting with a capital letter, as are most big feelings and situations in the Bible, written at a time people were not so used to words as nowadays, and might not know what's important without capitals to make the words stand out.

Not Awe. Something else. Awe is the Adoration thing, different, what you have to act when you look at the baby, a feeling I will never get right because all I see in the word Awe is a plastic doll in swaddling with flippy horror-film eyelids, a doll held in the arms of a friend who is not a mother and has only been on this earth eight or so years herself, and then I see my sister in a sparkly halo and wings, dancing around with too much enthusiasm. Awe is all mixed up for me now. But what is that long word? Never mind. Anyway, I am not sure it is OK to take words out of religion straight into life in a non-religion situation, so I might as well forget about it. Maybe if you take out the capital letter it is OK, I don't know.

'I'll get Harriet,' I tell Mum. 'She is a close friend of Sister Martha's. Harriet and me could go together, Mum.'

'Harriet and I,' she says gently.

'You'll come too? Great!'

'No, Jem. Harriet and I – not Harriet and me, remember?'

'Oh, right,' I say. I always get this wrong. There is so much to learn, bloody.

Going to the convent on a Saturday morning and wearing Saturday clothes instead of a uniform is a bit weird. I wonder if I will run into Mean Nun who will freak out even though she is not in charge of me on Saturdays, unless, of course, there are special rules about convent grounds and trespassing upon them in civvies. Maybe she is in charge at all times if I am on convent grounds. Oh well. I am not changing my shoes when I get there and she will just have to face the facts. It is the end of term and I am going on a ship, goodbye.

I think Sister Martha will like my clothes. They are pretty cool. I have my suede desert boots on plus my favourite jeans plus my BRITAIN IS GREAT T-shirt, all white except for those three words in black and the Union Jack below it which is our flag, depicting the union of crosses of saints, of St George (red) and St Patrick (red) and St Andrew (white). Nuns are quite keen to teach the flag story due to the saints part. The Union Jack has a blue background and this also has to do with St Andrew. I cannot remember why. Andrew was the big brother of Simon Peter, meaning the apostle skills and fishing skills clearly ran in the family. Andrew died by crucifixion, so maybe blue is for sky, the background against which he died, and for blue waters, because he was a fisherman and because he was a witness when Jesus was baptised in the river. Andrew did some good works in Russia, met his bad end in Greece and his bones are in Scotland. St Andrew is patron saint of Russia and Greece and Scotland. Saints have very busy lives and often do a lot of travelling.

I am wearing my best jacket, my General Custer jacket for special occasions. I love it, I mean it's lovely or whatever. It is coloured light brown suede, almost gold, a lot like Gus's hair. It has snaps for doing up and fringy suede on the underside of my sleeves and another nice row of fringes at the back across my shoulder blades. There is a silky lining, same as the borders of Harriet's ex-pink blanket. There are two problems with this jacket. 1) I once fell into a bog while wearing this jacket and it bears a small dark stain of bog on one cuff no one will notice except upon close inspection or else if Jude sees me in the jacket and reminds me how I fell into a bog while wearing this jacket. In a showy voice.

'Hey, Jem. Remember when you fell in the bog?'

'Yeh-yeh,' I usually reply, like who cares.

I do remember though. I remember trying not to cry, not because

I hurt myself and was going in for bravery or anything, but because this is my favourite item of clothing and I didn't want it wrecked, and I wanted to hide it, my grief over stains and possible rips in the fabric, because I know things are not important, that's what they tell you. People are important, not things, you don't cry over things. Still, when you own a suede jacket like General Custer's, it can feel quite important.

Everyone had quite a good time when I fell in the bog. I did not incur injury so it was permissible to crease up like this was the best comedy moment in my family's lifetime so far, especially in the case of my dad who loves this type of event, a person tripping himself up on the cuffs of his very own trousers or walking slam into a lamp-post while reading a book or losing a battle with a trayload of tippy objects, crash! Ha ha ha ha! This is quite an interesting reaction in my dad, seeing as he is the singlemost unsteady person I have ever met. It is possible he is just happy not to be the only one crashing into things. Now there is me to keep him company. Yay!

We were on holiday when I fell in the bog and Harriet needed some airing in a field because of throwing up all over Mum in the car on the way to a fishing village. I'm not sure there are cities in that country, only towns and fishing villages and rivers and fields in between, some of them with booby traps. It was raining pretty hard and Harriet had been staring at the windscreen wipers for some time, whipping her eyes from right to left like she was witnessing a duel about to start between two people in a frozen landscape. I felt a bit sick myself just watching her. We stepped out for some air, feeling bad for Mum who kept trying to make Harriet perk up and get back on the road to health, etc., which was very friendly on Mum's part, considering she was all covered in barf. That is when I fell in the bog, cheering everyone up no end, and that is also when I thought of Lawrence of Arabia crossing the desert with two small boy guides and one of the boys slips into quick sand, never to reappear, despite Lawrence's long white scarf and a lot of goodwill and encouragement, don't let go! When there is suddenly no more pull on the scarf and it comes away with no boy on the end, Lawrence drops his head in the dune. He is pretty depressed. He has one less boy.

Jude and my dad like to remind me of Bog Day, though for Harriet it is probably Windscreen Wiper Day, a day she recalls being hypnotised by two wipers making a groaning sound on glass and clearing up half-circles of space for Dad to see through, spaces obscured by rain almost as soon as they are wiped clean, a game with no winning in it and a bad sight for Harriet, maybe as if she were waking up on a Monday and wishing it were Saturday, opening and closing her eyes to change the picture, squeezing them tight shut with this high hope, but every time she snaps them open, it's Monday, still Monday.

Jacket problem number two. Growing. A day will come when I must pass on the Custer jacket, but not to Harriet, no, it will have to skip right on by Harriet and wait for Gus. She will not look seemly. She looks seemly in girl things. Why, she even has a little furry jacket and a furry bonnet and muff to match, and in this finery she resembles the child of a Russian king (tsar) and his wife (tsarina) which pleases her much when I tell her so as she has a particular fondness for Russian history involving finery and big chandeliers and revels in fine houses as well as the dark side featuring prejudice and the sudden uprisings of serfs, and the fleeing of Jews in ships, a dark side brought to her attention by my dad when he discussed his roots, some of which are in Poland where we are not headed, Poland that was once in Russia and once in the Austro-Hungarian Empire and now out there on its own. It sounds a bit dodgy over there and I am glad we are not going to Poland. Russian history, however, is now on Harriet's list of dear subjects and she is prone to questioning my dad thereupon, out of nowhere.

'Explain about the fleeing and the ships!' she demands, out of nowhere.

'When you're older! I'll give you a book.'

My dad has books on everything.

'Big fur trade in Russia,' says Jude. 'For hats and muffs and coats. Little animals jumping in the snow. Then nothing.'

'All quiet in the forest,' I say.

'Stop it!' says Harriet.

'Sorry,' says Jude.

'Yeh, sorry,' I add.

I see it for a moment, a Harriet vision of Jude's little animals jumping around in snow, scurrying across winter forests in a light-hearted manner, but leaving tiny footsteps for fur traders to trace, leaving footsteps when they ought to have fled in ships, to clutch the rails of tall vessels on billowy seas and take in deep breaths signifying safety, sailing farther and farther away from Russians waving angry weapons in the air and shouting terrible oaths.

'They ought to have fled in ships,' I tell Harriet.

'Yes, my dear,' replies my little sister in a small sad voice, patting my hand in a soothing manner like I am the one having the bad vision, not her.

It's kind of hot for my jacket today.

Maybe I should find Jude before I go. He will need to know where I am going and how long I'll be, even if he has no outright plans for us.

There are so many ways to leave this house, different paths, and it's weird now, how the house and all the ways to leave it seem like new things and not old things I have known all my born days. I don't know if we will ever come back, though Dad says if things do not work out over there we can come home, except he didn't use the word home, he said here, because this may be home for us but not for him, not really, his roots are in other places, he has to find them.

What does he mean, if it doesn't work out? I have dangers in mind again, things such as criminals in snowstorms and snow-blindness and our ship smashing up in a tempest and my having to learn to swim as fine as Harriet, to swim like a fish or die. And I think about boxing lessons, how they have come to a halt because of the too many questions I ask and how I am all at sea when it comes to facing up to dangers because of insufficient training in the ring. All I have is a stance and it is a bit out of date. I don't think Jude will box me any more. Last Christmas, which is a PAGAN HOLIDAY! according to Dad, Jude and I both got the same gift of red boxing gloves, one pair each, proper lace-up ones with black elastic on the cuff part and the rest all red, and such a blazing red, I believe I was more excited than Jude, though it was strange too, to get boxing-glove gifts, like we were enemies or something instead of twin types in a field of gravity. We have only had one match together. It's too hard fighting with Jude. Here's how it went.

'Here,' says Jude. 'Wear these.'

Jude passes me a pair of shorts from his drawer. They are navy-blue baggy sports shorts for playing rugby in. I feel special but I act normal, like I wear his clothes all the time. Well, sometimes I do, but only when he has grown too big for a thing and then it's not really his any more. This is different. He still wears these shorts. We change right in his room and take our tops off and then we gaze at our feet. We must have footwear. We are stuck. What we need are nice boxer boots, high boots with laces resembling the ones Victorian ladies stroll around in except without heels.

'What do we do now?' I ask.

'Football boots. Take the studs out.' Jude goes over to the cupboard for his boots and picks off clumps of mud, frowning. 'Studs don't come out of these. Forgot. Hmm.'

'We should clean that up, the mud. But, Jude? There's only one pair – so even if they did come out, what about me?'

'We'll have to pretend,' he says, real decisive, gathering up the clumps of earth and swishing the dirt into a little pile and staring at it. 'I'll fix that later,' he says.

'Are we bare feet, then?'

'Yeh,' says Jude. 'Bare.'

We sit on Jude's bunk and I watch him, do what he's doing. I pull on my gloves and we both have the same problem, gloves on and dangly laces with no fingers free for tying purposes. Jude hauls his gloves off by gripping them between his knees and does up my gloves and slips his back on.

'Hmm,' he says again. 'I'll ask Mum. Back in a minute.'

This dressing-up business is definitely taking a while and I'm kind of not in the mood any more and Jude looks all serious and spooky, like he's doing some hard labour or whatever, homework, gardening.

'Jude, let's not,' I say as he is leaving the room. 'Let's play something else.'

'We have to try,' he tells me, wandering off to get his gloves tied. When he comes back he has two rolled-up towels over his arm and he hangs one around my neck and the other around his. 'They always have that,' he says. 'Towels. Oh wait. We need dressing gowns. I can wear Ben's.'

We stop and look at our hands.

'We'll never fit through the sleeves now, Jude! And I'm not taking these off again.' My brother is cross, I am really letting him down.

'You wear it on the shoulders. No sleeves.'

'Jude, my hands are like a mummy's. I can't grip a thing, do we have to? Can we skip the gowns? Please.'

'Yeh, well, next time we do dressing gowns. It's realistic.'

'OK then. Do we fight now?'

'Yuh.'

'Where, here?'

'In the hall,' says Jude.

Jude starts jumping around on his toes and punching the air and breathing out in sharp puffs like a horse in a field, jumping all around his corner of the upstairs hall, doing the rope-a-dope I think, and I copy him, hopping up and down and jabbing my fists at nothing and when Jude flicks his towel away by jerking his shoulders quite sharply, I do the same. Now we are ready.

'Ding-ding!' I say, as I have heard on TV.

'Wait!' snaps Jude.

'What? That's what happens. Ding-ding.'

Jude stops dancing. 'You say our names first. In this corner – in that corner, you know. Then, let the fight begin, then ding-ding.'

'Oh. Isn't that just for wrestling? In this corner, in that corner?'

'Wrestling is fake.'

'I know.' Bloody. Everyone knows that. 'So what are we called then? What names?' I feel grumpy and I have a lump in my throat, I'm always getting things wrong, and this game is silly, it's not our usual game, I don't like it.

'I don't know, forget about the names this time, ding-ding!' Jude says, dancing towards me.

'Hey! I wasn't ready!'

'Come on!'

Jude cuffs me in the shoulder and I stumble slightly, my upper arm aching right away and pins and needles coming in a rush so for a moment I cannot wiggle my fingers or anything. This is realistic, he hurt me, I don't like it. Then suddenly I start to pull myself together and concentrate hard, running through all the instructions for boxing step by step, making a picture in my head and hearing my dad's voice in there.

Take a stance! I do it.

Be a moving target, not an easy one! Right.

Do the rope-a-dope! What is that, Dad?

Protect your face! Oh yeh.

I take it step by step but I am somewhere else already, I don't know where. I am not here, I go missing. I step outside. Back in a minute. And who is that? Like Jude, not Jude, some stranger. I dance, I do the rope-a-dope, my punches will hit hard, right on target, I'm ready. She's ready.

'What are you doing?' he shouts. 'Get close, you're out of the ring!'

I notice Jude's eyes, how they are not grey-blue like mine and Harriet's and Gus's, and bright in a different way from the blue in Ben and Mum, Jude's are a special blue, aquamarine, that's the word, I've seen it on the box of pastel chalks at school, the chalks you only get to use if you are good at Art, otherwise you can only look, don't touch. It is a beautiful box, flat and long with two rows of pastels in sets of colour, all the shades of one colour fading until the next colour begins fierce and dark until five or six chalks later, it is like a ghost of the first shade. I am allowed to use the chalks and I am miffed if I open the box and someone has messed with the order of things. I fix the order of things and then I draw and whatever colour I reach for is there in the right order of shade, dark to light, good. The box is wooden, it is oblong. A square has four equal sides. In an oblong the opposite sides are equal, and so a square = an oblong but an oblong ≠ always a square, that's the rule.

Jude is on the opposite side. Jude = my brother but my brother ≠ always Jude. Ha!

I am losing concentration. I feel silly in my shorts and naked body, suddenly unseemly, and I stop boxing to push some hair out of my eyes, my eyes that are greyer than Jude's, not aquamarine. I say his name real quiet. Jude? But he has not stopped, he is like a toy machine, a wind-up boxing man who has simply not finished fighting and so one red fist slams into my stomach because I have become an easy target, I've forgotten everything, all the rules for boxing. I crumple to the floor, feeling like I've swallowed a big stick, and I can't think a single thought and I can't speak.

'YOU STOPPED! JEM, YOU STOPPED!' Jude is angry, he is standing before me, stiff as a tree, yelling.

'I –' My breath floods back and I start crying and suddenly Jude is Jude again. He yanks his gloves off by pulling on the laces with his teeth and squeezing his fists between the knees and he flings the gloves so they fly through the air and slam against the bookcases in the hall as he falls to his knees.

'Jem? Where does it hurt, are you OK, you stopped, sorry, sorry, come in my room, come on, it's OK, you're OK, come on.' Jude puts his arm around me and walks me over to his bunk, pushing me down, pressing lightly on my shoulders. 'Now lie down, Jem,' he says.

'I can't. It hurts.' I try to stop crying, but the tears just fall, I can't help it.

'Back in a sec!' Jude says, scooting into the hall to gather up all our stuff, the towels and his gloves and the glasses of water and bath sponges we placed there for reality, for the splash a boxer needs between rounds. He scoops it all up like it is evidence of a crime or something, like mud stains, or sweet wrappers before dinner, broken pieces of crockery, dropped gloves, whatever's left when you've done a thing you wish you hadn't, when you stopped being careful, you stopped thinking.

Jude stashes our gear at the foot of the cupboard he shares with Ben and I watch him the whole time like he has answers for everything. I have given up for the day, and I am going to need instructions for all events until bedtime because a terrible injury has happened to me. Jude steps in the pile of mud and dirt he left for clearing up later, he'll fix it later, and he wipes his feet on his shins and slaps the dirt off his legs.

'Fuck-hell,' he says in a whispery voice.

'Bloody,' I say, to show support, though it hurts to speak.

Jude kneels in front of me and unlaces my gloves, gentle but serious, very determined, like he has a lot to do now and not much time and he doesn't want to forget anything, he aims to get things right.

Jude smells different from Harriet and I know Harriet's smell very well, we have a lot of close-up encounters. First off, she has this habit of dancing towards me and around me and then she has that other fancy for flying out from hiding spots behind a door or under a bed and then draping herself over me in triumph like a sporting star at the end of a race in which he has come tops. Also, she will come up behind me when I am reading and rest her chin on my shoulder and read as I read, going in for a lot of little reactions such as surprise and horror and amusement, etc., and I have to try very hard not to get annoyed, bearing in mind the time I shrugged her off and she bit her lip and it was pretty tragic. Even if I am merely a bit haughty she gets offended, limping around the

115

place for ages like some doomed person. I know her smell. Harriet smells like autumn grass and baby powder, she smells breezy. If a person can smell like windy days, that's how she smells, and Jude's smell is warmer, like rocks with moss on them, like earth, sometimes like butter and often like bonfires or smoky bacon crisps perhaps. I don't know how I smell. I'd like to smell like a binocular, especially when it is in the basket at Zetland's and I can make it out straight away in all the other scents there, just like I could find Jude in a whole crowd of boys, I could find him eyes closed the way Black Bob finds the Mountie in a snowstorm when everyone is stumbling around like mummies, arms outstretched, and snowblind.

'Can you lift your arms?' asks Jude. 'Are you cold?'

'Kind of. Yeh.' I sound a bit pathetic. This is permitted. I am a patient.

I lift my arms as Jude grapples with my sweater, forgetting about the vest I had on underneath before we became boxers and took our tops off. He struggles with the sleeves and I struggle with getting smothered, my head stuck in the chest part with only a bit of it poking through the collar where I can feel a welcome breeze, a little promise of open spaces. I try to be patient while Jude fights with sleeves and I contemplate death by smothering. I feel like crying again but it's not because of smothering, it's because of Jude working so hard to fix me and me wanting to help him and knowing not to, and because of this sudden surprise knowledge I have that he is spooked worse than I am about my terrible injury, about slamming his fist into my bare stomach by mistake, and there's a word for this, that long word again, the old painting word I can't think of, for arms raised aloft and fingers spread wide and large eyes, and an open mouth for sound to issue from, a strange sound of crying and laughing and no words.

Jude tugs off my shorts, I mean his shorts, and holds out my jeans for me to push my feet into and then I lie back on the bed, the big stick pain not so bad now, only a tired sensation in the stomach region. I lie back so I can lift my bum in the air and pull my jeans up the rest of the way, and snap the waist snap and do the zip, whereupon I sit back upright and stare at Jude, awaiting my next instruction. I feel like a lamb in a field, but never mind.

'Are you hungry?' asks Jude. 'I'll do fold-overs. And Ribena-milk. Yes?'

'OK,' I say, rising. 'It hurts, standing up.'

'Better soon. Better to move around. Come on, we'll go slow.'

'OK,' I say, thinking about war heroes with shrapnel wounds in their legs and arms, and gashes in the head from bullets that missed the brain by a hair's breadth. I think about an officer wiping the blood and gore away with an impatient swish of one hand so he can see clear to lead his men, showing the way with a wave of his pistol overhead, a man falling apart only when the job is done, and then calling out names of men he recommends for decoration, Victoria Cross, George Cross, Distinguished Service Order, calling them out as he is hauled off by stretcher to have a limb amputated and his dangling eye put out. I think about this all the way to the kitchen with Jude glancing at me like I am ready to collapse in a fainting heap right there on the stairs. I name you, Jude, for the VC, DSO. I name you for everything.

The kitchen has been hit. Big Bertha, Slim Emma. It is Lisa's day off and I picture her struggling over the football pools without me, placing her life savings on the wrong horse because of love and sex, while my dad passes through our kitchen for a tomato sandwich and causes destruction of epic proportions. Jude told me once that there was no field radio in the trenches and observation could be pretty dodgy in winter and messages about enemy placement faulty sometimes, or out of date, and so shells fell too short, gunners bombarding their own side. My dad has bombarded his own side.

The cutlery drawer is open. He has used three knives, one small one for spreading mayonnaise and two huge ones, one for bread cutting and one for tomato cutting. He needs different implements for different ingredients, I'm not sure why, but he has a particular craze for separate implements and it is a good thing we have a lot of implements in this abode. His two big knives are lying akimbo on the chopping board and the bitty knife is in the sink, signifying his contribution to clean-up operations. Why, thanks, Dad. There are crumbs and mayonnaise and tomato juice and seeds just about everywhere, on the counter, on the floor, on the seat of his chair, in a great field around his place at the table, in a neat path between there and the fridge, and on the handles of all the drawers and cupboards he opened for plates and tools. It's a battlefield.

Jude skids quite some distance in tomato fallout, slamming to a halt at the sink.

'Whoosh!' I say.

'Fuck-hell,' goes Jude.

'Yeh,' I say. 'Fuck-hell.'

'You sit, I'll clean up and do the fold-overs.'

I slide up on to a chair at the white oak table, seating myself like I am about four years old instead of ten, remembering how it was when the seat of a chair is a lot higher than your own waist and merely sitting down is an activity requiring some thought and strategic planning, not too bad a situation in your own home amongst friends and allies, but worrying in my first year out in the world, at the convent or the shops, say, where people might look at me strangely as I fight with a door that opens outwards, not inwards and is also on a spring and is going to slap me straight in the back causing me to fly into a room I mean to enter at a seemly stroll. This is why there are no grave decisions to make at the age of four. A kid needs time to learn about doors and furniture, the height and weight of things.

Jude swabs the decks in the kitchen and then he makes peanut butter fold-overs. I can see he is having trouble with the rye bread which has a tendency to snap, not fold.

'Jude?' I say, spotting a magazine Dad left on the table, smeared red.

'Yup.'

'Good thing Dad is not a criminal-on-the-run.'

'Why's that?'

'He leaves SO MANY CLUES. They'd track him in no time.'

'Ha ha ha,' goes my brother, chuckling softly. 'Now. Shall we go outside with these? Or do you want to stay in?'

'Can we have Ribena-milk inside and fold-overs outside?'

'Not a problem,' says Jude.

I wonder if he aims to feed me. Like one of Mum's wounded birds who have flown into windows and fallen splat on the terrace in a daze, or simply walked off the edge of a nest in an absent-minded manner before being awarded their pilot's wings. They are not yet distinguished in flying. Mum gathers the small bird and we settle it in a shoebox filled with hay, speaking very softly as she feeds it very very patiently by way of an eye-dropper. Once, there was a bird hurt beyond rescue and we had to go in for burial services but the worst thing about it was watching the bird ruffle up its feathers and stop resembling a bird at all, just disappearing into a ball with its tiny legs poking out, and so quickly, without suitable warnings such as peeps for help or agitation of wings or any such things. Harriet was speechless with grief and horror.

At school, older kids are sometimes called upon by Dining-Room Nun to feed stragglers, i.e. Babies who have not finished their slops, downing tools in misery and defeat, unaware, quite clearly, of the starving children in India who are of great concern to nuns. I want to put it to Sister Catherine that the little kid is not suffering from disregard for starvation in far-off countries but merely from oppression by spam and bangers and horror vegetables such as swedes which are more regularly destined for consumption by cows and other hardy beasts of the field who have one pastime only, the eating pastime. I saw a cow in a field chewing on a pair of socks and shoes one time. They are definitely not fussy.

I am happy to be called upon for slops duty when Sister Catherine is too busy as I have made a study of my mother's method of feeding wounded birds. I do not have an eye-dropper but I have patience, unlike Sister Catherine who is not a bad nun but is simply overcome by visions of starvation and gets in a muddle, looking deep into her dining room and seeing a workhouse full of scrawny kids, or a desert plain where no crops grow, crowded only by families with eight or nine small children each and no dinner bells ringing. The starvation problem is a mission with nuns and there is no reasoning with them on this matter.

This is why Sister Catherine has no time for waste and will hover over a small child who cannot finish her slops like the little kid has committed a criminal act. She stands there in terrible proximity, wielding a heavy forkload of leftover mush which must not go to waste while the four-year-old is still chewing like a maniac on the previous forkload of mush, eyes wide with oppression, swallowing in painful lumps and listening to the echoes of all the other kids who are running free after lunch, frolicking amongst the trees and squirrels and so on.

I feed the little kid with great patience, walking her over to the window seat with her napkin tied around her neck, and offering up tiny portions of peas the way I've seen my dad feed Gus, turning the fork into a racing car or aeroplane or other exciting mode of transport, and in between bites, I prod the window open a little more, so she can feel closer to home, and because I have the keys to the jail and I can tell the difference between a small kid and a felon. I know this kid is dreaming of home. The kid has a homing instinct. The kid is Harriet.

I remember it, how her eyes glazed over and she fell so quiet as I tried to feed her, I thought about the bird in the box, the one who had death throes and lost her bird identity and became a mere ball of feathers with stiff little legs and no life. I wanted to throw open the windows. Run, Harriet! But she had never worn that path alone. Later, I looked up *homing instinct*, in case of eventualities, in case my sister has to make her way home without me one day. Be prepared.

Homing instinct. 'See migration, animal.' OK.

Migration. 'The mechanism of navigation and homing is not completely understood. In birds it seems to involve sighting of visible landmarks, such as mountains and vegetation, as well as a compass sense, using the sun or the stars as bearings. Land mammals may lay scent trails for local direction finding.'

This may be an animal thing only, though humans are land mammals and this business of scent trails certainly reminds me of how I think about Jude, how I know his smell and so on. Sometimes you look a word up, a word or a person in history, and you get some bonus information, answers to things you did not even know you had questions about. I love that. Jude is a land mammal leaving scent trails for me and my sister swims like a fish. She may go astray but she will not go missing because when it comes to homing, Harriet reads the stars, Harriet is a bird.

'Jude? Where's Harriet? Where is everyone?'

'Oh yeh. Forgot. Mum was going to Jarvis. Took Harriet and Gus.'

'She did? Did she ask if I wanted to come?'

'We were busy. Did you want to go?'

'No. I'm with you. We're busy.'

'Right.'

I hate it though, when she leaves without telling me. I hate it.

'So we're having fish tonight,' I say. 'Fish pie or something. I hate fish pie. It's spooky.'

'You can have something else. I love fish pie.'

'Nice mashed potato, crispy on top and then WHO KNOWS what lurks below!'

'Same with shepherd's pie. You like that.'

'No. Lamb is lamb, there's only lamb in it. Have you seen how many fish bits come out of there? All different? It's like a whole aquarium! The miracle of the loaves and fishies!'

'Jem, what are you talking about?'

'Forget it,' I say, my cheeks hot. 'It's a joke I do with Harriet. You know. One fish, many fish. The miracle.'

'There's no such thing, Jem. It's Catholic, there's no such thing.'

'I KNOW! It's a joke. Why does everyone think I don't know anything! I'm not STUPID! I know things.'

Jude sits across from me at the white oak table, placing the peanut butter fold-overs in a neat tower between us. He speaks softly.

'You're just tired, Jem. Because of the boxing. You'll be OK soon. And you know lots of things. What was the year of the Great Raids?'

'1942 was the year of the Great Raids,' I say, staring at my lap and watching the tears spill there, big drops falling on to my jeans and bursting into smaller drops. Water plus salt. H_2O is the formula for water. I don't know the formula for salt. I don't know the formula for anything else.

'See? I don't know any other girl who knows that.'

'Really? Thanks, Jude.'

'OK,' he says, picking up Dad's sticky magazine and pitching it on to the counter, sending it through the air in a neat arc of flight. Jude is still clearing up.

'The DFC is for distinction in flying,' I say. 'Distinguished Flying Cross.'

Jude gives me his proud look, staring at me briefly and nodding slowly, real close to smiling, and I wonder how many other girls he knows, what other girls apart from Mum and Harriet and me? And what do they know, I bet none of them knows as much as Harriet even, Harriet who is only seven and has the low-down on slavery and ornithology and nuns, as I found out this term, she has the low-down on nuns where I do not. And on miracles. Harriet is not foxed by catechism.

I am waiting for Harriet after school. She is late. I am not worried, because this is not unusual. She gets waylaid. I lean up against the gates and pull out my new book, *The Lantern Bearers* by Rosemary Sutcliff, a very fine book about a Roman soldier in Roman Britain, a brave commander named Marcus Flavius Aquila.

Harriet would not be interested. I read the same paragraph three times, though I am not worried my sister is late . . . Here she comes!

'Hey, Harriet. What's all the stuff?'

Harriet is huffing and puffing and swaying from side to side as she walks like she is a Roman legionary herself, on a long march up a steep slope. The going is hard. She is carrying a paper bag, dragging it behind her in the dirt, and she is wearing her satchel with the straps criss-crossed around her neck and it looks downright ridiculous. She has a big book under her left arm, so big she can barely curl her fingers round the edge, her arm at full stretch. Her tongue is sticking out and her chin is high and she can barely see to walk, what with the strain of it all and trying to keep her straw hat from tipping further over her eyes. Sister Martha was clearly not in the cloakroom when Harriet packed up today. She looks a mess.

'Help! Help!' she says and I get to work sorting out the jumble of straps and gear.

'Harriet, I showed you how to wear this. AROUND your shoulders. Bloody. You look like a slave.'

'Why, thank you, my dear! I am a beast of burden. We learned it today. History of Agriculture. I need to know how it feels.'

'How what feels?'

'Tilling the fields.'

'Oh. What's the book? And what's in the bag?'

'Art,' she says, digging a glass ashtray free of a tangle of ballet clothes and her painting smock for washing. It's nearly the end of term. Our last. The glass ashtray is stuck with flattened pieces of coloured aluminium papers, old sweet wrappers.

'That's terrible,' I tell her. 'Disgusting. What it's for?'

'I am supposed to give it to Mummy. I hate it, my dear.'

'Harriet, let's chuck it. You give it to Mum, she'll be polite and think she has to keep it. We'll have to bury it, that's all. OK? Don't worry. Come on, let's go.' Harriet and I move along.

'I like drawing very much . . .'

'You're tops at it, Harriet!'

'. . . and I like painting. But I will not do sticky-paper ashtrays!'

'OK, forget about it. It's all over. Now what's the book?'

'A prize.' My sister is not happy.

'You won a prize? Yay! That's great!'

'An ART prize. For painting and drawing – not STICKY ASHTRAYS!'

Harriet hands me the book. Her prize is a book of Illustrated Bible Stories. Oh-oh. I flip through it and it's the usual, gishy paintings featuring Jesus standing on hilltops with his hands in the air, busy telling parables and so on to men in shepherd hats and ladies holding little kids, with sheep and donkeys gambolling in the vicinity. There are always donkeys in Bible pictures. This is because the donkey is downtrodden and not very lofty in the animal kingdom and the love of Jesus knows no bounds, etc. 'Harriet Weiss, First Prize for Art' is written in gold leaf on the first page of the book. The Catholic book. Are nuns crazy? I am beginning to think so.

'Harriet, we can't keep this book, you know that, right?'

'Catechism. Don't pay attention.'

'That's right!' I feel proud of my sister for remembering what I taught her, for remembering the word and everything.

'Let's bury it,' she says, perking up.

Not a bad idea. Harriet is smart.

'Jem. Sometimes they say catechism things in the halls. In the dining room. Jesus, Mary and Joseph! And Sister Teresa. Jesus wept! she says.'

'They're just expressions. Try to ignore it.' My sister is making me nervous.

'Jesus died on the cross –'

'Hey! Do not –'

'Do not –' says Harriet, repeating my exact tone.

'– say that at home!'

'– say that at home! And tickly under there!' she adds, tickling me under the chin and darting away from me.

'I mean it!'

'I just want to know – if Jesus can do magic, why did he die on the cross?' my sister asks, walking backwards.

'What magic?'

'The miracle of the loaves and fishies,' she replies, skipping ahead again and flinging a piece of paper into the bushes.

'Fishes,' I say, tired now and not sure how to do this one, how to tell her what's real and what's not. Mum would know. 'What did you chuck in the bushes?'

'Nothing.'

123

I peek in the bushes. I can see what it is.

'A green card. Harriet, you got a green card!'

'What larks!' she says.

Once you are no longer a Baby, a girl has to face up to cards, a regular Friday event at our convent, the doling out of cards and sweets and badges, and at the end of each term, prizes, there will be prizes. Nuns need to keep track of girls, they need to sort out what type of behaviour you are, it's important, and they have a special colour scheme for this. Cards come in three colours, in order of behaviour type. Blue = good. Pink = dodgy. Green = extremely rotten and headed for downfall in the great world.

A blue card comes with one boiled sweet. Your name is called and you rise up and stroll in a military fashion to the front of the class where your teacher is waiting. She is not alone. For the occasion, they haul out Sister Lucy, our Mother Superior we hardly ever see. She has the sweetie-handout job. She smiles. Her smile is on the spooky side, not the kind you match with a smile of your own without thinking, no. Her smile is tense and kind of crazed and I try not to look. Sister Lucy is a cotton top, a very old one, and on Fridays, I am always a bit surprised to see her there, smiling with the big tin, breathing in and out, sitting down and standing up, and shuffling to the door. She may be on her last legs. I have never heard her speak. She may be too important to waste words on a mere girl but my feeling is, she might be falling apart and is simply not good for much, aside from little official jobs such as perching on a chair in your classroom on a Friday afternoon with a big open tin of gruesome boiled sweets in her lap. I am quite worried even this is beyond her present capacities and she may keel over right in front of me. Or Harriet. Harriet is way too young to witness a real live death. The bird affair was bad enough.

Sister Margaret Mary stands next to her chair, possibly in case of imminent fatality, but chiefly in her guise as topmost nun in this joint, as was the fashion in olden times kingdoms wherein the king is a cotton top and is losing his marbles though he still sits on the throne and wears a crown and has all the accoutrements, etc. Everyone else at court hangs around waiting for death, his death, and discussing plots for the future in whispery voices. Meanwhile, someone does the ruling in the king's place, and hopefully it is someone brave and smart with many fine qualities, a sort of Black Bob of rulers who will put an end to plots and sow happiness in the realm. That is Sister Margaret Mary. We are all crazy about her, no holds barred.

It is quite unusual to see Sister Margaret Mary standing still. She stands still on Fridays at cards, and at assembly, for prayer leading, and she is not always available for prayer leading due to great demands and responsibilities and rushing about, attending to all that is involved in ruling the realm which is our convent. When she is not available, Mean Nun takes over and most of us get a bit depressed. Sister Margaret Mary is regularly sighted swishing past in a corridor in a tall rush of nun skirts and a clippety-clop of heels and I get an excited feeling as she swishes past, like I am watching a racing car or a firework flashing across the night sky. Sister Margaret Mary is a bit like Mum, elegant, that's the word. I'm not sure if I will get to be elegant, I don't think so, never mind.

When you make it to the front of the room, it is time to pluck the card delicately from your teacher's hand and curtsy for Sister Lucy, keeping your distance in case of tipping over of either party, one because of extreme old age and the other because of poor mastery of curtsying. Curtsies are mighty embarrassing but very important for nuns. My mother thinks a curtsy is fun and has done demonstrations to help me overcome my horror of curtsies. When Mum curtsys it is like the end of a dance and very impressive and graceful, etc. My curtsy, Ben said, puts him in mind of a person collapsing from shock or heat exhaustion. In the curtsy department, I am a lost cause.

After the curtsy, comes sweet selection. You must hope for the best. You hope for yellow, the only sweet in there that does not taste like medicine. A selection must be made, no pausing, you are not allowed to hover over the tin in a thoughtful and relaxed manner, this is not good convent behaviour. Good convent behaviour means not caring if you fish out one of those oblong sweets wrapped in paper with pictures of fruit on it and French writing, sweets that are possibly highly prized by French people but fairly gruesome to Harriet and me, hard on the outside and gooey within but so what! It doesn't matter how gruesome the sweet, not for a Christian, no! Say Thank you, Sister, and retreat. Unless you have also won a badge in which case you hang about a little longer for Sister Margaret Mary to pin it on your jumper, right over the heart, while saying something gentle to you in an Irish voice, something you cannot make out because shyness and close proximity to Sister Margaret Mary is making a blur of her words, like riding by car and listening to Mum and suddenly Jude rolls the windows down so that the words escape in a rush of air and speed, and that rush of sound is all I can hear, all I will remember.

Badges resemble miniature shields, the crested kind such as knights of the Round Table would carry around, tiny shields with a safety pin welded to the back and coloured in navy-blue enamel paint with a stripe across the front in a lighter colour so you can read the word written on it: Courtesy, Merit or Work. These are the three badges you can win if particularly distinguished that week in any of these special areas, whereupon you wear the badge for the entirety of the following week and everyone can read the word on your chest and marvel at your particular distinction of the previous week. I feel like a soldier except I have to hand over the medal one Friday later and soldiers keep theirs for life, sometimes even winning them after life, when they are dead soldiers, meaning they miss out on ceremonials before fellow men and officers, unless of course you believe in ghosts and can picture them rising up out of their dead bodies on a battlefield and strolling slowly forwards to have medals pinned upon their bleeding chests, strolling together without speaking, in gentle formation, very impressive and graceful, like the end of a dance.

The Courtesy badge is awarded for the doing of fine things such as standing to attention quick sticks when a nun enters a room, not like a jack-in-a-box or anything which would be a wee bit suspicious, but with no dawdling, no trying to finish a word you are writing or capping a fountain pen or reading up to the full stop in a paragraph, tiny hesitations that are disrespectful to nuns who are very sensitive on matters of courtesy. It's a good idea also to listen out for nuns in the hallways and be sure to hold the door open for them to pass on through ahead of you even though they are nearly three times your size and should not expect you to bear the weight of heavy doors. Next, it is important to add 'Sister' to everything you say to a nun, almost as if she won't know who you are addressing otherwise, even if there is no one else around for miles. Sister Martha is absolutely OK with lapses in official measures of courtesy, she is the only nun who understands I am not being rude when I leave a pause in the conversation. I'm still thinking. Most other nuns suppose you have come to the end of

your speaking and have forgotten to add 'Sister' out of discourte-
ousness. In every pause, they are prone to snapping 'Sister!' which
makes it impossible to think at all and rattles my nerves quite badly.
It is fairly easy to run into trouble when chatting with nuns, especially in reply to queries of any sort.

'Well . . .' I reply, gazing thoughtfully into the middle distance.

'Well, SISTER!'

Bloody.

Another way to win a Courtesy badge is to join in the hunt for
Brigitta's fallen-out contact lenses. Brigitta is very tall with short
blonde hair and a cross-eyed expression and she is the first person
of my acquaintance with contact lenses, as far as I know, because
it is possibly not always so easy to tell, it is possibly not always
associated with loss and trauma and national emergency. It might
also be a German invention, I'm not sure, and that is the other
thing, Brigitta is my first German person. Things are not looking
good for me when it comes to Germans, though I try not to muse
upon war and prejudice and anti-Semitism and grievous documentaries featuring Brigitta's countrymen. I try to have high hopes and
a friendly outlook.

Brigitta is not easy to like. She always looks upset for a start, a
frown on her brow and her mouth twisted up like she is tasting
something bad, all day, and it is no wonder, what with her contact
lenses falling out on a regular basis, falling, furthermore, from an
unusual height. I can't help it, she reminds me of Frankenstein's
monster in a film I have seen the first half of, and though
Frankenstein's monster was built in Switzerland, most of his parts
are probably German, in accord, I believe, with the population
count in Switzerland, which is part this and part that, but mostly
German at heart.

Several times a week girls sprawl across the ground, hunting
down Brigitta's contact lenses, with Brigitta hovering above us, her
hands held to her face, looking a bit crazed and helpless. Due to
her height and the hardness of the lenses there is a large area to
cover on hands and knees. When a tiny hard thing falls from so
high, it is likely to bounce and land pretty far from whence it came.
It is like a minefield all around Brigitta. Here's how it begins.

'Oh!' exclaims Brigitta. Or maybe 'Ach!' Never mind. It is the
alarm bell signifying fallen-out lenses.

'Nobody move!' yells whatever nun or teacher is in command.

Any time I hear Nobody move! at the convent, I know what's coming is something horrible, Mean Nun doing a pocket inspection, say, or me having to creep around on hands and knees in search of contact lenses, an activity I am mighty fed up with, and lately when I hear these words, I am prone to great agitation involving an urgent desire to shake a leg and move about in the manner of an athlete preceding a big race or the hurl of a javelin or some such thing, and I jump up and down for a moment or two in this manner of an athlete which is how I stepped on Brigitta's contact lenses one day. The main crime was not apologising straight off, being kind of cheery in fact, and this was definitely not courteous and might be the spark of a new world war even, no joke, like dropping a match in a forest when your mind is on other things, a war can start this way, just by letting a smile appear on your face when it is not appropriate and you are half-Jewish and Brigitta is German and she tells her mother that Jemima Weiss stepped on her contact lenses on purpose, though this is not true and I didn't even break them. Nothing was broken in the end. In my view, war is a state of affairs always waiting to happen and you have to look out for the signs at all times and be on your toes, because when war is not on, it does not necessarily mean peace, for which of course I hold out high hopes, but merely not war, and war can happen so quickly.

The Work badge is kind of a booby prize. It's a pity badge, a person wins it for what they are hopeless at, for great effort in the face of defeat. It's a nun thing. I won it for singing. Very interesting. Music Nun patted me on the head the week I wore the Work badge. Patting on the head is also a nun thing. They ought to get a dog.

Sister Clothilda approaches me and she looks lost, like she has stepped out of a lift on the wrong floor. She struggles with her physiognomy. She is so used to frowning at me in confusion and irritation, she just cannot do it, come up with a smile. She is having a very hard time.

'There, there,' she says, patting me on the head, in a show of pity, I believe, regarding my great efforts at music and my hopeless stand in the face of defeat by music.

'Thank you, Sister.'

'You are not Catholic,' goes Music and Directing Nun, 'but if you are a very good girl, you can be a Christian! I will pray for you. Now run along.'

Does she mean big C or little c type Christian? I think about asking.

'OK . . .' I begin.

'OK, Sister!'

Sister Clothilda looks quite proud of herself now, as if she deserves the Work badge also. I don't like her. She is a bad nun. And they ought to rename the Work badge the St Jude badge. Lost Cause badge. Bloody Stupid Bloody badge. I walk away slowly, my stomach afire and my knees wobbly. I don't run along.

Merit is the best badge and can come by surprise for a piece of work that was a breeze for you, maybe not even your best. I won it once for a dodgy poem I wrote about Lord Nelson, a poem illustrated by me, the words kind of floating in the middle of a smudge of blood-coloured fog, blood-coloured to signify the perils of war, etc. On one side of the poem I drew Nelson in his cocked hat and eyepatch and his no-arm-in-sleeve sleeve pinned neatly to his chest. On the other side were little drawings of naval equipment and the undergarments of a naval officer. I am quite interested in under-garments and find it quite annoying that in books of military uniform, they leave this part out, details of vests and undies and stockings and maybe personal items such as pendants and lockets containing curls of hair or a portrait of a soldier's wife or son or other favourite person. I made tiny paintings of all these things. I also drew the white neckerchief so you can get an idea of how it appears when unfolded and I tried to draw a diagram of folding operations but it looked too much like a dead seagull so I covered it up with some more smudgy red sky, no problem.

The poem was not that good and very short and I surrounded it with drawings so you would not notice straight off how not very good the poem is, you would be too distracted by Art. Most little kids think a poem = short lines with rhymes on the end, but my dad told me Not all poems have to rhyme, goddammit! when he saw me fighting with my poetry homework, and this was good news to me, my dodgy poem looking special suddenly, instead of plain dodgy. Here it is.

Horatio Lord Nelson
Fear could not stop him
Not as a boy,
Nor as a man.

129

One eye, one arm,
On board ship,
Came death
In victory, on the Victory
He took
A last breath.
In 1805.
Farewell.

I threw in a rhyme in case nuns are not apprised of the not-all-poems-have-to-rhyme situation in poetry. It is a good thing nuns have such a big feeling for Lord Nelson and are blinded by Art because that poem is frankly not a prize-winning poem, it is gishy and embarrassing. Never mind. It is how I won the Merit badge once.

Badges accompany blue cards. This means a two-sweets Friday. Two sweets to pluck from Sister Lucy's lap. One curtsy. I save my sweets as they can be swapped for playground privileges. Most girls at the convent consider anything wrapped in a twist of colourful paper a fine comestible. They are not all that choosy, in the way of CATTLE where brassicas are concerned. If Harriet is late to the playground and some fierce kid has staked her claim in my sister's favourite spot with no intention of sharing, holding on to it for dear life for no obvious reason and rendering Harriet wide-eyed with confusion, I note how the sweetie bribe works every time, the fierce kid suddenly waltzing off with the sweets no questions asked, confirming my doubts about the character of some girls and arousing anxieties in me regarding treaties of war and territorial rights and other matters I am learning from Jude.

Pink, green. Trouble. There are so many ways to trouble a nun. Too messy, too dashy in hallways, a wee bit rude or impatient or cross-looking. You smudge your homework and look a bit plaguey, with creeping black stains on finger and thumb, the fountain pen not yet your friend. You keep forgetting to fill in the top line on a ruled page, thinking it is a space for writing titles in, or a nice clear space where the eyes can rest, or a space to leave free just for the hell of it, as your dad would say. And never say Just for the hell of it. This is green card material. The rest is pink. Not writing on the top line is a poor show, same for nuns as cramming some sludgy peas and spam in that little free space beneath your neatly together cutlery. Hideaway food is pink, cutlery akimbo is pink, the latter not a problem for me as I learned this at home in a no-threat atmosphere, so it's a breeze to remember.

'Think of the starving children in India!'

Any old nearby nun will say it, except for Sister Martha who will give me a sly grin when spotting my under the cutlery hide-away peas, because Sister Martha was definitely a little kid once, unlike Sister Teresa who skipped out on that part of life.

The starving children. Would they like some paper and ink? Would they leave the top space empty or fill it in, maybe writing widthways first and then turning the page and writing across the length of it also, getting two pages out of one the way the Brontës did? I have seen photographs of it, pages of tiny slanting script criss-crossing the paper like bare skinny branches against white sky, kind of lovely, this invention that came out of nothing, from being poor with not enough paper to go round and a big desire to write everything down, making something out of nothing, which is cowboy-tough behaviour and close to heroism, I think so.

Cards are oblong-shaped, printed like little menu cards, the no-choice menu kind such as Dad brings back from aeroplane journeys, cards Gus gazes at for some long time though he cannot yet read, nodding slowly and stashing them in his new favourite toy, that blood-red domed record rack of Mum's made from spindly rows of wire. He carries it around and enters a room and perches on it, or else he files things away between the spokes, storybooks, or those menu cards printed so very nicely with destination and flight number, date and ingredients. Dover sole and potatoes, cheese and biscuits, *petits fours,* what's *petitis fours*, Mum? Pink and green cards are printed so nicely, date and ingredients, on this day, for poor comportment, for disobedience, and then the felon's name, written carefully by hand, Harriet Weiss. There are so many ways to trouble a nun, it makes me wonder about blue, how you are never permanent blue, but coloured week by week and you have to stay on your toes, pink and green always waiting to happen and blue not necessarily meaning goodness, but merely the space between, and pink and green can happen so quickly.

I am poised by the bushes where Harriet hurled her green card and she is staring at me, still and tight.

'Harriet. You got a green card.'

'I'm a helot! Jude said!'

'What is that?' I ask. 'Hclot.'

Harriet stares at me. 'Spartacus. He did a revolt. For slaves.'

'Spartacus was a gladiator.'

'I'm a helot.'

'Fine, you're a helot. Now look, Mum and Dad have to know, I mean, we should, you know . . .' Pull yourself together, Jem. 'What did you do, anyway? For green.'

Now my sister relaxes, doing a little Harriet crouch on the pavement, sitting back on her calves with feet flat on the ground, and little elbows on knees, her face in her hands. She says, 'If I could do magic, the loaves and fishies thing, I'd do it with chocolate.'

'Did you tell anyone that? At school?'

'I'd do it with chocolate bears and bunnies, the Lindt ones. Very nice.'

'You'd get sick of it. If you could have your favourite thing all the time, you'd get sick of it.'

Harriet looks up at me, a big slow gaze, like I am some crazy person. 'No, Jem,' she says quietly, in a voice full of know-how.

'Oh,' I say, hauling my sister up gently by the satchel straps. 'Come on then, let's go home.' I make a no-decision decision about the green card, pretending I am not even thinking about it. I'm not leaving it, I'm not taking it. I forget about it, that's all.

Harriet says, 'When we get home, I am going to change and do ballet all over the house.'

'Not in my room you're not.'

'Our room.'

'Yeh-yeh,' I say, distracted, worrying about the green card I must forget. 'Harriet? If you were a spy, you know, and captured by Nazis and there is torture and everything, would you give up the names of your friends, would you tell secrets, what do you think? In extreme pain, when you're delirious or something.'

Harriet scowls. Then she does her lamb act, dropping her head but keeping her eyes lifted to me and butting me real soft in the stomach, she butts me three times. 'Beh-eh, behhh,' goes my sister before standing up straight and walking like a regular girl again, the lamb act over.

What did she do for her green card? Did she say that magic thing? My sister is unusual but she is not bad. I am bad and I've nothing but blue cards ever. I have eaten the last binocular without sharing when very mad at Jude. I have stolen coins for tuck, stealing from Mum's purse lying open on her dressing-table stool like she knew I was aiming for it and was making it easy for me, easy to rob my all-out favourite person, the one least likely to say no to anything. Please may I have some money for crisps today? Just today? When I figure out why I did it, I'll lay cards on the table. It hurts to steal. My sister would never steal. She would ask first.

'May I please be excused?' my sister says at school, super-polite, knowing the nun code for comings and goings and permission to go to the loo.

The nuns let my sister go, even carrying her lunch tub with her, a special delight for Harriet ever since the revolution at the convent heralding days of home-packed lunches. OK, they think, she wants to carry it with her. They excuse her, they excuse her unusual ways. She takes a while to come back, they excuse that also. She wanders outside, not bothering with shoe changes, it never enters her mind. She finds a nice place to sit and then it begins. She opens her very own tuck shop, handing out nice bits of sandwich and carrot sticks to any passing fauna. Is that what Harriet did? Jiminy Cricket, what's bad about that?

I forgot to think like Harriet. I'm losing my mind and I was almost a traitor, thinking like a nun, seeing a green card and believing in what it has to say, this no-choice menu for the ingredients of Harriet according to nuns. Is there a colour for this? Is there a colour for crazy? Sorry, Harriet. I think it is time to move to my dad's country where they may not have nuns. May I please be excused from nuns.

'Harriet? Hey!' I run to catch up with her. She always does that, skips ahead of me. There she goes. Skip ahead, return, skip, return. 'Harriet,' I say in a spooky voice. 'The miracle of the bears and bunnies. THE MIRACLE OF THE BEARS AND BUNNIES!'

Harriet creases up. She snuffles and shivers and yelps like this is the funniest thing she has heard in a while. My sister has a big heart and she has the low-down on many things.

Jude is tops at mixing Ribena-milks. He is the Ribena-milk man in our house. He pours dark red syrup and white milk at the same time, holding the milk up high and letting it fall in a rush like a waterfall to swirl with the Ribena he dribbles in ever so slowly and it always blends into the best shade of pink and there is always a lovely froth at the rim. Well done, Jude. I have tried this myself but pouring at two different speeds is just too hard and the effort makes me a bit frantic. I leave it to Jude. Today, I leave everything to Jude because of my boxing injury.

He sets the drinks on the table and then he spreads out a paper napkin and rolls the fold-overs in it and places the package against his stomach and folds the waist of his rugby jersey over, making a pouch, which is our way of conveying foodstuffs into the outside world, leaving our hands free for important matters. Jude folds up the fold-overs. Do not try this with a flappy old jumper, it only works with a medium tight jumper. Too flappy and you lose your fold-overs. Too tight and you will have mashed sandwiches and maybe peanut butter ooze on your jumper due to compression. Compression = the squeezing together of two things.

Ribena is very useful wherever fake blood is required and Jude and I use it when we are Roman soldiers or commandos. World War II and the Roman Republic are Jude's special periods within his special subject of war, and by now we know quite a bit, Jude especially of course. Playing with Action Men or 34mm and 54mm Romans or being soldiers ourselves can often induce a grave feeling which is hard to explain to strangers. It can arise that a member of your own family can act like a stranger, even just for a day or one part of a day, and this is hard on one's outlook.

One time Ben hid in the cupboard under the stairs and recorded our war game on his little tape machine. Jude and I were camping on the first landing of the staircase as it makes a fine clifftop in Normandy when a clifftop in Normandy is needed. We had scaled the cliff in a night-time op, losing a few commandos in the attempt (all played by me) and when Jude spoke his big pre-raid speech to all his men (all played by me) it was what I would call a grave moment and quite moving. Later on though, Ben played it all back to us in front of Dad during that spooky part of the day when you are slipping out of being a British commando, say, and stepping back into your own body and gazing around at your family and thinking about them and supper and the night falling. It's not a time anyone should mess with, and Ben messed with it that one time, hauling out our commando selves when it was not fitting, and though Jude said nothing at all, my stomach hurt, because I thought he had spoken a fine pre-raid speech but Ben and Dad were creasing up like crazy so my cheeks blazed Ribena colour and the word traitor came to mind as I watched

Ben who had become a stranger for a day. Oh no, not Ben, why Ben?

'Good Ribena-milk,' I say to Jude who sits in his usual place to the left of my dad's place. I am in my unusual place. My place is in a diagonal across from Jude, in the seat to the left of Mum's, not bang facing him as I am now. At non-meal times, we are prone to swapping seats. Except for Dad, who never swaps seats. I look at his place where he is not and it is kind of alive with electrical charges or something, not an empty place at all, but a waiting for my dad space, like star-forming activity inside a nebula. Nebulae are my new thing, thanks to Ben who has a book with beautiful photographs taken by a floating telescope called the Hubble Space Telescope. Not floating. In orbit. It has to be right in space, beyond the Earth's atmosphere, because an atmosphere, says Ben, is obscuring. OK. I am stuck on one photo at the moment, 'Starbirth in M33'. I have never seen anything like it. 'M33 is just 2.7 million light years away from us.' Just, meaning not very far. Close.

'Light year,' I say to Jude. 'Distance not time! And, compression! The squeezing of two things!'

Jude laughs, snorting softly.

'Can we have straws? Are there any bendies?'

'No,' he says, frowning a little. 'I looked. Sorry.'

'I don't need it. I was just wondering. I'm not even in the mood for straws,' I tell him, worrying I am asking too much, like unwrapping a gift too fast on your birthday, eyes on all the shiny packages and coloured ribbons, behaviour that can seem like greed instead of plain rapture and greed is an outright sin, more than a green-card situation, with maybe no colour angry enough, not for outright sin.

'Harriet's the one, you know. She likes bendies very much. Even for water.' Most people hold off on straws for water. Straws are for fancy drinks.

'Bendy straws are good,' says Jude. 'And they don't fall in. If you have a Coke.'

'Oh yeh. Right.'

We are hardly ever allowed Coca-Cola in our house. It is a rare thing to see three little twisty Coke bottles queued up on our white oak table, one for Ben, one for Jude and one for me and none for Gus who is too young and none for Harriet who complains of headaches arising from the fizzing of gases that have travelled to her brain, etc. I was not all that worried about Coca-Cola until Mum poured a splash into a brass ashtray one day and suggested in an airy manner we let it rest overnight and, lo! next day we saw that the part where the Coke had been was scrubbed shiny as buttons on a military uniform.

'Corrosion,' pronounced Ben, taking up the ashtray and bringing it close to his eyes.

'Indeed' I said, in the same serious scientist-type voice. Then I went to look up corrosion and related matters and that's when my worries set in and I turned my back on Coca-Cola. I don't have a big thing for Coke anyway.

'Straws are good too if someone slobbery drinks from your cup,' I remark. 'You can just stick in a straw and skip out on the horror.'

'I hate slobber,' says Jude.

'Dad's a bit slobbery,' I say real quiet.

'It's Dad-slobber, it's OK.'

'I know. I'm just saying. I don't mind it one bit.' I have a sip of Ribena-milk. 'Yum. Jude? Let's not box any more. I mean, for good let's not.'

'It's a bad sport, Jem. A blood sport, gladiatorial combat. It's for slaves,' my brother says, glaring straight at me, no longer lost in his milk, like he has been gearing up to say this for hours, waiting and waiting for me to open up this subject of boxing.

'Dad loves boxing,' I say, frowning slightly.

'You don't have to go for everything he likes, I told you that before, you're separate from him!'

'Sorry, I forgot.' I hunker down and look at Jude through my glass, through a film of pink where my drink once was. I rest my chin on one fist above my left hand lying flat on the table and I feel like a statue on a statue column. Plinth, bust. 'Jude, is a bust always head and shoulders or can it be just head?'

'Not sure. And bust means bosom too. Breasts. It'll happen to you.'

'Yeh-yeh,' I say. I don't want to hear about it, why does he have to do that all the time, warn me about everything in life, I am separate from Dad, I'll be different due to bosoms, rah-rah-rah, and just when I have found something my dad goes for and I do not. 'Dad eats guts,' I say.

'Gizzards.'

'Right. Is that a Jewish thing, do you think?'

'You're Jewish too,' Jude says, kind of stern.

'Half. And in my half, I did not inherit the guts-eating thing. Yuck. We don't have to eat every part of an animal, you know. Vital organs. We're not in a famine!'

'Roman priests examined chicken guts for auspices.'

'Auspices?'

'Augury.'

'You said auspices.'

'Looking for auspices in guts is called augury, the priests were augurs. Auspice has Latin roots. Words for bird and observe. Augurs examine the guts and hold up signs. On the left, good will come. On the right, bad.'

'I don't get it. What gave them the idea to look for good or bad in chicken guts?'

'They also found auspices in birdsong. And in the flight of birds.'

'Right, well, I'd like to learn Latin.'

'Mmm,' says Jude, standing up and patting the fold-overs in his jumper.

Maybe Latin is a boy thing. Like science, and history books without illustrations and chemistry sets and Antarctic exploration and naval duty and sports writing and boxing, boxing too, though my boxing days are over anyway, not only because of Jude's red fist to my stomach but because of what he has seen coming, good or bad, I cannot tell, the two breasts that will happen to me, one on the left and one on the right, and so it will come too, I guess, this end of days of shirts off between us and everything his, mine.

'Let's go,' says Jude and we slink out the back door in that game we play, squashing up together and pressing close to the wall, crouching low, two special agents on the run passing through shadows and moving in one silent shape which is the best way to get around in a dangerous world.

The day of my mission of saying goodbye to nuns, I take a deep breath on the back-door step before setting off to find Jude who will need to know where I am going. It's weird today. I have to keep stopping because with every swish of my jeans and creak of my Custer jacket I hear someone calling my name quite softly. I stop. I undo some snaps on my jacket so it's less creaky when I move and it's cooler too, more Shane-like. I decide to rename this jacket. From now on it is my Shane jacket. I have been having some doubts about General George Armstrong Custer, b.1839, d.1876, dying in the face of defeat by Sioux chiefs, Chief Sitting Bull and Chief Crazy Horse, and largely because of faulty communications on the battlefield and not enough men and no cavalry support which is why he died in that helpless manner, a lost cause waving a sword and a pistol in the air with a heap of men lying dead around him near the Little Big Horn River. I don't know. At least Nelson died defending his country against invasion whereas it seems to me US cavalry and Indians were always fighting for no very good reason, for territorial rights and so on, fighting so often they got in a bad mood on sight and fell into battle on the spot, like Mean Nun and me, Brigitta and me, and where will it end? It's a good thing I'm on my way and it's a fine time to rename my jacket in honour of Shane, an all-out hero in my opinion, though he is not a figure from history the way Custer is, and I like that also, how Shane has unknown origins, b.? d. who knows? Whenever I choose. Maybe never.

Hey! Someone is definitely calling me.

'Jude?' I look up into our tree. Nobody home.

I stand still in the garden, listening so hard I get an earache. I don't hear my name, I don't think so. No sound is the noisiest thing. Same with smells. When we came back from our summer holiday from the place where I fell in a bog, I woke up very early on the first morning and raced outside for some desperate reason I could not make out, and I noted the smell of things and how different it was from the other place and how I had missed it without knowing, like hunting for something you are sure you lost but you can't remember what you lost, you don't know what you are looking for. The no smell of home was the biggest smell in that other place.

There are so many ways to leave this house. I choose the longest, scoping for Jude in the back garden and then crossing the terrace, saying Hey to the statues on my way, the statues of ladies and gents resting on one hip as they haul fish and sheaves of wheat no place with any pressing need for fish and wheat. I wander down the stone steps to the street instead of taking my usual commando route through the shrubs because I need to stay neat for nuns. I spot Jude before I hit the bottom where our no-garage garage is, more of a single-car car park, a grass and stone patch of ground behind fencing and big gates where Dad parks our light blue Renault after getting one of us to leap out and open the gates, action stations. The gates, the gates! He has to do this alone sometimes, when driving alone or with Mum as sole passenger and I bet he misses it, having one of us to yell at in an exuberant manner, and honk his horn at just for the hell of it.

I stroll over to the little gate, the person gate for people not cars and bearing the name of our house in iron letters. Jude likes to swing on this gate while looking out for Mum to come home from wherever and he fell off it one day, busting his head and spilling blood all over the joint, much worse for Ben than Jude because Ben was in charge of us that afternoon and blood is like the apocalypse for him, a word he taught me signifying the end of everything, a very depressing idea and one of many Ben has. He is very sensitive and should maybe choose less doomy and bloody topics to get devoted to, but you can't tell a person how to pick their devotions. I try to get my mind off war, for instance, and it's just no good.

'Hey, Jude,' I say. 'Remember when you fell off the gate?'

'Hey, Jem. Remember when you fell in the bog?' Jude opens his mouth and makes big pretend laughter, no sound.

'Yeh-yeh,' I reply. 'Ha ha, very funny. What are you doing?'

'Washing the car.'

'Oh.'

Jude is sitting by the car, leaning against it and reading a *World of Wonder*. There is not a lot of cleaning activity happening here though there are some rags and brushes and an empty pail roundabouts.

'Ben has to drag the hose all the way down here. I'm taking a break,' says Jude, flipping a page.

'I'm going to school,' I tell him, jamming my hands in my pockets with the thumbs dangling free, cowboy style. 'In case you're wondering.'

'Mmm,' says Jude. He does not say, It's Saturday, why are you going to school? or When are you coming back? or anything like that.

'I'm saying goodbye to some nuns I know. They're waiting for me and everything.'

'Taking Harriet?'

'Nope.'

I did ask Harriet. I said she could come with me, did she want to come with me? and she just raised her arms and did a pirouette or two. Heavens to Betsy.

'I don't feel the need,' she said, finally.

'You don't feel the need? What do you mean?'

This is an expression of Mum's. Any time we are about to settle somewhere for some time with no easy escape route, into cinema seats say, she will ask Harriet and me if we feel the need to pee first, asking Harriet and me especially because she knows convent-girlhood has messed with our timing in terms of activities we never thought much about before, such as eating and going to the loo, talking, and walking around in shoes. When it comes to peeing, for instance, we now believe it is brave to hold on to pee for dear life, as it is good for deportment! I have no idea what nuns mean by this. Sister Teresa also says that when we are mothers we will NOT be able to run to the loo whenever the fancy strikes, we will have a husband and children to look after! Whoa. This sounds hard. It is also a turn of events not coming soon in my lifetime and it seems to me a girl does not have to go in for training in everything all at once, but never mind, I am quite happy to pass up on going to the loo at the convent if I can help it, because they do not have proper loo paper there, it is slidy and akin to the paper Mum uses for wrapping sandwiches and bits of cheese except it has pinprickly holes across it for tearing purposes. Sister Teresa says we may use THREE SHEETS ONLY which is how I locked myself in the loo one day, for fear she might be peeking to check up on me and do a paper count. I use four sheets. Sister Martha had to rescue me and I was a pathetic wreck by the time she traced the cries for help. She gave me a close hug and made a few cracks in an Irish fashion. And the door was not locked, she said. I was pulling instead of pushing. I told Mum my story about loo paper.

'It doesn't work, Mum! It's slidy! Slippery! Not absorbing.'

'Not absorbent,' says Mum.

'Yeh – that!'

'It's to do with the war, Jem. And rationing. Dear oh dear.'

'We're in a war?'

'No, no,' she says, tickling me in the ribs. 'It's a hangover from the war, don't worry, Jem. We'll sort it out.'

My mother sorts Harriet and me out in the loo-paper department, tucking little folds of nice loo paper in our tunics or pinafores before we bash off to school, in folds of four sheets each.

'Thank you, my dear,' says Harriet.

'Mum?' I say, with great authority, 'I want you to know you can go to the loo any time you want. We'll be OK!'

'Thank you, Jemima. I'll be OK too.'

'Right then,' I say, having solved another problem in our house, just like that.

Asking to be excused at school though, when it is so nearly time to call it a day and turn our chairs upside down on top of our desks and pluck the grey balls of fluff from each chair leg in support of Clean-up Nun who is about to sweep into our classroom with rags and buckets, still seems like surrender. I hold it. Hold on! England expects! When the fluff is gone, girls say a prayer to the Guardian Angel which is quite a dreamy prayer, though it is largely to do with a request to Jesus to get everyone home in one piece without kidnapping or death by passing cars. Nuns are not very optimistic. I told Mum about the dust-plucking activity and the angel prayer and how one time my next-desk neighbour Annette Desarthe gave me a forlorn and desperate look before peeing in a long sad stream at our feet whereupon Clean-up Nun was called in for emergency duties. This was pretty terrible. Annette is very dashing and kind of resembles an angel herself, and furthermore, she is French, and they have different expectations over there and going to the loo whenever the fancy strikes is clearly not next stop to the waving of white flags on a battlefield without a fight.

Harriet has no patience for the rules of deportment and will ask to be excused any old time at school, and in a most charming manner, and she would never think to apply a convent rule to the world at large, laughing so hard one evening at home as I asked to be excused, Jude and Ben called out for stretcher-bearers in loud voices. And when Mum says, Does anyone feel the need to pee first? her suggestion is aimed at me, I believe, though she pretends it is aimed at both her girls, and I feel the need immediately as soon as she mentions it, whereupon I have a life crisis on the way to the loo in the cinema, not able to tell where it all begins or what is the cause of things, the need to pee or Mum's suggestion I might need to pee, and wondering if I am losing my faculties due to nuns and is it all too late for me, etc.

'I don't feel the need!' exclaims Harriet.

'But what about Sister Martha, you really like her, we may never see her again, well, not for ages at least!'

I think my sister ought to face the facts about goodbyes and related topics. I don't want her in a heap of tears on board ship in the middle of the night or anything just because she passed up on goodbyes. It is going to be tough enough what with no parks and gardens for ten days or so. I have already warned her about the paucity of flora and fauna, how there will only be sea, and fish beneath, and maybe birds when we are close to land, that's it.

'It's OK, my dear,' my sister says, butting me softly in the stomach.

'So you're not coming? Right, I'm off then,' I tell her, feeling confused, which is when I wander off to find Jude and tell him where I am going.

'I'll be washing the car,' says Jude, like he knows just how long I'll be gone. Not very.

'Bye!' I say, opening the gate and hoping for it to pass quickly, the moment that comes whenever I step out alone, my heart banging and lurching like an engine starting, it's weird. Maybe I have a fault in the heart and am doomed to perish out there in my nice Shane jacket and I should give up on this stupid old mission and stay home to mess with Ben and Jude and splash water all over our light blue Renault, light blue, sky blue, blue for good conduct and for veins to the heart and for Jude's eyes which are aquamarine.

The nuns are waiting for me. Lateness, pink. Gone missing, green. I picture Sister Martha leaning from a convent window, looking out for Jem with a telescope perhaps, like Captain Cook who was so famous for navigation and observation, the Royal Society gave him the command of a ship named the *Endeavour* and a mission to observe the transit of Venus across the Sun, which he did, as I remember Ben telling me, Cook pleasing everyone very much with the observation he made.

'Why, Ben?'

'Venus has a very high albedo.'

'Is that why?'

'There isn't a why for everything, Jem. It hadn't been seen before, that's all.'

'Oh. What's albedo?'

'Reflectivity. Venus is almost a twin planet to the Earth except it has this thick atmosphere and it's closer to the Sun so the surface temperature is very high. Lots of pressure. It is very cloudy and reflects 79 per cent of sunlight so it's the brightest object in the sky after the Sun and Moon. Close to the Sun, it's seen as the evening or the morning star – well, depending on the position of Venus and Earth in their orbits. OK?'

It strikes me Venus is no place to live.

If you live on Venus, and nobody does of course, you are under terrible pressure, and walking about in the clouds all the time, with no light ever and no cooling breezes. If you are observing Venus from the Earth though, from its nearly twin, Venus is bright as anything, the brightest, the evening and the morning star, very nice. It depends how you look at it.

Sister Martha will be watching out for me now, for the transit of me. I pick up the pace, but I feel fuzzy in the head the closer I get to school and I'm kicking at stones, I'm not slap-happy, I'm slap-sad. Harriet should be here, skipping ahead of me and coming back, skipping ahead and back. I do want to see Sister Martha, but I wonder if I can leave out the goodbye thing. I try to think about it, the goodbye thing, and all the ways to say it, because maybe Harriet knows something I don't and it is why she is not here today.

Bye! I just said this to Jude but it does not really count, it's not really goodbye, it's more like looking ahead to the next hello, a tip-off. I tell him where I'm going, he tells me where he'll be when I get back. We do this a lot in our house, everyone giving off a Weiss signal when leaving a room. I'll be in my room! I'm just stepping outside! Going to the loo! 'Be in the kitchen! 'Be upstairs, back in a minute! Each Weiss has a map in his head with a little x marking the place where every other Weiss is lurking. It's a good system, though I note some strangers find it weird, all this calling out going on in our family like we are in a maze and worried about getting lost and have to keep calling out to prevent it, each voice like a string you can follow with a Weiss on the other end, don't let go. What is wrong with that? Strangers give us that blinkety-blink of the eyes expression, meaning what on earth is going on here, what crazy behaviour is this, all these announcements to do with times and whereabouts like in a railway station?! Strangers may also think we have not discovered privacy or some such thing and they are wrong about that too. I can be in the same room as Jude and not talk at all, for a long time even. We can be private together in one same place, all of us can. We can do the privacy thing in separate rooms too, no problem, but being alone in a room is one thing and being alone in a room where everyone knows you are is much better. And that's how it is in our house.

Some goodbyes are breezy things and not fretful, a passing wave, a tip of a hat as in olden times, or a merry flap of both hands as my sister is prone to, like a bird taking off, and my dad has his own way with greetings altogether. He does not go in for hellos where they are usually called for. I come home from school and he has not seen me for eight whole hours and where a regular person will say, Hey, Jem! he pulls on my ears or bops me lightly not that lightly on the head with a rolled-up newspaper, making sure to remove my hat first in case I don't feel him properly. What he means by this is Hello! On a Saturday, on his way upstairs to the office to do some sports writing, he yells out Good–bye! leaving a big space in the middle of the word for full effect on us. It is a message from him to the whole house, loud and clear and we feel special because my dad does not have a big thing for niceties or speech itself. Why speak a lot of words all at once when we all know each other around here? When my dad shouts out Good–bye! I also wish him a pleasant journey in my head, a pleasant and safe one all the way to the top with no mishaps and tumbles or spills of tea and sticky lemon from his tea tray for me to crunch under-foot on my next journey up there myself, it's what I wish.

My dad also sings a goodbye song, one of three songs he knows, two of them to do with war and one with sports, the goodbye song being one of the war ones. My dad is pretty bad at singing and he knows this. Most people who know they are bad at singing will hold off in company and reserve their song moments for special situations, as I do, singing alone or for Harriet, upon request only. I sing OK for my sister, but otherwise I only move my lips in company, as I have learned at the convent. It's polite. If there are genes for singing, mine have come straight on down from my dad, no messing around. Genes are like ingredients for skills and behav-iour and things such as eye colour and vision, etc., and they come to you when you are in embryo form looking quite similar to a chicken, pig or fish. Some genes are dominant in the father, says Ben, and some are dominant in the mother. Ones that are not domi-nant are something else for which I have forgotten the word because it is a bit confusing. You might say, for instance, the no-good singing genes are dominant in Dad, knocking Mum's fine singing skills right out of the ring. Or you might say that singing skills in my dad are the other word for just not there, or faint as far-off bells. It depends how you look at it.

It is a pity Mum is not dominant or whatever in the singing-gene department, as things may well have been different for me and I would have one less battle in life, meaning the one with Sister Clothilda the Music Nun, a battle which is coming to an end due to travel by ship across the ocean, not a proper end at all, and more like a pause in the battle, Christmas Day in the trenches, a time for the exchanging of fags and schnapps and chinwags between enemies out in the middle before it is back to work and guns blazing. Music Nun and I require a treaty, that's what, and maybe a treaty is also a kind of goodbye.

When my dad feels a song coming on, he goes all out, singing loud, having a fine time giving everyone a headache in our house. He may learn some new songs one day, but these are the top hits so far, these are his songs.

Song number one. The SPORTING SONG. This is special as Dad requires a partner and there is a little torture involved. Torturing his kids is important for my dad and none of us minds, it's not a problem for us at all. One thing, though. He picks me quite often but there are obvious reasons why. I am the right size. I rarely have the heart to say no to my dad. I don't lose my mind the way Harriet does or get bored in the manner of Jude who also wins at games whereas I never win at games. Ben is too big and too sensitive. Gus is too small. Gus can wait. I also believe my dad is cramming in a lot of boxing, slap and sporting-song games with me while he can, not only for my training in cowboy-toughness, but because before too long, I will be an all-out girl with bosoms and so on and it will no longer be seemly, our games time is running out, he has seen the auspices same as Jude. Maybe later we can find some new games to play, grown-up ones. If I get to be a sports writer, for instance, we may hang out and swap sports-writing tips, or sit around in bars waiting for sporting heroes to show up for interviews and so on. Interviews very often happen in bars, as I understand. It is relaxing for both parties and makes a change from interviews in gymnasiums, where the sporting hero is likely to be a bit show offy because the gym is his habitat. You have to take him out of his habitat now and again, my dad says, for revelations, going to show that revelations can be dependent on physical deportment and the lie of the land, and quite variable, lying on the back and staring at the ceiling, for instance, being conducive to deep thinking in Jude, say, but deep sleep in my dad.

'Jem! Where are you going!'

Whoa. I cross a room in deep thought and my dad yells out like that and it's not good for my heart, or my bones even. I get a bit of a shock to the system plus whiplash.

'What do you want, Dad?' This is the standard reply in our house from Ben, Jude, Harriet and me. We are Dad's slaves and it is not a problem for us, and it did not take us long to learn it. Gus will learn too.

'Wanna play Take Me Out to the Ball Game?' Dad asks, kind of gleeful. He knows I'll say yes. I nearly always do.

'Um. Right now?' I ask, watching my dad's face fall. 'OK, Dad. Sure!'

'Great!'

My dad sits up straight. He really goes in for this sporting-song game involving the torture of me. Here goes. He sits on the edge of the sofa and I climb on to his lap facing him with my legs dangling by the sides. I cannot reach the floor yet but it's not a big drop. Dad holds my waist and does a little test bounce of me and I feel like I'm on some crazy ride at the funfair. Now comes the song part. My dad does all the singing.

> Take me out to the ball game,
> Take me out to the fair
> Buy me some pea-nuts and crac-ker jacks
> For I don't care if we never get back
> For it's root-toot-toot for the home team,
> If they don't win, it's a shame!
> Now it's one-two-three
> And we're out at the OLD BALL GAME!

The ball game in the song = baseball, the topmost summer sport where my dad comes from and a little bit like cricket, explaining Dad's peculiar bowling method in attempts at cricket, the target-practice method. Baseball is also akin to rounders, one of two horrible games girls have to play at girl schools, the other being field hockey. Field hockey most especially brings out violent streaks in convent girls who simply lose control of their faculties when offered a big stick and a ball of some kind, slashing at your ankles and other tender regions of the body instead of concentrating on the more masterly skills of ball and stick handling and the making of passes and the scoring of goals. Girls! I want to say, the big stick is your friend! Girls are not so used to sports and sticks as are boys and therefore give in to violence. When I play with Jude and his friends, there is peace on the field of play and no hard knocks for me because boys do not lose their faculties or undergo spooky personality changes as in *The Strange Case of Dr Jekyll and Mr Hyde*, a very good horror book lent to me by Ben, written by R. L. Stevenson, a Scotsman with a breathing disease that killed him when he was forty-four years and three weeks old.

As my dad sings, he bounces me up and down, rattling my brains, and at some point, you never know when, his lap opens like a trapdoor or the bomb flap of a Wellington bomber over Germany, and I hit the deck. It is in the spirit of this game for me to be in a frenzy of anticipation throughout. Anticipation means waiting for a thing you know will happen while feeling a bit giddy. I anticipate a crash to the floor in a cascade of limbs. It happens. It really doesn't hurt.

'Ha ha ha ha!'

'Let's all go bar-my and join the ar-my, see the world we ne-ver saw!'

This is song number two, the shortest of my dad's war songs and he prefers to sing it when one of his kids is nearby, especially Harriet who hates this song the most, clapping her palms to her ears and singing a song of her own, eyes closed tight to lock her song inside, so it's all she can hear. Bad move. Dad takes this as an invitation to sing even louder, unclamping her hands and singing straight into her outer ear which carries sound waves to her inner ear, sparking her nerves and impulses so she will reel around the house for a while in a state of woe and vertigo and drive everyone else a bit crazy.

'Harriet,' says Jude who is trying to read. 'Shut up or I will bop you on the nose with a rolled-up newspaper.'

'One day I'll be dead,' my sister replies in poignant tones, 'and you will miss me.'

'Not if Jude dies first,' I say.

'I say, old chap!' says Harriet. 'There is just no end to it!'

'To what?' I ask. 'No end to what?'

'To DEATH, dear sir!'

'Drop it! Both of you!' says Jude. 'Or bops on the nose. Coming up.'

'BARKIS is willin',' my sister says in a growly voice.

'Yeh, Jude,' I add. 'BARKIS is willin'.'

Harriet and I get a few bops with a rolled-up newspaper, the standard punishment for crimes committed by puppies, though it has never worked on either of the two dogs we have had so far. Our first dog was called Dog and he was a poodle who in no way resembled a poodle, being one shaggy crazed mess of a dog in a perpetual bad mood for whom Harriet decided the solution was grooming. This dog cannot see straight! This dog is too hairy and that is the problem with Dog! she announced, making a beeline for Dog with a pair of blunt scissors whereupon Dog lost his mind completely, biting Harriet in the knees and spending a very long time racing around the pond in the back garden chasing after her with the scissors hanging off his shaggy coat. I was pretty keen for that dog to pack his little bags and leave this family and that's what happened soon after Harriet's go at hairdressing.

Our next dog was a golden retriever named Shane who knocked us all down like bowling pins every single morning due to extreme youth and exuberance. On school mornings, Dad had to lock Shane in the scullery so that school-faring Weiss kids could make it out of the house in one piece, calling upstairs in a big voice when it was safe to come out and leave in a procession to the sounds of Shane scuffling on the tiles in a small room, waiting for Dad to let him out, only when Gus was somewhere beyond reach, aloft in Mum's or Lisa's arms. In the end Shane had to go too, let loose on the moors way up north in the keep of a sheep farmer and I bet he is a happy dog now, maybe even a sleuthing dog like Black Bob, a dog with fine manners and better judgement regarding who to knock over like bowling pins and who to leave standing. We were just not ready for Shane and it is probably a good thing we had to let him go as I am not sure a ship journey would agree with him, and I wonder how it would be for all those passengers having to stay locked in their cabins until my father calls out OK! It's safe! before they can take a stroll up and down the decks, holding parasols and tipping hats and nodding to each other in a genteel fashion as I imagine happens on ships, unless it is a battleship where not a lot of genteel strolling is likely to occur.

Goodbye, Shane.

My dad's other war song is the goodbye song, song number three.

> Goodbye, goodbyee
> Wipe the tear, baby dear,
> From your eyee.
> Though it's hard to part, I know,
> I've – been – tickled to death to go.
> Goodbyee, goodbyee
> There's a silver lining in the skyee
> Bonsoir, old thing,
> Cheerio, chin-chin,
> Root-toot, toodle-oo
> Goodbyee.

In two out of three of my dad's songs, there is a root-toot moment, making me a bit suspicious he has forgotten the words and is sticking a root-toot in the gaps. It doesn't matter though. I don't think he has left out anything very important. This song is sad. Here's why. A soldier is singing it. He is bashing off to war and maybe waving from a locomotive window to a loved one, his baby dear, trying to cheer her up like he is off on some big adventure and is coming back soon and there is no peril ahead, but he is lying of course, a white lie as it is called, because though his words are cheery, the man is falling apart, he knows he may never see his baby dear again, not ever, there is peril ahead.

This is an example also of how hard it can be, in trying times, to think straight in front of people you are crazy about due to worrying about their feelings and so on, or that you'll say something crazy or whatever. It happens to me all the time and I know now to go quick march round the pond or climb up a tree until it clears in there, the nebula in my head, a place with sparks flying and guns blazing. There is some thinking a person has to do alone, with no distractions, and not only for clarity purposes, but in case of coming up with something a bit doomy in the course of reflection, doomy thoughts bringing on doomy feelings, and feelings, in my opinion, are contagious. Fear, for instance. In the song, the soldier knows this and it is only when he stops waving and has pulled out of the station that he might realise he is a bit scared and he is proud of himself for not showing it at the station and passing on the jitters and causing a bad outbreak of nervous collapse on the platform. As long as he is waving and singing, he wants his baby dear to look ahead to fine things such as cheery reunions involving sharp hugs and flowers and silver linings in the sky above, etc. I am not sure about the silver-lining thing, what is fine about it. All I know from Ben's telescope book is that when a French scientist and a German scientist discovered how to line glass with silver instead of plain old metal, things improved in terms of reflectivity. Silver-lining mirrors reflected half as much light again. So maybe that is all it means, that if you look to the sky, which is what most people do when they are in a good mood, a sporting star who has won a race, say, or my sister Harriet first thing in the morning, all good-cheer type feelings will be reflected half as much again, which is kind of a bonus for people of hopeful disposition, and nothing to sneeze at.

What if you are a baby dear who is not foxed by songs? Jiminy, I am only ten and I can see the loopholes. How that lady might very well meet up with the soldier again though not upright and smiling, no, but stretched out and eyes closed with maybe a bronze cross on a crimson ribbon pinned to his chest, and those words engraved there. *For Valour.* This is the worst goodbye of all and even worse is how the only person who can help her out here is the soldier, he is the only one she wants, because that's how it is when something really bad happens, only one person will do, the person for whom you have the biggest feeling. In other words, if I were the lady in the song then the soldier could be Jude. Whoa. Or Mum is the lady and it's my dad . . . No, I'm the lady and on the stretcher is Mum, no . . . it's Dad. Hey. Stop it.

One day I'll be dead and you will miss me.

Not if I die first.

My head hurts and there are little silver flashes swimming before my eyes, like waves on the ocean under a bright sky. There's a silver lining in the skyee. My head hurts half as much again. I can't breathe. Sit down, Jem. Take a pew.

Not far to the convent, past halfway indeed, and here is the white gate and beyond the gate the path that is no longer paved, all pebbles embedded in earth and tufts of grass at the edges and my favourite part, I love it, it's lovely, especially in winter when the grass is frozen and the stones twinkle with frost, it's a fine thing, I concentrate on fine things. Harriet's Rock is a large rock near the gate, large enough to perch upon and where she will often take some time out, or a pausette as she calls it, the only word to survive her passing craze for adding this sound to all kinds of words ever since she learned the term for a small flower, floret, floweret, turning big things into smaller ones any time the fancy strikes her, cutting the world down to size, her own, with the help of one small sound. I sit on Harriet's Rock, I take a pausette. I have a lump in my throat, hard as a stone, rock, tombstone. I say, old chap! There is just no end to it! Why isn't Harriet with me today? There is some thinking you should never do alone.

Think up some jokes. Here's one.

I won't miss the Sands twins all that much. When I go. If they die. Rebecca and Heidi Sands are OK but weird, even Harriet thinks so, skipping way ahead of us and not coming back whenever the Sands twins walk our way. Rebecca is one half-hour older than Heidi. It shows. Rebecca is tops at sums and aims to be a scientist like her dad. Rebecca is very boring and she has scary limbs, skinny as twigs. Twiglets, says Harriet.

'I am going to be a scientist,' Becky tells me. 'I have a chemistry set.'

'Great. What about you, Heidi?' I ask, just to be polite. 'Any plans?'

'When I grow up,' says Heidi, 'I WANT TO BE A FISH.'

I am kind of lost for words.

'She does though,' says Rebecca, real serious.

'OK,' I say. 'Well, great.'

I have an urge to tell Heidi that there was a time in her embryo life when she was no stranger to a fish – or to a chicken or pig for that matter – and it was also maybe her best moment, the one time in her whole life when there was just no distance between her and hopes. It's all over for her now.

When I report the conversation to Harriet, she goes, What kind of fish? whereupon we both get pretty hysterical, running through all the types of fish Heidi might have dreams of being, and kind of losing our minds.

'A blowfish?' says Harriet.

'A goldfish in a bag at the fair?'

'Heidi, Heidi in the brook, Daddy catch her on a hook, Mummy fry her in a pan –'

'– BECKY EAT HER LIKE A MAN!'
'The miracle of the loaves AND HEIDI!'

If Jesus can do magic, why did he die on the cross?

Maybe if you are never really born, that is, your birth is immaculate and your origins unknown, same goes for death. It never happens to you. It's a possibility. Look at Jesus. He was never really there, so he never really died, just stepping out for a while, destination Heaven where the view is better and the albedo high. Look up.

When I get to school where Sister Martha is waiting for me to say goodbye to her, I scoot on to her lap and look around the parlour, a cool quiet room for special occasions only, for first meetings and goodbyes and chinwags between parents and nuns, and I spot the crucifix above the door frame and think a smudge of Ribena would do wonders for realism. Fake blood for a fake death. Ribena makes very good blood.

'Listen. Who's that?' says Sister Martha. She knows I recognise the footfall, a rush of steps I'd mistake for no one else's, not ever. 'Who is it?'

'Sister Margaret Mary,' I reply in a shy voice, and from the change in her breathing, I know that Sister Martha is smiling.

The rules are different today and I don't have to stand like a soldier, I can tell from the way Sister Martha still holds me close, but I slide off her lap anyway because it feels strange to sit before Sister Margaret Mary, as it would feel strange to watch a firework display anyhow but standing, and when I am upright, Sister Margaret Mary does something I've never seen her do, drop from her great height to perch on her heels, cutting herself down to my size, and then she strokes a rogue strand of hair from my face, tucking it behind my ear so I get that lump in my throat again. Mum does that. Sister holds up two little books.

'One is for Harriet,' she says. 'I've written your names inside. Do you know what goodbye means, Jemima Weiss?'

Yes. No.

'It means God be with you. You be a good girl and look after your parents now!' she adds, squeezing me tight in that Irish fashion and kissing my brows and Sister Martha kisses me also.

'Yes, Sister. Thank you, Sister.'

I walk away from them, listening to the creaking of my Shane jacket and the crunch of my desert boots on gravel and when I turn, they are both standing in the arched doorway of the front door girls hardly ever use, and they are both waving and I wave back, goodbyee. My throat hurts. Sister Margaret Mary, I'm half-Jewish, maybe more than half, did you forget? I want to run back and ask if that goodbye thing still counts, does it still mean what she says it does, will it work for me? Forget it, Jem.

Harriet's little book is a Book of Saints with paintings of saints and life details and related symbols, etc. Mine is the Gospel according to Matthew. That's funny. According to. Like he might have got it wrong. Sister did forget. More books to stash some-place or pitch in the bushes. No. You can't pitch books, it's bad. Giveaway box? I don't know. I flip to the end of the Gospel, I know how the story ends, it doesn't matter if I glimpse the last words, I just want to see how many pages there are, I always do that. Jesus says, 'Lo, I am with you alway, even unto the end of the world. Amen,' and that's when the tears finally come and I start running, because I can feel this is not true, not from anyone, no one is with you alway, it's not true and I need to get home, I need to see her face, time is running out and I have a new clock to watch, different from the one that began ticking the day Gus came home, one that winds down, I can see it, I'm not foxed. I am going to stay on my toes and look out for everyone, Mum needs me to, because of this peril that may come you never know when. Why did nobody ever say anything?

Now I have said goodbye to nuns and I have a new mission and I'm in a hurry. I race home, I can run this quick all the way, easy, as long as I choose the straightest line possible, remembering that acceleration, Jude says, is a change in speed or motion, and a straight line, of course, is the shortest distance between two points.

The soldier watches her leave, he watches from the balcony, she'll turn round in a minute and wave at him, he knows it. Sometimes she does it twice, three times. She always looks ready for adventure, her step is light and swift and he pictures her shoes, the shine in them. He buffs them, he does it nightly. You have a whole life ahead, there will be days and days of shoes, he tells her. Let me do this for you now.

You love walking, there is always something new to see. You walk by the Catholic church, prettier than yours, even the name is softer,

Catholic. Presbyterian, Catholic. Some days you step inside, you are not supposed to, it's not your church, though you go to the convent, that's different, it's for lessons. You like to wander but you are never late and you carry the music carefully, there are no creases in your sheets. Notes and chords, words, footsteps, sometimes you cannot tell them apart, you can hear music in anything if you want to.

Sister Clare lets you in and the convent is so cool, the lines sharp and unbroken, parallelogram. All the sounds ring clear in here, Sister's footfall, your own, on marble and stone, and then the light! Flooding through glass, and in the piano room, seeping in single streams through shutters, even light has a sound. This place is like no place you know, so quiet, a quiet with no fear in it, but something else, like the moment before music playing, full of things waiting to happen, fine things. Sister Clare is like no one you know, rarely smiling, barely speaking, different from Mummy. How can that be? How can rare smiles and few words in one person be frightening and not at all in another?

Begin. Sound! Everyone says how good you are at this. Sister Clare is so grave, she tells your brother Tom you have a gift and Tom tells Daddy, who nods, and Mummy who leaves the room, she is busy, it's not your fault. Tom pays for your lessons. He is so much older than you! You don't know anyone with a brother that old. He says there will be war. Coming soon.

Piano is so easy for you, like reading or dreaming, easy. You love touching the keys, the feel of them and the shape, the lines between, the black on white, all of it, and then the notes you never have to think about, playing a piece once, twice and it's there, easy. You could play for ever. Sister Clare is smiling, you can tell without looking. She smells like the convent, of flowers and rain, leaving the room in a swirl of skirts and a rush of air for your glass of water as she always does. This is when you look around, especially at that picture above the piano which makes you sad, like you want to do something, fix something, but you don't know what, you don't know how. Isenheim Altarpiece, centre panel. Mathis Grünewald, 1515. You are not sure how to pronounce this name. You might ask Sister Clare, but you are shy and you are not supposed to pay attention, it's for Catholics, for you there are no graven images. Why not? You want to touch the lamb in the painting, right there where the blood pours from his heart into a golden cup. You want it to stop.

Sister Clare comes back and she sees what you see. 'Behold the lamb of God,' she says, 'which taketh away the sin of the world.'

You say, Goodnight, Mummy when you slip into the sheets, saying it to the back of her head, did she hear you? Mummy smells like flowers, dried ones, you can put them in drawers, it's lovely in drawers, not here, it's sad here. Don't think about it. Dot is not in her bed, your sister has her own bed. She's late, there will be trouble and noise. It's so dark in here. Don't cry.

Begin. Light, the light show! You watch the ceiling, how the beams sweep across it from passing cars, slow, then quick, a searching wave of light with sharp edges and great purpose, fading and returning, covering its tracks, looking for something, for someone, not giving up. Light and music are the same you think, you cannot really see the path it takes and you cannot touch it, and it fills a space, filling it in all dimensions, spilling over, and suddenly you know what you have to do, in a quickening of the heart and breath. A mission. You will build a house out of straight lines, with a high roof and tall windows and light passing through it, and something else you know, that in this house there will be music and voices calling.

You see it, you hear it, and you close your eyes to keep the vision in.

Awe is merely a pausette on the way to Revelation, a long word from an old painting, and Revelation can come at any time, in any position, running, lying down, standing still, though Maimonides, or Rabbi Moses ben Maimon, b.1135, d.1204, that great philosopher and physician prone to administering remedies and commentaries from a lying-down position, being so very much in demand and often too weak to speak at all, may not have approved. Mental composure is a requirement, he wrote, for clarity of thought and valuable prayer and not all positions are seemly. Revelation does not come easy, though the rules may differ for him. For the rest of us, he prescribes lying turned to one side, standing or sitting, even riding a horse or just bumbling along a road, but as with good digestion, he proscribes the recitation and contemplation of prayer while face down or lying on the back staring at the ceiling, positions of a person asleep or dead, and no longer mindful of the clock built by God who called the light day and darkness night, therefore showing us the best times for sitting and standing and thinking alone in a state of composure.

Maimonides was a doctor of science and divinity, author of the Mishneh Torah in fourteen volumes and the three-book *Guide of the Perplexed*, a man of reason not above a sense of humour also, having patience even for the visions that came to prophets, sometimes coming courtesy of angels and their cherubic sidekicks, messengers the Rabbi called, respectively, the Imagination and the Intellect. Above all, though, he had faith in scholarship and in faith through scholarship, pushing a passion for books on all Jews, albeit for girls it was not so much a commandment as highly recommended, a pursuit through which they might earn merit. Maimonides hands out all the cards and badges and Merit is the best badge to win.

Revelations are not always good and ought to come in colours, I believe, pink, green, blue, as should signs in augury for those who cannot tell left from right. I can no longer tell left from right. Let me not be mad. Quarks and leptons are the ingredients for all matter, bearing labels for the purposes of distinction only, labels having nothing to do with their properties, merely analogies, like cherubs and angels. Quarks come in three colours, red, green and blue, identifying the electrical forces between them, according to the principles of symmetry in quantum mechanics.

The Rabbi would not approve of my colour scheme, no Merit badge for me, but he would have enjoyed the study of chaos, how pattern formations are universal, emerging out of this delicate balance between the forces of stability and instability, chaos a kind of health, call it something out of nothing. He would have liked this, I'm sure, how scientists see that the body is a place of patterns also, studying them in disorders of the respiratory system, and of the brain and heart, all of these, places of motion and oscillation in all dimensions, having a shape in space, you can hold a heart in your hand. My organs are dependent on a sensitivity to initial conditions and to subsequent electrical disturbances, to whatever advances or retards the breath, a brainwave or a heartbeat, such as revelation perhaps, which is why they ought to come in colours for the breathless and arrhythmic, just so we may be prepared, at the very least, for shock, for a change in the heart, a change of heart, because the laws of chaos apply to the body.

*   *   *

At Rosh HaShanah, the custom is to eat a fish with the head still on, something I could never abide, a custom based on the idea the head is powerful, and the seat of reason, and because the fish is a symbol of fertility.

And the Lord will make you the head and not the tail; and you shall be above and not beneath . . .

Aquamarine, blue waters, blue for good and for ocean only, with fish beneath.

I eat a fish with the head still on. Heidi Sands, is that you? Let me not be mad.

FIVE

*Holmes: What's the matter? You're not quite yourself. This Brixton
Road affair has upset you.*

*Watson: To tell the truth, it has. I ought to be more case-hard-
ened after my Afghan experiences. I saw my own comrades hacked
to pieces at Maiwand without losing my nerve.*

*Holmes: I can understand. There is a mystery about this which
stimulates the imagination; where there is no imagination there is
no horror. Have you seen the evening paper?*

A change of heart, a change in the heart.

The body is a complex system, I read, a place of cacophony and
counter-rhythm, of mathematical pathology or chaos, the study of
which demands something of an obsession with numbers and the
unlikely collaboration of physiologists, mathematicians and physi-
cists. Panting, sighing, arrhythmia and fibrillation, erratic eye movement in the schizophrenic or depressed, everything comes down to
the versatility of a complex system in a noisy world. Changes in
the heart are dynamical and non-linear. An electrical wave can be
traced through all three dimensions. Breakdowns in oscillatory
systems are dynamical diseases requiring a new *Guide of the
Perplexed* and a new Maimonides who might deem chaos an angel,
not of Death, but the Imagination, with cherubs in tow. All the
perplexed requires is infinite endurance.

Endurance, Endeavour! The names of ships are no accident, no
romantic thing. *Great Expectations* might be the name of a ship.

Good work, boys! When the commander and his six astronauts
return home in the *Endeavour*, having fixed the optics on the HST

and fitted a new camera, the pictures are clear, they see what has never been seen, but NASA can tell they are not looking back far enough. They need an even more perfect mirror in an even more perfect telescope, it's yet a new mission, and it will take years, but they'll get there. Eventually.

From the decks of his ship, Captain Cook sees what no one has seen before and while he is at it, he discovers and maps New Zealand and the east coast of Australia. Not a problem. He has endeavour.

I was thinking how these qualities of endurance and endeavour need to be right there, to be called up at will, innate things, like a kangaroo with the pouch facility, never having to waste any time searching her kangaroo home for where she left the baby. It's right there. I was thinking about this while studying some photographs of Ernest Shackleton's men trying to saw their boat the *Endurance* free of the pack ice on which they had been drifting for several months already by February 1915, and the men look as if they are on some merry outing in the wilds, sharing a few cracks and smoking on pipes and kind of larking about before cocktail hour, hacking at the ice with saws and picks, as hopeless an activity as cleaning city streets with toothbrushes, or fending off a firing squad with a polite sweep of the hand and a few words in a quiet voice, no thank you, not this, not today. These men do not appear desperate, their postures are fine and military, and in fact, two of the twenty-seven-man team Shackleton brought home alive in 1916, were killed within weeks of joining the Great War, a peril not even Shackleton could protect them from.

They called him Boss, and as long as he was leader, hope was not a problem for them, even as they waited on Elephant Island for Shackleton to bring help from the whaling station in South Georgia set in the shadow of impassable mountains. Maybe for a moment out there, their hearts gave out, not so much for their own fragility but for the potential loss of him, their own persons just passing stars to be swallowed by the black hole that is the terrible swirl of gravity left behind by the death of a massive star.

When Shackleton returns to Elephant Island in a small tug steamer, twenty-three men show no obvious surprise. Shackleton calls out Are you all well?

'All well, Boss!'

Now they are safe, now they are on their way home.

The SS *Pushkin*. Day one.

'Bloody!' I say.

Jude is busy opening all the drawers, doors and compartments in our cabin and looking out the round window. Porthole. I think of Tintin who often has cause to escape or infiltrate by way of portholes on ships. Tintin is always in peril and he is always OK in the end, never the worse for wear, merely strolling the fine city streets or the estate of Moulinsart with Milou in a relaxed manner, ready at all times, of course, to pack his little bag and embark on adventures, because being a hero is a full-time job.

'I forgot to check for the Plimsoll line!' I tell Jude. 'Was there one?'

I worry for a moment about the Plimsoll line and the loading of the ship. I hope someone is in charge. I can't do everything around here. It's bad enough with no Ben, meaning, the failure of my new mission of holding Weisses together before I have even begun, though this does not really count as failure as Ben is joining us later. Not a problem.

'Jude?'

'Yup.'

'I don't think I remember the way to Mum's cabin, Mum and Dad's.'

'Easy,' says Jude, unpacking his suitcase that used to be Dad's, made of chocolatey-brown leather with brass clasps and covered in old stickers, pictures of hotels or bridges and other monuments of distinction and the names of cities written below or in an arc along the top, names of important places in other countries my dad has seen, strolling the streets in a relaxed manner in the company of Mum. Jude is now the only Weiss who can uncatch the catches with one touch, a mere flick of two thumbs so impossible for my dad who has a hard time with three-dimensional objects seemingly invented especially to fox him and darken his days. You can give my dad a new thing and next thing you know, it is an old thing which is how it was with the brown suitcase, a gift from Mum he tried to look after with no success, fighting the clasps with such ferocity and dismay, they just stopped opening for him, so now it is Jude's case.

Jude strokes the scratches on the surface and peruses the stickers of far-off cities and then he releases the catches, with just one touch. 'We'll go in a minute,' he says. 'Then you can memorise the way.'

'I'll be with you most times anyway though, right? I mean, I can probably find it on my own, I wasn't really watching this time, that's all. I know you said to, but I forgot, sorry.' I slope off to the porthole with my thumbs in my pockets like I'm not one bit worried about getting lost without him. 'Hey. What happened to our boxing gloves? Did Mum put them aside for Giveaway? Or did we pack them, what?'

'Sold.'

'You SOLD them? At school? Did you ask Dad first? Whoa. You sold them.'

'Yeh.'

'I guess that makes us, um, conscientious, ahh . . .'

'Objectors.'

'Yeh. That.'

'They were really brave, you know. Some were stretcher-bearers. And doctors,' Jude says, placing his blue pyjamas under the pillow of the bed he has picked out for himself, and I do the same with my pyjamas, choosing the lower bunk opposite his. I don't go in for nighties for two reasons. 1) I feel like a bloody ghost in a nightie, or Wee Willie Winkie who was quite an anxious type and probably no fun to hang around.

> Wee Willie Winkie
> Runs through the town
> Upstairs and downstairs
> In his nightgown
> Rapping at the windows
> Crying through the lock
> Are the children all in bed?
> For now it's eight o'clock.

In my *Mother Goose* book illustrated by Mr Charles Addams, and like no other *Mother Goose* book I have ever seen, Willie looks like a cadaver, no two ways about it. I think Mr Addams has it right. Nursery rhymes are in the vein of party games, i.e. largely to do with horror poorly disguised in a party atmosphere of merry rhymes and trinkets for prizes. Mr Addams draws the truth. Willie is a loony and he has no friends.

2) I get tangled up when I sleep and feel panicky thinking about swimming lessons and drowning and that painting Mum showed me of the lovely lady dressed in a nightie and out for the count in a shallow stream, floating by amongst the lily pads in a mess of flowers and weeds. I say, old chap! There's just no end to it!

There are four beds in here but only three will be filled because Gus will sleep in Mum and Dad's cabin and there is no Ben here, no Ben in any berth. From a ratio of three parts boy to two parts girl, not counting Mum and Dad, the Weiss family is now in a ratio of 2:2. Ben taught me ratio. *Ratio.* The relation between things of a similar magnitude depending on how many times one contains the other. I am not sure girls and boys are things of similar magnitude but never mind.

'There's carsick,' I say, 'and airsick and plain old sick-sick and –'

'Seasick,' says Jude.

'Right. Harriet will get it, won't she?'

Jude and I go eye to eye for a moment and I can tell we are thinking the same thing.

'One of us has to sleep in a top berth, Jem.'

'Yeh. Or else we'll need umbrellas or something.'

'We should have put her in quarantine with the birds.'

'She can't even go see them, Dad said. It's the rules.'

Harriet is in Mum and Dad's cabin right now, trying to recover from the news about quarantine. Jude and I left her there moping because our two collared doves are in quarantine way beneath the Plimsoll line in case of animal diseases. She has learned they will have to go into further quarantine when we land, into a kind of refugee camp, Dad says, just until they get their health certificate or whatever. There is nothing wrong with our birds! goes Harriet, whereupon my dad tries to cheer her up by way of a joke. The birds are safer down below, he says, because the chef on board is Russian, and pigeon pie is a delicacy for Russians, ha ha ha ha! Harriet is putting two and two together when it comes to the Russian people who were once dear to her, and the Russian view on small creatures, i.e. that they are seen chiefly as fillings for pies and the stuff of warm winter wardrobes. Russians are more the hunting type than the zoology type.

My dad scoops Harriet off the ground and plops her down on the window sill. He tickles her, by way of saying sorry for the bad joke about bird pies. 'They'll be fine down there, my little chick-adee!' he says. 'It's not exactly the Pale of Settlement!'

Mum laughs, so this is clearly a joke too, though I don't get it and neither does Jude, and it's not really the time to ask, what with Dad joshing Harriet, and Jude pulling on my arm because he wants us to go and unpack, and Mum watching Gus stroll about in that investigative fashion, hands clasped behind him as he walks in slow circles, skirting the limits of the cabin, just as he used to wander round our pond in the back garden of what is already our old house. Ben told me a story about a boy artist in Renaissance times trying to join a studio of artists, and how he drew a perfect circle, a feat deemed impossible for the human hand and so amazing, they let him join right away and before long he was the top artist and very famous in all parts. A perfect circle may be impossible for the human hand but Gus walks them. He walks in perfect circles.

'Harriet!' I say, having a go at cheering her up myself. 'Jude says we'll see whales. How about that?'

No answer. She is still brooding about doves behind bars with no visitation rights. I'm not sure how she feels about large marine mammals, the only fish out here that are not always beneath. They come up for air. Harriet is not prejudiced regarding the animal kingdom, except for parasites, I believe, such as maggots. It is quite hard not to think about maggots since Mum took us to see *Mutiny on the Bounty*, maybe to put us in the seafaring mood, a film wherein sailors are forced to eat maggoty bread. Mutinies often come down to food matters, it seems to me. Take Oliver Twist in the workhouse for instance, or French people going on bread riots as Jude told me, because bread was too pricey, causing a whole revolution and, come to think of it, who knows what might have arisen at that wedding feast if Jesus had not done the loaves thing? Captain Cook got things right. The *Endeavour* was a happy ship with good food and no scurvy because he was well up on health matters. Before my dad met Mum, who is also well up on health matters, he had scurvy, which is very unusual, seeing as it was mainly a ship thing and a problem resolved by Captain Cook in the eighteenth century. *Scurvy.* 'A disease caused by deficiency of vitamin C, common in the past among sailors on long voyages and now rarely seen except in old debilitated people and vagrants.' I ruled out the first two and asked Dad if at any time he had been a vagrant in his days of poverty and he thought this was downright hilarious. Ha ha ha, etc. I ruled it out also therefore, and chalked his bout of scurvy up to fate and so on, something he might have foreseen in chicken guts had he been on the lookout, chicken guts with which he has a more regular acquaintance than most. Anyway, it won't happen again. No, sir. Not on my watch.

I saw *Mutiny on the Bounty* very shortly after the Case of Susannah Bonnington and the Maggoty Banger. I am very glad Dining-Room Nun is not hard-hearted and merely a bit crazy. Things might have been worse for Susannah. I don't care what anyone says about protein, etc., no one should have to eat insects, though Jude ate an ant once by mistake, dumping his jacket on the kitchen table and simply not paying attention to the ant that crawled from his clothes to his glass of milk creeping up the side to walk around the rim. It's a hazard with Jude as he is prone to lying on his back to stare at the ceiling, or the sky when outdoors. He ought to shake his clothes off before coming inside which is the sensible idea I had after Ben and I watched him swallow the ant, too much in shock to stop him in time, like watching a tree fall, I guess. There's nothing you can do. Ben and I breathed in sharply, our lower mandibles clattering down.

'Oops,' I said.

'What?' asked Jude, frowning.

'Nothing,' said Ben.

'Yeh,' I said. 'Nothing.'

An ant is not so bad. An ant is not a parasite, and more of a labourer insect concerned largely with the ferrying of crumbs overhead, sometimes straying to walk around the rim of a glass of Ribena-milk, say, strolling in perfect circles like Gus, only to meet a bad end inside Jude, maybe not even dying straight off but having high hopes of getting coughed up to safety in the manner of Jonah, who fled in a ship, and was swallowed by a large marine mammal as punishment for avoiding a preaching job or something, just like the ant in fact, the ant who ought to have stuck to the crumb job instead of going astray. It goes to show.

'Look after Jem, please,' Mum tells Jude as we head out.

I am not the one who needs looking after around here. My dad got scurvy in the twentieth century.

I try to stop thinking about parasites and eighteenth-century diseases. I am not doing so well. I try to think about exciting seafaring moments in *Mutiny on the Bounty*, but the maggoty moment is uppermost, I can't help it, and I have noticed this odd thing about remembering, how even when musing over some fine time, it is possible to get stuck on the single bad moment of that fine time, such as my boxing match with Jude. I recall what a great nurse he was and how I was like the most important person on earth for him and so on and then I remember his eyes right before the red fist to my stomach, I see his eyes and the look in them, a look saying I don't know you at all and that is the odd thing, how suddenly the rest is hazy, like listening to a bird singing, and then an aeroplane roars past and that's it, the roar stays with you for ages, mostly the roar.

'Jude!' I say, on the way back to our cabin. 'Remember *Mutiny on the Bounty*?'

'Maggots,' he says.

'Yeh! Maggots, right! It was a bad scene, wasn't it?'

'Very bad. Watch the way we're going from Mum's. You'll need to know.'

'OK – Jude, can you die from scurvy? Could we get it?'

'No. You have to be vigilant, that's all.'

'Right,' I say, as if I had not just learned this word.

Vigilance. Alertness to danger. *Vigil*. Keeping awake during usual time for sleep. Like Harriet! 'Eve of a festival, esp. eve that is a fast, watch kept on this; nocturnal service; prayers at such service, esp. for the dead.' Esp. for especially. Especially for the dead. Maybe a person who is vigilant regarding loved ones, etc., will not be in for vigils esp. for the dead or prayers said at such services, yet I see it for a moment, a vision of my dad laid out on a berth with his eyes closed, not shouting at his kids in a slap-happy manner but laid out still and quiet and his kids shouting at him, shouting and crying because he did not pay attention to vitamin C, something he ought to know by now, it's so easy to remember, and he messed up and none of this should be happening, not him stretched out and silent, not kids yelling at their own dad. My vision passes quickly though, nothing but a film moment with the words THE END coming up on-screen, wake up, go home, it's only a film.

Why do they do that, put THE END in huge writing at the end? Maybe for the doubtful, some type for whom last words, demises and embraces and the clattering of hooves to exuberant strains of music are simply not sign enough it's all over, some stray person sitting patiently even as the lights flare up and the curtains swish closed and people rise to fiddle with clothing and bash off home in a slap of cinema seats, waiting just in case there is more to come, something, coming soon, because these two words never came up to signify otherwise, these words THE END. That stray person might be me. So what, it's no crime.

Jude and I unpack. We tuck our pyjamas under pillows and figure out where Harriet should sleep. My pyjamas are white with a grey stripe which Mum says is very stylish though Dad seems to hold other opinions, handing me Mum's wooden meat pulveriser one evening, and pushing me outside, saying Why don't you have a go at some rocks, Jem! Ha ha ha. All you need is some ankle chains, ha ha ha. Everyone thought this was pretty funny. Jude's pyjamas, though, are blue and Jude told me once that in some cultures doorposts are painted blue to ward off evil spirits or whatever.

In some cultures.

The SS *Pushkin*. Day two.

'Jem. Jacket,' says Jude.

Jude means put on your jacket, Jem, we are going walkabout and it's cold outside. Jude is right. It's breezy up here on deck though it is summer where we came from and summer where we are bound and we are still in the northern hemisphere as I happen to know. Maybe the rules do not apply on the ocean, the ocean is a country with a special climate all its own. I wear my second-favourite jacket.

MY SECOND-FAVOURITE JACKET. Jude has the EXACT SAME jacket but we try not to wear them at the same times, as Jude gets cross and embarrassed like we are twins in a circus show or something. 'We're not Pinky and Perky, you know!' he snapped one day as I walked into the garden with the same jacket on as him. Whoa. Actually, I didn't know Pinky and Perky were twin pigs, but never mind. It's definitely hard to tell those pigs apart.

This jacket is navy-blue cotton with a fluffy red cotton lining and dark blue cuffs, collar and waist parts made of stretchy jersey material. Stretchy is good at the cuffs because it means breezes do not flow up the arms. The jacket is pretty soft in and out and it is covered in round patches which are badges showing the emblems of baseball teams. I am getting in the mood for New World sports.

Sometimes I have problems with the zip. If I am too hasty, I catch some material on the way up to my chin and get locked inside my jacket until I can find someone to peel it off me and then only Mum knows how to fix the zip. Likewise when that other thing happens. I do the zip to the top but the teeth don't meet and the whole thing flaps free except for at the collar, meaning I am a prisoner again in my own clothes. This is weird. Find Mum. Start again. This jacket is a lot like my dad's old suitcase, come to think of it, what with being all covered in emblems of places and requiring special handling skills.

The name of a baseball team = the name of a place + a nickname. The nickname is usually a type of Indian, wild animal or bird. Cubs, Braves, Redskins. I thought a Redskin was a kind of potato but I was wrong about that. Sometimes the nickname is just a friendly slang word for the populace at large, Yankees, Dodgers, Mets, and occasionally, just a word spelled wrong on purpose for a plain old item of clothing. Red Sox. In baseball the main thing is the nickname whereas in my country which can fit about thirty times into my dad's, the place name is the thing and that is down to space and lack of extra space and everyone feeling pretty fierce about the name of their town like in musical chairs, more and more people and fewer and fewer chairs and someone bound to get stranded with no place to be. Most party games are bad and depressing. Football teams often have the same nickname, kind of hopeful ones, you might say, for such a small island. Rovers, Wanderers. Let's face it, you cannot rove very far in a small place and maybe that is where the big thing for wandering and exploration begins, with growing up in a tight squeeze of a country where you cannot rove very far without bumping into some other rover or falling into the sea, frustrating, and Jude feels it, I can tell from the way he strokes the old brown suitcase with the pale scratches in the leather, and how he will gaze at the stickers of cities with a dreamy and grave expression, already in some far-off place where I am not, because there are some places you have to go alone.

'Jude?' I say. 'Don't you think I look like your suitcase?'

'Yup,' says Jude, with that lopsided smile of his. 'JEM! Come here!'

I scoot up next to Jude who is standing on his toes and gripping the railing, his arms bent at the elbows and poking straight behind like wings almost. 'What?'

'Whales,' he announces. 'See?'

I strain to see what Jude is seeing. I train my eyes on the horizon like I am on the lookout for enemy vessels, for telltale periscopes peeping up from the depths. No good. Maybe I will need specs. Or contact lenses like Brigitta's. Meaning my family will have to traipse after me on hands and knees searching for transparent slivers that pop out in any slight breeze, or whenever I move too sharply in all the excitement of my new clear vision. I can't see that either. I'll go for specs. That way no Weiss will have to be vigilant esp. for me and lens fallout.

'Wait! Yes, I see them, I do, Jude!'

I call this a no-lie lie because I do not want to let him down and because sometimes when a thing is that clear for someone you are crazy about, someone like Jude, his vision is as good as real, as good as mine own, good enough for me. But to be really sure of things and see it for yourself, sometimes if you say you see it, and are patient and hopeful, it will show for you too, it will. Sometimes, not always.

There they are. Wow.

'Wow, Jude! Whales.'

'Yeh.'

You see?

The SS *Pushkin*. Day five.

Things are not easy. I am on Harriet duty and Jude is with Zach. Jeremy is seasick. The Levinthals are emigrating with us! says Mum. Hmm. I thought emigration had to do with war and prejudice and subsequent fleeing in ships, but no, it seems it also has to do with roots and in Mr Levinthal's case, a new university posting. Posting. I thought that was a war thing too, for soldiers and battalions only. Wrong again, Jem.

I brought Jeremy a *Tintin* book yesterday (*The Secret of the Unicorn*) plus I gave him my very last Rowntree's fruit gums. Half a roll. I don't know what the sweets are like where we are going. Jeremy is definitely not up to sweets at the moment but it might brighten up his future just to behold the sweets. I hope so. Things are bleak for him. He patted my forearm and smiled faintly like that Greta Garbo woman in the film where she lounges about on the chaise longue in frilly dresses. *Camille*. She takes quite a long time to conk out and it's only when she starts smiling the way

Jeremy is right now that it is really all up for her. Harriet liked the film very much. I did not. And I do not want Jeremy to smile faintly. It should be a girl thing.

'You can save them for later,' I said. 'I don't have a full roll left. Sorry.'

'Come ON, Jem,' said Jude, anxious to explore and get out of the sick bay.

'I'm going to play with Zach and Jude,' I told Jeremy. 'I have to go now. Tomorrow you'll be OK probably and we'll be the four of us.'

'Thanks for the book, Jem,' said Jeremy, smiling faintly.

'Not a problem.'

'If you die,' said Zach, 'will you leave me your fruit gums?'

'FUCK BLOODY OFF!' replied Jeremy, which is more like it. He is on the road to health. Yay.

Jeremy Levinthal is three years older than I am and he has red hair, wild as flames.

I nipped around with Jude and Zach for most of yesterday but I am not invited today, partly as I am busy on Harriet watch and also because they are getting down to some criminal activities and I am losing my touch. Jude says I act too shifty and resemble a secret agent in a war film and it's a dead giveaway. I thought secret-agent behaviour was just the thing for activities requiring stealth. I am wrong about everything, clearly. Forget it. Zach is getting on my nerves anyway.

Zachariah Levinthal has dark thatches of hair sticking up in various directions like the hair on a wet Alsatian or Labrador dog. He has large brown eyes like my dad's, I suppose, except Zach never shuts his. Not in my experience. He has stary eyes, no blinking at all, I checked. I kept my eyes on him yesterday and forced them into a locked-open position for as long as possible so I could catch any Zach blinks. Not one. It is possible he blinked at exactly the same moment I did, but I doubt it, and then I had to give up my experiment due to getting an eye ache. The other thing about Zach is that he is not a still person, always shuffling on his toes or jumping out of a chair or off the floor like he wants to rush some-where, he doesn't know where, and for some reason he cannot figure, because of something he forgot to do or say, or something he left behind, or maybe to quash some emergency like a firefighter or something. Cool your jets, Zach. Everything's OK, Zach. Dad watched him do that shuffle in our kitchen one day before supper and he put down his drink to aim pretend six-guns at Zach's feet.

'Dance, partner!'

Zach looked so hurt and confused Dad had to wrestle with him and then we got to go across the road for Cokes to have at dinner and Mum sat Zach next to her at the table and he gazed at her most of suppertime without blinking at all.

'Shut up and drink your gin!' said Dad when we thanked him for the Cokes with too much enthusiasm. This is what Fagin says to his pickpocket boys in *Oliver!* when one of them complains the sausages are mouldy. Shut up and drink your gin! is my dad's favourite line from his favourite scene in the whole of the film, though he is quite partial to the scene wherein Oliver Twist is hurled down the cellar steps for rebellious behaviour at the under-taker's where he now works as an undertaker's boy, sold to the undertaker by the workhouse for not many shillings, just like a slave. My dad is not that interested in Oliver, he is interested in villainy, in Fagin and pickpockets with bright eyes and shocks of unruly hair and scruffy clothes and top hats and a lot of vim and vigour, which is something I kind of like about Zach actually, how he reminds me of one of Fagin's boys.

When Mum read *Oliver Twist* to us, she remarked, 'The portrait of Fagin is very disturbing,' whereupon I took a closer look at the drawing of Fagin in jail and I had to agree. He looks in need of a wash and there is something very wrong with his nose because Fagin resembles a bird of prey and not a human at all.

'I see,' I said in sage tones, fingering the picture.

'Mum means anti-Semitism, you dope,' said Jude, poking me in the ribs. 'In the writing!'

'I know it! I need to see the picture, that's all! I was just perusing!'

I think I may be falling for the wrong ideas in life and getting blind to reality. I simply did not catch that thing about anti-Semitism in time, and though I like all the scenes with the pickpockets I am definitely interested in Oliver also, even when he sings that song in the cellar about love and where is it and will he ever know it, and is it underneath the willow tree, and so on, a song that has Ben and Jude howling with mirth. I even feel great relief and some rapture when Oliver's perils are over and he gets to climb the steps to Mr Brownlow's house once more, a beautiful creamy house with wrought-iron railings in a sweep of such houses where on the top step outside the open door is Mr Brownlow's housekeeper ready to clasp Oliver in her arms and ruffle his dear blond head. Now he is safe. I fall for this too, I fall for it all, and it's a worry made worse the day Ben asked me in an accusing manner why is it Oliver is the only boy with fluffy blond hair and why do you think it is Oliver has a posh voice if he grew up in the workhouse and on the streets and all the other boys do not have posh voices?

'I think it's symbolic or something.'

'Of what? It's not realistic, Jem.'

'OK. Sorry.'

There is quite a lot that can pass unnoticed in films though it is plain unrealistic and maybe it's not a problem as long as you can tell the difference. I just need to remember not to do things that are OK in films but not OK in life, such as my secret-agent behaviour which is suitable for war films but a serious drawback on a day I want to hang out with Jude and Zach who are getting down to criminal activities while I am on Harriet duty, and Harriet is driving me crazy. I am a dead giveaway in life. Very disturbing.

'Jem! Your mother is tired! Take Harriet for walkies. I'll give you 10p!'

Harriet and I roll our eyes. And I don't need 10p. Jude won a whole pile of 10ps from the fruit machine yesterday and he had to hold out his jumper to catch the cascade of coins. Jude and Zach are loaded. Nevertheless, they are both shoplifting sweets at the moment, I believe.

'Come on, Harriet.'

'Cheerio, pip-pip, farewell,' she says, slipping her little hand into mine. She breaks my bloody heart when she does that. It's so hard to get mad at her. And no two ways about it, she is in a pesky mood today, though she does not let on until we are clear of Mum and Dad's cabin. 'Soon we will be in Russia,' she tells me. 'How delightful!'

'What? What was that?'

'What-what? WHAT is the meaning of all this!' my sister says in urgent tones.

Lordy.

'Is this going to go on all morning, Harriet? I'm just asking. What are your plans exactly?' I give her a pretty fierce look and she just giggles into her hand, squeezing her shoulders up to her ears.

My sister has two new voices she has learned off the radio since she spends an awful lot of spare time with Mum, who is a regular listener, most especially to news programmes and classical music programmes, Harriet's inspiration. The news voice means speaking like she is in a terrible hurry and in a state of emergency. She will also sound cross in that way newscasters do, because the world is falling apart and it is up to them to break the news about that, and it is everybody's fault but theirs, and this often sounds to me like a person trying to hold on to his hat in a fierce wind which is blowing dirt in his eyes and buffeting the body. Harriet is really good at this voice. Her second one is the music one. In classical music programmes, radio people speak in soft tones like there is someone sleeping nearby, and as if they are a little sleepy themselves or have just risen out of a bath and still have that floaty feeling. This is the sound of voices spoken in darkened rooms, when everything has the quality of secrets, making me wonder whether blind people always speak this way, like they are telling secrets, all day long.

'You know perfectly well we are not going to Russia. So I'm ignoring you, OK?'

'THIS,' says Harriet with a show-off sweep of one arm and her eyelids at half-mast in a show of disdain at which she is now expert, 'is a RUSSIAN ship. In Russia, I will dance!'

'There is no such thing as Russia for a start. Things are Russian, the place is something else. USSR. Union, no. United Soviet Socialist Republic. Or Republics. Never mind. And we are not going there either.'

'Who said?'

'Said what?'

'The United thing.'

'Jude.'

'Oh,' says Harriet, peeping through the fretwork under the railings and gazing seawards. 'Daddy says if they catch him, he'll have to walk the plank. I told Jude.'

'And how worried was he?'

'Thanks for the warning, he said . . . What's walk the plank?'

'Forget it. It's just a joke. Do you have any money?'

Harriet digs in her pocket and pulls out her furry mouse with

the zip on its belly. Her purse. She has 64p. I have at least a quid.
Not bad.

'Are we walking the plank? Planks. I mean, we are ON planks,
aren't we?'

'We should spend it, I think. It's no good where we're going.'

'Moscow!' says Harriet.

'Right, Moscow. Come on. Let's see what they have to buy in
this joint.'

I steer my sister towards the shops where we might bump into
Zach and Jude right in the middle of crimes, who knows. Then I
picture landing in my dad's country as I have seen in books, landing
on our sea legs to spread out squares of carpet and sit upon fancy
armchairs with Indians for company and a layout of old trinkets
at our feet, broken pocket watches and piles of tobacco and tins
of chocolate and rusting rifles we aim to swap for rivers and mountains where the Indians live. Braves. Redskins. When the Indians
cotton on, they start waving those rusty rifles in the air and I see
their point, though this is no excuse for cutting hair right down to
the roots, scalp included. I imagine holding out a handful of pence
to a bunch of strangers, swapping it for territory on which to build
a new Weiss house, going Oh all right then when they throw in a
mountain and lake to go with it for the measly pence I hold in my
palm as if it were the finest treasure. I don't think so. I'm no felon.

In the souvenir and sweetie shop Harriet starts furiously re-
arranging the display of sweet rolls and little packets and boxes
and so on and the shop woman glares at me. Me.

'So unattractive!' my sister says, quite cross. She's right.

'It's not stealing,' I tell the lady. 'She's making it neat for you.
Pretty. This is Harriet, my sister. It's OK.'

That woman carries on glaring at me while Harriet sings to
herself and fiddles with confectionery. I am having second thoughts
about our shopping spree. Maybe this woman does not have a full
grasp of the English language. Plus she is Russian and has probably had a hard life like many, many people in this world as Mum
keeps reminding me so that I will think twice about being rude
and impatient about their horrible bad moods. You never can tell
what hard times and disadvantages have befallen a person, she
says, making me think I have to be polite all my born days because
I am the only advantaged person on this earth, bloody. I have to
be tolerant, she says. Tolerant means not throwing this woman's

sweets all round the ship or yelling at her to stop glaring at me like I have just burned down her whole house with all her worldly goods inside. Glaring at me also like I am in charge of Harriet and responsible for everything she does just because I am about 2cm taller and a wee bit older. Harriet is her own woman! I want to say. She looks out for me in some areas, and I look out for her. That's how it is in our family. Age has nothing to do with it! I don't say a word though. I am tolerant. This woman has had hard times and disadvantages and she is in a lifelong bad mood. I want to say to Mum: You were poor and everything! That's hard! How come you are never in a bad mood?

'Hey,' I say to my sister, taking her right wrist in my hand as gently as possible so she knows I'm not mad at her, 'I think you should stop it. I mean, she doesn't want . . . she doesn't really, um, appreciate it. Stop. Let's just pick something and go. Something for Mum? For after her rest. Choose, Harriet. We can get two things if you want.'

It's definitely a sorry display. There are crisp packets still in their cardboard boxes like in railway tuck shops but instead of being crammed full, the bags are strewn in lonely as anything and look a bit scrunched and I bet the crisps are all broken inside. She has two depressing flavours. Ready salted. Salt and vinegar. Who cares. And instead of a sloping tumble of sweet rolls in neat rows, I see a mangy collection of mints and chewing gum and milk chocolate bars, everything looking fingered, perhaps longingly by Russian kids on whom hard times have fallen, kids cheery even for broken crisps or a tube of nasty Spangles. I see empty spaces also, fishy gaps between sweets that has me wondering whether Zach and Jude have breezed by and scooped up all the good things, meaning we can probably hang on to our £1.64, Harriet.

'That one, please,' says my sister pointing at a dusty bag with a ratty ribbon tied at the top and containing little squares wrapped in paper with swirls of navy blue and paisley shapes coloured green and red, but faded like a book left on a window sill too long. I cannot think why she has chosen this. She knows what's inside. Grey Russian chocolate.

'Harriet,' I say in low horror tones. 'Those are . . . disgusting.'

'Please,' she says, staring at the bag with great intent.

Yesterday there was a kid party on board to which ALL kids were invited like it or not. So many kids, where did they come from, all speaking different languages and messing about with party food and piling out at the end bearing a party gift of one HB pencil without a rubber on the end, a wee plastic mousie and a small see-through bag of wrapped chocolate squares tied up with a ratty ribbon. I could not wait for the end of the kid party and longed for freedom and stiff sea breezes. Harriet and Jude and I had a go at the Russian chocolate, spluttering it up on to the decks in no time. The chocolate is greyish from age or simply the wrong ingredients, as I suspect, the stuff smelling of dust and tasting of burnt toast with soap on top. Why does Harriet want it?

If we exchange our coins of the realm for grey chocolate, perhaps we will be doing a favour for the Russian people who are in a situation of few privileges compared to our situation of many privileges, and Mum will be proud. I try to picture it, this sorry universe she talks about, and I see bent figures walking nowhere special in a stark-eyed fashion, straggly-haired and wearing oversized coats with nothing but a few squares of grey chocolate in their sagging pockets and too many strangers to share it with, and then I see the Weiss family with merry unkempt hair and upright postures, striding across green fields and shiny streets and now the decks of the SS *Pushkin*, knowing it is impossible to get lost, and that wherever we hang our hats of an evening, there will be Mum with that smile, ready to tell you an amusing thing any old time the fancy strikes, and when she moves, she has the most upright posture of all, so easy, it costs her nothing, they call it a gift.

I pay the cross woman. I hand over 28p and grab for Harriet.

'Good afternoon!' says my sister in her news announcement voice, clutching her chocolates. 'Good afternoon.'

'Come on,' I say. 'Walkies.'

'Such clement weather!' exclaims Harriet, spreading her arms wide.

'Do you think Mum's awake?'

'Mummy is sick,' Harriet says in her regular voice.

'No, she's not. She's tired, Dad said. Not sick.'

'Oh yes. Poorly.'

'Don't say poorly, you sound like a nun. Only nuns say that. Hey. They gave me a book for you. Sister Margaret Mary and Sister Martha. They wrote your name in gold leaf inside.'

'How delightful!'

'It's a book of saints. You don't want it. I kept it though. For research.'

Harriet carefully tucks her chocolates into the pocket of her red mac and lines her two fists up in front of one eye in a telescope shape, twisting her hands like she is focusing. 'Don't say manger or the Little Lord thing,' she says.

'Right!'

Harriet lowers her telescope. 'Shiver me timbers,' she says. 'Thar she blows.'

'You had a pirate lesson. Was it Dad?'

'I saw five whales.'

'Where?'

'Yesterday. With Jude.'

'I saw two. I guess yesterday was Whale Day.'

'Blow me down,' says Harriet.

On the way to Mum's cabin, my sister slips her hand in mine again and although she sounds kind of tired, she tells me about whales, how they are large marine mammals who bear their young and suckle them at sea, and how they breathe through a blowhole on top of the head which closes when the whale goes under, and as she speaks I think how my sister has many moods, all of them good and all of them a variety of unusual and I tolerate them, each one, it costs me nothing, it's easy.

Jude is sprawled right outside the door of Mum and Dad's cabin, reclining on one elbow like a Roman and reading his big hardback book on Antarctic Exploration, the only book he packed for the ship, because it has everything, he says, tons of writing plus photographs and drawings and maps. We chose ship books and then all our other books went in crates, to join us later. Like Ben, who will come by air.

'Hey,' I say.

'Dad's gone out for some things. Mum and Gus are in,' Jude informs us.

'OK.' I try to step over him on my way to the door.

'You can't go in.'

'Why not? I'm going in!'

'No,' says Jude, grabbing my ankles. 'Just wait, Jem. She's resting.'

'Still?'

'Yup.'

'You look like that dog you told me about, the myth one, um –'

'Cerberus.'

'Jude. I wanted to remember by myself. Sometimes you don't give me a chance.'

'Sorry. Anyway, that would make Mum's cabin Hades. The underworld.'

'Oh. Well, forget it then.'

'Shiver me timbers,' says Harriet and Jude snorts, which is the same as a big laugh from a normal person.

'It was you. You taught her . . . Mind if I look at the book too?'

'And me! Sardines, sardines!' says Harriet, squeezing between us. 'Make room for the cat!'

I think Harriet is missing Ben. These are Ben games.

SARDINES. Ben is likely to call out Sardines! in urgent tones any time he sees Jude, Harriet and me in one place, shouting it when we are least expecting him to. Even Gus can play if we are careful. Ben shouts and we drop books, garden rakes, snacks, whatever we are doing while he commands us into some small space of his choosing where he will press his body into us with all his might, rolling us under a bed or into a cupboard or a wheelbarrow full of leaves, yelling out Sardines! Sardines! until we are all clapped out from laughing. Only Ben calls for this game, it doesn't work for anyone else, which is why we ignore Harriet now. She is missing Ben, that's all.

MAKE ROOM FOR THE CAT. At least two of us have to be sitting in a row for this game to work, otherwise the principles are pretty similar. Ben spots two of us on a bench waiting for a bus, or on a sofa watching our TV rations, and he might perch on the end of the row. This is not necessarily a dead giveaway. He plays only when he knows he can spring it on us, calling out Make room for the cat! and scooting our way so we are captives of his great body and all the air is wheezed out of our lungs due to mirth and compression. We don't play this game any more, because one day Ben was not thinking straight and he chose the wrong place to play it in. Never mind, Ben.

On Christmas Eve of our last Xmas holidays at home, we are kicking our heels because it is still day and too soon for all-out merriment and festivities and we are in a fever of waiting and also of recovering from the pressures of end-of-term homework projects, Nativity play performances and indoor school fêtes which are not too bad compared to summer ones featuring coconut games and sack races and pony rides and terrible prizes such as orange goldfish in plastic sandwich bags that make you think of Heidi Sands. Christmas fêtes are all about spending pocket money on trinkets and second-hand books and cakes and Xmas cards and raffle tickets. I never win anything, fine with me because it is usually a goldfish or a packet of biscuits. Raffle tickets are very important for nuns. Raffle tickets raise money for the convent. Good. Maybe they will buy proper loo paper, stuff that does the job and doesn't slide right off you. I made a sudden decision to buy a frozen-food knife for Mum last year. I had my duffel coat on and Dad was waiting outside to drive Harriet and me home so it was hard to think straight and it was the only thing I could see to buy for her when all the rest was junk. I think it was a wrong decision because a knife is not a pretty thing but it might be useful, who knows, plus it cost £1.10 and comes in a box. The handle worries me. It is plastic imitation wood unlike our knives at home which all have nice black wooden handles with metal rivets as they are known. The edge is not straight along either, but runs in small waves like a little kid's drawing of the ocean. I don't think Mum owns a frozen-food knife, though we do not have a freezer. Never mind. We do get bricks of ice cream on birthdays and Mum might be quite pleased to slice neat slices from the brick with a frozen-food knife, hey presto, it will be a right breeze for her! Maybe I'll hide it and not give it to her at all. It's not a pretty thing, Jem, she likes pretty things and flowers, and champagne and so on. My knife is a sad thing, it's no good.

We loiter in the kitchen. It is full of smells, smells of tonight and tomorrow. We hang around Mum with expectant looks. She'll tell us what to do, how to pull ourselves together. Tonight is Christmas Eve.

'Maybe you should all expend some energy,' she says, stirring things in pots large and small, a turkey and a goose sprawled nearby under kitchen cloths so Harriet does not stumble into stark realities regarding slaughter. Expending energy is an expression of Mum's and it means go outside and run around and climb trees, etc. Well, there isn't even any frost to play in, and I was hoping for snow, last year there was snow.

'We are too tired,' I announce, feeling free to speak for all of us.

Here comes Dad. Oh-oh.

'OK. Hats! Gloves! Hup-two-three! We need candles, potatoes, oranges! Last one into the car changes Gus's nappy!'

'Daddy,' I say, 'Gus doesn't wear nappies any more.'

'We'll put one on him! What the hell! It's Christmas! Everyone gets dressed up!'

'How about no presents this year? You always do that one.'

'Right! Thanks, Jem. Hustle, hustle! Into the car or NO PRESENTS THIS YEAR!'

Expeditions with Dad are quite interesting and almost always end up with a food reward. We shake into action, jostling each other accidentally on purpose as we run for hats and coats. We are gearing up for adventure with our dad.

Bye, Mum! Bye, Mum! Bye, dear!

'Don't get overtired, please. Tomorrow is a long day,' Mum says as she is mauled by hugs.

Dad seems to be heading for Richmond Park. Ben and Jude recognise the route, same one they take to school. Richmond Park, they murmur, exchanging glances. Dad is clearly expecting us to tumble out of the car like a pack of small dogs, excited beyond belief at the mere sight of shrubbery and woodland and stretches of wet grass. We want city lights! Maybe it's just a pit stop.

'OK!' he yells, parking the car suddenly in that way of his and giving us all whiplash. 'Everybody out! Expend some energy!'

We take our time opening doors and let out big old sighs, slithering out of our pale blue Renault like this is already too much work for us. And it's beginning to drizzle. Dad grabs us by the collars and gives us a few shoves of encouragement making me quite sure he cannot always tell the difference between his own kids and small dogs. We feel kind of on show and less inclined to gambol than if we were on our own, so we sidle up against trees like gangsters while he lights up a cigar and frowns at Harriet who is truly on top form today, doing her new Greta Garbo thing from that ridiculous film we all watched last night, three out of five Weiss kids falling over themselves with mirth and derision while Harriet took notes, I suppose, in her Harriet mind.

'Ah-heuh, ah-heuh,' she goes, clutching her heart and staggering a little.

'Did anyone bring a football?' asks Jude in a bored voice.

'Nope,' says Ben.

'OK, OK, everyone back in the car!' says Dad, mashing his cigar underfoot.

Harriet sits in front and gives my dad an embarrassing love gaze, fluttering her eyelids and smiling in a demented fashion.

'Do NOT watch the wipers,' warns Jude, worried about barf situations.

'YEH,' I add. 'Do NOT watch the wipers.'

'Leave her alone,' says Ben.

'Lord Protector! Lord Protector!' Jude and I chant at Ben, something we learned from watching the film *Cromwell*. Lord Protector, that's Ben. He hates that.

'Knock it off!' says Dad.

'Knock what off?' I ask. 'What DO YOU MEAN!' I add in Harriet's newsman interview voice.

'JEM!'

'Sorry, Dad!'

'Yeh, sorry, Dad,' says Jude.

'Sorry, Dad!' go Ben and Harriet.

We are definitely a bit hysterical.

My dad is impatient in traffic. Actually, there are practically no cars today because most people are riding buses to the shops in anticipation of traffic or they have holed up for the holidays and given up on motoring life until it is time for them to wander out on foot this evening and do Christian things in churches, singing and praying and general Adoration, etc. Mum says the singing is beautiful and she has records but we learn to say Xmas instead of Christmas as much as possible in respect of Judaism and Jewish types who come round for drinks and may be offended. It seems to me they are not bothered by our tree stacked with angels and tinsel, or big stockings hanging up and are excited by Mum's turkey and goose and even the ham which is not allowed, but words like Christmas or Jesus can definitely be a problem for them, making them a bit jumpy, as I keep trying to teach Harriet. Mum always switches her music off because there are plenty of Jesus words in the carols, there's no escaping it, though I don't think this is a problem either, it's words WE might speak, that's the problem, even by accident, as some of it rubs off, you can't help it. When I grow up, maybe the words will make me jumpy too, I'll see how it goes.

Dad is darting in and out from behind the car in front of him driven by a man in a peaked cap. He darts in and out and rattles my bones. What a *sheygets*! says Dad, whatever that means, probably not good, and Dad keeps making a move to jump the slow-coach car in front but the road is too narrow and twisty or some other car is coming the other way, straight for us. The fact there are only about three cars on the road, not counting us, has no calming effect on my dad. Everyone on the road is out to wreck his ride. He hates impediments, a person in front of him in a shop, some rogue car where he wants to park, toys on the floor where he wants to walk, anything in the way between him and a straight line to Mum anywhere, at any time. I can tell all these things are a nightmare for our dad. He likes a clear view. It's a cowboy feature.

'Move it, *bubeleh*! Move your ass!' he shouts, jerking the car this way and that, causing us to leap around in the back seat in exaggerated motion, yelping out Yikes! Yikes! and Move it, *bubeleh*, move your blooming arse! until Harriet feels so left out while the three of us leap around in the back seat she starts swaying and rolling her eyes like she is suffering from vertigo and it is possible we are pushing Dad too far, but we are on a roll and cannot stop.

'MAKE ROOM FOR THE CAT!' yells Ben, sliding into me and squashing me against Jude who mashes into the door which flies open for what seems like only a second before he slams it shut again, clapping his other hand over the lock and leaning back against the seat, breathing hard in shock, that's how it feels for all of us, shock, our four small selves frozen and speechless and waiting for Dad to lose his mind, Ben gripping my right hand and staring at his knees as if this way he can take us back in time and pretend it never happened, he can stop the storm from coming.

I don't remember the car pulling up, the usual helter-skelter parking job Dad does, the lunging forward of my body that always occurs, but we have come to a halt and it is very quiet in here. Dad grips the steering wheel and stares straight ahead and I don't know what he is seeing, something awful, and he scrapes his hands through the wilds of his hair maybe four times, right hand, left, right, left and then he scratches the back of his head, fast, the way a dog does. He doesn't say a word. He opens the door and steps out, plunging into the pockets of his sheepskin coat for cigars and matches, struggling to come up with the goods, and I want to help him and call out Left-hand pocket, Dad! because I know how much stuff is in there, receipts and keys and old shopping lists and notes from Mum, big balled-up hankies, paper clips, pens, coins, tomato stalks, lighters that don't work, notepads and empty matchboxes with phone numbers written on them but no names to go with them so that he will sometimes read them out to Mum with a frown on his face, Who do you think that is? he asks, and Mum will often have an answer for him, because she has a memory for so many things, even a thing heard once, in the distance. I know his pockets because he will send me there. I need a pen, Jem! Look in my coat! he says and I run there and pluck it free in no time, whatever item he needs, it's a gift I have.

My dad lights up, cupping his hands against the drizzle and wind, locks of hair tumbling over his forehead as he tilts to one side, making me worry he will light that too, but he flips his hair back with a toss of the head, flicking the match to the ground and inhaling deeply all at once, he's OK. Sometimes everything is so hard for him, firing a cigar up against the elements, opening a car door, carving a turkey, finding a pen, it can be a struggle. I'll do it for you, Dad. I'll find it.

He turns into his side of the car with his tum against the window and he lays his arms over the roof so we can hear the small thud of him and a little scrape of buttons, and he just smokes there like a cowboy leaning on a fence and thinking far-off thoughts to do with his woman maybe, and little glasses of whisky sliding across a bar and whether or not it is time to put away his guns and be a homesteader and build a fine home that can stand up to anything.

'Someone should go out there,' says Jude.

'No,' I say. 'He has to smoke for a bit. Leave him.'

'Is it bad, Ben?' asks Harriet sitting up on her knees to hug the back of the seat and look from us to Dad's tum pressed against the window, her lower lip quivering, her eyes filling up.

'Oh-oh,' I say, 'old wobbly lips.'

'Don't cry, Harriet,' Jude tells her, and I glance at Ben who seems frozen solid, his face pale and his mouth clamped tight. I am worried about him.

'I'll go, it's my fault,' he says suddenly, reaching for the handle, but Dad throws his cigar into the road just then with a big sweep of one arm we can feel through the car and he hauls the door open, crashing into his seat like a lunar module into the ocean when it has to break through the Earth's atmosphere, as Ben has tried to explain to me, and obey the laws of gravity on Earth which are different from the laws of gravity on the Moon where there is only one-sixth gravity, and life is easier, meaning landing there would be a gentle thing, like a feather falling.

My dad is not fleet of foot, he is not Gus who can make a circuit of the white oak table, hands behind his back, clearing the sharp corners, which are head height for him, without a glance, even as he takes the racing line as it is called, with no margin for error, and me watching him my heart pounding, foreseeing blood situations, each corner he passes, sharp and vile as a weapon to me, steel not oak, but nothing to him for whom the genes for fleetness have come straight from Mum, with no dilution, Gus can walk a perfect circle. Dad is not fleet of foot, he is a lunar module crashing to the ocean nearly everywhere he goes, the world rushing towards him with no time to gauge the distance between himself and the world, he just hopes for the best, but everywhere he walks there are tight squeezes and shifting surfaces and spaces that fall short of his estimation in size and touch, edges sharp and vile as weapons and rude as angry words spoken in a hurry, everywhere except in those few fields where the laws of gravity suddenly change for him, diminishing to one-sixth perhaps in the field of sports writing and torturing his kids, say, and above all, anywhere in sight of Mum, in the field of Mum where he is fleetest, and the laws his own, he is a feather falling.

Dad looks at his watch and then Jude looks at his watch and nobody speaks and I think how there is no time right now, we are all in a place where time doesn't count and maybe Jude's watch and Dad's do not read the same, Dad in a place where he had far-off thoughts and Jude in a place when the door flew open for a moment, and me in all those times and places. Dad has his own laws of gravity and of time also, like when he goes travelling for some story about a sporting hero and he rings Mum very often from whatever country he is in, making me think he is not doing all that much sports writing, no, he is running around looking for telephones to call Mum from foreign parts in a different time zone as the term goes, the time on his watch not the same as Mum's yet they speak to each other and have this one conversation, in a single place and time from separate places and times.

'Kids,' announces Dad, like he is explaining who we are and not calling us to attention. 'Kids . . .'

'We're sorry, Dad,' I say, real quiet.

'Sorry, Dad,' mumble Ben and Jude.

'Is it bad?' asks Harriet. 'Is anyone killed?'

'You know what could have happened back there?' Dad continues.

'Road pizza,' replies Jude.

'You got that right,' Dad says.

'Are we having pizza tonight?' asks Harriet very politely. 'I'm not very keen. So many things touching, you see.'

Heavens to Betsy.

Dad slaps his driving gloves over Harriet's head and she starts grinning and doing her fluttery-eyed Camille act and things are better around here already, it's a jumping joint again. Dad starts the engine and waggles his gear handle in that ferocious manner of his, like he is poking a big fire full of tumbling logs and lumps of blazing coal. We're off.

'You know what's wrong with you guys?' he says. 'Jobs. You all need jobs, when I was your age I had a job. No! I had two, three jobs!'

'Whose age?' I ask. 'When you were whose age?'

'What do you mean? Your age, Jude's, I don't know.'

'Well, how old were you?' says Jude.

'Ten, eleven, who cares!'

'What were your jobs then?' asks Ben, kind of grudging, like his time is coming, his time for hefting and hauling and tilling the fields.

'Right after school and weekends, I delivered bread for the baker –'

'Jewish bread?' I ask.

'Challah! Kimmel, bagels, bialys!'

'How did you carry it all?'

'In a basket! With straps.'

'I don't get it,' I say. 'Sending a boy out with the whole bakery on his back.'

'Just like an ant,' says Harriet, giving Dad a piteous look.

'Well, that's how it was! And I collected money for the butcher. In winter, I shovelled snow. And I helped in the scrapyard. Four jobs! Every day, something!'

'Every day, my dear?' asks Harriet, aghast.

'Damn right! Well . . . not Saturday.'

'Why not?' I say.

'The Sabbath,' whispers Jude, digging me in the ribs.

'The Sabbath, knucklehead,' says my dad.

'Oh right. Sorry, I forgot. No work. Day off, OK.'

'That would be Jude's favourite day,' remarks Ben.

'Every day is the Sabbath for Jude!' says Dad, shaking with mirth at his joke about Jude.

'Ha ha,' says Jude, unruffled. 'How much money did you make?'

'Almost nothing. *Bubkes!*'

'What DO YOU mean!' demands Harriet.

'Did you have to hand it over to your parents?' I ask, thinking of old films featuring poor miners with even their kids sent to work due to asperity. The kid comes home, all clapped out, a brave expression on his grimy face and his clothes falling apart but mended proudly, and a book he barely has time to read in a back pocket. He wants an education, he could be a sports writer. He is not just interested in scores and record feats but in battles heroic! He could fill whole books! He hands over a few coins to his mother who is stirring up a soup of weedy old turnips and swedes and other members of the brassica family along with a mangy bone. She takes the coins and drops them in a tin and puts it back on a high-up shelf. Clatter, clatter. That tin is not full, nowhere near. Thank you, son. She saws two thin slices of bread from the loaf on the table and cuts some Cheddar for her boy. Eat it slowly. Make it last.

'I kept the money! I needed it!'

'It doesn't sound too bad to me, you know,' I tell Dad. 'And what did you need it for anyway?'

'Girls!'

'You were ten,' says Jude, rolling his eyes. 'Or eleven.'

'Hey! I'm trying to tell you a story of my childhood, goddammit!'

'It was much worse for Mum,' states Ben, looking out his window.

'Yeh,' adds Jude, 'and she doesn't complain about it.'

'OK, OK,' says my dad. 'You know what? I'm going to sell you all, do a package deal, get some fresh kids who respect their old dad, that's what I'm going to do!' Dad parks the Renault outside the shops nearest to our house and Ben and Jude and I pitch forward into the backs of the seats in front. Bloody.

'We will all be slaves,' says Harriet. 'How delightful!'

My sister definitely has a big thing for slaves.

'ALL RIGHT, now LISTEN HERE! I am going to buy cigars. And potatoes and oranges –'

'Don't forget the candles, Dad,' I say. 'And they have to be the right ones, she likes the skinny ones. You can't just get any old thing.'

'I know, I know. Now look, I am going to be THREE minutes. Try not to cause a national emergency. You're not here when I get back, too bad.'

'No presents this year?'

'RIGHT!'

Bye, Dad! Bye, Dad!

My dad is a ruler, he is king, and not all kings are the same. Some believe all they have to do is go walkabout in a robe and crown and sceptre and a sheaf of papers of state, speaking a few words here and there in a calm voice a courtier will strain to hear and cannot ask to be repeated because he has to wait to be addressed first. Kings of this kind believe that a mere flash of kingliness is all it takes for your people to hop to it and swear allegiance and fealty, and feel safe in the realm, but this is not the whole story. Other kings, maybe not so usual, unusual kings who are not so sure of life or of their kingship, need to yell from time to time and issue threats in the voice a lion might have if a lion could speak, and that is the kind of king my dad is and this is not a problem for us. I lean back in my seat, my mind on kings and Christmas Eve. Xmas Eve.

'Ben, where is Orient Are?'

'What?' he says, extremely puzzled.

'Don't look at me like that! "We three kings of Orient Are, bearing gifts we travel afar –" You know, the carol!' I say, rushing through it, embarrassed to be singing to anyone but Harriet, and lo! there she is, touching her fingers to behind her ear and pressing her earlobe forward as she has seen Mum do in that game she plays with Gus, Gus cupping his ear also, both of them listening out for a sonorous bird.

'The rhythm is so lovely!' Harriet exclaims in her classical music voice. 'So many beats to the bar! Charming!'

'Shut up, Harriet,' say Ben and Jude, taking turns to bop her with a magazine.

'Well? Where is Orient Are?'

'Don't sing that with Dad around,' warns Jude.

'I KNOW THAT! I just want to know what it means, bloody!'

'Jem,' explains Ben in a slow quiet voice, like I have lost my marbles. '"We three kings of Orient – ARE BEARING gifts." Verb. Kings from the Orient. Not Orient Are. Get it?'

'Oh,' I say.

'What a dummy,' says Jude.

'It's the way they sing it then! The big pause after "are"! It's confusing –'

'For SOME,' says Jude, whereupon it is my turn for bops on the head.

'THIS . . . is a NATIONAL EMERGENCY!' declares Harriet.

When Dad comes back, he has more than just cigars and fruit and things, a heap more, he is bearing gifts. As well as the shopping bags, he has packets of crisps and little chocolate bars he hurls at Harriet and into the back seat, like it is feeding time at the zoo. The crisps are all the same flavour, never mind. He must have been paying for cigars and grabbed the chocolate by the till before glancing to his left and lunging at the nearest shelf in the crisp rack, he doesn't go in for a lot of time spent peering at items and making thoughtful selections in such matters, what's the difference? He wants to treat us. Grab, lunge. The chocolate bars are Cadbury's Milk, not very interesting, but Harriet will be pleased with all the purple aluminium wrappers, purple as the robes of Roman centurions. What does she do with it all? We stare at our laps, at crisps AND chocolate, and breathe out in surprise, a little laugh. Horn of plenty.

Dad pulls on his gloves, it's growing nippy, there might be snow. He starts the car. 'And it's for AFTER supper, AFTER supper. There'll be tons of goodies tomorrow. I don't want a houseful of bellyaches, got that?'

'Maybe just one tiny piece now,' says Harriet.

'What did I just say?' yells Dad, clamping her thigh in a pincer grip and pumping it until she wriggles like a fish. 'So listen. We don't tell Mum what happened back there on the road, everyone clear? Everybody heard me? Yes?'

OK, Dad. OK.

Crisps AND chocolate. It's a food reward but something else too, more than what comes our way for hanging out with him until that moment when he has run out of ideas and words and needs to sling treats our way, which he also enjoys, I can tell, laughing at the simple rapture we show him for a bag of crisps or a rare ice cream with rabbit ears. And this is more than a reward for giving him such a good time at the funfair, say, and surviving a round of bumper cars, his favourite ride, when he will ram into us quite gleefully until time is called and we climb out of our vehicles intact and still proudly walking this earth, instead of laid out in a row of hospital beds in casualty with doctors and nurses hovering, quizzing us in grave tones, and scrawling notes on clipboards.

'What happened out there?'

'Bumper cars,' we reply. 'Bumper cars.'

Crisps and chocolate. It's a reward and a bribe too. Don't tell Mum. Don't tell her. And now I know what my dad saw when he sat scraping his hands through his locks and gazing through the windscreen saying nothing at all, just breathing in and out. He saw all his kids on the road, mashed up and raising bloody forearms in the air, straining for something, for words, for someone, the way Messala does at the end of the chariot race in *Ben-Hur*, Messala who was Judah Ben-Hur's best friend and became his enemy because of war and prejudice and a lot of mixed-up feelings for Judah who wins that chariot race. When Messala is having death throes, his limbs mangled and bloody and due for the chop, he has one last desire and that is to see Ben-Hur and clutch his old friend's chest and speak nasty last words, which is what he does, his body leaping with energy from all those mixed-up feelings and Judah having to peel dead Messala's hand off his tunic, finger by finger. It's a bad scene, and may well be a case of anti-Semitism, I'm not sure, and anti-Semitism perhaps just comes calling for people who are open to persuasion, like a life of crime for the covetous, the covetous and not, of course, the desperate, like Fagin's boys, or the Robin Hood types like Jude. Coveting is very bad and Mean Nun is prone to spooky speeches on this subject, because according to her, covetousness is a mere step away from all-out felony and perdition. Crime, then, is a personality thing. It does seem to me Messala had a bad personality to begin with, and in boyhood when he was best friends with Judah, his dark side was in disguise, an early-embryo moment as when a pig and a chicken and a fish and a person are all one to the casual observer and who knows how things will turn out, if you will be scratching around with the fowl or swimming with the fish, the way Ben-Hur could not foresee that his best friend was a nasty type waiting to happen, a type so nasty he speaks terrible last words to him with ferocious energy and bloody digits.

When Dad had his vision of Weiss kids having death throes in the road alongside Richmond Park, seeing himself coming home to Mum and Gus with only one out of the four kids he took away with him, carrying Harriet piggyback, and entering our house with dark news, some very bad Xmas tidings, did he hear things too, things such as death rattles and last words?

Jude cannot be bothered with death throes. He is a goner and he faces the facts without tiring himself for no good reason, clawing the air and racking his brains for the right last words, what's the point. He lies flat and stares up at the drizzly sky, he's been doing this all his life. His toy telescope would be good right now, for a last glimpse of the firmament. Where did he leave it? Jem will know. Where's Jem? It's growing dark for Jude, dark enough for a telescope. A snack would be nice. Jem?

'I'll be back,' says Ben. 'Count on it.'

Ben is undead. He told me all about this matter one day and I found it so depressing, I don't recall much of what he said except for the no-dying part and how it applies to vampires only, but it's debatable. Maybe Ben is undead. He does not return by night, however, to terrorise people in their prime for no good reason, chomping at their necklines like a mad dog, no, not Ben who collapses at the sight of the merest globule of blood, he returns to help Harriet and Gus with their homework, explaining all the difficult words and ideas before tucking them in with laughs, make room for the cat! Ben is the worst and nicest vampire in the vampire realm. 'I'll be back. Count on it.'

Here are Jem's last words.

'I leave my Shane jacket to Gus. And I leave my second-best jacket to Gus too. The baseball one. Harriet can have whatever she wants. As long as she puts it back in the right –' Oh. That's no good. Start again. These are my last words. 'Take care of Mum. Please. Thank you. Over and out.'

My last words are the same as my birthday wish, the one I make every year, every year the same, holding a knife upside down and closing my eyes to keep the vision in, speaking the words carefully in my head, slowly, because you never can tell who might be listening and what have I got to lose? Long life for her, I say, health for her, always, no loopholes. And please let me die first. My last words are nearly the same as my birthday wish except for the last part. I don't need the last part any more because in my dad's vision, it happens, I die first, I don't get to see the worst scene in the world, I will never have to scream over her fading self, that scene is not for me, I skip it neatly, I am fleet of foot.

When Dad pulls up outside the house Jude and Ben tumble out and swing the gates open before he can yell The gates! The gates! and soon we are scrambling up the stone steps and bursting through the back door into the warm kitchen with Dad following and it feels like a party already and there is Gus doing his circuit of the oak table, hands clasped behind like Lord Nelson strolling the decks of the *Victory* and Mum is preparing spaghetti, no road pizza for us, not tonight! Dad pulls my hair and ears quite a lot, kind of pressing his luck, but I don't care. Go ahead, Dad. Mum laughs as he opens the champagne, because though she knows it's coming, she is always surprised and happy and then Dad hauls out a big bottle of Coca-Cola for Ben and Jude and me, generally forbidden of course, due to corrosive effects and nil nutrients, but not tonight, it's Christmas Eve and we made it through alive. We queue up clutching glasses, watching out he pours even shares and when he comes to Harriet, he pours juice instead and she says her routine thing, some line my dad taught her.

'And DON'T BE STINGY, BABY!' she growls, enjoying what she sees, awestruck she has this great power over him, nigh on delirious that these five words he fully expects to hear can cause such a tempest each time, a laugh big as a starburst I think, something like that.

'Sardines!' yelps Harriet. 'Make room for the cat!' she says, squishing between Jude and me and making a big old show of studying the pictures in Jude's Ernest Shackleton book, rubbing her chin with thumb and index finger and frowning as she has seen me do quite often, and will copy when the fancy strikes and she is in need of attention. Harriet is missing Ben.

Jude flips past a picture of Shackleton's ship stuck slam in the ice to a picture of men sitting around a cabin with cheery expressions and pipes in their mouths and their dogs nearby and a sign on the wall above with the words *God Bless our Dear Dogs* painted thereupon.

'God bless our dear dogs,' she reads, sounding chuffed. She likes these words the men painted on a sign, she might have painted it herself.

'They ate them,' says Jude who sits cross-legged with his left elbow on one knee and his head in his left hand, still able to speak this way, no problem. 'The five youngest first.'

'Really?' I ask, a bit worried about Harriet. 'Is it true?'

'Yup. They had to. For survival.'

'Whoa,' I say. 'Jeepers creepers.'

I can tell Harriet is upset because she starts singing quite softly, some tune of her own I do not recognise. She flips the Dear Dogs page over without checking with Jude or me. Usually if there is a joint reading activity going on, a person ought to say Ready? before flipping the page, it's good manners, but Harriet just flips it over to the next page, also a picture, all the pictures being in a clump in the middle of the book.

'Penguins,' my sister announces. 'Flightless. Aqua – aquatic . . . Good at fleeing enemies. Because of narrow wings. Dense plumage. For tolerating extreme cold. Highly gregarious.'

Wow. I pat my sister on the back with appreciation. In ornithology, she is tops.

'What's gregarious?' she asks.

'They ate the penguins too,' says Jude.

'What's gregarious! What's gregarious, what's gregarious!' Harriet is almost shouting now, she is mad at Jude and all his bad tidings she does not want to hear, and he is so unruffled, it makes things worse, I know how she feels, crazed, like screaming in a dream no sound coming out, and everyone passing you by.

'Come on, Harriet!' I jump up and pull on her arm. 'We're seeing Mum, we're going in.'

'No!' says Jude, grabbing the handle he can reach from where he is sitting and my heart starts thumping hard to see his hand there. 'Wait for Dad.'

'YOU'RE NOT BOSS!'

'Don't wake her!' he says so I feel ashamed and want to yell at him that I know how to take care of Mum, I wouldn't wake her, and anyway, she never sleeps this long, but all I can do is stutter, my tongue too big for my mouth suddenly, a feeling so awful I kick the wall and that hurts also, it really does. 'Come on, Harriet, come with me, back to our room. Cabin. Come on!'

Harriet slinks closer to Jude who was her enemy two minutes ago and Jude is reading calmly again, chin in hand. Bust, statue, statuary. Stop it, Jude. Harriet's eyes are fixed on me, she chooses Jude over me despite his bad news about explorers so hungry they kill their dear dogs to stay alive and eat the penguins they had been waltzing about with on the ice that has trapped them. She chooses Jude because I am in a temper and it's frightening for her, a bad temper is a journey, I think, a straight line, a short distance between two points and the end is always the worst place to arrive, like watching a horror film unto the end and there is no peace for a while, not even when the lights flash up and you know where you are again, no, not for a while, you need time to recover and Harriet will not come with me, why did I ask her to, I should never have asked, and my face grows hot with this stupid expectation I had, the blood rising like a fire in me, electricity, combustion. Don't make any noise. Don't wake her up. Walk away, Jem. Step lightly, do the rope-a-dope.

I dive on to my berth, somehow remembering the way alone, and I want to get under the covers but you can't do that in the daytime unless you are sick. Poorly. I am not sick. *Mum is*. On some schooldays, I act sick just so I can stay home and be with her, watch her, get little bed visits and dry toast cut in fingers with maybe a medium-boiled egg stirred up in a glass. I don't always win a day off when I act sick but it is important to feel at least a little bit sick on the day. You need something to build on, for reality. The routine goes like this. Writhe around in pyjamas when she comes to wake you for school. Frown and moan in a valiant manner, as if you are trying to keep the worst from her and this is only the tip of the iceberg. Now she fetches the thermometer and sits on the edge of the bed while Harriet flounces about taking too long to get dressed and gazing your way in a suspicious manner. A look from Harriet is like a pointing index finger on the end of an outstretched arm. Go away, Harriet. Mum smiles slightly and shakes out the thermometer. That smile may mean she is on to me. It does not necessarily mean you have to go to school though.

'Keep it under your tongue,' she says. 'I'll be back in a minute.'

OK. Now is the time to think hard, very hard, about being ill so the body might catch on and show signs of weakness and collapse. I hold my breath like I am a dead person, convinced the thermometer will now record fearful signs of imminent expiry. Imminent. Coming soon. I am not sure this works because Mum reads the temperature in a sly way, looking from the fine glass tube to me and back again, never reading the temperature aloud unless I am really sick, in which case I am not aware of much except for her mumbling some reading and calling out Yaakov! and pretty soon the doctor comes round and bottles of medicine are opened and Dad drops magazines on the bed in the late afternoon and chocolate for when you are back among the vigorous. Really sick is no holiday.

'Did you keep it under your tongue?'

I am not sure, I tell her. Maybe we should try again. 'Is it bad or good?' I ask.

No answer.

This is no help to me. If it is bad, then I should leave it at that. If it is normal, then I need to have a better crack at death behaviour and no breathing. I tried to test it out once, climbing on to the sink and stealing the thermometer from the medicine cabinet and settling on the floor of Mum's bathroom, clamping my tongue down just so over the glass tube, too loose and it pops free in a frustrating manner, too tight and your tongue aches and you are in danger of instant demise by poisoning, like a spy in captivity. Jude says mercury is poison and that's why you must not lick the back of a mirror. I have no idea who would want to do that, but never mind. The more perils a person is apprised of, the better.

I hold my breath and whip the thermometer out but I cannot read the bloody scale, straining to distinguish the little black rulings which keep disappearing from view like a trick of the light, straining to get a reading before the mercury goes back to normal, a place it maybe never left. And then I cannot recall the margin for ill health, or what kinds of sickness have no bearing on temperatures, or what a bad mark is, or just how high I need to get to stay home in my pyjamas and hang out with my own mother, goddammit. I've heard her say 'Oh, only 101. It'll pass by lunchtime.' And I've heard this too. '101. Let's keep him home.' Weird. Sometimes Dad is doctor in our house. He is not very good. First off, he makes a big deal of reading the thermometer, frowning at it near a window where the light is better and shaking it out, then pulling up a chair to press one great hand on your forehead and take a good long look at you, man to man.

'I don't know,' he says, ruminating. 'Stick out your tongue.'

'Why?'

'I'm looking for signs!'

Maybe the back of my tongue is a bit like chicken guts. 'OK, Dad.'

'Farther, farther!'

'Daddy, that's as far as it goes. I can't stick it out much. It's kind of connected underneath, I mean right to the end almost. See?'

'Gosh, Jem. You're right. Are you all like that?'

Are we all like that. Like we came off a factory line or something. 'No, only me. I checked. Why? Is it bad?'

'Well, look at mine! See? And your mother's is fine.'

'I guess it's just a flaw, Dad. Can we not talk about it?'

'Anything else wrong with you? Maybe I'll send you back! Get a cash refund! Let me count your fingers, ha ha ha ha!'

My dad examines my throat, peering into the depths of me. 'Hey. I'm going to ask your mother to make me some nice boiled tongue. Haven't had that in ages!'

'Dad! You are not supposed to look at me and think about dinner on a plate! You're supposed to say whether I go to school or stay home!'

'I don't know, Jem. How do you feel? How about a smoked meat sandwich? Or a large Scotch? Ha ha ha ha.'

Lord-a-mercy. 'I guess I'll go to school.'

'Attagirl. Put it there, partner. I'll see you at the bar at four. What'll it be?'

I shake my dad's big hand. I say my line. 'Mine's a champagne cocktail.'

Dad is not very good at medicine, he is best at the recovery part, when he will shower you with magazines and things. The illness part rattles him badly though, and Mum has to say everything three or four times, please take the tray away, please ring the doctor, bring me a wet cloth, please watch her for a minute, this last request being the worst for him, because it is not really a good time for cracks or stories and he has to sit there in your room looking edgy until you want to rise up and clap a wet cloth on him yourself. I wonder what he is up to now with Mum, if things are different with her and he knows what to do and is not just sitting there waiting for instructions from the one person who cannot give them, because she is sleeping, she is resting. I wonder if he looked for signs, examining her tongue and pronouncing it flawless, or is he just sitting there looking edgy and waiting for the recovery part, clutching fresh roses, I saw roses there yesterday, where did he get them, how do roses grow on a ship?

'Did you keep it under your tongue?'

Mum is very good at medicine. She keeps her cool.

After her thermometer test, when it is advisable to stare gloomily into the distance, forlorn and helpless, comes the body test, Mum resting her hand lightly on my forehead, first the palm then the back of the hand, glancing skyward. She is thinking. Then she curls her fingers and lays the back of them on the breastplate, right there below the top pyjama button. More thinking. Then comes the decision. 'Well. Why don't we keep you home today?' Or, 'Why don't you put on your uniform and step outside and take some deep breaths? Then we'll see.' Forget it. You lost. Deep breaths is code for Go to school, Jem.

In case you win though, it is advisable to do some research regarding dinner. You are not supposed to be excited about dinner on invalid day. A good day to be an invalid is fish pie night, especially when being even a little bit sick and facing up to fish pie can push a person right over the edge into fever and barf, what with visions of fleshy clams and wrinkly mussels with strange black lines on them and fish heads with stary eyes and all manner of things not quite dead beneath a nice blanket of creamy potato. I made the mistake of winning a day off on shepherd's pie night once, although Mum said she would save me a whole separate wee casserole for my recovery, but Jude came in to lord it over me and tell me how many portions he had (two and a bit) and how great it was (very). Thanks, Jude.

Is she hungry?

I am kind of worried about special properties and antibodies, which have to do with immunity Ben told me, when we did embryos, meaning resistance to diseases and infections, etc. I am worried about antibodies and does she have them, because of her unknown origins and how no one knows where she was in the first six months of her life and Ben says the two topmost important meals a person will ever eat are dished up before you are even half a year old and don't have much choice in the matter, when you are in the womb and at the breast. This is probably a good thing because, given the choice, a person is more likely to opt for cheese on toast and not so likely to want to mingle his own blood vessels with the mother's in this exchange of substances that occurs in a womb, of oxygen and nutrients and antibodies, the embryo feeding by way of an umbilical cord just like a built-in bendy straw you might say, and given the choice, a person is more likely to opt for apple juice in a glass, a lot less trouble than drinking straight through your own mother, but Ben says this milk has special properties and it is a once-in-a-lifetime offer and no other milk is any good to you, don't miss out. Who knows if she ever had mother's milk? I doubt it, I'm worried.

'Ben? Do all wombs come with antibodies?'

'Placenta.'

'What?'

'It's in the placenta, which is in the womb when you're pregnant. You have one.'

'One what?'

'Womb!'

'No, no. I don't think so. Not yet.'

'Oh yes,' Ben says. 'You do. You'll see.'

What is wrong with Ben and Jude that they have to keep threatening me with body parts and body functions like I am in some identity crisis or whatever and think I may turn out to be a fish or a chicken instead of a lady, goddammit? Never mind.

'So is Mum all right for antibodies and everything?'

Sure, said Ben that day. Of course. But I worry. Maybe she needs to make up for things now, that she missed out on then, special foods for immunity and resistance, etc., and I hope Dad is feeding her right, I hope so. She can't eat roses, Dad.

I think about Mr Shackleton and his men and I imagine them eating everything in sight, dogs and penguins and ice to help it go down, ice that is making them crazed, holding them all in a death grip. Soon they are hauling great wedges out of the white world with axes and picks, perhaps gnawing on their very ship called the *Endurance*, like woodpeckers, and then they look around for what is next on the menu, maybe each other, that would be next.

Has someone taken her temperature? Is it 101? 101 good or 101 bad?

I hold my hand in front of the light that nestles in its hole in

the wall. I switch it on and admire my hand as Ben once demonstrated for me, how the hand glows red and the red is your blood,
a substance of great interest to my big brother as long as it stays
where it belongs and does not drip from the body in untold ways.
Is Chris's family remembering to put out nuts and raisins for Ben?
In a bowl, all mixed together? *Why is she sick?* I stare at my hand
and the lovely red glow, I love it, but I see no movement, none of
the rushing sensation I feel in there. Blood does not always flow
the same, as I understand, sometimes slow as cream, or fast as a
river, running in small neat waves perhaps, like a little kid's drawing
of an ocean, the edge of my frozen-food knife, or in this mad rush,
fast as light and glowing right through me, so a small cut might
prove it, one to each palm, say, blood spilling as light also, my
hands like beacons!

I flick the cubbyhole light off and flip on to my stomach, pushing
the pillow against the headboard so I can lie flat, I like to lie flat,
and now my whole under-the-pillow stash spills out around my
head, my stripy pyjamas, criminal stripy and not blue like Jude's
or the Renault we had to leave behind because in our new country
they want your steering wheel on the other side, the left. Signs on
the augur's left, propitious. Good. Signs on the right, unpropitious.
Bad. I keep a torch under my pillow for reading at night in my
tent of covers, reading by torchlight so as not to wake anyone.

Don't wake her! I wouldn't wake her, Jude!

I have three books in my stash, the saints book and the according
to Matthew book I could not decide what to do with, and *The
Phantom Tollbooth* by Norton Juster, a favourite in our family
since Mum read it to us doing all the voices in that marvellous
manner. I don't understand it fully yet and have read the first part
three times so far. I am not sure it is OK to like something very
much and not fully understand it, but never mind. Milo is a boy
who goes on strange journeys and in the first part he meets a
watchdog who becomes his best friend and travelling companion
and this dog has an alarm clock built into his body and his name
is Tock. Milo is lost when they meet, he is stuck, he says. Can you
help me? Tock asks him why, why is he where he is, stuck, lost?

'I suppose I just wasn't thinking,' said Milo.
'PRECISELY,' shouted the dog as his alarm went off again.
'Now you know what you must do.'

'I'm afraid I don't.'

'Well,' continued the watchdog impatiently, 'since you got here by not thinking, it seems reasonable to expect that, in order to get out, you must start thinking.' And with that he hopped into the car.

'Do you mind if I get in? I love car rides.'

Milo began to think as hard as he could. He thought of birds that swim and fish that fly. He thought of yesterday's lunch and tomorrow's dinner. He thought of words that began with J and numbers that end in 3. And as he thought, the wheels began to turn.

'We're moving, we're moving,' he shouted happily.

'Keep thinking,' scolded the watchdog.

There is a lot you can do in a night if you are in the mood so it is wise to have a pillow stash. If a bad temper is a journey, taking you from one place to a different place, usually worse, maybe nighttime is too, with stops for reading and dreaming and the unexpected, such as sleepwalking, sleeptalking, surprises like Tock for Milo, like the ice that caught Shackleton, Sir Ernest Henry, a man who bashes off on a mission of exploration and has to change his mission from exploration to rescue. It's unexpected. And look at us now, headed for a new country and Mum sick and Ben not here and I'm failing at my new mission almost as soon as I thought it up. I suppose I just wasn't thinking. Start thinking. Travel is important, Jude says. Travel is hard, it is bloody, Jem says.

With my ear pressed to the mattress, I hear it all, the engine of the ship and my heart itself, every beat, beats that are jogging my body and making the mattress creak and for a moment, the rushing sound in my ears is the sound of everything, the way a wild rustling of leaves can sound the same as a bonfire, or driving rain, splashing and sparks, the roar of blood in my ears is the sound of everything. My heart is an engine, a clock, I feel it all, the pumping and bleating and swelling of veins and tissues, so loud in my head, I think how quickly it might come for something with so many moving parts – an engine, a clock, a heart. Failure, they call it failure.

Sit up, Jem. Start thinking. Book of Saints. St Crispin, I read, is patron saint of shoemakers, meaning he probably wore the right shoes at the right times in the right places and is Mean Nun's top saint. St Francis, Mirror of the World, what does it mean? Do not lick him! Mercury is poison! And who do we have here? St Catherine of Siena, Dominican nun, mystic and Doctor of the Church. Doctor of the Church. Like Sister Martha, Nurse Nun, nurse for nuns. Or like Mr Levinthal who is not a doctor of the medical kind, which is too bad because Jeremy is seasick and could do with some help. *My mum is not sick, she is resting.* Catherine, it says, experienced visions 'beginning at the age of six' and when she was grown up 'she felt the pains of the stigmata' and there are two pictures of her, one of her Mystic Marriage to Jesus, a wedding scene with angels and other guests identified in tiny writing below, Jesus's mum and John the Baptist and King David with a lot of musicians. The Israelite King David provides music, it says, which is very nice of him, I think, coming all this way to Siena many centuries after his death. It's symbolic, Jem. Of what?

St Catherine of Siena Exchanging her Heart with Christ Elevated in Rapture. In this second picture, Catherine stands on what looks like a heap of snow that is a special cloud of course, because she is elevated in rapture, and all around her are pink buildings with iron crosses on the rooftops resembling TV aerials, and amongst the houses is Jesus doing the heart exchange with Catherine who is holding hers out like a wet red sponge. I wonder what was wrong with it? Some flaw I guess, next stop failure, and Jesus doesn't need his because he has immortality, according to Matthew. *Lo, I am with you alway, even unto the end of the world.* Take mine, is what he means. Mine is flawless, and I don't need it, not where I come from. Not where I'm headed.

Is she still sleeping? What time is it? If different countries have different time zones, what time is it out here, does the sea have its own time zone, or no time, like an intermission at the cinema, time that does not really count, just a join between two rolls of film, a pausette, time out, time you might spend waiting for someone to appear, your favourite person, waiting for her to get better and play with you – play with me! – time that is a vigil with minutes like elastic, every tick loud and terrible and suddenly passing, snap, you dreamed it, and a dream is a journey that never happened.

I fling off my clothes, leaving my jeans inside out and my jumper in a tangle and I don't care what time it is, I slip into my stripy pyjamas and stare at the door, willing her to come through it and I start to cry when it flings open, though it is only my dad who tells me about the sandwiches and treats in Mum's cabin and how we are all having a picnic dinner in there and everyone is waiting for me.

'I'm in my pyjamas! Can't you see that!'

'I see that,' he says, pushing my feet into desert boots and my arms into baseball jacket. 'My little fugitive from a chain gang.'

'Chicago Cubs!' I say, crying harder and jabbing fiercely at my jacket, at the emblems here and there. 'Hank Greenberg, Detroit Tigers!'

'Jem,' he says, squeezing my ribcage and lifting me off the bed. 'Hey, Jem.'

It's late, he's not sleepy, he needs to move around, and a small whisky would be fine, whisky in a sparkling glass. Add three drops of water. Forget it. Fill your pipe. He finds his things where he left them, where he always leaves them, in his second-best jacket on the back of the door. He could make his way around this room blindfold and he steps lightly now, he can still do this, he's a soldier. Don't wake her. Even down the hall, past two closed doors, he can hear her shifting, shifting. Is she asleep? He can't remember the last time he slept with her, that time has passed, how did it happen, when did it? It's all for the best, all's well. She sleeps with Frances now. Frances. He named her, no one stopped him, even the sound is good. Frances.

The moon must be full tonight. He doesn't know about these things, he doesn't need moonlight anyway, this room is his realm, he runs it like a ship, stoking the stove, filling the tin bath, folding his bed, unfolding it, moving around like clockwork, this place is shipshape.

Out on the balcony with his pipe, the moon is almost too much for him, he doesn't look up, he does not want to see any closer than this, not like Frances, Frances would wish for a telescope. She showed him her book, she explained the word telescope, something in Italian, she says, meaning, to see at a distance, was that it? She showed him a picture of a man in a white beard and a little cap like Jews wear, and a lamp at his feet and a telescope in his lap. Galileo, Daddy. Lord Nelson, the soldier says, had a telescope like that. He suffered from seasickness, Daddy, isn't it strange? She knows so much, every day something new. Highest Honours. She won Highest Honours for playing a piano.

I have a medal, he tells her. Do you want to see?

He opens the cupboard and pulls it down, their secret suitcase he calls it, and he shows her the medal though she has seen it so often, turning it over and over in her hands. For Valour.

He can't remember valour, only noise and no thinking and moving with everyone else, his heart like a drum, a marching song, so loud it's all he could hear. He found this roar in the pub also, in his pub days that are now over, all the men there having one voice, he cannot tell them apart, it doesn't matter, and he speaks too, some words he can't hear in the rush of sound that is suddenly everything there, men, glasses on the bar, the splash of beer, the blast of wind when the door opens, a brush of snow across the floor, it's all one to him and he feels safe as houses, he gives himself up, like on a battlefield, he is not really there at all. Take one step, then another, it's all you have to do, for valour.

Of them which thou gavest me, have I lost none.

He heard that this morning, he's heard it before, other sermons, so many sermons. Jesus in the garden and his time is nearly up. Put up your swords! He doesn't want to lose any men. Not on his watch. He doesn't want to see it, loss of life. Take mine. I don't need it, not where I'm headed.

It's late, you're not sleepy, you can still hear it all, every note. Highest Honours! Mummy said nothing, never mind, she's not well, that's all. Highest Honours, and so nearly failure. You stopped. Something about the note you played, the right note but it never came from you, you couldn't feel it, you lost it, a flaw of timing, breath, pressure, feeling, it was not the note you heard in your head, it clashed. You stopped and stood up and closed the lid on that piano. I don't know you any more.

Everything that frightens you, a false note bad as the moulding in the kitchen, you hate it, lines not parallel that you stare at, willing them to straighten. On sad days, you extend them in your mind's eye, knowing that somewhere, at some point, at one end they will tangle like a clash of swords, like angry voices, Mummy and Dot, always fighting. Bad blood, Mummy said. What does it mean?

You walked offstage and there she was, Sister Clare who touched your shoulders in the wings and turned you round. Frances, she said. That's all. One touch, one word, Highest Honours and so nearly nothing. Sister gave you a book, The Revelations of Divine Love. *Dame Julian of Norwich. A man's name for a woman, isn't it strange? Hide this book.* All shall be well, *you read,* and all shall be well, and all manner of things shall be well. *Jesus is our Mother, writes Dame Julian. He suckles us, the sacrament our milk, we come to his breast through a wound in his open side. Our Mother Jesus, our beloved Mother, but Jesus is not your mother,* she said nothing today, you don't please her, not ever, and she smells of fading things.

All shall be well, and all shall be well, and all manner of things shall be well.

Hide this, hide all of it.

—It's nearly time, isn't it?
—We have three minutes.
—Tick, tock.
—You are very bloody-minded today. You are stuck, but you don't want to do any thinking with me.
—PRECISELY!

I want to tell you a cowboy story, Mrs Rosenfeld, but I get stuck and leave it too late because you might think I am talking about friendship and hopes and rescue and ridiculous soppy things of that nature when it's only a crazy story, who cares, I'd just be telling you a story and you might think I need you and I don't, I don't need you or anyone, so forget it, fuck off.

Start thinking.

I want to tell you about my favourite scene in *The Magnificent Seven*, John Sturges, 1960, and it comes around the eighteen-minute mark, a scene between two cowboys who have just met and are leaning on a fence together, acting all disinterested yet sizing each other up acutely in that cool cowboy fashion.

Steve McQueen: Where are you headed?
Yul Brynner: I'm driftin' south more or less. You?
Steve McQueen: Oh, just driftin'.

You might think this a slapdash way to strike up a friendship, but it is only code, and these two end up pretty close, enduring hard knocks together without complaint, and I don't think their friendship is a surprise to either of them or that it's some strange act of grace either, an accident of time, of drift. My feeling is that top cowboys can be downright rigorous when it comes to the selection of friends and travelling companions, under these wraps of cool, knowing from experience it is often better and safer to strike out alone than make the wrong choice of companion, and that is why I watch this scene sometimes and make a little shift in my mind, a transposition of time and place, just to see if it fits, and it always fits, the Steve McQueen cowboy standing in for any one of Ernest Shackleton's twenty-seven, asking, Where are you headed? to which Sir Ernest replies, I'm driftin' South more or less. You?

A famous biographer of Shackleton explained in a telly interview that having to change your mission from one to another of equal urgency is a change of direction that can break most men, it can break you, he said. Shackleton heads South to make the very first crossing of the Antarctic continent on foot, but he gets caught in a terrible trap, an ice trap, and now he has a new mission to bring all his men home alive and it seems to me he took on the new mission with even greater bloody-mindedness and devotion. He had a little help, though.

There is quite a well-known phenomenon concerning travellers *in extremis* and that is the phenomenon of the Extra Man, signifying a very definite sense of an invisible travelling companion more like a guide dog, there with you every brutal step of the way, there and not there. Take one step, then another. Thank you, don't leave me. Who are you? Shackleton later reported the presence of the Extra Man alongside him as he negotiated the awful passage across the mountains of South Georgia to the whaling station where he would find the help he needed to rescue his men from Elephant Island, all of them so close to the end.

—Are you all well?

—All well, Boss!

When Shackleton gets home he writes these words. 'Not a life lost and we have been through Hell.'

Had he been a visionary man, I think, and not merely a hero, he might have taken a moment to look back in time a little more carefully, and he would have seen he was no longer equipped for danger, for exposure to perishing cold and travel in high-risk territories. He might have called it a day and not set out on a vague fourth Antarctic expedition only to die on board ship of a heart attack in the very shadow of the mountains he crossed on his way to the whaling station and the writing of those proud words, Not a life lost and we have been through Hell. He might have spared himself this collapse, a cruel joke, this failure of the heart.

SIX

Black.

I have this persistent vision of the men Ernest Shackleton left behind on Elephant Island with little to do but scrape about on the ice, waiting and hoping, entertaining this single notion of endurance, playing this thankless role of survivor, out of time, time now their enemy and, in the absence of Boss, without direction. Waiting and hoping is one hell of a job and apt to make a person crazy.

Show no cracks. Cracking up is so easy, the smallest thing can send you there, as you pace a darkened room, say, doing this hell of a job of waiting and hoping, and what tips you over the edge is always a petty thing, a clumsy move, a stubbed toe, a paper cut, a glass you break, a dissonant sound, a tiny rent in the memory, a flaw in your vision and that impossible noise in your ears, like the grinding of knives.

Red. What is the name of the officer whose blood stained Lord Nelson's jacket, the last jacket he ever wore, a shroud? The jacket is preserved in a naval museum, the bloody evidence, so it seems, of Nelson's martyrdom but the blood is not his, it is the blood of another officer cut in half by a cannonball and cast overboard. Lies. England expects. What was his name?

Olbers' Paradox. Heinrich Wilhelm Matthäus Olbers, b.1758, d.1840. I have an obsession with numbers! Olbers was a doctor with a big thing for stars and mathematics and the influence of the Moon on the weather. He built an observatory on the top floor of his house in Bremen and he fitted it with telescopes, pacing the attic perhaps, between observations, as he calculated the orbits of comets and mused on ailments and diseases and puzzled at the darkness of the night sky. Why is the sky dark at night when it is so full of bright stars? Redshift is one cause. The Universe is expanding, galaxies fly farther apart, light weakens. Time is the main cause. There has not been enough time for light to reach us, not enough time to fill all the dark spaces with light, proof, they explain, that the Universe had a beginning, proof anyone can see with their own eyes. If the Universe were infinite, every line of sight would end on a star.

There they are then, Shackleton's men, beyond hunger now, sitting around and sucking on empty pipes, the mind wandering, no more sharp and defining edges, light weakens. A certain readiness is setting in, the mind yielding, not quite giving up. The body is famished for nutrients, beginning to feed on itself, a cannibal, looking to muscles for energy and sending it to the brain, yes, to my temporal lobe please, where memories live, let me have a field day, the man says, a tumble in soft focus, I want only the most sustaining views, the finest moments, a roll call of loved ones, stand in the light, just there, thank you. Wait a minute. What's that? A speck on the landscape at the edge of my dimming vision, is it Boss, or just my dammed eyes, the loosening jelly, the floaters imposed on every bright horizon, on every white and frozen space, a figure perpetually coming my way and never arriving. Better to wait in the dark, a person knows what's what in the dark.

Is it you?

Cracking up is so easy. Always a petty thing. What did I eat last night? Did I eat last night? Did I drink? Oh yes. Where is it, my photograph of you, Christmas, last year, you in your red dress? Sir John Herschel, b.1792, chemist, photographer, astronomer, he invented these words for photography, *positive*, *negative*, *snapshot*. What was the officer's name? Red. Blood red, Schiaparelli pink! Slow down! Giovanni Schiaparelli, b.1835, astronomer, student of Mars, he invented a name for the markings he saw there, *canali*, channels we now know are dried-up rivers. There was water on Mars. Was there ice? Reddening. Effect of dust grains on the light from distant stars. Dust scatters light, the shortest wavelengths first, blue, allowing the longer ones through, red. That's a sunset. Red penetrates dust and that's how maybe I saw you, I mean it, it was you, eleven years old or thereabouts, same as in that photograph of Yaakov's, the only one I've ever seen of you as a child, hand-tinted, Frances in her first red dress, too beautiful, I'm sorry, the black curls, the blue eyes so very much like Gus's, the goddam dimples, that smile. You spoke my name in a gentle voice at optimum pitch, like a wake-up call, and you said it twice. Jem. Jem! You had something to tell me and I stared into the dark, where did you go? Night to the short-sighted is so full of movement, of particles like dust. There was a reddening and then I lost you.

Cracking up, in my opinion, is a malady requiring isolation and a fine spirit of enquiry because the symptoms are so changeable. Pay attention. My heart, of late, has taken on a life of its own, its rhythms brazen and tearaway, protesting, and so they put a monitor on me, a twenty-four-hour tag, like I am some criminal. St Francis of course, b.1182?, d.1226, was subject to transports of the body and mind or what is called Illumination, though to be frank, he was a man so full of hopes and wayward to boot, usually starving and ailing, it is fair to say one man's lamb chop and potatoes on a white plate is another man's seraph with wings and stigmata. It depends how you look at it. Shackleton's men became visionaries too. Everyone needs vision for something, a vision of something. There's another thing. A doctor in the south of England taken up with research on the heart writes that the heart is a more powerful generator of electricity than even the brain. Isn't it strange?

Frances, I saw you.

TERRA NOVA.

A logbook is a diary but not a diary and I am quite interested in logbooks. When you see this word logbook, right away you start thinking about captains on ships, although other types can make logbooks, explorers and pioneers and military commanders and so on. I am beginning to think that even those According to books, or the Gospels as they are known, are also logbooks because these four men, Matthew, Mark, Luke and John, were like newsmen on the case of Jesus, reporting all his words and activities, often repeating things or describing one single event again and again but each time slipping in some new detail, which is OK, because a newsman has to be very careful about facts, he has to be very thorough and try to see things from all angles like a sleuth and not let his feelings get tangled up with his view of the facts.

This point about feelings is very important. A newsman or

logbook writer has to keep his feelings aside or no one will trust his news, his record of events, and this goes for the Gospels too. I looked up Gospel and note it is an Old English word meaning good news, and this is a problem as not everyone sees it that way, due to all the slaughter and prejudice and bad personalities in the Gospels. What they mean, I suppose, is that overall the news is good, but still, this is one place where feelings slip in, just by calling the report Good News instead of News. Oh well. I can't really blame Matthew, Mark, Luke or John who may not have chosen the title anyway. It was quite a big story with hard knocks at the end and they did their best as newsmen, though they were right in the thick of it and run a bit ragged what with following Jesus all over the country by day and night and trying to get some past history into the story such as, where was Jesus born, what was his schooling, etc., and all the while gathering the news in time, and reporting it, according to them, not an easy job in the light of miracles and otherworldly events which are hard to believe unless you can supply a lot of facts and physical descriptions, and times and places, and keep your feelings out.

For instance. At the end of the Matthew book Sister Margaret Mary gave me, the angel of the Lord comes down and tells the watchers of the sepulchre, which is a posh Bible term meaning tomb, that Jesus will rise from the dead, and this is a very tricky moment and hard to handle if you have a problem with angels and risings from the dead and such matters, but Matthew stays cool and packs in a lot of facts into a very short article. Here's how he does it. It is the end of the Sabbath, he notes, near dawn of the beginning of the week. That's the time. Mary Magdalene and the other Mary are present and the keepers of the sepulchre plus one angel of the Lord. These are the players. Next is place, including furniture and sound effects. The angel comes down and there is a big noise like an earthquake and the angel rolls the stone of the tomb right back and takes a seat on top and everyone is a little spooked. Matthew says the 'keepers did shake and became as dead men', but frankly, I think it is all the noise and messing around with tombstones that gets to them, not the angel who is very sensitive and patient, saying 'Fear not' which are typical angel words for the beginning of speeches of a portentous nature, a bit like saying Cool your jets, Relax, Excuse me for interrupting, I just want to tell you a thing or two I may not have time to repeat, etc.

I don't know why all this shaking goes on when an angel shows up in the Gospels because they have very fine manners and delicate patterns of speech and so many worse things happen here, stonings, crucifixions, nasty words and types with diseases lurking in the streets at all times, and none of this seems to cause any shaking and becoming as dead, no, but a very polite angel comes down, and mayhem ensues. It's perplexing.

Before the angel of the Lord delivers the tidings regarding the Resurrection and asks the two Marys and the keepers to pass on the tidings to the disciples, Matthew makes a note of some more facts to do with physique and haberdashery. The angel, he writes, has a 'countenance like lightning' and this is a nice thing, meaning he had a very bright and lively appearance, the kind that can put you in a good mood when you are in a bad one, reminding me of Mum, who can change a person's outlook on life from dark to bright again just by showing up and displaying her countenance. OK. Next, Matthew says his 'raiment' was 'white as snow' and that is the haberdashery moment. So now the reader has a pretty full picture of things and is not so stumped by miracles or big feelings and can face the facts of the story, no problem. Matthew's approach to reporting is a fine approach and my dad has the same approach. I have seen him watching some sporting hero do a bad job and he might thump the sofa and yell imprecations in more than one language: Knucklehead! *Pisher! Shnook!* and epithets of that ilk. He is also prone to depressed looks and mournful comments addressed to the nearest person, often me: He's past it. His heart's not in it. Etc. But when my dad comes to the writing part of his job, he puts his feelings aside so his readers are not distracted from the facts and can carry on trusting him and will not be confused by emotions, or start worrying about my dad instead of thinking about the sporting hero himself, the one who is having a bad day at the office.

Another important issue in logbook writing is truth. The low-down, my dad says. Cards on the table! Let's say a commander on a voyage makes a faulty judgement, a miscalculation of matters nautical. Whatever happens, he owns up. Write it down. A good captain will even own up to faulty judgements not his own, some fault committed by his right-hand man for instance. Record it. It's his fault because it is his ship, his watch so to speak, that's how it goes. He might have a terrible wound, he has not slept for days, never mind, every evening, he does it, he fills in the logbook. Captain Scott set out for the South Pole a second time in the *Terra Nova*, Latin words, Jude tells me, for New World though I knew this anyway, it's easy to guess, but here is what I did not know. Robert Falcon Scott, b.1868 wrote his logbook right up until expiring in his tent, perishing only eleven miles from One Ton Camp which was a depot with food and other bare necessities. Jude read me his last words and I recall them by heart. 'It seems a pity, but I do not think I can write more. R. Scott.' Then this. 'Last entry. For God's sake, look after our people.' Whoa.

Logbook writing is no sissy job and if you are not up to the job, skip it. I am going to try one of my own although I am not in a military campaign and I am not on a ship any more and this is already our third winter in my dad's country, this terra nova, but the thing is, I simply did not have the idea then, I have it now and it will be a better logbook perhaps, because when everything is new it is too hard to concentrate and keep your feelings out. My first requirement is a cover and I know exactly what I want to use. My notebook measures 22cm x 17cm and Harriet's painting of the Russian ship is 29.6cm x 21cm, meaning after I wrap it around there will be a little space left over all round the edges in the manner of a frame. Very nice. I need to find Harriet though, I need her permission.

It took Harriet a long time to come up with this painting, making me pretty sure she feels the way I do about being here, that at first everything was so new, it was too hard to concentrate on regular activities we knew so well and did without thinking, things such as filling in notebooks and, in Harriet's case, doing art. I am a bit honoured to have this painting as most often my sister hands them over in a ceremonial fashion to Mum or Ben, people quite like her when it comes to art and musing on art. Gus will no doubt join the art department in our family also. He strikes me as the musing type, whereas Harriet clearly considers Jude and my dad and me as a little rash and uncouth in the art department. She is not sure a person can have a deep regard for soldiery and sports and art also, but she is wrong about that and it is possible her gift of this painting is a sign, a sign she is changing her mind. It is more likely she gave it to me by fate. I am the first person she came across who saw straight off what was going on in her painting called *Mummy Resting Aboard – Shiver me Timbers*.

A person examining this painting might ask, Well? Where is Mummy? Where is that ship? These would be good questions. It's all there, though. This is Harriet's point of view of the ship and her nautical experience. She was always within, looking out, so that's what you get, swirly sea and night sky, very dark blue, and one bird flying overhead plus some spouty flows of water from whales. Harriet's spouty flows are very good and I like the sea very much, the way she mixed painting with stuck-on coloured paper and now I know why she wanted the packet of grey Russian chocolate tied up with red ribbon. Purple and blue paisley patterns can look a lot like night sea and sky. The red ribbon bits are reflections of light, I believe, something like that. Or maybe it is just art. Well done, Harriet.

When Harriet has made a piece of art, she traipses all over the house holding her art in a fearful grip like it is a brimming cup of blazing hot liquid and she presents it to each one of us, speaking no words and with a worn-out but lofty expression on her face. The day she finished the ship, a droopy old Saturday afternoon, she came across the three ruffians lying around in the study on her way to Mum and Ben, and Gus who doesn't really count yet but is sure to be very polite.

Harriet slips the painting between Dad's eyes and his newspaper.

'Hey! Cut that out! What do you want? What is that? Ask Mum! I'm reading!'

Harriet shoots Dad a disdainful look, her very best shot, and moves on to Jude who is reading on the floor.

'Mmm,' he says, glancing at it for barely two seconds without moving his head.

I feel bad for Harriet who is now felled by lack of art appreciation. I put down my King Arthur book and make a big show of my availability for art appreciation.

'It's the ship, isn't it? It's the ship, Harriet.'

How could I tell? I don't know, but my sister relaxes. She holds her painting to the side, delicately pinching one corner between two fingers and she butts me in the stomach three times, before stepping back and making her declaration.

'For you!' she says, handing me the painting, and I match her gaze which is kind of grave and hopeful all at once, as at the end of a tragedy by Shakespeare when some good soldier comes upon the scene and takes in all the carnage, noting the poor heap of bodies and launching into a quiet speech full of poise and plans for the future, i.e. how things are going to change, they are going to improve from now on, it will never again be as bad as this, not ever, and all the characters go speechless and stare into space with grave looks and great expectations and the audience must leave a respectful pause before claps and bravos and things. The End.

I accept the painting with two hands and leave a respectful pause, as is befitting, and then I give Harriet our signal for playing outside in the snow, something we picked up from a new song of Dad's.

'Baby, it's COLD outside!' I tell her.

'I really must go!' she replies, whereupon we both nip off for snow apparel.

First Entry. Weiss on Ice. This is the name of our hockey team. Ben made it up, though I was not all that keen at first, feeling we ought to have some name more in keeping with names of teams here, bold and jaunty names referring to Indian tribes or wild animals or special types of people, Yankees, Dodgers. We very nearly had nice team badges also, emblems sewn in neat stitching and a team name printed beneath but it did not work out so the emblem and the name are in our heads only, which is OK with us. Here's how it went.

Ben is on the floor of his room surrounded by patterns cut from white card, X-acto blades, a book of heraldry and scissors and sewing stuff and swatches of soft white jersey material, material that rings a bell with me, I'm not sure why.

'What are you making, Ben?'

'Team badges. We need badges.'

'Cool,' I say in an encouraging manner, staring at the fiddly patterns of heraldic motifs Ben is tracing on to white material. It's going to be hard to sew but I can't tell my brother this, he will think I am a ruffian when it comes to art appreciation, or maybe just too doomy, without enough faith in things, etc. 'Need help?'

'Great,' he says. 'Do you mind sewing?'

'Nope.' I bloody hate sewing. Oh well. 'Do we have a team name, then?'

'Not yet.'

'How about The Best Knights of the World?' I say.

'Jem, that's way too long, come on.'

'Oh. OK. How about The Dolorous Strokes?'

I had to put *Le Morte D'Arthur* aside for a while, for nearly three whole years in fact, because Ben was right, I was not ready and came to have dark visions of needing to reread those 997 pages not counting glossary sometime in my future. But now I am ready, and have reached the part when Perceval's sister meets Sirs Perceval, Galahad and Bors, leading them to a mystery ship though they don't even know who she is, and telling them a very long story on board that vessel, involving the low-down on the Waste Land and how it all came about because of a sword and the ship and a Maimed King who has to be healed, otherwise there will always be worldwide depression and pestilence.

The three knights have no idea who she is at first, but they follow her right on to the ghost ship, no complaints, maybe because she mentions Our Lord's will and so they presume she is on a mission from God and a person can't argue with that, or maybe they just have a good feeling about her, or it seems the best adventure going, who knows. It's a knight thing.

'*And when they came thither they found the ship rich enough, but they found neither man ne woman therein. But they found in the end of the ship two fair letters written, which said a dreadful word and a marvellous:*

"*Thou man, which shall enter into this ship, beware thou be in steadfast belief, for I am Faith, and therefore beware how thou enterest, for and thou fail I shall not help thee.*"'

Yikes.

Anyway, it's all very complicated, but the main feature of the story is this marvellous sword hanging over the fair bed on the marvellous ship, now a ghost ship, and this is the sword that can put things right in the world somehow, though it is the very one that killed the Maimed King's father with one dolorous stroke, whereupon things went downhill, ever worsening. I think this is a sacrifice-type story, meaning, to undo some really bad thing that has befallen the world, drastic measures are required to undo the bad thing and this usually involves blood and swordplay and a heap of bodies as in Shakespeare. No one seems to want to talk it over instead, but never mind, it's very symbolic, and surprising. Marvellous. Marvellous is a top word for Sir Thomas Malory and has many permutations.

Book XVII, Chapter 6: *How Solomon took David's sword by the counsel of his wife, and of other matters marvellous.*

This is definitely surprising. This sword is second-hand and it is the sword of Solomon. When Perceval's sister recounts the marvels of the sword, giving a detailed description of all parts and the origins of the parts, going into raptures like she is a world expert on arms and armaments or whatever, she rambles on in a lingering and passionate manner over the sheath, the hilt, the girdles and pommel, excited most of all about the pommel, relating how Mrs Solomon advised Solomon to bash off to '*Our Lord's temple, where is King David's sword, your father, the which is the marvelloust and the sharpest that ever was taken in any knight's hand*'. Well, that's all he needs to hear, though she is not finished with instructions:

'*Therefore take that, and take off the pommel, and thereto make ye a pommel of precious stones, that it be so subtly made that no man perceive it but that they be all one; and after make there an hilt so marvellously and wonderly that no man may know it; and after make a marvellous sheath. And when ye have made all this I shall let make a girdle thereto such as shall please me.*'

OK, dear, says Solomon and off he goes.

And that's how it gets the name, the Sword with the Strange Girdles with a separate name for the sheath, Mover of Blood, and the thing I find surprising is the King David thing. Renaissance painters, it seems to me, are clearly not the only ones in Christendom with appreciation for King David who is Jewish, or perhaps they are merely confused, explaining why David shows up with his orchestra at that Mystic Marriage party of St Catherine's and why, according to Malory, he will play his part in healing the Waste Land, just by virtue of his sword, and another dolorous stroke perhaps, a dolorous stroke to undo the other.

'So how about it, Ben? The Dolorous Strokes? Or Weiss on Ice?'

'Absolutely not,' says Ben. 'And Weiss on Ice sounds like a cocktail! We could call ourselves Martyrs of Jesus.'

'Forget it! Are you crazy?'

'Ha ha ha,' goes Ben, slapping me on the back. 'You're so gullible, Jem.'

'Yeh, well . . . Hey! That's Jude's cricket top. Isn't it?'

'Maybe.'

'Whoa. You cut up his top. You didn't ask first, did you?'

'He won't need it any more.'

'I'm glad you're undead, Ben, because Jude is going to be very mad at you. I am very glad you're undead.'

'Hide us from the face of him that sitteth on the throne, and from the wrath of the Lamb; for the great day of his wrath is come, and who shall be able to stand?'

'Am I supposed to say something here?'

'Book of Revelation,' says Ben. 'You should read it.'

'How many pages?'

'Very few.'

'Well, I don't know. It sounds depressing. But I'll thinketh about it.'

I help with the tracing and cutting and sewing but those badges never worked out for us, falling off our jerseys after the very first wash, dangling by single threads like baby teeth that are ready to be yanked from kid jaws and when Mum offered to sew them back on for us, properly, I guess she meant, though too polite to say so, I put my foot down, no thank you, I said, because I can see there is too much to do around here and we don't have Lisa living with us any more, and some sacrifices must be made such as wearing ice-hockey tops without emblems or even the team name printed thereon, OK with me, because our ice-hockey days are numbered anyway, we are downright hopeless at ice hockey. It is possible that emblems and a printed team name would be an inspiration to us but inspiration is kind of a private thing, requiring no emblems. Emblems are a bonus element, decorative.

Weiss on Ice is a four-man team plus Gus who is boss. He is manager and coach due to not being strong enough yet for pushing himself around on skates and wielding a big stick, but the time is not far off for such exploits in Gus and then we will be five and Gus can be player-manager. In the meantime, we build a mound of snow for him, right behind the boards on the side of the rink where pucks are least likely to whizz his way and cause unhappy disfigurements, though I devised a rule that Gus must wear a helmet all the same, which he does, just in case, wearing it jammed over his brown suede cap with the small peak and the ear flaps that tie up in a bow under his noble chin, looking even more like a small king in this extravagant head gear, perched there as he is with such composure on his throne of snow.

We lay Ben's big coat on the throne before seating Gus or else his bum might freeze. Ben's coat is the best as there is quite a lot of coat and quite a lot of Ben so one damp patch will not irk him much, the ratio of damp to Ben is pretty favourable and insulation for Gus is important as he barely has any bum at all, only a mere covering of smooth flesh to protect his bones, meaning he reaches freezing point fast if we do not insulate him carefully. Gus is very finely made, very finely wrought, an expression Mum uses regarding art and music which I decide suits Gus, the fineness of him and how he has always been lovely to gaze upon and touch, ever since the day he was revealed to us from within Harriet's old pink blanket. Everyone feels this way about Gus, and Dad still yells at us when, according to him, Gus is being manhandled beyond seemliness in some game of our devising.

'Gus is NOT A TOY!' is what my dad yells, leading me to suppose he never had any good toys because Gus is a toy, our favourite, and if my dad could rustle up some good toy memories, he would know that a person pays the utmost respect to a favourite toy and is likely to be more vigilant and mindful towards it than his own self. Gus understands toys and respect for toys, so he never minds being mauled, even sporting a shy pleased expression on his face when we have finished up with him, knowing it is a top honour to be so singled out for torture. In winter, we pitch him quite regularly into banks of snow, but only the deepest and freshest, banks that have had no time to frost up or gather grit and we always dust him off afterwards in a cheery fashion while Gus chuckles to himself, his eyes shiny with glee, and that is the difference in the Weiss family between hard knocks (bad) and torture (good).

I look at my little brother from time to time as I circle the ice and there he is, calm and serious, his chin high in the air so he can see us from under the peak of his cap which is slipping a little over his eyes under the weight of the red helmet. Now and again, this requires adjustment, also a good moment to receive tips from Gus who is not the kind of coach apt to yell out criticisms or look exasperated and drop his head, covering his face in his hands in a big show of coaching despair, no, and we do have problems as a team. Harriet and I pose the worst problems. Harriet is not keen to skate with any particular purpose, such as the scoring of goals, say, and is prone to pausing fretfully any time the puck skims across her path before moving on gratefully, like she is crossing a busy road and has just had a brush with perdition. Even this Gus handles thoughtfully, making sly and tender suggestions in the manner of Mum, telling us the flaws he sees and the vision he has of our future sporting prowess, so I always skate away from him frowning with determination and braced with fresh hopes, which I would not if Gus showed me up as the pathetic hopeless wreck of a hockey player I surely am.

Here are my two chief problems. 1) Falling down. 2) Playing with strangers. My two problems are closely connected, that is, my problem number one (falling down) gets much worse when I am in the throes of problem number two (playing with strangers), and playing with strangers is what you have to do if you are on a team. Teams play other teams, that's how it goes in sports. Often though, when we make it to the rink, waltzing our way there slowly, hockey sticks over shoulders like rifles, kitbags hooked by the blades and dangling on behind, there is no one there and the ice is ours, I pray for it, this is how I like it. Great. We shed our gear and get busy building Gus's throne and stuffing feet into skates, making sure socks are not twisted or bunched at the toes or pretty soon we will lose circulation and be in for amputation of digits like Antarctic explorers. Ben laces for Harriet and me because he has strong and dextrous fingers, he works with speed and dexterity, a word from the Latin for right, and the opposite of sinister, left, which is confusing because in augury signs on the left are propitious yet sinister behaviour is dark and shabby and not worthy of celebration at all. I have tried lacing my own but my fingers freeze quickly and my lacing is too loose so my feet wobble within the skates leading to problem number one, falling down. I blow on my fingers and concentrate hard but I am too stuck on having each tying end the very same length, meaning I have to adjust each little row of lacing, incurring blisters and an urge to kick my skates off and swing them by the laces far from sight with a violent sweep of my arms and a vow to renounce the game of ice hockey for all time. I am beginning to notice I do not have a tight grasp of my feelings, I need some dexterity in the feelings department, like Ben with laces and Gus in coaching and maybe it is something you have to be born with and it is already too late for me which is a bit depressing but there you are. Forget it, Jem. Skate. Wait!

White. There should be another name for this kind of white, the special whiteness of ice I see also in the Moon and snow, white with so many shades of grey and blue and pink it seems there is movement and change right before my eyes, these are the clues, icy patterns that are the very proof of shifting things, of tides and winds and fading light, nothing like the plain white of Q-tips and

Kleenex and paper and school shirts, and if spirits were real they would be coloured white of the ice kind also, white of the Moon kind, I love it, it's lovely.

Before stepping out, I have this brief moment always, just long enough to close the eyes and breathe in, a brief pause for the awareness of ice and the feeling that comes with it, of everything new and all possible, and in this moment I can forget how my body lets me down every time, I believe my ankles are strong and will propel me across the ice wherever I want to go, with perfect timing and in clean, straight, exciting lines, a path with a sound of its own, decisive cuts in the ice like a locomotive along rails, I believe this and forget what is so likely to happen instead, my ankles splaying, my pace sluggish, angry pains shooting through my shins and an awful ache in the sides of my feet that within twenty minutes or so is close to unbearable. No, I am fleet, let me be fleet.

Whoa. Look at Ben. I am so proud of him, I have never seen him take to a sport so keenly, and in his keenness he has forgotten about blood and the spilling of blood for which there is great potential in this game involving high speed + big sticks + sharp blades, making me grateful his keenness is uppermost and he is suffering from a happy memory lapse, otherwise he would hang up his skates and down sticks for all time, and we would have to play without him, meaning, it is quite a good thing not to recall all things on all occasions.

Jude plays this game fierce and strong and determined and when he is in a good mood, he lays off passes for me so I might have the joy of scoring, of slipping the puck past Harriet which is a breeze as she has no intention of getting in the path of a puck. Jude passes to me even though he is pretty sure I will fall down due to the sheer excitement of receiving a pass, the ensuing responsibility almost too much for me. Don't mess up, Jem. Score. And I do OK when it is just the four of us, most of the time I am capable of a few startling instants of sporting prowess, earning me cuffs on the shoulder and thumps on the helmet from Jude and Ben and smiles from Gus and an ice pirouette celebration from Harriet who is not one bit downhearted about letting my puck pass her by on its way to goal, watching it glide by her and finding it newsworthy, barking some observation in her newsman voice. 'WHAT is the meaning of this!'

Jude has already grown out of one pair of skates and I wear them now, which is great, I don't have to wear girly white ones any more like Harriet's. White figure skates have this little toothy part at the tip, same as a saw for wood cutting and that's how Harriet does her little pirouettes, jamming one toe into the ice and swivelling round and it's also how she comes to a dainty stop, dragging one foot behind as a seaman might drop an anchor, a graceful stop so unlike the kind I aim for but never quite manage, that marvellous sudden turn to one side, stepping on the brakes, cutting to a stop at a perfect angle to send a spray of fine ice chips into the air, my body leaning, not quite falling, like a trick of gravity, fantastic. I can do the sudden turn part then I fall down. Slam. I tell Ben this is due to *la loi de Newton* I have just learned about at my French convent and rules regarding momentum.

'How come no one else has that problem?' says Jude.

'You have to allow for it, for the change in speed,' Ben explains. 'Pull back, compensate with your body.'

'OK. I'll try,' I say, rubbing my sore knees.

'Don't think too much,' suggests Gus who is coach. 'You won't fall down.'

'Maybe you could just play hockey lying down,' says Jude.

'Maybe you could just shut up,' I tell him.

Oh-oh. Here come strangers. Problem number two. My heart works faster and harder as these boys arrive, flooding the ice like a silent troop of commandos, dropping on to the rink one by one in swift succession and without looking down, there is no pause for them between land and sea. I watch them swoop around the rink, always making the corners in time, crossing one foot over the other, easy, the ice, I believe, their fondest surface, home to them, moving more freely here than on pavements or across rooms, I know it. They glide round and round, doing their warm-up circuits, not talking, and the air is turbulent, buffeting my body as when walking to school with cars rushing past, or as a tree sways in an angry wind, something having to give, someone having to pay for the terrible motion of things.

I am sort of marooned out here in the middle and I try to look cool, as if I have no fear at all of being run over and trampled like a charioteer in *Ben-Hur* whereupon I will lie dying in the snowbank near Gus's throne, clutching at Jude's hockey jersey and choking up some last words. 'May the best team win. The game must go on!' That's what I'll say. 'I leave my favourite jacket, etc., etc.'

These boys are French. French boys are very good at ice hockey, which means we will have to leave Harriet out, no use to us in her regular role as decoy and commentator and occasional net-minder of the lackadaisical kind. With friendly and chatty strangers, she can play and make time, getting in the way and allowing us to dig the puck out from a scrummage just because no one wants to bump her or rush her and Harriet might even engage the opposition in conversation, a tactic you might call cheating, never mind, something they all fall for in different ways, halting a moment and saying, Pardon? or, Excuse me? by which time the puck is ours. Pardon? is an expression over here, confusing at first, giving me instant pictures to do with confession and Hail Marys, not to mention a desire to bless people with one touch to the forehead and a tap on the shoulders, pronouncing forgiveness, but I barely flinch now. Pardon? = Sorry, what? and the French say it too although it sounds OK in French and not so weird, more of a formality I find quite poetic. For instance, you say *Pardon!* with a slight flourish and a heartfelt expression to which the other person replies *Je vous en prie!* meaning, No worries, and this is very poetic, even if the person says it in a grudging manner. Poetry is not always comforting, thems the breaks.

Suddenly the French boys break out of their perfect circles, maybe on a signal that passed between them, I don't know, but they arrive at centre ice one after the other, and it's like music I think, this roll of sound they make, cutting to sharp stops one by one in a cloud of icy spray, the little chips anointing me same as fine snow blowing off a snowbank. Meeting in the middle is like no man's land on Christmas Day, the boys pulling off their gloves and shaking Ben's hand and then Jude's before nodding gravely at me, and I nod right back, standing there with my weight on one hip, I'm cool.

Harriet glides by, trailing off towards Gus with one foot poised behind like she is making an exit from *Swan Lake* or something, saying *Bonjour! Bonne chance!* in urgent tones as she goes, which is quite odd considering the romantic style of her exit, and it is possible Harriet is making one of her favourite points concerning sports and gravity, and how they do not go together, but she is wrong about that and will maybe come round in time. Sports is indeed a grave matter or sporting heroes such as racing-car drivers would not dice with death, and my dad would not shake his head in a forlorn fashion when a favourite player messes up and my heart would not be pulsing so hard right now that my skates keep skidding out from under me, so loud I am sure everyone can hear it and I can feel the beat in my ears, a drum roll, a call to arms, *En avant!*

The Weisses do not get split up today and that's good, it doesn't always work out like this and I hate playing against Ben who will make mistakes on purpose for my sake or against Jude who ignores me, even if I crash to the ice, acting like he doesn't know me, whereas all I want to do is watch him, all I want is for him to do well and make some goals, swooping away from the net and getting taps on the legs and bum from the sticks of French boys on his team, taps that are a top form of congratulation, breezy but dashing.

I do not do well. I am a flurry of nerves whenever the puck is anywhere near me, I simply fall apart and lose my sight, digging furiously at a puck tangled up in my own skates as if I were two players, Jem and some enemy Jem, or I cannot stop in time and fish wildly for the puck in an empty stretch of ice when it is already trailing on behind in my wake, fishing wildly for a puck not there. And, of course, mostly I fall down, the puck a gunshot. If I am still standing and can manage a pass at all, slashing the puck away instantly towards Jude or Ben, the only men on my team I can recognise without stopping to check, I misjudge acceleration, meaning, speed + direction, so the puck jams up in their skates or they have to flail at it to scoop it in, or make a U-turn for it, awful, and I imagine my dad watching and looking all depressed, because I am that sporting hero who is letting him down, so baldly you might suppose I am reaching out for failure with arms wide open. Sorry, Dad.

I pause. I want to give up, I want to tell Ben who is skating my way I feel sick and I am going home, and then it happens. I am in the right place at the right time, how did I get here? Suddenly, a French boy passes to me and I stop the puck quite neatly without thinking at all, surprised to see it there in my path and swiping it away gently into Ben's path whereupon Ben scores and now it is me getting taps on the legs from everyone on my side, the French boys making sure to steer clear of my bum out of courtesy and respect for sex matters. Whoa. I made an assist, it's called an assist, with more glory attached due to the skill required, the timing and vision, all sporting fans know this, that the goal part is easy and the assist is the thing.

I play OK from then on, more than OK, I can do no wrong, although I am relieved when the shadows fall and it is too dark to play any longer. There is a lot of handshaking and the French boys bash off, vanishing almost, leaving only Weisses on the ice unlacing and packing kits, and it's a fine end to things when your last moves are glorious with no time left to start messing up again. I make a note in my head for the logbook, that maybe the giving-up feeling is not all bad, maybe the one good thing in it is how the body and mind go all loose instead of tight and edgy and you can do things and see things a little better, you can be a bit more fleet, which is probably all the angel of the Lord means when he holds up those two fingers and says Fear not.

'Good. You were good,' says Jude who is pulling off my skates, his old scuffy brown ones, most of my double-sock arrangement coming off with them. I haul the layers of sock back up, not fussing too much as we are almost home and it feels right to fling the doors open into the warmth in a state of soggy cold disarray, like war-weary troops with days'-old stubble looking ahead to baths and beers in big old glasses.

'OK,' I say, frowning slightly, accepting this high praise of Jude's with a suitably grave expression and acting all distracted by socks, good behaviour in a sporting hero, it being most unseemly to pay direct and close attention to praises, to break into a grin, say, or other transgressions, such as asking for details of one's prowess, a glorious breakdown in words from Jude's-eye view, or expecting a bear hug or a high loft above his shoulders and a crown of laurel leaf as in ancient times, though none of this will ever come from Jude, and I don't care, his 'Good. You were good' enough for me, the same as prizes and trumpet blows.

'You look down too much,' he says. 'You have to look up more. Look ahead. Skate. Don't think.'

'Yeh. Gus said that too, I look down too much, don't think.'

'Gus is Coach,' says Jude.

'Coach-man,' I add. 'Gus knows.'

Harriet has been clapping away for some time without any of us taking any notice and so she speeds up, slapping her mittens together hard, her alligator mittens with the jaggedy white teeth and the red leather palms that are the insides of an alligator mouth.

'Bravo, bra-VO!' she shouts over and over in that posh opera manner she has heard on the radio. We thump her a lot and yell Shut up, shut up and then we load her down like a pack horse, making her heave all our gear up the hill to the house in punishment, all of it, sticks, helmets, skates, hockey gloves and shin pads.

'I'm a slave,' she declares quite happily. 'A beast of burden.'

Ben takes a long sly look at Gus who starts quivering straight away. 'Coach,' he says. 'Time for a coach ride.'

'Yeh, time for a coach ride,' says Jude.

Now Gus squeezes his eyes shut and chirps like a trapped mouse, waiting for torture to overcome him, and Ben and Jude drag him up the slope by his boots with Gus screaming and giggling although snow creeps into his clothing, bringing him perilously close to freezing point.

I move along with that weird weightless feeling that comes upon the removal of skates and the shift from ice to ground, foreign to me now, as strange as the end of a Moonwalk might be, the earth too close to my feet, the contact a shock, this surface too plain and rude, unlike ice which is marvellous, marvelloust. Ben says nothing is solid or unchanging, nothing at all, and as Ben always has two fields of study in mind when he teaches me things, the Gothic field and the science field, when he says everything is changeable and in motion, everything, I believe he is thinking about vampires and types like Dr Jekyll and also about science, I believe so. All matter, including humans that is, has a freezing point for instance, and a boiling point. All matter is atoms and molecules in a sea of electrical forces which determines its shape and make-up, its very life form and characteristics. A person contains around 10^{28} atoms, meaning an incredible amount of atoms, close to the amount of persons that would fit into a star. 10^{28}. This is a very interesting way to see the world and I imagine it as I traipse after the boys and my sister who is calling out remarks about asses and donkeys or something. I stare at the snowy darkening ground and think how if I had the most perfect telescope in the world I could see motion, atoms and molecules teeming in electricity, I could see the ground is not a plain and solid mass but a dizzy shifting one.

Look up, Jem! You look down too much. I am going to get better at ice hockey, I will hold my head up and trust my body to do the right things and manage without a lot of brain activity, and for more than a passing moment, that's my plan. I look up and recall how Ben taught me we are star material, made from the fallout of stars, how all the elements in us are star elements, and it all began up there, so I wonder does it all return there, seeing as everything is changeable and in motion, and I picture it, all the dead returning, 10^{28} to a star, standing erect as soldiers, their bodies shimmering white, whitened from their last shocking tussle with life on Earth, white as the whiteness of ice, and now there they all are, back whence they came, and I marvel that the firmament must be so heavily peopled, make room for the cat! I marvel that the spirit world is such a populous place.

I look up and see the light glowing in our house, spilling on to the snow and trees, and light is wholly motion, Ben says, carried by streams of particles called photons in a jiggling field of radiation, electric, magnetic, oscillating, everything in motion in a spectrum that includes the invisible to me, ultraviolet, infrared, radio waves and X-rays, and the visible to me, something in wavelengths measured in nanometres, or what we call light, he says, and I watch it, light spilling out of the windows so my house seems alive, 10^{28} + 10^{28} + light + 1 dog alive! How many atoms in a dog?

'What's for dinner?' I shout. 'Who knows what we're having?'

'Chicken old-ladies-on-the-bus,' says Jude as we bundle into the basement and step around Gus who is lying on the floor in a pool of snow, giggling quietly, his limbs flung out to the sides.

'Gus,' I say. 'You look like a sacrifice.'

Here comes our dog, our German shepherd, Weiss family dog # 3. He scuffles down the basement stairs, first off barking softly from the top of the stairwell, announcing his arrival in his regular manner, with one single hello bark. He is a polite dog in some ways, but not all. Pretty soon, for instance, he is leaping all over Gus and chomping his wrists and ankles, all parts of Gus that are easy to clap his fangs around and that resemble bones with meat on them, as I suppose. The polite part involves not actually drawing blood, or leaving indelible scars or causing rabies, etc. Our dog reminds me of Harriet sometimes, the way he launches himself into a fighting frenzy right at the end of our revels when the energy has dipped and we are ready to move on and there is our dog nevertheless, making crazed snuffly snorting sounds and clamping his jaws around us and jerking his head from side to side with a firm grip on some Weiss body part, going in for the kill just as if he might get things going again, start the party up. Harriet does this often, taking a running jump and landing on top of us when our game is sewn up, Ben and Jude and me sprawled on the ground with a football or rugby ball roundabouts, a ball that has a whole new aura now, no longer a prize and the only worthwhile possession in the western world, and now Harriet hurls herself our way, snatching at the lifeless ball and going through all the motions she observes in sports types, including that quick noisy panting style of breathing, a wild flapping of arms, hunched shoulders and sharp turns of the body, Harriet does all this alone as we watch her from our idle sprawl. It is a bit ridiculous and before long she gives up, suddenly stopping short and staring at us with big eyes and I wonder whether it is no accident my sister picks the end of a game to pitch in and do her stuff, I wonder is it one more Harriet-fashion of displaying her feelings regarding sports, i.e. that the sporting life is not for her, she is not very keen, the sporting life is not a serious or lofty endeavour unlike Art and the making of paintings that are hard to understand, such as ones featuring swirly green and purple paisley patterns called *Mummy Resting Aboard – Shiver me Timbers*. Where is the ship, Harriet? Where is Mummy?

When our dog gives up, facing the fact that revels are over for now, he lets go of Gus and takes a long dog look at us all, at Ben sitting up on the clothes washer with one boot on, one off, and Jude draped over a chair in a state of undress, and Harriet cross-legged on the floor near Gus with all the sticks and skates and stuff still kind of attached to her by straps and laces and so on, making me think of a one-man band, a type in a top hat with instruments hanging from his body, harmonica, drum, flute, ukulele, and hand-held clackety things and the man can play every single instrument, some of them even at the same time. If I had money in my pocket, I'd hand it out to a one-man band if I were passing, I would, though a one-man band cheers me up in no wise, depressing me and giving me an urge to ask how it happened, how was it he began his days with a big feeling for music and the ability to play every instrument in sight and ended up by himself with no band of players and all these instruments to hook around his lone body in an intricate arrangement, all these instruments to play alone in a top hat, on shuffly dancing feet.

'Donkey,' declares Harriet to no one in particular. 'Stronger in hindquarters than forequarters. Bears load over pelvis.'

'And Mum made soup,' says Jude, thinking hard about food. 'Leek and potato.'

'Asiatic wild ass,' continues my sister. 'Dark bristly mane, dark stripe. African wild ass. Ancestor of domestic donkey.'

'Harriet,' I ask. 'Did you say wild ass?'

'Yes, my child,' she says, smiling and doing that fluttery eyelid thing.

'Harriet! You are not a nun on an African mission! Stop that!'

'Bless you, my child! God bless our dear dogs,' she says, making some weird point, I guess, about how being blessed cannot always save you from doomy situations, such as being carved up for dinner even if you are a dog and man's best friend, etc., and not therefore a regular recipe item in cookbooks. Or maybe like Jude and me, she is thinking about comestibles and her ideas are mixing up perilously in her brain, which is quite a common side effect of starvation.

Our German shepherd scuffles his way back upstairs, probably to carry on what he was doing in the first place, his topmost favourite pastime of following Mum around all the livelong day and settling down in a decorous heap some ten paces away from her, raising his head sharpish, ears stiff, ready to up sticks and move camp if she strays too far out of his field of vision. They don't converse much and I have rarely seen Mum stroke him or scritch him behind the ears or anything, but when she does go in for such ministrations as strokes and scritches or is ready to speak to him, almost always his name alone, uttered in different intonations, our dog is simply a mess of dog emotions, ears folding back and paws lifted and a real pathetic look in his eyes which is pretty close to lovesickness, I believe. He is quite a dignified dog, he has dignity, except in these two departments of shadowing Mum and fighting with the Weiss kids, his two favourite activities.

He is not really a sporting dog in the strictest sense so we are on our own mostly when we go down to the lake for ice hockey. He used to amble along and perch next to Gus on his snow throne and venture on to the ice, but now he leaves us to it largely, too confused by all the rushing around and the sweeping of big sticks and the slippy surface he can't get a grip on, his legs splaying out from under him in an unseemly fashion, and I don't think his dog sight is all that acute, things moving too fast for him so he cannot figure who to protect if necessary, which one of us is a Weiss on ice. Because that is another thing with our dog, he is protective, a guardian dog of the Cerberus kind if you forget about the Hades part, and in situations involving strangers, our dog is vigilant, sensitive to even the slightest jostling of one of his own. If a friend of Jude's, say, cuffs Jude on the arm or ruffles his hair in some boy greeting, anyone but Zach or Jeremy that is, the friend will be in serious trouble with our dog and at risk of trampling, biting and all-out bark assault, altogether different from his trespasses against us which are more akin to Gus-torture, an extreme form of affection and very reassuring.

There is one sport he is quite keen on and that is tobogganing, a Micmac word for sledging. Micmac is the name of an Indian tribe and it is the name of a language also. There is no baseball team or hockey team named for Micmacs, which is too bad in my opinion, especially since they invented a word for sledge, a practical and sporting item which furthermore brings out crazed sportiness in our dog. Tobogganing drives him wild and allows him to indulge in his second-favourite activity of mauling Weisses. Here's how it goes. He sits at the top of our driveway in that wonky position he favours with us, meant to mislead, one hip slung out to the side in a show of casual behaviour he puts on though we are well aware he is all charged up and ready to leap into the air, loping like a reindeer in the snowbanks alongside us until choosing his moment to hijack the toboggan, clapping his jaws around the wrists of whoever is at the helm of the sledge, and growling like a maniac dog. It's a long, steep, curvy driveway and this job of being at the helm can be quite painful and a rigorous test of one's mental faculties and resistance to pain and slaughter. Don't lose your mind. Don't let go. This is why we usually pick Gus as helmsman, knowing what a fine gent he is and how he will carry on steering no matter what, inspiring a touch of respect in our dog, and in us also, because Gus is so very in command and, moreover, so used to torture that only towards the finish line, before we all pitch forward or topple sideways in a smash-landing, will Gus begin screaming and laughing and yelling Pax! Pax! which is our dog's name and a very apt one, and a name Gus chose by accident.

Second Entry. How Gus saw a dog coming to himward, and chose a name, and of other strange dogs.

When Pax! first came to us in puppy form, following closely

behind Jude one summer day in our second year in our new country, nipping at Jude's heels in a bewildered fashion, he arrived name- less, and quite small, not having grown into his ears, tail or paws which were all still a mystery to him, impediments, not yet friends, giving him general difficulty in locomotion and a tempestuous air. This dog was my dad's idea, and Jude's. They decided we needed another go at dogs in our family after our misadventures with Dog and Shane and they locked heads together in thought, batting and bowling pros and cons for a while and coming up with this dog decision. The conversation went like this.

'Dad. Zach's dog had pups,' says Jude, flipping through a maga- zine and sipping on a banned Coca-Cola on our terrace overlooking the lake. I sit right next to him with my feet up on the wall, reading that Antarctic explorers book Jude passed on to me. It's a lazy day.

'Don't let Mum see that,' I say.

'Mmm,' goes Jude, setting his can behind a huge flowerpot, not really stashing it out of sight so much as putting it in the shade. Warm Coke can make a person throw-uppy. 'Five pups,' he adds, glancing at Dad.

'We'll talk later. To Mum. Now, you want to do something for your old dad? Go in and get me a tomato. On a plate with a knife.'

'In a minute, Dad,' replies Jude, flipping a page.

'What was that? IN A MINUTE? You trying to finish that article, my son?'

'Yup.'

My dad plucks Jude's magazine away, ripping it in two neat parts before handing it back politely, a favourite trick of Dad's and one he finds very funny indeed.

'Thanks, Dad,' says Jude, giving up on the magazine and letting out a big noisy yawn, stretching wildly like he doesn't know I am right here, so he can bash my book out of my hands accidentally- on-purpose, which is no real surprise to me, knowing that torture is kind of a contagion thing in our house.

'Hey,' I say, fishing for my fallen book.

'Jem and I could get the dog tomorrow,' Jude says, staring out at the lake.

'Whose book is that on the ground?!' my dad shouts.

'Jude's,' I tell him.

'Jem's,' goes Jude.

'Tomato! On a plate with a knife! At the double!'

'So it's OK then? Dog?'

'Fetch!'

'THANKS, DAD!' we say, bashing off indoors, making dog plans, thinking up names and dog necessities while I worry to myself about Mum and wonder if this dog will be too much for her, so I aim for this dog to develop fine manners on our watch and be a good friend to her, maybe as fine a dog as Black Bob the sleuthing dog, one with few needs except for a nice tin of dog food tipped into a bowl of an evening, daily roaming and some swipes with a dog brush, all things we can take care of without her. She gets tired, I've seen it, ever since the ship, just a wee bit tired, maybe she caught something there, not scurvy, nothing perilous, something else, a passing thing. Don't think about it. I try not to think about it, about signs of tiredness in a favourite person, a person who is never tired, never sick, and so I think about dogs, and what type might suit Mum and be a gentle companion when called for. Milou, for instance.

Tintin's dog Milou is a top dog although subject to high jinks, such as keeling over drunk due to a predilection for Loch Lomond whisky, or being felled by food, stuffing himself silly on stolen links of sausage or entire roast chickens whereupon his stomach inflates to at least twice its normal size and he is one helpless heap of a dog, no good for anything or anyone. *Gourmandise* is the French word for this problem and I am glad of it because the word greed is just not right, suggesting an ugly scramble for all things, probably a chief characteristic of beasts before there was much evolution at all and no one knew any better. Milou, though, has evolved and gourmandise merely causes him to lose control when face to face with good things, a fine roast chicken, handmade sausages, charcuterie, tinned crabmeat, single malt. It's a problem, not a crime, and is maybe just the other side of his bent for heroics, although even in the field of heroics, things are complicated for Milou. Household spiders, for example, give him the shakes and an urge to flee, creating in him a state of terror involving flying beads of sweat and a petrified expression because of a strong feeling about that spider that is not strictly bound to reality, i.e. that the spider has the power of life and death over him, but when it comes to Tintin and the rescue of Tintin, Milou is fearless and a very quick thinker. He is a devoted dog. For Milou, a world without Tintin is no place to be and, frankly, regular life-saving of your favourite person is a demanding occupation and a drain on your emotions and mental capacities. You have to conjure up gruesome images of death situations featuring the loved one in order to develop fine reflexes and quick thinking, and so falling back on gourmandise and mild drunkenness now and again is merely relief for Milou and not really a problem, that's how I see it. Sleep it off, Milou. It's no crime.

Bullseye is an interesting dog case. He belongs to Bill Sikes in *Oliver Twist*, a book that is not a favourite with my mother due to anti-Semitism, of course. In the musical *Oliver!* there is a scene depicting the extreme closeness of Bullseye and Bill. Bill has returned from a hard night's larceny and what you see of him first is his black shadow in an alleyway moving slow and heavy as a Panzer tank in the steppe, Bill with his hands in pockets, a thick walking stick under one arm, his crushed and wonky top hat at a jaunty angle, but the very first thing you see is his shadow's shadow, and that is Bullseye. Nancy watches the shadows from outside the tavern where she works and where Bill and Bullseye are headed for refreshments. She is not scared or depressed because she is blinded by love for Bill. She wears a blood-red dress and you might call this ominous, an augury of the right-hand sort, bad. This dress shows a lot of cleavage, a lot of bosom exposed to the elements. It is a very cold night, everyone is busy rubbing hands together over braziers, wearing gloves with cut-off fingers just like Dining-Room Nun in my old convent. Nancy does not feel the cold because she has love-blindness and this is very poignant if you know the story, even when you have read the book twice and seen the black-and-white film three times and the musical nine times. Some kinds of poignant situations do not wear off.

Cleavage. I am not sure about this word but I am not all that worried, as I am unlikely to call upon it often, I simply do not foresee myself remarking on bosoms aloud in a room filled with strangers, which is the topmost worst place for getting a word wrong. The thing is, I looked up cleavage and read something quite complicated to do with the division of cells in fertilised eggs and the different types of cleavage depending on the amount of yolk in that egg. Bird eggs are yolky and so only the yolk-free region divides. This is meroblastic cleavage. Frogs and mammals are not very yolky when they are at the fertilised-egg stage so the whole thing divides. This is holoblastic cleavage. I have no idea what this means. Unexpected findings like this are extremely confusing and induce a mild crazed feeling in me akin to doing a sum over and over and getting it wrong every time. Bloody. Now I don't know what to do. I can only think of one person to clear this matter up for me without giving me any strange and lingering looks of the piercing variety, and that is Mum. Walk a straight line to her and spit it out, Jem. Is the word cleavage to do with bosoms, please? Thank you! Some day I'll ask her.

Here is the scene depicting extreme closeness between Bill Sikes and Bullseye. Nancy starts up singing when Bill enters the tavern. Singing is regular behaviour in musicals when you are felled by emotions such as love-blindness, even when you are not a singing tavern waitress by profession like Nancy. Musicals are not real-istic, otherwise, in life, everyone would be doing this, breaking into song when a feeling is simply too much for words. My dad, for instance, would take up singing as a full-time occupation in place of all activities which are bigger than words for him, yelling and torture, and being with Mum, and tussling with everyday house-hold objects, and this would give us a mighty full-time headache, making me glad for this reason alone that musicals ≠ real life. While Nancy is singing, she dishes up for Bill who settles in at a remote table as far from the revels and merry singalong as possible. Revels are not his big thing, his big thing is crime, especially night-time larceny. *Larceny.* Felonious taking away of another's personal goods with intent to convert them to one's own use. *Felony.* Grave offence such as murder, rape and larceny.

Bill shucks off his wonky top hat and lays it on the table brim-side up right next to his stick, as if ready for a magic act. Bullseye is on the table too. Nancy brings one implement and two wooden bowls, a bowl of bread and a bowl of slops, which are the chief items on the menu for downtrodden types according to films and musicals set in Victorian times, stews of slops, jagged hunks of bread and old cheese, mouldy bangers, gin and beer. Bill knocks back the beer and scoops the brown mush of stewy beans into his mouth with swift strokes of his knife which is all Nancy brings in terms of cutlery. This is not an oversight. Downtrodden types of the felonious sort do not go in for cutlery, displays of fine manners or the reading of books in musicals. Nancy does not call out Bill! Wash your hands, supper! in a cheery fashion, or unfurl a big white napkin on his lap although Nancy is a gentle type with good intentions. There is no point. Bill is beyond everything, especially words spoken in full sentences. He gobbles. Quite a lot of stew falls by the wayside en route to his jaws. Then he does this thing. He exchanges a look of comradeship with Bullseye who is a very ugly dog and is licking his chops in an unappetising way. Bill scoops up a knifeload of slops and feeds Bullseye. Bullseye slobber and Bill slobber is all one to Bill and the mingling of slobber is only ever OK in two situations. 1) Starvation situations, such as in prisoner-of-war films or Antarctic exploration stories wherein there is little choice in the matter what with no time and not enough cutlery or comestibles to go round. 2) Love situations, such as the one involving Bill and Bullseye up to the night Bill crashes his thick walking stick against the body of Nancy causing gruesome injuries a person cannot recover from.

The death of Nancy is what it takes for Bullseye to turn on Bill, to hesitate a moment, and read the signs that were always plain to see but invisible to the dog because Bullseye was lovestruck. And Bullseye does more than run from Bill, so outraged is he by felony. He leads the police to him, bringing on the end of Bill, showing just how far outrage can take you, even when you are a dog. I am sure Bullseye felt a song coming on just then and it is a pity we do not get to hear it. A dog in a state of outrage should have a song to sing, one with a chorus so everyone can join in, I think so.

These are interesting dog cases, Milou and Bullseye, but too complicated to be fine and gentle companions for my mother. When you are a complicated person yourself, a person with full-blown human emotions and a taste for non-stop deep thinking and worrying desires like being at the top of the queue for that first public transport rocket ride to the Moon, then it is probably a good idea to have a graceful dog for a companion, one who can be counted on to perform simple acts of protectiveness and vigilance, lying nearby, calm and steady, with an eye out for calamity, anything from air raids to paper cuts, a dog to be counted on for traipsing after you at a polite distance, a friendly not a hounding shadow, there and not there. A guardian should not make you edgy or else you will come to expect calamity and walk straight into calamitous situations, making me think of my dad who is a keen guardian of the nervous sort. Let's say I am on some project and cutting things up with sharp blades, creating a battlefield to place soldiers in, a battlefield mapped out with scraggly trees, manholes and heaps of earth, shell craters and a maze of trenches, my dad will snap 'Hey! That's a sharp knife, knucklehead! Watch out!' repeating this four or five times until I am so rattled by premonitions of disaster called out in a loud voice, I do it, I cut myself. 'What did I tell you!' says my dad, kind of satisfied, rising up in an earthquake of newspapers to hold my hand under freezing cold water before wrapping a plaster on me, applying it all crooked and wrinkly and smudgy with newspaper ink and with the end sticking up in the air, because he wrapped me up so quick it folded back on itself. Bloody. I hate that. I hate a messy bandage job.

A guardian should stay cool. Mum says, 'That's a very sharp knife, little goose,' and she says it in passing, not even looking at me, adding, 'Are you sure that's the one you want?' It's not a pressing question, not one I am expected to answer outright, but I am supposed to do some thinking about things, and I do, gazing at the knife and having visions of severed limbs and dolorous strokes from marvellous swords, and then I put the knife aside for some smaller one or I just concentrate better on the job or whatever. Mum is not edgy, she is cool in her job as guardian and I believe that is the kind of dog she needs herself. Everyone needs protection from something.

Keeper might be the dog for Mum. Keeper was Emily Brontë's favourite dog. Emily Jane Brontë, b.1818, d.1848. Emily was definitely a complicated person. She was not a very sociable type and often in a bad mood so it is lucky for her she got on fine with dogs and kept busy marching across moors and writing books or else she would have been a downright depressed cross person with nothing to do and no company, heading all alone for that untimely death at 2 p.m. on 19 December 1848.

Emily was a little reckless when it came to health matters although she was mindful of dog troubles and very sensitive to their needs at all times, making me think had she bashed off to the Antarctic with Mr Shackleton she would have passed up on that meal of the five youngest dear dogs, she would rather have perished, the only casualty on the team, one frozen and starving woman, maybe not all that mourned due to her complicated personality and tempestuous manners.

Emily could not always think straight in the face of dogs. One time, she spied a dog dashing past her house, a parsonage, not a very cheery place and maybe not so conducive to straight thinking. The dog has a disturbed expression and a flapping-out tongue and a dodgy gait. Whoa, thinks Emily. A thirsty dog. Bring that dog a glass of water. OK. Chomp! Now Emily is in a blood situation and only now does she start thinking about rabies, etc., signs of which most regular types can recognise in a dog, no problem, and at quite some distance. And this is what Emily does next. She grabs red-hot tongs from the fire and sears her very wound, this dangerous mess of blood and dog slobber, killing any infection that might lurk in her bloodstream. Emily was cowboy-tough.

On her last night on earth, 18 December 1848, Emily is causing a lot of anxiety and maybe even some exasperation amongst her family members. She is not steady on her pins, she is falling apart, anyone can see that, but she must feed the dogs. Feed my dogs, I must feed my dogs. Emily moves into the stone passage, the feeding place for the dogs and she is felled by wintry air, nearly keeling over in a final death heap. Sisters rush her way and Emily brushes them off. *Leave me alone. I am fine, I am not sick, I am not dying. Feed my dogs.*

She rises at 7 a.m. the next morning and sets about combing her hair and the comb flies out of her hands into the fireplace. Never mind. She is trying to think. *Something Charlotte did last night, she gave me that flower, what is the name of that flower? Work now, get to work. Get dressed, don't lie down, lying down is so close to dying.* By noon, Emily is having death throes and last words. All right then. Time for the doctor. Keeper stays next to her bed until she is dead. Keeper leads the funeral procession and follows that coffin to the vault and hears out the funeral service from the family pew and when he gets home to the parsonage, he stretches out by the door of Emily's empty room and starts up howling and does not stop for days and days.

Heather is an evergreen, a shrub with scaly leaves and purple flowers in bell shapes and it can grow to a height of sixty centimetres and it was Emily's topmost favourite flower. Heather is the name of that flower, Emily. You couldn't even remember it. You remember dogs. *Feed my dogs.* The more I read about this family, all those sisters with not enough antibodies within, and one brother who scratched himself out of the family portrait he painted himself so that he is really the most there there, a face I stare at like it might come clear to me, he might appear for me, reminding me of

Harriet's ship picture with Mum resting on board and no ship visible and no Mum visible, the more I think about the Brontës, the more I see it, how some types cannot live long, it's just too hard for them.

Is Tock the best dog? I vote for Tock the watchdog, though he is prone to abruptness.

Chapter 2: Beyond Expectations.

'Can you help me?'

'Help you! You must help yourself,' the dog replied, carefully winding himself with his left hind leg. 'I suppose you know why you got stuck.'

'I suppose I just wasn't thinking,' said Milo.

'*PRECISELY*,' shouted the dog as his alarm went off again. 'Now you know what you must do.'

Birds that swim, fish that fly, yesterday's lunch, tomorrow's dinner, words beginning with J, numbers ending in 3, Milo thinks of all these things, seemingly unconnected, and suddenly they are moving, picking up speed all the time, 'And the dog,' writes Mr Juster, 'his nose in the wind, just sat back, watchfully ticking.'

Our dog Pax! is nothing like these dogs, and he turned out fine in the end and he was named by accident, by Gus on that summer day the German shepherd came home to us, charging in after Jude, nipping at his heels and covering him with slobber, licking his ankles and wrists like Jude is the best thing he has tasted so far in life, better even than his mother's milk which should probably come tops, due to rarity, and how it is specially designed for a pup at this specific time in life, a once-only offer for the very beginning of things, a time you are not supposed to remember, everyone will tell you that and they will not trust you if you describe the flavour to them when you are thirteen or so, as I could, in a manner suggesting authority and no doubts, how I could say it was the best flavour in the world, I remember, something like binoculars or toasted bagels with Cheddar, my new favourite comestible, no, they will look at you as if you are ready for the spooky building behind high pointy black iron gates with the rusty sound, and the white jacket with long sleeves tied up at the back.

Maybe for Pax! Jude's wrists and ankles are the closest in taste to the milk he'll never drink again and maybe also he is still a little baby-blind, and chasing after Jude, licking those parts of him like a maniac dog is simply what he has to do to feel safe and know he is not some lost puppy of unknown origins, but in a good place where he can settle down and start learning some rules of behaviour in fine company, and acquire balance, growing into his ears, tail and paws, those oversized features that are causing him such mayhem, this dog with no name careening into table legs, sliding like a baseball player, tripping up like a clown in a circus for all the sudden change around him, for all the chaos in his young dog self. Cool your jets, puppy. Everything's OK.

'Let us call him Dear Dog,' says Harriet with a polite look on her face.

Lordy. Harriet is tenacious when it comes to slights and disturbances, meaning she will not let go of things, not until she has changed an enemy notion into one she can live with, one that is Harriet-sized and -shaped, and no longer fearsome. She is not angry with Jude any more for his communication about Shackleton's dear dogs, she knows she may well have come up against this sad story by herself, but she does want her old relationship with dogs back, she wants to gambol with dogs in an open-hearted manner with no cloud between them, only trust from the very outset, it stands to reason. She thinks, Dog, you will never be dinner for me, not ever, and this thought rattles her, she is all distracted, worrying about this suspicion she is sure the dog is carrying around, a weight on his dog shoulders. She needs to do penance for that sacrifice of dogs for the survival of men, and her way is through tenacity and open-heartedness, everyone having their own way with slights and disturbances, bringing to mind my boxing match with Jude and how, afterwards, we shook the fear out of that red fist to my stomach with a little nursing and a powwow regarding gladiatorial combat and Roman augury, and a snack of fold-overs, carefully prepared. You have to find a way, or a dark matter can oppress you for all time, so Harriet has tenacity, she calls upon it.

'Forgive us our trespasses as we forgive those who trespass against us,' is what she took to saying to our dog # 3 in close conference with him, right from those very first dog days.

'Hey!' I say in my sternest tones. 'Don't let Dad hear that.'

'I'm talking to the dog!' she replies, all lofty. 'It's private.'

'Yeh, well, watch out.'

'Yes, my child.'

'So,' says Jude to Harriet the day Pax! arrived. 'You're really going to stand in the middle of a field calling out DEAR DOG.'

'Yes. Why not?'

'Well. I say we call him Karnutzel, then,' says Jude, stroking the dog who has slid into a clapped-out dog heap on the kitchen tiles, his four big paws splayed out like the points of a star.

'How about Binoculars?' I add. 'Or Toasted Bagel with Cheddar on Top!'

'Loaves and Fishies!' offers Harriet. 'Chocolate Bunnies and Bears!'

'Pillar of Salt,' goes Ben. 'Vial of Wrath, Blood of Saints!'

Jude and I go stony and speechless like Mum or Dad has called out, Bedtime! in the middle of revels.

'Ben,' says Jude, real quiet.

'What?'

'That's really depressing. No one wants to call a dog that. Not even in a joke.'

'Sorry.'

'Try not to be so depressing,' I add, patting Ben on the back.

'OK, sorry.' Ben is really cooperative, glad I believe, for us to take over at times and tell him what to think. Being the oldest is a strain and he needs time off or he gets mixed up and carried away, that's all. 'Nuts and Raisins! Jelly on a Plate!'

'Not bad,' we tell him in an encouraging manner, but it's too late now, those words blood and wrath having given us a gloomy feeling that is bigger than us.

'Dear Dog is really quite good,' says Harriet thoughtfully.

'So is Pain in the Neck,' says Jude, opening up the fridge and glaring into the depths, frowning deeply like he is reading some serious article in a newspaper.

'I turn the other cheek!' my sister replies in her finest martyr tones. 'See me turn the other cheek!'

'Yeh-yeh,' goes Jude, farting quite slowly.

'Whooh! What a smell of sulphur!' says Harriet, quoting her favourite line from *The Wizard of Oz*, a film she finds quite distressing, though she has an abiding fondness for Glinda the Good Witch who appears in a bubble of rainbow colours to the tune of tinkly violins, strolling about with great swoops of her arms and a lot of manic blinking, signs of behaviour I have observed in drunken persons, but never mind. Harriet will quote from Glinda quite freely, especially that line about sulphur she utters when the Wicked Witch comes and goes in her whirl of fiery smoke and a crashing sound which Glinda waves away with a loopy smile and long fingers and a flutter of eyelids, Whooh! What a smell of sulphur!

Harriet stares accusingly at Jude, the master farter in the Weiss family, in other words, stealthy and cool, and pretty annoying. At least you know where you are with Dad who farts just about every day of my life, but noisy and angry with it, leaping a little off the sofa or chair with a cross expression, sometimes barking aloud in protest like there is some world plot going on causing him to fart in this thundery manner, thus disturbing his concentration. Jude, though, is not one bit bothered and accusing stares from Harriet are no odds to him, so he gives her a slow, disinterested look, the kind he gives to strangers who enter our house. Who are you, what do you want, don't talk too much.

Watching Jude gaze into the fridge is clearly making Gus peckish because he reaches for the bread box and fishes out a sesame seed bagel, ambling across the kitchen with it, taking graceful small bites whereupon the puppy charges at him, fierce as a soldier going over the top, blind to everything but the officer's signal, that pistol in the air, this way please, gentlemen, and Gus is sprawling now, getting his very first dog-mauling, waving his bagel aloft for dear life.

'Pax!' he yells, 'pax!' calling out this word we use in all games, a password meaning lay down your arms, call off hostilities, bring on stretcher-bearers, I am in serious trouble, a speck in the eye, a stitch in my ribs, a genuine affliction, and everyone stops, it's an honour thing, pax!

'Pax!' we all say, nodding slowly.

And that is how Gus named our dog by accident.

Third Entry. Of a communication between Jude and Jem, and of the sorrow Jem made, half sleeping and half waking, for the war between herself and her sworn sister, and of other matters marvellous.

Harriet said no.

It's late. Weiss on Ice. Chicken old-ladies-on-the-bus, I had two pieces, a wing and a breast, it's not my favourite dish, I love all her food but this recipe is not hers, I love it less. Tomatoes and onions, some recipe she overheard on the bus from two old ladies speaking Italian, another language she knows though I've never heard her speak it, she knows so many things. She learned it before I was born, from days in famous cities with famous monuments, days spent strolling down a runway being beautiful in beautiful clothes, something she now does in our own house for free. Runway. Like in airports. Maybe this is where it came to her, her thing for flight, right there on the runway when waltzing along ready for launch, a thing for flight not just to other famous capital cities with glorious monuments, but to farther reaches, to the stars and planets, why not.

When it is late at night and you are not all that sleepy, and your outlook needs improving upon, the best thing for it is fine reading material and *Tintin* books are best, but they are across the hall in Jude and Gus's room and she'll hear me, every tiptoe and glide, even though I have memorised the pitfalls, the wonky boards, the obstacles of furniture, the creak factor in doors, I have a map in mind, I move like a minesweeper. She'll still hear me. I don't even rustle the sheets, she'll know I'm reading and it is way past my bedtime. One floor away, a whole set of stairs, Goodnight, Jem, she'll say in a special quiet voice reaching only me, rousing not one single sleeping Weiss and I will close the book thinking, Bloody, foiled again. I close the book and then I yank the little chain on my lamp which goes ping! A dead giveaway. Now she knows she was right, she is always right. I resort to torchlight, but thumbing it on and off is same as slamming a door it seems, I am sure she can see it all, hear it all from the foot of the stairs where she smiles a little, one hand on the newel post maybe, fingers like in that painting by Mr Lippi, Filippo, b.1406?

Gravity has a very long range, it can be infinite, that's the principle. On Earth, it holds everything in place and the gravity of the Sun keeps the planets in orbit, and the gravity of everything in the Galaxy holds the stars. Gravity can even cause the collapse of spacetime, as it is called, right into a black hole which has a field so strong it can curve spacetime right round on itself so nothing can escape, not even light, a black hole is everything and nothing, there and not there, going to show that gravity may well be the weakest force in nature, but its influence can be infinite. Ben says there are ripples in spacetime caused by the motion and orbits of things and this is known as gravitational radiation and it travels at the speed of light, having a kind of domino effect out there, the merest vibration of one body creating vibrations throughout, with all other bodies reacting to it, a sensitive business and quite complicated, and I grasp it now, just for a moment, half sleeping and half waking, as I flip a page, p. 332 to 333 and she feels it, a slight breeze across her face, a whole set of stairs away, something like that. *Goodnight, Jem.*

Harriet said no.

Logbook. Chicken old-ladies-on-the-bus. *She makes it when she is sad, there and not there.* Perceval's sister . . . Perceval's sister. Did Sir Thomas forget to name her? Maybe he ran out of names. Sometimes he just goes Red knight, White knight, damosel, gentlewoman, etc., and it is possible he aimed to come up with names when he had finished the 507 chapters in twenty-one books and two volumes and then he forgot, and it was too late, the printers printed. Or maybe he was fed up and could not be bothered. Or this. The most important thing about the damosel is that she is Perceval's sister, that is her distinguishing feature, like a birthmark, her truest thing, her name.

Perceval's sister brings Sir Galahad to Sir Perceval and Sir Bors who have all gone questing in a rather hopeless manner, in sore need of guidance, and they have been apart, enduring hard knocks and perils and one-man tussles with grave danger. It is a timely thing they run into her, because, frankly, they are more or less lost causes until she reunites them and gets things organised, pointing the way to that ghost ship and the Sword with the Strange Girdles. Here we are. Here you are, all well. Sir Thomas writes 'the two knights received them both with great joy and every each knew other' and I have this fine picture in mind of the damosel standing by with a shy proud feeling, watching these three men, fellow knights and adventurers, this clash of armour and chain mail and raised visors and shiny noses, dusty chins and happy tired looks, all of them taking their time because this is important in a greetings situation, as important as words, coming before words and the swapping of stories, and if this were a musical and not an old book in 507 chapters published in 1485, it would be a song moment, most definitely it would.

Every each knew other. No. Perceval does not know his sister, not straight off.

'*Perceval, wot ye what I am?*'

'*Certes, nay, to my witting.*'

'*Wit you well, that I am thy sister, which am daughter of King Pellinor, and therefore wit ye well ye are the man in the world that I most love; and if ye be not in perfect belief of Jesu Christ enter not in no manner of wise, for then should ye perish the ship, for he is so perfect he will suffer no sinner in him.*'

You have to be a bit patient when it comes to mistaken identity in olden times books. I can only suppose that as sleuthing was not very developed, the populace at large had not yet acquired a suspicious nature, or the art of detection of the art of deception, so most types were easily hoodwinked by the merest thing, even rudimentary techniques of disguise. A king or a duke in a Shakespeare play, for instance, can sling a cloak over his shoulders, a cloak with a little hood, and stroll about in broad daylight amongst his trusty ones and nearest and dearest and no one is the wiser. A person's very own sister or beloved can swap a dress for a pair of trousers and roam the joint quite freely having close-up conversations with the beloved or brother and she is a complete stranger to them, and her best friends walk right on by, not one single person seeing the light, or even that she is a girl and not a boy. It is likely all this is meant to be symbolic because it is definitely not realistic, even allowing for bad eyesight in most characters and how spectacles, in some cases, were not invented yet.

I change from my convent kit to trousers five days a week in my house and I do not fox a soul. Everyone recognises me, no problem. Plus my whole family has bad eyesight except for Jude and my dad, but specs on or off, not one Weiss needs to do a body search or take fingerprints or anything to ascertain my identity, they know me. I am Jem and I am an all-out girl, no two ways about it, but in the old books, things were different, and also poetic, and that is the symbolic part and quite interesting.

Some plain old differences have to do with time and inventions. On the back cover of my Penguin copy of *Le Morte D'Arthur*, I read this: edited and first published by William Caxton in 1485. Printing was a pretty new thing and not all that refined and it improved with the invention of spectacles and the acceptance of spectacles as a recommended instrument for seeing what the bejesu you are doing and getting things right. Mr Caxton learned printing techniques from Gutenberg, Johannes, b.1399?, d.1468. Caxton's works, it seems, 'are not usually regarded as being of the highest aesthetic quality', meaning, not very lovely, but never mind, he worked hard and printed nearly one hundred volumes on his press between 1476 and his death in 1492? Why don't they know when William died? I am worried about this. Did he die all alone, clapped out from a hard day's printing, falling in a heap right there on the floor of the press room in Westminster, his fingers all inky and his eyes strained from printing that hundredth volume, one volume too many? Maybe he lay on the floor a few days before anyone noticed, OK, but getting the year of his death confused is very weird. Which brings me back to specs.

The very first specs had convex lenses for close-up work, helping out cotton tops who have a hard time with close-up work. Some cotton tops, nevertheless, are still struggling with inanimate objects, gripping a road map or a handful of coins and messing about, poking their faces into the map, say, and then snapping it away at arm's length with a startled expression. Then comes all that fiddling with specs, lifting them up and down, up and down, and peeling them off to scavenge for dirt on the lenses and putting them back on again, then looking around like everything is just a mirage in the desert, even though there has been some progress since the thirteenth century and the invention of convex lenses, meaning, this is a behaviour problem and not a specs problem. To point this out, however, would NOT be courteous. My dad, for one, has the inanimate object problem though he is not yet a cotton top and he can see fine. I know this because I have the job of cleaning his close-up-work specs and they are permanently coated in lemon juice and newsprint smudges and there is no way he can see through them apart from the two minutes they are clean after my cleaning job. They are for show only and for struggling with inanimate objects and getting help from his kids. OK.

Next came concave lenses for myopia, which is what I have. All the Weisses have this excepting my dad and Jude, so there is a myopia to good sight ratio in our family of 5:2, quite bad, and I am the worst case, I deduce, because everyone else can go walkabout pretty freely without specs if they feel like it without any bad accidents though this may be down to a finer sense of direction and sheer courage, I don't know. Myopia is for distance and this is a little confusing because I have noticed that my idea of distance is not what you might think of as distance. You might think distance is somewhere across a big room. Not always. I held a ruler between my eyes and one of Jude's old *World of Wonder* mags and I cannot see beyond 27cm. 27cm = distance. Many things are not worthy of close examination, but a thing or a person I really want to see does not have to be all that far from me to be distant, that's how it is, and I keep this information to myself, however, because people get quite worried when you confess to problems of vision, as if it might be contagious, or you are doing it on purpose, bringing down the side with your dodgy vision and posing a threat to humanity or something.

Myopia. 'Spectacles with concave lenses appeared and spread with the introduction and widespread distribution of printed books.' Very wise. I feel relieved to read this. I am not the only one in history for whom near is far. I also note that the first recorded sale of specs to correct myopia occurs in Florence, 1451, making me wonder why there was still all this muddling in the Middle Ages, over time, all this head scratching over years of birth and death unless there were a lot of types with bad eyesight roaming around and not facing up to the need for specs, due to that lingering anxiety over the properties of lenses, how they alter the appearance of things, something a Franciscan friar named Roger Bacon wrote about in the thirteenth century, describing magnification and the marvellous transformations created by different shapes of transparent glass, writings that caused him to be accused of sorcery, no light matter in olden times. The need for specs led to a lot of deep thinking of the tenacious sort, after the manner of Harriet, and a theory to shake the fear of sorcery out of transparent glass and accommodate the need for specs. Here it is. Before Eve came along, making Adam realise how lonely he had been, etc., which is when he made that rash move and ruined everything, he was perfect and required no specs, but since his rashness, man has had a lot of problems and frailties and now we need specs to approximate the perfection of Adam, a lifelong quest apparently, and very improving for a person. Of course, nobody knows what kind of eyesight Adam had at the time, what with the world so small and all things to hand and only Eve and a snake to witness his butterfingers, and neither of them very reliable witnesses at that, but it does go to show how the need for specs to correct myopia led to thinking of the tenacious and practical sort, hopefully bringing an end to this muddling of dates arising from fear of specs, bad eyesight and no electricity, in other words, shaky handwriting in poorly lit rooms, ink blots and smudges and question marks next to numbers, question marks around the very recording of time. Jem, you are a right sleuth.

This business of vision is complicated and it is a mistake for people to count on this one out the five senses as they do, for the most accurate information and the last word on things. For example, if you are a stranger and observe that my dad is wearing two socks more or less related in pattern and colour but not matching exactly and the left sock has a great big hole in it with his big toe poking out, you will think, Oh, he is colour blind, or, Oh, he does not see very well and has come to grief in the matter of socks. Wrong. My dad does not have much time for socks, whether they fit or belong together in a pair. My dad sometimes forgets to cut his big toenails and there is a mighty high ratio of holey socks to non-holey socks in his drawer, reminding me of Dining-Room Nun and her gloves with cut-off fingers, making me think perhaps my dad should have special custom-made socks with cut-off toes, why not. And this is an example of how over-reliance on visual evidence can lead to faulty vision regarding some other person's vision.

What if a person cannot count on this sense at all, even for faulty judgements? In films featuring blind people, it seems there is only one thing on their minds and that is blindness, a condition that makes them very soft-hearted with extra skills such as mind-reading and telling the future or else it makes them very bad-tempered and intelligent like Miss Helen Keller, but all of them tend to walk arms outstretched like mummies, patting the air and walking in a ramrod fashion, chins in the air, which is not too smart if they are worried about bumping into things and crashing to the ground, because if you are worried about this, you ought to let your body go loose and carefree and you will not end up in a broken-limbs situation, a tip I have gathered from drunken types such as one or two sports-writer friends of my dad's who are often keeling over but walk free in the end.

Another strange thing about blind people in blind-people films is how they can either hear a pin drop and so on and recognise a friend or relation by a mere sound due to their special skills, or else they make a big palaver of the recognition process, never going in for any straight questions like Who is it? Who's there? thus getting to the heart of the matter in no time, but stumbling over to the friend or relation in that horror-film method and fingering that friend or relation's face with both hands, staring like a zombie no blinking, and looking everywhere but right at the person's face with their no-seeing eyes, always aiming over the person's head or shoulder, which strikes me as unrealistic, looking everywhere but at what you want to see, like the blind character is anxious the audience will forget he is blind, quite hard to do when a person is fingering a person's face in that studious manner not considered appropriate in regular circumstances. I decided to try out this recognition method myself. I tried it out on Jude.

'Hey, Jude.'

'Hey.'

Jude is lying on his bed with a book open on his stomach and his eyes closed, but he is not asleep, of course, he is reading.

'What's the book?' I ask. 'Mind if I sit here?' I add, sitting on the edge of his bed.

'Don't jog me, I'm reading.'

See? 'I won't. What's the book?'

'It's about a plane crash in the Andes. Survivors ate some of the dead.'

'Oh. Going to tell Harriet that?' I am worried. She has been stuck on those dear dogs for two and a half years now and there may be no end to our troubles if she latches on to this story, though perhaps people eating people for survival will not be such a problem for her.

'Probably not,' says Jude. 'Unless.'

He means unless she is a big pain in the neck and drives him to distraction.

'What are you eating, what is that, yuck! And Mum's making lunch for everyone soon.' There is a plate on the bed that looks like prison rations, a tin of tuna sitting in a pool of oil and still in a tin shape on a clump of lettuce that Jude must have ripped out of a whole lettuce in one hasty move. 'You're supposed to wash lettuce, you know.'

'Not iceberg, you don't. There's no dirt,' he says. 'And I'm on a diet.'

'Jude, you're slim as anything.'

'Kosher diet.'

'But Dad's not even Orthodox any more, and is that kosher tuna? How many ways can you kill a fish, goddammit?!?'

'There's no ritual for fish. And I'm a separate person from Dad.'

'Yeh-yeh.'

'It's not just about ways of killing, you know. It's about thinking. And purity. Respect. Animals who are not predators, who are herbivores and have cloven hooves. A cleft –'

'Cleavage!'

'What? Yeh. So they can't hold prey. And no blood, you can't have blood. Even in an egg. The soul is in the blood. And *milchig* and *fleischig*, no mixing. *Thou shalt not seethe a kid in his mother's milk.* Exodus. I told you to read that, have you read it?'

'I'm about to.'

'You should know these things, Jem. It's important.'

'I know some things. But why can't you seethe? Oh. I see. It's kind of a transgression, right? The mother's milk is sacred when the kid is alive, and his first meal, with all those special properties and so on, so when he is mutton on the plate, it's not very respectful, mixing them, is that it? It's sort of depressing, right? Life and death right there on your plate. A glass of milk and a lamb chop is like the saddest meal in the world. The beginning and the end. Is that it?'

Jude stares at me. 'Have you finished?'

'Yup. Sorry. Go ahead. I'm listening. What else?'

'Nothing diseased. Or even dead of natural causes. No hindquarters with the nerve still in. And no fish without scales, there have to be scales, though since microscopes, some forbidden fish are probably OK. They just couldn't detect the smallest scales before then. Before microscopes. When the rules were drawn up.'

'So are they permitted now?'

'No. It's about thinking, Jem. I told you. It's not science.'

'What about blessings then? You can't have any old tin of tuna, can you? You need a special fisherman or something. What if that tuna died from an injury or hypothermia, or a heart attack? It's a natural-causes dead tuna but caught in a net with all the others or maybe washed up on a beach with all the regular murdered tunas and clapped into tins all the same. The rules are iffy, Jude.'

'Jem. I am trying to read.'

'OK. Sorry. Anyway, I have to do an experiment, um, for school. About blindness and sensory perception. I need to do a Helen Keller thing, I need to touch your face, I won't touch your neck, I promise, I know you hate that, you can carry on reading and stuff, it won't take long. Please?'

'How long?'

'Ahh.' I do a count in my head, imagining that fingering job blind people do in films. 'Nine seconds.'

'Helen Keller's books were burned. In the Nazi book burning.'

'Really? Why?'

'And she donated her royalties to blind German soldiers. First World War vets.'

'Wow. How do you know that?'

'Dad.'

'He tells you everything.'

'No, he doesn't. And anyway. Then I tell you, so it's no problem.'

'Yeh . . . So can I do it? The experiment.'

'All right. Hurry up.'

I get prepared. I make friction, rubbing my hands quick sticks along my jeans, my thighs, my hindquarters if I were a beast, making friction so I do not freeze Jude's face with chilly fingertips. 'Hindquarters,' I say, still rubbing, 'what's wrong with hindquarters?'

'It's a respect thing. It can be OK if the nerves are out, all the blood vessels and sinews. It's about Jacob and his fight with a stranger in the night. How he was left with a limp, a thigh injury.'

'Whoa. Like the Fisher King.'

'What?'

'You know. In *Morte D'Arthur*. The Maimed King, wounded in both thighs and then came the Waste Lands, that whole thing. It's symbolic, I don't know,' I say, beginning to frown and mumble because I am so unused to speaking such things aloud, not having enough knowledge for conjectures and pronouncements, unlike Jude and Ben. 'I'm probably wrong, it's just – I thought – how injuries can be symbolic, that's all. It's probably stupid, forget it.'

'No. You're right.'

'I am?' I can't help smiling now, just for a second, then I frown and rub my hands again, working up friction. *Friction*. A force between two solids that retards motion between them, caused primarily by the two surfaces interlocking at the microscopic level. Microscope, invented 1590, Zacharias Jensen! Who could detect scales! Who might have expanded the fish menu for Jews, had he been so inclined, lifting the sentence on some forbidden fish, thanks to microscope vision.

'Come on, Jem. Do that face thing now,' says Jude.

'Yup.'

I close my eyes and reach out for Jude and start fingering his face, touching him lightly and trying to be organised about it, taking in every feature of him, beginning with his forehead, but there is some kind of tussle going on within me, like I am having two experiences at once, one part of me realising I have never felt Jude in this way before and wanting to learn him, to know him, and the other part of me working hard to forget this is Jude and play out the experiment, and see if I could recognise this face as Jude's if I were blind, by the fingering method alone, the fingering method as favoured by blind people in blind-people films.

I am so amazed by the softness of his forehead and temples, I can't think straight about Helen Keller and so on, Helen Keller who was deaf also, and this is a softness like nothing I have ever touched, not cashmere or fur or clean sheets or even Mum's hand and you might suppose all soft skin to be soft in the same way, but I think different now, or is it just because I know this is Jude and not Mum? Experiment. You are blind, Jem, you are blind. His eyelashes flutter in my palms and I almost leap in the air with the shivery feeling and I can hear my heart loud and echoey, like it has swapped places with my brain and suddenly I want this over with. Nine seconds. Move along. Nose, cheeks, the faintest scratchiness, what's that? I think of Action Man, my bearded man, and now I feel for an Action Man scar, I am searching for a scar Jude does not have. Lips, whoa! Kid gloves or something, and warm, a pulse there, a tiny heartbeat. Chin, scratchy and firm, and the end of the line, don't touch his neck, all change, please.

'I wouldn't know you from Adam,' I say, recalling this expression of Mum's out of nowhere. 'Who's Adam?'

'Adam and Eve, dummy.'

'Oh right. Bloody. What an eejit.'

'That was eleven seconds by the way,' says Jude, staring at me. Aquamarine.

'Oops – sorry.' Blink, Jude, you stopped blinking.

'No worries,' he says, raising that book off his stomach, his book with the glaring red title against a frosty background of blue and white, *ALIVE!* Blue, the colour of hot young stars, what is wrong with me, I am not thinking straight. Straight line, the shortest distance between two points. Stop it.

'Jude?' I say, getting up and hovering by the door.

'Mmm.'

'Hope there were not any Jewish types in that air smash. Jewish survivors, I mean. On kosher diets.'

'They'd have had some problems,' he says.

'Definitely. Oh hey. Mum's making croque monsieurs, I forgot to say. But I'll tell her not for you, right? A lot of seething in a croque monsieur. And pig, that's top of the list bad news.'

'*Terefah*.'

'What?'

'Forbidden. Tell her I want two.'

'Please.'

'Please. I can eat two. I'm just finishing this chapter.'

I wander off, jamming my blind-person hands in my jeans pockets, hands I decide are not much good when it comes to the science of deduction and analysis, and when I arrive in the kitchen, although my mother is making a cheery racket, whipping up croque-monsieur sauce in a bowl, and listening to classical music on the radio with her back to me, she says, Hello there, Jem, just like that, and I decide that, sometimes, the closer you look at a familiar thing, the more perplexing it is, and that recognition between nearest and dearest can be the simplest thing also, there in something small, even microscopic, a matter of sound alone, half heard, a shuffle you know, a swish of clothing, a footfall, something to do with pace and pressure or the quality of breath, simple. Hello there, Jem.

Microscope. Before Galileo started working with the spyglass, *perspicillum*, *telescopio*, pointing it at the sky to find new stars there, and mountainous regions on the Moon and other strange discoveries, he recommended the telescope for the art of detection in wartime, for staying one step ahead of the enemy, just like Harriet who has taken her painting away from me and is pretending to be asleep, rising now and again to aim her pretend telescope at me and utter a few words in her pirate language, keeping me at bay because I am her enemy, inimical to her, due to an offence of what might seem a microscopic nature with unforeseen consequences. Even before Galileo and his telescope, came Zacharias Jensen and his microscope invention.

Zacharias made spectacles and played with lenses concave and convex, coming up with the microscope invention nobody knew what to do with until many years later when this new idea was accepted, that all big things, all phenomena, depend on the union of tiny things in motion. Particles, atoms. Robert Hooke writes a book called *Micrographia* and in it there is a folding plate, an engraving measuring 35cm, a blow-up of a flea and its hairy scaly legs, a plate so amusing to some people, a play is written in which Mr Hooke is turned into a joke for his genius for minutiae, and he goes to the theatre one day, a mistake, if you ask me. When you are exploring new realms, you must have faith and stick to your guns, or else you will fall apart in an audience of people shaking with mirth because they think you are a big joke for writing a book and producing close-up views of fleas with scaly legs. As Robert sat there, buffeted by all this hilarity, hanging his head maybe, I wonder did he shut his eyes for a moment and see these laughing people in his mind's eye in microscope vision, with crazed expressions and gaping mouths, faces gruesome with follicles and pores and tongues rolling like a bad storm at sea, tongues in hideous close-up, papillae ugly as disease? Maybe he saw all this quite suddenly and felt better for that moment, I'm not sure, but when Robert arrived home, I do know this, he wrote in his diary and came up with a name for that audience, Damned Dogs, he wrote. Damned Dogs. Dear Dogs. *Harriet, give me my painting back, I want it back*.

Breath. I know all the breathing styles in my family, half sleeping and half waking, I know them by breath alone. Wot ye what I am? Yes. Spectacles, microscope, telescope, I don't need them. I hear Harriet across the room and the big barrier she has built, the Hindenburg line of our little war, and I know the wee sound of her, soft as a bird, private as dove breath and I know dove breathing also, I've held our collared doves against my ear, one by one, to see if they sound the same, holding them firm, not too firm, firm enough the bird knows you won't let go in dangerous places, not too firm he feels trapped. Holding a dove, I can feel everything bleating inside, all the works of him, and it's kind of shocking, like watching Gus, the map of his veins and the muscles moving across his fine back and arms, and his chest changing shape, making room for what his heart and lungs are doing with every step he takes, all the parts of him so close to the surface I have an urge to clap chain mail on him until he is older and stronger, a suit of armour with a helmet and visor and a pair of high leather boots with spurs and pointy metal toecaps for special protection, yes.

There is one person in my family I can recognise by breath alone even when my hearing is impaired, when coming in from extreme cold in a state of mild vertigo, say, or out of Ben's room where he has just played me some weird music or when stepping out of a shower with its eardrum-bruising rush of water, and that one person is my dad who goes in for three kinds of breathing. 1) Really Mad Breath. There are many occasions for Really Mad Breath, and here are some examples. The wind is blowing his hair around, obscuring his vision so he cannot fit the car key in the door without a lot of trial and error. Someone has eaten the last of the butter, there is no room-temperature butter left in the dish, only a mean scraping mixed with sesame seeds from a bagel. JUDE! Something is in my dad's path, foxing his direct line to the sofa at the end of a long day. What is it? It is a face-down reference book with a fresh crease in the binding! And who has separated the sections of the newspaper before him? This is the worst. Dad has to separate the sections first, everyone knows that. It is OK for HIM to leave the newspaper all swollen and wrinkly with none of the pages meeting properly, requiring a major refolding job before you begin to read, and a preliminary shake of the paper over the kitchen floor where you can gather crumbs and other debris with a whisk and pan. My dad, however, must have an off-the-press newspaper. And although he can only peruse one section at a time, he must have all the sections in a tight circle around him like a ring of covered wagons in a Western. Do not reach out for one. He is a quick draw. Do not sneak one away if he leaves the room for a snack. These are the conditions that must be met if you do not want to see him go into a Really Mad Breathing episode, which is not scary but quite distracting and nobody can concentrate as long as it lasts. You just have to wait it out, suspend all activity.

There he will be, inhaling great swathes of O_2 as he stares straight ahead, his hands rising and falling a little at holster height, as if priming for a high dive in the Olympics, though this would not be his sport due to his problem with total immersion in blue waters, a problem I share with him, like the headache problem. My dad is a sports writer, not a sporting type, fond of imparting its history and finer points to me, largely to me, Jem, particularly on the subject of boxing, a sport most dear to him, like tobogganing for Pax!

My dad tells me there is a fine long line of Jewish boxers, Daniel

Mendoza being only one bright star in the boxing firmament. He tells me Jewish boxers were excluded from the German Boxing Association in Nazi Germany and all Jews excluded from German swimming baths and then from the Berlin Olympics of 1936, only one German all-out, both sides Jewish sporting hero allowed to compete in the Winter games, for instance, a hockey player by the name of Rudi Ball. My dad tells me things, he gives me tidings, not all good, and in small parcels, because a great rush of history is unseemly and it is so important, this legacy of mine, of boxing and headaches and trouble with water and other matters, that it must come by degrees. So I am patient.

He is prone, also, to passing on the same item of news he has imparted a few times already, such as what Hank Greenberg, the famous Jewish baseball player, said to his commanding officer in wartime, a snappy remark I keep forgetting because I do not get the joke, just as he will repeat the same few stories of his childhood, telling me again and again how in his house loo paper was ripped up in time for the Sabbath, because the tearing of loo paper counts as work and there are thirty-nine types of work you cannot do on the Sabbath, and that some boy, a boy like my dad, would have this job of running through the streets on a Friday afternoon, a town crier, warning everyone to finish cooking, shut up shop, down tools, it's almost time, the Sabbath falling eighteen minutes before sunset and ending the next evening as soon as three stars are visible in the night sky. Or he might tell me the same story about the village his family came from on the Weiss side, a *shtetl* as it is called, stopping short round about where he left off the last time, with perhaps one or two tiny variations each time.

I am patient. Listening to my dad is a bit like collecting hockey cards, what with the waiting part and the repetition of things, how each new packet of cards may yield the same old cards I already own. I do not have this mania for collecting every single card, instead giving away players I am not interested in and holding on to favourites, even in multiples of five, which is not how collecting works. You are supposed to swap one for one until you have the whole set. You are not supposed to be chuffed, as I am, with five Guy Lafleurs, each card the very same to the casual observer, a photograph of Guy with his stick aloft, a Frenchman with chestnut hair flying on behind, the ice his home, his finest surface, every picture of Guy having tiny variations of detail and light and colour, every one worth saving.

My collecting days are over now. I make my own cards, drawing portraits of players from photos or paintings in my dad's sporting library, the very tall Mr Greenberg of the Detroit Tigers and Sandy Koufax, and Daniel Mendoza putting up his bare dukes. I stick the drawings on to cut-up oblongs of shirt cardboard 7 1/2cm x 10cm, writing in vital information in tiny black print on the back, items such as team statistics, marvellous feats and whatever personal details I can find, favourite comestible, name of wife and, of course, dates. Birth, death.

I want to make things up. Hank played the pianoforte well into the night, esp. the works of J. S. Bach. Before lights out, he would pick out a volume by Charles Dickens from his fine library, any volume except *Oliver Twist* which depressed him due to anti-Semitism. I want to make things up but I do not, because if you do not stick to the evidence, you will not be trusted as a chronicler, sports writer, journalist, logbook writer, gospel man, no one will trust you when you lay cards on the table regarding the more alarming truths and miraculous events you have seen. *I remember how it tasted. I remember the red dress, my first sight of her. I do.*

I don't make things up and I don't make copies, swaps, doubles, duplicates. Duplication. I am not sure about this word, if it means twice only or any number of times again, and when I consult the dictionary, there are so many definitions I feel dizzy, taking note of what surprises me, things to do with Genetics and Anatomy and Catechism. *Genetics. The existence of two copies of a particular segment; the process by which it arises.* And this: *Anat. Folding, a fold.* Then this: *Eccl. Celebration of the Eucharist twice in one day by the same priest.* Bringing to mind that genetics item. As in the Father, the Son and the Holy Spirit, the Son and the Spirit being two copies of a segment and the last arising from the first. And finally my question answered. *Duplicate a. & n.:* Exactly like some other thing (with any number of copies or specimens). Any number of times again. I say old chap, there's just no end to it!

Duplicate. *Genetics.* Of genes: indistinguishable in effect. Trouble with water, Mr Mendoza, headaches, vigilance, my dad has been duplicated within, into my Jewish side, esp., perhaps, in the quality of vigilance, in effect, if not in style, a quality indistinguishable between us, born of a once pressing need to flee the country and find a new home in a nest of trees, perhaps, with water all around and enough provisions to withstand a siege, which is why my dad may buy four dozen bagels on a Friday, though he is likely to return to the Bagel Factory one week later. Be prepared.

Before the Nazis, before and after, my dad says, there were enemies everywhere, Egyptians, Greeks and Romans, Iberians and Russians, Italians, Austrians, Prussians, Hungarians and French, Swiss and Norwegians and Poles – Poles, my dad's very own countrymen – making me think if there were an Olympic sport befitting him, boxing is it, as it is for me, and after boxing comes running, we are gold medallists, we keep moving, boxing and running, travelling fast, and travel is important, I see it now, Jude, I get your drift.

My dad told me something truly new the other day, about the *shtetl*, something new that I felt I had heard before sometime, the same way I know about Mum and the piano without being told, I don't know how. He says that in Jewish law the dead cannot be left alone in a new cemetery and when one was built in the *shtetl* and the first dead person was buried therein, someone slept right by him every night until the next dead person came along and that first body had some company, bringing Keeper to mind, Keeper who kept watch outside Emily's empty room, maybe waiting until the ghosts of Anne and Charlotte could join her, and then I think how death is the end of breathing, which is why I do not mind my dad is so noisy, breathing for his country, Olympic class, he is all parts alive, listen up!

Activity Breath is breathing kind number two. Dad is in this mode whenever not sleeping or really mad, when opening a tin, say, or scratching his head in thought, walking around, turning a page, typing, gearing up to speak to one of his kids; in all tasks, he lets us know just what effort is involved, how his breathing apparatus is taxed for our sake, the machinery I have sketched in Biology, bronchi, alveoli, bronchioles, trachea, larynx, pharynx, how the airways and walls of muscle are pulsing in him and if my dad could sing well, he would be an opera all to himself, with non-stop tunes and no dialogue, unlike in musicals where singing is attached to big feelings only, because for my dad most everything is worth singing about, even standing up and sitting down, and tucking in his shirt, which is why there is no disguising him, I'd know him anywhere, with stick-on moustachio, hooded cape, on a shadowy street corner, I'd know him. Hello, Dad.

Ben set up his tape recorder one day while Dad was in Sleep Breath mode, breathing kind number three. We played it back to him later on, standing across the room with a trembly feeling, a mix of mirth and fear, ready to scarper in case he started up yelling and pitching things at us, pillows, whatever comes to hand. He looked at us all for a moment, grunting and frowning and then he went right on reading, looking at us as if to say Haven't you anything better to do? because, for him, the thunderous sounds he makes when napping are not unusual, they are wise, as in prehistoric mammals with their sensible ongoing policy of no trust, this manner of heavy breathing in sleep being an indication of readiness. There are enemies everywhere.

My dad had a boxing dream one night, tossing and turning in bed and waking to give Mum a knockout punch, a black eye we all considered mighty glamorous, Mum felled by love and Dad the champ, though he scratched his head all week in perturbation and filled the house with white flowers, the colour of conscientious objection, and opened champagne and applied great kisses to her eye as gently as possible, to her badge of courage as she called it, Mum going on to tell me a story that very week, out of her past, about Brownies and Guides and the seemly way to stand, legs and spine aligned ever so neatly, and about badges, so many badges in her case, there was no room the length of her sleeves for further decoration. She told me this story in quiet shy tones and I listened without moving or blinking because stories out of her past are such rarities I think she never had a past, though she did, of course, it is merely unknown.

Orphan, stray, Oliver! When Mr Brownlow brings Oliver home for the first time, after Oliver has been cleared of pickpocketing him, Brownlow glances at the portrait of his dead and beloved niece who died in her prime in mysterious circumstances, as far as he knows. He rubs his kindly chin. There is something about the boy he recognises, it stirs him, though in my opinion he did not need to glance at the portrait, just as he does not really need the evidence that arises later on, the locket stolen from his niece's body in a workhouse, a locket he gave her. The painting is for the doubtful, for all those who cannot imagine that Mr Brownlow loved his niece so keenly, that sleeping or waking, he is alive to any trace of her in sound or gesture, and this live vision of her in Oliver, this duplication of things, is a dead giveaway, quite literally, Mr Brownlow's dead niece giving herself away in the son she only beheld for a moment. Recognition can be so easy.

I have weighed it up, this business of time and inventions and how the differences between now and olden times might explain cases of mistaken identity between friends and relations, and I decide there is no excuse for it, not really, it is all down to symbolism in the end, to symbolism and complicated feelings. This can work a bit like myopia in some people, ones for whom near is far and 27cm a great distance. If Mum is not there when I get home from school, even if she wanders off into the garden or upstairs for a ten-minute rest, when she reappears, I greet her like she has just been rescued from shipwreck or avalanche, a sole survivor. My dad hates this.

'OK, OK, that's enough! Leave her alone!' he says, pulling me away by the collar.

I am not so anxious when my dad wanders off, especially as Jude explained to me how wandering is in his nature, in our nature, our Jewish side, though it seems to me the kind of wandering that has to do with fleeing enemies and finding a cheery home with the table set and your family all round it, these days are over for my dad, or on hold, at least, in readiness, of course, because history, Mum says, REPEATS ITSELF, by which I am pretty sure she means the doomy things only.

My dad's wandering days are on hold, furthermore, because he has roots, and origins, known ones, with a birth date and place and facts regarding where his father was born and his mother and grandfathers too, and the name of the Weiss *shtetl*, and when a person has roots, he is less prone to make worrying comments regarding passenger ships to the Moon, and being first in the queue, an idea as crazy as everyone thought Cyrano de Bergerac, for the books he wrote about travels to the Moon and Sun, involving transport by way of a flight of geese, beyond the Earth's atmosphere, exactly in the manner adopted some three hundred years later by *le petit prince*, another person of unknown origins with a wandering spirit and rash notions of interplanetary travel. *Je crois qu'il profita, pour son évasion*, writes M. de Saint-Exupéry, *d'une migration d'oiseaux sauvages*. He is on a mission. It's a worry.

There are other times when a reunion can resemble a case of mistaken identity or sudden amnesia. Once, I misplaced my favourite Action Man who was dressed in the uniform of a No. 12 Commando trained in Arctic warfare for raids in enemy-occupied Norway, 1943, a kit complete with special commando sleeve badges, furry cap, snow goggles, skis and poles, Bergen rucksack, white windproof trousers, assault harness, 9mm Sten machine gun with silencer, and Finnish boots, less old-fashioned than the earlier Arctic commando boots, big white ones with many straps known as 'Shackleton boots'. I hid my man too well. I hid him because everything was messed up in our house what with our *migration* only a month or so away and two systems of packing going on before my very eyes, Dad pitching everything close to hand into crates and Mum quietly undoing all his work, organising material into themes and consulting with us over our immediate shipboard necessities before repacking things very neatly, making me think she must have won a Brownie badge in packing. I hid my favourite man in case of sudden pitching into a crate to be nailed up with the whack of a hammer by my dad, buried alive so to speak. But where did I put him?

When I found him in my school sock and knickers drawer, I stared. I took in the sight of him, feeling so much rapture and confusion, Harriet stopped everything and stood nearby, half dressed for school, glancing swiftly from me to the open drawer, me to the drawer and so on.

'Is he killed?' she asked. 'WHAT is going on here?!'

'*Ecce Homo*,' I told her, recalling these Latin words Catechism Nun was explaining to the girls the other day when I ought not to have been paying attention, not then in my old convent and not now in my new convent, raising my head that day, however, at the fine sound of these words, Behold the Man. And that is what I said to Harriet the day my commando came back and I beheld him with an intimation of how it might be for the baby dear in that Goodbye Song, if the soldier does come home, whereupon there is all that staring and speechlessness and no smiling on the platform amongst nearest and dearest, the behaviour, you might suppose, of complete strangers, when in fact *every each knew other*, it's just that for that moment, everyone is in some other moment of contemplation, an unknowable moment like that one before the Big Bang Ben told me about, between 0 and 0.0001 seconds when none of the laws of physics apply, a missing moment of unknowable violence perhaps. Missing in action, buried at sea, unmarked grave. It never happened, but everyone pictures it and so there is a lot of staring and toe shuffling, and watching the soldier now is like seeing him arisen. *Ecce Homo.*

Fourth Entry. How Harriet took back her painting, and of the war made to Jem her sworn sister, and how they overcame the battle, and other matters.

'Let me see now,' begins Harriet with a very sweet expression on her face. 'You want to FOLD my painting, fold it over? Have I understood correctly?'

'Yeh. That's what I said. Asked. To make a cover. For my logbook, I told you.'

'Fold it in half? As if – with a HINGE in the middle, my child?' *Anat. A folding, a doubling, a fold.* 'Yup.'

'So there would be a CREASE in my painting?'

'You know it, Harriet. Yes, yes, yes! Fuck-hell!'

My sister plucks *Mummy Resting Aboard – Shiver me Timbers* right out of my hands, using two fingers only so as to avoid any horrid mingling with me, any physical contamination.

'We are a long way from being made in God's image,' she says, quoting from her new favourite film, 'but there has been some progress since then! Such things as art – as poetry and music – DON'T . . . don't hang back with the BRUTES!' she says, doing a pirouette and swanning off to stash her painting, carrying it like it is the most fragile thing on this earth.

Bloody.

I fold my arms and stand where she left me. I watch little Harriet, a tower of strength now, toiling like a slave, hauling furniture, dragging and shoving and lining it all up with a ferocious slap of wood, brass and upholstery. It's all there, standard lamp, armchair, wooden stool, bookcase, the ship's trunk she has covered in a patchwork of cut-out pictures of flora and fauna, the chaise longue.

'Hey! That's both of ours!' I say. 'I like to go on that! I read there! Put it back!'

Harriet does not glance at me, she doesn't speak, she presses on, even tossing a spare blanket over the most alarming gaps in the wall, the Hindenburg line I call it, after the line built by the Germans in the winter of 1916, right behind the Somme battlefield, a wasteland by then, a place Jude says nearly 420,000 British soldiers died, a number too hard to grasp, though I try, closing my eyes to see this many men perishing in so short a time in such a small place, too hard to grasp until I place Jude there with a Lee–Enfield rifle, Jude not coming home, and there it is, 420,000 in one.

I watch Harriet and see that she is in this for the long term, although she will have to crack soon as Christmas is looming and everyone buries the hatchet then. I retreat to my sector and think up some tactics.

Don't hang back with the brutes! is what this woman Blanche DuBois says to her sister Stella in Harriet's new favourite film. Stella = star. Blanche = white. These are symbolic names if you are interested in symbols. I am not sure why Harriet has fallen for this film and is not spooked at all by it whereas *The Wizard of Oz* has her running for cover, but never mind. It is possible my sister merely changes the picture in her mind when Miss Vivien Leigh is carted off to a loony bin, and this scene is not a problem for her because she takes comfort in knowing Miss Leigh is a great survivor also, as can be seen in *Gone with the Wind*, a film wherein she is on the point of death because of starvation and civil war and all manner of calamities, yet comes out on top, shouting brave things skywards in mighty tones. 'As God is my witness, I will never go hungry again!' she screams right before the intermission, shaking one fist at the heavens while clutching a mangy old member of the brassica family she has just hauled out of the cold and muddy wastelands.

When I beheld the falling apart of Blanche, I was wide-eyed, I must confess, my heart beating in an irregular fashion as I looked around at my family sprawled in the study in front of the telly, checking for any matching signs of waywardness between Miss DuBois and them, just in case. I want plenty of warning, so I can fix things in time, because here is a sight I aim to pass up on: a Weiss being carted off by strangers ready to slap on the white jacket with the long sleeves tied up at the back.

For Blanche, Stella's husband Stanley Kowalski is a brute. Stanley is not a symbolic name. In this film he is played by Marlon Brando who also plays a lost-cause boxer in *On the Waterfront*, a film inducing in me a strong desire to take the boxer home following a simple marriage ceremony, and introduce him to some good books because this was an oversight in his education and not his fault.

I have to forget all this when he is Stanley. I also try to overlook his connections with my dad. He wears T-shirts with rips in them. His parents were Polish. He did not go to finishing school. One night over a pork-chop dinner on Blanche's birthday, Stella is edgy, she wants this terrible meal with her sister over with and asks Stanley to clear the table whereupon he flings his plates against the wall.

'My place is cleared!' he says. 'You want me to clear your places?'

Pork chops. *Terefah*. Stanley's links with my dad involve T-shirts, erratic table manners and ancestral home, but they end there. Stanley is not Jewish and he has a bad personality and I believe if his family and my dad's family had stayed in Poland instead of emigrating to the New World, Stanley would be the Pole chasing my dad into trees, pointing him out to Nazis, spitting on the ground my dad walks upon, and laughing at trains going nowhere good, nowhere a person is likely to return from, and never with postcards or souvenirs anyone wants to see.

Bedtime, nightfall. I have drawn up my tactics. Tactic # 1. Lurk outside bathroom. Listen out for Harriet to stop splashing about and singing to herself. Pound on door like Mr Kowalski when he is really mad at Blanche for lolling in bathroom in scented water for hours on end.

'Hey, canary bird! Toots! Get OUT OF THE BATHROOM!'

Harriet flounces out, eyelids so low in disdain, I marvel at how she makes it around the corner to our bedroom without crashing into anything. Not a flicker of a smile, not a crack in her resolve. Retreat.

Tactic # 2. Wait for lights out. Assume Mexican peasant look by draping hand towel over long unruly locks. Remove bouquet of dried flowers from bathroom dresser and clutch in both hands. Stroll along Hindenburg line and chant in spooky voice like funeral-flower-selling Mexican woman in film.

'*Flores. Flores. Flores para los muertos . . . Flores.*' Repeat.

After the edgy pork-chop dinner, Stella feels her baby coming on and bashes off to the hospital and Blanche is left alone. Her disposition is not good. She hears voices in the dark, some real, some not so real. She opens the door and watches the Mexican woman (real) roaming the streets of the Latin Quarter of New Orleans peddling funeral items in lugubrious tones, a strange night-time occupation, but there you are, and sadly it is the funeral posy that pushes Blanche to the confines of reason and deportment, etc.

She should not have opened the door. Blanche has had it with deaths and funerals and she is clearly not well now, leaning in the doorway of her sister's house with a cross-eyed expression and mumbling about flowers and decay, legacies, drunkenness, death and desire, *regrets and recriminations . . . And other things such as blood-stained pillow-slips*. It's a very bad moment for Blanche and all-out collapse is not far off. Harriet and I are wild for this scene and on our way to school, I might pluck a straggly old autumn flower and do the *Flores* Walk to perk us up, traipsing after my sister with stary eyes and floating steps, as if moving under water. *Flores. Flores para los muertos*, I say while Harriet displays signs of total despair according to her, involving a waving about of arms and a little speech indicating dementia.

'Broccoli tops and no more chocolate . . . Jude farting . . . home-work and nuns . . . and dear dogs . . . and other things such as blood-stained pillow-slips!'

Tonight, though, Harriet does not join in and I strain to hear that telltale snuffly sound signifying mirth and forgiveness, and Harriet and me, sworn sisters again. I think I hear it, but it is more akin to what I think I hear in the shower as soon as water beats down on me, I think I hear my mother calling and it just didn't happen. Blanche spends an unusual amount of time in the bath and maybe she hears voices in there too, not urgent ones, but soft and kindly as the water licks and laps at her body and the steam rises, she hears it, a voice calling, an invitation from a gentleman to drink fine wine in elegant glasses and eat marvellous titbits before strolling down the avenue in moonlight. It didn't happen, Blanche, and to make matters worse, Stanley yells at her for steaming up the bathroom, and she falls apart that night of her pork-chop birthday dinner, shouting right back at him for the first time, a dam bursting. 'I've said I was sorry THREE TIMES!' she yells, and that is tactic # 3, my last.

'I've said I was sorry THREE TIMES!'

Nothing. Go to bed, Jem. Fall back. Tomorrow is another day. Christmas, Xmas, Hanukkah, days from now. *Maybe it will be all too much for her this year*. Chicken old-ladies-on-the-bus. My mother rides the bus. She listens to two old ladies talk about chicken, a recipe involving tomatoes and chillies. Red. Soon she will wear the red dress. On Christmas Day.

I slip out of bed. I am wearing my old BRITAIN IS GREAT

T-shirt. It still fits. Yay. Sometimes I think my growing days are over, no more growing pains to come, this is it, this is me. I have no bottoms on, just white knickers. *Blanc, blanche.* White. Weiss on Ice. I try to stand tall like a Brownie, a Girl Guide or whatever. I try to stand the right way. Was there a badge for standing properly? I think so. Stand at attention, everything lined up neatly. Legs should touch at the knees, and at ankles and calves, making three neat spaces between. I look down and it's all wrong. I have one space only, running from my knickers, my crutch as it is called, to my heels. Bloody. I cannot even get my ankles to meet, they are supposed to meet, ouch, it hurts, I can't do it, bloody. *You look down too much.*

Book XVII, Chapter 4. Perceval's sister is on a mission. She points the way, she has badges in so many things, decision-making, map-reading, navigation. She leads the three knights, Perceval still scratching his head, who is she? She is patient, she has a badge in that. She stops, standing beautifully, with all the right lovely spaces and she spies the ghost ship and makes a decision.

Go we thither, and there shall we see adventures, for so is our Lord's will.

Travel is important. *Terra nova.* I wish I were her, I'll never be her, why are you crying, Jem? I stare down at my legs. Something familiar about the way I am standing. Dad, my dad. I have cowboy legs like my dad. Is there a badge for that? Yes! Sheriff badge. I do a quick draw, two guns, turning sharp to my left, knees bent, back straight, and I see Harriet's eyes on me through a chink in the wall of furniture between her sector and mine, her eyes across the Hindenburg line, and I think about wolves, the stillness and readiness of them, their eyes flashing in the trees, the trees creaking and groaning in the cold, calling out, making that lonely plaintive sound as they do on winter nights. Shiver me timbers.

'Reach,' I say. 'Reach for the sky. Bang.'

'Pax!' replies Harriet, real quiet. 'Pax!'

And thus endeth the Fourth Entry, which is of a war between Harriet and her sworn sister, and how they overcame it.

It's almost time. The soldier looks up at carriages, at boys hanging out of windows and waving, he knows some of these boys, but the names come slowly and in a jumble, like he is drunk and he is not, no, the uniforms confusing him, that's all, the uniforms so clean, no creases, no stains, buttons dazzling, he has seen this before and that confuses him too. He has been here before. It is so hard to breathe this morning.

He stares at his son, everywhere but Tom's face, he takes it in, dress the colour of mud, shoulder title and straps, waist belt and shoes without scuffs, the bag at his feet. Goodbye. He stands an arm's length away and sees his own reflection in Tom's buttons, five mirrors, the shocking detail, the Sunday best of him, startling, but then he has always had keen eyesight, the eyes of a marksman, a gift, fifteen rounds a minute, and extra pay for marksmanship, a badge he won. That time. Before. Lee–Enfield.

Tom turns from him and hugs his mother, once, tight, quick, and she says his name, Tom. She hands him two pieces of pie wrapped in paper, two triangles, and he lifts the packages to his nose and breathes in, smiling. He slips one in each pocket. He winks.

For the journey, she says. Formal.

Yes, says Tom.

The soldier remembers yesterday, how his wife moved about the kitchen making this pie, moving around in the light from counter to stove as if this were her realm, not his, and he watched her, drawing on his empty pipe, don't smoke inside! and drinking tea, and he thought maybe she'll sing, anything is possible today, she might sing a hymn, he doesn't care, any song will do. It is Saturday, he thought, and there she is, his wife, his Emily, there she is, his pal, and he wished it always be like this, and with no dead son in their lean shadows, no baby swap, all three children their own and no bad blood, no darkened room and separate beds, none of this. He is a king and a soldier and everyone close to him is safe.

Tom cuffs Dot in the arm. Don't do anything I wouldn't do.

Don't forget to write, she says, rolling her eyes.

He lifts Frances off the ground. Fluffy, he says. Highest Honours girl!

The soldier stares at her two white gloves on Tom's back, white handprints on dark uniform, and he can't help it, he thinks of the head on a pint, and white crosses in mud, white flags. Surrender. He remembers the hymn this morning. 'The Call'. He held the book open, he cannot read the words, but he has memorised them, he has a fine memory for some things, not all. Come my Way, my Truth, my Life, such a Way as gives us breath. *And then a line* with the word *killeth*. Such a Life as killeth death. *He stops. They've got it wrong, they have it backwards he thinks.* The Call, *The Call-up! Such a Life as killeth breath. Ha! He wants to laugh. And another joke. He only ever made one child, a son, with enough breath in him to last barely a minute, and in the blink of an eye and a flutter of blankets came the living boy, like a magic trick, and all that for the soldier to see in this moment on a railway platform how his one son may die two deaths. Ha! They should have walked away. He blinked. It seemed right, like magic. His dead baby, the dead mother in the next bed, the living son. Walk away! Everyone close to him dies. Not Frances, though, please not Frances.*

His town crier! That's what he calls her. She has so much to tell him, stories, items in the newspaper, she reads about war, everything. She has new friends with strange names, Grünewald, Hoffman, Gold, Jewish, that's all right, it's no odds to him. And she is so busy, her books, they lend her so many books, and her lessons at the convent, Brownies, cinema on Saturdays, swimming and ice-skating, Dot says she swims like a fish, she skates like a bird. And her work at the Grünewalds, going on two years now, two whole years, babysitting, bookkeeping, shop-minding, she is so good at sums, she is thirteen next month. She hands him money in an envelope, he gives her back one-third.

Don't buy me things with it. Stop buying me things, he says.

He knows her every step. She comes home from school, she puts down her books and goes over the road. She brings in the groceries and prepares the tea, rolling up the slices of ham and arranging leaves of lettuce, he watches her. She cuts a tomato and presses it lightly, it fans out on the plate, more magic, where did she learn that?

Mummy won't eat it, he wants to say. He can't. She knows.

And on Sundays, they walk, they walk for hours, the soldier and his town crier, but not today, today is different. He pats his son on the arm. He hands him a parcel, his old tobacco pouch inside.

To keep it dry, *he says.* Your smokes.

Yes, *says Tom.*

The soldier imagines Frances in Tom's place. The day will come for trains and ships. He will give her his old suitcase, the secret suitcase. No. He will give it to her soon, before it is time, easier. And he doesn't need it, he doesn't think about trains any more, he is a watcher of trains only.

He is so thirsty now, there is no end in his view, no limit to the number of pints he could drink, line them up, Mister Man! Fifteen rounds a minute.

Numbers and signs, clues, foresight, invention! Everything is observable. There is mystery and then there is good detection, signs in accidental things, patterns everywhere, you follow the signs, like Sherlock Holmes and Sherlock Holmes is your favourite.

Make something out of nothing. A test. No vanilla ice cream this Saturday, no thank you, Daddy! and now there is enough money for next week's film. Easy. And this. Drawing with light. To draw with light, that is what photography means, you read that, and you do it, every night, making something out of nothing, drawing with the light, beams that cross the ceiling, enough to build a house with, count them.

Numbers. Take a number! Five. You had a dream and there were five dogs in it, all different, jostling each other, pairs of skates attached by the laces hanging around their necks, how strange, how silly! And this morning, the first snowfall. Amazing. It's too early for snow. So today's number is five. Five o'clock, Sister Clare. Five in your family, five blocks to the Grünewalds, you are invited to supper, Mummy said yes, you can go – cross, sad, don't think about it. Five buttons on your coat, five pairs of eyes in each shoe, nearly there, five times five steps, five birds on the way, all robins, five senses, fifth column, bad, five red ribbons, good, you tied a plait in your hair, you don't need a mirror, pretty, for supper tonight, you are ready. Five Books of Moses, says Mr Grünewald. Five wounds, stigmata, Sister Clare, quintet, five-finger exercise. Play.

You tell Sister about the train and the uniforms, the waving. You ask about wounds, you have read all about this and Sister Clare says things that make you feel hot, it is hard to sit still and still- ness is easy for you. Red Cross, Lamb of God, Light of the World, she says, I am the good shepherd and know my sheep. She says the word sacrifice.

Yes, Sister.

You picture Tom with one leg only, you know that will not be enough for him and you look for signs in Sister's words, something close to a promise, it's what you want. Explain sacrifice. Please.

Think of your mother, she says.

Mummy?

Sister says these words infertility, adoption, making something out of nothing, the sacrifice she had to make, the blessing that came, look at you all, look at you. It is difficult to hear, there is a ringing in your ears.

No, Sister. Not me. Only Dot. Mummy made me. And Tom.

No, Frances. Oh, Frances, she says.

And your tears are awful.

You try to see the painting above the piano. Mathis Grünewald. Same name. Amazing. The lamb with one paw in the air, the blood pouring into a cup. Good blood, bad blood. Mummy screaming this at Dot. Bad blood! Daddy hitting Dot, his belt coming away like a snake, all the horrible noise.

Stop it!

You keep out of this, Frances!

You can't move, you watch it all and you make a decision about slights and disturbances, about displays of ill feeling and billowing grief. Everyone must find a way. Never again, you decide. Not in my lifetime. I will run so far from this and I will not need much. A small suitcase, a fine pair of shoes, I can walk for hours.

Mrs Grünewald. Call me Anne! She could be your mother, anyone could. Sister Clare. Are you my mother? At supper Anne brings a loaf to the table, you've never seen bread like this, golden, plaited, pretty, it tastes lovely, melting. You try to pronounce it, you're shy. Challah. You add this to your house of light and straight lines, a plaited loaf on a white oak table in a large kitchen, and outside, chattering dogs, all different, loping in snow, skates hanging around their necks by the laces. Five of them.

Holmes: I'm a consulting detective, if you can understand what that is. Here in London we have lots of Government detectives and lots of private ones. When these fellows are at fault, they come to me, and I manage to put them on the right scent. There is a strong family resemblance about misdeeds, and if you have all the details of a thousand at your finger ends, it is odd if you can't unravel the thousand and first.

Watson: But do you mean to say that without leaving your room you can unravel some knot which other men can make nothing of, although they have seen every detail for themselves?

Holmes: Quite so. I have a kind of intuition that way.

* * *

Francis, mirror of the world, mirror of pain, and perfection. Don't you see my house has collapsed? Go and repair it. The most perfect mirror in the world. A fleck of black paint 2mm wide, everyone blaming everyone else, how could this happen? Let's go fix this thing! An astronomer says it is like putting a pair of glasses on the Hubble. Good work, guys!

Eyes. I'm looking for my postcard, you sent me another post-card, with no date or message. Where are my glasses? Play hunt the specs. Is this work? Eighteen minutes to sunset, thirty-nine forms of work, three stars at night, what if I can't see them? Blurring: spherical aberration. Colour fringes: chromatic aberration. Is that me in the mirror? Jem, wot ye what I am? *Certes, nay to my witting.* You look like a loony. Comb your hair for a start, your comb is your friend. No, not tonight! Thirty-nine forms of work. Show no cracks, cracking up is so easy. St Francis calls his favourite friars the Knights of my Round Table and he has rules for them, rules with bare concessions. From the Rule of 1223: *And those who are forced by necessity may wear shoes.* Why, thank you. And he tells them this. Don't look depressed, there must be no open displays of grief or depression, please, that is the lot of the devil. No, that can't be right, because even Jesus had a devilish moment. *O my Father, if it be possible, let this cup pass from me.* I don't blame Jesus for this, it's his last night of freedom and it's a fair complaint. Must we go quite this far?

Don't you see my house has collapsed?

Numbers and signs. Chemistry and optics, maths and philos-ophy, what I see and what is true, speculation and evidence, hypoth-esis, assertion, belief, perplexity. I have one hundred trillion questions. To pass the time, let me pass up on time. If it be possible. No. Stick to your guns, have faith! *If ye be not in perfect belief . . .* Yes, I will find you. *Whither thou goest.* Start with five senses, add philosophy, apply reason, examine the alternatives, as Galileo did, making a no-decision decision, because so much is possible, esp. the unknown. Galileo, a hat on like a yarmulke, the long beard, the *telescopio* in his lap, the lamp at his feet, Light of the World. Galileo went blind, so did St Francis. Nelson suffered from seasick-ness. Shackleton writes *The Heart of the Antarctic*, he dies of heart failure.

Take a number.

San Damiano, 1206. Francis is twenty-four, maybe twenty-five, b.1182? He steps into a small church, it's a wreck, he notices this, and he has trained as a builder. Geometry is one of the seven liberal arts, he also knows Arithmetic and Astronomy, Music and the three fundamentals, Grammar, Rhetoric and Dialectic. In Dialectic, three sources of proof: reason, authority, experience. His mother has taught him to sing in three languages and she has taught him about heroes, the Christian saints and King Arthur's knights, and Perceval is his favourite.

Good Friday. Perceval is clapped out, he has been fighting in the Waste Land and stops at a hermitage. He says, I've been wandering for five years, I know nothing, I'm a mess, and the hermit says, Eat what I eat, do what I do, penance, stay two whole days. OK. And that is the end of Perceval the wanderer and knight, his wandering days are now over, he is a hermit too, things change.

San Damiano, 1206, a wreck of a church. Francis looks up at the altar, at Christ with a dreamy expression, his legs together, two straight lines, no spaces between, demure, though there are little fountains of blood spurting from his hands, knees and flank, like a whim of the imagination. It can't be happening. Five wounds, one voice, the voice is polite and Francis hears these words, *Don't you see my house has collapsed? Go and repair it for me.*

Now Francis gets busy with hammer and nails and two-by-fours, and hands out so much money for lamp oil, the lamp in this church will never go out. He has paid attention to instructions from the altar, Francis is a practical man, though restoration is expensive and pretty soon he is stealing from his father the cloth merchant, bolts of cloth, a horse, anything and his dad is really mad, you are not my son. Francis is on the run, in hiding, working overtime, falling apart a little, forgetting to wash, food doesn't matter to him, he is on a mission. Fix my house. And that is the end of Francis the troubadour, gourmet, travelling man, partygoer, hunter, soldier, things change.

Five wounds, fifth gospel, five-a-side, Weiss on Ice. Numbers, Book of Numbers, Exodus, too many Jews, Pharaoh has a fear of numbers! Into the wilderness with you. Three. Three stars at night, three Brontë sisters, not counting the dead ones, feed my dogs. Christ makes three appearances to his disciples before the Ascension, he breathes on them, Receive ye the Holy Ghost. Feed my lambs, he says it three times. Three kinds of breathing, really mad, activity, sleep, go to sleep, Jem, stop walking the planks.

Seven. *Shivah*. Forgiveness, you must dole it out in sevens, Jesus tells Peter, according to Matthew 18:22. Seven times? asks Peter. No. *Until seventy times seven*. Christ speaks from the Cross seven times, last words, there are seven names for God in the Hebrew Bible, seven is perfection, like a circle, the Round Table, that's enough knights! Seven astronauts on the *Endeavour*, magnificent seven, *The Magnificent Seven*, Where are you headed?

Driftin' south more or less. You?

Just driftin'.

Monday 4 August 1914, mobilisation day. Shackleton is still in British waters, he has just set off. He offers his services. Call us up. The Admiralty declines, the voice is polite. 'Proceed.'

Shackleton moves along with his twenty-seven men and sixty-nine sledge dogs, only to drift in floes and be trapped in ice eighty-five miles short of his destination.

I found the postcard. No return address, no message, no instructions. Feed my lambs. Go and repair it, let's go fix this thing, feed my dogs. Nothing. Just this picture of St Catherine holding her heart, oh Frances. The postcard marks a place in my book, there are books all over my floor, rock formations, my landscape now, my *terra nova*, and in this place is a photograph of Frank Wild, Shackleton's right-hand man, and a photo of Frank's dog. I marked the place because I want you to see how I have found a dog for you, this is the dog for you, a white streak in his dark hair, a thoughtful gaze, something to do with composure and fortitude. His name is Soldier.

I found a dog for you.

Come back now.

SEVEN

William Herschel, b.1738, his father is a soldier, an army bandsman in the Hanoverian footguards and William takes after him, playing the oboe in the army until coming to England as an organist and composer with a fascination for numbers, for the mathematics in music, studying a book called *Harmonics* by an astronomer named Smith. And this is it now, cosmology his big thing and he brings his sister overseas from Germany to assist him, Caroline sacrificing a singing career to help William build telescopes and plant them in freezing winter fields, so devoted to her older brother, she feeds him by hand while he works, so fixed on him and her job of assistant, she falls in a heap of melting snow one New Year's Eve, cutting her leg on a rusty hook and later writing these words in her logbook, 'I had, however, the comfort to know that my Brother was no loser through the accident, for the remainder of the night was cloudy.' She uses a capital for the word brother.

William understands the reflecting telescope, he knows it has a power greater than mere magnification, which is the power of light-gathering, and so he increases the aperture and polishes and perfects his mirrors, knowing the more light he gathers, the farther he can see and the more stars he can count. He is a starman and a scientist and pride is not a problem for him. 'I have seen further into space than ever human being did before me,' he writes, more than thirty years after he and his sister discover Uranus, the seventh planet out from the Sun, a planet with at least eleven moons all its own.

Chemistry and optics, light and reflection, microscope, telescope, spectroscope, camera. William's son John is a pioneer of photog-

269

raphy, inventing these terms for the new technology, *photography* and *snapshot*, *positive* and *negative*, and picking up where his father and aunt left off, drawing up catalogues of nebulae and clusters of stars, playing with light and time, with exposure, and taking his place in that line of visionaries, of chemists and musicians, theologians, navigators, soldiers and mule driver, all of them asking the same question, where are we now? and going beyond magnification, beyond the image itself and into the light, visible and invisible, knowing an eye is a camera and it is not enough. More light!

George Ellery Hale, b.1868, his father is a lift man, an engineer, fitting lifts into all the new Chicago skyscrapers built after the great fire of 1871. George is an engineer too, building three telescopes and three famous observatories, but he shows a lot of cracks, falling apart at regular intervals and, in the very darkest times, receiving visitations from an elf who is something of a slave-driver or maybe a godsend, who knows. The elf yells at George. Get up! Get back to work! Gather more light! George calls these episodes 'nervous breaks', his nerves are breaking, he is taking a break for his nerves, a pausette, not a bad idea, he is on a mission and a mission can break a man.

His third telescope is the Hooker on Mount Wilson, the great telescope through which Hubble and Humason see nebulae beyond the Milky Way, separate galaxies travelling fast, *speed increases with distance*, galaxies move apart, the Universe is expanding. The 100-inch Hooker has a light-gathering power 160,000 times the human eye, what a person would need to spot a candle 2,400 miles away, yet George is still calling out More light! because for him near is far, never near enough. Distance, look-back time, the Universe is always unfolding, the farther you look, the earlier you see, and newborn stars are hot, ultraviolet, explosive, *son et lumière*, the film that keeps playing for me, the end my beginning, where are we now, where am I, not here, not there, but then.

I've said I was sorry three times.

Three days until school, summer almost over, my final year at the convent coming up, cool with me, I am well fed up with nuns, *kindly excuse my daughter Jemima from nuns*. This is the year of their last big push and my last stand, they have only three terms left to achieve their battle plan and gather me into the arms of *le Bon Pasteur*, who is likewise *l'Agneau de Dieu*, shepherd and lamb, one and the same, indistinguishable in effect. I put up my dukes to Christianity and I shake the fear out of words. *Pasteur*: a scientist with a trim beard and a fascination for germs who invented chemical processes, including a vaccine for rabies, mad-dog disease, too late, however, for Emily Brontë who preferred the cowboy method. *Agneau*: a fine dish cooked by Mum, lamb with a lovely flaky crust and an aroma of rosemary and garlic served maybe once a month in our house and every Passover. Ha! Clearly those nuns have some fight on their hands, I will force them back to their last line of resistance, their Hindenburg line, and even nuns have to crack, just as the Germans did in all the stories Jude has told me.

November 1918. The Kaiser meets his generals. They tell him to bury the hatchet, Please, sir, the men are falling apart and want to go home, we are all falling apart. The Kaiser is shocked. What about the oath, he says, what about our oath? He means the *Fahneneide*, an oath a soldier swears on regimental colours, by which he pledges to die before he will ever disobey. General Groener, a name I recall as it is a word for a colour like our own name, replies, Today the *Fahneneide* is only a form of words, and this is it, total surrender for a German, same as a nervous breakdown or something. Worse.

There will be no ground given in this battle with nuns, I saw it in their eyes at exam time before the summer break, the time of the Objectif Lune Incident for which I am now very famous. Ever since then I see a reflection in their eyes that is me and not me, a new version perhaps, a vision inducing a whirly feeling of flight and freedom. The vision I have comes straight out of the Jewish cookbook Mum peruses now and again due to love-blindness for my dad, flipping pages with a perplexed expression, amazement and disbelief, mirth and gravity showing up on her face in quick succession, before she goes about the cooking of Jewish dishes for my dad after a fashion, Jewish food according to Frances.

My mother makes chopped liver with a scent and texture so lovely there is rapture all round. Occasionally, she will treat us to latkes and there is a true party atmosphere in the Weiss house, all of us yapping at her, waiting on each batch like a pack of puppies. The latkes are golden and slim and crispy with lacy edges resembling the stars in those watercolour paintings in *Le Petit Prince*, Gus's topmost favourite book, written and illustrated by M. de

Saint-Exupéry, a reconnaissance and courier pilot in World War II who disappeared on a mission. *Au revoir*, Antoine. Goodbye. When Mum reads this book to Gus, he is such a mess of nerves and quivering lips, seeing the trouble coming for *le prince*, I am sure of it, that there was no point in Mum dissembling as she did the very first time she read it to Harriet, so that *le prince* makes it home to his planet, his rose and his sheep courtesy of some useful travel instructions from snake, instead of the truth, that is, a false promise of safe return by way of snakebite, bringing on a death scene wherein *le prince* falls softly to the ground, his hands over his eyes and a golden star like a latke shining above, a star that might well be his own planet. '*Il tomba doucement comme tombe un arbre.*' And in this reading experience between Mum and Gus she explains the business of planets and flight with extreme confidence and clarity, as if interplanetary travel were always on her mind, she knows the ins and outs.

Aside from chopped liver and latkes, Mum really ought to give up on Jewish food and stop trying to make it harmonious, because this is food that should strike a light, it is drum-beating stuff, getaway and on-the-run food for wanderers and the besieged, for the cowboy-tough, the soldier, boxer, hero. I remember watching her one evening last winter preparing a speciality for my dad's return from some sports-writing trip. I am in the kitchen with a book, my chin in one hand, glancing up at her from time to time and fighting an urge to express my feeling to her regarding Jewish food and harmony, and how it is food befitting plastic tubs from the deli, tubs stacked in paper bags spotted with grease and packed with extras such as pickles and karnutzel and skinny hopeless paper napkins definitely not up to the job, and it is all right that we should eat it in unseemly haste, felled for hours thereafter, sprawled across the living-room floor in a daze, happy casualties of Jewish food. I don't say anything, though, because I think she knows that all this is befitting and what she is doing is not quite befitting. Something else is at stake here.

I watch her marinate a goose neck, tenderising the meat and the wrinkly bumpy skin she has plucked with tweezers by bathing it in cognac and such things where it will lie for hours, stuffed with a mixture of goose meat and herbs and vegetables she chops so fine I cannot believe my eyes, next unfurling a length of silken thread from a spool and sewing everything in, tracing a fine even line of stitches along the neck like she is making a tapestry and all the while she has this dreamy and purposeful look, there and not there, and I begin to worry.

'Mum, are you OK? Would you like a glass of wine? Mum? Should I put some music on? Bach? Billie?'

She is OK.

Soon my dad comes home, a great wave crashing against our shores, strewing his last few days over the premises, end to end, a trail of kit he must unpack THIS MINUTE, little heaps of shirts and boxer shorts, tangly socks and scrunched hankies, and his sponge bag spilling its contents all crusty with pink tooth-paste, and then the flow of newspapers and magazines and envelopes from the mail he has just torn apart, his scuffed overnight bag gaping there, all he ever needs, no matter how many nights he leaves her for, as if by taking an overnight bag only, he believes he is not away for three nights but for one plus one plus one, and to him, sitting in his hotel room at night after he has called her for maybe the fifth time that day, far becomes soon, I think so.

'Bartender! Sommelière!'

That's me! I bash off to fix him a drink, jostling members of my family aside like a rugby player on a winning run and it's a wild time, like every homecoming of Dad's, Weisses racing about, it's a jumping joint. I have to run back from the bar clutching an empty whisky glass and get him to indicate a Plimsoll line because a coming-home drink is not the same as a regular after-work drink, the Scotch requirement is a variable thing. And after the drink, Mum makes her presentation, her gentle offering of this speciality first course which has been roasting quietly in the oven guarded by Pax! the gourmet dog, whose habit it is to lie by the stove in a decorous manner as long as dinner is simmering within. Mum stands by my dad and speaks in a shy manner.

'Helzel,' she says. 'Helzel.'

We cluster around him at the table, Ben, Jude, Harriet, Gus and me and we pass this word around, *helzel*, and we clam up as he goes in for the first bite, a feeling of awe and ceremony looming in the dining room.

'Well, Dad? Well?' we say, whereupon Dad begins to crease up, laughing and falling into his plate just about.

'*Pâté de foie juif!*' he declares, clapping his arms around Mum, pressing his great head into her, Mum kind of giggling and crying also, and making little helpless gestures with her hands.

'Helzel de Coco Chanel!' I call out and now Ben is loping out of the room and charging up the stairs three at a time, and back in seconds flat, wielding a camera.

'Pop art!' says Ben. 'Art for Pop!'

'Is it OK to use mustard?' Jude asks quite calmly, ignoring all the commotion and pulling Dad's plate his way to carve fine slices off the helzel, feeding himself and Gus with the same fork, reminding me of Bill Sikes and Bullseye.

'*Poivre vert* is the nicest. Not the *moutarde de grains*, please,' suggests Gus with composure and urgency, very thoughtful as is now his custom when it comes to culinary matters, despite extreme youth.

Harriet stares at Jude and Gus in disbelief, fully aware that the helzel was once something to do with sensitive parts of bird anatomy, the offence of it so startling she must overcome it by calling up that old sporting instinct all her own which has everything to do with joining in and nothing much to do with sports, timing or any rules known to man. Harriet plucks a carrot stick from the clay jug in the centre of the table like she is drawing the sword from the stone and she shakes it at the heavens.

'AS GOD IS MY WITNESS,' she exclaims in momentous tones, 'I WILL NEVER GO HUNGRY AGAIN!'

I step up on to my chair in the spirit of things, and because I feel Tiny Tim coming on, a song-type moment except I do not go in for singing. 'God bless us EVERY ONE,' I say in a meek manner, indicating shy triumph over asperity and doom, things such as dire poverty and polio and no education and imminent death, nothing to me in the face of home and Christmas and family affections.

Helzel night is the night Mum more or less closed up that book on Jewish food, the one with the photo in it that had me mirth-stricken the first time I saw it, and is now the image I see reflected in the nuns' eyes at my French convent ever since the Objectif Lune Incident for which I am now exceedingly famous.

This is a very old photograph from the pioneer days of photography when people just stood around I guess, same as posing for a painting or sculpture yet looking less real than in paintings, kind of stiff and suspicious and stuck in a lonely setting of bleached-out pools of light and smudgy brown shadows. Under this photo

are the words 'bagel peddler' and there is an explanation alongside to do with the symbolism of bagels which were invented in
south Germany, and about this job of bagel peddling, an occupation requiring a licence, being quite a popular activity in the Polish
shtetl and not only there, I know now, thinking back on my dad's
early life before he sought opportunity and the sports-writing life.
Bagel means bracelet in German, a bagel is a ring, having no end
or beginning, therefore making it a symbol of the eternal cycle of
life. This expression is a problem for me. I simply do not perceive
the circular or the never-ending in this business of being born and
ending up under a heap of earth with maybe a faithful dog lying
atop and howling for days. Life strikes me as more of a straight-
line situation, but never mind. Bagels in olden times were symbols
of eternity and, furthermore, handy things for warding off the evil
eye and bringing good luck, all of which is a downright bonus if
you are a great fan of bagels, like discovering a loved one has
untold marvels in his past, my dad for instance, who was not only
a baker's boy peddling symbols of eternity, but an amateur boxer
with a fine left hook. I look at my dad sometimes and see what
might have been, I see a stooped man in a leather cap with tufts
of hair sticking out around his ears, and a straggly beard and a
worried look, wearing bashed-up floppy boots and what appear to
be pyjamas under a heavy rumpled overcoat, and around his neck,
a taut strap, the ends attached to a basket big as a military drum,
and it is filled with bagels. He is the bagel man.

I like to haul out the bagel man for my family, especially at
Xmas time when I worry Dad is feeling swamped by Christianity
and events such as the Nativity and the Epiphany and the playing
of carols featuring ecstatic endearments suggesting love-blindness
for the Lord and perhaps some confusion over the identity of the
Lord, who is King, my liking, my dear Son, my Sweeting, my dear
Heart, mine own dear Darling and sweete Lording, etc. Very interesting. In Judaism, I believe, we tend to skimp on endearments,
meaning it may not be such a cheery vision of spiritualities as the
nun vision of spiritualities, but at least there is no mistaken identity when it comes to the Lord. We *wot* what He is.

I slip into Jude's battered work boots, his Kojak boots as they
are now known since Gus mistook the word Kodiak for Kojak,
preferring to believe such fine and venerable boots are named in
honour of a great television detective and not some stranger by

the name of Kodiak, and looking forward also to the day his feet will have grown to Kojak boot size. The day will come, Gus, for Kojak boots of your own. I slip into Jude's boots and clap his suede cap on my head and wrap myself in Ben's greatcoat which is some three feet too long for me and oversized in all measurements. I tip the fruit out of the wicker fruit basket and fill it with bagels and there is always a fine stash of bagels in our house at Christmas time, sesame seed (my favourite) and poppy seed (my second favourite). I wait for peak time, just before a meal when Weisses are hovering in one place, restless and slap-happy and peckish, all veering eagerly kitchenwards though mindful not to pressurise Mum in an unseemly fashion, everyone excepting Dad who has a look of profound affliction when he is hungry and is a bundle of nerves. Now is my time. I shuffle in, wending my way in the crowd with a scrape of Kojak boots and a droopy expression, mumbling in a depressing manner and moving along like I am headed before my time for that hole in the ground and no company expected, not even a dog.

'Beigels. Beigels. Nice beigels. Not warm, but who cares. If you don't want, it doesn't matter. It figures. Who cares. Beigels. Beigels.' Etc.

I'm not quite sure why, but there is a big feeling for the bagel man in my house and I get calls for him on a number of occasions, sometimes from Harriet when it is most inconvenient, like at three in the morning after a bad dream.

'Do the bagel man,' she says, sitting up in bed, her covers a mess of nightmare rumples.

What a palaver. I can't say this to Harriet though. 'Um. Tomorrow I'll do the bagel man, OK? How about cards?'

'Bagel man, please.'

'No, Harriet. Cards.'

'OK,' she says, making her way to my bed, her ship to my ship. 'Shiver me timbers,' she adds by way of greeting, smiling fondly in remembrance of pirate days.

'Ahoy there,' I reply. 'Welcome aboard.'

And Harriet and I settle down to cards, any arrangement and set of rules will do, games I invent to coax my sister back to bed, to a better kind of sleep, a place with no dangers.

I have been thinking a lot about the Objectif Lune Incident because I recall coming home from school that day and telling Jude the story more or less straight off, not even changing out of my uniform, but heading for his bedroom to sit on the floor and lean up against the wall, with Jude lying on his bed on his side watching me and kind of chuckling now and again, and both of us drinking Ribena-milks as in olden times. I also remember how the first time I clapped eyes on that photograph of the bagel man, I was hysterical with mirth and traipsed all over the house hunting out Jude because I needed him to see it too, like his eyes and my eyes are just one pair of eyes, but pretty soon I will not be able to do this, seek him out straight off, as he is going away, for a whole year he says, a span of time I just cannot make sense of, a science problem with too many imponderables, a problem too far.

Jude has already been away for most of the summer holidays, seven weeks of it, weeks when my days took on an irregular shape and quality, some spent in a frenzy of intense activity, making fiercely accurate drawings of British commandos 1940–45 complete with front and back views, or reading up a storm of novels, all the old ones with bumpy leather bindings the colour of night or of dried blood, and with leaves so fine they hover a little in mid-air before falling as I turn them, days spent reading these and that massive tome on European Jewish immigration to America my dad handed over to me with great ceremony, and other days spent wandering around lost, days of hours and minutes loose and strange as our days at sea, between shores. What country, what time zone is this?

Jude was at a mining camp for seven weeks, the youngest member of a seismic crew, and although I am not too clear on what this means, I do know it did not involve canaries and the heaving of coal carts along rail tracks, or the collapsing of tunnels with terrible screams ensuing from man and beast, screams no one is likely to hear in time. Jude went to a mining camp to earn *isolation pay* for his great expedition, isolation pay being a lot of pay in little time, what you get for very hard labour and for being stranded somewhere in a rocky mining-type place far from patisseries, cinemas and museums, and also for living in a huddle of men only, no girls at all, making me wonder what would arise if Mum, Harriet and I packed our little bags and waltzed out, slamming the door behind us, would someone come along with moneybags for Dad, Ben, Jude and Gus, bags of isolation pay?

Jude told me something about the seismic crew I find quite

interesting. Last thing at night, he says, and no matter what, even all the men wobbly drunk due to isolation, etc., the tables had to be set for breakfast, someone having this job of shuffling out cutlery and cereal bowls and cups for coffee and glasses for juice, and most often this was Jude's job as he was the youngest. I like this story very much and picture miners hurtling across the landscape all day and climbing in and out of lorries, wrestling with great items of machinery and explosives and falling rocks, miners who need to wake up in the morning, however, and see the table set neatly, knowing someone was thinking about them the night before and moving around in the dark with purpose, someone looking out for them.

Jude brought me a gift from mining camp, a rock encrusted with sparkly bits and wrapped in a fold of soft cloth he unfurled for me so carefully, flipping back one corner of the cloth at a time, I knew not to ask any questions but just to take that rock in with suitable gravity and a sense of occasion.

'Thank you, Jude. Thank you for this rock, it's really a good rock.'

'Keep it in the cloth,' he said.

OK, Jude.

Three days until school, one Jude night.

Tonight we had a barbecue for Jude, a going-away dinner, and he could have had anything he wanted on this night, even that roast chicken with the little mushroom and truffly herby bits under the skin and the tagliatelle spilling out, or even osso bucco, his all-time favourite, but he chose a barbecue and that's what we had and it is also probably the last barbecue of the summer, which is fitting, I suppose.

First off we drank champagne on the terrace and the lake was so busy with boats, I think everyone set sail today including half-hearted types, weekend sailors, everyone pushing the boat out for a final fling on the waters before autumn and satchels and brief-cases and jackets and falling leaves, and I hoped those sailors remembered their right-of-way rules because the lake resembled the bumper-car ring at the funfair, with mayhem and crash situations and a lot of shouting in store, it wouldn't take much, just one false move. It's a question of gravity.

Ben says most of the Universe is dark matter. We know it is

there because of mass, and we know there is mass because of gravity and the gravitational attraction of things, meaning how fast something falls towards some other thing, and without all that dark matter and the extra gravity it brings, stars would just fly away, galaxies would fly apart! Stars are in orbit same as planets, but quicker, Ben says, nearly ten times quicker, and things in orbit are always falling, even the Moon and the Earth in the Solar System, and the faster something falls, the faster it moves in orbit, with all the stars under the influence of all the other stars, and just as the Moon is always falling towards the Earth, always falling, no crashing, the stars behave likewise, as collisionless particles, Ben says, in elliptical galaxies. That is a fine word, elliptical, though our Galaxy is not elliptical, it is a spiral galaxy and in a spiral galaxy the orbits of things are speedier at the centre than at the edges, in the halo as it is known, something I can easily grasp if I think about us, our house a tempest of Weiss activity, yet in the great world as I see it, Jude on his expedition, say, or Mum out shopping, I imagine less speed and more caution at the edges, due to the unknown in the halo of things. And now, sitting on the wall at the top of our hill, I watch boats swarming around in the breezes and my family milling about on the terrace and I feel like a traffic cop, a lollipop lady, orchestra conductor, navigator, night pilot, Antoine de Saint-Exupéry, my job, the preventing of collisions, and I declare there will be no collisions, not on my watch, hold your course!

This is a champagne feeling. It comes quick and I know why, I have read how CO_2 in champagne fizz expedites alcohol into the bloodstream and I close my eyes for a moment always as this feeling is coming on, picturing my circulation and the expedition of things in my veins as I recall Ben explaining womb to me, and words such as placenta and how the blood vessels of the mother and the embryo mingle in this exchange of substances, of nutrients and oxygen and the antibodies required for resistance to disease and the rejection of foreign tissue, the foundation of immunity. I remember all this and think there may well be antibodies in champagne too, champagne which is the goodbye drink, the antibodies making Jude's farewell barbecue a fine evening and not a sad one, for the immunity they bring.

'Do we have lift-off?' asks Jude, pouring out seconds of champagne, meaning are you there yet, in that champagne moment?

'All systems are go!' I tell him whereupon we launch into the tune from *Thunderbirds*, and Jude refills my glass.

'Well done . . . Parker,' I say to Jude in the thoughtful manner of Lady Penelope, posh heroine spy in *Thunderbirds* to her hero chauffeur named Parker, bumbly, yet brave. Heroes are complicated and can be a bit remote.

'Thank you, Milady,' says Jude in a bumbly brave manner.

'All is for the best in the best of all possible worlds,' I remark, all lofty and in French.

'Voltaire was an anti-Semite,' Jude says, moving away with the bottle to perch on the end of Mum's deckchair, right by her feet which are crossed at the ankles in a manner I have tried to imitate with horrible results, looking not one bit like a painting of a beautiful reclining damosel and more like the victim of an ambush, in pain and trussed at the ankles and left to roast in the desert sun and be pecked to death by vultures.

'Really, Jude?'

'Yup.'

'Bloody.'

Not more enemies, I think, blaming the convent and wondering is anywhere safe for Jews, anywhere at all, and adding Voltaire and his book *Candide* we studied last term to my list of crimes perpetrated by nuns against me.

Jude pours champagne, usually my job, we all have jobs, beginning with Dad. Apart from the job of sports writing, there are four or five roles and activities my dad considers all his own, fields in which he will allow no challengers, even though in some of these fields his qualifications are distinctly dodgy. The division of responsibilities in a family can be a sensitive thing, a job thrust upon you quite by accident, or as some kind of distinction, or sometimes to shore up crumbling confidence when it comes to skills, and now and again, a job is yours due to supreme natural ability. For instance, I am the dustman in our family, but only where Dad's rubbish is concerned. No housekeeper or other Weiss has this honour of emptying my dad's wicker bin of scrumpled pages of sports writing, cigar butts, twisted paper clips, shirt cardboard and cellophane, tomato stalks and seeds, business cards, old magazines, tea bags, empty boxes of chocolate raisins and soggy Kleenex. No. This is my job. I struggle, but I don't complain. Is this a shoring up of confidence job or a special distinction job? I don't know. Maybe it began as a shoring up job and ended in distinction, making it, really, an accident-type job. It's complicated, but there is one job I know is mine for supreme natural ability and that is my role of sommelière in the Weiss family, a job quite close to a vocation, and one I relinquish tonight because Jude has a craving for a whirling dervish of an evening on this night before he leaves, which is clearly why he hit upon this choice of a barbecue dinner, definitely the least sedate of family meals in our household, and on that list of activities my dad considers all his own and for which his qualifications are distinctly dodgy.

If I had not given up on my logbook around which I wanted to wrap Harriet's painting, giving it up to mark the armistice between Harriet and me, then the barbecue would be an entry in that logbook, Entry Number Five, a monograph on novel things in my dad's country, including ice hockey, French boys, showers and bagels, all these things requiring a slight change in world view, which is how it must have been with Horatio, Lord Nelson, when he was suddenly a great hero with only half his expected share of arms and eyes. He had to adapt and make choices and there is only so much change a person can take. Picking up a lamb chop one-handed is irritating, but dancing with only one arm for the loved one is call for grief. If change is a problem for you, it is wise to learn the difference between novelty requiring adaptation and novelty that is a threat to life and sanity.

Change is certainly a problem for my dad. Every year he gets a new pair of leather slippers at Christmas, slip-ons with no backs, plus one new pair of blue espadrilles with backs, backs that he mashes down with his heels in the summertime, turning them into slip-ons. Do not say 'Dad, they make blue espadrilles with no backs' because he does not want those, he will never wear them, he needs to mash down the backs. Why is it OK to have leather slippers without backs, why doesn't he require slippers with backs to mash also? Do not ask.

When my dad opens the fridge in search of mayonnaise, the very jar of mayonnaise that is always on the top shelf right in front and on the left where he can see it, mysteriously replaced there by Mum, in its usual place and usual state, i.e. with the lid twisted on all wonky and a wee waterfall of crusty yellowing mayonnaise down the side mixed with flecks of tinned salmon and chopped onion, clues of snacks past, and he does not see it, he yells out for me, always me, another job for which I am specially distinguished due to supreme natural ability.

I drop whatever I am doing and make my way Dadward. I do not fish out the jar pronto even though it is plainly visible, I display a measure of perplexity, meaning I understand his distress and know that for him, if something is not exactly where he expects, it is not somewhere else but NOT THERE AT ALL, and this is a feeling close to horror.

'Hmm,' I say. 'Let me see . . . oh! Why, there it is! Here, Dad.'

And now he does not want me around any more, just because I saw this fissure in him, a fissure being the sharpest of cracks, a cleft in a rock, and also, as I have read, a medical term to do with wounds, a wound in the shape of a line, a straight line.

When the mayonnaise is not where Dad expects it, I believe he thinks about Frances without even knowing it and this is why he gets so rattled. When he wants Mum, which is just about always, and she is not there right before his eyes as he enters the house or a room he expects her to be in, he loses his mind and starts calling out her name over and over in the manner of King Arthur avenging the stealing of his Queen by the traitor Sir Launcelot and storming his way to Launcelot's castle called Joyous Gard with the loyal Sir Gawain *and an huge host where he laid siege and made strong war though his heart was never so heavy for pure sorrow* (Book XX, Chapter 10).

When he is not yelling out FRANCES! FRANCES! many times over in quick succession, giving her no chance to respond at all, Dad collars whichever kid crosses his path, demanding 'Where's Mummy? Where is your mother?' in accusatory tones, and no matter how strong the urge, you must not reason with him, you cannot say, 'Dad. In our old country, we lived in a house with three floors and a garden. Now we live in two houses, one country house with three floors and a lake, and one city house with four floors and a garden, territory a regular human being can negotiate without too much palaver, unlike crossing a desert with only a dribble of water in the flask, or hacking your way through the Waste Land or riding the high seas in a tempest. It will be OK, Dad. Calm down. Thank you.' No, you do not say this. Here is what you do. You start running around and calling out 'Mum! Mum!' and opening and closing doors and charging up and down stairs, adding to the general atmosphere of air-raid hysteria and impending doom, and pretty soon, lo! Mum glides our way, gazelle-like, cool as anything, like nothing unusual is happening at all. Well, hello.

'There you are,' says Dad every time, kind of aggrieved and cross. 'I was looking for you,' he adds, aiming for casual now, scraping his hands through his hair, recovering from this great adventure of search and rescue which he has accomplished once again with banners waving, sword raised and a battle cry loud as thunder, as if without even a passing thought regarding unspeakable loss. He has laid siege and made strong war, and this when there are enemies everywhere. Everywhere. Well done, Dad.

I am tempted to remark that barring rocket trips to the Moon, she could never go missing, but I do not. It is not possible to go missing for any worrying length of time in our household due to the elaborate tracking system we have established and which is still going strong, growing more and more elaborate as we grow up and begin to embark on short solo journeys on buses, in cars and on foot to meet up with friends in little networks of our own, going thither and seeing adventures, etc. The tannoy operation works fine, still, with its regular travel updates concerning departure times and destinations and estimated times of arrival and round-trip information of course, including all projected stops on the way, outgoing, incoming. 'Going upstairs to do my homework,' I might announce. 'Calling at: Bathroom. Ben's bedroom. Harriet's and my room. Down in time to set table.' And if I had a whistle, I'd blow it right then, the sound of a train whistle and the ensuing slam of carriage doors echoing like no other sound I know, terrible and thrilling at once, what with the shock of freedom and separation and fears of forgotten things, such as belongings left behind and unsaid words, a shock altogether too great for my body, a sensation close to euphoria, I think, and to mourning, not quite grief. Travel is important.

Tannoy announcements, though, are not enough now, so we go in for notes offering up travel details of varying usefulness, Harriet, for instance, having a special way with hours and minutes which can be a problem to interpret. I try to cajole my sister into sticking to essentials in notes – whereabouts, names and compass points – and to forgo this pesky business of time. Once we are apprised of the essentials, we can work out the times for ourselves, totting up journey times, factoring in possible diversions and unavoidable pit stops, and coming up with a fair estimate of when she is likely to return and whom she might bring on home with her.

'Mum,' I say. 'I'm setting the table for eight. Harriet's with Kath and they are ONE this month. Like this,' I add, holding up two crossed fingers. 'She'll definitely bring her home.'

'Well, don't put her next to me,' says Jude who is helping me out. 'She leans. And she drools.'

'That's true! Kind of like a dog!'

'Yeh. Probably why they are bosom buddies. Maybe we should set her place under the table. There's a spare dog dish.'

'Let's do it!'

'I don't think so,' says Mum. 'And they'll be late. Café Zweig is on the way from Kath's.'

'Oh right. *Sachertorte* pit stop.'

Jude says, 'Harriet should be on a leash. One we can yank from here.'

Jude's notes are not very helpful either, but quite reassuring if you know Jude. He has communication in mind, that's the main thing. 'I'll be back,' he writes. Or, 'I'm out.' 'See you.' Messages of that ilk. Words explaining just where he will be and for how long and what for are not important. Jude is not shifty or secretive, not one bit, he just needs to wander freely, which is why he is headed outbound with Zach, Zach who has made some progress since our Russian ship days, though he still dances around in a quick two-step foot to foot, his gaze wild and open as if there were an excess of electricity in his body, or he has some special knowledge of things to come, and this dance of his keeps him at the ready always for doomy eventualities and unusual demands, the need to escape, to run fast as a leopard from such possibilities as earthly tremors, flash lightning, or enemies in the hills, cold-eyed crackshots every one, which is how I know that on this expedition, Zachariah will be the man with the watch on his wrist so that Jude does not have to fret about time, Zach will have spare woolly items in his kit when Jude has lost a jumper too many, and Zach will be the one to chase up a penguin or dog to roast if the necessity arises, and shield Jude from fire, stepping neatly between him and a bullet, because he sees Jude is a leader of men, Nelson, Shackleton, Cook. Behold the man.

For the last week or two since Jude returned from mining camp, he has been leaving a different variety of note around the house carefully addressed to Ben, Gus and me, notes full of instructions, going-away notes. I do not believe he has addressed any notes to

Harriet. I do know he has summoned her to his room to deliver private instructions of the verbal kind, because I have spotted my sister in the halls doing a slow march before pausing outside his door to pronounce the gladiator oath while raising her right hand in a gladiator salute, a poignant gesture she picked up from breezing through the study one afternoon when Jude and I were watching *Spartacus*.

'*Morituri te salutant*,' she declares in grievous tones, loud enough for Jude to hear, the only three words of Latin she has been willing to learn aside from the names of flora and fauna, thanks to her expertise in slaves and slavery, and the heartbreaking reaction she had listening to gladiators speak this oath to their Roman masters, uttering what might very well be their last words in voices proud and alert, showing no cracks at all. *Those who are about to die salute you.*

Notes issued just short of imminent departure are a bit spooky and solemn, I find, even if the words themselves are bold and plain with no shadows. 'You can wear my rugby top.' 'The socks under the bed are for the wash.' 'There is emergency money in my Cherry book', by which he means *The Worst Journey in the World* by Apsley Cherry-Garrard, a favourite book of Jude's which I aim to reread pretty soon. All these messages, these small white squares with a quick dash of Jude-writing in black, animal prints on snow, just the sight of them is enough to cause a squeezy sensation in the throat and a pain like swallowing a stone, a musical moment almost, and Jude knows this, keeping the notes bold and plain, and away from Harriet who might wave one about at the dinner table, which would be very bad for Mum who believes in travel and adventure, but maybe not solo journeys, not yet, not for us, I don't think so.

These notes of Jude's are making Ben crazy. There is no end to the craziness of Ben due to this very bad experience of receiving notes full of instructions and reminders and lists of household tasks to perform in Jude's absence, and although Ben would not dream of complaining to Jude, he has a strong need to display outrage to me, Jem, on the morning of Jude's farewell barbecue, and he does this by shaking his fist skywards, Jude's note scrunched in his hand with little white edges of paper peeping from between his long fingers and as I watch him, I think about Dr Jekyll in that moment he is stepping into his dark side, becoming Mr Hyde, a man not in control of things and with strong impulses for murder and larceny.

It's hot out here.

I unfurl my towel, the ice-hockey emblem towel my dad gave me with some fanfare two years ago, with its white background and the emblem in the centre, a big C with an H inside it, H for the French word *habitant*, a throwback to a history of trapping and hunting and settling in a frozen place full of wild things plus Native Indians, and English types mighty suspicious of French types and French types mighty suspicious of English types as is customary in history.

'Maurice Richard,' my dad says, showing me old photos of hockey players and pointing out a man in the same battle pose as every other player in the team, facing the camera, knees bent, hunched over his stick with the blade flat on the ice, this man Monsieur Richard having an enormous head and a lot of dark hair greased back in the manner of Bela Lugosi in *Dracula*, something I choose not to remark upon to Dad.

'The Rocket,' he says, expressing awe and reverence. 'His nick-name.'

'Whoa,' I say. 'Thanks for showing me, Dad. May I borrow the book?'

'But put it back after. It goes right here,' he adds, poking his finger at one scrawny gap in his shelves not even wide enough now for a magazine, a space boxed in by tomes of all sizes stuffed in at dodgy angles so that pulling one out is akin to a game of pick-up-sticks, one false move and you are standing in a landslide of volumes with a shuddery helpless feeling and bruised limbs. My dad's library arrangement and general state of affairs in his office universe brings to mind that missing moment of creation Ben explained to me, wherein conditions were too extreme for us to apply the laws of physics, but behold what ensued! A whole universe of intricate rules and laws misleadingly called chaos.

'OK, Dad. Right there. Fear not. And thanks for the towel. It's great.'

I anchor two corners of my towel with the black plimsolls I always wear on the walk down the hill from terrace to dock, ever since I clapped eyes on a grass snake lurking in readiness in the cool of the stone steps, and another in the long grasses where the dock meets the low wall at the water's edge. My black plimsolls are my anti-snake shoes. 'Snake, snake, go away, never come again, any other day.' That is my anti-snake chant, now a famous chant in the Weiss family. You can add 'thank you' at the end if in the politic vein, though this is optional and will depend largely on your state of nerves. It is advisable to do the chant at all danger spots while stamping on the spot with anti-snake shoes. Any shoes will do except sandals, of course. Chant and move along at a brisk and forthright pace and hope for the best. Look straight ahead, no blinking and think not about snake encounters and ensuing horror, but about heroics and soldiers such as Lord Horatio who had his own way with fear and lost a lot of blood in combat, as well as highly prized parts of his anatomy, but never his nerve, he never lost his nerve.

I haul off my T-shirt to reveal my bathing suit which is actually an old ballet leotard of Harriet's. I don't go in for regular bathing suits you have to try on over your knickers with all your other things in a horrible tangle on the floor in strange and suffocating cubicles in shops. No thank you. I fold my T-shirt into a pillow shape for head protection on the dock, otherwise I will not be able to concentrate on my book for fear of the squashing of my nerves and blood vessels and impending dementia and brain damage.

'How did it happen, sir?' the surgeon asks my dad, both of them observing my pitiful struggle with basic skills of coordination, computation, language and memory. It's a bad scene.

'She was reading on the dock. That's all I know.'

I sit up to give Ben my all-out attention, Welcome, Ben! and little silver fish swim before my eyes because it is a hot day and I skipped lunch and I have made this sudden move from lying down to sitting up. I watch my brother have his Dr Jekyll into Mr Hyde moment perilously close to the edge of the dock, and I note that the Sun and Moon are in the sky this afternoon, proof once and for all that they are not the same, that there is no nightly trans-formation from Sun into Moon, a conviction I held until an alarm-ingly late age, well past my twelfth birthday in fact, something Gus is very fond of resurrecting for general amusement in his graceful teasing manner. I don't mind.

'LOOK at this!' screams Ben, flapping Jude's latest note in my face. 'READ it!' he yells, which is quite hard, seeing as he keeps whipping it beyond my grasp in a crazed fashion.

'Ben,' I say. 'Cool your jets. Tomorrow is another day.'

Emma Richler

Ben crumples to the dock beside me in a mess of long limbs in the manner of a dromedary, a type of camel and beast of burden quite dear to Harriet due to its place in the pantheon of slaves and slavery in the animal kingdom.

'Dromedary,' she announced one afternoon after a hard day's schooling, dumping her heft of a satchel in the doorway of our room and doing a belly flop on to her bed. '*Camelus dromedarius*. One-humped Arabian camel. Long-legged breed. Cannot store water but can drink nearly sixty litres at one go. Hump shrinks when hungry.'

'I say, old chap,' I declared. 'There is just no end to your trials.'

'I know it, my dear.'

'You are a slave to education.'

'Bless you, my child,' my sister replied, reaching into her chocolate and treasures drawer and selecting a florentine she broke in two very neatly, crossing the room to hand me half. 'For what you are about to receive . . .'

'I am truly thankful, Harriet.'

'Fiddle-dee-dee then.'

'OK.'

I unscrunch Ben's note. Here are Jude's instructions for Weiss 1, i.e. Ben, his elder and Lord Protector.

1. You should not do drugs. You can't handle it. If you do, don't let Gus or Harriet see. When you get the munchies, clear up after. If you finish the butter, put out more. Dad freaks out at hard butter.
2. When you go out, take your fucking keys with you.
3. You should go to uni. Fill out applications. You can paint in your spare time. Life is not a dream.
4. If you move out, get a job first. FIRST, right?
5. Help with the shopping on Saturdays. Go with Mum, it's too crowded and she gets tired. Don't wait for her to ask you. She won't. Just go with her.
6. Rubbish nights: Tues, Thurs. Slam the lids on tight, fuck, or the squirrels and cats get in. The guys won't collect if it's all spilling out.
7. Make sure Harriet gets her homework done before Monday morning.
8. Help Jem after dinner, washing up, stashing stuff, other-

288

wise she'll do the martyr act. If she does, get the hammer
and nails from the toolbox and tell her to lie down with
her arms spread. That always cracks her up.

9. Rag Gus about his inhaler and his medicines. Shocks can
    collapse the lungs, he almost died that day. And keep cab
    money for the hospital if you take him out.

10. Snow. It falls. Shovel the fucking path or Dad will do it
    and slip a disc and be a drag for weeks.

11. Wash your things. Clothes in, then soap, close hatch,
    normal-normal, low-heat dry, ON. Not complicated.

12. Keep the bass down when you play music at night.

13. Don't leave food out in the basement, or we'll have the 4th
    plague down there. Bugs, right?

14. Walk Pax! in town last thing at night. You stay up latest.

15. Go to the cottage most weekends, or Mum worries. Stay
    together, it's important.

OK, man. I'll try to make it home for Christmas. Over and
out.

Love, Jude.

'Hmm,' I say to Ben. 'He left out the part about forty lashes
and maggoty bread for messing up.'

'Yeh. FUCKING unbelievable,' goes Ben, slapping his knees.

'FUCKING unbelievable,' I say, gazing out over the water. 'Plus
he used the word fuck three times in one page. COULD do better,'
I add in headmistress tones.

'Yeh!' says Ben. 'Right!'

'That boy will not go far! He is going nowhere fast! I cannot
recommend prison too highly.'

'Right,' says Ben, softer now, picking at the seams of his black
jeans. 'Seal not the sayings of the prophecy of this book; for the
time is at hand. Revelation.'

'Indeed.'

I think about Jude's note and how it is true that Ben is dreamy
and a bit hopeless at household tasks, but some facts are hard to
face and so I stay with him in his state of outrage, letting it simmer,
joshing him out of it gently, because everyone needs a little indulgence with extreme feelings and bald truths, why, even Jude does,
though you might suppose that boy is so calm he can take any
kind of truth at all with no special measures of the soft-shoe variety

required to help him face those truths, but you would be wrong about that. Here is an example from just the other day.

Jude is in a pretty bad mood due to hard labour. He has to mow the lawn finally, as he is headed for exotic lands and has managed to put off this lawn-mowing job for ages but the time has come, the grasses are high, something which fills me with particular dread because of the snake situation. Tall grasses are a favourite hangout for snakes. They are all waiting for me in there among the tall grasses, I know it. I wait inside until it is all over. Here is Jude. He has mowed the lawn and is scowly and sweaty and anxious for snacks. I watch him scour the bread bin for bagels that are not there, as if there might be some secret compartment within. He cannot believe his eyes although I told him twice since breakfast we had run out of bagels and each time he gazed my way and blinked, nodding gravely, but I see now he simply did not take in the truth about bagels because of his bad mood over the forthcoming terrible job of lawn-mowing. I break the news to him one more time.

'Jude, we have run out of bagels,' I say in a forlorn and sympathetic fashion from a safe distance across the kitchen, whereupon my brother bangs the bread bin shut and bashes the chopping board with both fists, sending a lot of crumbs flying. Yikes.

'GODDAMMIT! DID YOU EAT THE LAST ONE?! WHAT IS GOING ON IN THIS HOUSE?! FUCK-HELL! I'M GOING AWAY AND NOBODY FUCKING CARES!'

And that is an example of delayed reaction to truths and how people have different ways with the telling and receiving of truth, some requiring extremely special measures of the soft-shoe variety, beyond a person's capacity for indulgence, even a sister's, even when willing.

When Blanche has lost her mind due to abuses and misunderstanding and Stanley has arranged a blind date for her with a man prepared to hold her coat, yes, but a jacket with long sleeves he can tie up at the back, Stella and her neighbour Eunice carry on an edgy conversation with Blanche to do with grapes, speaking in sad and gentle voices, cajoling and guilty, helping her dress for the terrible date, distracting her from the real peril of her situation, hoping to keep her in a safer place of mild craziness instead of all-out craziness, which is where she is headed, it is only a breath away.

SCENE ELEVEN

STELLA [handing her dress]: Is this what you –
BLANCHE: Yes, it will do! I'm anxious to get out of here –
    this place is a trap!
EUNICE: What a pretty blue jacket.
STELLA: It's lilac coloured.
BLANCHE: You're both mistaken. It's Della Robbia blue. The
    blue of the robe in the old Madonna pictures. Are these
    grapes washed? [She fingers the bunch of grapes which
    EUNICE has brought in.]
EUNICE: Huh?
BLANCHE: Washed, I said. Are they washed?
EUNICE: They're from the French Market.
BLANCHE: That doesn't mean they've been washed. [The cathe-
    dral bells chime.] Those cathedral bells – they're the only clean
    thing in the Quarter. Well, I'm going now. I'm ready to go.

I try to distract Ben from craziness. I try to point out some
wisdom in Jude's note, but that instruction # 9 is clattering about
in my hot head.

'That was a bad day at Black Rock, wasn't it?' I ask Ben in our
Weiss family code for calamitous times, coined from the film of
that name starring Spencer Tracy in which he is a one-armed sleuth
uncovering crimes of war and prejudice committed under a blazing
sun in a bright blue sky that can bleach the faculties.

'Which day?' says Ben.

'Gus Day.'

'Oh . . . Yeh.'

I think about this day Gus fell in a heap at the karting track
where Ben and Jude and I had taken him for a treat, to satisfy
Gus's very big thing for cars, especially of the racing kind, and I
recall how the scrapy breathing we have grown used to in Gus,
something that comes and goes with him, suddenly grew noisy and
rapid, like skates cutting into the ice as I imagine it now, and how
as in all the happiest films, the ones that come out right, there was
a doctor amongst the crowd, a doctor, happily, who also had a
very big thing for cars of the racing kind.

There were a lot of doctors after that, and a lot of testing and
speculation and auguries to do with performance and dangers, and
so many fine needles stuck into my brother's tender forearms leaving

regular rows of perforations, that his limbs resembled cribbage boards, a game I cannot fathom for the life of me, and it is possible Gus felt like a car of the racing kind himself, perched in the pits under the eyes of mechanics and engineers and designers in all his fragile glory of technology and near perfection, and near perfection, I think, is most susceptible of all to cracks and small failures, flaws that might pass unnoticed in a vehicle of less sophistication.

There is no formula for Gus, and all the doctors and specialists could pronounce upon with any real authority was that Gus suffers from frailty in the lung department, something hereditary perhaps, going on to prescribe calm and caution because alarms, they say, and full-blown emotions can kick-start disaster, causing an irregular flow of oxygen in the bloodstream, a shock to the heart and brain he may not support. I don't know. I am not keen on this prescription for inner peace, not one of us is, and although we are vigilant, keeping stashes of pills and inhalers, telephone numbers and cab fare in our pockets, we pursue our policy of torture, singling Gus out, as ever, for special assault and ambush, and we carry on exposing him to the thrills of karting and the dodgy mix of speed and dust, petrol and noise that is so inadvisable for Gus according to science and medicine, but clearly so restoring also, as I have witnessed, watching my brother with his hereditary frailty just about electrified with rapture caused by racing cars, despite his famous grace and composure, and Jem the one needing recovery time back home, wet cloths, aspirins and a hard mattress in a darkened room, which goes to show what a weird science is this business of auguries and prescriptions, and also has me a bit worried I am evolving into a fainty consumptive type as in old films featuring ladies prone to collapsing in a heap of billowing skirts in the slightest of breezes and the faintest beams of sunlight.

It's hot out here. I'm hungry. I can't move for silver fish swimming in the corners of my eyes, goddammit.

'Ben? Remember home? I mean home-home, you know?'

'Yup.'

'The chippie down the road. Across from the 85 bus stop. It had a white sign, right?'

'Yup.'

'OK. Four words in two lines. Was it SILVER FISH HAKE BAR, SILVER HAKE FISH BAR, or SILVER BAR, FISH HAKE?'

'I know what you mean. I used to wonder myself.'

'It's a puzzle,' I say, pleased Ben is coming round.

'Yes, indeed,' says Ben. 'Up there with Olbers.'

'What's Olbers?' I ask, reclining again. 'Want to share?' I add, scooting over on my hockey emblem towel, making room.

'It's OK,' he replies, but I stay where I am in case he changes his mind once he has finished being mad at Jude and wants a bit of cushioning. When you are mad at a person, it is quite hard to lie down or close your eyes or do anything of that nature. Olbers' Paradox. A puzzle that was not a puzzle at all: why is the sky dark at night?'

'Is that a puzzle? Why is that a puzzle?'

'Jem! God's teeth! One day maybe you'll join the human race and have a grasp of reality and science and general knowledge!'

'You think so?'

'Probably not,' says my brother. 'Anyway. Olbers. The point is, everyone should have known better. The speed of light was measured by Rømer in 1676. Newton knew it. The Church had even dated Creation from 4004 BCE, but astronomers were still puzzling over the darkness of the night sky!'

'Oh,' I say, not understanding one word so far.

'They all supposed the Universe was eternal and unchanging, see? Meaning that every line of sight should finish on a star and the sky would be a blaze of light – like standing in a forest and seeing trees in every direction and no gaps, no darkness. Kepler knew there was something wrong here but he only got so far, realising that darkness is proof the Universe is finite – are you with me?'

'Um, yuh. But could you trickle some water on me, please? You can reach.'

'Sure,' says Ben, scooping up some lake and dumping it over my face.

'Trickle, I said. Thanks anyway.'

'OK. So that's it then. The Universe may be infinite, but not eternal, not unchanging and the darkness proves it. It's partly a redshift thing –'

'Stop! Redshift?'

'Light stretches. Red light has longer wavelengths than blue, so a star moving away from you will show a redshift in its wake, right? And if it's coming your way, the waves get squashed and shorter, and the light blueshifts. Astronomers can work out how fast stars are moving in space that way. Spacetime expands, the Universe evolves, I taught you all that, galaxies move apart and so on, remember? So as I was saying, the dark sky is partly a redshift thing but mainly a time thing. Light years. The Universe would have to be about a million times older than it is for every line of sight to end on a star. We can't see farther than light can travel in the age of the Universe, well, the observable Universe. Imagine a sphere and the radius is the age of the Universe times the speed of light –'

'Wait. Don't do maths. That really messes me up. I was with you until the radius thing.'

'OK. Just think that beyond the age of the Universe, light has not had time to reach us yet, it hasn't had time to get here from the beginning of everything, so when you look into space – and remember, stars are nothing compared to all the space between –'

'The dark matter?'

'Right! So when you look out and back in time, you see the darkness that was there first, before stars were born, get it? It was never a puzzle at all.'

'A no-puzzle puzzle. Like SILVER FISH HAKE BAR.'

'It was a puzzle because the assumption was wrong. That the Universe was eternal and unchanging. They were asking the wrong question and all they had to do was look. Darkness is proof. That's called sense evidence. But you mustn't be hasty there either and invent instant theories. That's called *saving the appearances*. Before the telescope and Galileo, everyone thought they *saw* the Earth was still, and at the centre of the Universe, even though there were clues suggesting otherwise, right? Save the appearances! Big mistake,' says Ben, hauling off his shirt, which is quite surprising as he is keen on swaddling in all weathers, reminding me of cotton tops and deranged types on warm spring days, all kitted out for a snow-storm you might think, in tight folds of woolly items, hats, coats and scarves, bending into the no wind on their desperate pilgrim-ages to shops and parks while the rest of the populace is stripping off in a merry fashion. Cotton tops and deranged types have a beady eye on weather systems. They are not very trusting about appearances, I suppose, because they are no longer up to the elements and sudden changes, which is quite poignant, and depressing also.

'Ben,' I declare, as is the custom. 'I haven't seen your flesh in a long time.'

'Yeh-yeh.'

'Although I know it is there. DARK MATTER!' I add, as Ben flops down next to me, going in for much unnecessary jostling and digs in the ribs and blows to my lower limbs, a sign of recovery in my brother and a happy return to his Dr Jekyll side.

'You know how else you can tell dark matter is there apart from gravitational pull on galaxies and so on?' asks Ben, not waiting for an answer. 'It bends light. Stars and galaxies in the background show up in arcs of light, like when you look through a magnifying glass, the image stretches. Let's say a piece of dark matter crosses in front of a star, well, the gravity works as a lens and the star flashes brighter and then dims as the dark object passes. That's gravitational lensing.'

'Lovely,' I say. 'Now shut up, please. Time for forty winks.'

'OK.'

I close my eyes. I think about the bending of light and the halo of light that is the rotation of stars in the halo of black that is dark matter. Ben said stars would simply fly apart without this extra gravity to hold them together and it's weird how something you cannot see without special detection, without measurements of the speed of stars and occasional flares of light, how the invisible can be so important, and how a dark thing passing in front of a bright thing can make a bright thing brighter, bringing my dad to mind, Dad in the vicinity of Mum, crossing her path, and how things brighten and change, how there is a flare of light, making me so very glad for the love situation between them for this reason alone, and because Ben says dark matter in the Universe may amount to nearly three hundred times the bright stuff. We are all thankful for Frances.

'Enough winks,' I announce, rising up. 'Barbecue tonight! Yay! Chaos! Jude's idea. His night. The Last Supper, ha ha! Hey, Ben, let's follow Jude around later and do a lot of household tasks in his wake, you know, sweep behind him, whisk his plate away before he's finished and just hover, you know, awaiting command and instruction. What do you think? Yes?'

'Yeh,' says Ben in a sad voice, summoning up Jude's note, no doubt, and the grievous feeling it gave him. 'Yeh. Good one.'

'And what did he mean by the way? In the note. If you move out, get a job, etc. Ben?'

'I told you. Ages ago. I said I was moving out. Before university. If I go.'

'No you didn't. You said one day, one day you would.'

'It's one day, Jem. One day has come. I also said you could help me look. For a place, I mean. Remember?'

'Oh yeh. Mmm. Hot! It's hot,' I say, frowning in the sunlight and staring at the dock so hard I can make out every grain and knot in the wood, foreseeing all the places where splinters will arise under pressure of the elements, of heat and summer storms, wood being alive almost, expanding and contracting, roughening and smoothing and changing colour and shape, so there are gaps now between planks where I can see straight through to water, gaps that were fine lines not so long ago. Then I find the spot near the end of our jetty where there is forever a pile of dried white bird poo because this is the top-favourite spot for the big duck meeting that is held early each morning before any one of us is fully awake. They gather on this spot and have a duckbill wag about their day, and iron out problems and make plans, decisions to do with fishing prospects and weather conditions and family matters, and then they leave a pile of white poo, always in the same place, which is quite considerate really, as we know to avoid that spot now without even looking down, sidestepping it neatly, so used to it we forget to warn strangers and this can seem careless or rude, though it is merely a lapse of mindfulness regarding the many things that are understood between Weisses, so many, that it is only when a stranger steps into our world that I see it, just how very many things there are between us, how very much there is in this private language I cannot translate, and do not wish to translate, such as why we might forget to indicate a friendly pile of white bird poo, or explain why we never scrape it away, and how it is we come to sidestep it quite cheerfully, sometimes even depositing the corner of a sandwich thereby, or some biscuit crumbs, right near that whiteness, a sign from Weisses to ducks, this is your home, any time you need it, your depot, One Ton Camp for ducks, only eleven miles to go.

'Ben, I'm going in the drink. Will you come, will you swim?' I ask, expecting a no, because Ben is no swimmer, yet I raise my arms in that way people do in displays of resolve and acts of courage, hoping to infect my brother with a desire for swimming.

'Sure. OK,' he says.

'You will? Blow me down! Do you have to go up for trunks?'

'Got them on.'

'You mean . . . you were actually INTENDING to swim?'

'Well, actually, no. I ran out of undies.'

'Fuck-hell, Ben! Wash your stuff. Clothes in, soap in, close hatch, etc.'

'Ha ha. Hey. Know what Jude did with the dosh Dad gave him for clothing?' Ben says. 'He bought fourteen pairs of undies.'

'No.'

'Yuh. So he doesn't have to worry so much about washing.'

'But that means Jude will be walking this earth every fourteenth day with thirteen pairs of dirty knickers in his rucksack. Yuck!' I say, making my way to the end of the dock.

'That's if he wears a pair a day.'

'Oh, right. Double-yuck, then. Coming?'

Ben stands up and pushes his jeans down, whipping them off so fast the lower legs are inside out with his dark socks still attached and I think about undies for a moment, remembering my first year at the French convent when Mum took Harriet and me shopping for regulation kit and accessories. I am increasingly worried about rules and conviction for rules, being quite preoccupied with Nazis and the German people and wondering just what happened that they stopped thinking about the meaning of rules, and will it ever befall them again one day. One day, two words I used to assume meant never.

Nevertheless, in my early days, I took on these convent regulations with some fascination, enjoying the pleasure most of all, of shopping for kit with Mum and Harriet, something that always gives me a sensibility for things military and a vision of a queue of fine men stripped to underpants, forearms extended in readiness for the neat pile of clothing and stores that will turn them into commandos, Norway 1943: 1 fleece-lined cap, 1 pair snow goggles, 1 Bergen rucksack, 1 skeleton assault harness, 2 pair windproof trousers, 1 pair Finnish-pattern boots, 1 Mark 2 Sten 9mm carbine with silencer.

Harriet and I hover near Mum at the counter in the school outfitters, two growing heaps of kit before us, the sales lady checking items off on the convent list and marching off now and again with a look of deep concentration and gravitas to ferret in shelves and drawers for all the proper accessories according to the rules, a serious bloody business that is driving Harriet to quiet distraction, I can tell, her mind on chocolate and Mum's promise of tea at Zweig's, a place serving borscht and cucumber soups and tall glasses of Viennese coffee and dense aromatic cakes and those little wafers of dark chocolate studded with cracked hazelnuts and raisins that Harriet eats with an expression of rapture.

Here comes the shop lady, a person for whom the selection of colours and sizes is clearly a vocation.

'You can have these in green or navy, madam,' she says, holding aloft what remind me of the large pants we wrapped on Gus over his cloth nappy.

'What ARE they?' I ask, horror-struck.

'BLOOMERS!' the lady snaps as if to say, you have a lot to learn, my girl, and it is a good thing you are going to school soon and will be off the streets.

Mum smiles in that sly fashion of hers while Harriet gazes at the bloomers navy and green and flutters her eyelashes, fingering the garments with an air of studious application.

'No thank you, my dear,' she says very politely.

'It's regulation!' says the shop lady, quite rattled.

'Deliberate cruelty is NOT FORGIVABLE!' adds Harriet, assuming a crazed look and her very impressive Southern accent, whereupon the two of us become a bit giddy with mirth and a desire for *Sachertorte* and Mum decides quickly on one pair of gruesome bloomers, just to wrap things up and for the sake of regulations, though her left eyebrow is raised in cheerful resignation as she signs her name with a flourish, and I think how she is kind of magnificent.

'But you have two girls, Mrs Weiss and –' protests the lady, all thunderstruck, and pronouncing our name without the V sound, something Harriet corrects sharpish.

'Weiss!' she says to the lady before turning to me and speaking in low tones. 'Blooming hell!'

'Please don't worry,' my mother says real cool, taking the parcels from the lady, 'It's big enough for both of them, thank you.'

And that's it, Harriet and I are downright hysterical now, not even able to walk a straight line to the door, slamming into each other and keeling over like drunks outside the shop while trying to keep up with Mum who is giggling and loping ahead in graceful strides, same as Harriet skipping ahead of me on the way to school.

'Harriet!' I growl in my Wild West voice. 'These bloomers sure are BIG ENOUGH for the BOTH OF US!'

'But are they WASHED, honey?'

'They're the only BIG THING in the Quarter!' I reply.

'Mummy, wait!' calls Harriet so that Mum stops and turns to face us.

'Move your BLOOMING ARSE!' says Frances.

'Whoa!' I say. 'Mum! You said arse!'

'How delightful!' declares Harriet.

It takes a while to get to Café Zweig.

Three days before my fourth and final year at my French convent, my second convent where I now have a more reckless way with rules, subjecting them to a spirit of enquiry in the same way Gus was briefly devoted to the tablecloth trick as a baby, a failed magic act Mum observed with such indulgence for Gus's scientific deliberation on motion and gravity that we soon had a small cupboard full of broken crockery Mum kept for good drainage in new plantings, an operation she takes charge of with Gus during our group gardening activities, activities keenly supervised by Harriet who is quite drawn to horticulture except for the work part, the dirt and the elbow grease, though she will select the most fetching pair of gardening gloves and for no useful reason except for the making of horticultural pronouncements to no one in particular.

'Roots. Root system. Anchors plant to earth and conveys nourishment. Used as food or in medicine. Roots draw deep for nutrients in well-drained soils. Thank you. Thank you.'

'Harriet,' says Jude. 'Shut up and shake a leg. Draft dodger!'

'Sticks and stones!' she says.

'OK. Coming up,' he says, plucking a big stick from the pile of winter debris he keeps shifting from one part of the garden to another and staring at, shuffling tools around while he thinks what to do about it all, the debris in the world, and the arsenal of tools, this array of secateurs, hoes and trowels at his feet, often giving up altogether to watch Mum and Gus, as I do, watching them pack shards of cracked bowl and cup into terracotta pots of earth taken from special bags, arranging all this around a fine mess of roots, as grisly and weathered as the beard on the bagel man, and handling those roots with the kind of sureness and gentleness that always reminds me of a wakeful night I spent in Jude and Ben's room in our old country on a night Ben was at Chris's house. She entered our room on her nightly watch, or on a whim, a random thing, I don't know, maybe she was only passing, but I saw her move Jude's way, noiseless, and lift his stray arm to tuck it back under the covers with the rest of Jude, tucking him in so tenderly he never woke, he never even shifted, though perhaps she entered his dreams, like Perceval's mother for Perceval.

When heard ye tidings of your mother?
I heard none of her, but I dream of her much in my sleep.

My reckless way with rules has made me famous, of course, famous for the Objectif Lune Incident, an episode arising in last term's Art & Catechism class, a study of devotional paintings full of perplexities that induced a feeling in me quite close to anarchy as the term went on, beginning with a fixation on that pair of pants in the painting by Piero della Francesca he made in 1450? called *The Baptism of Christ.*

Soeur Rosa is Catechism/Art & Latin Nun and looks so much like Mussolini I am sure he is in her ancestry, Benito Amilcare Andrea himself, b.1883, shot and hanged upside down, 1945. Soeur Rosa prowls in front of the classroom, strolling in and out of the light of the slide show so that I can see jigsaw pieces of *The Baptism of Christ* on her deathly white broad face, which is quite disturbing. She talks about composition and harmony, the human and divine, and she uses this word divine in a pointed fashion, glaring my way, meaning as long as I am Jewish, this divine place, this realm of salvation is beyond my reach, no entry – HAZCHEM! – HaShem being a word Jude cleared up for me one day by accident.

I walk with Jude in the city and I see that sign in large black letters against a yellow background, a sign I have seen on enough gates and doorways by now to require an explanation.

'Jude? What is that, what does it mean, Hazchem?'
Jude's eyes slide to the left, where I am walking. 'It's Hebrew.'
'Oh,' I say, feeling a bit suspicious.
'It means GOD: NO ENTRY.'
'Oh.'
'HAZARDOUS CHEMICALS, DUMMY!' yells Jude, giving me a body check into the fence and creasing up with mirth, meaning

there is just no end to my idiocy but we all have to live with it, etc.

No entry. Hazchem.

I am getting a headache watching Soeur Rosa and trying to fathom composition and harmony in this painting by Mr della Francesca featuring an angel in a red dress and tricolour wings to the left of the picture, looking concerned and uncertain, one hand raised as if to stop the show, and a man in the background at the water's edge hauling off his clothes and getting all tangled in them the way Ben does when stripping off, a man wearing a pair of knickers VERY MUCH LIKE MY OWN, plain and white and snug, and then, in the foreground, behold Jesus being baptised, Lamb of God, *Agneau de Dieu*, his skin the chalky white of statuary, and around his loins, which is the seemly word in Art for hips and genitals, is a graceful swathe of white material, see-through, diaphanous, a word from the Greek meaning to show, and this is what it shows, that some types are more special than other types, bright and morning stars, and this is just one way to show it, courtesy of undies of distinction, the wearing of divine pants that remind me of Mum's.

My mother's undies are fairly extraordinary, bare morsels of haberdashery I have seen draped over the edge of her bath, because items such as these are too fine for regular washing in brutish machines and require hand-washing and special soap and air-drying in temperate conditions. Mum's underwear is close to Art, I believe, slips of divine linen or silk, some resembling boxer shorts, for girl boxers, and others being mere wisps of material with frilly edges and seams of lace and embroidery, and still others, tiny sheathes covered in leopard print, most of them, however, coloured pure black or white or cream, and all of them confections surely not up to a lot of wear and tear and the regular vicissitudes, but undies of awe and mystery, light years from me and my pants, and light years = distance, not time.

Ben swims with me. In his trunks that became pants and are now trunks again. Swimming with me is a camaraderie thing. What with Jude's farewell night looming, this is a hard day all round and that is why Ben swims with me, despite a dog-paddle technique that even Pax! the unsporting dog improves upon. Ben swims with an expression of sheer terror in his eyes, gulping wildly at the air as if these might be his last breaths on this very earth. He does not travel in any decided direction, so there is a zigzag trail of a wake behind him and a great deal of froth to boot, due to the crazed scooping of lake water he hurls to each side with his large hands and the furious thrashing of his size eleven feet. Swimming for Ben is definitely an ordeal. For me it is an adventure. I am not a good swimmer, creepy-crawl slow, my mind too often on slime and weeds and aquatic life of the alarming kind to build up much steam, but swimming with Ben now, grateful for the camaraderie, I realise just what a marvel it can be, how marvellous, merely to stay afloat.

My body is so weak today, a heat or a hunger thing, or maybe an end-of-summer thing, I don't know, that I need to tread water for a while and I call out to Ben, scoping the horizon for him, a horizon which, without my glasses, is only a few strokes away.

'Hey! Ben! Lunar Bob time?'

'OK,' he yells, thrashing my way and nearly causing me to plummet to a watery demise in the suction of him, in the manner of the shipwrecked not clear enough of the sinking ship to avoid the pull, clapped to the hull for a few dying breaths, a demise of violent suddenness that is all down to some terrible law of physics and gravity. Buried at sea, The End.

The Lunar Bob is an endurance game and quite ridiculous, invented following Ben's explanation of re-entry and splashdown of the lunar capsule, a piece of knowledge he surmised might help me overcome my fear of diving. Ben says the Earth's atmosphere is very small and the lunar capsule has to enter it just right on the journey home, there being a precise angle set for re-entry between 7.2° and 5.2°. If entry is too steep, the capsule will pitch too fast and burn up. Too shallow, and it will bounce off the atmosphere like a trampoline effect and head back into space. This is all very interesting and I listened to Ben with suitable attentiveness but diving is still not for me. I simply cannot enter any kind of atmosphere head first, especially water, a manner of immersion that strikes me as brazen and foolhardy. I do accept I entered the world head first and to some, therefore, diving may seem a natural progression of things, but I would remind such types that there was help around on the day and my mother right there, and nurses and emergency services to hand, and I have decided this first birthday will stand as my one and only head-first appearance of all time. Thank you.

Ben and I do the Lunar Bob, treading water with as little arm aid as possible, bouncing in a lunatic fashion, a lunar fashion, like cork buoys in rough waters, lolling crazily side to side, sinking and shooting upwards, even braving our fear of leeches and weeds to touch bottom and use the muddy lake floor for extra leverage. The Lunar Bob is quite amusing as a pastime, especially on days when one is already limp and giddy and open to hilarity, a game that makes no demand whatsoever on the mental faculties. Harriet and Gus are best at this type of game, launching into it with immediacy and conviction, not because they find it easier to let go of their mental faculties but because of extreme youth, and how they are free of inhibitions and the full-blown kid pressures that encompass wariness and caution regarding appearances. Wariness is one of the drawbacks of greater age and of seeing yourself as a grown-up might, knowing he is likely to appraise your behaviour differently once you hit the age of fourteen or so, when, for some reason, allowances for doubtful behaviour are no longer granted so readily, in the same way that howling and screaming in babyhood is quite charming, yet alarming thereafter, and definitely wayward, the first steps on the slippery slope to vagrancy and derangement, signs of which the edgier variety of grown-up is forever on the lookout, making me very grateful for parents who are not so easily rattled.

'I think I'll go up now,' says Ben.

'Up-up? To the house?'

'Dock,' he says. 'I'll dry off, wait for you.'

'I just want to float for a bit, OK? Cover me?'

The back-float is pleasant, and recommended for deep thinking in troubled times, but it is also perilous. In a dark leotard and more or less motionless, a bather can be mistaken for an old log and be sliced in two even parts with bloody gaping ends by a passing speedboat. Get someone to cover for you. I do not want to wash up today on Gus's Beach, torso preceding, enacting my second and final unplanned head-first appearance, my legs following on separately, still lively, as it is said to be with a chicken who has had his head lopped off in preparation for becoming a roast chicken or a dish of chicken old-ladies-on-the-bus, etc., its little bulbous body scrambling around under the influence of some fine spring-chicken memory of strolling the farmyard in a sociable manner and pecking for seeds, just as my legs might still be kicking feverishly, driven by the memory of swimming master yelling, forever yelling, Kick! Kick, kick!

Gus's Beach is a miniature inlet at a break in the wall at the water's edge, a half-moon of sandy territory we cleared of rocks so that Gus could get on friendly terms with the lake and enter it at his leisure, without fear, from his very own honorary patch of land, but he has never been in a hurry to swim, unlike Harriet who is amphibian at heart, slipping into the water like a platypus whereas Gus prefers to stand with his feet on the shore, his slight and coltish shins lapped by miniature waves on his miniature beach, his hand in Mum's, gazing out upon the waters and having some quiet Gus thoughts. It is a reflective place and therefore a sorry one for me to end my days washed up in two terrible parts, thereby marking this last Friday of summer not as the day Jude packed and Ben prepared to pack, the night of Jude's Farewell Barbecue and last supper for some long time beyond my contemplation, but instead, the day Jem was mistaken for a log with gruesome consequences, entering a happy place which is Gus's Beach and marring it for ever, turning it into a place of mourning and darkness and the strewing of white flowers, and of weeping.

I float like Ophelia in that famous painting, the one wherein it is clear she went swimming without anyone to cover for her, not at all wise when in a state of turmoil. Ophelia is doing the back-float in a mossy stream under a canopy of depressing foliage and reedy twigs and her hands are out to the side, palms up, which is supposed to bring crucifixions to mind, as I suppose, though by her physiognomy it seems she perished in mild exasperation, due to extreme weariness and a bad lonely feeling. It's all me, she is saying, it's nobody's fault. Her eyes are open and her mouth also, and her lips are rosy, meaning she was full of life and urgency in her last moments, with some important point to make, some kind of conviction of regarding the state of world affairs, I believe, a conviction of great poise and certainty. Ophelia is said to be crazy and therefore not necessarily accountable for things such as decisiveness and purpose, but I have my doubts about her crazi-ness, which is why this painting by Mr J. E. Millais, b.1829, d.1896 is not quite right, because he shows Ophelia alone, as if crazy begins and ends with one person, a solitary pursuit instead of a terrible warning to others regarding world affairs, and, in her case, a presentiment of war and heaps of bodies and the demise of loved ones, and Mr Millais ought to have painted this in somehow, by messing the foliage around like it is bent by a ferocious wind, by change and so on, or by placing a person on the bank of the river, a person grasping the message in Ophelia's sacrifice and tearing at his hair and rending his garments or whatever, I think so.

There is not a lot of helpful information about Ophelia in the play by Shakespeare in which she figures, unless you are a suspicious type like myself, prepared to mistrust and re-evaluate the somewhat dodgy reports concerning Ophelia's behaviour leading up to her back-float in the brook, reports even her brother Laertes falls for, no questions asked. I don't think he knew her at all, I believe he would even have had problems recognising her in a line-up of other fine-looking girls in flouncy dresses clutching flowers and reciting poetry, two topmost favourite activities of his sister's. He watches her dance into a room wielding a bunch of herbs and wildflowers and rattling off a list of related medicinal and symbolic properties, and breaking into song here and there, and Laertes decides she is crazy, a downright hasty assessment of the evidence, if you ask me, especially since their father has just bled to death from multiple stab wounds to the abdomen, and you would suppose any kind of apparently wayward behaviour quite acceptable in the circumstances, and for some time thereafter, as grief and mourning can push a person right over the edge in all kinds of ways, Hamlet himself being a pretty good example of this. And what about dancing into a room, bearing flowers and singing ditties? My sister does this very often and no one around here thinks she is crazy. My sister is keen for ballet and horticulture and experiences many musical moments in her life wherein mere speech without tuneful accompaniment is just not enough. I wish I could be a concerto of instruments for Harriet, or a heavenly chorus if I could sing, or a corps de ballet, and this is where Laertes lets his sister down, as her father did also, having no grasp of Ophelia and her nature, and not encouraging her in her keenness for poetry and music and horticulture, maybe just seeing it as some kind of girly thing, not serious, and this led her towards a lot of solitary confinement for the sake of personal freedom, and a bad end.

The Queen, Hamlet's mother, not a very reliable person in my opinion, what with her murderous inclinations and taste for rash sexual activity with close blood relations, the Queen is the one who reports the death of Ophelia. Ophelia was messing around with *fantastic garlands and weedy trophies*, she says to Laertes. IN THAT WAY OF HERS, if you get my drift. She was climbing trees, the Queen explains, and looping the fantastic garlands around flimsy boughs and then she fell into the stream, happy to do the back-float for a while and call up verses from favourite songs, her flouncy dress kind of like a Lilo, until it absorbed too much water whereupon she drowned. I don't know. First of all, was the Queen watching the whole time? Why didn't she cover for Ophelia and go in for life-saving techniques if she thought things were getting a bit out of hand and death imminent?

I blame them all. I blame them for not looking out for her, because although she may have been headed for an early end regard-less, due to an edgy personality prone to extremes of sensitivity and neediness perhaps nobody could tend to, and feelings she kept to herself for lack of encouragement and the right sort of compan-ionship, and though her mission in life may well have been martyrdom, meaning a death that is OK in plays and paintings because of the improving effect it is supposed to have on other people, it still makes me crazed, because Ophelia should have had a little more time, goddammit, she should have grown up a scien-tist if she wanted to, a botanist maybe, or a poet, a dancer, or a woman married to Hamlet with a house full of music and little kids and floral arrangements, good garlands, not awful and fantastic ones that lead to depressed feelings and crack-ups as with Blanche DuBois, another woman inclined to horticulture and poetry who lost her mind, or Perceval's sister, who also had martyrdom in mind and a final journey by water in a prone position, dying in her brother's arms with a request he float her dead self downriver and let her go *as adventure will lead me*, she says, having this notion her end will have a healing effect on the world and the Waste Lands it had become. And all of this is a great pity, and why I want wind in that Millais painting, some sign, anything but that stillness, the not a whisper, only the end of things and the beginning of nothing, the one-day-never that has come.

One day feels so far, a view from a telescope, and Ben says the farther we can see, the farther back in time we are looking, and Ben says looking back can help us determine the future, Big Bang to Big Crunch perhaps, the final state, and Big Crunch will not be the same as the Big Bang because of cosmic evolution, he says, and how if the Universe collapses again into a fiery state, it will not be as simple as the Big Bang, but bumpy and wild and full of complexity. Most likely, though, the Universe will expand for ever, faster and faster, growing thinner and cooler, with fundamental matter decaying or falling into black holes, the Universe dark and empty and running out of energy and gas, and gas is what you need for new matter and the birth of stars, and matter and stars mean gravity and light and magnetism, all the elements that make the Universe a jumping joint instead of a dark and empty place, cosmic winter Ben calls it, that time might come.

One day you'll have breasts, one day Pax! will grow into his paws and ears and tail, and it happened, both these things, one day, however, always a surprise, where did it go, the space between? One day I'll move out, one day you'll have breasts, and children, days you don't wait for, days you shrug off. One day you'll forget Jude slapped you, impossible, remember it, Jem? Oh yes. Late last term, a Friday night, Mum and Dad out to dinner, no marshals left in Tombstone. Jude eats quickly, he has a date, he won't help clear up, he spills ketchup. Stanley Kowalski, that's what I say. *Pig, Polack, disgusting, greasy* and the slap is awful, messy and naked, so unlike a punch or a shove, and I bash out into the road and run for a while, tears hot and ferocious and no shoes on, what are the right shoes for such an occasion, are there any right shoes for this? I'll never forget this, I hate you, go on your expedition, I don't care. Take for ever. This blooming town ain't big enough for the both of us.

The following afternoon, Jude wanders into a room I am in and I pay him no attention at all. I frown at my book, bringing it even closer to my face and flipping back a page or two as if to check some vital piece of information and submit it to special scrutiny, so preoccupied am I, so blind to him, yet the whole while my heart is beating fast and I will my face not to flush beetroot red, not because of the horrible thing Jude did, a slap right out of a black-and-white film, no, but because I am ignoring Jude and it feels so unnatural, such an undesirable journey. Jude! I want to yell from my train window as he stands on the platform, the details of him more and more blurry to my eyes, my near so far, the heft of him, my nearest so far.

'Hey,' he says from the doorway of the study. 'Bite?' he adds, holding a bagel aloft. 'Vintage Cheddar, Jem. Thinly sliced.'

Don't be a pushover, Jem. You are not my brother, I'll never speak to you again, I can't see you, go away. Think about torture, the plucking of fingernails, eyelids sewn open under a blazing sun, slow roasting at the stake. Don't answer him. It's all over.

'Hmm,' says Jude, and he leaves the room.

See? He doesn't even care. I am going to leave home, yes. I will run so far from this and I will not need much, a small suitcase, a fine pair of shoes, I can walk for hours.

Now Jude is back, with a hammer in one hand and nails in the other, nails he tosses up and down in his open palm like he would a cricket ball or something.

'Arms to the side!' he says. 'Pick a wall, any wall!'

And that's it, I crease up, I can't help myself, even falling forward and banging my head on the coffee table in the midst of hysterics.

'Hallelujah,' remarks Jude, sitting astride me and counting the nails out quite slowly. 'One, two, three, yeh, just one for the feet, that'll do. Right.'

'Pax! Pax!' I shout.

'Forget it,' Jude says, raising the hammer. 'No truce. Say your prayers.'

'No, wait! Um . . . Into thy hands, I commend my spirit!'

'Yeh-yeh, that's what they all say.'

'I'll be your slave!'

'OK then,' says Jude, downing tools. 'Pax.'

Whereupon we both rise up and head for the kitchen and Jude opens a beer, pouring a little out for me in a washed-out yogurt cup which the Weiss kids still use around here for spare drinking vessels, a hangover from extreme youth and days of imperfect coordination and a calamitous run on glassware.

'Do you thirst?' asks Jude.

'I thirst.'

'Give up the Ghost then,' he says, handing over my yogurt-cup beer.

'You know not what you do, etc.'

'Thems the breaks,' goes Jude, and we sit quietly for a while, on the same side of the kitchen table, side-saddle in our seats, his feet resting on the struts of my chair, right there between my feet, his knees inside mine.

'You want me to clear your place?' says Jude in Stanley tones, lifting our cups off the table and eyeing the wall while I grin at him.

Don't go, Jude. Stay.

I swim to the dock, flipping over and out of my back-float and when I reach the end where there was once a wooden ladder with slime-green steps and splinters poking out, I dangle for a bit, gathering strength, which is what I will need to launch myself high out of the water on to the dock, high enough to land one knee safely without scraping half the skin off and requiring plastic surgery, especially hard for me as I do not use the lake floor for extra launch power except when doing the Lunar Bob and in a state of carefree giddiness and forgetfulness regarding the lake floor which is home to leeches and lasso-like weeds and gruesome lower-depths-type fish such as catfish, and catfish definitely belong in that nun list of All God's Creatures along with the amputees, dwarfs, aardvarks, Africans, felons and Jews, etc.

We do not have a ladder any more because Jude wrenched the whole thing off one day before leaving for mining camp, and pitched it into a bonfire, a Jude-decision for the Collective, a decision with one startling feature, i.e. no need for consensus of opinion, no gathering up of thoughts and feelings from any other Weiss family member, Jude thinking and feeling for all and acting thereupon, making it a Jude-decision.

'Hey!'

'It's ugly. It's splintery. Mum could get hurt.'

'She never swims, Jude.'

'Yeh-yeh. She might! She used to.'

'Well, how am I supposed to get back up?'

'Use your arms.'

'Thanks a lot! Guess I'll have to borrow Zebedee!'

'Ha ha,' says Jude, stalking off with the ladder.

Jude has taken to working on his arm muscles by hauling on what looks like bed springs with handles on the end, bed springs as on those puppets in *The Magic Roundabout*, a kid show in our old country I never understood, involving a polite woman called Florence and a dog called Dougal and a man with mad mustachios by the name of Zebedee who resembles a Russian Cossack. The three of them have nothing at all to say, just shooting the breeze in dozy voices like people in a bus queue or something, and they hover around on their bed-spring legs in the vicinity of a round-about, with Zebedee the worst of all, springing into view for no good reason apart from bossing the others about, bouncing up and down, going boing! boing! and everyone exclaiming Why, it's Zebedee! Hello, Zebedee! etc. It's weird.

'What the hell is going on here?' I asked my sister one time in my early years.

'It's French, I believe. It can't be Russian,' Harriet replied.

'What do you mean it's French, it can't be Russian? It's English.'

'I'm not very keen,' she pronounced, frowning and blinking furiously. 'It's not very – illuminating,' she added, whereupon we closed the door on *The Magic Roundabout* for ever, thereby saving up valuable TV watching time for more improving programmes such as war films and that cartoon about King Arthur, only documentaries being free viewing in our household, of course, something for which I am now quite grateful, although because documentaries are most often to do with Nazis, even my memories of *The Magic Roundabout* are heavily clouded by sensitivity to anti-Semitism, in this case, a fear of Russian Cossacks committing terrible purges against Polish and Russian Jews, sweeping through villages on swift horses, wielding blades and rifles, and with them, a hero of my dad's, Mr Isaac Babel, a writer and sometime soldier and a very young man at the time, suffering even then from poor vision, going into battle with little specs in skinny wire frames and a feeling of confusion regarding war and prejudice and his Jewish identity, calling himself Russian, Russian first, and changing his name in his Cossack days, to a less Jewish one, which is very sad seeing as he perished in a Russian prison in his prime, leaving behind an unfinished novel, my dad says, about *shtetls* and Jews, going to show that roots draw deep, as Harriet explained, because Isaac died a writer and a Jew, Jewish first and Russian next.

Whenever Ben and I hear the huff and puff and clang and boing! of Jude performing arm-muscle-development exercises, esp. in these days leading up to his grand expedition, we creep into the room he is in and make a big show of bouncing up and down as if doing the Lunar Bob on solid ground, while singing out 'Why, it's Zebedee! Hello, Zebedee!' until Jude is so mad, we need to run fast to escape the hurling of missiles, nearby shoes and books, unfinished snacks and bits of haberdashery.

'What are you doing down there?' Ben says, peering over the edge of the dock.

'Just driftin',' I tell him in my cowboy voice.

'Well, mosey on out. You're going to shrivel up like a prune,' he says.

'Then I'll look like Fang!'

'Fang!' Ben shouts, lying back down on my towel. 'Bride of the night!'

Fang is the name we gave the wife of one of our ex-gardeners, a woman with shrivelly old skin and almost no teeth excepting incisors, vampire teeth, who used to roll up our driveway in her two-seater tractor at speed, trampling the ground cover and rare herbaceous items every goddam time en route to collect our ex-gardener Phillibert, Mr Fang, my least favourite of all Mum's hopeless cases. Between Fang and Phillibert, there was a lot of damage done and our gardens were at risk of suggesting Arras and Vimy in 1917 following rain and sleet and bombardment by heavy artillery, and even Mum could see that, persuaded finally to give them their walking papers for this, but chiefly for another reason, and despite the fact Fang and Phillibert did not grow up with the privileges and affections we are accustomed to and must be forgiven all trespasses, etc, etc. Trespasses is a pretty lame word, in my opinion, for the havoc Fang and Phillibert brought into our lives, words such as onslaught, siege and invasion coming more readily to mind, but then I am not such a pushover for hopeless cases, Mum being very close in spirit to St Jude in this department, St Jude whose cause, according to that Book of Saints, is desperate circumstances, quite worrying to me since most saints I know of share this feature of going a little too far for their causes and meeting bad and spectacular ends, often in the full bloom of youth, meaning I must look out for my mother, in case she is that way inclined.

Most of Mum's hopeless cases are OK with us, especially Mike for whom Mum clearly has a soft spot, remarking to me one time how Mike has arms like her father's, slender, she says, and sinewy, and lined with muscle.

'Corded, Mum. Corded with muscle.'

'Is that the word?'

'Oh yes,' I say with the rare authority of knowing a word she does not know, unless she is being polite of course. Mostly, I am curious she should be commenting on any man's physiognomy and musculature aside from my dad's and I wonder also just who this man is, the man she calls her father when she is of unknown origins and does not really have a regular father. Next time she mentions Mike's arms or some such thing, I might pop a question or two, who knows.

Mike and his friends have skills of an uncertain nature. They mess around with tools and paintbrushes and are partial to heavy machinery and heroic tasks involving major gymnastics, because heave-ho work is where they are happiest, I think, digging pits and hauling trees, and laying our dock in the water in late springtime, anchoring it with chains connected to blocks of cement, and stowing it away again in autumn so it does not break up in the ice. As for the finer tasks, with a lot of coaching and coaxing and many pathetic trial runs for which the men are always paid, things eventually get done around here, though at great expense, so that I am beset by anxieties to do with impending bankruptcy and incarceration, and Weisses doing forced labour and all of us recalling it, how Mum told us so, HISTORY REPEATS ITSELF.

These men are pretty devoted to Mum and she has a way of encouraging them to improve their outlook on life and their hopeless skills, and to show up on time, without actually saying very much, or spooking them the way a regular boss might, a boss who will say, for instance, 'Be here at 9 a.m. or else!' No. Mum goes, 'Well. What time would you like to start, Michael?' Whereupon Mike shuffles his feet and clears his throat before suggesting 9 a.m., like this is an epic struggle for him, committing himself to a time and place in this manner.

'Lovely,' says my mother, turning away and getting on with things. 'You wouldn't let me down, would you, Michael?' she adds with a quick glance over her shoulder, and that's it, Mike is never late, no matter what shape he is in, and he always scrubs up neatly for her and stands at attention like a soldier when she speaks to him, even bringing her posies of wildflowers some days or funny-looking vegetable matter from his kitchen garden, overgrown and misshapen and heavily encrusted with earth, poignant offerings my mother accepts with the grace and charm for which she is widely renowned.

'I'm not eating that!' I announce. 'Forget it!'

'Jem, it's organic!' says Mum.

'So are my guts! Doesn't mean they're good to eat!'

'Well, they're from Mike's garden,' says Frances, making some decisive point I suppose, about courtesy and tolerance although I can tell by her expression she is ready to crack.

'I like my vegetables on the clean side, you know. Washed. And regular-shaped. I don't need to see the origins of a vegetable, goddammit, earth and dead wrigglies and all that, no thanks! Yuck. I mean, what do you call this? Is it a brassica thing?' I ask, waving what might be a carrot at Pax! who sniffs suspiciously before trotting off in disdain. 'See? Even Pax! won't eat it.'

'Actually,' explains Gus quietly, 'he simply doesn't like crudités.'

'Oh. Well, anyway.'

Jude prods the vegetable matter on the counter. 'It looks like shrapnel,' he says.

'Or an experiment in genetics,' suggests Ben, just as Harriet grabs a tuber of some variety and shakes it at the heavens, spraying dirt around and we all join in, 'As God is my witness,' we shout, 'I'll never go hungry again!' repeating this a few times and stomping about the kitchen until Dad yells at us to 'Cut it out!' and 'Set the table! Where's my dinner?' Etc. etc.

When Mike first showed up at our cottage looking for work, Mum found him hunched outside on the basement steps with his back to the door, trying to figure out just what to do next, I guess, now that he made it this far to the house of the new family he heard about in town, and Dad gave Frances the low-down that evening following her interview with Michael.

'He's a drunk! A layabout! A *shiker*! He'll never show up! He can't even walk a straight line! All he can read is a bar bill!'

Pretty soon, though, my dad was drinking with Michael at weekends, and at Christmas time, after too many beers and Scotches, he would traipse into the woods with Mike and saw off a little tree, something I wanted to tell my dad is a fine old Christmas tradition a father is supposed to carry out with his kids, not drunks his own age, but never mind, we are Jewish and can change the rules, not a problem. And every year Zach and Jeremy, who have a cottage nearby, rattle off the list of break-ins, just about every place in the area stripped of worldlies, notably bottles of spirits and wine and the less unwieldy items of electronics, portable television sets and pocket radios, nothing too foxy to negotiate when tipsy, and every year the Levinthals and the Weisses are untouched, which is downright peculiar, especially in our case, seeing as most of our doors do not fasten properly, great sliding sheets of glass with unworkable locks, the house losing wall space by degrees, brick and wood sacrificed to glass due to Mum's craze for light, always more light, our cottage a very Crystal Palace and an open invitation even to the most hopeless case of a criminal on this earth. Step right in, pour yourself a drink.

More light! calls my mother, changing more and more wall into glass and hanging curtains solely in bedrooms, filigreed flaps of lace that serve no useful purpose, being diaphanous and translucent, meaning, through which light passes, and everything else too, goddammit, all very well in deep winter but in summertime, not only is there no sleeping in, but no privacy, what with Michael and his men either repainting the window frames so hopelessly we have to prise them unstuck with chisels afterwards, or else they are looming in the trees like marsupials, lopping off dead branches, an event this summer I was quite alarmed to see one morning upon waking, wondering just how the bloody-bloody I was going to get out of bed without revealing all my girly nakedness, and having to eke the top sheet free and slink to the floor, slithering out of the room like a snake, and then all the way downstairs because there are no curtains in the upstairs bathroom.

'Fuck me!' exclaims Harriet from the dining-room table where she perches with Gus, watching me slither by as they eat their Swiss muesli with extra raisins in Babar bowls, rye bread toast on the side. 'What the HELL is going on here?' she adds, my sister swearing quite freely in the mornings, her most jubilant time of day.

'*Il tomba doucement comme tombe un arbre,*' recites Gus in a thoughtful manner, recalling the snake moment in *Le Petit Prince*, still a favourite book of his, a story whose sad truths he faces with regret and fortitude, and from which he can quote impressively in French.

I stand up when I reach the kitchen where more Weisses are milling around, taking cover in my see-through sheet as amongst trees in a forest, my mother flipping through cookbooks and Ben making toast and my dad singing aloud, pausing in his song only long enough to perform his favourite cooking ritual with unfailing application and the usual havoc, this rinsing out of his teapot with boiling water TO WARM IT, you have to warm it, he says, even though these are the hottest days of summer and the kitchen, the warmest room in the joint. In goes a splash of boiling water which my dad swirls around the pot with some ferocity, shoulders and hips shaking, his brows tightly knit in concentration before he tips it out, aiming for the sink but splashing most of his immediate surroundings, including innocent passers-by, Weiss 3, for instance, clad in a skimpy sheet.

'Well, hey, Dad. Good morning.'

'Let's all go BAR-MY, and join the AR-MY!' he sings. 'Hey, Jem.'

'Mum,' I say, clutching my sheet, aware this is possibly not the most dignified and authoritative garb in which to hold forth and lodge a complaint, but there we are. 'Mum! It's like a PEEP SHOW in this house! A Roman slave market! Men in all the windows! It's a *cauchemar*. A *cauchemar*, I tell you!'

'Darling, you could wear a nightie while the men are working.'

'Mum! They're always working! And it's too hot for nighties!'

'It's too DARN HOT,' sings my dad. 'It's TOO DARN HOT!' And he moves towards Mum in a threatening manner, which is how he appears when in the vein for some kind of dance shuffle involving Mum, like a large beast going in for the kill.

'Plus I hate nighties, I get all tangled up and panicky, you know that! Are you listening to me?'

'Like Ophelia?' says Ben with relish, clearly thinking of the Millais painting, quite dear to him because of the Gothic elements of dead damosel, very long flowy hair, elaborate haberdashery and fantastic garlands, etc.

'Oh God!' I declare, heading for the bathroom. 'I mean, maybe we could get the men to do something like fix the downstairs shower, Mum, how about it?' That shower is a problem, only the holes in the perimeter of the shower head releasing any water, so that you must flatten yourself against the walls and flap your arms in the air wildly to get rinsed off at all, making me understand just how it feels to be a pigeon caught in a belfry. 'Mum? I mean it. Everyone needs a bit of wall. The roof might fall in. That's enough windows.'

'*And the building of the wall,*' chants Ben, '*was of jasper . . . and the street of the city was pure gold, as it were TRANSPARENT GLASS!* Revelation,' he adds, chomping toast.

'Oh, STOP THAT, Ben! Cut it out! I mean it,' I say.

'Sorry.'

'But, Jem,' says Mum, 'isn't the light lovely, don't you love it?'

I look at my mother in the kitchen, Dad mauling her now in his dance shuffle, and I cannot answer her, remembering our ship days, shiver me timbers, and how ill she was well before we caught sight of land, and how she recovered only to grow worse suddenly, beyond our first Christmas here, beginning with a wilting, my mother unable to face the light, turning pale and somehow luminous, almost too dazzling to behold, and my dad calling her back to us with her favourite comestibles, smoked salmon and champagne and thimbles full of glossy black Russian fish eggs, the aromas sickening her in early months, though she tried to pretend otherwise with laughing apologies, mere fluttery things I felt crazed to see, thinking how terrible it was for a favourite thing to become a sickening thing, as with Lord Nelson and the high seas, and how strange also that wine and fish and light, these features of miracles, should make her so ill. And so I look at her now and think, if light is what you need, then tip your hat, Frances, meet the sky, blow the walls down, let there be light.

When Frances ran out of wall space, she went through the roof, fitting glass where there used to be insulation, rafters and tile, starting in the kitchen with Michael messing up so badly, he forgot that a skylight ought to open, and he sealed us in for all time by way of nails and licks of tar and frames of wood so that, looking up, I was mindful of Galileo and Zacharias Jansen and the *Micrographia* of 1665, of 35cm folding plates and the minutiae of the common flea, and I wondered just what might be made of a Weiss under the great eye of Mr Robert Hooke, a starman not only interested in the magnification of tiny specks but in the movement of light, the first to propose, I read, how it moves like a wave.

In high summer, that glass acts as a reflector, the beams of light and heat actually visible to the eye, swirling and thickening, strange and exotic as hypnosis must be, and Jude and I navigate the kitchen with caution and forethought and the specialised rigour of U-boat crewmen, *Kriegsmarine*, May 1943, stalking the depths on a mission of stealth, foxing depth charges and direction finders, with the air thinning and time running out, we are losing kilos in sweat alone. Enigma is cracked and the tide of war has turned, but we do not give up. It's hot in here.

'Ping,' goes Jude.

'Ping,' I reply, sliding two paper napkins his way, because reaching high for plates we then have to wash up is a reckless waste of energy, as are superfluous words and moments of hesitation. In the *Unterseeboot Waffe*, speech is a luxury and a risk, a peacetime thing. In times like this, signals are unspoken, sent in a flash and decoded as quickly, at the speed of light maybe, no problem for Jude and me, language moving like a wave.

'Ping.' Pass the butter, Jem.

'Ping.' No butter on mine, Jude.

'Ping.' Pour the juice, grapefruit for me.

'Ping.' I know.

Jude told me once that by the end of the war, nearly 29,000 out of 35,000 U-boat men died and that signifies 80 per cent of U-Boat men, or eight men from every ten, and I like to assume there were fewer all-out Nazis in the *Unterseebootflotille*, many Germans choosing the ocean not just for the pleasure of boating, but because the sea is a separate country, and plumbing the depths is as far as they can run in a time of peril while still performing heroics in the name of *Heimat*, and though this assumption might be the wrong idea to have, wishful, I stick with it for now.

It was hard to get mad at Mike, even on those Saturday afternoons in late July, Michael sitting in our engine room of a kitchen with his end-of-the-day beer, no glass, thank you, the first beer of the countless beers he will drink after leaving us, sitting here so military straight, Harriet settles across from him with her little face in her hands grinning with pride, the two of them sharing this secret of fine posture, the soldier and the dancer, and then Mike speaks his few words, words some might consider a wee bit provoking, Mike always choosing the steamiest of days to utter them, days when we cart in the industrial-strength fans we were forced to buy, aiming them Mum's way, and to either side of her so she can cook for us without keeling over from heat exhaustion.

'Hot enough for you?' he says to Weisses at large, squeezing his eyes shut and chuckling into his chest while we stare at him, though not one of us is mad. And round about that summer Michael sealed us in, turning our cottage into a microscope or telescope depending on how you look at it, a telescope trained forever on the same patch of sky, Mum decorated Mike, her finest hopeless case, for the heroism he performed in the name of Weiss, so it seemed he had invisible badges the length of his arms, those arms corded with muscle covered now in golden stars and anchors and white wings and black crosses, and red chevrons maybe, special insignia signifying the place he took up in our family, keeper, guardian, watchdog, knight, for going into battle against Phillibert and Fang.

Phillibert and Fang made me come to grips with the murder instinct. Whenever I was anywhere near Phillibert in his brief reign as our hopeless case of a gardener, I had visions of arms and armaments and fatal blows to the nether regions, and vials of poison causing extreme agonies, esp. when I caught him smoking while gardening, the one single thing my mother asked him not to do, and in such a gentle voice, I was pretty miffed at her too, not just for asking so nicely but for her enduring faith in the human capacity for reason and thoughtfulness and so on. I want to break it to her sometimes, how there are types who dwell on the dark side, and that is where they choose to lurk for all time, it is home.

'Please, Phillibert,' my mother said. 'I'd rather you not smoke and handle the plants. It spreads disease. Blight. Please, Phillibert. It will make me very sad.'

Lord-a-mercy.

'Righty,' goes Phillibert with a slight smirk, putting out his fag with two wet fingers and slipping it behind one ear.

I have never seen a man take so long to do so little, staring at a hedge, say, for a half-hour or so, walking all around it with a fag hanging from his lips and then stepping up a ladder to go in for aerial assault, mauling that hedge to death and causing a lot of grief for Mum who persisted nevertheless in gardening instruction, and in preparing croque-monsieur luncheons for him, arranged just so on a pretty plate with a sprig of watercress decoration, and always my job to deliver, elected by my mother for improving purposes, as if I might soften up somehow in this act of dishing up to Phillibert, the way taming a pet is supposed to give you a big feeling for humanity and communion with all the creatures of the Universe and so on. Bloody. Forget it, Mum.

I place Phillibert's lunch on the steps where he is doing some vague horticultural activity, weeding I believe, although I note an alarmingly naked patch of flower bed at his feet, no growth at all, Waste Land.

'Lunch,' I say. Feeding time.

'What do you call that?' he asks. 'What's in it?'

'Croque monsieur,' I reply, knowing I am not helping, and moving away quickly, like I am real busy and have done him this big favour, making time in my day to bring him lunch on fine crockery. This is dodgy behaviour. Not charitable. Too bad.

'Is that – Jewish?'

I stop. Whoa. The way he said that. Turn back, Jem. This could be good.

'French,' I say. 'It's French.' *Milchig, fleischig. Terefah.* 'Ham. Cheese. Béchamel sauce.'

'A beer would be good with that,' says Phillibert, fiddling with a roll-up. 'I work. Up at five every morning. All my life. You people. You kids. Always reading books. You were my kids, I'd give you all a hiding. Take my belt off. Then you'd work. Hah! And where is it you go, what do you call it, church, where you people go. What do you call it?'

You people. Whoa. My first train-waver. Star-spotter, window-smasher, book-burner. There are enemies everywhere.

'Synagogue? Or – *shul*?' I say, sweet as Harriet, my heart pounding.

'Yeh, that's it. That first thing,' he says, and then he mutters something to himself and shakes his head before lighting his roll-up, and I blink with every gesture, taking snapshots, I am making my documentary about Nazis.

'I'll ask Dad about the beer. And synagogue is a GREEK word, by the way.'

'Righty-right, heh-heh. A beer would be good. It's hot. I work. Up at five every morning.'

OK, Phillibert. Righty. Coming up. One beer and one set of walking papers, but before I find my dad, I go in search of Mike because I know he will act quick, this will be no fumbling matter for him, such as painting moulding and skirting boards without running over the edges, or sanding wood smooth enough to stroke, no, this will be a breeze, easy as a scamper across our rooftops in quest of holes through which mice and chipmunks might pass, easy as trapping racoons whose favourite pastime is to churn up the rock garden, and burrow great craters near the wall at the water's edge, laying booby traps for us to fall in, and creating havens, as I suspect, for snakes. Without the vigilance of Michael, our grounds are in danger of a ravaging, battered as the face of the Moon with its highlands and mountains and impact basins, Crisium, Mare Tranquillitatis, old scars dating from its very formation in the Solar System nearly four billion years ago, and with no healing to come, no smoothing over, because the Moon is airless and inactive and not subject to weathering. Some scars never heal.

When I find Mike, I skip lightly over the 'you people' part, not sure he will understand, and he listens to me keen as Pax! hearing Mum call his name, whilst I elaborate on the threat part, the part to do with hidings and the loosening of belts, and off he goes like a shot, slapping me on the shoulders first off, and repeating that exclamation of his, 'Heavens! Oh, heavens. Heavens!' and I think of two things right then, of detective stories in which the sleuth offers up a scent of felon apparel, all a sleuthing dog needs for the tracing of footsteps, and I think of Harriet's Book of Saints wherein I read that Michael's cause is doorkeeping against the entry of devils, doorkeeping which is surely Mike's finer point whereas the sanding and painting of doors is not. Goodbye, Phillibert. Goodbye, Fang.

One evening before supper shortly after that day last summer it was decreed Phillibert and Fang would never darken our doorways again, Jude sat up on a kitchen stool while Gus and Harriet and I helped Mum with dinner preparations, some of us busier than others, i.e. Gus and I busier than Harriet, and Jude told us how Mike slugged Phillibert in the village bar, how it happened right before his eyes.

'KO?' I ask, frowning at Harriet who is making origami out of paper napkins, a pretty smart way of shirking the heavier tasks such as emptying the dishwasher or washing up stray afternoon dishes.

'Yup,' says Jude. 'Left hook.'

'Is he a southpaw?' I say, calling upon my sports-writer sensibilities.

'You don't have to be a southpaw to have a left hook, Jem.'

'I know that! Bloody-jeepers! Hey, Harriet. Listen. We are having CHILLI and maybe corn on the cob. MESSY meal. How about just slapping those napkins in half or in triangles or something and helping me out here, how about it?'

'We are a long way from being made in God's –' she begins.

'Yeh-yeh! All right! Do art! Fine with me, Jiminy. So then what?' I say, turning back to Jude. 'Tell.'

'Blood poured out,' says Gus who is standing on a chair at the Aga stirring the chilli around with both his slender arms and his top off so I can see all the tendons and little muscles flicking under his skin over his ribs and shoulder blades which are like little wings. There is something so bare about Gus.

Mum scatters more herbs and spices into the big pot and asks Gus was he in the bar, was he there too, although there is no surprise in her voice, no alarm at all.

'Ma!' goes Jude. 'He had a soft drink. Straight, no chaser.'

'Cherry Coke,' adds Gus. 'Sometimes I have plain Coke, never Pepsi. And no ice.'

'Gus,' I say, 'If they let you into Paradise, are you going to ask for the menu first, or what?'

Gus thinks this is funny and he does his new Mike-laugh, no sound, eyes squeezed shut, chin into chest, a mirthful reaction I appreciate in Michael but I want Gus's old laugh back, the one where his whole body is electrified and his eyes flash and he gulps in excitement, giggling and yelping like a small furry animal. It is likely this new laugh has to do with hero-worship, giving me a strange left-out feeling, shifty and sad, especially now with this picture in mind of Gus and Jude in the bar together watching Mike slug Phillibert, a knockout punch, left hook, an act that is probably my doing yet had to happen without me in a place where I am not welcome, due to girlhood, this congress of cowboys simply not my domain, not according to Jude, Hazchem!

'Jude?' I say, fishing cutlery out of the cutlery drawer into which Mike fashioned dividing frontiers of wood from Mum's delicate design that in Mike's hands turned out so bulbous and clumsy there is barely any room for cutlery, the reason also that our implement drawer has no divisions at all. Don't bother, Mike, we told him. Thanks anyway. 'Jude, he didn't just slug him, right, I mean, what happened?'

'He said a very rude thing,' mumbles Gus, glancing at Mum quick sticks.

'Phillibert?'

'Yeh,' says Jude, pouring white wine for Mum without asking her first, making a Jude-decision. 'I was getting the drinks in, we were at the bar and Phillibert muttered this thing, um, well, he goes, "Sometimes I wonder why they didn't put all those bastard Jews in the oven." So Mike punched him out.'

'That's amazing,' I say. 'Are you sure?'

'Have you told your father?' asks Mum.

'Not yet,' says Jude. 'And yeh, I'm sure. Anyway, it was a great hit.'

'Right in the kisser!' I declare. 'And blood pouring out!'

'What larks!' exclaims Harriet. 'Was he killed?' she adds, where-upon Jude and I roll our eyes and Gus starts up laughing again. 'I need to know,' she says, kind of affronted. 'Michael might have to go to Australia and be a slave on a slave gang.'

'Chain gang, Harriet,' I tell her. 'And there are no penal colonies any more.'

'Thank the Lord for small mercies,' she says, eyelids fluttering.

'Harriet, come here,' says Jude. 'I'm going to tie your sleeves up at the back.'

'You and WHOSE ARMY?!' she growls and we all stare at her in shock because she has used this fierce expression and spoken sharply in plain and angry words, so unlike Harriet, there is a great silence in our kitchen, and Gus is clearly moved. He lays his spoon in the scalloped spoon rest and climbs off his chair, approaching Harriet who rises up immediately in readiness for their greeting scene as in plays by Russians featuring impecunious aristocrats with a lot of mournful feelings. Gus and Harriet fling their arms out to the side at shoulder height and gaze at one another briefly, with a countenance denoting grief and forbearance, and thereafter, they embrace, pressing cheek to cheek and patting shoulders and suddenly they disengage and fling arms out to the side again, repeating the embrace on the other side, right cheek to right cheek. Depending on the gravity of the circumstances, the weight of afflic-tion borne by either party, they will go in for a third embrace, left to left again, and with prolonged back-patting, which is the case today. It's quite poignant, and we observe them with poise and respect, as is befitting.

'You OK now, Harriet?' I ask quietly. 'Do you want a glass of water or something? With a straw perhaps?'

'Why, fiddle-dee-dee, Jem,' she replies in her finest Southern. 'Why, yes, please! A long cold drink always gives me a brand new outlook!'

God's teeth.

Here come Ben and Dad, my dad pounding up the basement stairs and breathing hard in triumph and achievement, clutching a great paper bag of sweetcorn to his chest, every arrival of my dad's a homecoming, with a feeling for trumpet sounds and flag-waving and the popping of corks, Hello, Dad! noblest knight, right wise king, yes, *ye may enter the ship and begrip the sword, and who that draweth me, wit ye well that he shall never be wounded to the death.*

'Corn!' he announces. 'Just picked!'

To meet my dad now, to hear him, you might suppose the bundle he bears to be the result of months of toil, Dad the farmer staring into the night skies in spring and observing the lunar phases, selecting the finest day to sow the seeds he will watch over in the growing season, right through his fears of frost and up until harvest time when he works his way proudly down each row, snapping off tender ears of corn and pitching them into a bag to hurry home with before the sugar has turned to starch, hurrying home to his hungry kids, though all my dad has done, in fact, is jump into a fast car with Ben for company and race seven minutes along the road to the village farm where piles of sweetcorn are laid out on trestle tables for dads round about, and for the especial glory of mine, a dad with a *shtetl* in his ancestry and a ghetto in his very lifetime, and present dreams of green fields to call his own. My dad's way with farming is close to his way with gardening, which is to burst on to our terrace at the end of a day's sports writing and yell out 'Frances! Frances! Are you still out there?' in exhausted tones, as if he had done all the hard gardening himself, in her place, the weeding and pruning, the landscaping and beautifying, the something out of nothing, just by virtue of missing her and calling out 'Frances!' into the summer stillness, reminding me of what Jude told me once, how before the Jewish calendar was devised, time was measured by observations of the Moon, witnesses reporting their sightings of the crescent to the High Court in Jerusalem so that it might proclaim the new month with these words, 'Sanctified! Sanctified!' whereupon bonfires are lit on mountaintops, a message to the farthest reaches of Israel from the highest watchdog of them all. And so my dad marks the time and place, Frances! Are you still out there? You have to come in now! Frances! Frances! Sanctified!

Jude is keen to tell Dad his bar story.

'Dad?' says Jude.

'Just a minute!' he says, shoving Mum aside in a playful manner, tickling her in the back of the knees as he crouches down to stuff the corn into the upper right oven, his one contribution to dinner preparations for which he will expect great acclaim, involving short speeches and expressive murmurs to do with the perfect timing of the cooking and the sweetness of the corn, and the felicity of weather systems, the very phases of the Moon perhaps, the bounty on the Earth below. Well done, Dad.

'OK,' he says to Jude, scraping his hair back with both hands and letting out a big breath. 'Wait. Where's my drink? Oh, there. OK. Shoot. What?'

And Jude tells him the bar story right then and we all listen, some of us for the second time, but as if we never heard it before. It's a big story.

'Phillibert will go to Hell,' pronounces Harriet in a small voice. 'He will go to Hell in a handbag.'

I flop on to the dock in a spume of water and check my toes right away for leeches even though I can barely focus, a whole smelt run in my poor vision now. I feel queasy also. Bloody. I don't feel well today and this day is Jude's last, a faraway idea. One day, never.

'Ben? Aren't some days now and far away, know what I mean?'

'Some infinities are bigger than others! Did you know that? A single infinite universe is not big enough to realise all its possibilities, that is — there'd have to be an infinite number of infinite universes for that to happen, for all possibilities to be realised. Isn't that great?' Ben says from where he is standing, all ready to go up to the house.

'Yeh,' I say, kind of weak, too weak for curiosity and enthusiasms.

'Are you OK, Jem?'

'A bit throw-uppy. Hot. Forgot to eat. Need a minute, I'll be fine.'

Ben collapses neatly right next to me and drops the hockey towel with our spare clothes he has wrapped tightly within like a soldier's bedroll, a swimming-baths habit from our old country where a person learns to be compact due to paucity of land mass. I don't know what else Ben can do for himself when it comes to personal management. He is going to be dependent on courtesy and I don't know how much there is of that out there in the great world.

'You don't have to move out,' I say. 'Ben? There'll be tons more space now.'

'That's not why, Jem. It's not about space.'

'I know it,' I mumble, picking at a splinter on the dock and sweeping it into the water. 'I'll be OK in a minute. I already said that, sorry. Hey, Ben. Sun and Moon. Look. NOT the same, ha ha.'

'Ah, Jem. You're so dumb,' goes Ben, flinging one infinite arm over my shoulders. 'What will you do in life? That's my question.'

'Solo act. Singing and dancing, top hat, cane. I'll call myself the Dumb Bunny. No. The Miracle of the Dumb Bunny.'

'Pity you can't sing or dance.'

'That will be the pathos part. You must have a pathos part. They will cross my palms with silver for all the pathos of me.'

'Right,' says Ben.

'How about you then? Jude says get a job, I don't think there are jobs out there for wizards and so on. Not paying ones anyway.'

'I rest not from my great task, to open the Eternal Worlds, to open the Immortal Eyes of Man inwards into the Worlds of Thought, into Eternity!'

'That doesn't sound like a paying job either . . . and what is that? Not that horrible Revelations again, I bloody hate that,' I say, rising up carefully, hands on knees, deep breaths, take deep breaths.

'Revelation. And no, it's Blake.'

'Oh, right. Well – how about this: Every man is a king,' I say in my quotation voice. 'And don't you forget it!'

'Um. Leibniz?' says Ben, gathering up our things. 'Voltaire?'

'STANLEY KOWALSKI!' I yell and Ben bops me on the head.

'I could piggyback you,' he offers. 'Unless you're going to throw up on me.'

'I won't!' I say, taking the towel from him and draping it around my neck, boxer style. 'I swear!' I add, my head alight with a whole mess of thoughts. Why is the sky dark at night? Light stretches, Ben says, *the Universe evolves.* Redshift, blueshift, radio waves, Ophelia waves, why didn't she wave for someone? For someone dressed in blue! Blue – short, coming closer. Do not wave to anyone in red. Too late. Red – long, moving away fast. Jude's notes. *You can wear my rugby top. 3. Life is not a dream.* It is, it is! Faraway-now 9. *Rag Gus about his inhaler.* Gus Day, *il tomba doucement comme tombe un arbre. OK, man, I'll try to make it home for Christmas. Over and out.* Mike the Archangel, Phillibert and Fang, Hazchem! . . . and something my dad said, the night of Jude's bar story when

325

we sat down to sweetcorn and chilli, he said it laughing, 'Remember what Amalek did unto thee!' and Mum bowed her head, smiling, a moment between them, Ping! Don't ask, Jem, this is not the time to ask, not sanctified! Questions you save up, signals that are unspoken, Ping! Things you tell straight off, to Jude, mostly to Jude, such as the Objectif Lune Incident, a day I am threatened with expulsion for writing these two words on a blackboard, next to a slide projection of one of the silliest pictures I ever saw, *The Ascension of Christ*, Albrecht Dürer, b.1471, d.1528.

'His last appearance on earth,' Soeur Rosa says.

One night only. Roll up, no concessions, no returns. Custer's Last Stand.

'These are his miraculous footprints, this is the Mount of Olives,' she says. 'What do you think, Mlle Weiss? What are your feelings?'

My feelings. Ascension. The apostles gathered round, a huddle of outstretched arms and waving hands, all eyes skybound, and at the top of the picture, in a puff of cloud, Jesus disappearing, his bare feet poking out below the hem of his garment, feet that leave miraculous footprints on a mountaintop in a swirl of smoke. You have lift-off. All systems are go.

I walk to the front of the classroom and write two words in white chalk, *Objectif Lune*, and there is a feeling within like the shifting of gears in a fast car, violent but sure, because the genes for driving have come straight on down to me from Dad, undiluted, indistinguishable in effect, and I see not only that familiar expression on Soeur Rosa's face – you are the bagel man, I slap a star on you, a yellow one – but so very much more, all reflected in her eyes, a new and populous vision of Daniel Mendoza taking a stance, protecting his face, and Hank Greenberg, soldier and baseball hero, and Jude with the battered suitcase only he can open, and my dad remembering Amalek who, I now know, attacked him, attacked all of us, by surprise in the wilderness at least thirteen centuries BCE, not to be forgotten, history repeats itself, and finally me, I see me, Jem, bearing a stick of white chalk, *the marvelloust and the sharpest that ever was taken in any knight's hand*, knowing that some battles, some stands, can be the making of you.

Ben makes stirrup hands so I can ride up the hill in style and then suppertime comes, Jude's Farewell Barbecue, don't go, and I sit on the wall and close my eyes, awaiting the champagne feeling. Be nimble, be quick.

'Do we have lift-off?' asks Jude. Are you there yet, in that champagne moment?

Jude pours seconds of champagne, assuming my job tonight, though I pour the first glasses and open the bottle, turning it, not the cork, and letting the pressure escape, bang! just so we can play out our Western scene from *My Darling Clementine*, as is customary, a scene wherein he always has the Wyatt part.

'Mac,' he says. 'You ever been in love?'

'No,' I answer, filling flutes. 'I've been a bartender all my life.'

The soldier covers his face with both hands, it's dark out here on the balcony, and so late, his hands are wet, a man might drown this way, in tears, like gas, keep your mask on, don't take it off, gas lies longest in the hollows, don't forget that, lachrymatory, chlorine, phosgene, mustard, he doesn't know many words, he remembers these.

Everyone close to him dies, anyone he loves grows ill, leaves him, and this is the worst thing, how he hit Frances today, there can be no worse. Don't touch! His ears ring, for nearly thirty years now, tinnitus they call it, more words, always hard ones for things he does not want to know, or say, and a sound in his ears like the grinding of knives, the rattle of equipment, helmet, belts, Lee–Enfield, fifteen rounds a minute. He hears it, and then he sees it, and then he closes his eyes. What he can't see might not hurt him. What cannot be touched can never be taken away. He hit her.

Saturday morning, and Tom home tomorrow, the war is over now. Over again. Tom sent letters, many coming at once, not always in order. The soldier sits with Frances and watches his wife, making a cake again, a cake with lemons and spices, vanilla. An essence, she says.

—*Read that one again, Frances. The one about the painting.*

—*That's such an old one, Daddy!*

—*I know it.*

Frances finds it easily, it is always on top of the pile, Mummy reads this one again and again. Tom sees a painting on leave, Picture of the Month. They put all the paintings away, he says, hidden someplace, because of the bombing. All but one a month. He joined a great queue, the painting is by Titian, Noli mi tangere, it's called, from John. Touch me not. Mary Magdalene stops a man she thinks is a gardener. The tomb is empty, where is he, she asks, where have you taken him? Tom describes the picture, how the ground is brownish, except for under the gardener's feet where the grass is lush and green and how Mary wears a red dress. Then Tom writes about the decision he made, to take holy orders when the war is over, when he is home, then.

—*He will go to the lost sheep of Israel, says the soldier's wife. 'Provide neither gold, nor silver, nor brass in your purses, nor scrip for your journey, neither two coats, neither shoes . . . And when you come into an house, salute it.' Matthew, she says. Chapter 10. It's time, Bert. Frances. I'll get my hat. Where is Dot?*

—*Daddy, why lost sheep? And will Tom move out? Will he live with priests?*

—*Shush, you. It will make her so happy.*

—*No. Never, she'll never be happy.*

A flap of the hand, no thinking at all, and the stillness of her, the great blue eyes on him. Frances!

Saturday night. It's so dark out here. Tom tomorrow. He remembers his own demob. Good luck! And thanks for all you've done! A handshake and a ration card, a small packet of money, fags, now what? I'm a marksman, a soldier, I'm no good for anything else. Pack the case, have a pint, two, three. Buy a ticket, cross the ocean, run. They say it snows every day over there in wintertime, the sun shines all summer long.

He never-hit-me-only-once.

When you leave this house, salute it.

—It's very difficult for you to talk to me today.

—Excuse me, Mrs Rosenfeld! I was daydreaming!

I speak to you in my Sherlock Holmes voice, full of purpose and crazed vigour, because there is something else I want to tell you and I can't find it for all the noise in my head, an underwater sensation, and, as I happen to know from my U-boat days, underwater, sound is magnified five times. Excuse me, I was daydreaming! says Holmes coming out of a reverie, a place he goes for the sifting of clues, and sleuthing is home for Holmes, everyone has a home. When the case is closed, he needs the feeling back, he wants lift-off, so he tries all-night chemical research, even intravenous, why not? And he plays the violin, in a dressing gown, sleepless, he tries everything, but he cannot get the feeling back, it's never the same.

In my reverie, I am a telescope, I follow the light and the colours change in time, I read this, though the mix is always the same, light revealing its source, remembering the early Universe. All the clues are there. In the Big Bang, the centre was everywhere and nowhere, because everything was present, it's so simple. And in an expanding universe, this is still true, but for new reasons, because although from wherever a person stands, things are flying away fast, don't go!, the centre is not that person, never that person. The centre is everywhere and nowhere. *I have looked further into space than ever human being did before me*, writes William Herschel. Except for your sister, William, your sister did.

There are things I want to tell you, Mrs Rosenfeld, but I don't know if you can help, and I don't trust you to stay, I don't trust anyone, not any more, there are enemies everywhere, and in moments such as this, all I can do is count. Three Brontë deaths in nine months, Branwell, Emily, Anne. Three weeks before the third anniversary of Emily's death, Keeper dies. Three years after Keeper dies, Anne's dog Flossy dies. Charlotte dies three days before her thirty-ninth birthday. I say, old chap! There's just no end to it! Let me not be mad! Count!

The paces between the bus stop and your house, running, walking, a different count. Stitches in my wrist, the left of course, I'm no southpaw! Sixteen. *Mezuzot* on your side of the street, including yours, seven. The doorways in the tiny vestibule where I sit waiting for you, seven, and counting your footsteps, various! The cuts on my wrist, four, dolorous strokes, ha! *Who that draweth me, wit ye well that he shall never fail of shame of his body, or to be wounded to the death*. Which part of this statement is false? No answer. The colours of my experiment in escape velocity, three. The mix always the same. Blue. Fine veins, della Robbia blue streams, lovely, hot young stars, little blue Renault, Jude's eyes, aquamarine. Red, beautiful, the red dress Frances stops wearing the Xmas Jude does not make it home, though he said he'd try, the dress I saw her in the day I first opened my eyes, I remember everything. And finally black, my vision dimming, curtain down,

The End, not quite. Not so fast! *Je tombai doucement, comme tombe un arbre.*

And here am I now, doing the back-float on your couch, with my weedy trophies and fantastic garlands, singing snatches of old tunes and daydreaming, excuse me! because I cannot find it, the something I wanted to tell you, it's so hard to hear myself sometimes. Is it time? Wait. There is one thing, there is always this one thing.

My mother built a house, I tell you, *and the street of the city was pure gold, as it were transparent glass.*

EIGHT

Don't you see my house has collapsed?

One evening in late October 1915, the night before Shackleton orders his twenty-seven men to abandon the leaking, groaning *Endurance* which is cracking up beyond repair in the frozen Weddell Sea, eight emperor penguins march right up to the ship and take in the sight of it, shuffling quietly, as I imagine, doing a two-step from web to web before sending up a lament, wailing in such an eerie fashion, the crew is rattled quite badly, though they carry on pumping out, all through the night until the next afternoon when suddenly the decks start shattering and the keel breaks away. Jock Wordie, geologist turned glaciologist, a well-liked science man in a friendly beard and little wire-rimmed specs, writes these words. 'Everything has come too quickly to make us pause to regret. That will come in the future.'

Shackleton is ever mindful of his dogs and they disembark first, the men making slides out of canvas so the journey of the dogs to the ice is swift and comfortable. After you, Dear Dogs. Boss is last away, and before leaving, he raises a little blue flag which his men salute from the ice, shouting out three cheers, and noting a strange thing also, how the emergency lamp on the abandoned *Endurance* turns itself on, and although the circuit is fragile, causing a persistent flicker, it stays lit one whole night, their first night on the floes that are splintering fast with a naked and terrible sound like thunder and the rolling of great boulders, cracking beneath them so unpredictably they are forced to up sticks and move house three times in that night of temperatures way below freezing, the men lying on leaky groundsheets in tents of linen so thin, the walls are

331

transparent and the moon shines through the walls. This is a vigil for an ailing ship, and it lasts three nights.

On the day they set off in two parties in search of safer ground, somewhere less shifting, Shackleton limits his men to one kilo each of personals, meaning they must discard luxuries and even the ship's Bible, out of which Ernest tears a few pages from Job before going ahead with Wordie and Hudson the navigator and Hurley the photographer in a pioneering party to smooth the way forward through frozen ridges and hummocks for the sledges to follow, and it is the same damned day Crean the dog man is obliged to shoot three of his puppies, because this is now a journey permitting no excess baggage, no needy creatures, God bless our Dear Dogs.

Out of whose womb came the ice? And the hoary frost of heaven, Who hath gendered it?

There is a photograph in my Shackleton book taken by Mr James Francis Hurley and it is an over-the-shoulder shot of six dogs in harness, perched in the snow and ice at a cautious and respectful distance from the wreck of the *Endurance*, and five of the dogs are watchful, alert, waiting and hoping, perhaps, for a sign, a waving, something, and one dog is slightly adrift, lying off to the side, wound up tight in a coil of dog-sleep. *Excuse me, I was daydreaming!*

Much later, Shackleton writes a caption to this photograph. *The End*, he writes, which, of course, it was not, because all twenty-seven men came home, and Ernest too, *Not a life lost and we have been through Hell*. I believe he was telling some separate truth about things when he wrote these words, something to do with what he sensed in October 1915, how these were his great days and nothing would ever be the same, nothing would ever compare, these two words *The End* possibly coming to mind also on a night in January 1922 when he dies of massive heart failure on board his last ship, the *Quest*, anchored in the shadow of the same mountains he scrambled across on his way to the whaling station in South Georgia, a January night he tries to shrug off the attentions of his old friend Macklin, surgeon on the *Endurance* expedition, another Scot in wire-rimmed specs and a friendly beard who only wants to wrap a second blanket around Boss because the night is cold, and his resistance is not what it was, it will never be the same.

—I can stand the cold! he snaps, but this is not true, not any longer. The ice, his realm, is now killing him.

—Maybe you should give it up, says Macklin, meaning the ice, saying this quite gently, though it is still outrageous to Boss who grumbles and turns to the wall, as I picture it, how he turns to the wall as Macklin leaves his cabin, and then, too quickly to allow anyone pause, within that hour, at ten minutes before three in the morning, Boss dies.

Everyone has a home.

My days are numbered, I can see that now. Numbered and signed. This way, calamity.

Everything's messed up in my house again, everything different, even the path to school with Harriet today, like some path I have never pounded before, and the journey this morning, only six days since Jude left and Gus rode his bike off the dock, is downright arduous, an obstacle race, a veritable nightmare, a *cauchemar*. I keep halting and staring up at street signs which are harder and harder to read because of short-sightedness and how my far is growing nearer and nearer.

I recall a fierce and blowy afternoon last winter when Gus and I stepped out on a job for Dad, a job of collecting hockey tickets from a friend of his living eight or nine twisting blocks away, and we shuffled out quite merrily into the snowstorm, but pretty soon we are lost, due to collective myopia and dreaminess and whippy snow sticking to street signs and interfering with vision in every way. And to the fact I left the map Mum drew for us on the kitchen table, bloody.

'Gus, my man! Number 71, right? Was that it? But what's the name of the street we are looking for, again? Was it Hillcrest? Yes, Hillcrest. Does it say Hillcrest up there? Can you read that?'

I look down at my brother who is rapidly approaching me in the height department, my days of looking down on him certainly numbered, and I think how he resembles a World War I dispatch rider in his brown suede cap with the ear flaps and leather chin strap and racing-car-driver gloves with the leather palms, and his little wire-rimmed spectacles, frames he chose at the optician's without hesitation as they are exactly the same as Ben's, and Ben is a hero in Gus's firmament of heroes, which includes Jude of course, Jude who has perfect vision and does not wear specs. I am not sure if I can be a hero in the firmament for Gus, due to girl-hood, but this does not preoccupy me. A person cannot set out to be a hero, the hero state being a condition that falls upon you.

Gus says, 'Binoculars would be handy.' And I realise that the distance between Gus's eyes and the street sign is still greater than it is for me, although not by much. Not by much.

'Periscope up,' I say, and Gus nods sagely as I scoot close to the lamp-post and plant my feet firmly as possible and make stirrup hands for my brother, making sure to keep my face clear of the post as my dad says skin can freeze to metallurgy and a person must beware never to lick a lamp-post, etc., or else he will be in for an emergency situation of paramedics bearing boiling water and heat blankets, and an eventuality of skin grafts and lifelong speech impediments. I cannot fathom the desire to lick a lamp-post in any kind of weather, but never mind. I take no chances.

Gus clambers into my hands and straightens up slowly, hugging the lamp-post and craning his head back to call out all the letters he can distinguish with certainty.

'H, definitely,' he says. 'Plus a double l. Oh, and there's a c.'

'Great. That's enough. Well done, Parker.'

Once Gus and I find Dad's friend's house and the envelope of hockey tickets, we shake hands in a solemn fashion. Mission accomplished. As we head home, Gus rattles off the names of parked cars, not just names but numbers and letters that usually go along with names of cars, things you know if you are a car man like Gus. When he comes upon a car of particular distinction, he pauses and imparts details to do with horsepower and tyre pressure and the span of time required for that car to accelerate from nil kph to very many kph. It's quite interesting and I say 'Whoa' or 'Blow me down' and other such remarks, and now and again I knit my brows in a display of appreciation and thoughtfulness regarding the details imparted to me, inspiring Gus so much, he digs out his change with a scoop of racing-driver gloves and holds the booty up for my inspection, proposing a pit stop at the slot-machine arcade where, he tells me, they have a new Formula One game.

'Gus, are you allowed in there? It's gambling or whatever. There are rules.'

'Jude knows the manager,' replies Gus. 'Shall we then?'

'OK. Walk on!'

Gus runs through the rules for me and operates the paddles and gears so all I have to do is handle the steering wheel yet still I veer off the track at every corner and chicane, only managing to stay on the track long enough to find that slick of oil and mow into every other car in sight, this hysteria of sheer speed and power simply too much for me. My race at Magny-Cours ends in no time. *Nul points.*

'That was pathetic, right, Gus?'

'You were pretty hopeless,' he says, taking over and playing with skill and composure and winning bonus games before sliding off the car seat suddenly, worried I may feel left out. Gus is a gentleman, no question about it. We pool our coins and decide on apple strudel at Zweig's where Mrs Zweig is so pleased to see my brother, she cleaves slices of strudel of epic proportions, wrapping them carefully against the elements, and slipping Gus a cellophane bag tied up with a ribbon for Mum, a packet containing those discs of dark chocolate studded with cracked hazelnuts and large raisins, and I decide that Gus would make a fine saint, and a healthy one to boot, in no danger of attrition, never having to raise that wooden bowl hanging from his sash, as people would shower him with delicacies and offer up warm garments for his body with great willingness and immediacy because of these qualities of gentleness and tranquillity and quiet wisdom, and the slightness and grace of his frame and face, a fragility of the inspiring kind. Gus looks like a man with a cause.

'What's the matter, honey? Are you LOST?' asks Harriet, observing my wayward stagger on our way to school and stopping to pat my hand and give me a pitying look as if this were really it for me, and soon time for the small white room with barred windows and soft furnishings.

'Harriet,' I say, sitting on the grassy verge at the edge of the pavement, 'I don't feel very well. I have to head home, I think.'

'Are you vomity?'

'Kind of. You go on to school, OK?'

'OK, dear,' says Harriet, sitting down next to me in her regular display of fine deportment, straight ballerina back and straight ballerina legs and little feet waggling from side to side, her expression cheery and hopeful like she is waiting for some nice surprise to come her way any moment soon, a surprise she can dance to.

'Go on, Harriet. You'll be late. Nuns all cross and everything.'

'*Bonjour, ma soeur! Bonjour, ma soeur!* Fucking-bloody!' she says, not budging.

We sit quiet for a little while, pirates on a rum break, shiver me timbers, and I think about Gus and how he rose up out of his convalescence and bashed off to school today, though it is Friday and there is practically nothing left of the schooling week, what's the point. I waltzed into the room he shares with Jude, expecting the same strange scene of Jude's neat and empty bed on one side and Gus on the other in his billowy sea of white covers and storm-tossed books, me strolling in all casual so as not to draw special attention to convalescence, as if I were only passing, see you later, need anything? And there he was, standing in front of the door-length mirror, dressed for school and tying his tie in that apparently breezy way I have observed in all male members of the Weiss family, neck stretched taut, chin high and hands busy in a frenzy of tying activity, ends flipping and looping wildly as if speed will somehow eliminate error, reminding me of the high-speed flight of stars, and how the Moon is always falling towards the Earth, always falling, not crashing.

'Harriet. Why did Gus go to school today, I thought he was supposed to stay home all week, it's Friday, what's the point?'

'Lemming,' replies Harriet. 'Norwegian lemming, arctic and tundra mammal. Thrives on grass, berries and roots. Travels south across bodies of water when food is scarce. Amphibian, although prone to drowning through exhaustion. Thank you.'

I frown and turn my head towards my sister, and she does the same, raising one eyebrow slightly and inviting the same in me, it's a chain reaction in our family, we all do it, this raising of eyebrows, and it can mean different things at different times, a communication of varying gravity, always indicating, however, an agreement of Weisses, a collective sigh in the face of worldly strife, as when clustered around the study of an evening, awaiting the news broadcast and imminent announcements to do with threats and consequences of fire, blood, massacre, engine failure, incendiary device, war and prejudice, all the evidence of rash and vengeful behaviour and regular human frailty, the news, it seems to me, always eyebrow-raising, an expression of the collective signifying, in this case, extreme gravity, a sinking of the heart beyond words and an instinct for the rending of garments, an ancient practice, Jude tells me, still observed at Jewish funerals.

I have not been to a Jewish funeral, or any kind of funeral, though Jude has, and he says there is a name for this procedure of rending, *k'riah*, a word easy to remember as it sounds like crying, of course, and he also told me there is left-side rending and right-side rending, that if a parent dies, the kids rend on the left, over the heart region, and all the others, on the right, which goes to show that, even in a funeral situation, there are still rules in Judaism, an order of grief for instance, and kid-grief for a parent clearly comes tops in that order. I think it is a very good idea to have rules in a funeral situation because things are desperate, I imagine, and everyone has crazed feelings and a need to get organised, thankful for some direction in the haberdashery department, for instance, and in matters of prayer selection and candle-lighting, say, and also in matters of timing, such as for the rending of garments and so on, otherwise a funeral will be like a madhouse or something, with a lot of mayhem of howling and screaming and rending and everyone out of time with everyone else and making things worse than they already are. In dark times, it is recommended to sort yourself out with rules so there is energy left over for thinking about the grievous circumstances that have befallen. That's my opinion just from listening to Jude.

I am not sure which side you are supposed to rend if you are a grown-up and your kid dies, and though I am pretty sure it is the left, I did not ask Jude, because when a person is afflicted the way Jude was this past winter the day of Jeremy's funeral, he ought not be pestered with unnecessary questions, he should be allowed to recount things in his own time. I think a parent might rend right and left, rending on both sides maybe, to mark the horror of things, though this matter of rending is just one of the dark matters Zach's parents had to face up to after Jeremy killed himself out of love-blindness.

Suicide is definitely a dark matter and frowned upon by most parties, being a criminal offence in Judaism and Christianity in past times and a criminal offence still in Islam, Jude tells me. Not so long ago in my old country, a suicide would be forbidden a burial in nice hallowed ground and might be pitched into a public highway with a stake through the heart, treatment which strikes me as harsh and careless and a display of bad thinking, rabbis and priests convinced, I suppose, that a proper funeral for a suicide will encourage types in the congregation with inclinations towards this unseemly end to things, as if the denial of a nice party were the single deterrent they require to stop them hurtling towards death with great impatience and a do-it-yourself approach, the mere knowledge they will be pitched over the city walls or slung into an old pit with a stake through the heart not quite enough to change their outlook on life, but a ban on festivities definitely tips the scales.

I don't believe suicidal types are swayed much by the promise of festivities. Ophelia, of course, perished in a party dress and a halo of fantastic garlands and so on, and before Jeremy Levinthal slit both wrists, no messing around, cutting vertically, Jude says, because the blood runs quicker that way, he dressed up in his finest, his one going-out suit, a charcoal-grey dinner jacket with matching trousers and a tie-it-by-hand ribbon bow tie and well-polished black brogues, just the right shoes for your finest, one-and-only going-out suit, but they were not dressing up for festivities, or to spite those who would deny them festivities, I don't think so.

'Did Zach find him, Jude? You never said – who found him.'

No questions, Jem. In your own time, Jude. I watch my brother from bed where I am busy reading, propped up on an elbow to gather the pool of light from my desk lamp when Jude comes strolling in, Jude clearly a bit drunk and woozy, heading for the desk and sweeping aside my books and papers because that is where he wants to sit, right there where all my things are. OK.

'Hey, where's Harriet?'

'Kath's house.'

'Old slobber-lips,' says Jude.

'Yeh!'

I watch and I wait, and I note how long Jude's hair has grown and how the snow has made his curls lush and unruly and sparkly in the light, like melting frost on fir trees. He is still wearing his big coat, that old sheepskin coat of Dad's with the rip in the left pocket seam because my dad had one fight too many with all the stuff he crammed in there, a coat that has since been replaced for Dad by another sheepskin coat, same as the old coat as change is a problem for my dad, same as the old coat though slightly fuller now that he is slightly fuller himself, his days of scurvy and poor nutrients well behind him, courtesy of Frances. Jude grips the edge of the desk and his gaze is caught by his own swinging feet and the little drips of water falling from his socks where the snow is still encrusted around the ankle folds, meaning he must have been wearing shoes out there, he forgot his boots again, or left them at the Levinthals', he did not wear the right shoes for a trip home from a funeral in winter.

'Oops – sorry,' he says, staring at drips.

'It's only water. Hey, Jude. Take your coat off.'

'Baby, it's cold outside,' he mumbles, making a wee throaty sound, akin to the start of a laugh, and then he stops swinging his feet and looks straight at me. 'Yeh,' he says. 'Yeh.'

'Yeh what? Oh. Zach found him, it was Zach.'

Jude raises one eyebrow quite slowly, his left, whereupon I raise my left likewise and we look at each other, no blinking, for what seems a long time, but is probably only a second or two, no more, before Jude gazes at his dripping socks again, which I do also, and I think about Zach walking into Jeremy's room, and wonder did he dance from foot to foot in that crazed fashion of his at the sight of his brother's body laid out all neatly in his finest with no blood left within, did Zach do his two-step of readiness for all things, for danger and the impulse for rescue, or was he still for once, as Jude is now, Jude who told me that according to the laws of *kashrut*, kosher rules, blood is *terefah*, forbidden, it has to be drained for an animal to be kosher, meaning ritually fit, and in modern times, the way Jude sees it, the rules are symbolic, taking the measure of you and your spiritual purity in all departments of life, and I see it too now, deciding that although Jeremy did a bad thing, frowned upon, he did a good thing also, a pure thing, that is what I decide.

'Was he buried in the suit, his black suit?'

'Charcoal grey. Used to be his dad's. No. In a shroud, you have to be in a shroud.'

'Oh,' I say.

'It's Jewish, Jem. About being equal and not shaming the poor and all that.'

'Oh,' I say, not sure this rule is right, and thinking Zach's brother who was only fifteen months older than Zach who is the same age as Jude, the distance between Jeremy and me exactly twice the distance between Jude and me, between Zach and me, which is like no distance in the scheme of things, I think Zach's brother can still be equal to all Jews and not one bit shaming to a single poorer Jew if buried today in the right clothes, ones that are symbolic to him, marking the finest time in all his born days, Jeremy Levinthal in his black, no, charcoal-grey going-out suit, clothes he wore to take his girlfriend on dates, the girl who left him, causing Jeremy to let his own blood, more than a dishful, because he could not foresee better days, he could not see any farther than this, his finest time, he cannot fix this thing.

Jude rummages in his right pocket, pulling out small bottles of Scotch, aeroplane-type bottles, miniatures Dad calls them, wee bottles he loves to arrange at my breakfast place on his return from sports-writing trips, waiting for Jude and me to shuffle down to breakfast and play that scene from *My Darling Clementine* that creases my dad up every time.

'Mac, you ever been in love?' says Jude.

'No,' I reply, moving the little bottles around in an ever more elaborate show of industry and embarrassment, 'I've been a bartender all my life.'

Tonight Jude breaks the seal off a miniature malt, trying to read the label in the lamplight, which malt is this? but he gives up quick sticks, because twisting and bending and eyestrain is too much for a person in a state of affliction and drunkenness.

'Fuck-hell, forget it,' he says. 'Malt, malt, malt – words, words, words. Sip?'

'I brushed my teeth.'

'You shouldn't drink spirits anyway. Girls shouldn't.'

'Why?'

'Fucks up your womb, Jem. I mean it.'

'Oh. Jeepers creepers. What about wine then? I like wine a lot.'

'I know. Wine's OK. Minerals and stuff. Iron. Stick to wine.'

'OK, Jude.'

Jude tells me now about all the food he ate at the funeral party, how there were bagels, poppy seed and sesame, and boiled eggs, symbolic foods signifying the cycle of life, still a problem notion for me, life surely a straight line and a straight line is the shortest distance between two points, one of maybe three things I remember from geometry along with obtuse and acute angles, designations I recall because Mum uses these words for people, obtuse and acute. 'How obtuse!' she might say on the subject of the latest crazy mishap in building and decorating inflicted upon our cottage, and only when especially agitated and done-in. 'How acute!' she will remark of an observation offered up by some Weiss at dinnertime, most often Ben or Jude. And I recall this third thing in geometry, that in a square, all sides are equal and the opposite sides are equal, and in an oblong, only the opposite sides are equal, meaning a square is an oblong but an oblong is not always a square, and I suggest that a square can be a coffin, for a bird, say, but a coffin is not always a square, the square does not always meet the requirements of a coffin, the requirements are more likely to be met by the oblong.

I think also how bread and symbolism go together, the way bread and revolution go together, and that although my dad exclaims again and again, 'I'm not Orthodox any more, Jem! We are not Orthodox!' I note that every Friday afternoon before there are any stars in the sky, he seems to find the time and desire to bash off to his favourite Jewish bakery so that upon my return from the convent, pushing open the back door into the kitchen with hello-weekend abandon, I am slap-happy at the marvellous sight of great paper bags filled with bagels, poppy seed and sesame, and two loaves of golden challah lying right there on the white oak table we shipped all the way from our old country, and every Friday before changing out of my uniform, I nip in on my dad who is messing about with newspapers on the living-room sofa.

'Hey, Dad. Thanks for getting bagels!'

'AND challah! AND challah!' he says, cross not-cross that I appear to have overlooked the sheer depth and breadth of bounty he has hauled home for his kids.

'Yeh, AND challah. Thanks, Dad!'

'Should keep you all going for a day or two, ha ha ha!' he goes, slapping his knees with the newspaper, enjoying this conviction he has that his kids are the only ones who do any eating around here, a pack of ravenous hounds invading his house, with appetites beyond satisfaction.

And on Friday evenings my dad will tell me about Fridays in his extreme youth, how before the Sabbath comes at eighteen minutes before sunset, not ending until three stars are counted in the night sky, a story I have heard many times, I don't care, I never tire of it, he tells me how loo paper was ripped up in readiness because no work is permitted on the Sabbath and the ripping of loo paper is work, as is the switching on and off of lamps, or the lighting of fires, a job for which they would pay a local kid, Irish, Scots, something I marvel at also, this hiring of strangers to light your stove so there is warmth in your house on a Friday and Saturday, and the food stays warm.

'What about the washing up, Dad, and cooking?'

'Ahh . . . well, women do that.'

'But it's work, I don't get it.'

'No, no, no. It's fine, it's OK,' he says, frowning a little over the rim of his drink.

'What do you mean? OH! I SEE! It's girl-work. It doesn't count, right?'

'Ha ha ha!' goes Dad, gearing up for his topmost favourite joke to do with girls in his house where the ratio of girl to boy is 3:4. 'That's right! Under the sink with the rest of the pipes!' he declares, heading for Mum and clapping his arms around her, burying his great unruly head in her neck.

Bloody.

And every Friday evening in his extreme youth, my dad tells me, for the first of the Sabbath meals, there would be challah at the table, because challah is symbolic, and his mother would say a blessing over it, which is where my dad's Sabbath story always ends, right there at the blessing moment, as if the mention of his mother puts him in a mood that brings an end to memory.

'Symbolic of what, Dad?'

'Look it up! There are books all over the house!'

And I do look it up one day, seeing straight off that challah is a momentous bread and not to be eaten lightly, which is maybe all my dad wants to do now that he is grown up and no longer Orthodox, Jem, a man with a house full of kids and a lot of work to do and less time for symbols and symbolism.

I read that challah is a word for share, denoting the commandment to offer up a share to God, something Jewish bakers are supposed to do still, pitching a knob of dough into the fire whilst speaking a blessing, meaning there is an awful lot of blessing going on when it comes to the baking and eating of challah whose very shape, oblong, round, triangular, whose braids and humps and seeds or no seeds, all have special significance to do with tablets of the law and the cycle of life, with love, truth, peace and justice and that double helping of manna that fell from Heaven on a Friday for the Twelve Lost Tribes of Israel during the flight out of Egypt and slavery, a very bad time for Jews, forever mindful of the rules from thence, even in the darkest of days, so grateful for the manna that fell on a famous hungry Friday, they mark the moment for all time. *Please, sir, I want some more.* Thank you, sir! And this piece is for You, any time I bake it, any time I eat it, there is a piece for You. I remember.

'Bite?' says Jude, hauling a stick of karnutzel from his pocket.

'I brushed my teeth, Jude.'

'Oh right.'

'How is karnutzel for my womb? Safe?'

'Ha ha.'

'You always keep karnutzel in your pocket?'

'Sometimes. It doesn't squish. Can't really go off. Great pocket food.'

'No life cycle in a stick of karnutzel though,' I say.

'You got THAT right,' goes Jude in Mike's voice. 'And it gives you hell-breath. Oh, hey. Listen to this. On the Sabbath, souls are let out of Hell. There was even some debate, in the laws and commentaries, you know, about water. How we should not drink water then, but leave it all for the dead souls. They cool off at the fountain at the Gates of Eden, and drink until the Sabbath is up –'

'Time, please, gentlemen!'

'Right! And then they head back to Gehenna – Hell. Isn't that great?'

'So it's like bail. Or whatsit. Parole. For good behaviour. Or a Sabbath thing – I mean, does everyone get let out? Is this a joke, Jude?'

'No joke,' he says.

'I bet the women have to stay down below, they don't get let out, they have to cook and wash up.'

'Under the sink with the rest of the pipes!'

'Yeh . . .'

'Zach likes you,' Jude tells me in a small, serious voice.

'What do you mean?'

'He says I have a beautiful sister.'

'Harriet.'

'No, Jem. You.'

'I have cowboy legs! You're supposed to have three spaces between, I have one long space, that's it, I don't have the right spaces!' I reply, quite heated and with what feels like tears coming on.

'Cowboys are fine,' says Jude. 'Are you crying?'

'I don't know, I don't think so. Jude? Is Jeremy there, will he go – there? You know.'

'Go where? Oh. Gehenna. No. I mean, everyone goes for a bit, but Jeremy is OK, he'll be OK, I'm telling you, I'm saying so.'

'OK,' I say, possibly too quiet for anyone to hear, and Jude slips off my desk, stuffing the debris of drinks and snacks into his pockets, even into that left pocket with the rip along the seam, karnutzel ends and empty miniatures, all of it, and he kneels by the bed for a moment before climbing up to drop his body on to me, and I think he cries though I cannot swear to it because everything is so noisy so suddenly, and Jude bashes his chin into my shoulder, his damp curls tumbling on to my eyes and cheeks and mouth, the weight and softness a surprise to me as I take in the slowest breath possible so as not to startle him with movement, with the rising and falling of me, and I smell Jude's smell of autumn earth and mossy rock mixed up with this night's karnutzel and Scotch smells, and my dad's old sheepskin, and something else, an aroma of something like the end of a party when it is time to clear up. *My place is cleared. You want me to clear your places?*

Jude sits up and grips my shoulders, squeezing and releasing, squeezing and releasing, and gazing at me with clenched lips and an expression of gravity and growing resolution, like he is about to do battle and the enemy is great, but the time has come and there is no turning away from adversity as long as you have a dream of return and safe houses, and Jude, Jude is a leader of men.

'All right,' he says, real soft. 'OK. Sleep now. Get some rest, Mac.'

I watch my brother leave the room, padding out in his wet socks and I am not sleepy now, I want to tell him, no, I'm a bartender, there will be no rest for me, never again, not really, for all my life, a bartender. Open all hours.

Lemming, prone to drowning through exhaustion.

My sister scrabbles around in her satchel and hauls out her Biology/Ecology notebook. *Cahier de Biologie/Écologie.* She has clearly applied herself to the decoration of the front cover with great skill and devotion. I behold an exotic array of fauna depicted in their natural habitat of grasses and shrubs and fronds, complete with a subtle expression of weather systems represented by a stuck-on frill of white bandage gauze around the sun to suggest shimmering heat. It's fine work, and I say so.

'Fine work, Harriet. I shower you with laurels. Crown you, I mean.'

'Fiddle-dee-dee,' she murmurs in a modest fashion.

Harriet flips her *cahier* open to a centre spread of mammal drawings.

'*Mammifères*,' she announces with some authority, and I take a look at these pages with the four separate boxes on each page containing all the types of mammals that there are in the great world, arctic and tundra mammals, temperate and forest ones, tropical grassland and tropical forest, fresh and salt water, desert and temperate grassland. Harriet points out the Norway lemming and shoots me a sly glance, but I find myself quite preoccupied with the Philippine tarsier in the tropical-forest box, a small mammal resembling a tiny bear with a long skinny tail and a grief-stricken wide-eyed look. Harriet takes note of my preoccupation.

'Nocturnal creature. Gripping pads at ends of digits. Arboreal. Family, Tarsiidae.'

'Why thank you, Harriet.'

'*Je vous en prie*,' she replies, bowing her head slightly. Harriet has a formal way about her when it comes to her fondest subjects and the dissemination of knowledge.

Next she shows me a drawing of a bird, all coloured in with coloured pencil and shaded very nicely, and pierced by a veritable quiver of arrows indicating the various parts of bird, suggesting a casualty of ancient warfare and famous battles involving prowess in archery, such as the battle of Agincourt wherein French losses amounted to some six thousand men as opposed to six hundred Englishmen, an English victory chalked up largely to prowess in archery. I don't tell Harriet this as she is highly sensitive on matters of warfare and would not appreciate the mingling of warfare and ornithology. War is not among her fondest subjects.

At the tip of each arrow poking into Harriet's bird, is a name for that part of the bird and some names are educational while others strike me as downright obvious, and possibly insulting to a student of the natural sciences of Harriet's rare sophistication. Harriet rattles off the more complex terms for me, such as coverts and rectrices, medians and submoustachial stripes, and then calls out parts of bird requiring no identification to anyone over eighteen months of age with all the expected mental faculties, parts of bird nevertheless requiring the inscription of terms in neat writing according to convent rules for the instruction of *Biologie/Écologie*.

'CLAW!' she says. '*Griffe. Front! Poitrine!*'

'Harriet, you should be able to skip this class, right to the next level, or the top level, even, it's ridiculous!'

'Darling, it's absurd!' she replies in Mum's voice.

'Obtuse of them, don't you think? How obtuse!' I declare as Harriet starts pointing out more parts of bird.

'Back,' she reads, glaring at me with big foolish eyes, slapping her knees in outrage and merriment. 'Chin – *menton*. Eye! Fucking-bloody!'

Eye, *oeil*. Optics, microscope, spectroscope, telescope, I should have been watching him, I should have been watching, it's all I was asked to do, I blinked. Falcons, Harriet told me once, have eyesight eight to ten times more acute than humans. How acute! All birds see in colour. Colour, I have read, studying the definition in my dad's encyclopaedia, is a sensation occurring when light of different wavelengths falls on to the human eye. White light contains all seven colours in the visible spectrum, wavelengths running long to shorter, from red to violet. When light passes from one transparency to another, from air to glass, say, the waves change speed and if they cross a surface at an angle, entering and leaving at different angles, this change of speed happens twice, double refraction as it is known, light splitting into a rainbow, as can be seen in prisms which are used in optical instruments to change the direction of light in cameras and binoculars, and the eye is a camera too. Colouring is an effect of absorption and reflection between light and matter. If you shine white light on to a red book, the book accepts everything but red, it reflects red, it rejects red. Red, white. Red, Ben tells me, is a very useful colour for superstitious types, being prized for this property of keeping devils away. I reject you! I reflect you. On a bad day at Black Rock, Jem, a day like this, you ought to wear something red, you forgot to wear something red.

I remember Jude telling me about the scapegoat ritual on Yom Kippur, the Day of Atonement, a ritual involving two goats, one for outright sacrifice and the other sent bashing off into the wilderness with an encouraging shove, as I suppose, a symbolic goat representing collective sin. A red ribbon is tied around this goat and following his walkabout in the wilderness, he is pushed off a cliff whereupon, miraculously, someone announces to the congregation that the red ribbon has turned white, signifying purity, a message from God meaning He is feeling better about goings-on in Creation and He is appeased and accepts the atonement of all parties. This ritual story had me a bit worried and a pretty stupid question came to mind.

'Jude. Um. The goats thing. That's only in olden times, right?'

'You will be cleansed! You will be cleansed! That's what the High Priest says,' goes Jude, cracking up softly. 'No Jew I know is a goat-killer, Jem. So fear not.'

Remembering this now, I have a Harriet moment of anxiety about the animal kingdom, and recall another Yom Kippur story, a story of my dad's wherein he recounted this business of swinging roosters overhead whilst uttering some verses to do with atonement, every man swinging a rooster and every woman swinging a hen, and praying and then clobbering the chickens, according to kosher rules of course, and giving them away thereafter to the poor, but seeing as my dad was poor and everyone around him was poor, I imagine there was quite a lot of unnecessary chicken swapping going down and a lot of chicken dinners to end the fast. I think about all these elaborate methods of making amends and realise how very complicated is this business of apologising, and how very hard it is for a human to consider himself forgiven, a problem leading him into symbolic acts involving many casualties of atonement in the animal kingdom, sorry goats tumbling to a rocky death and dizzy doomed chickens enduring a terrible state of vertigo before that fatal loss of blood. I am happy to hear from Jude these times are passing, and my dad's rooster-swinging days are over, and then suddenly I picture Soeur Rosa pointing out those five wounds of Christ in Art & Catechism class, favouring especially that grievous folding altarpiece painted by Mr Mathis Grünewald for the Order of Antonines at Isenheim, the centre panel depicting the Crucifixion. This is a very realistic portrait and goes to show that pain was definitely a problem for Jesus and things are not easy for a scapegoat who is not a goat but a man in his prime. At the foot of the cross is a white lamb with a skinny cross of his own slung over one shoulder the way a soldier marches with his rifle, and the lamb has an intellectual expression and a calm demeanour despite the alarming jet of red haemoglobin flowing in a neat stream out of his fluffy chest into a golden cup.

'Behold the Lamb of God which taketh away the sin of the world,' quotes Soeur Rosa, sauntering up an aisle of the classroom in that threatening Italian fashion, checking me out as always for signs of surrender, foreseeing a manic charge perhaps, hands high, straight across no man's land and into her territory, into Catholicism, wherein some people, as I perceive it, feel let off and carefree, all their atonement now done for them, though others feel downright depressed for all time, because this sacrifice of Jesus Christ's is one terrible burden, and something they never asked for and cannot repay, convincing me that the method of individual yearly reckoning, the goat and chicken method that is, like the rending of garments and the offering of dough and the regular adherence to rules, etc., all of this strikes me now as preferable, even fine and wise and certainly not so hysterical and wayward as might be a path to sainthood in Christianity, say. I make this choice, even though I myself am not seeking atonement just yet, no, merely a victory over time, strongly desirous as I am, of a turning back of the clock to the moment I blinked and Gus rode his Ferrari-red bicycle off the dock, suffering possibly the last shock in his allowance of shocks to the respiratory system that he is expected to survive.

Colour is a sensation.

Ferrari red is an official colour, says Gus. He has a biography on the designer at Ferrari, a man by the name of Pnin Farina, so Gus can attest to such things. He has a very big thing indeed for well-designed vehicles capable of great speed and finesse in movement and navigation. Bicycle manufacturers, Gus explains, often went on to apply their design skills to the production of cars, Morris, Peugeot and Rover being cases in point. The trend for bicycle riding in the nineteenth century, furthermore, led to improvements in road surfacing and the development of helpful road signs. Lane control ahead. No thoroughfare. Cul-de-sac. *Keep off the water.*

I see in rainbows now, something that no longer surprises me, because a tear is a transparency and if your eyes are brimfull in a beam of light, light spilling around a door frame at night when you are sleepless in bed, say, or this morning with Harriet in the September sun, light entering my eye at an angle, a tear acts as a prism, colour definitely a sensation, and crying the only luxury, and luxury is a word with a Latin root meaning light.

I tell Harriet about the spectroscope, I tell her the story of Joseph von Fraunhofer, a German maker of spectacles with a perfectionist streak, a man always fretting over the quality of glass and testing prisms in sunlight, until one day in 1814 he noticed hundreds of dark lines in the colour spectrum and kept measuring wavelengths and finding those same dark lines in moonlight, and moonlight, he knows, is only reflected sunlight. Joseph moves on to the study of starlight, this time shining it through a telescope on to a prism, which is how he invented the spectroscope one year later, although he died aged thirty-nine without fully grasping the meaning of the dark lines, a discovery left to another German, a physicist named Gustav Kirchoff who realised these lines were evidence, fingerprints of the elements themselves, the chemical make-up of stars, and so a New Astronomy was born, mingling the camera invention with the spectroscope invention, starmen from thence pointing the new telescope into nebulae and photographing the spectrum of stars, and reading the lines and concluding that the chemistry of stars reflects the chemistry of humans, so I love this story, it is so full of answers, and I tell it to Harriet.

Harriet looks dubious and slightly cross.

'We are a long way, then, from being made in God's image! FULL STOP!' she says. 'Unless He is a chemistry set too. Blow me down.'

'Hazchem!' I say. 'Whoa, Harriet! HaShem, you know – God! Hazchem, hazardous chemicals! Oh, forget it.'

Jude. I want Jude to hear my joke, he'd like it, I want Jude, where is Jude? Red, orange, yellow, green, blue, indigo, violet, I see in rainbows.

'Honey,' my sister says, plucking a hanky from a compartment in her satchel and placing it on my knee. 'It's washed.'

'But it's the Flopsy Bunnies!'

'Oh yes,' she replies in a breezy manner as if this hanky were nothing to her, and not a hanky of moment and stature, hand-washed weekly for my sister, and the very hanky she waved at total strangers on the docks from aboard the SS *Pushkin*, clutching the handrail of the Russian ship she could barely clear with her chin, waving the hanky and shaking her head slowly with a lugubrious expression as observed in old films featuring ships full of soldiers pulling away from docks laden with crowds of mothers and fathers, baby dears and sisters, except that Harriet had things backwards, she did the left-behind-beloved wave instead of the outgoing cheery-brave-soldier wave. Never mind. In a performance situation, liberties may be taken, and Harriet opts for the big emotions as a rule, horror, fear and dread, grief, awe, rapture and outrage. My sister has a great feeling for tragedy.

'I'll just use the edges, OK, not the Bunnies part,' I say, flicking the worst of my crazy tears away by hand before unfolding the hanky and noting how it has been murderously ironed, certainly not Mum's work, this deep cross mark right there where the Flopsy Bunnies are leaning up against the only lettuce they have left standing in Mr McGregor's garden, their eyes closed and paws aloft, felled by food. 'Slithers?' I ask Harriet, displaying the hanky.

'Slithers,' she says, in tones of resignation and forbearance.

We have not had much luck in the housekeeping department since Lisa left us for love-blindness and Portugal and her large family of scowly dark-haired men standing in the sun against bleached white stone walls, and Slithers is our latest hopeless case, though in my opinion her time is nearly up, housekeeping for a family of seven definitely not her calling in life as I believe it was for Lisa. Leave-taking was sorrowful and I recall how Lisa squeezed each one of us, crying the whole time, even hugging my dad with Portuguese heartiness and gravity, and last of all, taking hold of Mum's hands and kissing them and pressing them to her cheeks with her eyes shut, a moment of such poignancy, Ben and Jude went all shy and shuffly-toed. Lisa began the process of leave-taking, however, with Gus, going walkabout with him once her cases were piled neatly by the front door, making a circuit of the back garden with Gus in her strong arms, a scene we all watched from the kitchen window, Harriet and me kneeling on the counter for a prime view. Gus looked fine, I always marvelled at his grace and elegance from his very first days, and how he would perch on a forearm with a trusting expression and an air of calm, the art of balance and movement simply never a problem for him.

Lisa had a lot to say to Gus that day of leave-taking, and I am not sure how much he understood, or what language she spoke in, though maybe it didn't matter what language she spoke in. I remember how they paused for a moment before coming back inside and I could clearly see Gus patting her softly on the shoulder blades in that gesture he borrowed from Mum, a gesture on her part designed to ease burps and hiccups and other internal eruptions of the baby kind, a gesture he began to return, patting Mum softly and gazing at her with a thoughtful look just as he did that day on his leave-taking tour with Lisa, a gesture on Gus's part so much like the offering up of consolation and absolution we smiled to behold it, and I remember carrying Gus around myself and patting him for no good reason but for him to pat me right back, holding my breath in expectation of the very pleasant feelings to come.

After Lisa, we had a wee stream of hopeless-case housekeepers, most of whom simply collapsed under the weight of numbers, the number of Weiss kids, and the number of floors and rooms in the Weiss domain, facts that must have eluded them during interviews in the harmonious and distracting presence of Frances. The comings and goings in the billowing dust and disorder was difficult for Mum, Mum who was still pretty weak from the sea crossing, though always cheerful and busy, only giving in to wee ten-minute naps when yelled at by my dad and chased upstairs, Mum leaving us with an expression of amusement followed by frustration, because illness is an enemy and not an accident, and there should be no surrender. 'Why are you sick?' Mum will ask, as if a cold and mild throw-uppiness were not mere quirks of fate and nature but evidence of wilfulness and a headstrong rush towards that space in the ground and the oblong that is not always a square. Nothing falls upon you, there is a reason for everything, a chain to everything, that is what Frances believes. 'Why did you cut yourself? Why are you tired? Why are you cross?' My mother plays the Why game and she does not give up.

Why did I blink?

I try to smooth away the deep cross mark from the Flopsy Bunnies and I wonder who will do it tomorrow, who will take over Jude's specially ordained Saturday-morning task of ironing out the horrifying and uncool central creases Slithers has forged into our freshly washed jeans with mighty strokes of the iron, making me think there must be blacksmiths and foundry men in her ancestry. Elena who = Slithers, our most enduring of hopeless-case housekeepers, comes from Budapest, Hungary, where there have been many uprisings and crushings of uprisings, accounting, no doubt, for her ferocity with steam irons. She has crushings of uprisings in mind when ironing.

Jude and I invented this name Slithers for Elena, a name so fitting we struggle not to say, 'Hello, Slithers. Goodbye, Slithers,' in a blithe and natural manner, just because of how fitting it is. Slithers never uses the front door for her slithery entrances and exits, she likes the back door only, a door I have to remember to open up for her at 0830 hours on Mondays, Wednesdays and Fridays, because she has a problem with doorbells and knockers, which may be down to revolutionary events in Budapest and the need to slither around like a ghost, evading noisy instruments of torture, or the alarm of guns and loud signals announcing the toppling of regimes and the heralding of new regimes and the shouting of names of new leaders of new regimes, I just don't know. I do show Slithers the doorbell each time, just in case she has a change of heart, but she merely smiles at me in that creepy fashion reminding me of enemy agents and master criminals in spy films.

Slithers wears mud colours, orange and brown clothing in shiny stretchy material, and she brings indoor shoes in a plastic carrier bag, slip-on ballet-type shoes the better for slithering around in, and a cleaning hat also, a see-through plastic cap like the shower caps Mum brings home from hotels all folded up in little cardboard pouches with the hotel name emblazoned thereupon in florid script. Interesting. When I first clapped eyes on Slithers in her shower cap, I wondered if perhaps she once enjoyed more pecunious circumstances and travelled the world in her glory days, sipping bowls of coffee on the balconies of fine hotels, visits she commemorates with a fine collection of shower-cap souvenirs in emblazoned pouches. Mostly, I was cheered at the sight of Slithers in her plastic hat. This woman, I thought, is going to raise a veritable dust storm in our house, she is going to get cleaning and things will be shipshape indeed, and Mum will have a fine rest from housekeeping! I had the wrong thought. Slithers does not do any cleaning at all, she only slides around the house with a duster in hand and a creepy smile, moving objects about and putting them back in the wrong places, just to mark her journey, leaving a souvenir of herself so to speak, before slithering off to some other location in our house, giving me a strong desire to strap some dusters to her feet so at least she will gather up some dirt on her travels. On Monday, Wednesday and Friday afternoons, everyone now has this extra job of shifting furniture and replacing objects, and hunting out missing items of haberdashery, usually to be found inside the washing machine which has not been switched on.

I have observed, furthermore, when home from school on sick leave or on holidays, that Mum has another extra job on Mondays, Wednesdays and Fridays, of serving Elena lovely sandwiches cut neatly in three triangular shapes and laid out on a pretty plate with a sprig of greenery for decorative purposes. Clearly all that no-cleaning and waltzing about the house gives Slithers a sharp appetite, meaning she is largely to be seen lurking in the kitchen eating up Mum's nice sandwiches while bemoaning aloud in strange slithery tones tainted by desperation, What-shall-I-eat, what-shall-I-eat, what-shall-I-eat? three times always in quickfire succession, a foible all to do, I believe, with memories of oppression, uprisings and wartime asperity, and perhaps nostalgia, also, for goulash and cabbage rolls and schnitzel from Austro-Hungarian Empire days, nostalgia which is a malady, from a Greek word meaning pain, going to show you can suffer from nostalgia for bad and good things, uprisings and schnitzel, or even for things you are too poorly to recognise when death is imminent, as it was with Emily Brontë and her favourite evergreen, a shrub with scaly leaves and purple flowers capable of growing to great heights of up to sixty centimetres. Heather, Emily. Heather is the name of that flower.

And so I observe Mum taking on these extra jobs of furniture rearrangement and soup-kitchen chef, and I say to her one evening, 'Mum? Why don't you just go ahead and open a hopeless-case diner or something? No, I mean it, things are getting out of hand. Can't we hire a regular-type housekeeper, you know, someone with cleaning abilities and no war trauma, how about it?'

Mum found my protest very amusing and even when Slithers stole the ring, Mum would not issue walking papers. In the case of the missing ring, there was only one suspect. The services of Black Bob were not required.

The Adventure of the Missing Ring, how St Anthony was not called upon, and how I look back on a life of crime, and other marvellous things.

It is a school morning, a Wednesday, and I am in search of Mum. I need her to write me a note kindly excusing me from PE, because I have had it with wooden horses and I refuse forthwith to hurl

myself over the hard leather back of a wooden horse four-fifths my
height with two iron hoops I am supposed to grip as I leap off the
ground into oblivion, eyes shut and hoping for the best, i.e. no crash
landing and permanent injuries and a hasty excursion to casualty
rooms. It is a horrible exercise and I won't do it and there is only
so much untying and tying of gym shoelaces and circling to the
back of the queue with pretend cramp a person can do without
being spotted for desertion by PE Nun and marched to the front
of the queue at finger-point by sports master, so I call for official
representation in my case against wooden horses. I call for Mum.
I am not in training for the Special Air Service, a division famed
for heroics and acrobatics and formed in North Africa in 1942 by
Colonel Stirling, and I do not foresee any situation in life wherein
there will be this lone choice of perambulation open to me, that is,
to leap over a rock-hard obstacle four-fifths my height, limbs
akimbo. I have checked out the situation with the boys and they
also have wooden horses in their PE classes and a lot of forced
marches and awful shouting going on, shouting being a property, I
believe, of sports masters as a breed, possibly because sports are
deemed good preparation for wartime wherein there is a lot of
shouting and marching. Or because it strikes them that what they
are demanding of little kids is unseemly and ridiculous, and shouting
and marching will prevent clear thinking and gentle voices of protest,
even on the part of sports master himself. Why am I asking this of
little kids? It's ridiculous and unseemly. No. He cannot hear himself.
No one is heard. Listening to Ben and Jude discuss PE practices at
their school, I decide this wild hurtling over leather headless horses
is a crazed phenomenon of my dad's country, which may be down
to war guilt and overcompensation for tardy involvement in World
War II and extravagant self-congratulation for victory on all fronts.

Jelly on the plate,
Jelly on the plate,
Wibble-wobble,
Wibble-wobble,
Jelly on the plate.

In my old country, PE training began with exercises geared to
develop coordination, concentration and teamwork, exercises
performed in pairs to the tune of ditties such as the above, until

we were ready for hardier stuff like ballet, with pirouettes, jetés
and mastery of the five positions surely deemed good preparation
for minesweeping and the scaling of sheer rock faces in deepest
night. Then came field sports and what I now see as the venerable
sports of rounders, field hockey and, above all, cricket and football, sports responsible for skills of teamwork and invention and
quick-fire response to orders, in other words, PE sensibilities and
skills clearly prized in wartime and enough, for the people from
that small island that was once my home, for the fighting and
winning of two World Wars, and not one leather horse required,
as I recall. I tried out this argument one day on PE Nun who sits
watchfully on the side with some knitting in her lap plus a little
booklet in which she records and evaluates our ability to leap over
wooden horses and come out alive, but she was not sympathetic
to my argument, no doubt because she comes from Italy, a country
suffering from confusion and identity crisis in wartime, switching
sides and fighting amongst themselves to boot, fascists and anti-
Semites, socialists and communists and partisans, good nuns and
bad nuns. There are enemies everywhere.

I stride into Mum's dressing room but she is not there. Slithers
is there, flapping a duster at nothing in particular and smiling in
a creepy fashion reminiscent of double agents. There is simply no
escape from this woman.

'I'm looking for Mum,' I announce.

'Not here.'

'Right. Well, thanks.'

I deduce the following things from my swift observations in the
dressing room. Mum is not fully dressed. Mum is in Gus's room,
or downstairs with him, and slightly distracted due to anxiety over
health matters.

Watson: How in the world did you deduce that?

*Holmes: It was easier to know it than to explain why I know
it.*

I try. I explain to Watson in my 7 per cent solution cocaine high,
that my mother never removes her wedding ring, but last thing
at night, she slips off the first ring Yaakov gave her, not putting it
back on until the next morning when she is out of nightclothes and
FULLY DRESSED, leaving the ring right there on her dressing
table near the tiny pillbox she always carries downstairs to breakfast, a box containing gelatinous capsules oozing a mysterious

substance resembling the capsules Harriet pitches into her bath, leaving behind a treacherous oil slick for the next Weiss kid in need of immersion. Mum always carries this pillbox downstairs unless DISTRACTED. Gus is suffering a spell of respiratory disorder so I expect Mum to be with him, in his room, or downstairs in a state of distraction due to preoccupation with health matters, and dressed in a silk nightie and matching gown with one ring on the fourth finger of her right hand.

Watson: You have an extraordinary genius for minutiae.
Holmes: I appreciate their importance.

Mum is downstairs making a coddled egg with chopped herbs for Gus's breakfast. I greet them and bash off upstairs again to fetch her potion box without being asked, I know she won't ask. She will say, 'Oh Jiminy, I left my pills upstairs! What a silly!' whereupon there are likely to be five volunteers for the fetching of pills, because though she may not be surprised by the help at hand, she is always so grateful and moved, it gives one a keen proud feeling of achievement and distinction to help her. Mum has a knack for inspiring devotion and selflessness, whereas I do not. I try it out on my brothers and sister. I go, 'Oh bloody. I left my book upstairs on my bed,' or, 'Fuck-hell, I forgot my gloves. They're on the shelf in the cloakroom!' I say such things and my brothers and sister ignore me completely. I do not have the knack.

I fly upstairs, suddenly worrying about Mum's need for capsules and the substance of capsules, a worry just as suddenly cast aside when I reach Mum's dressing room and behold one pillbox, no ring. No Slithers. A crime, I tell myself, is not always a mystery, something missing, not always lost, so I do not call upon Black Bob the Sleuthing Dog, and I do not disturb St Anthony whose causes are shipwrecks and lost things. Dogs and saints are always busy, often overtaxed. Before you call upon them, set thy house in order.

I cannot be the one to tell Mum about the Adventure of the Missing Ring and related suspicions, because she will mention hardship and education and wartime attrition and then she might refer to that old chestnut of casting the first stone, etc., though she will do all this in a charming manner with a little smile of bemusement on her face, quite unlike the manner of nuns, especially Soeur Rosa who will respond to an uncharitable remark on a girl's part by bearing down on a girl, like that's it, you have just booked your passage to Hell, no refunds. Bloody. Nuns are a threatening kind and cause a lot of fear and despair and premature moral decay and hopelessness in kids because of their nun view of the afterlife which is based on a barter system of good works for time out, and a barter system is open to question and abuses, it is a system vulnerable to the sleight of hand.

First off, Purgatory is a special invention of Catholics, a halfway house on the way to Heaven, a kind of pit stop where a person gets cleansed and purified and goes in for a little suffering of the tolerable variety, no real rough stuff, no Hell-type ordeals or anything. Then there are Indulgences. I looked up Indulgences. This is a racket. An Indulgence is time off from Purgatory, something you earn by reciting prayers, sometimes in front of special paintings or relics, or paintings of relics, such as the Veronica, which is a hanky named in honour of the nice lady who wiped the face of Jesus the day he hauled his very own instrument of torture up that slope to the Crucifixion, a form of punishment reserved for slaves and the very worst of criminals. When Jesus handed the wipe back to Veronica, the print of his face was impressed upon it and that surprised Veronica, it really did, and she kept that hanky for a souvenir, no more hand-washing and careful ironing, not ever again. Jesus was very depressed the day of the long march with a cross over one shoulder and he muttered from time to time, telling the women who were following him to stop crying. 'Weep not,' he said. 'Weep for yourselves, and for your children.' In other words, you will all be very sorry when I am dead. Then he pulled himself together and forgave everyone and accepted his destiny as scapegoat for all sins, for all time, and gave up the ghost, etc., and this is how the Veronica became such a big thing and the most famous souvenir in the realm of souvenirs in Legend and/or History, depending on how you look at it. In 1216, Pope Innocent III allowed FORTY DAYS off from Purgatory for praise of the Veronica. Later on, a person could win 10,000 years off for praise of the Veronica. I don't know. It's all a bit fishy.

There is no Purgatory for Jews. Jews get Hell, Gehenna, and no fooling around, everybody has to go there, due to equality of man and so on, everybody goes right away, at least for a spell, the soul lurking near the dead body, Jude says, not sure where to bash off to, where its final destination might be, hovering for a whole year while loved ones of the dead person, especially blood relations, do a lot of special thinking and praying for eleven months of that year, with high hopes of raising the dead soul from level to level in Gehenna, no soft job, seeing as there are seven levels in that place, according to sinfulness, and ranging from regular bad behaviour such as being in a bad mood or something, to downright unspeakable acts like massacre and pillage with no remorse, and even then a soul gets a day off, a Sabbath day wherein he can do a little self-reckoning while cooling down and taking a long drink at the Gates of Eden, so not all is lost, not as long as he keeps thinking. I wonder what is the ratio amongst dead souls, of Gehenna-bound to Eden-bound, and just how many get raised all the way and will a person have any idea where he is headed by the time loved ones are eating symbolic bagels and boiled eggs in his name? Not knowing may not be a bad thing. When you are Jewish, although you are likely to be oppressed by enemies and continuous anxieties to do with the final destination of your soul, it is better than that barter system, because being in the dark means you are in a lifelong quest for self-improvement, doing the rope-a-dope with your own pathetic failings, ever hoping to come out on top, leaving no casualties. *Set thy house in order.*

My life of crime was brief, but spectacular, due to sheer perversity. My crimes were not random or stealthy and I had one lone victim, which is why I say I suffered, as a criminal, from perversity. I chose Mum, singling out the gentlest and most benevolent person of my acquaintance as sole object of my criminal activities, a person for whom I have an immense feeling. Perhaps this was not perversity at all, and merely good sense. Perhaps some part of me knew my victim was not likely to bear down on me, wild-eyed and threatening in the manner of nuns, but let me flirt with felony instead, and discover for myself there are just too many pressures involved in a life of crime, and happier paths to follow.

Once a week, for maybe eight or nine weeks when I was eight, I strolled into Mum's bedroom somewhere between breakfast and school-departure time, calling out 'Mum? Dad?' in casual tones as if I were looking for them instead of making sure the coast was clear before plucking a 10p coin from Mum's handbag, still not realising she was on to me even by the third visitation when she removed her change purse from the handbag and placed it helpfully out in the open, right there on the dressing-table bench, all the better for plucking from, which goes to show

how blinded I was by the life of crime sprawling before me, into Eternity.

10p was a good haul in those far-off days, affording me enough tuck for a week with room for largesse, something I could not lavish on Harriet though, as she would be suspicious and blab. Crime leads to cold-heartedness and calculation. It's a bad scene, and quite tormenting and I was eager to give it up, but I was caught in a trap. 10p from a handbag = three packets of roast chicken flavour crisps at 3p each and 1p left over for a liquorice pipe with little red beads in the bowl representing embers. I will go to Hell in a handbag. I purchased my booty from Tuck Nun who set out her cardboard boxes in the cloakroom at break time, or in the playground in clement weather, before a queue of girls spending their legitimate pocket money, Tuck Nun like a black marketeer in war films hastily purveying stockings and fags and bread and sausages from the backs of lorries to shifty types in cloth caps and dark circles around their eyes. Types like me. I wheel away from Tuck Nun and scan the horizon for Harriet, clutching booty wrapped in a fold of my pullover, crisps and liquorice that are no compensation for my new qualities of cold-heartedness and calculation. Someone, please, shine a torch my way. Cast a stone, your first, I don't care.

Before long I began finding notes in my blazer pocket, sometimes with a coin attached by Sellotape, or a square of posh chocolate wrapped in green or gold foil. These were love notes, and it was awful, and a turning point in my life of crime. 'Not too many sweeties before supper, darling!' I read, or 'See you later, little goose!' or 'Gus and I will meet you at the gates at ten to four!' And one day, that did it, though I could not say quite why, my conversion accompanied by a state of very unusual pain I feel sure was nostalgia, if you can suffer nostalgia for things not past, not missing, the conversion coming with the sight of Mum behind Gus in his pushchair, Gus lighting up the moment he claps eyes on Harriet and me at the convent gates, his feet rising off their pedestal, a levitation. 'The girls! The girls!' he exclaims, and I think now that home is not always a house, but maybe like colour, a sensation, a matter of absorption and reflection, and on that day nearly seven years ago I had absorbed all the criminal waves I could stomach and reflected something else, not anything close to saintliness, but stand-up and cowboy straight, my black-market days surely over. This is my house and

I will keep it clean, the best I can do, I am my own hopeless-case housekeeper in a lifelong quest with no heavenly promises, those are the facts and I face them. This is my house. I am my house.

The morning of the Adventure of the Missing Ring, the ring that went missing, not quite lost, Mum asked us to be mindful and on the lookout, before turning to Elena with an air of slight distraction and explaining how Mr Weiss bought it for her when they were poor and struggling, and how much sports writing he had to do to buy it and how there were three babies by then with me the latest, and we lived in a small flat near a heath, and then Mum laughed, adding how I napped in an orange crate on the balcony, but there were tears in her eyes as she told this story and lo! the ring came back, reappearing on Mum's very pillow before Slithers left for the day, such a pathetic confession of guilt I knew we were stuck with Slithers for some time to come, which is what I said that evening at supper when my mother reported the case closed.

'I guess we're stuck with Slithers, then.'

'It's a cross we have to bear,' sighs Harriet in a mournful voice, and Jude picks up the baguette from the table and bops her on the head with it.

'Shut up and drink your gin,' he tells her.

'Mum?' I ask. 'Dad? What do you mean by orange crate, what do you mean I slept in an orange crate? You couldn't afford a crib? Did I have a little cushion at least?'

'Nope,' says my dad, real pleased. 'We laid you right on the splinters. Sometimes we left you out all night, ha ha ha!'

'Yeh-yeh,' I say. 'But, I mean, how poor were we exactly?'

'We nearly sold you,' Dad replies, spearing a roast potato.

'Into slavery?' asks Harriet, all excited.

Slithers stayed and we carried on with furniture rearrangement and clothes-hunting and supplementary catering on Monday, Wednesday and Friday afternoons and Jude carried on with his specially ordained Saturday-morning task of ironing away the uncool and murderous creases in our jeans, all of us gathered in the kitchen in our tops and pants watching him work, mashing at the offending creases with a very hot iron, spraying a lot of water over the legs first and smoothing things out and handing them back, pair by pair, instructing us to hop into them quick sticks so they mould happily to the body. When Jude goes a little heavy on the water, we have to grab reading material and lie down near a radiator in wintertime, for evaporation purposes, a scene that confused my dad every single Saturday he stormed downstairs from his study on a tea break, to behold all his kids splayed about the living room with books held aloft and steam rising.

'What do you think this is, a DOSSHOUSE?!'

'Hey, Dad,' we say, quite calmly, letting him stand there for a spell and gaze at us in disbelief and perplexity before moving off in search of Frances, Frances! because, of course, she may well have been kidnapped, or packed up and left in the hour or so they have been apart. Keeping track of Frances is a twenty-four-hour operation for my dad, and full of perils.

'Where is your mother?'

My dad needs to see and hear Frances to be sure she is there. He needs sense evidence and no conjecture in any matter of import, even in what might seem a lesser matter, such as the barbecue. No matter how many times he is advised by Mum and Jude, and most intently by Gus, to PLEASE hold off cooking until the coals have turned from fiery flashing red to almost white, he just can't do it, he cannot trust whitish embers with glowing red cores to harbour enough cooking power for his hamburgers and frankfurters and lamb chops. No. He needs to see and hear it. Flames. Yaakov stands by the barbecue, a vigil, and then the frenzy begins, the flapping at coals with wild sweeps of folded-up newspaper at the sight of a first spark, until flames leap high and mighty.

I am also quite partial to staring at coals. I am forever gathering clues to do with the life cycle of stars and how they evolve differently according to mass, burning up their nuclear fuel and enduring gravitational collapse, and exploding into red giants, supernovae and maybe even black holes, or into neutron stars, white dwarfs and nebulae and sometimes pulsars. I am especially interested in pulsars at present. There is so much to learn. I stare at coals.

'Watch out! Watch out!' Dad snaps in official tones if I come anywhere too near during the conflagration he is encouraging, sometimes even halting me with sharp prods of newspaper like he is an air-raid warden in the National Fire Force separating anxious civilians from their burning houses. My dad the fire warden, my dad the Keeper of the Flame, high priest of the outer sanctum, the Holy Place. Dad has a book I examined because of all the things Jude said the night of Jeremy's funeral and in this book there is a floor plan of the Tabernacle which is the sanctuary in the wilderness God designed, handing instructions, as it is written, to Moses, along with a great many particulars concerning measurements in cubits, specified construction materials, furnishings and knick-knacks, etc. I tried to read this passage in Exodus in one go, but kept drifting off and frowning over cubits and my disappointment regarding God's qualities as chief architect and His serious lack of charm, not to mention the uncertain abilities of Moses in his new and specially ordained guise as building-site foreman. I thought about Mum and Michael and how she is both designer and foreman, and how she has charm in both departments whereas God and Moses do not, and the job was tough enough in the wilderness what with a paucity of construction materials and a lot of tired people far from home, making me wonder just how many hopeless-case builders and decorators there were out there listening to boring instructions and fumbling hopelessly with floor plans, and trying to erect a sanctuary with the best will in the world, but worrying the whole time they might mess up again and Moses will get really mad as he did over the Golden Calf Incident. When your boss is grumpy and lacking in charm and prone to fits of bad temper, your work is likely to suffer, that's how it goes.

The Tabernacle is divided into three sections. 1) The Outer Court. 2) The Holy Place (outer sanctum), and 3) The Holy of Holies (inner sanctum). The Outer Court (1) is reserved for twice-daily lamb sacrifices and libations of wine, and the Holy of Holies (3) is the topmost sacred part, housing the Ark with the law tablets inside, but I am most of all interested in (2), the Holy Place. In the Holy Place there is a Table on the north side for the 'bread of display', the dozen loaves of the Sabbath, a table measuring 1.5 cubits in height, while the Menorah is on the south side, this lamp stand with three branches hammered out of one ingot of pure gold to form six lamps + one lamp, the central one, which is used for lighting the six other ones, all seven lamps being decorated to resemble almond flowers, which are very symbolic, having to do with nature and the life cycle and other matters. I am most of all interested in (2), the Holy Place, because of Dad, and ever since I saw that ground plan of the Tabernacle, I look at him in his frenzy of concentration and watchfulness over fire and food, and I put him right there, in the Holy Place, doing his specially ordained tasks according to law. OK.

I stare at coals and suddenly Dad starts slinging all the meat on to the grill, never in shifts, meaning pretty soon he is calling out our names in a ferocious manner and there is a veritable relay race of kids clutching plates and cutlery because all the orders are more or less ready at once, one of the reasons a barbecue is such a calamitous and sprightly event in our family, one ending in stupor and altogether hard on the emotions, especially on this night of Jude's Farewell Barbecue, or the Last Supper as I call it.

'Jem! Your frank! Jude, your burger!'

'Dad, you forgot cheese. I asked for cheese, please.'

'Tough bananas!'

'Daddy, I don't want a chop, thank you. I'm not very keen.'

'Give it to Ben, goddammit!'

'But my plate is bloody.'

'Give him your plate! Use your noggin!'

Dad dishes up franks and burgers, some with licks of flame still rippling across the surface, never mind, the franks kind of blackened and wrinkly outside and pinkish inside, the burgers a bit crunchy without and not all that far from the abattoir within.

'Dad,' I declare. 'We could get rabies or something.'

'Salmonella, dummy,' says Jude.

'Yeh – that.'

'It's like steak tartare,' suggests Gus. 'Very nice.'

'Gus,' I announce. 'Many moons ago, we invented FIRE. For heating our houses. And for COOKING.'

'Discovered, you mean,' says Ben.

'Right, discovered. But what I mean is, we are a long way from being made in God's image, rah-rah, but no one needs to eat tartare any more, OK? Tartare = RAW.'

Gus starts giggling, his nose nearly in his plate now. Gus has a lovely nose, I must say, and it looks an awful lot like Mum's. That boy resembles her in many ways and it is probably no accident I have a rare feeling for gazing upon him, and I am not much given to the gazing upon and fingering of human beings, meaning when it comes to Gus I am like my dad when it comes to Frances, having a need to see and hear, to have all-out reassurance in the realm of sense evidence, a need no doubt OK and highly recommended for Yaakov and Frances who are in a love situation that is not a blood situation, but possibly not OK for me, who knows.

Dad offers to pitch my burger back on to the grill. This goes to show what a fine mood he is in because he does not take criticism lightly, even in culinary matters wherein his skills are rudimentary, making us mighty thankful his adventures in the kitchen are few and far between. He is known for four specialities.

Speciality # 1. Chopped liver. If my dad decides it is a chopped-liver day, largely choosing a day of rain or snow, he chuckles to himself and rubs his hands together from early morning so everyone at breakfast can tell what is afoot, a chopped-liver day is afoot, always falling, furthermore, at a weekend or holiday, when there is plenty of full-time staff available, though I note everyone scarpers, suddenly very busy and muttering about mounds of homework and overdue assignments, everyone except me, because I am a pushover. I am the lone recruit on chopped-liver day. Some call it press-ganging.

'What a good day for chopped liver!' muses Dad, rubbing his hands together and chuckling to himself.

'Oh no, darling, please!' exclaims Frances.

'Ahh yes! Chopped liver! What do you say, Jem? Who's my favourite child?'

On chopped-liver days, it is definitely me.

I gather ingredients and implements while Dad puts on an old jazz record, one with a lot of growly singing and trumpets and banging piano and Mum glides about the kitchen quickly covering her books and fond items with sheets of newspaper for protection from flying shmaltz and then she heads for the hills, hiding in her bedroom until it is all over.

'What does she think I'm going to do? Make a MESS?! Ha ha ha!' goes Dad.

I run through the rules with Yaakov, reminding him to keep within bounds of the oven and chopping block and on no account to stray out of bounds before I inspect his extremities and digits for chicken fat. Mishaps are not uncommon on chopped-liver day, Weisses all over the joint dropping things my dad has touched, skidding on tiles and floorboards, and unable to get a grip on those light switches or door handles that have crossed his path. I am his right-hand man, doling out pots and pans, knives and mixing bowls, eggs, chicken livers and onions, and a one-man band, also, of rags and dishcloths, mop and broom, so that by the end of the after-noon, I am somewhat delirious, though the chopped liver is very good and I am relieved of galley duties for the night, everyone grateful in their own fashion for my exertions, some nodding sound-lessly and others clapping me on the back with congratulations because I have done it again, I have come through another chopped-liver day one small hero.

Speciality # 2. Plastic eggs. These are served on occasions my dad deems Mum too tired to make supper. She is banished from the kitchen. I am quite fond of plastic eggs, which are an acquired taste, I believe. Mum has not acquired it, but she puts up a great show. Plastic eggs is a one-dish dish involving a sea of mashed potato with a central concavity containing an egg. Sometimes my dad digs the little well for the egg with such purpose, he misses the centre, the egg is off-centre, so that after he has scraped his fork across the potato in an attempt at decoration, the one-dish dish of plastic eggs reminds me of Moby-Dick, the great white whale with his terrible open eye and the map of scars across his body. To sum up, plastic eggs is always a one-dish dish though it can be made in multiple dishes, i.e. in individual casseroles for indi-vidual pleasure, meaning everyone has an egg to call their own, and if you don't mind mashed potato with lumps and bits of potato skin, and egg which is soupy below and tough as plastic above, not to mention spooky thoughts of Moby-Dick, then this dish is for you.

Speciality # 3. Salmon mixture. Cards on the table. This is pretty bad. You can never be sure quite what is going crunch-crunch alarmingly between your gnashers when chewing on this speciality of tinned salmon + salad onions + celery + mayonnaise. You hope for the best, it's all you can do. You hope it is vegetable matter and not bone. Mum says cheerfully how bones are good for one, due to calcium which provides resistance to disease in your very own bones, apparently. Bones, however, small, large, mine or other mammal bones, simply do not rate high on my list of preferred comestibles. The trouble with speciality # 3 is how my dad is not all that thorough when it comes to fishing bones out of a tin of salmon and it is not uncommon to find actual segments of salmon vertebrae in a mouthful of salmon + salad onions + celery + mayon-naise, a danger not always visible to the eye, what with pale pieces of celery and onion lurking therein and how offended Dad is if you start poking at the salmon mixture instead of brazenly raising a forkful, no qualms. I have qualms. I have a plate of salmon mixture set before me and think of mass graves. It's a bone-yard.

Speciality # 4. The barbecue.

'Jem! You want me to put that burger back on or not?'

'Um, well, thanks, Dad. I'm not so hungry any more. I mean, I had two franks. Sorry,' I say, tapping the crust of the burger I have cut open. Tap, tap. Impact basins, I think to myself. Craters of the Moon. And something else. I prod the reddish heart of my burger with the point of my knife and I am reminded of something, what? I don't feel well, everything is mixed up in my head, and this is too close to carnage for me, my bleeding burger bringing to mind visions of animals gambolling merrily in fields with this one heedless notion, of a life without end, eternal, unchanging, but suddenly there is change and a crazed herding into strange and noisy places, and all the rituals of slaughter, the inspection for signs of abnormality and disease and finally the unwitting sacrifice, courtesy of one single stroke of a knife. Make it clean, maybe painless. *Jack be nimble, Jack be quick.*

'Darling?' My mother speaks softly. 'Don't play with food.'

'I know, I know. Sorry. Think of the starving children in India, right?'

'I'll have yours,' says Jude. 'I like it rare,' he adds, reaching for my plate. 'Plus I'm starving.'

'And soon you will go to India,' chimes Harriet. 'You will be a starving child in India. How delightful!'

I watch Jude press my burger between slices of rye bread, the juices running free, and then I have it, that's it! Sacred Heart of Jesus, le Sacré-Coeur. Art & Cathechism. *Prayer sheet with the Wounds and the Nail*, the print hanging in the stairwell that leads down to the refectory and cloakrooms. The *Prayer sheet* is a new acquisition of Soeur Rosa's, Soeur Rosa who is becoming slightly deranged by her big thing for Art & Catechism and her particular keenness for gore and sacrifice. I am a convent veteran by now and increasingly worried for nuns and their keenness for gore and sacrifice. They call it the Passion, which is a clue, if you ask me, to derangement, that they find passion and not disgust or despair and horror in the Stations of the Cross, in this business of trial and murder and fatal torture by scourging, piercing, prolonged exposure in a mere slip of diaphanous material, and bare untended wounds doused in vinegar. Be prepared! Was he prepared? I don't think so. Was he downhearted? Yes, Sister. I think so. For a moment. He wore a ribbon, and it was red. Sacred goat.

There was very nearly an uprising the day that *Prayer sheet* appeared in the stairwell, a great crush of girls on the steps in a fever of physical proximity and agitation, a feature of uprisings that I happen to know is quite typical in the history of Budapest.

'Hey! *Sapristi et tonnerre de Brest, etc.!*' I yell from the top of the stairs before letting loose in my mother tongue, well aware French girls are deaf to any language but their own and prone to zombie looks if you speak in English, a feeble demonstration of superiority on their part and one I endure with magnanimity, having a soft spot for French girls. 'Coming through!' I say. 'Move your bloomin' arses!'

Simone and Marie-Laure pull me by the hands until I am right in front of the engraving. *Prayer sheet with the Wounds and the Nail*, I read. German, late seventeenth century. Germanischer Nationalmuseum, Nuremberg. Whoa. I bite my lip. I am already in trouble due to heresy and the Objectif Lune Incident. There is a momentary hush amongst the girls as they look from me to the print, me to the print. I see three drawings one on top of the other in oblong boxes outlined in black plus a lot of fancy decorative motifs as they are known, and much Teutonic script in between, instructions, no doubt, concerning prayer and penance. The top and bottom engravings are the Wounds, with tears of blood flying out, like the beads of sweat on Milou confronted by a spider, and the middle engraving features the Nail, giving rise to further thoughts, not only regarding the Nail itself, but also regarding just what those open wounds resemble. The further thoughts are sex thoughts. No question about it, that Nail in its oblong box is a penis with intentions. It is also a circumcised one, I note, realising how it is quite possible to be well up on the subject of penises with almost no real live experience of penises aside from rare sightings in my immediate family, which does not really count. I am certain that every single girl in the scrimmage around me is having vagina and penis thoughts also, except for the circumcision part, of course, as they are Catholics and most likely doomed to a sorry future of no-circumcision penises, undignified ones of a sharp and pointy variety I prefer not to muse upon, and so unlike my family's own, more akin to arrowheads, in fact, to wooden stakes, knitting needles and accusing fingers. Behold the Man.

I turn to face the girls. I cannot help myself.

'Girls,' I say in the manner of Soeur Rosa. '*Les filles! Voilà le Sacré-Pénis!*'

My pronouncement causes all-out mayhem in the stairwell, and a swelling of bodies as girls keel over in Gallic hysterics, howling and clutching each other with teary eyes, a habit, I observe, peculiar to French girls, as if mirth were a contact sport, a group activity requiring a lot of hugging and general exertion. This is how it comes to pass that Simone and Marie-Laure pitch headlong down the last five steps or so, with more girls tumbling after them, falling like mountaineers on a guy-rope until there is a veritable heap of hysterical girl on the tiles down below for Watchdog Nun to scream at in her fond torrent of French and Italian, glaring at us white-faced and hands on hips, which is not one bit spooky, because we know Watchdog Nun is a pushover for larks.

All the best nuns are down here in the lower depths, all the best nuns and all the best smells, aromas of espresso and baking and tomato sauce with chilli and although heat rises as I have learned in Physics, it is energy never lost, and here it never seems to escape the lower depths at all, but to linger in defiance of Physics, swirling about in the lower depths, the best place to be, especially in wintertime, a refuge between classes, this engine room of our convent realm, with the ovens going and busy nuns bashing about, keeping the warm air in happy circulation. Everyone likes Watchdog Nun who is in charge of policing and security and office duties, we like her even though she shouts at us regularly and waves her arms about in a delirious fashion. She shouts at us and then she cracks up, because the job of shouting and policing does not come naturally to her and because, I believe, she finds the mere sight of us downright risible, but poignant also, her laugh full of prescience and knowing, as if Watchdog Nun can tell we are in for knocks big and small in our lifetimes, that we are one gaggle of messy humanity and all in it together, nuns and non-nuns, so we might as well do a lot of shouting and laughing and rushing about in warm places while the going is good.

We flip and flop in a helpless fashion at Watchdog Nun's feet in an effort to right ourselves and recover our seemliness. It is slow-going. I reach out to adjust Karina's tartan skirt, mindful not of her modesty but of her dark secret, that is, how she uses her thigh as a memo pad in case of surprise tests, inscribing thereupon key dates in history, chemical formulas and ridiculous geographical niceties of knowledge no one will ever require, such as the names of towns a person can mine for bauxite if so inclined. If you have fine eyesight, it is recommended to sit close to Karina in case of surprise tests. Sadly, she is no good to me as I have discovered from willing those blurry lines to come clean and turn into the formula for velocity or the chief industry and natural resources of the Republic of Suriname, staring as I did at Karina's thighs one afternoon of a surprise test with such concentration and intensity, I became liable for arrest on suspicion of sex mania and perversion.

Watchdog Nun yells at us, mostly in Italian now, and even Slave Nun has paused in her duties to witness the commotion, standing there in a state of wonderment, her trusty mop and industrial-sized bucket by her side. She is never seen without them and is forever swabbing the decks and scrubbing stairs, maybe even deep into the night when girls are home and boarders asleep, girls who are no longer bashing about and scuffing up her handiwork. I say 'Hey, Sister' in a spirit of companionship any time I pass Slave Nun on the stairs or in the muddy cloakroom and she always looks up in surprise and confusion, and without responding in words, like words are just not her thing and swabbing the decks her sole purpose in life, and although this worries me, I also want to take her home and offer her up to Frances in place of Slithers, because I think she is a top candidate, being a lost cause but not entirely hopeless, at least when it comes to hard surfaces of all natures and the application of mops and cloths. Soeur Rosa tells me that Slave Nun cannot read.

'Why don't you teach her then?' I ask, whereupon Soeur Rosa gives me that Italian Catholic look, sly and suspicious and pitying all at once, as if to remind me I am doomed to perdition and were I Catholic, I would understand there are many paths to Salvation meaning some types are ordained to scrub decks while others are ordained to terrorise by Art and a special keenness for gore and sacrifice.

In my opinion, Soeur Rosa is scared. Scared of uprisings.

'According to their works, ye shall know them,' she says in her New Testament quotation voice, and with a wary expression suggesting premonitions of revolt and fear of uprisings and the toppling of world order. Soeur Rosa is Roman and it is possible she is having ancestral memories to do with Thracian gladiators.

Remember Spartacus. Soeur Rosa has a vision of Slave Nun rinsing out her mop and emptying that industrial-sized bucket, all done swabbing for the day, and heading not for chapel and bed, but for the convent library, *la bibliothèque*, to work her way through the shelves from the bottom upwards, level by level, filling her bucket and hauling a few volumes back to her cell where the dust is gathering because there is never enough time left to clean her own 6 1/2 feet x 11, and she has no visitors. Slave Nun is not shamed by dirt, she is dust, dust is her. She is reading up on saints, it is her present subject and her favourite is St Anthony, a Franciscan and patron of the poor and oppressed, of prisoners and travellers, a saint whose causes are shipwrecks and lost things. St Anthony had visitors. The Blessed Virgin and Baby Jesus show up in Anthony's cell one night while he is reading and that is why he is portrayed in art with a washed-out face from too much reading too late at night and the surprising things he saw, and it is why he is painted with an open book with a tiny Jesus lolling about on the very pages as in those pop-up books in the library reserved for little kids in lower school. *Not everyone can read, but everyone can feel.* And so Slave Nun marches right out into the great world in a straight line which, she now knows, is the shortest distance between two points, and she moves at speed. With *velocity*. Velocity = speed + direction.

Velocity.
   The speed of light through space is an absolute constant, but its velocity is not, light can change direction at one same speed.
   Escape velocity. Escape velocity is the minimum speed required for something to keep moving away from a star or a planet, to evade the gravitational field of an earthly or celestial body and not fall back on to it, or into an orbit around that body, and the escape velocity depends only on the mass and size of the body it is flying from, the dimensions of the projectile itself having no bearing on things. The escape velocity at the surface of the Earth is 11.2 km/sec, meaning this is all Mum requires for her rocket trip to the Moon, and it is all Gus required for lift-off from our dock on his Ferrari-red bicycle, and it is far more than Jude requires to pack up his navy-blue hockey bag with fourteen pairs of pants, and Zebedee for the strengthening of his arms and chest and neck. The bust of him.
   You can wear my rugby top.
   When you go out, take your fucking keys with you.

Rag Gus about his inhaler and his medicines. Shocks can collapse the lungs.

Farewell, Jude. I look around at nearly empty plates and the scattering of crusts and rings of onion and chop bones and brackish juices, mustard, ketchup, blood. Marne, Ypres, Somme, Verdun, Passchendaele. Five Wounds. I was hungry before, I'm not hungry now, I'll never go hungry again. I'll never be hungry again. Only Jude is still eating, he has finished my burger and is scooping up coleslaw with rye bread, groaning a little in that manner of his and knocking his teeth with his fork, a habit of his that makes me wince for him, as if it were happening to me, this assault of metallurgy on crown and neck with root below, on enamel and dentine concealing nerves and blood vessels, clearly too scanty a carapace in my case, and a hereditary failing perhaps, my dad susceptible also to toothache.

'Jude,' I declare. 'Your FORK IS YOUR FRIEND!'

'Actually,' goes Ben, 'when Italian nobles made forks fashionable in the, um . . . eleventh century, the Church banned them. They said fingers are godly and forks are man-made, therefore not godly. The use of forks is blasphemous!'

'Really,' I say. 'Maybe we shouldn't use sponges and facecloths, then. We should just lick all our dirt off, paw ourselves clean. Like dogs and cats.'

'Dogs are definitely godly,' says Harriet. 'God bless our dear dogs!'

'Did you know that most household dirt is human particles, dead skin and follicles and so on?' adds Ben.

'Which makes it godly, I guess. And Dad SUPER-GODLY!' I say. 'He keeps it on! Hey, Dad. Had your summer bath yet? Nearly time for your autumn one!'

'My *mikveh*!' says Dad, which is how he refers to his rare total immersion in water, an operation he tends to perform as rarely as possible.

Mikveh. This, my dad tells me, means gathering of waters, a *mikveh* being a ritual bath with special waters, not any old tap water but the natural running kind, from streams, as I suppose, and immersion therein has to do with spiritual purity, and with sex matters also. Men might take a dip on Sabbath eves or eves of festivals, etc., but this bath is chiefly for women who run a higher risk of impurity because of blood and sex matters. This worries me. I hit the books.

In Judaism, I read, sex is recommended. It is recommended for sanctity. OK. Sex has sanctity but a woman has to do an awful lot of washing regardless, taking a proper dip in the *mikveh* before her wedding, for instance, and after she gives birth, and on the seventh day of her menstrual cycle. Throughout the cycle she is officially in a state of impurity and has to keep checking herself out for the slightest stains and changing her clothes and sheets and she cannot touch her husband or even pass him the newspaper or take a bite of his apple or mingle with him in any way.

Sex has sanctity, but a woman has to be clean as falling snow, she has to stock up on soap and have as many spare pants as Jude, and go in for this rigorous personal inspection, and though the book stresses how the impurity is a spiritual issue and not a regular old dirt issue, I am not convinced. I worry about women who are still Orthodox, unlike my dad who is no longer Orthodox and is a man, and would not have this problem anyway, of growing up with an over-the-shoulder feeling, edgy and guilty and uncertain, a girl in a body bound to betray her any moment, what with these particles of haemoglobin, detectable only by microscope, yet enough to condemn her, like a no-scales fish, *terefah*, so that she stands in a bedroom with her loved one, and no fruit bowl in sight in case of impetuous sharing of apples when the time is not right, and she gazes at him without ever feeling quite sanctified, she can never be sure. She shuffles from foot to foot, hearing awful words in her head. 'Honey? Are you washed?'

Mum says menstruation is cause for celebration. I am unconvinced about this also. I do know that for Soeur Rosa, menstruation is cause for prosecution. Clearly she does not see Passion in this type of bleeding, she sees only mess and intimations of criminal behaviour, and last term she told us with a dark smile that in this bloody time we must change our swaddling just about every two minutes and wear extra deodorant and wash our hair every night, threatening to line us up on random days and whiff us one by one, dispatching offenders on a quick march to the showers I have never even seen, showers in some lofty part of the convent reserved for the handful of boarders. Yikes. I now count the days and study my cycles, heart palpitating, praying for periods to fall at weekends and holidays, oh please. Save me from pointing fingers and strange showers.

Sanctity, spirituality, impurity, celebration, prosecution, I am not sure about any of this, especially since the advent of Sex Class. Madame Robuchon, our Sex Mistress has come to us to instruct upon blood and sex in a brief course of lectures the nuns are forced to introduce by law of the land, an imposition that makes Soeur Rosa very jumpy indeed, leading her to hover outside our classroom waiting to quiz us as we pile out of class, whereupon we lord it over her as politely as possible, marvelling at this gulf between us and the power of knowledge beyond the realm of nuns, Hazchem!

Madame Robuchon is full of cracks and fond examples of sex matters from her family history and all the girls laugh, me included, though so many of these cracks are perplexing, giving me a lost and anxious feeling so close to despair, an apprehension wholly new and terrible of something unreachable, of which Madame Robuchon is the very embodiment, perhaps, what with her husband and three teeming sons and her trophy bosom, her joviality and ampleness, signs testifying to an ease and dexterity in sex matters I cannot foresee for myself, another wooden horse, I can't do it, I won't do it. And must there be blood? She says there is blood. And Judaism says there is washing, there is all that washing. *You will be cleansed, you will be cleansed.* I want another note from Frances. Kindly excuse my daughter from sex and blood matters. Oh please.

Boys, says Madame Robuchon in jovial tones, are easily aroused and to make matters trickier, they sport their chief sex organ on the outside of the body, swinging loose and exposed to the elements and flying objects and fleeting human contact and all manner of unwitting provocation. There are four men in the Robuchon household and Sex Mistress has seen it all. Anything can spark it, lingerie ads in a magazine, passing glances, instant reveries arising from the haphazard, such as warm toast plummeting from plate to lap, the brushing of the nether regions against door frames, window ledges, tables and tight clothing, and everywhere they roam in that house, there she is, the wife and mother, Madame Robuchon and her great bosom. Lo! Pop-up. Again and again. It's exhausting, maybe even awful, but the way Madame tells it in her warm and jovial tones, it is a plainly wondrous state of affairs and not a *cauchemar* at all, which is how it strikes me, to be in this perpetual state of sudden arousal and at the mercy of landscape and weather systems, and assault by household items and furniture and haberdashery, boys so love-blind, love-bent, the whole world is a woman, suggestions of my dangerous gender to be found in every curve and aperture, every gentle prominence and soft touch, in the folds and embrace of things, every single day another twenty-four-hour obstacle course of arousal by light bulb and door handle, table leg, eggcup and light switch, by the yielding of sofas and armchairs and the slide of drinking straws into glasses, of legs into trousers and hands into gloves, one, two, go gently.

Arousal by photograph or painting is not the same, it is for the dull-witted, but the running of taps, the trickle and gush, the lighting of candles and smoothing of creases, this is sweet, and for the blessed and initiated, such as Dad, who felt compelled to explain the word *fuck* to me lately, because words are his province, though communication is not, and the reason, I see now, he chose Mum's bathroom for our brief powwow, so he might explain better for feeling her presence there, Frances in the snowy porcelain and curves of the bath and bidet, Frances in the soft white light and familiar glass bottles with their pearls of bath oil and perfumed tendrils and silken tassels at the neck. And when Yaakov steps out later, head bent, she will be everywhere there too, in a slight breeze, in the groaning of trees, the wild blast of wind, everywhere the promise and delirium of her, the whole world is a woman, this woman, I can see that.

Frances!

NINE

Jeremy Levinthal was three years older than me, but soon I will catch up with him in age, because he has been dead for eleven months so far. Jeremy Levinthal had red hair, wild as flames. And he was blessed and initiated, his whole world a woman, one who left him, thus ending his world.

Jude told me that for a whole seven days after Jeremy's funeral, in this time called *shivah*, the Levinthals were not allowed to do any special washing, any lolling about in baths with nice bath oils, say, because that would count as vanity-type washing, involving pleasure and self-regard and so on. They can only splash at the sink in cool water, just so as not to get too crusty and disgusting and they have to wear the same outer garment for those seven days, the one with the rend in it over the heart region and if that garment gets too crusty, it is permissible to change it for another but it must be rent also, in the same place. The Levinthals cannot shave or get haircuts or anything like that and then there are rules to do with shoes, and with mirrors and seating arrangements. There is a no-sex rule and a no-music rule and this is because of the unseemliness of joy and revelry, as if there were only joy and revelry in sex and music and no shadier feelings such as violence and woe, feelings plain to see in the love situation between Nancy and Bill Sikes in *Oliver!*, say, wherein Nancy has a lot of mournful-song moments relating to the sex matter between herself and Bill, a sex matter that became a blood matter beyond repair just as it did for Jeremy for whom sex and music were suddenly woeful only, because the single-most girl he ever wanted to dance with gave up on him to dance with others. The no-sex and no-music rule require revision.

Shoes. Leather shoes are not the right shoes for a grieving person. Jude says a grieving person has to be close to the earth, in a vertical position, forming as direct a link as possible with his ancestry and his offspring to come, with no impediments of hard shoe leather, and standing in a straight line, as I suppose, because it is the shortest distance between the past and things to come. The right shoes, therefore, are no shoes.

Mirrors. Mirrors have to be covered up, due to the dangers of pleasure and vanity and self-adoration. This rule cannot be right. It seems to me that in the midst of days of beard and straggly hair and crusting garments with rends in the heart region, and hard-boiled-egg and toasted-bagel stains, and stark grieving bloodshot eyes, a glimpse of one's falling apart self in a mirror could only magnify the stricken feeling and would not be connected to pleasure or vanity at all. I say, Uncover the mirrors. Take a good long look. See Jeremy there. I reflect you. I cannot reject you.

So there is vanity-type washing, and bare-necessities washing of the kind my dad chiefly favours, and *mikveh*-type washing. OK. Before they wrapped Jeremy in a shroud signifying equality, they washed his body according to ritual and I think how Mrs Levinthal might well have had a *mikveh* after giving birth to Jeremy, her first son, and how that is not fitting in my opinion, a *mikveh* for Mrs Levinthal would be more fitting now, after his suicidal end, now that she needs to feel it is not her fault, and she is not responsible for all things in her sons, and I believe also that Mr and Mrs Levinthal should go in for a lot of sex and music during *shivah*, a word meaning seven, sex and music altogether seemly and not carnival-like, because they know what fuck means and want to remember how Jeremy was made and that it was better to have him for seventeen and a half years than for no years at all. And I say there should be music for Zach too, David Bowie and Peter Gabriel and Johann Sebastian Bach, his favourites, to transport him and open his immortal eyes inwards, into the world of thought, into Eternity, and maybe see his brother wandering there, walking up and down in Eternity, walking to and fro in it, there for ever. *Lo, I am with you alway, even unto the end of the world.*

You will be cleansed.

'The redcoats are coming! The redcoats are coming!' *Les Anglais descendent!* This is how French girls at my convent announce the onset of blood days, revealing an enduring hang-up regarding military defeats and tortured feelings of subjugation, most especially following those military defeats at the hands of the English, *les Anglais*, and in particular, one fine day in September 1759 when the bluecoats were defeated by the redcoats on the Plains of Abraham, thereby losing supremacy in what was to be my dad's country and never really his parents' whose roots were elsewhere, in the Pale of Settlement, a September day with both proud commanders expiring on the battlefield, exhausted as lemmings, and likely dreaming of home. What a palaver. Because of this hang-up regarding military defeats, and a Gallic excess of emotion, not to mention the loss of 1,700,000 men in the First World War, the French have since shown a marked reluctance to engage in military matters, which is why they had a Resistance in the Second. When your whole country fights back, you do not need a Resistance, something I remarked upon in a reckless and lofty manner one afternoon to Mlle Aragon, our gruesome French and Spanish mistress, whereupon she accused me of *dilettantisme* and *désinvolture*, and asked me was my mother Jewish and do we have a kosher diet, this string of accusations and queries confirming my view that Mlle Aragon suffers from a form of dementia. I never heard this word *désinvolture*. I looked it up, believing it might have to do with Count Alessandro Giuseppe Antonio Anastasio Volta, inventor of the battery in 1800, a marvel he demonstrated for the Emperor Napoleon who found it so marvellous, he bestowed decorations upon Alessandro Giuseppe, including the Légion d'honneur and the title of Count, but the word *désinvolture* has nothing to do with Count Volta and electricity, which is measured in volts in his honour.

I turned against this word and decided never to use it in my lifetime due to antipathy. Nobody likes Mlle Aragon who is a nonnun with a lot of knowledge hard to absorb by girls because of her bad personality and because we strongly suspect her of sex mania when it comes to girls, clues to which perversion are evident in her habit of holding unnecessary private conferences on the subjects of marks and personal progress in *littérature*, *grammaire*, *rédaction* and *conjugaison*. She held an unnecessary conference with me one late end of day, catching me in the halls and taking me to task for my new attitude to Voltaire, addressing me in hushed tones at alarming and unnecessarily close quarters whilst caressing the black kid gloves she held in the palm of her left hand in a sly and furtive manner suggestive of sex maniacs and Gestapo officers in torture cells. It is possible that Mlle Aragon is love-struck, it is possible that for her the whole world is a woman, this convent full of nuns and girls a wondrous and terrible place, the hell she chooses, like Lord Nelson on the high seas and Galileo in his moonlit garden. Lord Nelson was seasick, Galileo went blind.

'*Les Anglais descendent!*' Marie-Laure confides to her inner circle, a warning to us that, as she has learned from Madame Robuchon, for five days or so, although not impure, according to her faith, she will be prone to alarming fits of temperament, the charming Marie-Laure we all know henceforward likely to be a veritable grab-bag of spooky moods and emotions. Marie-Laure is a good student in all subjects except Art and she has listened carefully to Sex Lady. A brief reign of terror is her aim and duty. She aims to be something less than warm and affable, to be downright ratty as it is written in sex and blood pamphlets handed out by Madame Robuchon in a jovial manner, pamphlets with rallying captions, 'How Marvellous to be a Woman!' a call-up to the colours. Red for blood and black for mood. For five days, Marie-Laure tries not to help lost causes with their late prep, she tries not to come tops in Physics and History and Chemistry, she tries to be mean with her packed lunch and not go in for handouts to the needy, girls who have left their lunch at home, right there on the kitchen table next to the letters they promised to post for Mum on the way to school, girls like me. Being ratty comes hard for Marie-Laure, the heartiest, most equable and charming French person I have met in all my born days. She is also very fetching, as my dad would say, and Jude likes her, he likes her in the way he tells me Zach likes me. I know this from the way he frowns and growls hello at Marie-Laure on the rare occasions I bring her home, as if she has disturbed his one-track concentration on impending transglobal exploration with Zach by her appearance alone.

I think about Zach with his arm flung around Jude, Zach ruffling Gus's hair and swinging Harriet around in circles by her hands in a game they play, leaving her dazed and walking like a drunk well beyond the bounds of verisimilitude regarding how long it takes for a regular person to regain equilibrium. I see Zach cuffing Ben on the upper arm, a little uncertain with Ben, but full of purpose, and I see Zach pumping my dad's hand, proud to have overcome his days of vulnerability to cowboy cracks and to be standing so very nearly nose to nose with him now, and I see Zach kissing Mum goodnight on his way out, kissing her with great momentum and a subsequent affliction of blushes and I realise how much I like to watch him, the dance of muscle and sinew in his neck and forearms, arms which are corded, Zach all movement and velocity, and I realise also that I am the only Weiss he never touches. Sex and blood matters.

Like Marie-Laure, I wait for the Mr Hyde of me to emerge on blood days, this monthly outrage, yet all I undergo is something paltry, a mild and diverting transformation involving a higher than usual rate of minor injuries to the self caused by the self, toe stubbings and paper cuts and mystery bruising, in addition to a pronounced appetite for curses, all of which symptoms mark me out, Ben decides, as a victim of Tourette's syndrome and not of sex and blood matters at all. Chiefly, though, in these five days, I experience a horror of Soeur Rosa and forced marches along echoing corridors to communal shower rooms, a horror that may well account all on its own for extravagant cursing and minor injuries, but might also be a shadow of an ancestral horror that has come to me in a direct and shoeless vertical path through Yaakov, a horror surely mine to pass on, of Amalek and Phillibert, and the building of shower rooms not meant for washing.

Three days until school, one Jude night.

'You'll probably have to do a lot of washing in rivers out there, Jude,' I tell him. 'They may not have the proper facilities. You'll have to stand in the rain and stuff. In India, I mean.'

'If he's there in the rainy season,' says Ben.

'What larks!' goes Harriet.

'I'm not only going to India,' Jude snaps.

'We know it,' I say.

'Remind us then,' says Ben. 'Of all the places.'

'Yeh, Jude. Where are you headed?' I ask in my *Magnificent Seven* voice.

'Just driftin',' he replies, smiling again.

And then Gus speaks up, in a soft and solemn voice, raising his chin a little and not looking at anyone in particular. 'San Francisco,' he says. 'Hong Kong, Bangkok. Kathmandu, Nepal, Karachi,

Baghdad, Jerusalem, Haifa, Tel Aviv, Cairo, Athens . . .' and everyone is quiet as he speaks, because it's like a song, Gus's song, and Gus hasn't done any singing for years.

In his early singing days, Gus was not sure of his voice, or, rather, his impulse for singing surprised him perhaps, so when he felt a song coming on, he would seek company, not so much an audience as familiar faces, so that if his song felt strange to him, at least he could draw comfort from familiarity. Gus would enter any room where there was likely to be a significant gathering of Weisses, usually the kitchen, or Jude and Ben's room in our old country, and perform brief song preparations, Gus being not quite four when he started having song moments, and an indoors singer by nature until travel became his inspiration, not the subject of travel, but the mere fact of it, velocity some kind of muse for him. Travel is important. Gus's song preparations were wordless, Gus making an entrance wielding either Mum's blood-red record rack, emptied of his aeroplane menu cards, or that orange crate that sat by the fireplace with bits of kindling within, the crate once my bed when we were but one step from the workhouse and debtors' prison. We are in for a song, that's what we all knew when Gus entered thus, stopping in our tracks out of respect for him and the song that was coming on. He turned the crate over and perched upon it, or the record rack if he felt like strumming on the stiff red spokes, and launched into song, no prologue required, always that one about flowers and ablutions and medication, his only number in those early song days.

> I wash my toes every MOR-ning!
> I wash my toes every MOR-ning!
> Dah-lia, dah-lia, DAH-li-AHH!
> Baby AS-pirin! Baby AS-pirin!
> Dah-lia, dah-lia, DAH-li-AHH!

The way he sang that song, 'Dahlia' as it is known, an appreciative round of applause was definitely called for, appreciative but thoughtful, as his tone was rousing and intense and so very different from the later style we came to know, one of softness and solemnity and absence, Gus singing in a voice so private, his gaze so distant and absorbed, we were careful not to react especially, or even look his way, because we did not want to make him self-conscious, and we did not want him to stop. Singing is a delicate business and sometimes very close to breathing and private thinking, like being naked out loud, and so although it may still have felt strange and surprising to him, Gus just had to sing, but did not need our say-so any more, our familiar faces, not really, that song bigger than him, and there he was with it, travelling the world in our light blue Renault and then the decks of the SS *Pushkin*, Gus in backs of cars, Gus riding the waves, recording his impressions of the Universe without judgement, except for in his very voice, awestruck and mournful at once, full of celebration and farewell, as if to say, if you look real hard, there is grief in all things, in all places, even in the uttering of words, and the echoes of them.

> Sticks and old ladies and fishing rods,
> Mountains and grass and rocks.
> Sky and fish fingers and fried eggs and chips.
> Binoculars.
> Sea and clouds and whales.
> Yogourt and honey and Meccano.
> Cars and cranes and birds, and Mummy.
> Handkerchiefs.

I think of these two voices of Gus and the difference between them, the new voice, soft and solemn, against the old voice for the old song, intense and rousing, and I wonder if maybe Gus's old song was a warning to us, an intimation he had of future difficulties with respiration, with lungs and breath and the shortness of it, and the wheezing to come, the constriction and swelling of the bronchi, and the asthma caused by allergies, making it extrinsic, and by infection, making it intrinsic, and by the malfunction, also, of the autonomic nervous system, meaning asthma, therefore, can arise in all things, in all places, at any time. And maybe it was no warning, just Gus singing the world as he saw and felt it, because he had to see and feel it, and on his mind in those early singing days were flowers and aspirins and washing, that's all, simple things, or hard, like breathing and thinking, it depends how you look at it.

'Shall I get the camera?' says Mum.

Jude's barbecue is definitely an occasion! We do not go in much for photography around here. We are not snap-happy like some

families I know. I visit friends on holidays or at weekends and see
parents roaming the house of an afternoon, skulking in plain view
around door frames, sneaking up on their kids like hopeless-case
spies, snapping them at every opportunity, before walking off in
smug triumph, chuckling softly to themselves because they have
captured one more piece of evidence for that file they will slap in
front of their grown kids some fine day in the future, or on a Bad
Day at Black Rock, evidence for prosecution or defence, who can
tell. Here's what you were, what you did. I saw you.

It's weird behaviour, and responsible, I believe, for alarming
quirks of personality in those of my friends with snap-happy
parents, some girls muttering excuses and running for cover at the
mere sight of a camera and others displaying signs of showman-
ship and extravagance more befitting circus acts than casual gath-
erings involving glasses of sparkling apple juice and grilled cheese
sandwiches in family settings. And so I understand how the Church
became frantic about the use of optical aides in the thirteenth
century, associating the wonders of lenses with corruption and
sorcery, although hypersensitivity in fifteen-year-old girls in the late
twentieth century was perhaps not the terrible state of corruption
and sorcery they had foreseen. Just as the Church sat up in horror
when, thanks to posh Italians, the fork came between godly man
and his daily bread, the magnifying and clarifying properties of
convex slivers of glass could not be right and seemly, only magical.
What we cannot see clearly should remain obscure, as is ordained,
and like the bending of light and the birth of time, no one should
see this far, as far as a Universe maybe not God-made, not God-
designed, but born in a bang and evolving in clouds of gas and
dying stars and supernovae explosions, and this continuous flow
of elements light and heavy. But what could be godlier, I wonder,
than being made from stars? If God exists, He is a dying star.

Roger Bacon, the Franciscan friar from Oxford, b.1214?, d.1292,
was known as Doctor Mirabilis. Doctor Wonderful. His study of
stars led him to criticise the Julian calendar. He is thought to have
invented the magnifying glass and he had many visions of the future,
predicting spectacles and microscopes and telescopes until he was
jailed for heresy, dying shortly after his release, depressed, I am
sure, oppressed for his vision. *Damned dogs*, he might have written,
in the manner of Robert Hooke.

The Church taught that failing eyesight and dimming perception, your near becoming farther and farther, is all evidence of sin, just another knock to be endured because of that sex situation between Adam and Eve, how they fell for each other against regulations, quite understandable in the circumstances, in that empty world, Eden not Eden, Adam and Eve decided, without a family, and a house maybe, no doubt their next move, the building of a house of straight lines and tall sheets of glass, the better to view Eden from. In Christianity, this sex situation is a doomy event with no let-out clause, a green card for unspeakable deportment as issued by nuns, condemnation not for a week, but for all time, not negotiable. You cannot fix this thing. Jews are less hysterical when it comes to sex matters, apart from that washing business, of course. Sex is recommended. In Judaism, the chief consequence of that situation between Adam and Eve is our present state of mortality. We are not immortal. OK. This means Jews can get on with things and not waste a lot of time fretting over the seemliness of visits to the optician, even very fretful Jews, such as Isaac Babel, who wore little wire-rimmed spectacles quite like my own.

Jews do not fret over the use of forks either. In kosher homes, in fact, the case can be made for Jews having a very big thing for forks, and for cutlery in general, separate sets being required for the consumption of *milchig* nutrients and *fleischig* nutrients, and a topmost special set of cutlery reserved for Passover, with any brand new forks and knives and spoons, not forged by other Jews, having to go in for ritual washing, a *mikveh* all their own. Your fork is your friend! Your knife is your friend! *You will be cleansed.*

'Well? Shall I get the camera?' asks Frances. 'Will I need a flash?'

'Mum! We all know what the sky looks like! No more photos!' I declare, and everyone thinks this is pretty amusing, even Mum. Whenever Mum snaps a family photo, the main feature is sky with maybe the tops of heads below, sometimes only the hair part but often also foreheads and pairs of eyes, bespectacled and unbespectacled, so that a peruser of the photo will have a fair idea of the weather systems and celestial motions on the day that photograph was snapped, and not much else. People not so well acquainted with the tops of our heads definitely have trouble making out just who is witnessing the exciting events happening in the sky that day. It would be an exaggeration to say there are no photos snapped by Mum featuring anything more than sky and our ruffled heads, as we are in possession of a tiny collection of photos with more anatomy within the frame, sometimes right on down to the knee region, and once there was the whole of Jude's upper body in close-up, tossing a football round and white, that football with the signatures of Gary Sprake, Johnny Giles and Alan Clarke of Leeds United FC scrawled across it in suspiciously similar handwriting, and plain to see, because Mum snapped that close-up of Jude at the precise moment the ball covered his face. Oh well. We all know this is Jude because his hair is in the picture, his curly dark locks floating above a white football. I would know those locks anywhere.

Wot ye what I am?

Yes! You are my brother, nearly my twin.

In fact, I have come to prefer those photographs of Mum's featuring a lot of sky activity and our topmost extremities only. They are clues, and proof that Frances is forever looking up in life, a reflex, Frances searching the skies, trying to see beyond the edge of the Universe, beginning with the Milky Way and lingering over the Moon in all its phases and reading the signs to be detected even in a seemingly bland patch of sky, because what may appear plain to a casual observer is fraught with change and fascination to anyone for whom the sky is a calling, home, like ice for Shackleton. And just as the ice photos Frank Hurley took for Shackleton include the remains of his ship, or a scattering of dear dogs, or tight huddles of frostbitten men, Frances includes our dear heads, her eyes are sky-bound but she is doing a headcount, always.

Are you all well?

All well, Boss!

'Very amusing!' says Mum in her over-the-shoulder fashion, skipping up the terrace steps into the house for her camera, and before little over a minute has passed, my dad begins to fall apart.

'Where is your mother?!'

'Dad!' I say. 'Cool your jets! She's getting the camera, she'll be back in a sec.'

'Achh, she's probably doing other things on the way!' he says, kind of disgusted and despairing, like there is just no controlling his wife and mother of his children, and she is betraying him yet again by her very absence, her daily flits, prolonging the agony of separation by lingering, maybe, over an open book, and picking up stray kid clothing or going to the loo on her way to the camera, leaving Yaakov helpless, edgy and uncertain, and with a growing doomy feeling. The world might end right this minute and look how she has left him amongst strangers in a strange land, because stripped of Frances, he is always alone, even tonight in a crowd of his own children, children who are shadows of her, her but not her, the worst thing of all, how can she do this to him?

My dad falling apart in the absence of Frances is all science, something I have learned from my study of binary systems, something scientific I am sure Frances understands and my dad does not. Nearly half of all stars are binary stars, fellow stars in binary systems that orbit each other in periods lasting from hours to thousands and thousands of years. Some binary stars are born together from a proto star, which is an embryo star, or else one star will capture another after birth, more of a mating-type binary situation. There are different kinds of binary stars depending on relative mass and, above all, relative closeness, and in order of closeness, these are: visual binaries, spectroscopic binaries, eclipsing and cataclysmic binaries, and novae. A person can spot visual binaries by telescope or even binocular, making it a visual binary. Spectroscopic binaries require detection by spectroscope, a word that always fills me with awe and sadness because of Joseph von Fraunhofer, the optician and physicist whose science career began with one miracle and ended in another, yet before he could fully grasp the meaning of his own discovery, the revelation in the black lines he saw in white light through a prism. Joseph was poor and when the roof fell in on him one day at work while he was busy polishing eyeglass lenses, he made it out of the tumble of plaster alive, receiving many slaps on the back from his fellow opticians for this feat of survival and also a big pecuniary reward so that he was free to pursue science and invent the spectroscope and measure wavelengths and puzzle over black lines, only to die aged thirty-nine, in his very prime of scientific endeavour, which is why his gravestone bears this epitaph in Latin words, *Approximavit sidera*. He approached the stars.

Joseph died from tuberculosis, an infectious pulmonary disease. Death by pulmonary disease and respiratory disorders is considered quite romantic, and portrayed in films by types with pallid demeanours spluttering in a pathetic fashion into extravagant flowy handkerchiefs before expiring gracefully on to a heap of pillows, arms akimbo, the lovely hanky with its terrible revelation of pulmonary disease spilling decorously upon white bedclothes, blood on snow. Veronica.

In films involving the tubercular type, there is always a fine linen hanky in pretty good shape, not at all disgusting as one might suppose, aside from that telltale spotting of haemoglobin the tubercular type does his very best to hide from loved ones in a furtive manner, the study of scarlet for his eyes only, betrayed merely by that flicker of private despair and a reckless toss of the head, denoting fearlessness in the face of doom and demise. My days are numbered! I do not know the meaning of fear! For the romantic victim in films there is usually an interesting bed, a bed that is now home. Sometimes it is hard and unyielding, sometimes soft and billowy, or may be a chaise longue if the tubercular is a girl in the nineteenth century. Camille, for instance. Camille has a chaise longue. The interesting bed is a place for decision-making, decisions to do with sacrifice. You might think that waiting for expiry from fatal disease is sacrifice enough, and that the tubercular type ought to be in a very bad mood and not in the least in the sacrificial vein, but these would be the wrong thoughts to have. In films, sacrifice is uppermost. Tubercular types in a selfish bad mood is just too depressing to behold and no one would go to the cinema where films are playing featuring fatal pulmonary disease. That's how it is.

Camille is a famous case. She is famous for infectious pulmonary disease, sacrifice and sex. She is a nice woman whose chief flaw seems to be merrymaking. Party-going and party-giving. In black-and-white films, a mania for parties is symbolic. Parties = sex. Disease, of course, is very symbolic though the symbol is various and extremely dependent on character, being a first prize or booby prize dependent on how very nice or very bad you are, which is kind of confusing seeing as the end is the same, the end is death and burial. Camille has a prize-winning death. She has a dodgy reputation in society due to sex matters but she gives up her beloved, who has a fine reputation in society, so he will not be infected by her dodgy reputation in society. Go away, I don't love you! she says, which is a lie and is what makes her famous for sacrifice. In life, there is simply no *mikveh* big enough for Camille, but never mind. Death is so rewarding. Always plan some nice sacrifice before you go, just in case of flaws of character in your lifetime.

I leave you my Shane jacket.

Films are not always good on reality. They are more symbolic. I do not think respiratory disorder was all that romantic for Mr

R. L. Stevenson, a real-life writer and travelling man and son of a lighthouse engineer. This I deduce because Robert Louis is famous for a book about a doctor clutching his throat in agony before turning into a tortured person with murder in mind. Emily Brontë was certainly somewhat edgy on her dying day, as per usual, being quite prone to edginess as a rule. Pulmonary disease did not put her in the sacrificial vein. She remembered her dogs though. Feed my dogs. And if Joseph von Fraunhofer had not caught tuberculosis, he might have come closer to the stars, and delighted in binary systems, especially, of course, of the spectroscopic variety, but he died in his very prime, for no good reason, for reasons of tuberculosis, right in the middle of his great work of approaching the stars, and this is why there can be no realistic film about him that would not leave an audience stark-eyed with gloom and frustration and hopelessness in the face of disease, and wanting their money back.

Eclipsing binaries, cataclysmic binaries.

Some pairs of stars are odd couples, a cool giant and a hot young star orbiting each other in such an intimate fashion you can only tell them apart in an eclipse when there is the greatest dip in the light curve, with the closest pairings of eclipsing binaries known as contact binaries, some pairs so tightly bound, a white dwarf in a pair will draw gas from its companion and grow into a neutron star, or a pulsar even, a pulsar being a spinning neutron star, my favourite, like a lighthouse. Finally, amongst the inseparable pairs, there can be cataclysm. This involves flashes and surges of brightness, and the spiralling of gas with explosive results, the outer layer of the white dwarf blowing off into a nova, dwarf nova or supernova, and supernova remnants are made up of neutrons, some of which are pulsars, and of black holes, and interstellar gas, the birthplace of things, the heavy elements swept up into new stars and rocky planets, and into humanity itself, as Fraunhofer would surely have seen had he not died of romantic disease before he could swear to it, what he came so close to recognising in those black lines in the spectrum of light, that all the elements of life are here, from the aqueous humour in his eyes and the calcium in his bones that withstood a collapsing roof to the fragile tissue in his willowy lungs.

There is another clue to understanding Yaakov and Frances in my study of binary systems. *The wider the separation between bina-*

ries, the longer the period of orbit. And this is what Frances knows and my dad does not, and why Yaakov is frantic just now that Mum is in the house longer than he expects, whereas she knows it is a good thing, it is good for the period of orbit. Frances is well up on stars and celestial motions and my dad is not.

'Where is your mother?!'

Dad is really quite jumpy now, and I know the feeling. My jumpiness in the absence of Frances has to do with visions of a ship journey and something lost at sea and her subsequent sojourn in hospital and my new and most telling mission of looking out for Frances, not an easy job because she will never let on when in need, she will not go in for helpful signs of swooning and near death throes or the ringing of bells in the manner of Dad, an expression of need he goes in for even when he has a mere case of sneezes or something, reminding me very much of Sir Urré in *Le Morte D'Arthur*, Sir Urré the wounded knight of Hungary.

Book XIX, Chapter 12: *How Sir Launcelot was commanded by Arthur to handle his wounds, and anon he was all whole, and how they thanked God.*

Sir Urré had a problem with wounds. He was a fine knight and well liked and generally very preoccupied with slaying and jousting and rescue call-outs and other marvellous things until the day he slew a knight of Spain and endured very hard knocks, coming out of this bout with seven wounds, three on his head and four on his body, including one on his left hand. It is not reported how grievous was the hand injury, or whether or not he was a southpaw, but in the scheme of things, he was in altogether bad shape. It is possible also that Sir Urré was Jewish, a Mr Isaac Babel of his times, what with being a knight in a period of uprisings and a bit of an outsider, hailing from parts of what was to become the Austro-Hungarian Empire, and not all that far from Odessa on the Black Sea, the birthplace of Isaac.

Unfortunately for Sir Urré, the Spanish knight's mum was a great sorceress and she was understandably in a very bad mood after her son's death in battle and so she condemned the Hungarian to fester and bleed until the unlikely time 'the best knight of the world had searched his wounds'. Sir Urré knows where to go. He bashes off to the Round Table where all the best knights abide. One hundred and ten knights search his wounds. No luck. He is still festering and bleeding. Arthur is anxious but he does not give up, even though these are hard times at the Round Table, Arthur having just lost his top knights Perceval and Galahad to the Grail quest, Sir Bors burying Perceval right there alongside Perceval's sister and Sir Galahad in the spiritualities, just as she predicted before bleeding that dishful of blood, etc. Sir Launcelot is the best knight left in the world. So far. The palaver with Guenevere and the sorrow and lamentation of the king for the collapse of things and for the strong war made against Launcelot at his castle called Joyous Gard is all to come. Yet Arthur is on the slippery slope. Here is what he says.

'Mercy Jesu, where is Sir Launcelot du Lake that he is not here at this time?'

Where is your mother?

And lo, Launcelot arrives and quick sticks gets busy searching Sir Urré. Arthur asks the Hungarian how he is feeling.

'My good lord, I felt myself never so lusty.'

This is very interesting. You might think Sir Urré would seek out a sorcerer to undo the spell of the Spanish lady sorceress if he was that inclined to fall for sorcery. You might think he would simply fetch up in some doctor's office. No. He is a needy knight and highly strung and quite suspicious of doctors, and it is just possible that festering and bleeding is largely in his imagination and that he is just too susceptible to curses and spells, meaning what he really needs for recovery is a lot of attention. He wants to be amongst his own and go in for dramatics and get searched by all his friends. He wants the best knight in the world. My dad is like this.

Where is your mother?

Dad suffers from wear and tear in the lower back and knee departments, recurring injuries of varying gravity I fancy are down to his days of amateur boxing and scurvy, and no doubt also to an ancestral legacy of wandering and exile and self-defence in the face of generations of enemies. When it is all very bad with him, Mum sends him to bed so we can have a little peace and get on with life, moving freely about the house without being at the mercy of Dad and his endless needs, especially for fresh drinking glasses, a different one each time, out of which he will swallow maybe half a teaspoon of water in order to take his tablets bang on the hour according to the rules, making you stand there while he does it so he can hand the glass back to you and force you to witness the horrible agony involved in swallowing water without single malt in it.

'You can take it away now,' my dad says, swooning into the sofa and waiting until I have nearly cleared out of the living room before asking me for some other thing.

'What, Dad?'

'Come here.'

'I can hear fine from where I am, Dad.'

'Come here, Jem.'

'OK.' I move close, stamping the path between us. 'Right then. What now?'

'I need you to push those magazines a bit closer.'

'Are you serious?' I say, aghast.

'What do you mean? Oh, and switch off that lamp. I have to nap.'

Mercy Jesu.

When my dad is wounded, the whole house resembles a field hospital in World War I with exhausted nurses and orderlies running to and fro, nerves fraying, hunger gnawing, no thought for themselves, and that is why Mum made that fine decision to confine Dad to his bedroom in particularly bad spells, giving him a little white porcelain bell to ring in case he needs her. Big mistake. It was terrible. The bells, the bells. One Christmas time he twisted his knee ever so slightly hauling supplies out of the car boot, my dad always choosing holiday times, I note, for injury and convalescence so as to be sure of a full house of on-call nurses and orderlies, especially in winter when we are more likely to be indoors for long periods and within earshot. I stole that porcelain bell from him when he scuffled out of bed on a loo break. I hid it in the samovar. Well done, Jem. I received furtive pats on the back all round.

Then more bells. A different pitch. I know that sound.

'Dad! Where did you get that bell?'

'Ha ha ha ha!'

I recognise the bell in his hands. It's that wee iron bell of Mum's, worn and a little rusty and misshapen, probably downright old and antique and rare, etc. It hangs in the tree outside her bedroom window, making haunting echoey ringing noises in the winter night, very nice.

'Mike got it for you, didn't he?'

'Ha ha ha ha!'

'It has to go back in the tree, you know, Dad.'

'Well, give me back the other bell, then!'

'One for one,' I say.

'OK,' he replies, handing over the rusty bell.

I run off with this bell also, stashing it in my room and ignoring his hollers, which is when he storms out of bed despite his grievous injuries to take the cowboy ranch type triangle off the hook in the kitchen, the triangle Mum gave him as a fond cowboy-type joke present, a triangle he is overfond of banging to wake us up at week-ends or call us in to dinner, clattering away at it with increasing gusto the closer we get to him, having a really, really good time watching us wince in pain and clap our hands to our ears, Mum included.

I try again to do a deal with my dad. I stand in the door of his bedroom and think about redcoats and bluecoats, no difference between them when it came to that shameful spreading of blankets and the awful swapping of ageing firearms and cheap plugs of tobacco and broken pocket watches for beautifully woven throws, for furs and jewellery, and for land, our small and passing pleasures for your very roots. Fair? Not fair, so what. I forget about shame. I spread out my blanket.

'Dad. I will give you the white bell back if you hand over the triangle. Fair?'

'You said that last time. Bell first.'

'Dad! I don't have time for this! I'm helping Mum with dinner! It's nearly time! Triangle, please!'

The word *dinner* is a bribe. My dad goes all grave and attentive at the mention of this word *dinner*, same as Pax! who still perks up in readiness when dinner is announced although he has grown quite dignified with age and education, not always joining in on every sledge ride, for instance, but gazing upon us from the heights of our driveway, almost stately and solicitous, showing a lot more restraint and composure than in his extreme youth, and I wonder if it crosses his mind to feel the loss of those days, his all-out gambolling days. Harriet says dog time is different from human-being time, kind of high speed, making me think of pulsars again, pulsars that eventually slow down because something has to give, something has to pay for the powerful radiation that spans the entire electromagnetic spectrum, radiation responsible for that great sweeping beam of light, a beacon flashing at regular intervals until, but for sudden sharp changes in speed known as glitches, the rotational energy is drained away and the pulsar slows down. Pax! has glitches too, racing alongside us as in olden times, barking with the same old ferocity, loping in the snow and clamping his jaws around Gus's wrists, but only at random now, maybe every third toboggan run on a sledging day, Pax! slowing down, it's visible, I see it.

'Give me the triangle, please.'

Dad has an expression of deep concern on his features over this matter of dinner and he surrenders the triangle no problem, a boxer dropping his gloves.

'What are we having, Jem?' asks Dad.

'HAVEN'T THE FOGGIEST!' I reply, making off with the triangle, helter-skelter.

'HEY! The BELL! JEM!'

My dad won the white bell back in the end because after he lost the cowboy triangle, he bashed off upstairs for the hand-held air-raid siren Jude bought him from an army surplus store so Dad could gather Mum in from the garden in the summer months without roaming all over the grounds calling out 'Frances! Frances!' in that frantic manner, causing panic stations for the entire Weiss family, something he preferred to do regardless, as it turned out, only once cranking up the air-raid siren, only once until this time of the Stolen Triangle Incident, the Christmas of his slightly twisted knee when I robbed him of bells.

I have since changed my mind about bells. I want to assign a bell to each Weiss, Pax! included, bells with a varying pitch each one, a bell for ringing in case of dark days or calamity even, a falling roof, an ambush, a blood situation, anything, a bell useful also for the signalling of comings and goings and announcements to do with discoveries and revelations, a bell, of course, not one bit useful in cases of fatal disease when no amount of bell-ringing can summon the succour required, not even from the best knight in the world, powerless over days of swooning and festering and the ache of ringing bells that can bring only a fresh supply of extravagant handkerchiefs and the presence of familiar faces.

Until I find the right bell for Frances, I need to look out for her, she must never get tired again. And so before that summer Jude went to mining camp and came back and left again for all the places in Gus's song, and Gus rode his bike off the dock, before all that, and as soon as I realised Slithers and other such hopeless cases were fated to stay because of Mum's charity and compassion and so on, I draw up a list of kid tasks, with days of the week written along the top and names of Weiss kids in a column down the left side in order of primogeniture as it is known, and in the spaces where a name meets up with a day, I inscribe a task. I think up ten tasks, two each, and then I write these words right above the days of the week, writing them in capital letters with thick black ink for due emphasis, **TEN COMMANDMENTS**. I am quite pleased until Jude comes along beside me, propping one elbow on the table and resting his head in that hand, the better to peer at my handiwork.

'613. There are 613 commandments,' he tells me.

'Ha ha, that's ridiculous.'

'I'm serious, Jem.'

'Well, I never heard that before,' I say, a bit worried now.

'They're sort of subdivisions,' he continues. 'Positive and negative charges. 248 imperatives and 365 prohibitions. But they are commandments. That's how it is.'

'Forget it then!' I shout, scrunching up my page and starting all over again, thinking up a new title in the process and writing it in on top in a thick and more hasty scrawl of big letters, in a hand freed by despair and frustration, **BY THEIR WORKS (YE SHALL HELP HER)**, I write and underneath I put in a subtitle, just for the hell of it, in skinny capitals: SHAKE A LEG!

I don't bother about the number ten any more. I am freed from the tyranny of number ten. I concentrate on making sure everyone has tasks they do not mind, as close to specially ordained as possible, because a task you do not mind does not really feel like work, which is why I write 'ironing: jeans' in the space where the across line leading from 'Jude' meets up with the down line from 'Saturday'. Jude likes this job. This is my private feeling about the Sabbath matter also, and those thirty-nine forms of work you are not supposed to do. Prohibitions. If it does not feel like work, maybe it is not work at all, but that is not the main idea according to my study of the Sabbath, the main idea is to free yourself up for praying and deep thinking and reading up on laws and rules, etc., and remembering how God is tops at everything and you are not, you are a mere mortal and a bit haphazard when it comes to work and creating, and even God required a rest on the seventh day and you have to respect that by not carrying on working all seven days like you are better than Him. Things are hard for God. He made the world in six days and then He packed up His tools and that's it, He never really did anything else. And now He is fretting up there, especially on the seventh day when some of His people might be carrying on with works and creativity. He is worried some Jewish person, maybe even a girl, will come up with something better than He did, a cure for fatal disease, say, and then He will get depressed about His prowess in all things, and about how He is diminished, how He has let us down. Thems the breaks, if you ask me. This is the price He must pay for working one single six-day week in His whole immortal life.

Thirty-nine sounds like a lot of prohibitions, a lot of works not to do, but as I understand it from running through the list of no-go fields of work, unless you are a baker, dressmaker, or in the fur trade, and definitely in the mood for hard labour on the seventh day, skinning and scraping pelts for instance, you will not run into trouble, and really need only be mindful of basic prohibitions, such as not carrying burdens or switching lights on and off and chin-wagging on the telephone and other tasks that have been updated to modern times upon the advent of electricity and the motor car and so on. In other words, a person can loll about for twenty-five hours with a fair supply of snacks and reading material, breaking off every so often to gaze thoughtfully into the middle distance before and after a good night's sleep, and this is deemed restful and respectful, and is more or less what Jude does all weekend anyway, apart from that ironing job on Saturday morning. And I note another thing in this list of prohibitions. There is a let-out clause, an imperative, in fact, whenever there is a life at risk, to indulge in any form of work on this earth you might think neces-sary for rescue of that life. To save a life on the Sabbath, you can do anything, you must do everything. Carry a small burden, light a fire, ring a bell, ring all bells.

Harriet prefers work not involving direct contact with dirt. Dry dirt is not too bad for her but wet dirt is bad. Dust and crumbs are OK, but splashes of toothpaste in sinks are not OK, and very bad indeed are food particles on plates. This induces horror in my sister and when I put her on washing-up duty, she was pathetic to behold, and fit to be tied as my mother might say. Even wearing enormous maximum-strength rubber gloves, Harriet will only hold a plate in a loose grip between finger and thumb and run it briefly under the tap, swiping at it vaguely with a dishcloth, likewise held between two fingertips because she cannot abide a wet dishcloth, and all the while she is looking away from her work, staring straight ahead in horror and disbelief, as if she cannot fathom what is happening to her, how this strife and misery have befallen.

'Think of slavery,' I tell her, hoping this might cheer her up.

'Think of the slops inside you,' says Jude. 'You are just one dirty old dish.'

'NOT helpful, Jude,' I remark, glancing at Harriet frozen in horror.

'The overall surface area of the digestive system,' says Ben, 'is four hundred square metres. And you know what else? "Death lurks in the large intestine." I read that.'

'Well, thanks, Ben,' goes Jude, rolling his eyes.

'Yeh. Thanks, Ben,' I add, watching Harriet slip yet another dish in the washer with a lot of particles still on it, so it is plain to see what we had for dinner, lamb chops plus broccoli plus *pommes Anna*. We are supposed to douse the plates before putting them in our washer or they do not come out properly, Mum says. I think we are the only family amongst families with dishwashing machines to do this, like ours is a kind of hopeless-case washing machine, merely a finishing school for crockery, meaning plates and glasses come out more or less the way they go in, just a bit sparklier and disinfected or whatever. Every time Harriet slips a plate in the machine, I have to remove it and rinse it properly and now and again I frown and make a wee tutting-type noise in the manner of bad-mood cotton tops, just to see if Harriet will take the hint and swipe a little harder at the plates without my having to tell her so, but she is in a horror trance and ignores me completely. I tut louder and toss in a big old sigh for good measure.

'Fuck-hell, Jem!' says Jude. 'You're being so – um – Goddammit!'

'Fastidious? Punctilious?' offers Ben. 'Crabby?'

'Yeh! All that!'

'You can't just leave all the gunk on the plates!' I protest. 'Mum says! They won't get clean! Oh, forget it, everybody fuck off out of here! I'll do it myself!'

'Whoa,' says Jude. 'Martyr, martyr! Ben! Quick, hammer and nails.'

'SHUTUP! Leave me alone!'

'Fuck off?' says Harriet, suddenly returning to general conscious-
ness, perking up and giving me a sweetie-pie smile. 'Does that mean
I can go now? May I, my dear?'

'YES! Go ahead! Abandon ship! You know what?' I say. 'Maybe
we should all have one dish each. Like Pax! One dish for all things
and it's up to you to wash it or not, like a mess kit. How about
it?'

'Does anyone ever wash Pax!'s dish?' asks Harriet with deep
concern.

'Well, YOU bloody don't,' says Jude.

'Fiddle-dee-dee,' goes Harriet, swanning off with Ben.

'Actually,' says Jude, handing me stray wine glasses and bits of
crockery Harriet never bothered with, 'I had an idea lately, an
invention. For a table. At every place, there is a sort of dug-out,
built in, a built-in dish. All you have to do at the end is scoop out
and swab the deck. No plates.'

'That's disgusting,' I say, smiling.

'Yeh, well.'

'Pretty soon we won't have any plates left, anyway. Not at
the rate Slithers is smashing them. We wash up before the machine
does. We wash hand-painted bloody plates by hand. Hand-
painted in Italy! *Fait à la main!* And now we wash up before
Slithers gets anywhere near a plate . . . what the hell is going
on here?'

'Slithers,' moans Jude. 'Shape up or ship out, that's what I'd tell
her!'

'That would be CRITICISING. Slithers didn't have privileges,
rah-rah.'

'Do you think she had plates?'

'No. They had an uprising for plates. For equality. In case
someone had nasty old plates and someone else nice hand-painted
ones. That's why she's so mad at plates and keeps dropping ours
all over the tiles, mercy Jesu. Harriet should go and live with her,
she'd never have to wash up! Slithers and Harriet finish eating,
they just drop the plates on the floor. There. My place is cleared,
fucking-bloody!'

'Mum dropped something the other day,' says Jude, hoisting
himself up to sit by the sink where I am busy scraping the lamb
rack with a wire brush. 'Let it soak, Jem,' he adds, turning the
taps off. 'I'll do it later. Come on. Stop.'

'Yeh,' I say, perching on the wooden stool that used to be Gus's kitchen seat before he made it to chairs. 'So what do you mean, Jude? What do you mean she dropped something, she never drops stuff. She was probably just tired. Or thinking.'

'I don't know. It was different. A bit weird. She was putting a glass down and – well, she kind of missed, you know? And went a bit dreamy. And made jokes. I don't know.'

'That's nothing. It's OK, Jude. I mean, I do that a lot.'

'But you're a bit clumsy, Jem. She's not.'

'Yeh. I know. I just don't see what –'

'Forget it. I'm just saying. Maybe it's nothing. She can't get sick again, that's all. Hey, look. There's a glass left in here,' Jude says, raising a wine bottle to eye level. 'Half-half?'

'OK.'

O, *my Father*, I think suddenly, *if it be possible, let this cup pass from me.*

Pretty soon after the evening Ben informed us death lurks in the large intestine and Harriet hung up her rubber gloves, I put her on new duties, ones she could face without causing a scene and going all bilious and mutinous. I assign her nicey-nicey jobs like table-setting where she can indulge in a lot of origami-type napkin folding, and sweeping, a task she has taken to with some ferocity and devotion even though it is a job involving dirt, albeit of the dry kind. Harriet is very keen on sweeping, going in for great flourishes of broom in open spaces and deft scratchings in corners, and it occurs to me sweeping may remind her of her ballet days in our old country, a discipline she has since forsaken for the less rigorous forms of dance and motion, in the style of Isadora Duncan, a style she adopted after we watched an entire film about this woman who was much influenced by Greek goddesses and flowy Greek clothing not recommended for outings in fast cars. She met a bad end in a fast car whose expert design was most likely influenced by the bicycle craze of the late nineteenth century, whereas notions of appropriate apparel were not. Isadora was too chic and romantic to bother with the influences of the bicycle craze on modes of dress, notably the invention of knickerbockers, known also as bloomers in honour of Amelia Jenks Bloomer who was famous for knickerbockers and uprisings, uprisings of women from under the sink with the rest of the pipes, etc. Amelia would not have worn a long flowy scarf in an open-topped fast car, no.

I certainly hope the Isadora phase is a passing phase of Harriet's, because I have rarely seen dancing quite so ridiculous and embarrassing, everyone swishing about in flimsy diaphanous material and a hopeless expression and flailing arms as if they were at the mercy of sudden chill breezes on a blustery day. I wish I had not seen this film because now I have a new fear in my list of fears regarding my mother. Any time I see her wearing a long flowy scarf, it crosses my mind she might be aiming to go for a fast ride in an open-topped automobile and this is a ridiculous fear to have. It is possible I am losing my mind due to fear and responsibility regarding my mother, which is what Jude keeps warning me about these days, remarking in an offhand manner how people will be coming for me shortly, to tie my sleeves up at the back and confine me to a small space, maybe only 6 1/2 feet x 11, a place where I can no longer do any oppressing of siblings out of responsibility and fear. Where I am fit to be tied.

I am having a hard time with this tasks business. Too many household tasks are plain boring and arduous and highly unlikely to be specially ordained, meaning I just have to assign them to siblings and swallow my qualms, etc., and I am beginning to feel like an Egyptian slave-driver lashing out at the Twelve Tribes and forcing them into exile and wandering, plainly inviting horrible plagues to come upon me. Ten of them. I have a powerful intimation Harriet is trying to tell me something by sweeping in this increasingly demented fashion, more in the tragic vein of Isadora Duncan, and not the romantic vein, Harriet rising up right in the middle of mealtimes to bash at our ankles under the table with a hard broom.

'Cut it out!' says Dad. 'I'm eating!'

Harriet moves into the open with great heave-ho motions of broom like she is building the Trans-Siberian railway or something.

'Harriet,' I say. 'There'll be more crumbs when we've finished eating. Can't you wait? Stop it. Please, I mean.'

'Here, Harriet,' goes Jude, dribbling bits of baguette on the tiles. 'Mush!' he adds, cracking an imaginary whip. 'Mush!'

I take Harriet off sweeping duty. I decide to let her do whatever she feels like, whenever she feels like it, though I don't quite know how to write that in my **BY THEIR WORKS** chart. Never mind. She is quite fond of helping me unpack the groceries, albeit only the stuff for which she has appreciation and is happy to see in those bags Ben and Jude haul home from the shops at week-ends, items such as fruit, muesli, raisin bread, milk and butter, and anything at all with chocolate. Harriet will pluck a packet of chocolate digestives from a bag and cradle it carefully to its resting place in the larder, but she will ignore all complicated items such as cleaning materials, shoelaces, light bulbs and sundries, leaving them spread out on the floor for someone else to deal with, an expression of vague distaste and confusion on her face.

'Harriet!' I say, falling apart while staring at an abandoned heap of Kleenex and loo paper. 'One day you'll have to grow up and get married and be a PERSON! What are you going to do when the time comes, goddammit?!'

'Deliberate cruelty is NOT forgivable,' she says.

'Ha ha ha! I mean it! What are you going to do? Have a pile of servants?'

'YES, my child,' she replies. 'Ones who can CLEAN!' she adds, waltzing off out of the kitchen, whereupon I turn on Ben who has clearly been let loose again in the aisles because there are an awful lot of weird and useless items emerging from shopping bags.

'Ben! What the bloody-bloody is this?'

'Food dye. It's all natural.'

'Who the hell needs it? It's not a nutrient. You buy this just about every time. It's not on the list, you are supposed to get what's on the list! It's OK to sneak a bag of crisps, but not this! We use dye once a year, not even. You know when?'

'Easter,' he says.

'Right! And when's the last time we painted eggs at Easter?'

'Years ago.'

'Right! So forget it. And this, why did you buy this funny soap again?'

'Soap's on the list.'

'Yeh! Regular soap! Here I spy horrible orange soap and horrible black soap. That's not regular at all. People wash with the orange stuff, the whole joint smells like nuns! It's got petrol in it or something –'

'Coal tar.'

'RIGHT! Disgusting. And this black stuff? It's very expensive and it's no good. People wash around here, they want to get clean, they want white suds on them, not grey suds. Got that?'

'But Mum likes it. It's handmade. Spanish.'

'Oh. Did she ask for it?'

'She wouldn't. It's expensive.'

'Well . . . I don't know,' I mumble, running out of steam and filching noisily in grocery bags, and feeling Jude's eyes on me, Jude who is staring at me from where he is sitting on the floor eating unwashed grapes.

'I'm unpacking the fruit,' says Jude, glaring. 'I'm helping.'

'Sorry, Jem,' says Ben, a bit forlorn, reminding me of Slave Nun.

'Ben,' I say, gentle as possible. 'Why don't you buy that Pears soap next time? It's a nice colour and it's see-through also. And Mum likes it definitely. It's special, but not weird. OK?'

'OK, sorry.'

'No worries. I'm just in a bad mood, sorry. Lots of homework to do. Hey, didn't Mum want you to hang pictures with her today?'

'Oh yeh!' he says, sounding quite restored. Ben is very enthusiastic when it comes to hanging pictures with Mum, for when it comes to picture hanging, Ben is specially ordained, something for which I am most grateful as picture hanging is not my thing. There is more solid wall space here in our town house than at the cottage where wall has increasingly made way for glass, and yet in both places there is a great deal of picture-hanging activity because Mum is pretty keen on swapping new art for old art, or shifting old art from wall to wall, or to a different place on one same wall, to change the perspective, as she puts it, and achieve harmony and impulses for reflection and so on, and this can take a very long time to achieve. I have helped out once or twice, traipsing all over the house with the best will in the western world, wielding frames large and small and leaning up against walls raising pictures aloft for Mum to gaze upon from varying distances while issuing airy instructions involving minute adjustments up and down, to the right and left, so that pretty soon I have an awful armache and a hot head.

'Mum? How's the perspective out there, is it good?' I ask hopefully.

'Well . . .'

I do a lot of groaning and sighing and Mum gets a kick out of this, like Jem is being so hilarious, exaggerating as per usual, but actually, this groaning and sighing is pure heartfelt, a genuine physiological reaction to pain and exertion, all natural! It occurs to me also that picture hanging might be a good form of penance for art criminals perhaps, for criminals and oppressors of all kinds even, the 10p-coin-pinching criminal I once was, for instance, and the oppressor of slaves I am becoming, and penance, I know, is torture with no blood involved, and a reward at the end, improving.

It is possible that a change of physical perspective can give a person a brand new outlook on a painting, and I think how Soeur Rosa says that many devotional paintings of the Passion, i.e. of gore and sacrifice, particularly the *Isenheim Altarpiece* by Mr Mathis Grünewald, b.? d.1528, were hung up for the edification of patients, so they could recall and contemplate this situation of suffering and atonement on their behalf, and it strikes me those patients in the Antonine hospital at Isenheim ought to have had a hand in the hanging of art and choice of perspective, they ought to have been given a hammer and nails of their own, and little hooks, yes, even in their feeble and hopeless condition, so they could feel part of this new perspective, this view of suffering and atonement, and not merely victims of it, of wounds doomed to fester and bleed for lack of the best knight of the world, victims of fatal diseases not one bit romantic.

I am no longer surprised by all that arguing and mayhem over the issues of icons and images leading to war and prejudice between religions, and within same religions. It seems to me that devotions to do with words is a lot more sensible and less bloody, even where there are 613 rules to remember and blessings over bread and light and just maybe some whirling of roosters, yes, I think this is less crazy-making than devotions before paintings of handkerchiefs and nails and of a baby kissing and touching his mother, fingers feeling for lips and reaching out for breasts in a forthright manner that would surely cause all-out alert amongst boys and men in the house of Robuchon. The Little Lord Jesus lays his cards on the table. His whole world is this woman. And in these mother and baby paintings, I note also how the baby has a burden of knowingness, another message for his mother, how things will never be so perfect as this, never safer, an augury in his expression that is a vision of a man in an appalling state, bleeding from five places until giving up the ghost along with a few last words reported in trying circumstances and pandemonium, words that will be open to question therefore, and to crazy-making devotions. What the baby knows is how that man is him, he will be me, Mama, Man of Sorrows, and acquainted with grief. Sex and blood matters.

Can such devotions be good for a patient?

St Francis says yes. Yes on two counts, the counts of Incarnation and Atonement. God became man, he explains, to suffer just like us and go through all the vicissitudes of growing pains and accident and emergency situations, and this is supposed to make us feel better and not so alone in the vicissitudes, etc. St Francis is not all that reliable when it comes to pain, however, especially as five wounds in all the right and telling places were found on Francis's body when he was laid out after a lifetime of suffering from stomach ulcers, liver trouble and trachoma, the most common cause of blindness, and from malaria and irregularities of the heart, leprosy, depression and hallucinations, these no doubt arising in part from a condition of self-inflicted starvation, Francis finally giving up his ghost after a lung haemorrhage, a typical symptom of tuberculosis which is, of course, a romantic disease. When Francis contemplated the Man of Sorrows in paintings, he felt better and not so alone. It's understandable.

Atonement. Francis says the suffering of Christ is our fault, but it is also a show of love on his behalf for our behalf. This is tricky. The more we mess up, it seems, the more blood he sheds, blood shed for sheer love in a one-off repayment plan for sin Jesus has taken upon himself for our sake, a job of atonement for which he is specially ordained by God the Father who does an awful lot of delegating if you ask me.

God does not think things through. Those are the facts and I face them. To make matters worse, He has one single idea when it comes to instruction of humanity and that is the pain idea. Build My Tabernacle. I don't care if you are clapped out from oppression and wandering and there are no building materials within easy reach. Shake a leg! Then there is the matter of Job. God frets about Job, He wants to make of this man a kind of beacon of faith and obedience and resistance to vicissitudes, but He simply does not think things through and in the middle of His musings, lo! He hands the matter over to Satan, which is downright lazy and irresponsible.

'Whence comest thou?' asks God all airy and casual, and open to distraction.

Satan: 'From going to and fro in the earth, and from walking up and down in it.'

This is not a straight answer. It's a very fishy business altogether. God and Satan run through this dialogue twice, no doubt in case of spies and other witnesses, both God and Satan mindful of the future and what is going to rain down upon Job, and mindful of alibis, how God can claim temporary insanity or something and Satan can say he was just following orders, etc. The Devil is an opportunist, he knows God only ever worked six days in His whole life and has lost His touch and something has to give, someone has to pay, beginning, according to nuns, with His very own son. But for glitches, a pulsar will eventually slow down.

The *Isenheim Altarpiece* is a triptych, but there are diptychs also. Soeur Rosa says diptychs were made popular by the Franciscans, something I already know due to my close study of St Francis, a study I am careful to pursue in private so as not to offend my dad with Christianity, although I cannot keep it from Jude who needs to know what I am reading at all times, strolling up to me wherever I might be and plucking the book right out of my hands for inspection and guidance purposes.

'Franciscans were terrible anti-Semites,' says Jude.

'No!'

'Yup. They spread blood libel.'

'You mean – that Christian baby blood for matzoh business Dad told us about? That?'

'Yup,' goes Jude. 'And they started pogroms. Incited. Dominicans did too. Know what Dominican means? In Latin.'

'Um,' I say. 'Lord – um –'

'Dogs of the Lord. *Domini canes*.'

'Is that bad, Jude?'

'What do you think?'

'Enemies everywhere, I guess.'

'Even some Jews are anti-Semites, Jem.'

'Whoa. What a *cauchemar*. There is just no end to it, old chap.'

'You got THAT right,' Jude says in Mike's voice, before wandering off.

A diptych is a takeaway-type painting, in two folding panels with a hinge down the middle for closing up neatly and slipping into a suitcase so it is available to a person at all times for private devotions, no excuses, and very handy to a Christian person for

whom travel is important. In a non-Christian way of course, this
is what would have become of Harriet's painting *Shiver me Timbers*
had she let me use it to cover my logbook, a desire of mine that
sparked a famous war between Harriet and her sworn sister and
other marvellous things, a war we overcame. Maybe if I had said
her work would become a 'diptych' in its guise as cover for my
logbook, with the red ribbon as the hinge part, etc., she would
have seen past the offence of folds and creases and there would
have been no battle to overcome. This is a problem in history. How
you can see a way to sidestep a war some time after there have
already been untold casualties and terrible oaths. For instance, all
that handshaking in no man's land on Christmas Day in World
War I irks me, it hurts me right *dans les tripes* as French people
might say, right in my very guts. If soldiers on opposing sides can
handshake and chinwag and pass around tenderly handrolled fags
and nips of schnapps on one given day, they can do it on any given
day, on all days. Bloody. We have a lot to learn.

The portrait that Branwell Brontë painted of himself and his
three sisters, Anne and Emily on the left and Charlotte on the right,
the picture wherein he is now absent, from scratching himself out
in a fit of self-disgust, is kind of a diptych by mistake. There are
many creases in this painting, in fact, because it was folded up and
stashed on top of an armoire for years and years before its restoration, but the most prominent crease, in what strikes me as a cross
shape, is the vertical crease running right down the centre of the
painting where Branwell once was, the no-Branwell part being like
the hinge in this painting. In a diptych, the hinge is a topmost
important part, although you might not think so, you might suppose
the picture is the thing and the folding-up part in the middle is just
a handy travelling feature. Wrong.

The earliest known folding devotional diptych was painted
before 1300 by an artist in Umbria, the home-town region of St
Francis himself, clearly a region of spiritualities. The artist of this
earliest known diptych is not known. In the left panel is the
mother and baby scene, the knowing baby with the sensual fingers,
and in the right panel is the Man of Sorrows, that inspiration to
the sick, and the thing to be mindful of is how you are meant to
look at this painting slightly folded inwards, not spread out flat,
and then to envision it folding completely like a peanut butter
fold-over, both halves face to face in a mirror image, because the

whole story is here and the hinge is a symbol, the hinge = the Incarnation.

If you look closely at Mary, you can tell she too has special knowledge, that she is dignified by augury, the augury in her son, and although he is not floppy-headed and wriggly as are regular babies of my experience, apart from Gus of course, yet she has to support him, and the way she supports him, protective and loving, is an augury on the left side of the diptych, of how she will support him later in life on the right side of the diptych, when the baby is the Man of Sorrows and the Deposition has happened, Jesus taken down from the cross out of respect for the Jewish Sabbath, and into her arms before the washing and Entombment according to rules, Jesus lying in Mary's arms one last time, in a state of *pietà*, an Italian word meaning piety, and pity also.

Augury on the left, propitious. The whole story is here. For Jesus, life is definitely a perfect circle, a cycle and not a straight line. It is not your fault, Mama. You are not responsible for all things in your son. I was born to this. Remember Gabriel, his two pointing fingers? Human and divine, this is my nature. We'll meet again. I do know where. And you won't need much, not where you're headed. *Lo, I am with you alway, even unto the end of the world.*

Some things only ever happen once, and at such times, experience is of no use to you. You can call on experience but it won't be there. At your own birth, for instance. You just have to muddle through. Head first. As at other times, the birth of the Universe, cataclysm in a binary, Jude's red knockout punch, Jeremy Levinthal's fine straight lines etched by knife, his body a totem of last words. Last Supper, farewell.

When Mum reappears at the top of the terrace steps holding her camera aloft, it is beginning to grow dark, it's late, and I elbow Jude and prompt everyone for that music-hall greeting we do for Mum when she has been absent a while, longer than expected. I whisper 'Hello-my-baby' in urgent tones, a cue for Ben, Jude, Harriet, Gus and myself to fling arms out wide in a haphazard and exuberant manner before breaking into our welcome song, a greeting that really cracks her up, and Dad also. It's a night of songs.

'HELLO MY BABY! HELLO MY HONEY! HELLO MY RAGTIME GAL!'

Mum reappearing, it's definitely a musical moment. She comes up behind Gus now and tickles him in the neck which is a secret sign to him, one we can all read, a sign to fetch out the cake from indoors, cake we have only on birthdays and special occasions, brought to the table from a hiding place in the kitchen, a place everyone knows, and with great ceremony always, to be received furthermore with appropriate awe and delirium. A cake at the Weiss table is a no-surprise surprise.

Fetching out the cake with great ceremony is Gus's job, except on his own birthday of course, Gus's job because it is a culinary matter and an assistant-chef-type duty for which Gus is specially ordained. Assistant chef, that is Gus.

I gave up on **BY THEIR WORKS (YE SHALL HELP HER) SHAKE A LEG!** just a few weeks before Jude bashed off to mining camp this summer, taking the chart down from the fridge where I had attached it by magnet and ripping it up in small pieces because it was now a mess of arrows and amendments I had scrawled in tiny writing in an effort to accommodate Harriet's way with household tasks and reassign Jude's duties in a fair and reasonable manner until stumped, stumped by jeans and Saturdays and the ironing out of creases. Forget it, Jem. Some jobs simply cannot be reassigned. Time was up, then, for **BY THEIR WORKS**, something I had known since that winter's day Dad strolled into the kitchen and yelled at me for oppressing my siblings, the same dark winter Jeremy Levinthal left us for ever, emigrating one last time, and without us.

'Hey! Jem! What do you think this is, a PENAL COLONY? A WORK CAMP? *Arbeit Macht Frei*! Jem the *Kapo*!'

'Don't SAY THAT!' I screamed, tears flying. 'I'm NOT a *Kapo*! I know what that means! Don't say that, it's not FUNNY!' I slap my rubber gloves to the floor, pushing past my dad in a hysterical flurry, straight into the larder in fact, slamming the door on him, on them all, and hearing my sister through it, though my ears are ringing and I am crying like an eejit. Any time I lose my mind, it seems, I hole up in small rooms and slam doors, it's ridiculous.

'Has penal colony anything to do with penis?' asks Harriet. 'I'm just wondering.'

'Shut up, Harriet,' says Jude.

'OK, dear. God willing.'

As God is my witness, I'll never go hungry again. Not here in the larder. Ha! *Death lurks in the large intestine.* And in small rooms and oblong boxes. Into the earth, buried at sea, my body sprouting into sheaves of wheat, or fed to the fish, a miracle of loaves and fishies, life is a cycle, isn't it lovely, I am the Ghost of Bagels Yet to Come! Dark in here. A spill of light around the door, a murmur of voices. Light, effusion. St Francis retires to small dark rooms, for rapture and private devotions, and his companions note a spill of light around a closed door, effusion, gradually intensifying, glowing fierce as any sun. An emanation, yes. In the spectrum of the Sun, Fraunhofer counts 574 black lines and science men have since counted over 30,000 and they know what it means, how the whole story is here, the make-up of everything, all the elements in these lines like little creases, shimmering, light of the world. God is a dying star.

A bed would fit in here, easy. This larder is oblong-shaped, maybe 6½ feet x 11. A bed, a ship. I say, old chap! *Great Expectations* might be the name of a ship! *Victory, Endeavour, Endurance,* I'll be OK in a minute. My endurance. Barring ice floes – sea like a snare, a death trap – I could sail far. By dead reckoning, that's what sailors call it. 'Navigation is an art,' writes Shackleton's Captain Frank Worsley, remembering how he pointed his sextant at a darting Sun in a stormy sky, from a 22½-foot boat. There are twenty-two men left on Elephant Island, waiting and hoping for rescue, eyes on the freezing waters, they have a dream of return.

Navigation is an art, travel is important, *by their works ye shall know them. Kapo.* In the *shtetl,* my dad says, the Germans announce a journey, Jews get ready. Where are we going? Don't worry about that, don't pack much, you won't need much. *We'll meet again, don't know where, don't know when.* Everyone packs a wee suitcase for this journey. *Go we thither, and there shall we see adventures.* I'm not a *Kapo,* Daddy, I am a cowboy, a wanderer, maybe there is no such thing as home. Everything's not OK, I have a dream of Passion, of gore and sacrifice and no return, I want to go like Jeremy, I get his drift, some things only ever happen once. But please, kindly lay me out in my Shane jacket, and may ye go unwashed and pray for eleven months and eat bagels for me, because life is a cycle, and Merlin likened the Round Table to the world.

Dark in here, and so noisy in my head, a spill of light and sound, *son et lumière.*

Gus only ever had one task, but when that list was still stuck to the fridge in our town house and a variation upon it at the cottage for weekends and holidays, he would march right up to it each day and carefully run one index finger along the line of his name and the other index finger down the line of days until they met in one place over those words 'assistant chef', whereupon he would nod and step away a pace or two, clasping his hands behind his back, after Napoleon.

'Assistant chef,' Gus says in a quiet and thoughtful voice, as if marvelling at the distinction that has surely come too suddenly for someone not yet in his prime, this responsibility he aims to bear with grace and gravitas, a distinction to live up to, which is what he does, what he always does.

On the night of Jude's Farewell Barbecue, Gus places a cheese-cake on the round white wrought-iron table with quiet ceremony, as only Gus can do, and he cuts seven slices in slightly varying sizes according to taste and appetite, and as he passes the plates, something else shows up in his face, something new and fleeting and easy to mistake for nothing at all, a shadow passing quick as blinking, too fast and too small for pause. I stand up in my chair to speak my regular commandment for special occasions, God Bless Us, Every One! and then I sit down to squash up with the others, posing for Frances and the camera she raises ever so slightly at the very last moment, taking all six of us into her scope but with a view to the sky, approaching the stars.

Book XIII, Chapter 8: *How great sorrow was made of the king and ladies for the departing of the knights, and how they departed.*

It's so late, Harriet and I will be so late.

I hand my sister her Flospy Bunnies hanky with the deep creases, the fold marks in a cross shape as in Branwell's portrait of his living sisters with himself scratched out, and I think how it is like a Veronica also, because the shape of Branwell is still there and he was a man of sorrows, and acquainted with grief.

'There's no nose-blow on it, just tear gunk, no nose gunk.'

'Thank heaven for small mercies,' says Harriet.

'Sorry. Thanks . . . Gus will be OK today, right? At school, I mean. I wasn't watching, you know. Saturday. I took my eyes off him – and he was so tired on Friday night, the barbecue and every-thing, I saw that, I noticed and then I forgot, there was so much to – I forgot, so it's me, it's my fault.'

'You know what I shall die of?' says my sister in her Blanche DuBois voice. 'I shall die of eating an unwashed grape one day out on the ocean!'

'You know all the words, all the speeches, it's amazing! You should be an actress, play one part only! Travel the world playing the one part! London, Paris, Vienna, Stockholm!' *Fourteen pairs of pants. How many pairs so far, Jude?* 'HARRIET WEISS IS BLANCHE DUBOIS! Standing room only! Roll up!'

'Poor lady, they'll say, that unwashed grape has transported her soul to heaven!' continues Harriet, staring at me now in that full-on way she has. She is trying to tell me something, still trying to tell me something.

'What, what is it? It was an accident, not my fault? Is that it? He was . . . so tired. Exhausted . . . as a lemming! Harriet?'

My sister butts me in the upper arm in that lamb fashion from where she is sitting alongside me on the grassy bank overlooking the pavement and then she does a lot of crazed ruffling and scrab-bling in her satchel, as if it were some bottomless pit of treasures and hidden things, and finally hauls out her lunch tub which contains, I know, all the makings of a sandwich, a sandwich same as the one I now realise I left behind and forgot to slip into my pocket where it would fit quite neatly. Not for Harriet, though, a sandwich that is handy for travellers. Harriet's tub measures maybe 6 1/2 inches x 11. She peels the lid off. I see a roll of baguette and ingredients in separate wrappings of cling film, slivers of cucumber, a curl of Black Forest ham, slices of Emmenthal fanned out like a hand of cards. There are cherry tomatoes with the stems intact, as she likes it, and sticks of celery and carrot, and a chocolate biscuit in waxy paper. Cling film is no good for chocolate, everyone knows that.

'What-shall-I-eat, what-shall-I-eat, what-shall-I-eat!' demands Harriet after the manner of Slithers who suffers from nostalgia.

'It's not lunchtime.'

'Fiddle-dee-dee,' she says.

'Well, I forgot mine. God, we'll be so late. You'll have to do Camille, you know.'

'Yes, my child.'

Whenever we are late for school or Harriet wants to bash off home early or something, she does her Camille act for nuns, going in for eyelash-fluttering, a wobbly gait and a lot of leaning into walls with a distant look on her face, and a doomy expression from visions of blood-stained pillow-slips and all the charms and romance of fatal disease. The nuns fall for the Camille act every time. They fall for the charms and romance of Harriet.

'For what you are about to receive –' says my sister.

'I am truly thankful.'

'*Bon appétit* then.'

Harriet makes a picnic cloth of her white paper napkin and she shares out each part of her lunch, half-half, beginning with the baguette, and I want to cry again, for everyone, for everything, for my sister's picnic, for that binocular roll I wanted us to share out in the garden in our old country, for God's tearaway piece of challah – His share, a blessing, an offering – for Jude's gift of the mining-camp rock, my wee splinter of the planet he will roam for a year, though there may be no end to it, and for Gus's cheesecake last Friday night, the careful slices he handed round in varying sizes according to taste with the usual grace and ceremony, and something else too, something like a shadow in his eyes, a burden of knowingness maybe, something too small and too fast for pause in his expression, and in a voice I think I heard, a small murmuring sound.

Fear not. I was born to this.

I am the bright and morning star, the beginning and the end.

Frances calls him when his wife dies and the soldier's heart bangs like a drum. She rings from London and he pictures her looking beautiful in beautiful garments as in the magazines Dot collects for him, magazines so dear he is afraid to finger them. He keeps them in the secret suitcase. It is hard to hear her, the soldier's ears hurt all the time now, mostly the left, a sound like wind, like bells, the rattle of equipment, and echoes of things he is supposed to forget, everyone says this is better, to forget.

He'll never see Frances again, he has a feeling about this, and it is his fault, it has always been his fault. When she left that first time, years ago, crossing back over the sea he once crossed, never to return, he gave her three things, she took only one thing. A medal, a suitcase, his bullet-hole Bible. She chose the medal.

He told her the story so many times, of how it happened to other men and not just him, the hole in the Bible, the life-saving book in the breast pocket, amazing, who would believe it? A book he could not even read with a tunnel in it deep into Job. He has learned the words because of that, some of the words. Hast thou entered into . . . the treasures of the snow? Or . . . the hail – hast thou – *entered, no. Seen?* seen the treasures of the hail, which I have . . . reserved against the time of trouble – *yes! against* – against – the day of battle and war? *Ah, yes.*

Some things he remembers, but he cannot understand them. They enter into him, that's how it feels. The eleventh hour of the eleventh day of the eleventh month. He remembers that. And he remembers choosing Frances. Some things only ever happen once. A sound in his ears like wind, like winter. He is just an old soldier, and full of days.

Whoa, the Moon.

The Moon has no atmosphere and so it is open to impact, it cannot protect itself, its surface scarred by ridges and deep craters, a map of troubles so easy to forget in the beautiful glow it imparts, light that is all reflection. Always keep your left hand in front of your face! Unless of course, you are a southpaw. 4.5 billion years ago, when the Earth was 50 million years old and nearly fully formed, not quite, an object the size of Mars smashed into it, causing a shower of debris that cooled to form the Moon, a planet similar in size to the Earth itself and that fell into orbit around it, slowing the Earth's spin and fixing its angle of rotation, so lengthening its days and securing its spot in the Sun, making it habitable, more than that, a marvellous place, with seasons and tides and regions tropical, temperate and polar. *How goodly are thy tents, O Jacob, thy dwelling places, O Israel.*

Memory is a sensation! Everything has a sound. Play! How Sister Clare fought for you, for the music you should be making, in London, Paris, Rome, you were born to it. You win scholarships, Mummy says no, a girl must work. All right then, I'll work, let my body be my bread, my blessing, and I might have been born to this too, though I am only moonlighting. And I will never touch the keys of a piano again, but I will have music. Noli mi tangere. *What cannot be touched cannot be taken away.*

411

When you leave home, you take only Daddy's medal, a bronze cross on a red ribbon. For Valour. *And now you have his letter, Mummy is dead, the handwriting is shy, the words spindly and uncertain. 'I've lost my pal,' he means to write, though he spells it with a double l. 'I've lost my pall.' Yes.*

Smell of death, lavender, Mummy was born to it, and then Daddy follows her so quickly, for valour! Albert was a soldier and you cried for him, his town crier, because there were things you wanted to tell him, your not-father father, and nobody warned you in time of his impending demise, not dear Dot with her bad blood, always late, always forgetful, and not Tom the priest, because you are a stranger now, out of the fold, and a woman of display, and pious men, you have learned, can be so unforgiving.

You wanted to tell Daddy a story about a house and of a dream you once had with snow falling, and five dogs all carrying skates around their necks and sticks over their shoulders, five dogs of varying sizes with an awful lot to say. You think there is a circle in this story and a story in the circle, beginning with a soldier who makes a choice and signs for you with an X, a mark like a leaning cross or a small star perhaps, and ending with another man full of decision, a fighter wearing an invisible star, a yellow one.

You meet a man with a deep frown, a man out of place nearly everywhere, not yet fully formed, spinning wildly, a man with a mess of curls and a twisted collar, in a coat with a tear in the left pocket where he has crammed in too many things. He is clearly a southpaw. This is a man used to fighting, wired as a boxer in the ring, his ears alive to the sound of bells. Ding, ding! Round one! Gentlemen, come out fighting and may the best man win!

Yaakov's brown eyes are full of days although he is so young. He is lean, almost scurvied, if that were possible, and his bones are prominent, a message part archaeology, part intent. He has been wandering a long time, you can see that. He doesn't speak, there are no words for a meeting like this. Wot ye what I am?

Yes. You are my beginning and my end. You are my house, I am your house, I salute you, enter me.

Count!

In a Jewish wedding ceremony, before seven honoured friends speak a benediction each, the bride circles the groom seven times. Frances does much better than this, she locks into orbit for ever.

Due to the laws of gravitational attraction in a double-planet system such as the Earth and Moon, there is a continuous push-me, pull-you motion, an infinite two-step with a gentle transfer of energy, something having to give, with nothing quite lost. Here is what happens. As the Earth slows under the influence of the Moon, its days full as never before, its seasons rich and changeable, the Moon drifts a little, by nearly four centimetres a year, just enough to grow a little smaller in our view, a little less visible in our sky.

Where is your mother?! Frances! Frances!

According to Talmudic tradition there is a ritual for nightmares wherein the suffering dreamer sits up in bed, say, and calls upon three close friends, three confidants to visit him and utter a special recitation seven times over, and the idea behind it is alchemical. Body into bread, blood into wine, it happens. *And with his stripes, we are healed.*

The friends gather round with an air of formality, as is befitting. They do not cajole, they don't tell the dreamer 'Hush, it's just a dream, forget it'. No. They implore him in a ritual manner to find some good in the terrible vision afflicting him, the propitious in what is not, order out of chaos. Energy is neither created nor destroyed, any science man will tell you that. Alchemy.

The dreamer begins with a lie. 'I have dreamed a good dream!' he says, according to ritual, wide-eyed with night terrors. He does not believe it. That is why there are three confidants in his room, and they are patient. The dreamer looks down too much, that's his problem.

'May the merciful One transform it to good,' they say. 'May heaven decree upon it seven times, that it become good and always be good. It is good and may it become good.' The confidants recite this seven times in unison, which is a little excessive but symbolic and also quite necessary, due to the terrible state and despair of the dreamer.

THE SCIENCE OF DEDUCTION AND ANALYSIS.

Come now, and let us reason together, saith the Lord, though your sins be as scarlet, they shall be as white as snow.

—I have seen a good dream!

—Mmm. Do you want to tell me about it?

—I keep telling you! What I saw, I saw it all! Frances gets sick, she leaves us! It's my fault. Gus drowns, I killed him, I gave him his last shock, shocks can collapse the lungs, he has the lungs of an old soldier. I blinked! I am an old soldier, everyone close to me dies.

—You must be a very powerful person.

—Not for long! I have arrhythmia. And tinnitus in both ears. And hyperacusis. *A sound like chains, like bells, like someone approaching, never arriving, for ever. Everything has a sound.* I am losing my sight. Blepharitis, myopia, conjunctivitis, floaters, it's a classic punishment, isn't it? For the breaking of oaths. *Fahneneide. Death before disobedience.* I am a soldier. I was supposed to look out for him. I blinked. Zedekiah rises up against the Babylonians and they kill his children before his eyes and then they put out his eyes. Zedekiah, Lear, let me not be mad! I don't want to see any more. Some things should remain obscure, it is ordained! I want to go home, nobody there. Where is Jude? Always travelling, I should have seen. Travel is important, he told me, and I was not paying attention, not really – things you miss, clues you pass over – Gus's song. Gus knows everything. Big Bang! Whooh, what a smell of sulphur! Galaxies fly apart. Faster and faster, it's Hubble's Law, speed increases with distance. Redshift. Frances! *Don't you see my house has collapsed!* I can't fix this thing, you can't fix this thing! I don't want anyone, I don't need anyone, everybody fuck off. Fucking-bloody, fuck-hell, nobody there, nowhere safe, nobody anywhere, so what!

—I am here.

Sometimes crying feels like bleeding, it feels the same.

With my stripes, I dream of healing.

May it become good, and always be good.

TEN

Watson: You have an extraordinary genius for minutiae.
Holmes: I appreciate their importance.

Son et lumière. What is that sound? Why is the sky dark at night?

The Universe is not eternal, not unchanging, it is changing and violent, and most of it is invisible to the naked eye, dark matter, though there are clues everywhere.

Let me not be mad!

Everything has a sound.

Jansky's hiss. 1932. Karl Jansky is a twenty-six-year-old radio engineer from Oklahoma, busy in New Jersey investigating interference in ship-to-shore communications for a telephone company, and in all the noise of the Earth's atmosphere, the familiar frenzy of storms near and far, he hears something else, a persistent hiss, a rush of sound coming from everywhere at once, the sound of stars, he discovers, stars from the heart of our Galaxy, electromagnetic disturbances moving at the speed of light. Sound is light.

Telescope, camera, radio. More light! Light is distance. For a star, now is there. The more light you gather, the farther you can see. In 1800, William Herschel is observing the Sun and he applies filters to protect his eyes, slivers of differently coloured glass, each one, he notes, with a different feeling of warmth on his skin. Now William holds a prism up to sunlight, breaking it into the spectrum he knows so well, violet to red, but this time he takes the temperature of colour, recording a rise in heat beyond the red visible to his eye, finding radiation in the invisible. Light is energy, colour a sensation.

Hiss. Karl Jansky is only a telephone man with a physics degree, an outsider, and it will be up to proud starmen to make something out of this moonlighting job Karl did of being an accidental pioneer in radio astronomy, listening to what turned out to be everything in what seemed nothing, just as the Hubble Space Telescope looks into a seemingly bland patch of sky to find over 1,500 separate galaxies there, many of them four billion times fainter than can be seen by the human eye, some, palest blue, the blue of hot young stars. The HST can spot a star a trillion times fainter than a bright one, the Hubble has look-back time, it reads the light and light can tell you everything, light remembers its source, it is revelation, and so much of it is invisible. An eye is a camera and it is not enough.

When Karl Jansky dies of heart disease aged forty-four, I wonder does he hear a rush of sound then, the noise of early light, and of redshift, things racing away from him in every direction, and does he recall, also, the feeling he had when he first heard that sound without knowing the meaning of it, a moment when the sound itself was enough for him, startling, marvellous. He marvelled, and then he asked himself a question. What is that sound?

Paris, 1631. Pierre Gassendi is holding out for the transit of Mercury, keeping vigil in a darkened room. He points a telescope at the Sun through a hole in a blind and captures the image on a white sheet, tracing the motion of something moving too quickly for a sunspot and too small, surely, for Mercury. But it is Mercury. A friend remarks of Pierre's observation that the planet was of 'an entirely paradoxical smallness', meaning there are clues everywhere and it depends how you look at them and some are too small, too fast for belief.

You have an extraordinary genius for minutiae!

Not always. There are things I missed, clues I passed over, I think so.

Gus is a baby with a burden of knowingness and sensual fingers, and my mother wears a moonstone, she is all reflection. Jude's favourite thing is a small battered suitcase only he can open, a legacy. The Grail, he knows, is not an object, it is the journey itself. Shackleton knew that, all explorers know that. My dad, barbecue man, keeper of the flame, pillar of fire. Yaakov eats the centre of a loaf, he cannot be bothered with ends, tapering crusts, no, he neglects the beginning and the end, he is the beginning and the end and he has so much to do. So he jabs a hole in bread wrappings, tearing at paper and plastic and hauling out the centre, taking his share. Challah. I marvelled at this all my days without knowing the meaning. Now I know the meaning. *HaShem. Let them make me a sanctuary that I may dwell among them.*

Where is everyone? They were only passing through, don't you see that? I am an old soldier with cowboy legs and I know the rules of boxing but I am no good in the ring, I am a hopeless-case boxer! I forget to protect my face, I always forget to protect my face, a pushover for the knockout punch.

Play the Why game!

Why is the sky dark at night? You know this one. If the Universe were infinite, every line of sight would end on a star. The Universe is not eternal, it had a beginning and it was marvellous. Some things only ever happen once.

Why am I still here? Four cuts, not quite fatal. *With my stripes, I dream of healing.* As a reward for his willingness to sacrifice his own son, Abraham is granted the survival of his people. You see, Jem? God is the Invisible Third, the Extra Man to the traveller *in extremis.* As a reward for his obedience, no, for his endurance, *the Lord blessed the latter end of Job more than his beginning.* I am still here.

What is that sound? The sound of the shofar on the Day of Atonement is a call to repentance for all Jews, even hopeless-case Jews. The Divine Judge remembers everything, nothing escapes Him, Satan walking to and fro in the earth, every mistake, all of it, everything, but He never forgets the binding of Isaac for which He is forever a soft touch and, despite everything, merciful.

Always plan some nice sacrifice, in case of flaws of character in your lifetime.

I keep vigil then, in a darkened room, 6 1/2 feet x 11, and I watch my great picture show with the starry cast, a spectacular, *son et lumière,* and visible light, I know, is only a curtain raiser, so much is invisible. My show is private, like devotions. George Ellery Hale is a man prone to nervous breaks and visions of an elf with a bossy nature, a slave-driver, or George's Extra Man, willing him on to gather more light, more light! because light means distance, it is memory, and for George, for me, near is too far, never near enough. More light!

I am holding out for something, something maybe too small, too fast for belief, and for a latter end more blessed, a dream of return and a nightmare that may become good, and always be good. *Of them which thou gavest me, have I lost none.* I watch this same moment over and over, my let-out clause, because wasn't what happened always beyond me? All the clues were there, and I missed them, forgetting that some things should remain obscure. It is ordained. Gus rides his Ferrari-red bicycle off the dock and achieves escape velocity ever so briefly, a moment passing too quickly for pause.

I saw it. Gustavus, one small king. *He approached the stars. Objectif Lune.*

Some infinities, Ben said, are bigger than others.

Book XII, Chapter 8: *How great sorrow was made of the king and ladies for the departing of the knights, and how they departed.*
Gus is acting weird.

'Gus,' I say. 'Can you NOT ride your bike on the terrace? I feel like a circus man! You know, top hat, jodhpurs, whip – whatsit!'

'Ringleader,' says Gus, circling, circling.

'Right! Plus if you keel over, it will be messy, goddammit! Gore, blood, all over the shop! Come on, my man. Cut it out!'

'*Il tomba doucement,*' goes my brother, '*comme tombe un arbre.*' And he carries on riding in rings on the slate terrace, narrowly missing wrought-iron chairs and the barbecue with its field of ash, the embers of last night's feast.

'Gus? I mean it. And Jude's leaving in minutes.'

'Yeh-yeh,' he says in the manner of Jude, meaning he will carry on doing his own thing as long as the fancy takes him, though he follows me to the edge of the terrace all the same, to where the driveway begins, the slope that is our sledge run in wintertime and where everyone is now milling about in a slap-happy fashion and talking in overlapping voices about nothing in particular, avoiding any lingering looks at Zach, who has arrived to fetch Jude for the first leg of their journey to town and to so many other towns, or at Jude, above all we avoid lingering looks at Jude who is making grunting noises while pitching his voluminous blue hockey bag into the boot of the Levinthals' car and thumping at bags and cases like the most hard-pressed baggage train porter on this earth.

Gus stops right there at the edge of the terrace and leans in the saddle against the antique lamp-post Mum had Mike install in the corner, Mike doing a lot of grunting of his own and shaking his head in fond dismay at the sheer folly and waywardness of Mrs Weiss who considers some old iron pole with a fancy glass casement housing a green light bulb with a persistent flicker from antique wiring a truly necessary accoutrement for the Weiss estate. 'Heavens!' Mike had said, chuckling into his chest. 'Heavens!' I watch Gus slink over in the saddle for balance, slouching like a cowboy resting his horse after a hot day on the range, perched high, however, just taking in the sight of things and musing on his place in this new world and the big country before him. Where are you headed? Oh, just driftin'. But even drifting, a good cowboy knows, is a serious business, you need guts.

Zach is staring at me and doing his wee shuffle, the new version of that crazed hopping he was prone to in early days. He has changed in these strange months since Jeremy died, though I do not chalk it all up to Jeremy, I don't believe things are so neat as that. I think little changes occur in people and then events come along to show them just how right they are to go in for little adjustments. If everything had a direct bearing on behaviour, it seems to me a person would not keep messing up in one same manner. Shackleton would not have carried on bashing off to Antarctica when he had already seen so much peril in those nether regions. Some changes never happen, no matter what, and some changes are bound to happen, no matter what. I believe Zach was always aiming to settle down a little, from crazed hopping to steady shuffle, and Jeremy dying like that just gave him permission to get there sooner, to be himself in a new version, the way Pax! grew into his outsized ears and paws and tail in time with the shedding of his more frenzied puppy ways and his new acquaintance with grief and experience, such as rash duelling with creatures three times his size. Pax! was always headed for composure and for the outsized in him to gain stateliness. Bill Sikes loves Nancy, but it does not change him, he has dark impulses for love and felony he can never tell apart, as Bullseye can, which is why Bill meets a sorry end in a doomy Victorian street. He was always headed there.

Jude tells me there are rules for Jews regarding felony and offences of any kind. This does not surprise me. There are an awful lot of rules in Judaism, though I maintain this to be a more sensible approach to morality than the barter-system approach which is more of a free-for-all system and quite cushy. The rules approach is especially good for difficult times when a person wants to do right but is just not up to decision-making and self-regulation. The main thing to remember, Jude says, is how God is the Invisible Third, because everything and everyone belong to Him. This means that if you are in a really bad mood and curse Him and use His name in vain or whatever, God will be miffed but not so miffed as when you are crabby and horrid to a fellow man, whereupon you are committing an offence TWICE OVER, to Him and to one of His own. OK. And there is more. Open theft is better than stealthy theft. If you rob a person in a sneaky fashion, covering all your traces and so on, then clearly you have more fear and respect for man's retribution than the divine kind. Very bad. I was definitely a hopeless-case-type thief, plucking coins from my all-time favourite person right out in the open for all to see and Heaven to boot, and always headed for reform, surely, the clues lying in my obsession with felony and morality and sleuthing, courtesy of Mr Charles Dickens and Sir Arthur Conan Doyle, but I do not count on the permanence of godliness, I stay on my toes. A person can slip up at any time.

Zach stares at me. He is struggling, I can tell, to focus on a seemingly bland patch of me, his eyes trained somewhere between my organ of birth with its cycle of reproduction, blood and sex, and the two breasts that Jude augured for me many moons ago in our old country over glasses of Ribena-milk. Zach is not doing too well. I try not to think about Sex Mistress and her house full of men in a state of perpetual frenzy and torment. Jude says Zach likes me, but I cannot concentrate on this today aside from the fleeting anxiety I feel to do with the look of me, the straggly blonde holiday hair, the Farewell Barbecue stains on my Lord Nelson T-shirt, and the full-on view of my poky knees and cowboy legs, legs with none of the right spaces between, a look befitting this final weekend of summer when I am having my last fling with shorts and reckless country-girl apparel, but perhaps not befitting the love encounter, I'm not sure. When you are a girl nearing your prime, you hope for a better sort of knee, one with a silky feel and a flowing line, as opposed to angry scrapes and scars and undue prominence like knots in an old tree or carvings in totem poles symbolic of legend and times past. Oh well. My mind is on superior things just now. I try to rise above the blight of sorry knees and lower limbs more suitable for a cowboy than a girl nearing her prime and being scrutinised by her brother's best friend who likes her.

Invisible Third. I think about Jude's book of Antarctic exploration with the emergency dosh within. I think about that passage regarding this phenomenon, as it is known, of travellers *in extremis*, i.e. in extremely bad shape and at risk of perishing in extreme conditions. This is the phenomenon of the Extra Man whereby a ghostly companion acts as a heavenly escort for the traveller. Shackleton felt the presence of the Extra Man as he crossed the mountains in search of the whaling station in South Georgia. Much later, Sir Edmund Percival Hillary saw the ghost of Shackleton when he embarked on the Commonwealth Trans-Antarctic Expedition in 1959. Very interesting. Everyone needs an Extra Man it seems to me, and I wonder will Jeremy show up for Zach any time Zach finds himself in a perilous situation. I hope so, though Zach may be the type who needs convincing this is indeed his brother alongside him, just as when Jesus appears to his disciples, when he 'shews' himself, as it is written, before the Resurrection and Ascension, yet after the trial, scourging, crucifixion, Deposition, *pietà*, *mikveh* and Entombment. When he shews himself, the disciples are all dumbstruck and dithering about mistaken identity, same as Perceval is when first reunited with his sister after long separation and transfiguring trials of the questing kind, and she asks that foxy question, Wot ye what I am? The disciples, however, really ought not be so dumbstruck and dithery beyond, of course, a little shock and surprise over this matter of Resurrection, which not everyone is disposed to accept no questions asked, because the fact is Jesus has been gone barely two days.

Jesus gives up the ghost on the Cross late Friday night and his friends obtain permission to depose him according to the rules of Judaism and how he should not remain upon the Cross on the Sabbath day. Jesus is deposed and wrapped in the right shroud for equality, and entombed in a new sepulchre in a nice garden and then, lo! He goes walkabout on Sunday morning and everyone suspects a case of grave robbery, as in horror films, and Mary Magdalene is *in extremis*, doing a lot of weeping and even having a conversation about grave robbery with two cool white angels sitting atop the tomb with the gaping door and the empty linen shroud in a suspicious heap on the floor. These angels know exactly what's up and, to be honest, the signs are all there for Mary also but she is felled by grief and confusion. That is when Jesus makes his very first appearance and shews himself to Mary who mistakes him for the gardener, and he says those words, *Noli mi tangere*, whereupon Mary sees the light. Jesus then explains he has not made the full Ascension yet, that he is shewing himself to his loved ones, which is pretty thoughtful of him, though he also has to impart a few last-minute instructions to his brethren, the disciples, reminding me a bit of Jude's note to Ben with those fifteen imperatives. When Jesus has shewn himself and organised his HQ on Earth, so to speak, then he will do the full rising all the way to God, to be One with Him, etc., but meanwhile he has an unexpected task on his hands. His brethren do not know him.

According to John, most of them are won over that evening once Jesus lets them peruse his sacred wounds. Now they know him. Of course it's you! Silly us! Then Jesus breathes on them and says, Receive ye the Holy Ghost, meaning they are absolved of sins and so on, just like that, another excuse, it seems to me, for the subsequent invention of the barter system of morality involving visions and prayers said to pictures of wounds and handkerchiefs, etc. He breathed on me, I swear it! Never mind. Jesus and the disciples carry on with their evening, swapping stories, I imagine, and catching up with recent events. One disciple, though, not counting Judas, of course, is missing that night. Thomas is missing and he is no pushover. Forget it, he says, listening to everyone. That was not Jesus. I need to finger those wounds, filch around in his side, that's what! Did you all finger the wounds? I bet not. Think I was born yesterday? Ha!

After eight days, Jesus shews himself again, marching right through closed doors as per usual since his Deposition, pressing the point a bit, but he does let Thomas poke around in his side, because Jesus is an indulgent man, although not without rancour, lording it over Thomas and passing off some lofty remark about faith, about speculation and assertion and the marriage of philosophy and sense evidence, and how a true investigation should not really begin or end with one or the other, but with both, a view shared by Galileo I might add. Jesus is not being mean to Thomas when he says, Blessed are they that have not seen, and yet have believed, and he is not advising blind faith or anything, but it is a slight. And I do not blame Jesus for being a bit uppity, seeing as he has been through hell and taken it quite well all in all, aside for the one brief moment in the garden when what he foresaw was simply beyond bearing whereupon he said that thing about the cup, asking God please to let it pass from him, and for the other moment on the Cross, when he demanded of his Father just whether this was not a bit excessive and did He not think He had let things get out of hand, etc.

After eight days. What was Jesus doing in those eight days? John does not say. I believe he was busy walking to and fro in the earth, gathering clues for his great task ahead of sorting things out from above in the manner of a good general walking amongst his troops, knowing that if he aims to issue impossible commands from an invisible command post, he must never forget what it is like to lurk in a trench in a state of ill health and desperation with lice and rats for unwelcome company, while ready to go over the top and fire fifteen rounds a minute into clouds of smoke at complete strangers.

The third occasion Jesus shews himself to his brethren is on a night trawl, a fishing expedition wherein he stands on the shoreline and tells them to pitch the net over the starboard side of the boat and lo, a bad night in the nets becomes a fulsome one, a catch of 153 fishies all told. Jesus is in an odd mood over their late open-air barbecue dinner of fish and bread, and three times he needles Simon Peter, asking Do you love me, do you love me, do you love me? like he is a bit delirious or something, and reminding me of Slithers who clearly had more than the menu in mind whenever she sat in our kitchen, things such as uprisings and nostalgia, which is why she asked that question three times, a question not as simple as it seems. What-shall-I-eat, what-shall-I-eat, what-shall-I-eat? Do-you-love-me, do-you-love-me, do-you-love-me?

Simon Peter does his best not to act alarmed. Yes of course I do, you know I do, he replies, or words of that ilk, which is when Jesus says, Feed my lambs, a famous saying of his. If you are not apprised of this, and read too quickly, all you will think of this passage According to John is, Blow me down, what a strange conversation. The lamb saying is famous, and it helps to remember also that Peter is very well meaning but not very smart, so it is likely Jesus felt the need for special emphasis without too much explication, in the hopes Peter will realise Jesus is not merely referring to small furry animals when he keeps saying 'Feed my lambs' in that edgy manner, just as in early days when he told his disciples they would become fishers of men, he was not merely referring to man-overboard situations in shipping mishaps. OK. This may also be why he shews himself on a fishing trip, to jog their memories, and help them put two and two together regarding lambs and fish and the symbolic side of things.

John runs out of steam at the end of his Gospel, wrapping things up in a terse fashion like an investigative reporter suddenly called out on a new and more pressing assignment. Or maybe he was overcome and lost for words. Here is how he wraps things up. 'And there are also many things which Jesus did, the which, if they should be written every one, I suppose that even the world itself could not contain the books that should be written. Amen.' This is a cagey ending, and quite weird.

Matthew, however, goes in for the full rising scene, the one depicted in that woodcut by Mr Albrecht Dürer named *The Ascension of Christ*, the woodcut that inspired the Objectif Lune Incident for which I am very famous, a piece of Art & Catechism showing this scene According to Matthew wherein the sacred footprints are left on the mountain top before Christ rises aloft in a puff of smoke while reminding everyone to do as he told them and observe all commandments, before finally leaving his people with a shady parting promise of epic proportions, the cause of so much trouble in terms of hopes and devotions in history, and last words are a breeze when you are not around to be held to them. *Lo, I am with you alway, even unto the end of the world.*

Harriet steps forth. She is making a presentation to Jude, clutching a small navy-blue oblong box tied up with a red ribbon. I know this box. It has pride of place on her bedside table and is a repository for revered titbits of a highly personal nature and illustrious legend, ends of favourite coloured pencils, decorative crowns of champagne corks from Christmases Past, two or three wafers of hazelnut-studded chocolate from Zweig's, folded-up notes from Mum she has saved from many a lunch tub, and a few tiny lambs from the herd my sister wrought out of wood, carefully painting eyes on each one, eyes with an amazing expression of ferocity and mournfulness. Harriet gave me one of these lambs and I prize it, perpetually astonished at how much life she could impart to a chip of wood barely the size of an almond.

'Do you mind opening it now, my dear?' my sister says to Jude. 'I need the box back, you see. Please. Thank you. Isn't it pretty?'

Jude rolls his eyes and tugs at the red ribbon, plucking a small magnifying glass from Harriet's box. 'Mmm,' he says.

'For specimens,' she announces. 'You must always bring back specimens. And may St Anthony be with you, my child. And don't hang back with the brutes. Amen.'

'Very handy,' Jude says, slipping the eyeglass into his jean-jacket pocket and giving Harriet a squeeze before turning to Ben. 'You read my note, man?'

'I must create a system or be enslaved by another Man's!' exclaims Ben, clapping his wild arms around Jude. 'William Blake,' he adds, breaking away.

'Blake. Right. So, I'm the other man?'

'Yup. Until I create a system. I'm your slave. Yeh, I got the note. Walk the dog, don't forget keys, get a job, soap in, normal-normal, no-heat dry –'

'LOW-heat dry.'

'OK, low-heat. Shopping, washing, rubbish, rah-rah-rah, don't worry.'

'Mush!' says Jude, cracking his invisible whip.

'Rest not from your great task!' I declaim in Ben's Blake voice, eyeing Jude.

'To open the Eternal Worlds? Um, the immortal Eyes?' says Jude, fumbling for Ben's latest favourite saying from his latest favourite sage.

'NO! OF BEING BOSS AROUND HERE!'

'Into Eternity,' says Ben. 'Jude is boss for ever.'

'And *in absentia*,' goes Jude, chuckling, enjoying this idea of being boss and slave-driver, even *in absentia*, as it is called, a word sounding to me like a place, a country with fjords and long nights and a mournful Nordic language and mammals of the tundra and arctic family.

My go. I cram my hands deep into my shorts pockets and cock my head to the side, feeling like a kid when I am not, and I know it. I am nearing my prime and my clothes are not quite right and Zach is staring and Jude is going and all I can do is cram my hands into pockets and frown in the early sun. Jude purses his mouth in that way of his, the left corner of his mouth curling upwards, which is close to grinning for Jude. He raises both eyebrows, both of them, and I do the same, it's a reflex, I can't help it.

'Ping!' *Don't go.*

'Ping!' *You'll be all right, Jem. I'm not going to war or anything.*

'Ping!' *I know it. Fuck-hell, though. I hate this day.*

Jude blusters into me like a rugby player and raises me a foot or so off the ground, jarring my ribs, his curls muffling my ear though I cannot hear properly anyway for the jumble in my head, of sounds and pictures. *Objectif Lune!* I think. I have lift-off. All systems are go. I must create a system. Let me down, Jude. But let me not fall too fast, or too slow, anywhere between 5.2 and 7.2 degrees will do, angle of re-entry is so important, and so slight, so easy to miss. Too steep and I burn up, too shallow and I bounce back, to rove in space for ever.

Gus's turn. Your go, Gus.

'Hey, Gus,' says Jude. 'Hey, man.'

Gus slinks out of the saddle and wanders Jude's way, burying himself in jean jacket and getting his hair rumpled and an application of Jude knuckles to the scalp in the Knuckle Torture and pretty soon Gus is giggling, everyone giggles, making me feel better all round, especially for Gus who is acting weird today and whose top lip is pale, and left ear burning red, that flaming red that afflicts him mostly in the dry cold air of wintertime even if his ears are well muffled by suede cap with World War I dispatch-rider ear flaps, afflicting him otherwise on days of sheer excitement, one or both ears aflame and see-through like a hand held up to torchlight. Maybe it's the sun today, September strong. One red ear, it's not serious, everything's OK.

'Jude!' says Dad, grappling him in a bear hug, with a lot of groaning and squeezed-out breathing and bursts of back-slapping going on between them, as if a regular old gentle hug without bodily harm and noise involved would simply not do the job right, this farewell job of theirs. Now my dad pushes Jude to arm's length, clamping him by the shoulders to take in the sight of him while saying 'OK, OK' three or four times before they kiss on the lips, and then it's all over and it is Mum's go, a fluttery, heartbreaking business, with Jude looking stricken and shifty thereafter and everyone staring at the ground as Mum veers away to do a little pruning, suddenly spying a dead shoot on an overhanging branch and snapping it off carefully and with great attention, like this is the most urgent thing, and pruning is her calling in life.

The rest happens too quickly, a flurry of shouts and the slam of car doors, and the roll of tyre across earth and stone, and Dad clapping his hands and issuing warnings about the time of departure of our wagon train tomorrow for our journey back to town on the eve of the new term, 11 a.m. ON THE DOT, no messing around, pack up tonight, 11 a.m. tomorrow, all aboard, OR ELSE!

'Keep an eye on Gus, please,' Mum says as she heads for the terrace steps under the weight of my dad's arm flung around her. 'Jem? He's very tired from last night.'

'Not a problem,' I reply. 'Hey, Dad! Or else what? You said, or else.'

'I LEAVE YOU BEHIND!'

'Fine with me,' I tell him. 'I can quit school. I learn more at home anyway.'

'Same here,' says Ben. 'I quit.'

'I'm not very keen either,' adds Harriet. 'And the weather is so clement!'

Dad turns on the steps, releasing Mum for a moment to flap his arms about and address us from the heights like Caesar to his troops exaggerating the might of the enemy as per usual. 'My family fled the *shtetl*! They crossed over in stinking ships and worked in sweatshops so YOU could go to school! You LUNKHEADS! 11 a.m. ON THE DOT!'

'What is a lunk exactly?' asks Harriet. 'I'm just wondering.'

'We who are about to go to school salute you!' I say, giving Dad a gladiator wave.

'Hail, Caesar!' goes Ben.

'That's the spirit! OK. Now I'm going inside with your mother.'

And Jude is on the road, I want to say, barely ten minutes away, time no real distance yet, nowhere near a year, 'I'll be away a year', a light year! Distance, not time, no time at all.

'We'll be down at the dock,' I say, filling in the map of things we must have in our family. Nobody gets lost around here.

Picture a fork, ungodly, with three prongs bent out of shape, all veering right. There is a fork at the foot of our driveway with three prongs, three ways to make an exit, three different exits. Know where you are going. 1) Carry on at the foot of the slope that is our sledge run in winter, choosing the far-left prong and you're off, straight out of the property and into the great world. 2) Stay in the loop. Pick the rightmost prong, turning back in on yourself, around and around, down and around, like a racing car, beep-beep!

You might think this is like making no exit at all, but as long as you are on the move, you are always leaving someplace for somewhere. Every step a person takes is an exit from somewhere. 3) Pick the middle prong, veering right but not so gently as in 1 or sharp as in 2. This is the long way to the lakefront, for thoughtful ramblers and for vehicles, unlike the quick and reckless clamber down the grassy snake slope below the terrace, or the dignified path leading offstage left, as it is known in theatricals, down mossy slate steps between ageing stately hedgerows where your dignity is at risk, however, if you are leery of assault by spiders in smothery cobwebs. Dignity is not for everyone. In terms of topography, then, the terrace is a plateau with an incline to front and rear, one falling off to the lake and the other, if you so choose, to the great beyond, and whenever I reach the terrace from the lowlands at the lakefront, or when piling out of our car at the top of the driveway at the end of a journey in from town, I step up with a sudden desire to plant a small flag and sing a lofty anthem with poignant undertones, mindful also of that demand made of King and country by Robert Falcon Scott in case of outright peril, in the name of God, a divine imperative, surely a *mitzvah* had Sir Robert been Jewish, and top of the list of the 613 Jude told me about. *For God's sake, look after our people.*

Jude and Zach pick exit number one. Harriet chooses dignity, and mossy steps, the slow road. She will be a while reaching the lake, due to minute observations she will be making of flora and fauna, the specimens in her path. Gus is back on his bike and takes exit number three, giving me a prickly feeling and an impulse to issue warnings, an impulse I squash because it might embarrass him and because I have this new fear that the issuing of warnings is imperilling by nature, or an augury. I see it, it happens. Be nimble! Be prepared! It's supposed to be helpful, envisioning the pitfalls ahead, but I just don't know any more, meaning visions may well be wise and helpful but are very exhausting, and a cross I have to bear, as Harriet would say.

'You know what?' says Ben, tumbling down the grassy slope with me. 'Let's sit right here.'

'Not on the dock?'

'Well. It's kind of choppy out there.'

'You think? OK.' My big brother is prone to motion sickness. Even a glance at passing clouds can do it some days, so I agree to settle in the grass, with stipulations. 'You'll have to check for snakes, then,' I say, whereupon Ben does the Anti-Snake Dance for me. 'Thanks, Ben.'

'Not a problem.'

Gus rides circles around Ben and me, sunlight flashing off the spokes of his bike. It's annoying but I can't stop myself staring at spokes and I am reminded of Jude's ant in olden days, the one he swallowed by mistake, an ant in a strange land, circling the rim of Jude's glass of Ribena-milk in a headstrong manner before rushing down his throat, this Jonah in the realm of ants.

'Gus! You're like a hamster today. You know one thing only, how to go round and round. I'm about to lose my marbles. Will you cut it out, please-thank you.'

'It's kind of like a voodoo ritual,' offers Ben.

'Is it? Oh. Well, I feel like Tintin. You know – on the cover of *Tintin en Amérique*. Tintin tied to the stake and the Indian chief dancing round and round. It's definitely a bad feeling. Gus! Hey!'

Gus has a spurt of giggles causing him to wobble in the saddle and then he veers off suddenly to ride across the lawn and into the thicket of trees near the beach named in his honour. Gus's Beach ought to go down in cartography like all territory of special distinction, such as that sliver of shoreline on Elephant Island where twenty-two men awaited rescue for twenty-two whole months, a place discovered by second in command Frank Wild seven miles from where the twenty-eight-strong *Endurance* crew first alighted after 170 days on drifting ice that was cracking up beneath them. Cape Wild they call it, in honour of Frank who is left in charge of the waiting party when Sir Ernest bashes off in the 22½-foot open boat with his five chosen men in search of the whaling station in South Georgia. Pretty soon the sailors change the name of this place to Cape Bloody Wild, which goes to show that hope may have become a problem for them but jokiness had not, not even when they had just about lost control of their faculties because of exposure, malnutrition and frostbite. Cape Wild is not a suitable place for habitation. No doubt it cannot be mined for bauxite or any such natural resource, but it is more than a place, it is a landmark of things rare and lofty, of heroics and a crazed faith in rescue despite conditions of *extremis*, faith inspired by a man named Wild and his daily wake-up call to men in a state of near dementia. 'Lash up and stow! The Boss may come today.'

I can't see well today. Worse than yesterday. A kaleidoscope for eyes. Weird.

'Ben, I'm all blinded. It's Gus's bike doing it, I think. Like sunspots, I have.'

'Actually, sunspots are dark patches –'

'OK, OK! I know what they are!'

'Whoa. You're in a bad mood.'

'I'm not. Sorry. I'm just – not in the vein for knowledge right now. I need a break kind of thing, OK? Man! I've got silver fish again. Fuck-hell!'

'Did you eat breakfast?'

'Not really. I mean, I look at breakfast and all I can see is my burnt burger last night, raw inside. One step from the abattoir, goddammit.'

'Mine was fine,' says Ben, picking at grass. 'Hey, maybe your silver fish are a sign.'

'A sign I'm hungry or a sign I'm crazy?'

'Sign you're a visionary.'

'Yeh, right. Dumbest one you know. Grumpiest! Is Gus EVER getting off that bike today, do you think?'

'It's a Christ symbol.'

'Gus is? The bike?'

'Very funny. No. The fish! There's an acrostic. First letters of: Jesus Christ Son of God the Saviour. In Greek, that's *Ichthys*, meaning fish, and the early Christians were still, well, Jewish enough to avoid idolatrous images, right? So they portrayed Christ in letters and symbols, namely the fish, in the catacombs –'

'Catacombs! We've learned that. Last term.'

Soeur Rosa shows us pictures of underground burial places, the catacombs as they are known, explaining how there were celebrations in these burial places and that they were decorated for this purpose, the celebrations and decorations all to do with waiting for resurrection and so on, and I stare at the photographs of rows of tombs stacked several storeys high, trying hard to see it her way, as something worthy of celebration and not mourning and rules for mourning, etc., but all I see is a barracks, and the neat bunk beds there, and an army hospital with rows and rows of men and boys waiting hopefully for something, any kind of resurrection will do, even standing up again might feel like a party, maybe a party like in that painting Soeur Rosa also shows us, an example of Art & Catechism called *Paradise*.

This painting by Giovanni di Paolo di Grazia, b?, d.1482, depicts famous saints and martyrs greeting each other in the woods in a long-lost fashion, with some being congratulated for their fine deeds back on Earth by very well-dressed angels with delicate sparkly wings as in Nativity plays. It's a cheery scene and it makes me smile, it really does, but it's kind of a trap painting. You look at it and get all this reassurance about Paradise, clearly a place of distinction though not mapped in cartography, and definitely habitable, and not just because of eternal life but because it is one long reunion party in a lovely stately garden at twilight, forever twilight, with fluffy rabbits bounding in grass coloured British Racing Green, and rare specimens of wildflower and an elegant row of fruit trees on the horizon against an azure sky, with elegant deer strolling amongst the greeting couples and not nibbling at coat-sleeves or vegetation or anything, but poised gracefully amongst those greeting couples clutching each other in this fervent fashion, making up, perhaps, for the absence of their Host. He may well be there, of course, but Invisible, or else Giovanni's idea was that the painting is God's point of view, as if He were taking a photograph, which is why He is out of the picture, of course, and the saints and angels are acting all posh and excitable, as is often the custom when a photographer is lurking, people trying to act natural and unawares and ending up looking downright show-offy and feverish.

I don't know. There is certainly something a little too feverish in all this hugging and hand-holding and chinwagging in Paradise and it must have to do with knowledge and unspoken things. They know this party moment is poor compensation for being dead and losing all their friends and being caught up in an endless reunion scene with the gracious host they expected to greet them with warmth and fine words and tall glasses of champagne, absolutely nowhere in sight. It's a let-down and they have to make something out of nothing, which is how it was for the twenty-two men on Elephant Island every morning they heard those words 'Lash up and stow!' and put off their doomy thoughts for one more day.

Cape Bloody Wild. Waiting and hoping. *The Boss May Come Today* might be the name of their ship. *We'll Meet Again, Great Expectations* are good names for ships and houses. Or paintings of ships and houses, or of Paradise even, not for everyone a garden party with an atmosphere of fever and extravagance but a picture of twenty-two men raising crazed toasts over meals of boiled seal bone to the tune of banjo music, toasts of the alcoholic brew Frank Wild distils from a mash of spirits intended for the preserving of specimens, with sugar added, and water and ginger, a party drink he calls Gut Rot 1916.

Wild, there's a ship.

Picture it. A party of men in a state of disrepair and decay, tumbling on to a beach to light a fire and hoist an old wind-torn jacket up a flagpole, eyes trained on the sea for the tugboat with a man in the prow, shape of a man they know well and who is staring at them through binoculars and counting aloud, doing a headcount. Two, three, four . . . seven . . . They're all there. Paradise, this is Paradise all round.

'There's a lot of fishy stuff in the Bible, isn't there, Ben? Fish, fishermen.'

'And water. It's their habitat, right? And there's baptism, of course.'

'And loaves and fishies.'

'And then there's St Christopher.'

'Oh, right. Ferryman. I don't get that,' I say, lying back in the grass. 'Some saints have an easy ride, I mean it! What did he DO, exactly, for sainthood? Ferry people across rivers. And a little kid who is strangely burdensome and turns out to be Jesus in disguise. According to some. So? I've had it with saints and their symbols and things, how they get to be patrons of stuff and have causes barely even related to anything they did in life!'

'It's really not important, Jem.'

'I KNOW IT! I'm just saying. Hey – did Harriet give up on us? She went inside, didn't she? Ben, I don't want to go back to school. Nuns are a *cauchemar*. And they have a vendetta on me. Against me. An Italian thing, Mafia, vendetta. Catholic.'

'You have to go. It's your last year there, anyway.'

'Jude says you might skip out on uni. And he's taking a whole year off. Is he even going to university afterwards? Are you?'

'Haven't decided yet,' says Ben. 'Oh look, a wild strawberry. Want it?'

'A snake probably slimed this way, it might have snake juice on it.'

'I'll wipe it. Open up,' goes Ben, dropping the tiny berry in. 'Body of Christ,' he adds, sniggering.

'Hey, it's very nice actually. Tastes fake though, like fruit gums.

I miss fruit gums. Anyway. Ben? How is it you and Jude get to choose about school and things, and I don't? Because I'm a girl? Under the sink with the rest of the pipes and so on?'

'Have you said you don't want to go to university? You still have to finish school, though, there's no choice in that.'

'I know. And I did tell Dad I might not want to go, and he says OF COURSE YOU'RE GOING! Plus I got the schmatte-trade and *shtetl* speech. And the soup-kitchen speech.'

'Hmm.'

'Plus . . . Harriet and I aim to be pirates. We're passing up on song and dance and going in for piracy. Harriet is turning her back on dance for now. She says the world is too VULGAR and she is waiting for progress.'

'Harriet can't be a pirate, she doesn't drink.'

'She can be a temperance pirate. All the rest of us are drunk and reeling, she'll steer. Navigate. Navigation is an art, I read that.'

'Right,' says Ben. 'Sounds good. Especially as you hate travelling.'

'They had girl pirates, you know. In case you were wondering.'

'Great,' my brother says, losing interest.

I think about Mary Reade, famous girl pirate of the eighteenth century, and the picture of her wherein she is lording it over an enemy pirate upon whom she has inflicted a bad head wound. Mary has a pistol in her right hand and the enemy pirate's cutlass is at her feet, the man disarmed in all ways, real and symbolic, but Mary is not interested in murder, no, she is interested in lording it over the enemy. She is taking a stance, feet firmly planted, and she is wearing tartan breeches and a fetching red frock coat. She has a fierce expression on her face and has ripped her coat open, displaying fine bosoms, no bra, which is why the mouth of the enemy pirate is ajar in shock and disbelief, and not because of the pistol in her hand. Lingerie was not on the list of kit required for pirates at pirate-ship outfitters, though bloomers were, original-style bloomers resembling knickerbockers and clearly worn by Mary Reade long before the days of Amelia Jenks Bloomer and the craze for bike riding in ladies. It is likely Mary still owned a bra from her pre-pirate days, but she is not wearing it. Frilly accoutrements are no longer her style. A naked bosom is a powerful show-stopper and a fine way to end arguments while forgoing unnecessary fatalities, and I feel sure Mary knew that. When Mary was put on trial for piracy, a fate that might beckon for Harriet and me, she was let off execution because of pregnancy. Very interesting. I believe Mary was born with a tempestuous spirit and prone to frustrations leading to fisticuffs and, finally, a career on the high seas for lack of opportunity and understanding, as it was for Ophelia, because in other times Mary might have been a sporting hero, the first gentlewoman boxer, say, bare-knuckle. In the end, the tempestuous spirit was a good and bad thing for her, meaning she had no fear of hand-to-hand combat, although, in tiffs with her loved one, father of the embryo, she knew how to drop the gloves and summon up the finer feelings just by ripping open her upper garments and exposing her fragile parts, the cushiony soft tissue covering the heart region, reminding me of another kind of rending of garments over the heart region, the *k'riah* kind Jude explained to me last winter, the night of Jeremy's funeral, most mourners rending on the right but Zach and Mr and Mrs Levinthal rending on the left where the heart is, showing how very close they are to their grief, how there is room for nothing else. I see it, though I was not there.

'What's the point of visions, Ben? Who's to say a person is not plain bonkers, or making it up or something? Or plain starving? And who's to say it's holy? I mean, St Clare for instance, she had all these visions, more than the regulation amount for a nun, so she gets to be a saint with BLINDNESS for a cause. And know what she is patron of? Guess.'

'I give up.'

'TELEVISION! She is the patron of television! Heavens to Betsy!'

'Well, Blake was a real visionary. It's divine inspiration.'

'Oh, Blake, Blake!'

'You're definitely crabby today,' my brother says, jabbing me in the ribs.

'Is a crab a fish? No, a crustacean. Is that a fish? Hey, let's say I see little baguettes swimming before my eyes, nice ficelles with vintage Cheddar inside and a little mustard, what if I see that and not silver fish? I mean, bread is symbolic. Am I still a visionary?'

'Nope. Just hungry.'

'OK. How about little flashy knives?'

'Killer. Or pyschotic.'

'Pyschotic? Stark-raving? Fine! They have a saint for that! Dympna, St Dympna! Famous for sex and blood. I have no idea why she gets to be saint. All she did was run away from her father who had sex mania for her, his own daughter, yuck. He chases her across Holland to an oratory and tries to haul her home for sex purposes and she puts her foot down, no! So he chops her head off. And lo, she gets to be saint of insanity and nervous diseases –'

'Disorders.'

'Yeh – that. Saint of insanity, nervous disorders, and – hey, you'll love this – possession by devils! And she gets two symbols in art, a devil on a chain and swords. Flashy knives!'

'Jem, you're well up on sainthood. It will take you far. I salute you.'

'I think I'll go in for sainthood myself. Forget piracy. All that travelling, what a *cauchemar*. I could be patron saint of, um, the Bagel Factory. Oh wait. That's not right, Jude says no saints for us. Is he right? We have martyrs, though, don't we? Anyway, my art symbol is bagels and baguettes.'

'You're kind of a bread saint. Or martyr.'

'Right. And bread is VERY important. It covers everything, all causes and things. Life, death, rah-rah, the lot. Plus I love bagels and baguettes. Devotion is important, it's a requirement.'

'Well, you also have to die to qualify. For your causes.'

'No problem. I'm working on it,' I say, sitting up. 'There's starvation for a start. I'm definitely hungry. Where's Gus? Fuck-hell, I've still got sunspots, it's driving me crazy! Let's get Gus and go up for snacks, hallelujah. Want to? Gus! We're going up!'

'GUS!' yells Ben.

'Don't shout at him, he hates that!' I say, blinking hard and rubbing my eyes and opening them wide, willing my vision to clear the way I do at the cinema these days once the curtain drops and the lights snap back on and Jude and Ben start jostling me while I fumble with coat-sleeves and fish around on the floor for a pretend lost thing when really I am just playing for time because I don't want them to think how weird it is my eyes take this long to adjust to the world again. Come on, Jem! Let's go, they say, jostling me, pulling at me, same as Ben is doing right now.

'JEM! Get Dad. GET DAD! RUN!'

'What? What is it! Cool your jets!' I say as he hauls me to my feet and bashes off so quickly I am left clutching at air because of the sudden shower of stars I see, a whole nebula, and the rush of sound in my ears like sleigh bells, coming or going, I don't know, until just as suddenly I see and hear with that strange clarity of marvellous things not seen or heard before and passing too quickly.

I marvel at it. There goes my brother, isn't that Ben? There he is, one of the best knights in the world racing along the dock, a flurry of limbs, the dock lurching and slamming in its moorings as Ben runs, flinging his shirt away and leaping to the water which is not his habitat, it is the habitat for fish. Ben is the worst swimmer in the Weiss family.

I saw it. Gus, Gustavus, our small king, *where are you headed?* It happens too quickly for pause, a slight boy flying off the dock on a Ferrari-red bicycle, ready for launch and approaching the stars, one hand free of the handlebars and raised aloft as if waving at someone and with a few last words to say, something calm and graceful for which he has all the time in the world, and takes all the time in the world, because parting words, he knows, can be so perplexing.

For God's sake, look after our people.

In the brief moment before Gus splashes down, falling much too slowly to my eyes, I swear it, to hit the water with all that fury, this terrible commotion of boy and machinery, I have a feeling that is nothing to do with calamity and terror, but still and strange and close to awe. Look! Look. That is my brother, he's my brother.

Il tomba doucement comme tombe un arbre.

Sixty to 65 per cent of childhood asthma cases worsen. Treatment of all childhood cases is necessary. Established asthmatics may experience attacks following exposure to sudden changes in temperature or humidity, or both, and to exertion, and to emotional stress. A person experiencing a prolonged attack that is resistant to drugs is said to be in *status asthmaticus*.

9. *Rag Gus about his inhaler and his medicines. Shocks can collapse the lungs.*

Keep an eye on Gus.

Not a problem.

I do not sleep this whole night, that's how it feels. I wonder how it is for the others. I can make out the small heap of Harriet across the room but I don't know if she is asleep. Even if she is just lying awake or reading or playing with small inanimate objects, animate to her, she always makes a little home in her bed, like a burrowing animal. She is a burrow-maker. I do not want to call out to her yet. I am not in the mood for a powwow, not yet. I need to look back. I need to figure things out. I wonder if Jude is awake. Jude is not here, Jem. He left with Zach this morning. Try to get it straight in your head. A straight line is the shortest distance between two points! Where are we now? Where are they now? Is Jude still on his first pair of pants? Jude and Zach are not travelling a straight line. They are taking the long way round. Gus was thinking a lot about that last night. He felt it and he sang it and this morning he was distracted by it and went on a journey of his own, a journey of epic proportions that so nearly made a Waste Land of all of us for ever, had Ben not come up out of the lake with Gus in his arms, fighting the waters, taking giant strides towards Gus's Beach, and laying Gus down with his head upon that smooth flat rock where he is fond of sitting to watch us swim and play the Lunar Bob and other ridiculous games. Gus's Rock is a feature of topography in Gus's Beach, which is a place of distinction and a landmark.

'IS HE KILLED? I mean – Ben! Is he –'

'Run, Jem. Get Dad. Get EVERYONE. Find Mike!'

There was so much running and shouting yesterday, running and shouting and sudden murmurs, it reminded me of the day Gus came home in Harriet's pink blanket and the door opened on all our noise and rapture and we traipsed upstairs after Mum and Dad, nipping at their heels, cuffed like puppies all the way to their bedroom where Mum sat on the bed holding the baby whose name we didn't yet know, whose name she spoke for the first time before Dad let us peek at him one by one, single file, not too close, not too close! *That's enough knights*, I thought, I remember that, how I felt that life truly began right then for all of us, a holiday befitting certificates with red ribbons dangling from red sealing wax, it all began then as it might have ended today, and possibly has in some way although Gus is OK and not dead and sleeping now in Mum and Dad's room, ending in some way because of what I see now, that a lifetime is not only measured by my own beginning and end but by someone else's, or by some fine adventure never to come again, never so fine, 1942 was the Year of the Great Raids! Everything is different now, everything is messed up in my house, here comes change again, big as ships, monstrous, and change is not for everyone.

I don't want it. I look back on the day Gus first came to us, with a grievous feeling where there was only ever a great one, because of what I saw today and what I know now. Maybe it was thus for Hudson the navigator of the Imperial Trans-Antarctic Expedition of 1914 when he recalled the happy words he wrote the day he headed out to sea aboard the *Endurance* with high hopes of glory and a fever for unknown things in spite of that warning in bold print, SAFE RETURN DOUBTFUL. 'What a glorious age we live in!' writes Hudson that day, and he has one single feeling, but when he looks back on it, he feels grievousness also, akin to a malady.

I do not sleep this whole night, that's how it feels, no part of me quite ready to believe sleep is a good thing and what I want, maybe because I no longer believe this either, that sleep is a state of safety or that it will be natural, ever again, to drift off with the full expectation that everything will be OK when I wake up, it will all be here when you wake up. My nights are numbered! They were always numbered, and I have slept them all, perhaps, my drifting nights.

I listen to September breezes and watch the trees sway in that mournful fashion through lacy curtains, trees still with a full head of summer foliage though some of the leaves have turned already as my dad pointed out the other day in that way of his, satisfied and knowing, like he is making some point about humanity itself and the whole bloody Universe or something, a truth he has been apprised of all his born days, the evidence so plain, clear to a lunkhead even, how summer is a brief fantasy and before you know it, lo, there is autumn and the very next thing, winter, and time to slide around on ice and shovel snow and drive us between town and country along the motorway with that winter grip on the steering wheel and shoulders hunched, alert to sudden spins and the seduction of snow, the hypnosis of flurries in a darkening sky, a soft white patter on glass like piano playing, like one touch of Frances maybe, and dizzying as a rush through space right there amongst the stars. Hold tight, Dad!

'See that, Jem?' my dad says the other day, for the second time in two days, as he does every summer, standing up from his chair on the terrace, a crumpled newspaper in one hand and pointing out trees like he is identifying perpetrators of crimes. 'The leaves are turning! How about that! It's August the – what?'

'Twenty-ninth, Dad.'

'Ha!'

And I look out for it too now, every summer, as soon as July, scouting trees for that telltale sign of things to come, the evidence so slight, a spark of flame, an illumination, burning like Gus's ear, a tiny lick of leaves coloured Ferrari red.

'Look, Dad,' I might say, sitting next to him in the car, bashing back from the village shops. 'There. Did you see?'

'Ha!' he goes, and I make a chuckling sound also, satisfied and knowing, same as him, and with a hint of bitterness for good measure, even though I crave autumn and the coming of winter, I love it, I dream of ice. 'AND there,' he says. 'See?'

'Yup,' I say, and Dad elbows me and we share a glance and a nod. My dad and I, we are in the know. It's a cowboy thing. A good cowboy may be a pioneer in all things, homesteader, herdsman or sheriff, and hope is not a problem for him, but he is always in the know, he reads the signs. He is apprised of truths.

I watch the trees sway this tenebrous night and listen to breezes and to that tinkly bell of Mum's, the beat-up antique one that rings all night in a shy and persistent manner, a winter sound for me, even in summer, and a sound connected to one same vision always of someone calling out from a distance, standing in the trees at the edge of a big white field, a person with great composure and a graceful demeanour and grave words to impart, for my ears only, words I strain to hear though the person is patient, because the message is so perplexing and may take a lifetime. A ringing sound, a vision.

Seeing and hearing.

That quote of Jude's! Words from the Talmud, companion volume of the Torah, which is the Bible part, meaning Talmud is kind of an instruction manual, I believe, full of rules and discussions and arguments to do with rules. OK. The seeing and hearing quote, however, is a favourite of Jude's for threat purposes, not instruction, and delivered, always, in ominous tones whenever he wants to spook me for some bad flaw in my personality or some small crime committed against him, such as scraping the last smear of crunchy peanut butter from the jar for my own self, or refusing to fetch an item he requires from some far-off room, or, as on one afternoon last winter, for refusing to swaddle myself upon demand and brave the snowy evening and do that last-minute message Mum asked of him, of purchasing a packet of unsalted butter in time for dinner, French, please, it must be French, thank you, darling.

'Come on, Jem. Do it. I'm tired. You love snow. Go on.'

'No. I'm reading. Forget it.'

'Did you say no? My sister, my twin, Jem Weiss, third in line, vassal, serf, minnow, GIRL? No? You said no?'

'You got THAT right,' I reply, flipping a page in that official manner indicating great purpose and concentration on the offices of learning, and other lofty things. Kindly do not disturb.

'And to think of ALL the things I do for you in life,' Jude says, settling in at one end of the sofa and mashing his feet against me, squishing me into the other end. 'I'll remember this, you know,' he adds, eyes large and stary.

Here it comes.

'Know what is above you,' my brother says in his best ominous. 'A seeing eye, a hearing ear, and a book in which all your deeds are recorded!'

'Very spooky,' I say, unruffled. 'Shiver, shiver. Shake-shake.'

'Book of Life! Book of Death! What's it going to be?'

'Book of Shackleton! Book of Tintin! Book of Shutup!'

Jude sighs. He is working up to a bribe. 'I've got chocolate. Toblerone.'

'Wrong slave. You want Harriet. Get her to go.'

'Always remember that you were a slave in the land of Egypt!'

'Right. That's why I need a rest just now. I'm reading. Shhh.'

'Wrong, wrong, WRONG as usual,' says Jude, swinging his legs off the sofa to sit bent over his knees with his forearms crossed and his curly head to one side, one eye on me. 'It's not about rest, eejit! It's BECAUSE you were a slave and then a stranger in a strange land that you must never oppress another stranger.'

Kapo, I think. *Kapo*. 'What are you talking about? You're the oppressing one, how am I oppressing you exactly? And anyway. You're not a stranger, you're Jude.'

'A SEEING EYE! A HEARING EAR!' he says, bopping me on the head with a sofa cushion.

'I am trying to read. Cut it out! Pax!' I say, holding up two crossed fingers whereupon Pax! bursts into the room, Did I hear my name? Have you started a fight without me? 'And furthermore,' I add loftily when Jude stops hitting me, 'I don't see how you can be the Seeing Eye God person AND a stranger.'

'Technically speaking,' Jude says, scritching Pax! vigorously behind both ears, 'I can. You oppress the stranger, you oppress me. God, that is. The Invisible Third, remember?'

'Well, thems the breaks,' I say, flipping pages. 'It's not all cushy being boss, is it? You have to go down with the ship and all that. Have a little oppression. Know what it's like for the rest of us joes. Fuck-hell. I've lost my place. Forget it. I'm not going.'

'We could go together.'

'OK,' I say, slamming my book shut. I am a pushover for Jude. Those are the facts and I face them.

Outside, the snow is still blowing but feathery now, billowing in the air from all quarters, it seems, falling upwards and down and across, and on to my lashes and white of the eye, white on white, to melt there with that surprising coldness that is like no other. The sky is dark and the few cars around move slowly, gingerly as Mum would say, and the tyres make that muffled creaky sound because the snow is deep in the road, and new, and I love it, how at the end of a snowstorm there are so few sounds and they are all different and separate with special pauses between, giving me a deep private feeling and a sudden conviction there is all the time in the world, for everything you want, and thoughts are crisp, your voice is crisp, there is nothing but time and clarity.

'Jude? Do you believe in God, then?'

'I BELIEVE in karnutzel. I believe in smoked meat sandwiches, medium-fat!'

'I'm serious. Come on! Is it a gishy question? Do you mind it? Oh, never mind.'

'I believe I was a stranger in a strange land,' Jude says, softly now, attentive.

'You could be that again, it could happen again. What does it mean?'

'Yes,' he says. 'Again and again.' And we go quiet for a while, kicking gently at snow, scuffling along in the quiet world, because words are so big on snowy nights, words and motion also, everything is bigger in echoing places. Then Jude says, 'Hey. Let's buy a beer at Robinson's. Drink it on the way back.'

'But there's beer at home. We'll have wine with dinner.'

'Jem. Ever had a beer in the dark, in the snow? It's good.'

'I like the one with the gold top and the black label, will they have that kind?'

I shuffle like Zach in the strange brightness of the shop while Jude gathers butter, French, unsalted, and other sundries called for in Dad's urgent tones as we traipsed away from the house, every short hop to Robinson's of a winter's night like a last chance at One Ton Camp for my dad. We could be snowed in for all time. Mr Robinson knows us well and he is not that bothered about the beer but Jude buys four bottles anyway so that it does not look fishy, the way one beer would. A single bottle purchase is definitely an on-the-way-home beer for two kids some way short of eighteen. Ever had a beer in the dark in the snow? I wonder if maybe there is something wrong with me that I am not eager for new things, or new places, unless I am with Jude or another Weiss, that I like the old things in their right places, the old ones, and my own room, and books everywhere, all the books, and these six faces I know and the one dog named Pax! by accident for an oath which is a password amongst us, meaning as long as we are together, any time there is distress, a Weiss is ensured all-out attention and rescue courtesy of a word in Latin and the raising of two crossed fingers. This is my country.

Jude opens the beer with his penknife a few paces from Robinson's.

'That's the one,' I say. 'That's the kind I meant. Thanks, Jude.'

Jude and I bash off home and he carries all the stuff in the crinkly paper bag under the arm farthest from me, and although the snow has no sound to speak of, I swear I can hear it falling, and that everything has a sound, and that sound comes before everything, before vision even, but maybe it is only the faint and persistent ringing I hear lately when things go quiet in the world, brightest in my left ear, a sound like the swish of skates on ice or far-off sleigh bells, or maybe just the sound of listening out too hard for something not there, not coming. Jude and I pass the bottle to and fro and he doesn't wipe my slobber and I don't wipe his, we never do, we mingle our slobber, no worries. And Jude is right. Beer in the dark, in the snow, it's good. It's all good.

Seeing and hearing. Book of Life, Book of Death.

The Talmud threat of Jude's against me to do with all my deeds being recorded and weighed up, etc., with two possible verdicts only, life or death and no halfway-house-type punishments such as a really bad cold or a limp or anything of that ilk, makes the whole card business of the nuns in my old country a mere whimsy. Measuring a girl's seemliness according to colour codes is slightly off-putting, but not likely to dissuade a girl from a life of crime and cheating. In fact, it is bound, largely, to give a girl nothing but an uneasy feeling for certain shades of pink and green, the heart sinking at the proffer, say, of a sweetie wrapped in pink aluminium, or a nice helping of creamed spinach. It is clearer to me than ever before just why Harriet pitched her green card in the bushes that day in my past. It was a case of contempt. Harriet meant to show how she is above the grading of behaviour by colour code, aiming even then for a life free of judgement by nuns who do not understand her, free of prejudice towards certain shades of blue, pink and green, which was a great show of wisdom in someone not yet fully formed and quite new to matters of morality, making me wonder now if born in other times, would she have pitched a yellow turban in the dust, or ripped a yellow star from a fond lapel of a favourite jacket, would she have risked life and breath for a life free of war and prejudice in the manner of heroes? Yes, I think so. Harriet has so much dash.

This Book business, then, is quite different. Life or death, no messing around. This saying regarding the eye and the ear and the Book is Jude's favourite since last September at the Jewish New Year when Dad explained over dinner about the Days of Awe, proving to me quite finally just what a powerful word this is, awe, covering many issues, from Adoration to reckoning and judgement, and all of these issues, godly.

'Dad,' I begin. 'One moment, please. I need to get this straight –'

'Oh God,' says Jude.

'Oh God,' says Ben.

'Don't mind them, my child,' goes my sister in a soothing voice. 'Go ahead, *je suis à l'écoute*. The world is your oyster.'

'*Les huîtres*,' says Gus who is remarkably proficient in the French language, particularly when it comes to culinary terms. '*Huîtres mornay.*'

'Dad? Are you listening? OK. There are three books actually, right? I mean the all-out good book and the all-out bad book and then the in-between one, kind of temporary, where God hasn't made a decision yet and just about everyone is in this temporary book, except for killers-no-remorse, on the dark side, and saints on –'

'We don't have saints,' says Jude, twirling spaghetti. 'I told you that.'

'OK, OK! Martyrs then, we have those! Saintly types. Let me finish! So, Dad. Unless you're a clear-cut case and so on, you get hauled up in judgement EVERY year, you go up for review even if you passed the time before, is that it, every year at Rosh HaShanah? Yes?'

'THESE are the Days of Awe!' my dad says in his poetry voice. 'Ha ha ha!'

'Which are?' I ask. 'The New Year days plus Yom Kippur? The three days or the ones between as well? The whole ten? You said there are ten Days of Repentance.'

'I am beginning to think you have an obsession with numbers,' Ben informs me. 'It could be a problem.'

'It's not the only one she has,' adds Jude, elbowing Ben and raising his brows at Gus who starts giggling while Harriet looks around with an airy expression, like she would rather not have anything much to do with any of us, she would rather some fresh topic of conversation altogether.

'Rashi called Rosh HaShanah one long day,' says Dad.

'Rashi? Wait. You said two days, it's two.'

'Yes. One long day –'

'But –'

'A day of solemn rest,' my dad continues, kind of ignoring me and speaking in a weird far-off manner, like the past is a story he might tell but a place he must sometimes go alone, a place too sad and too funny to explain. I think how Mum also has a strange and private way with the past, how she hardly ever speaks about it, and when she does, she is real quiet and fragile and party-merry, as in that Paradise painting, merry, even though the stories she tells strike me as a bit desperate and I listen with a fierce desire to rescue the girl in the story, the girl with the gift for piano playing and a love of straight lines and books, and a depressing mother who is not her own mother and a father who cannot read or write, an old soldier gassed in the First World War. I want to rescue this girl with scholarships in everything and no permission to do anything because she is one step from the workhouse and because she is a girl. It makes me mad, it really does, and then I remember quite suddenly how this girl is Frances, my mother, and she is right here, safe. Looking back on life is no breezy thing, I can see that. It requires fortitude and easily accounts for this slight derangement in grown-ups such as I observe in Yaakov tonight, my very dad who is reciting Talmud and Torah things in a poetry voice and a far-off manner. 'A day,' he says, 'of sounding the ram's horn –'

'Shofar,' says Jude.

'Did you know,' begins Ben, 'that demons hate loud noises, which is another reason they sound the shofar?'

'I hate loud noises,' I say, a bit worried.

'What larks!' declares Harriet.

'It's not the MAIN reason,' says Jude with disdain.

'Still. It's one reason,' goes Ben, kind of huffy and staring into his plate while Dad carries on with recitations, talking right over our voices.

'In the seventh month, on the first day of the month, you shall have a holy gathering, and . . . ahh . . . You shall not do any manner of work –'

'Yay,' says Jude, raising a glass.

'– and you shall sacrifice an offering . . . a bull, um, a ram and SEVEN YOUNG LAMBS without blemish!' says Dad, looking round at us all with large and hungry eyes, and just before he comes to that favourite quote of Jude's regarding the three things to consider to escape the clutches of sin, ominous lines of poetry about the eye, the ear and the book that my dad intones in Hebrew and then English, he tells us stories of extreme youth, new and old, stories to do with the swinging of roosters and the counting of stars and the sprinkling of bread into running water, preferably water with fish swimming therein, the littering of bread symbolic, he says, of casting off sins, going to show, once again, how bread is not only a feature of uprisings and revolution but covers everything, all causes and things, life, death, rah-rah, the lot. I listen to these stories new and old and reflect how I know the words to many but hear them differently, old ones, say, about the numbering of three stars in the night sky to mark the Sabbath, and new ones about the reciting of prayers by my dad in extreme youth amongst nine other boys and men, anyone over thirteen, which is how it must be for full prayer-power, because some prayers cannot be said alone, you have to gang up, and little kids do not really count, and girls do not count at all, girls simply cannot make up the numbers in a quorum, no, sir. Why? I do not know. Maybe because we have no special distinguishing mark as is bestowed upon boys by a specially designated person wielding a blessed knife from the appropriate set of cutlery reserved for *fleischig* only, a mark of special distinction bestowed eight days after birth.

Harriet has heard enough. She has had it with rams, kid, fish, roosters and lambs in sacrifice situations, lambs and kid especially, what with being struck down before their prime, and so she claps her hands to her ears and starts singing that new hit song of Dad's, a very embarrassing song that appeals to Harriet, I believe, purely for the wildlife connotations.

'Bingo-bango-BONGO, I don't want to leave the JUNGLE!' sings my sister.

'Congo,' says Gus, correcting her quite politely. 'Not jungle, Congo.'

'Zaire,' says Jude.

'I thought some of it is still Congo,' goes Ben.

'Two separate countries,' explains Jude. 'Republic of Congo, Republic of Zaire. They're separate.'

'Oh, right,' says Ben. 'Well, thanks. *Ago maximas gratias tibi.*'

'Look,' I say, getting a bit crazed. 'Can I just ask one more thing. May I? About the Book. Dad? Are you listening?'

'Will you be dropping in, my dear?' Harriet asks Jude. 'To the Congo?'

'It's not on the list of places,' says Gus. 'I've seen the list. And the maps.'

'Why thank you. I see. And, *ago maximas . . .*' muses Harriet, batting her lashes at Ben. 'I am sure that is not Russian. What language is it?'

'*Le langage,*' quotes Gus, '*est source de malentendus.*'

My little brother can quote freely from *Le Petit Prince* and it is always quite telling when he so chooses, a special moment he shares with Mum, the rest of us mere bystanders, same as that Russian aristocrat hug is special for Harriet and him, something private happening in public by mistake almost, because the urge is there and there is nothing you can do. Whenever a *Little Prince* in the French language moment comes upon Gus, such as when Mum empties a vase of some fading bouquet and he remarks '*ma fleur est éphémère*', we pipe down for it and there is a seemly hush, as there is right now when he says that thing about language being the source of misunderstandings, etc.

'Quite right, darling,' remarks Frances and Gus nods and frowns, and smiles that little upside-down smile of his, the one suggesting deep thought and sensibilities in the French language.

'*Ago maximas gratias tibi*,' explains Jude. 'Latin for thank you. I extend many thanks to you. Latin. Which is NOT for girls.'

'Hey! Whoa there,' I say. 'I'm in my fourth year of Latin. Just because Harriet doesn't take Latin does not mean it's a boy thing. PLUS she knows a lot of Latin words, all those animal families and species and things, and names of specimens. *Biologie*, *Écologie*, words in those subjects. That's Latin! So stop ganging up on us.'

'Jem, Jem, no one's ganging up,' my dad says, patting the air with both hands, like he is bouncing two balls or something. I bloody hate it when he does that, and now Harriet strokes my hand, possibly in gratitude for sticking up for her, but more likely because she thinks I am about to lose my marbles. It's extremely annoying and although Harriet's touch is soft, it feels wild to me, scratchy and alarming as someone stroking your sunburn, like all the nerves are on your outsides.

'Votes for women!' declares Harriet. 'Votes and rights!'

'What rights do you want, Harriet?' asks Jude. 'Rights to take out the rubbish? Shovel the snow? Bring up logs from the boiler room? Rake leaves?'

'Just a cotton-picking minute, bejesu,' I say. 'We do logs, we rake!'

'You don't do logs any more.'

'That's because of spiders. It's a spider thing.'

'Exactly,' says Jude, satisfied.

'What I'd like,' begins Harriet quite slowly, 'in my rights, is . . . at the library, there is a book. Ornithology. I want to keep it longer than three weeks. I explain and explain. I need it for a project, I say. No, Harriet Weiss! Three weeks only, we stamp it and you can take it out again. Return, stamp, borrow. Return, stamp, borrow.'

'Maybe you would like that book for your birthday,' suggests Mum.

'How delightful! But, you see, I sent Jude one day. To the desk. And he said the same thing, I need it for a project and they let him take it for six weeks.'

'Harriet,' I say. 'That's because Jude is grumpy and scary.'

'But, my dear,' replies Harriet, patting my hand again, 'you are grumpy and scary and I made you ask for me and it didn't work. Three weeks only!'

'Oh yeh. I forgot. So it might be a girl-boy thing. Hmm. I don't know, is this really rights for women though?'

'It's rights for Harriet,' offers Gus politely, like a peace pipe.

'Hear, hear,' says Frances, tapping the table with two fingers. 'Quite right!'

'And there is no ganging up! Everyone is EQUAL in this house!' says Dad.

'And I wouldn't say Jude and Jem are scary,' adds Mum. 'Thoughtful, yes. Serious. All my children are serious.'

'Some of us are just scarier than others,' mumbles Jude, breaking off a piece of ficelle.

'WHY do you have to DO THAT?!' I shout. 'Like I'm your ENEMY! Like you don't know me any more! And I can't say anything right! Not ANYTHING!'

Jude looks stricken, holding the bread in mid-air and staring at me, frowning a little, no blinking. In aquamarine.

'Please,' I say in a small voice. Jem, be seemly, Jem, be calm . . . it's a girl thing, be a girl. 'I'd like to finish, please. My question. About the Book.'

'Go ahead,' says Dad, leaning back in his chair like a great general, ready for it all now, the petitions and dispatches, tactics, maps and numbers, ground won, ground lost, dead, captured, missing, deserted, wounded, shell-shocked. Perplexed.

'Well,' I begin, aware of all eyes on me. 'Two things. First off, why do you have to go through it every year? The test, I mean. So you don't get lax, is that it? You can't be trusted? And secondly, when do you know if you've made it out of the temporary book into the life book? After the ten days? Or on Yom Kippur? And what if you are suddenly dying of a car smash or fatal disease, how do you know if it's just an accident, when it might be a judgement, because God put you in the death book for sins and sinfulness? When do you know? How do you know? You can't see the books, right? So, does someone come and tell you? How does it work exactly?'

'Excuse me, God,' says Jude, eyes bright with hilarity. 'Please, Sir, my sister Jem would like to SEE the books!'

Jude and Ben collapse now, flopping around in their chairs and generally going overboard in terms of mirth and derision and my dad explodes with laughter while Harriet and Gus wave their arms about in the spirit of things. It's quite raucous.

'Children, children!' says Frances. 'I think everyone should take a DEEP BREATH! And Yaakov, you must explain to Jem. Patiently, please. It's difficult.'

'Consider three things,' my dad recites in Hebrew and then English, in his doomy Bible voice, 'and you will not come into the clutches of sin. Know what is above you: a seeing eye, a hearing ear, and a book in which all your deeds are recorded!'

'KNOW WHAT IS ABOVE YOU,' Jude chants.

'And the tenth day of this seventh month,' says Dad, 'is the Day of Atonement –'

'A seeing EYE, a hearing EAR!'

'– and you shall afflict your souls, and you shall bring an offering –'

'STOP IT! STOP IT! BOTH OF YOU!' I yell, shooting up out of my chair so suddenly, it slams backwards to the floor and I carry on screaming, banging both hands on the table, driven by the rising fury within, too big for my body. 'STOP IT! It's because I'm a girl! If Jude asked the same question – or Ben – I'm not stupid! I'm not CRAZY! And I'm not a baby! I'm fourteen nearly fifteen! I'm just trying to understand! Leave me alone! You think it's so funny, I'm so funny! Go away! I'm not coming back!' I say, more and more ridiculous, fleeing the dining table to jam myself into a far corner of the living room, grabbing *Tintin* books from the low childhood shelves on my way, managing to recognise my favourites though my vision is clouded, like heatstroke. *Objectif Lune, On a Marché sur la Lune.*

Before stepping out, Tintin stands in the open doorway of the red-and-white rocket ship and he is in awe, a word covering many issues, even applicable to Tintin gazing upon a lunar landscape that is nightmarish, he says, a deathly place, desolated, making him afraid, but like that other hero Horatio Nelson, enabled also. And ennobled, distinguished. Tintin is the first man on the Moon.

C'est . . . comment vous le décrire? . . . un paysage de cauchemar, un paysage mort, effrayant de désolation . . .

I know all the words, all the pictures, I remember everything. Words are like rescue sometimes. Book of Life! I know this place. I flip pages and concentrate hard, chasing other words, other pictures I know so well. Words are like peril, I know this place too. From other books, such as books about Brontës. Book of Death! Three deaths in nine months, Branwell, Emily, Anne. The Reverend Brontë has already lost his two eldest daughters and a wife. He keeps a manual of family health and scrawls notes in it, all manner of personal comments and analysis scrawled in margins next to entries on 'Nightmare' and 'Insanity or Mental Derangement', afflictions causing his one and only son to hurtle towards death, his son who is raving due to alcohol and opium addictions and a feeling of failure.

It must be hard to deduce the causes when faced with the impending death of a loved one, to tell just what came first, derangement or addiction. Which comes first? I don't know. But I know this, how the Reverend Brontë made not one single notation in the family health manual next to the entry on 'Consumption' though he lost four out of five daughters to consumption. I read that the Reverend showed much grief when his son died. Anguish. I read he did not show anguish for the girls, maybe because he had so many, or maybe he showed anguish for the girls in locked rooms with no witnesses for the recording of his anguish, yet I wish I had not read these words, because they linger and I have doubts now where there were no doubts before, about love and so on, and whether it is equal. I wonder about the equality of love for sons and daughters, and this is a bad doubt to have. It is possible I had the doubts first and that is why the words flared up on the page when I read them, seeming so much bigger and bolder than other words on the page. Words or doubts. Which come first? Forget it, don't cry. Remembering or crying. Which comes first?

Everyone mills about that night of Rosh HaShanah, making little overtures of the heart-melting variety, my mother tucking a strand of hair behind my ear in passing, a wayward lock dangling between my eyes and Tintin in the nightmarish landscape, and Harriet does a dance in the manner of Isadora not three paces away, and Jude leans up against me on the sofa when it is nearly time to watch the news, joined quickly by Ben and Gus, make room for the cat! I try to hold firm and take a dignified stance but I am a soft touch for peace pipes and the burying of hatchets. I watch my dad disappear up the stairs to his office, coming back down shortly thereafter with that sure and heavy tread of his, a footfall like a sign and a message also, even if only to say he has been walking a long time and is responsible for so much, and he walks for all of us, do not forget this. He stops at the foot of the stairs with his two large tomes and calls my name and I unsquish myself from the clutches of Ben, Jude and Gus and step up to my dad.

'Hold out your arms,' he says, and I do, squeezing my elbows tight to my ribs with my forearms and open palms straight before me in what we call the Forklift, a topmost useful hold for the ferrying of folded towels from washer-dryer to linen cupboard, and logs from boiler room to fireplace, etc., and also a joke for when asked just how hungry we are for dinner or what we want for our birthdays. There is no end to it, old chap, there is just no end to our desires. That's what the Forklift means in a joke. And there is a joke inside the joke, because greed is truly not a problem in my family. Not one of us will go into the Death Book on account of greed.

Dad holds up his first tome before laying it across my wee fore-arms.

'Five Books of Moses,' he announces. 'Torah!' he says, and then he raises the second volume. 'Talmud. Traditions, laws, debates. The works! You'll see. Any questions, you come to me. Right? Right!'

'Thanks, Daddy. Thanks.'

'OK. Now how about a hug for your old dad!'

This is not a question, it is a command, and OK with me. My dad does not go in much for hugs and regular demonstrations of affection, except where Frances is concerned, so that when he opens his arms wide like that and commands a hug, I always feel this is how it must be for a soldier stepping up for the VC, Victoria Cross, highest decoration for 'bravery in presence of the enemy' though I cannot think who my enemy is or what brave thing I did tonight apart from yell at the boys and Dad and generally show signs of Insanity or Mental Derangement.

I put the books down, forgetting to remove my specs, however, so they get mashed against my skull as Dad presses and squeezes my small person into the great body of him and I come out of this hug in a state of cheery disrepair, gravely winded and nursing glorious injuries to the head and skeleton, the costs of bravery. *For Valour*, for my valour. I walk off with the two books, glancing over my shoulder in search of my mother before bashing off to my room for a moment alone with the tomes I lay on my bed, sitting there next to them, the books I will study with a whole new attentiveness following the winter night, so very soon after this Rosh HaShanah, when Jude comes home from Jeremy Levinthal's funeral and snow drips from his socks, a whole new attentiveness worthy of Sherlock Holmes himself, and marked by fever, just as it was with the great detective, the fever of his race against time and evil, and the imperious clutch of fate.

I do not sleep this whole night of the day Gus nearly died, that's how it feels. One long day. One long night. One long day of forty-eight hours. Dad! Who is Rashi? Rashi, b.1040, d.1105. Rashi is a sage and there are a lot of these in Judaism. Most sages are rabbis, types with special wisdom who spend just about all day well into the night reading and studying and making little notations and having reveries and deep thoughts related to books, which is more or less what everyone in my house does, though we do not quite qualify as sages, probably because we also go in for sporting activities and film viewing and ridiculous games plus we have a dog. It is a good idea to have a dog in life if you are a person with sage inclinations, a dog who cannot open the fridge or a tin by himself, let alone a cutlery drawer, and who needs a human-being escort when he is out strolling in the city, because this reminds a person with a big thing for books and reading that he is in the world amongst people and dogs who might need him and desire a chinwag every so often on a subject of levity. A sage ought to have a dog, and a favourite sport.

A beard is a topmost requirement for a sage. Yaakov had a beard once. Before he met Frances. But he also had scurvy, so I am not sure if it was a beard of wisdom such as sages have. A sage beard is a no-vanity beard quite like that of the U-boat man, marking long days at sea, *untersee*, and those of transantarctic explorers, marking long days trapped by ice. The beard of a rabbi is a beard of knowledge. It has brushed the crumbs from large open tomes, a beard of deep thinking and isolation in small rooms full of books, a beard of long-seeing. In all these cases of bearded men, of sage, soldier, explorer, there is a notable paucity of female company. A no-vanity beard can be so sad. For seven days Zach and Mr Levinthal keep away from razors and scissors, they must not cut or trim or shave, and for those seven days they are relieved of grim reflections in

mirrors because they must not look in mirrors. These are the rules
and I grasp them. Seven days of this is seemly, a lifetime is cause
for treatment of Mental Derangement.

A sage's mission in life is to impart wisdom and clear up the
rules and laws attached to the Torah, so that people know what's
what and how to be, and it is a tough job that can put a person
in a very bad mood, Moses being a prime example of this, leading
everyone out of bondage and then going walkabout to take further
instructions and revelations from God while his people are losing
their minds due to exhaustion and abandonment and lack of leadership, and giving up Moses for lost. It's a communication problem.
Moses ought to have left a note the way the Weisses do. 'I am on
the mount doing research for my project. I may be a bit late for
supper. See you soon.' Moses does not leave a note and his people
are in a state of disarray and go in for false idolatry, a bad move
but understandable in the circumstances, though Moses does not
see it this way, coming back down from the mount and crashing
his two tablets to the ground in a rash manner, yelling and breaking
the false idol and scaring everybody quite badly before bashing off
up the mount again in a big huff and putting God in a bad mood
also because now He has to make those tablets all over again. It
is a great palaver and largely down to the strains of leadership and
the imparting of wisdom without the niceties of communication
skills and tolerance and so on, and this is why I recommend girls,
dogs, personal grooming and sporting activity, etc., all of which
can be very improving when it comes to matters of charm, honour,
good conduct, spirituality, overall deportment and outlook.

A rabbi studies the laws and rules and writes commentaries,
sometimes swapping these commentaries with other rabbis and
sages, in a spirit of companionship perhaps, and no doubt also to
steer clear of duplicating the same thoughts and commentaries,
which reminds me of the hockey-card business in my recent past.
The writing, swapping and discursing of commentaries can go on
for years, as I understand, and even from generation to generation
if the rabbi has rabbi sons. Frankly, I spy a flaw in all this and
have a small suggestion to offer which is no doubt disrespectful.
It seems to me, if some one rule is causing big headaches, confusion and a great deal of commentary, not to mention rash behaviour amongst sages, and even from generation to generation, maybe
there is something wrong with the rule in question. I'm just saying.

A sage ought to have a dog and a favourite sport, for purposes of perspective and so on. Take a wee break! Look up, you look down too much! When you live with a rule a very long time, it can be downright hard to abandon it, which is why everyone got so mad at Roger Bacon and his spectacles, and at Galileo for pointing out that the Sun is the centre of our Galaxy and not the Earth at all, because nobody likes this, being told to start again and entertain a whole new vision of things knowable.

I am still not happy about the rules concerning women and washing. Honey, are you washed? I want to separate this business of monthly blood and marriage and childbirth from the business of sacrifice and the scapegoat story Jude told me about with that red ribbon turning white and the promise of atonement spoken in ominous tones. *You will be cleansed.* If I had not blinked, if my blood could run white, sparkling as streams. I'm so sorry, Gus.

Mikveh. A Ferrari-red bicycle, Gus's ashen face, his blazing ear and blanching lip. Red into white. Here is a good rule, I am happy about this rule. You may, you must violate the Sabbath to save a life. St Christopher was a giant, with giant ways.

A seeing eye, a hearing ear. I could not see, I could not hear, just for a moment. I said I was sorry three times.

One long day.

It seems like one long day since Ben stood on the dock and shook his fist at the skies, Jekyll into Hyde, clutching that note with Jude's fifteen commandments to him therein. One long day with a Farewell Barbecue and a morning after when Gus rode his bike in tight circles, near perfect, and Zach and Jude piled into Mr Levinthal's car taking driveway exit number one leading straight out of the property into the great world. And then all the running and shouting, running and shouting, and sudden murmuring.

I fall in and out of sleep and ponder dashing downstairs for the book I left there. Outside Mum and Dad's door, I believe. And I ponder those words Frank Hurley wrote about the men and the landing of the two open boats on Elephant Island after seven days on the winter seas and 170 days on drifting ice. It has been 497 days since they stood on solid earth. 'Many suffered from temporary aberration, walking aimlessly about,' writes Frank observing the men staggering on the shore around Cape Wild, Cape Bloody Wild, and that was definitely the case with us in the cottage this day and evening following the relay race of doctors with small suit-

cases, Ben, Harriet and me staggering about and loitering outside
Mum and Dad's room where Gus is, until they close the door on
us for a little while, and we do not close doors in this family.

*How Gus came into the house for to be healed of his wounds,
and how the King would begin to handle him, and after him many
other knights of the Round Table, and anon he was all whole, and
how Jem required forgiveness.*

Dad emerges around suppertime and hustles us into the kitchen,
assigning tasks of peeling and boiling potatoes, cracking eggs,
opening tins of salmon and cutting up vegetables, my dad singing
a medley of his best hits the whole while with pauses for criticism
of our handiwork and cuffs on the head of the exuberant kind. He
sets the table himself, spilling a flurry of cutlery and unfolded
napkins on to the table from a dizzy height and so causing an
unseemly clatter and then the four of us sit down in a scrape of
wooden chair on hard tile to a heap of Plastic Eggs and Salmon
Mixture, two of my dad's top specialities in one go. I relish the
egg, slippery below, hard above, and the potato lumps and eyes
and flecks of skin and I'm not bothered by the crunch in a mixture
that is part onion and celery and part bone. A fish is a vertebrate.
We listen to Yaakov tell some bad jokes in a bigger voice than per
usual and he repeats that old story for the umpteenth time, the one
about being alone with me at the cottage one time, everyone else
due on the early-evening coach from town loaded with last-minute
Xmas supplies, and before we jump in the car to meet them, he
tosses up two mushroom omelettes, but there is only one small box
of mushrooms and he uses all the mushrooms, not leaving me one
bitty stalk, so that I have a mushroom omelette with nothing inside
but wobbly whitish streaks from inadequate beating, streaks which
always freak me out. My dad beats an egg with abandon but he
doesn't fold, you have to fold or you will have wobbly whitish
streaks suggestive of wounds doomed to fester for ever. The gathering and cooking of food in the absence of Frances is a helter-
skelter affair with my dad, marked by merriment and subsequent
exhaustion and tummy aches and I decide this is an ancestral thing
in him, a legacy of wandering and being on the run, of racing
against the clock, against time and evil and the imperious clutch
of fate, and of being thankful, as Harriet might say, for small
mercies, such as bread on a Sabbath day, bread falling like snow.

I play along with the mushroom omelette story and act out my outrage and misery of that famous occasion which is such an endless source of glee for my dad. I act it out for the umpteenth time, to the usual huzzahs, and there is a lot of noise in the dining room as the sun sets but still I see Gus in mid-air, a pioneer of aviation with a special purpose, a vision all his own. Navigation is an art.

I am relieved of mess duty tonight, no doubt because I am deemed unreliable and not to be trusted with crockery and glassware, not on a day I have let my one small charge slip from view, from my ordained care and attention, standing rooted to the ground instead, in a state of dreamy paralysis I can only think of as awe. These are my days of awe. I bash off to the living room and hover outside Mum and Dad's bedroom where Gus and Frances are and I walk aimlessly about, fingering and rejecting books, longing for the others to join me because sometimes a commotion is so restoring.

When Dad leads out the galley slaves, Harriet looks especially aggrieved and worn out due to close contact with dirty dishes and wet rags, and after a while of thumbing books and flicking the news on and off, we are allowed to say our goodnights to Gus, one by one, not too close! Then it is Yaakov's time to do his lamp-lighter job. My dad is keeper of the flame. When passing by on dimming afternoons, he will switch on a lamp or overhead fixture if ever he spies one of us reading in what he considers to be inadequate illumination.

'How about a little light on the subject!' he will say. This is not a question.

'Thanks, Dad,' is the expected response, even if you do not want the glare of electricity beaming at you. Do not switch off the lamp, as that would be insulting. Dad knows better. There should be light, let there be light.

And now, same as every night-time he is ready for bed, he marches through the house, switching off as he goes and pitching us all into sheer darkness, no matter what anyone is up to, lingering long enough to enjoy the startled shuffles and the chorus of Hey! because he loves to be the cause of uprisings. Hey, Dad! I'm reading! Hey! I'm making toast! Hey, someone turn a light on! I'm halfway up the stairs, bloody!

Tonight there is no uprising, there are no Heys of protest.

Ben whispers, 'See you in the morning, see you, girls.'

I crouch on the stairs where I am stranded and clutch the banisters, getting that jailbird feeling. I am waiting for my night vision, for my retina cells to get sensitised to the dark and through the banisters I can just detect the large mass of Ben shuffling from the sofa to his room, and I can hear Harriet breathing somewhere down below, waiting also. The eye is a camera, it works the same, with an opening for light and a lens that changes shape to focus, and a plate at the back for the gathering of light. The plate is the retina and it has two types of cells, cone cells and rod cells, the rods largely doing the nightshift, being insensitive to colour but most sensitive to low light. Night vision is black and white, as in old films, and old films are my favourite.

Clearly, Harriet's rod cells are more quickly adaptable to night than mine, because pretty soon she is scampering past me on the stairs, going Beep-beep! Beep-beep! which is how we deal with traffic in our house, impediments in the form of a Weiss sprawled in one's path or standing in a doorway, a stairwell, an open fridge, or generally lolling about and impeding one's progress in life at a critical moment. Beep-beep! is what we say in varying tones of urgency or courtesy, beep-beep! like we are a houseful of rally cars.

That was a bad day at Black Rock, wasn't it, Ben? I asked him yesterday, recalling that day at the karting track when we nearly lost Gus, his air passageways, bronchi, simply not equipped for the excitement of cars of the racing kind and the rousing tempest of happy clouds of dust and petrol and cheering.

Which day?

Gus Day.

Oh yes . . . Yeh.

9. *Rag Gus about his inhaler and his medicines. Shocks can collapse the lungs, he almost died that day.*

And today, Jude. Right after you left, today too. He almost died.

10^{28}. This is the approximate amount of atoms in a human body. I remember this number, no doubt because of an obsession I have, though there is not always clarity in an obsession, uncertain as I am just how many noughts there are in 10^{28}. What I do know is that it is a huge number, because the book says how to envision it, how it is approximately the same as the number of people who might fit in a star, something I also remember because of the vision I had of ghosts in stars, packed tight as sardines. How many life-times in Gus? Maybe 10^{28}.

When I am a sports writer, not a girl job, I will make motor racing my speciality. Formula One will be my province, in honour of Gus. Grand Prix racing is an exceedingly glamorous sport and a poignant one, featuring dashing daredevil types with no beards, considered bad luck for racing drivers and not very aerodynamic. Racers are dashing in all ways, in guise, and in passion for velocity, and they would surely have been RAF fighter pilots had the time been right, instead of which they hurtle along in racing cars, dicing with death for no good reason, maybe trying to hit upon a reason lap by lap of a circuit, and this may well count as a spiritual matter, who knows. In my opinion, there ought to be some seating in the grandstand reserved for sages and rabbis, so they can sit huddled together in their long coats and covered heads and flowy, complicated beards, clutching crinkly paper bags containing karnutzel snacks and sesame seed bagels. When a person is on a lifelong mission of study and the imparting of knowledge regarding the human condition and the rules and laws pertaining, he will need nutrients. Snacks. The rabbis observe the race and they write up commentaries, determining for us whether the laws in hallowed books have any bearing on the sporting life, and whether there are any revelations regarding spiritualities to be found in motor racing and other sports, such as boxing and baseball, cricket, football and rugby, sledging, hurdling of wooden horses, sailing, riding, natation, fencing and archery, and ice hockey, field hockey, running and leaping, and field games involving big sticks, such as pole vaulting and caber tossing, and maybe in sports to come, not yet invented, like bicycle riding for non-swimmers where there is no solid ground beneath, only an expanse of water, which is the habitat for fish. There ought to be Sporting Commentaries.

Commentary number one. How it is imperative to have physical fitness and an aptitude for mountaineering in the event of being chosen as leader of men. Moses goes up and down the mount, up and down the mount, no pit stops. Clearly, physical fitness and climbing skills are top requirements for the getting and imparting of wisdom, and the ferrying of heavy oblong tablets of testimony containing vital news and instruction. Look at Jude. He packed Zebedee along with books and fourteen pairs of pants and Harriet's wee magnifying glass. Jude might be a sage.

I need to tell Harriet something before we call it a day, but I have to wait until she settles down and turns her bed into home, a warm burrow. It will take a few minutes. Firstly, she has to go through her little protest against darkness and shadows, shooting me a sharp glance as she rearranges the bedroom door just so, the door I closed too far, leaving it open less than her regulation 10cm. Next, she switches the night light on and off three or four times to be absolutely sure it will not fail her in deepest night, and then she leaps into bed from a distance so as to fox the clutches of evil demons or the slithery rush of snakes, whatever might be lurking in the nether regions below the bed. Finally, she flaps around in an extravagant manner, fighting her sheets and blankets like she is caught in a trap until she has burrowed them into shape from within. It's exhausting and no surprise to me that my sister usually falls asleep so quickly thereafter.

'Everything OK in there?' I say.

No answer.

'Harriet? You asleep?'

'I'm not sure I brushed my teeth,' she replies. 'The memory eludes me.'

'You did. I saw you. Do you need anything from downstairs? I have to go down again, I left my book, I'll be back in a minute.'

'Jem?'

'Yes, old chap?'

'Remember when Jude was sick that time, when he was in his dressing gown for days and days and didn't go to school and we had to keep away from him and he was horrible, fucking-bloody grumpy?'

'Last October. Yeh. Mononucleosis,' I say, heading for the door.

'Well, Kath said it's a kissing disease, from too much kissing, is that true?'

'I've heard that too, but it can't be right. Look, do you really need to know now? Because I can look it up tomorrow. It's late.'

'Tomorrow then. And hepatitis, too. Mummy had that. Can you die from these? I'm just wondering.'

'NO. I don't think so. Anyway, I'm going downstairs. Back in a minute.'

'Why isn't there a word for it?'

'For what?'

'You can be an orphan, a widow. What if your brother dies, what are you?'

'No one's going to die around here.'

'There should be a word for it.'

'Yeh, you're right. Look, are you going to be OK? I'll be back in one minute, one and a bit. And I'm not turning any lights on but I'm taking the torch, so don't get all hysterical when I come back in, please. I'm warning you now. You'll see a beam of light, the door opens, it's ME! Right? Right.'

'Did someone put his bike away? Gus likes it parked at night, in the shed,' my sister says and I can hear little snuffly sounds and her voice is small and sad.

I walk over to Harriet's bed. 'Ahoy there.'

'Welcome aboard,' she says, as in olden times. 'Shiver me timbers.'

'Harriet. Mike took the bike away, remember? In his pickup. Some spokes got bent and the paint was scraped and the chain came off. He's going to fix it up.'

'It must be the right shade of red. Will you tell Mike? Maybe we should find it ourselves. It's a special red.'

'I know. Ferrari red. Yes. We can look for it in town, after school, this week. I'll ask Mike to hold off on the paint job.'

'And let's buy him a bell, a pretty one, in case he's going too fast and nobody's watching –'

My heart jump-starts like an engine so I pitch forward over my knees and am slightly winded, speaking to Harriet in a strange whisper beyond my control. 'You're blaming me. Harriet, are you blaming me?'

'Going TOO FAST CAN'T STOP!' she says, thumping me in the upper arm over and over with soft little head butts. 'Not your fault, not your fault, not your fault, Mummy told you.'

'OK,' I say. 'OK.'

'And Mike goes too fast. In his pickup. There is a great incidence of animal mortality on the roads! Thank heavens Pax! is still alive. Look right, look left, look right again – and if all clear, quick march! I taught him.'

'You remember! The bobby, when he came to the convent. At home – I mean, in our old country. Teaching us the right-of-way rules, road crossing. I liked him.'

'There is a great risk of mortality in the police force.'

'Probably. You're having a death moment, aren't you, Harriet? I can make it go away, I think. You want me to?'

Harriet nods slowly.

'I want you to try and think of very nice things, favourite stuff, like writing a list. I'm going to sit right here while you do it. Come on. Christmas, things like that. Chocolate. Say them aloud. OK? On your marks, get set, go!'

'*Death Comes for the Archbishop*,' my sister says in her small sad voice.

'What?'

'It's on your shelf. In here.'

'Oh right, I haven't read it yet. It's Jude's, I borrowed it, he had to read it for school. What about it?'

'*Death of the Heart*. You have lots of death books.'

'Books with death in the title?'

'Yes.'

'You want me to take them away. Is that it?'

'Yes, please. Just for tonight, I think. Please.'

'I'll have to check all the titles. It could take a while.'

'I know where they are,' says Harriet, taking my torch and scrambling out of bed and dragging a chair over to the shelves where she begins pulling at books and handing them to me one by one.

'Wait a minute,' I say, returning *Book of Saints*. 'There's no death here. No death in the title.'

'I know,' she replies, leaving me waving the book in the air.

'Well, could you put it back, then?'

'But, my dear,' Harriet says, 'saints is ALL death. Death, death, death.'

'Oh. Right, of course. Sorry.' I add the saints to the reject pile.

'So much French death!' my sister remarks, rather cross, tossing out Céline, Gide, Maupassant, Montherlant.

'Yeh, it's bad,' I say, thinking of Mlle Aragon who is possibly guilty of sex mania and will very soon be following me down convent corridors in her dark glasses and black leather gloves. 'It's poetic. Romantic, I mean. In an official way. It's a rule of tragedy. Oh, never mind, let's not talk about it.'

Harriet shines the light into the cupboard while I stash the books and cover them up with a T-shirt. 'How's that, then?'

'The one next to your bed.'

'Harriet, I'm in the middle of that!'

'You're always reading it.'

'It has 997 pages plus glossary! Look, I'll put it in my satchel, you won't see it.'

'*Morte D'Arthur!* There is no "e" on the end of "mort"! And Arthur is not French. He's English,' says Harriet, waltzing off and grumbling as she scampers back into bed.

'Ready then?' I ask.

'For what?' she says, all gloomy.

'The list of good things. I'm listening.'

'Mummy,' goes Harriet, a bit uncertain.

'Good, that's the way!'

'Hepatitis.'

'NO, Harriet. Try to separate things. A good thing without a bad thing attached.' Red into white. *You will be cleansed.* 'Come on. Try.'

'Zweig's. Everything at Café Zweig. Especially the discs with nuts and raisins. The light ones. And *Sachertorte*.'

'You like the dark ones.'

'Not as much. Not as much as you.'

'Well, anyway. Next!'

'Ornithology.'

'Yes! No fast cars up there, right? Not much bird mortality! On the road up there! Things are looking up! Hey! That's a joke, Harriet! Joke,' I say, but my sister frowns at me. 'Never mind. Go ahead.'

'Slaves and slavery.'

'What's good about that exactly?'

'I'm quite keen on the subject.'

'OK, then. Next.'

'Kath.'

'Are you sure you want Kath?'

'Because she drools? We are ALL God's creatures, my child,' replies Harriet.

'Doesn't mean we have to have her over for dinner all the bloody time. We have to mop up after!'

Harriet buries her chin in her chest and squeezes her eyes shut like a small bird ruffling up in a breeze and she makes a different kind of snuffly sound now, the laughing kind. Harriet is recovering from death.

'I'm going to nip downstairs now. All right? Back in a minute. You carry on.'

'Jude,' says Harriet when I reach the door. 'Jude.'

'He'll be back too,' I say, real quiet.

'Not for Christmas.'

'We don't know that. He'll try, he said. It'll be OK, everything's OK.'

'Holidays!'

'That's good.'

'The bagel man! Oh, do it! Please!'

'Harriet, I need my stuff. Coat and basket. Kojak boots. And it's better spontaneous, you know . . . I have to be in the mood. Do you mind? Soon I'll do it. Anything else?'

'Lady Penelope!'

'When I get back, I'll do her. If you're still awake.'

'Baby, it's cold outside!'

'I simply must GO!'

'Ben says you're moving into his room in town,' Harriet says in a rush.

'He did?'

'When he goes.'

'I don't have to. You don't want me to?'

My sister stares at me, sitting bolt upright and reminding me of old films wherein little kids are dying of romantic diseases, and one moment before expiring in a small heap on to a mountain of pillows, the child lurches into this bolt-upright position, wide-eyed and brimfull of energy, and it is definitely a horror moment with a lot of spook power. Is this true to life? I cannot tell, but it is too late for me now, too late for happy dissuasion because I have seen it in old films and played it out in my head, and am now destined to be on the lookout in the ailing for small signs of agitation that herald the awful moment, the terrible lurch upright from a bank of pillows and the prompt expiring, no last words. Be prepared! There are some things, I believe, for which there is no readiness. Sometimes my sister will do this for fun, the Romantic Disease Trick, as we call it, Harriet springing up in bed like a fish out of the lake on a calm day, whereupon I simply fall apart, screaming at my sister, and storming about the room in a desperate manner while she scampers after me, going 'There, there, my dear' and asking do I need a glass of water, and why don't I take some deep breaths, etc.

The Romantic Disease Trick as inspired by old films is not what is on Harriet's mind tonight. My sister is not trying to spook me. She has had a death moment and all her thoughts lead her one place only, to a vision of sudden change and calamity she wants

me to fix, turning her bad dream, somehow, into good, finding
something kind and familiar in this land too strange. Everything
is messed up in her house and this is why she is sitting bolt upright
and looking at me like she is no longer chief pirate and master of
the ship, temperance pirate, navigator, no, her bed is a slight and
sorry raft tossing on angry night-time seas when her light-gathering
power is poor, her eyes sensitised to low light and no colour, and
my sister has no uneasy feelings for colour, colour films are her
favourite.

'I'll stay as long as you want. In town, I mean. Our room. I'm
not moving out.'

'Maybe I should come downstairs with you,' says Harriet. 'What
book did you leave? Why do you need it? It's sleepy time.'

'Shackleton book. I need it, that's all. It'll be quieter just me.
And sooner I go –'

'Sooner you're back!'

'Right!'

This is a thing I do with Harriet on days she pulls up short
halfway to school, dragging her feet like she is a slave hauling
bricks in the land of Egypt. Sooner you go, sooner you're back. I
tell her that each step she takes, every hour she survives in classroom, gym and refectory, she is not farther from home but one
step, one hour closer, and it usually works, she perks up and will
even skip ahead, casting impatient backward glances in my direction, as if merely by desire she can speed us both through this part
of our day, this stretch of a journey less scenic.

'I'll time you,' says Harriet. 'I'm counting from – now!'

'OK.'

'Wait! Did I wash my face? I'm not sure I did.'

'Harriet, you're not going to a Russian ball or anything, you're
just going to sleep,' I say, although, who knows, maybe dreaming
for my sister is like party-going, and sleep the invitation to evening
garden parties of the reunion kind, with all her friends in colourful
garments and rabbits and deer round about like this were the most
regular thing in the world, rabbits and deer and people mixing at
parties as in that Paradise painting. If dreaming is quite close to
Paradise for Harriet, then I can see why nightmares shake her so
badly and why she is so rattled tonight, when the knowable has
given way to the unknowable in this diminishing ratio, which is
the character of the Universe, as Ben explained, and if you do not

have a scientific bent, you have more of a Russian-ball bent, this is not very reassuring, I can see that.

'Honey,' I say. 'You're the ONLY CLEAN THING in the QUARTER!'

And my sister suddenly stands up in bed and raises her hands to her chin, head up and eyes heavenwards, as if counting the stars, making me smile because here it comes, Harriet's famous imitation of Blanche's single moment of rapture, when she is kissed on a date before her man turns brute, a moment Harriet is prone to act out any time, in acknowledgement of favours large and small, if you pass her the butter, if you save her from death.

'Sometimes,' she declares in tones of rapture, 'there's God – so quickly!'

There it is. My book in a spill of light right outside Mum and Dad's door where I was reading earlier, hoping to be called upon, to be needed, or just to keep vigil, and I remember another vigil in another time, involving Jude and this very same book, Jude on the Russian ship outside Mum's cabin, guarding the door like a watchdog. Some things are so very much the same as other things in other times, they simply do not come to mind, which is strange, as if only differences have the power of surprise and alarm, as in that puzzle on the puzzle page of comics, with the two identical portraits, of a boy, say, tying his shoe, identical but for some minute difference easy to recognise straight off because everything feels wrong in the pit of you, though it might be down to one tiny flaw, a missing eyelet in a lace-up shoe, an extra fine line on his forehead. What is wrong with this picture? It's a no-puzzle puzzle. The real puzzle is this, how I sat outside Mum and Dad's door with a Shackleton book earlier, keeping vigil, exactly the way Jude did five years ago yet I do not recall it till now, and I wonder which comes first, doing the same as Jude because we are one, or being one because we often act the same. What is wrong with this picture? That one is a girl. And for that girl, travel is not so important.

I make a little coughy sound so Mum and Dad do not think I am creeping about like a demented person or a felon or spy, but that I am on a mission of a practical and seemly nature. I am here to retrieve my book.

'Jem?' says Frances, real soft. Mum knows all the sounds, all the sounds of each one of us.

'Yeh,' I whisper, poking my face through the gap in the door. 'It's me. I left my book. Sorry, goodnight.'

I take in the view of Mum and Gus on the chaise longue Ben and Dad hauled in there this afternoon. Mum and Gus are propped up against a bank of pillows, Gus swaddled in sheets but for his naked upper body tucked under Mum's wing, and turned into her where she sits with one long leg beside him and the other draped over the side of the chaise, her foot trailing on the floor like an anchor.

Dad rouses himself in the half-light under the white duvet where he is dozing over a mess of books while waiting for Mum to join him there, and he speaks to me in his night voice, a voice I love because it is full of private things and gentleness, as if this were his truer side, his low-light self, the trace of gruffness having only to do with being roused from sleep, a passage he never makes easily, waking often with a great shake of dark locks, a deep growl and a loud bark that always has Pax! eyeing him with alarm and wonder. What is wrong with this picture? Ruff! That man is not a dog. But he has a mighty fine bark.

'Jem! Go to bed! It's late!' Dad says, flipping over in bed so there is a cascade of reading material to the floor, and I marvel at the back of him, thinking this is how the mountain ranges and noble glaciers must have appeared to Shackleton and the five men with him when they landed on South Georgia Island, mountains they had to cross to reach the whaling station in the foothills, six frostbitten men in tangly beards and the wrong shoes taking on a journey through an interior considered impassable, one never crossed before by any man.

'I'm going! I'm going!'

'You can stay for a minute,' says Frances in a voice like music, the start of a song, that secret radio voice Harriet loves to use for passing remarks regarding weather systems or some such thing.

I slide down the wall near the door, hugging my book to my chest, wound up tight with a feeling of gravitas, as when watching a tragedy in the cinema or theatre, as if seeing and hearing a tragedy were an accomplishment of will and inclination involving all the internal organs, all of them, another rule of tragedy perhaps, a rule of deportment for the audience. Mlle Aragon says there has to be a death in tragedy, it's a main rule, along with the human flaw one, otherwise the play does not qualify as tragedy, it is the main rule, but my commentary on the death rule is that it might be faulty.

Maybe there is no word for it yet, as Harriet said there is no word for losing a brother, and there should be, as there should be a word for no-death tragedy, an epic featuring awe and danger, sudden change and violent imaginings, the possibility of death causing temporary aberration in even the most cowboy-tough, a feeling tenebrous and final, in spite of there being no dead body, no, only a small boy with a bare chest revealing a fragile map of sinew and bone, a boy not quite asleep although his eyes are closed, and he is reaching out for Frances, touching her mouth with two delicate fingers as if expecting a message from thence, a story, a song, something to which he knows all the words, all the words and all the notes and the timing also, it's a double act.

A small boy with reaching-out fingers, a stroke of the lips, a gesture so minute, it's a signal. Begin.

'My time of day,' my mother sings, and Gus wheezes, his breathing still broken and faltering, but this is a wheeze of pleasure and excitement, he loves this number.

Show tune, number. There is a tiny moment at the start of a show tune, if you listen out for it, a pausette at the very beginning that follows the first few bars of music, the first few words, which I believe is a mark of consideration for the listener who might love this number and require a tiny moment, just the time it takes to recognise his big feeling and pull himself together because pleasure and excitement can be so blinding, so deafening, and without this moment, sometimes too small for belief, but there, the song will play on regardless, leaving the listener chasing, always chasing, fretting over that part of the song he missed due to the blindness and deafness that comes with an excess of feeling that is so close to rapture.

All-out rapture, a famous condition of saints and visionaries, must feel like that tiny moment for ever, and probably why saints do not live very long and are a general cause for concern and controversy in their lifetimes, their rapture unknowable and open to question, like that missing moment in the Big Bang of such alarming change and violence it does not obey the rules and laws of physics, it is outside the laws. What happened? Starmen just do not know and so they call it a singularity. This is a scientific word for rapture, rapture of the Universe, an end and a beginning. I am the beginning and the end! Some things only ever happen once. Ben told me what Dr Jensen said today, how Gus's heart stopped, how it failed him, meaning there will always be a missing moment in Gus's life where he fell out of time, and out of step with me, so that I am forever older by this one moment of time he never lived, his rapture, my singularity of alarming change and violence that made everything different, so quickly. What happened?

Regular rapture is merely a small shock bringing on a flood of feeling and an urgent desire to utter innermost thoughts, even to passing strangers, like the song moment in a musical when a character suddenly stops speaking and bursts into song and no one is the least surprised, because in a musical everyone suffers from this same peculiarity of breaking into song. It's symbolic. That is to say, for characters in a musical, songs are symbolic of highs and lows of feeling, and you just have to accept that and not be surprised. The same goes for death throes in tragedy. You are not supposed to be surprised by long speeches from the dying, and I often hang back with the cadaverous and their impossibly long death throes, so that when they rise up at the end, and stand all in a row waiting for applause while observing the improving effect they have had on you courtesy of death and tragedy, they are as ghosts to me, and brave shadows, which is why I am so wound up now, as Gus gears up for his duet with Frances, I still see the body he left behind, his limp self in Ben's arms on the landmark beach, a place of rapture.

'My time of day . . .' sings Frances, pausing in a show of consideration for the listener. 'Is the dark time, a couple of deals before dawn . . .'

A wheeze from Gus, a shiver. He loves this number, they have been singing it for years.

'When the street belongs to the –'

'– cop,' says Gus, whose job it is to fill in the missing words.

'And the janitor with the –'

'– mop.'

'And the grocery clerks are all gone. When the smell of the rain-washed pavement . . . comes up clean . . . and fresh and cold, and the streetlamp light . . . fills the gutter with –'

'– gold,' Gus adds, slipping further under the sheets alongside Frances so that his head rests in her lap, and his arm is flung across her waist, taut with pleasure because he knows what's coming, the chorus is coming, and the chorus is the best part.

'That's my time of day. My time of day. And you're the only GUS I've ever wanted to share it with me,' sings Mum, stopping there and waiting for Gus to pick up where she left off, as he always does, it's his job, but I worry he is just too short of breath tonight and well beyond regular rapture, so I lean in close, listening out for the sound of him with all my internal organs, wound up tight, as if the answer to everything were here, the remedy for everything, in the power of Gus to finish a funny old show tune about a love-struck gambler with a fondness for shadows. Sing, Gus. I stake my life on this song.

'That's my time of day . . .' A voice small and shy, innermost, sad as an echo. 'And you're the only doll I've ever wanted to . . . share it . . . with me.'

Gus died, and then he came back. I saw it and I heard it.

Sometimes, there's God. So quickly.

The Science of Deduction and Analysis.

William Blake dies singing.

Watson: This is indeed a mystery. What do you imagine that it means?

Holmes: I have no data yet. It is a capital mistake to theorise before one has data.

When doctors of psychiatry hit upon electricity as a remedy for the depressed and wayward, the man of sorrows acquainted with grief, they were hoping, as I suppose, that a wee dose of electricity might light him up like a lamp, reviving emotions of the cheery variety and inspiring an urgent desire to speak innermost thoughts, to sing them even, what with this sudden brand new outlook on life thanks to voltage and Count Volta, Alessandro Giuseppe Antonio Anastasio. Very interesting. In my opinion, however, all the doctors need is a fine collection of show tunes, choosing only those numbers loved by the grieving, songs causing a jolt to the heart in that tiny moment following the first few bars, the first words, a jolt to the heart which is the chief generator of electricity in the body, no battery required, rapture will do. I love this number! the grieving will say. And this is just another way to have an obsession with numbers.

The Book of Numbers was originally known as In the Wilderness, being an account of Moses' leadership in the wilderness and the comportment of his team under that leadership, and playing away, so to speak. Sporting Commentaries.

Before a match, you might see a footballer reach upwards in the players' tunnel at the entrance to the pitch and touch the arch above his head, with the emblem of his team there, touching it with his fingertips for extra sporting prowess and protection from injury, and for luck, maybe, though he is not really a gambling man. Before entering the room I pace some nights, I might touch my mezuzah according to the rules (optional), though I know it is against the rules to believe in a mezuzah, or touch of mezuzah, as protection from evil or any such pagan thing, just as it is frowned upon to dangle a mezuzah in the back of a car, in place, say, of a hard plastic doggie with fuzzy felt skin and a wobbly neck on a spring. For luck. This is kind of peevish on the part of sages, and so some days I reach out with a touch of fingertips according to the rules and believe in protection from evil in spite of the rules, a touch of two fingers like Gus to Mum's lips before the start of their number, and like in that first panel of the famous diptych painted around 1300 by an Unknown Umbrian Master, featuring the mother and child with their burden of knowingness. What is wrong with this picture? Nothing. Nothing and everything is wrong with this picture.

Blake dies singing and it is no mystery. Blake dies singing because he is rapturous and free, and where he is headed, he will not need much, not even shoes, and a small trick of velocity will take him straight there, to the eternal worlds, safe return doubtful, never mind, these are the true regions of reminiscence where he sees and hears everything, he remembers everything.

Holmes: Where is the mystery to all this?

Watson: It is as clear as daylight. I should have had more faith in your marvellous faculty.

ELEVEN

A Study in Scarlet.

Holmes writes an article he calls 'The Book of Life'. 'So all life is a great chain,' he writes, 'the nature of which is known whenever we are shown a single link of it. Like all other arts, the Science of Deduction and Analysis is one which can only be acquired by long and patient study, nor is life long enough to allow any mortal to attain the highest possible perfection in it,' meaning, there is just no end to it, old chap, to this business of knowledge and the writing of commentaries and rules pertaining, and it is what Edwin Hubble meant when he wrote that the history of astronomy is a history of receding horizons, the answers to things leading to further questions about things, there is just no end to it, so it is not surprising that the pursuit of the highest possible perfection can bring on the dark side in a person.

Holmes: I get down in the dumps at times and don't open my mouth for days on end. Just let me alone and I'll soon be right.

Doctor Watson does not ask questions on this matter. He is not that kind of doctor, he is not that kind of man. He can only watch Holmes in this passing state of decline and paralysis, his friend lolling on a sofa with a dreamy expression, hardly moving, hardly speaking, in the eternal worlds maybe, where he sees the chain in things, in all life. Watson lets him be, but he does not leave him alone. And he writes commentaries of his own. *A Study in Scarlet* is his first commentary, and in it he begins his long and patient study of his friend who is the only unofficial consulting detective in the world. 'SHERLOCK HOLMES – his limits', he writes, numbering the limits from 1 to 12. Here are some examples of his limits.

2. Knowledge of Philosophy – Nil.
4. Knowledge of Politics – Feeble.
5. Knowledge of Botany – Variable.
10. Plays the violin well.
11. Is an expert singlestick player, boxer, and swordsman.

What surprises Doctor Watson are the strange gaps in his friend's knowledge, but Holmes's dark side is not a problem for him, the Doctor makes no comment upon it, which is quite interesting, as a dark side can kill, same as romantic disease.

Life is a great chain.

William Blake is an engraver, a prophet. He is moody. Like Moses.

Lord Nelson goes to sea aged twelve. When he is a Lord and an Admiral with decorations, he remarks of the boy sailors in his charge that they are too young. They are too young for seamanship and wartime. I go to sea aged eleven, going on twelve, and on board ship, Jude reads a book about Shackleton and keeps vigil outside a cabin door with light spilling around it, an emanation.

St Francis has a dark side but he never shows it. Show no cracks! Displays of bad temper and depression are unseemly, an invitation to the Devil and to the distraction of vain pursuits such as singlestick playing, perhaps, and boxing and swordsmanship. The Devil, Francis knows, is an opportunist and Francis is the mirror of perfection, so he is not fair game.

Frank Wild is fair game. Winner of the Polar Medal, hero and brewmaster of Elephant Island, he ends his days a lost-cause bartender in a Zulu mining camp, on four quid a month, waiting and hoping for something, a taste, his favourite, Gut Rot 1916, but no amount of beer, wine or whisky will do, nothing comes near, it is a vain pursuit. Forget it. Everyone has a home. A place, a person, a time of day, you lose it and you wander for ever.

Buzz Aldrin has a dark side and he shows it. In 1969, sixteen years after Tintin, Buzz lands on the Moon where there is one-sixth gravity. He is never the same again. There is too much gravity on the Earth. He wants one-sixth gravity and he cannot have it and his own land is now strange to him, he has to wander it for ever.

Shane falls in love with a woman and her family of homesteaders, but she is married and he cannot have her. He does his job of protection and heroism on their behalf and then he has to go and wander for ever. Goodbye, Shane!

Forgetting is exile. I remember everything. I will not be a stranger in a strange land.

After eight days, when I am not circumcised because I am a girl, I open my eyes and see a woman in a red dress, scarlet, and a flash of silver chains with a cross amongst them, a cross with a moonstone at the heart of it, no graven image. I hear the soft murmur of chains and a still small voice. *All shall be well, and all shall be well and all manner of things shall be well.*

How Jem had a vision and entered into Gehenna, and of a fair bed therein, with other marvellous things, and of a king, and of bagels.

I don't know who did it, who took my shoes off and placed them very neatly over there by the wall under the chair by that spooky old painting of Mr Grünewald's depicting Jesus in his death throes, but it was probably either Nurse Nun or Slave Nun. Or was it Watchdog Nun? Whoever it was, one thing is certain, nuns of all nations and job descriptions have a mighty big thing for shoes and rules to do with shoes. No shoes in or on bed, no matter what.

I am laid out in the sick bay down here in the lower depths where the fine scents of arrabbiata sauce and espresso cannot reach me because of the bigger smell of nun soap, the orange stuff, whatsit, Ben? Coal tar. You would think coal tar soap would be black and you would be wrong. Black soap is posh and expensive and fragrant whereas coal tar soap is for slaves, nuns and the poorly, and must smell strong not fragrant, it has to be bigger than smells of slavery and endless devotions and romantic diseases, not to mention hopeless-case injuries such as mine. I lie under a scratchy blanket more suitable for beasts of the field or Roman legionaries heading off to war, men who have just downed gardening tools and said goodbye to loved ones and are therefore not in the complaining vein, they are too sad to quibble about the quality of blankets, due to what is uppermost in their minds. Doom, terrible absence and all-out calamity are the issues uppermost in mind. I get their drift. I lie in this small room, maybe only 6½ feet x 11, under a scratchy old blanket and it is no odds to me. I have other things in mind, namely how did it all happen exactly and has someone called for Harriet, and did someone sew stitches in me before wrapping the cream-coloured bandage round me like a turban, and am I going to be expelled, and just who was it who took my shoes off and placed them so very neatly over there by the wall?

No shoes in or on bed, no matter what. I can see how fretting over rules arising from a special contract with God, by which I mean, of course, the Ten Commandments and the 613 sub-commandments positive and negative, the *mitzvot* Jude apprised me of, I can see how these are worth fretting over, etc., but I note that fretting over rules not to do with the Decalogue can cause problems in a person's world view and nuns have a very bad case of this. For instance, a girl might be bleeding to death, with but a few digits on one hand hanging by a mere thread of gristle and sinew, or one eye lolling dangerously from a socket, or maybe the girl is rising bolt upright from a bank of pillows and going in for that last gasp in the romantic fashion, and yet nuns would be busy applying the shoes rules, removing shoes instead of tackling the more pressing issues with needle and thread and chemical substances, or even the spiritual necessities of rites and ablutions, which is their speciality. It's definitely a worry and I am grateful for the opportunity to grasp this today in my bare socks under a scratchy blanket, because I am quite interested in rules myself, and can foresee how the contract of rules I have drawn up with myself could mean the end of days, and before my very prime. My rules are largely concerned with washing. This is down to Mme Robuchon and to Art & Catechism and my Battle with Nuns, and to the books Yaakov gave me, in other words, to sex and blood matters in general. This is uppermost in my mind this Friday afternoon, and I can see it, how it is imperative to demand the reason for rules and apply them with wisdom and discretion, otherwise you may come to grief just because of an unreasonable commitment to rules. Death by air raid is an example.

You might be a person with an unreasonable commitment to washing last thing at night, no matter what, face, hands, feet, teeth, knees, underarms, ears, the lot, though you have been through the wash once already during the day by shower or bath and only a gentle swab and brush-up is strictly called for. There is an awful screeching of Heinkels aloft the attic bathroom you share with a younger sister who is wisely flinging toothbrush aside and scrambling for the dugout and calling your name, but you are stuck, being committed to washing the lot last thing at night, no matter what, even an awful sound of bombs falling, and the end of days. Demand the reason.

When you are a nun, the show must go on. This is a main rule and, like the personality-flaw-leading-to-death rule in Tragedy, you do not qualify as a nun without it. The show must go on. This is why there must be school even in blizzards of such ferocity, not a soul in the great world is making his way anywhere on two feet, or in a vehicle, unless in thraldom to nuns for whom the show must go on. Here is how it is at my convent on ferocious blizzard days.

Harriet and I tell Mum we will be home by lunch probably, and there is no point in ringing up nuns to ask if there is school today, because of course there is school today. You might expect Italian nuns, aside from Alpine Italian nuns, to be wary of snowstorms and have empathy for girls in storms and call the whole thing off, what with blizzards and hardiness to blizzards not being in their roots, but that is to forget they are nuns and do not conform to Nature and regular conditioning of *Biologie* and *Écologie*.

'*En avant!*' I say to Harriet in my World War I French officer voice, prodding her out the back door. 'Unto the breach, etc. *Pour la patrie! La gloire!*'

'And *Dieu. Pour Dieu* too, dear Sir,' says Harriet.

'Right! And for croque-monsieur! Home by lunch, I say! Sooner we go, etc.'

We face up to the tempest, then, the lashings of freezing wind and the assault of snowflakes sharp as knives. Safe return, doubtful. What a glorious time to be alive! It takes a lot of nun power to hold the cloakroom doors open against the gale-force winds, but in we troop, a sorry stream of girls in a state of near snow-blindness. We strip off to indoor things and gather in classrooms, hands clasped on desks, waiting and hoping for release as in that famous meeting of 9 November 1918 when war-torn commanders, bound by an oath sworn on regimental colours to die rather than disobey, gather with their vain Kaiser still unwilling to concede defeat before the greater enemy and the cards on the table regarding defeat, how it has come, no two ways about it.

What about the *Fahneneide*? asks Wilhelm II.

Today, says General Groener, the *Fahneneide* is only a form of words. Groener is a brave man, but he demands the reason for rules. It is all over. It is time for his soldiers to go home and for the Kaiser to face the facts regarding folly and defeat.

Armistice between nuns and blizzard is in the air and we can hear the yelps of release from the lower-form kids, *les petites*, even before Soeur Rosa saunters our way to utter words of defeat in the face of snow. She is not happy. She is cross. She wants the show to go on but she is surrounded by deserters and yellow-bellies. First, comes the news, always the same: Not one non-nun teacher has made it to school. They are not in thrall to nuns. They have stayed home and are no doubt doing what Harriet and I will soon be doing, eating croque-monsieur with cornichons on the side, and a pile of nice books to hand. After a grave pause, comes demob.

Now it is time for girls to queue up for the telephone in the great hall under the eyes of Soeur Rosa who stands in close in the Roman Imperial manner, one hip slung out to the side and arms folded, the toe of one black shoe tapping the floor and a wised-up look in her eye, ever suspicious, as we dial home requesting right of return, of pretend conversations with nobody on the other end, or pretend smiles if somehow refused the right of return. Which is another rule. A girl cannot simply bash off to her own home upon release by nuns after making it to school alive in the worst snowstorm for eighty-five years as pronounced on the radio. She cannot even go home on a day she has had a vision and incurred a head wound in a fit of fainting, no, she must ask permission of her parents, the very two people who made her in a love situation, a matter of sex with no anxiety for washing, only the soft sound of murmuring, and laughter, as I suppose, and the naming of names. Yaakov. Frances! Frances! They made me, they made Harriet, and they aimed for us to stick around in their house and live with them and come and go free as we please, goddammit.

I am reeling due to frostbite, earache and subsequent vertigo, and now the crazy fear Frances and Yaakov might refuse me the right of return. No! You stay with nuns! Or find a soup kitchen! A workhouse! We don't want you! Goodbye! I reel from cold and confusion and a wariness of the telephone I know Harriet accepts, no questions asked, aware that a telephone call with a Weiss gives me a strange sad feeling of a person twice removed, speaking in my ear from a place beyond reach, a strange sad feeling worse than plain absence, lonelier than imagination, and causing a sudden failure in me involving comprehension problems and speech impediments.

I nudge Harriet towards the phone and she dials in the jaunty and elegant manner she has observed in Mum, using the end of a pencil to spare her long nails, though Harriet's fingernails are as short as mine, short as boy nails.

'Well, hello, my dear!' Harriet says, ringing through to Frances. 'The weather is SO inclement, *n'est-ce-pas*? Jemima and I are coming home, we would like to drop in! IF it is CONVENIENT,' she adds, batting her eyelids at Soeur Rosa. 'Why, thank you, my dear! Luncheon? How delightful! We may take the scenic route but we will see you shortly. Pray for us!'

Before we head out, we get to huddle in the refectory in our duffels and boots as nuns pass around bowls of *chocolat* in compensation, I believe, for all the chaos the High Command of nuns has caused due to the application of rules without wisdom or discretion, and for the risk they have run of meetings on the morrow with anguished parents, their arms full of frozen convent girl no amount of tears will thaw.

I watch the passing of bowls and have a last-chance-Antarctic-explorer moment.

We were dreadfully cold till after our supper of cold pemmican and biscuit and a half pannikin of cocoa . . . All our feet are getting bad . . . Amputation is the least I can hope for now . . . blizzard bad as ever – tomorrow last chance . . . we are getting weaker, and the end cannot be far . . . For God's sake, look after our people.

Harriet, meanwhile, is having a fine chocolate moment. She is quite keen on convent *chocolat* which is Italian and very nice and served to us by Kitchen Nun who is soft on the Weiss girls, especially Harriet of course, even though we render her a bit misty-eyed because of perdition and Jewishness, etc.

'For what we are about to receive,' my sister says sweetly to Kitchen Nun, 'don't be stingy, baby!'

No shoes in or on bed, no matter what. Demand the reason! My feet are cold. Thirty-nine forms of work. What are the words? I can't – oh yes: *Remember that you were a slave in the land of Egypt and the Lord your God freed you with* – a mighty arm – no. With an outstretched hand – no, Jem. *With a mighty hand and an outstretched arm!* How many pairs, Jude? What pair are you on now? *Therefore the Lord your God has commanded you to observe the Sabbath day.* Thirty-nine forms of work. Number thirty-nine: Carrying. Children may not be carried. Kindly excuse us from rule #39. Not a problem. You must violate the Sabbath to save a life. See, Jem? Sometimes, there's reason. So quickly.

My feet are cold. Watchdog Nun! It was Watchdog Nun, I remember now, how she carried me downstairs right past the *Prayer sheet with the Wounds and the Nail*, late seventeenth century, or *Le Sacré-Pénis* as it is known in my circle, and into the sick bay in the lower depths with this other print on a wall, hanging here, as I understand from Art & Catechism, for my edification and speedy recovery, kind of a Get Well Soon! print. *Guérissez vite! Bisous, Jésus et les Soeurs.* Bloody. It's definitely confusing. Since the end of last term, before the summer break when Jude left with Zach and Gus flew off the dock and died for a moment, I am famous for the Objectif Lune Incident. The autumn term is only four days old, Tuesday, Wednesday, Thursday, today, and now I am also Famous for Visions and Famous for Wounds, and possibly for Fainting, even more famous for fainting than Harriet, because as I dropped to the floor I bashed my head, incurring a wound. My fit of fainting is something grave and historical, not romantic, unlike the poignant gasp and shimmy my sister goes in for, crumpling gracefully to the floor in such a plain play for the heart, no nun can deny her simple desire to be absolved of failure to do her homework, or gambol in the open air, or see Frances without delay and be home again where things are ordered according to a happy system all her own, simple desires expressed quite plainly in a graceful fit of fainting. Harriet has a winning way about her and a lot of wisdom and she will go far. Not I. This is my Last Stand, like Custer's, and General Custer was a hero according to the rules of Tragedy as taught by Mlle Aragon, with a tragic flaw that was, in his case, the vain pursuit of glory in the face of doom, and with death at the end, there was death at the end, death all round. This is my Last Stand.

I stare at the Crucifixion panel by Mr Grünewald and I am supposed to feel better. The bloody wound on my head, lunkhead! is a mere trifle compared to scourging and nail holes and spearing. He suffered so much, Soeur Rosa says, because he loves us so much, despite, I suppose, that dark night in the garden at Gethsemane when no one would stay up with him and he had to go to and fro in the garden, wondering Why me? and, Do I have the right stuff to be the Lamb of God and make a horrible spectacle of myself and heal everyone with my stripes? etc. *Let this cup pass from me*, he said. It was a moment of doubt, that's all, and the same thing happens to Ernest Shackleton the first night he spends on the shifting floes. Ernest goes to and fro in the ice watching the emergency light twinkle on and off in that persistent manner on his abandoned ship, knowing he has already failed in his mission to cross the Antarctic continent without ever really beginning, and wondering does he have the right stuff to take on his new mission of bringing his twenty-seven men home safe.

These two men both have a dark night, and make big decisions, and in the end they both say it. *Of them which thou gavest me, have I lost none.*

Jesus makes up his mind to drink from that cup, and just in time, because suddenly the garden is a jumping joint. Priests and officers come wielding lanterns and big sticks and pointy weapons, and jostle the disciples in a provoking fashion, trying to figure out which one is Jesus so they can clap him in irons, not easy when they are not sure of his countenance and it is night and there are all those beards and everyone is a bit excitable. Jesus stops the rumpus. Put up your swords, he says, meaning Cool your jets, and he definitely has a calming effect on people even though Simon lops some soldier's ear off. Simon is a bit rash and not all that swift when it comes to instructions and so on, but for the most part, everyone gets off lightly and there are no casualties. Jesus will be the only casualty, yet until that time, he has a contract with God. *Of them which thou gavest me, have I lost none.* Well done, Jesus.

When Shackleton has rescued all his men from Elephant Island, reaching out for them, you might say, with an outstretched arm and a mighty hand, he bashes a letter off to Mrs Shackleton his wife, from a port in South America on the long road home. 'I have done it. Not a life lost and we have been through Hell.' He uses a capital for the word hell, which is not strictly necessary, but quite understandable. Well done, Ernest.

And something else. When Jesus makes his showy comeback, appearing first off to Mary Magdalene in a nice sky-blue cape and bearing gardening tools, which is a bit of a red herring, of course, and then shewing himself to his disciples by breathing on them and going, Receive ye the Holy Ghost, while walking through doors and letting Thomas fiddle around in his wounds, etc., in a general display of exhibitionism, Jesus is actually covering up for insecurity. He is downright anxious. He is anxious no one will recognise him just because everyone saw him give up the Ghost, and now he might get the brush-off, and get nowhere with those last-minute instructions to his brethren for all humanity, etc. But he is patient, and it's the same with Ernest who has come so far but has to go all that way back again for those twenty-two men, and he needs a ship, a ship for Elephant Island.

When he strolls into the Norwegian whaling station with Crean and Worsley after crossing the famously impassable mountains of South Georgia, even sliding down a rock face arms around each other, a human sledge, sliding because their shoes and makeshift studs had worn out and there was no time to lose, Ernest knocks on the door of the manager's hut and complicates things a little.

'Don't you know me?' he says, waiting for the poor manager to see through the straggly beard and stricken face and torn clothing to the man he met two years before and had given up for lost.

'I know your voice,' he replies.

An old Norwegian whaler is there at the time and reports later how the Boss then introduced himself in a still small voice, going, *My name is Shackleton*, whereupon the whaler is clearly overcome, adding, 'Me – I turn away and weep.'

A leader of men is a complicated person and a bit of a gambler and sportsman, because just when he has come so far and yet has everything still to lose, he might go in for a mad flourish and hold up proceedings, just like the sporting hero who has rounded the last defenders and a sprawling keeper and takes all the time in the world before scoring an elegant goal. What is going on here? The strange pause is something of a gamble. Ernest and Jesus play the Why game. 'Do-you-love-me, do-you-love-me, do-you-love-me?' asks Jesus and let's face it, it's very annoying, especially in a ghost. It's fair to expect a little more composure and purpose in a ghost. 'Don't you know me?' asks Shackleton, holding up proceedings.

A leader of men is complicated and prone to anxieties, extravagant behaviour and fits of temperament, but it is only the strain of leadership as exhibited also by Moses who had his own dark night in the wilderness when he crashed those two tablets to the ground and stormed off up the mount in a huff, thinking it was all for nothing, the whole bloody Exodus, until he pulls himself together and takes dictation again, writing out those rules with even greater decision and fortitude.

Shane, too, has a dark night, and a big decision. He knows a hero has to be on the move, always wandering, or else people fall in love with him and give in to hero-worship and simply cannot get on with their lives, which is how it is with the homesteading family he works for, Shane building fences and felling trees, clearing spaces for tilling and gardening, and generally doing a lot of DIY around the joint. It is not easy for Shane to remember the wandering rule of heroism because he is tired of gunfighting and he is in love with this family also and that is the dark night he has before achieving heroism by fighting off the cattlemen so the homesteaders can stay in the homes they have built and have some peace, and get on with their lives in the big country. Shane folds his blue-jean gardening clothes and puts on his buff Shane jacket and now he is a gunfighter again, a protector, that is his job. He wins the fight just when you think he will never fight again, and now he is on the move, though with a single sad vision in mind, of standing in the rain at night looking in through an open window at a woman looking out at him, a beautiful wife and mother with a young son in the bedroom behind her, and a husband nearby, both man and boy confused by hero-worship of Shane, and the woman by a feeling for Shane she cannot express because of an older feeling for her two men named Joe, and for the job she has, and this is her dark night, a night only as long as a glance in a window, yet one that may last for ever.

'Don't just stand there, Shane,' is all she says in a still small voice. 'You'll catch your death of cold.'

I have to close the window, Shane. You have to move on.

Every hero has a dark night, a kind of Gethsemane, I think so, and this is what I realised upstairs in Art & Catechism before I became Famous for Visions and Fainting, seeing this is what happened to Gus the day he rode around our land in tight circles on his Ferrari-red bicycle and flew off the dock, approaching the stars, I see he was not merely in a state of confusion and despair over the departure of Jude, but achieving heroism, with a flourish. At Jude's Farewell Barbecue, Gus sings a song full of geography and wandering, and he hands round seven slices of cheesecake of slightly varying sizes, according to taste, and a shadow passes over his face, too fleet to question. The next morning he drinks from that cup and makes a horrible spectacle of himself, so calling our attention to the real peril, to some greater danger, because Gus is a small king and leader of men and he understands it this day, how the break-up of the Round Table, a perfect circle Merlin likened to the world, is not caused by departure, by mere comings and goings, but by outright loss. Let me show you, he thinks, gambling on flight and safe return. Well done, Gus.

And that is what I realised upstairs in the classroom in the vexing light of the slide show and all those graven images, it is all I meant when I told Soeur Rosa that Jesus is Gus.

JEM'S LAST STAND.
15 heures 23 minutes. Nearly go-home time. Yay.

This is a veritable nightmare. *Un vrai cauchemar.* I am beginning to hate this nun rule that it is OK for me NOT to participate in Art & Catechism, I can do whatever I like, read, do homework, etc., but I may NOT leave the classroom. What is the reason? Nuns are trying to brainwash me with Catholicism, that is the reason. They will not get very far with the brainwashing of me. Brainwash, brainpan, my brain hurts today!

I have pins and needles in my head. Very weird. It must be down to thoughts, all the thoughts rushing around in there, chaos, even though Ben says chaos is really a kind of higher order or something, and full of patterns. I don't know, it still feels bad to me, the chaos in my head, like uprisings of thoughts and nobody listening, uprisings in Eastern Europe with everyone screaming their revolutionary ideas, speaking all at once and generally forgetting their finer manners, which is how things were for Slithers in her extreme youth and why, according to Mum, we have to excuse her appetite for crime and larceny and cabbage rolls in our very own house. As Harriet says, it is a cross we have to bear. Cross, crucifix. Lord-a-mercy.

Soeur Rosa is having a field day, summing up the whole of last term for our recollection in a slide show of epic dimensions, and clipping all her favourite prints to the blackboard frame and round about the classroom, a Hit Parade: Nativity and Adoration, Epiphany, baptism and miracles, Ecce Homo, death march, and that two-for-one painting by an Unknown Umbrian of Mary and

Little Lord on one side and the Man of Sorrows on the other, plus
that ridiculous painting of the empty white sepulchre with the door
wide open and Roman soldiers leaning up against it in a druggy
sleep, same as the Flopsy Bunnies and the lone remaining lettuce
in Mr McGregor's garden as depicted in Harriet's special hanky.
Veronica, my Veronica.

15 heures 27 minutes. I have not eaten since my picnic with
Harriet this morning but I cannot decide if I am hungry, what with
all the clamour in my head and the spooky symptoms I have
incurred since Gus's accident last Saturday, his *mikveh* as Dad calls
it, symptoms involving a sharp ringing in my ears, and now these
fiery red bumps on my hands and knees, like pinpricks of light,
and which I keep forgetting to show Mum as I do not want to
have to go to the doctor and I do not want her to ask me, Why
do you have these red bumps, why are you sick with bumps, do
you suppose? like there is some great philosophy behind all symptoms, involving a person's own will and bloodiness, which is her
general view when it comes to sickness in a child of hers. This
tenacity in the face of symptoms is down to Frances's mother, I
believe, a woman who was a full-time casualty, embracing a life
of feebleness and dark rooms, and tapping her foot impatiently for
that fade-out of the great world into Paradise, and without ever
asking why, why can't I have both, the great world and Paradise
to boot? Mum says she had to share a bed with her, due to poverty
and to being the youngest and so on and this is quite depressing
although Mum tells me this story with a gentle smile, in a light
and airy voice, making it unseemly for me to venture a suggestion
regarding the sleeping arrangements in her far-off past it is too late
to do anything about, so I move the furniture in my head, pushing
Dot's bed into the kitchen and tucking Frances into the soldier's
foldaway cot there, arranging it just so with hospital corners and
the edge turned down as in fine hotels, and then I move the soldier
into the sick bay with the mother, where he belongs, and where he
can whisper bedtime stories perhaps, about the Lee-Enfield and
VC, Victoria Cross, and other marvellous things. The End.

I remember having a snoozette alongside Mum the day we moved
into our cottage for the summer, that year when we suddenly had
two houses not one, and the new beds were not yet assembled and
my dad was bashing around in the car for tuck and supplies and
the rest of us kipped on the floor on pillows and towels but I could

not rest at all, staring at Frances's face and her closed eyes and smelling her smell and memorising every detail with no effort required, as it would be, say, for memorising the location of bauxite mines in Suriname and the production figures for aluminium for which bauxite is the main source, but staring and memorising in a confident manner, like I am a camera, every blink a picture taken, *positive, negative, snapshot*, and all I have to do is close my eyes to keep the vision in.

My red bumps are hot and scratchy, giving me a woozy feeling in my tripes. *Dans les tripes*. Maybe if I stroll up to that Crucifixion painting with faith and awe in my heart, I will get redeemed and the bumps will go away, like in *Ben-Hur* when Judah Ben-Hur's mother and sister come out of the Valley of Lepers and traipse after Jesus for some healing. They already have faith and awe so, really, the job is half done, and lucky for them, because unfortunately Jesus is on that death march and will not be available for long chats and healing sessions. Never mind. It's not very timely, but Jesus makes a mental note of the mother and sister when he sees them traipsing after him along those Stations of the Cross and he thinks, I must do something about leprosy and other skin diseases, I must, I must, he says, repeating it three times, as I imagine, in that way he has. When he is giving up the Ghost, there is a great storm, which is very symbolic, of course, and a manifestation of God the Father with whom he will soon be One and a Ghost too, which is also symbolic, or simply a matter of genetics, it depends how you look at it. In the torrents of rain, Christ's haemoglobin is washed on to the ground and goes to and fro in it, right up to the feet of Judah's mum and sister and lo, no more leprosy. Actually, they did not have too bad a case of leprosy. They had the nicest possible leprosy, consisting of little warts on their faces such as I once had seared from two fingers in my early days courtesy of our family GP poking at me with a little stick fizzing on one end very much like the sparklers you wave about as a kid on Guy Fawkes' Night. It was a simple operation requiring no anaesthetic or lying down or anything, and no doubt all that was necessary for the Hur girls before they were flung rashly into the Valley of Lepers for lack of medical knowledge in the environs, and things certainly did not improve for them there. Christ's blood improves things for them. The girls roll their sleeves back and unfurl headscarves and then they pat each other's physiognomy with rapture and awe and there is a big Hallelujah chorus to wrap things up. The End.

Harriet and I collapse every time they show this film at Easter time. We have rarely beheld anything so hilarious as this miracle healing scene and after it we examine each other close up for old bicycling and sporting scars and scabs of vicissitude, singing out Hallelujah! in awestruck and rapturous tones until Dad yells, Hey! Girls! Cut it out! meaning the Miracle game, and Dad yelling at us is part of the game.

Harriet. Harriet and Dad. Coming soon.

I keep looking at my *Tintin au Tibet* watch and then I forget the time I saw there. Weird. *15 heures 29 minutes*. OK. And this is weird too. How I have this crazy urge to speak aloud in a big voice, to Marie-Laure and everyone else in the classroom, to tell them all it is nearly time and my dad is coming for Harriet and me, he is coming in the car to take us home by the scenic route up the mountain by way of the Bagel Factory where we will buy one bagful of sesame and one bagful of poppy bagels and a challah also. He will be here in no time. At *16 heures*.

Read your book, Jem. Head down.

Book XIII, Chapter 8: *How great sorrow was made of the king and ladies for the departing of the knights, and how they departed.*

This is their Farewell Barbecue. What-did-they-eat, what-did-they-eat, what-did-they-eat? Bread, surely. Bread of distress! That is the name for matzoh in the Torah, to remind us of the hurried departure out of Egypt when Moses was plain fed up with getting nowhere asking Pharaoh very nicely to mend his ways regarding slavery and oppression, whereupon he called for uprising and hurried departure in which there was no time for a lot of packing or notes to the milkman and all that sort of thing, and definitely no time for Jews to bake regular bread for the journey, bread with natural leaven causing the bread to rise and develop a fine flavour, something you have to wait for in the case of bagels and challah and baguettes, etc. Matzoh has no leaven. Nor is it very nice, in my opinion, although my dad is keen, even crumbling it up in chicken soup at all times of the year and eating it in a horror state of mush, quite possibly in the tradition of his ancestors in the Pale of Settlement, previously part of the Austro-Hungarian Empire and now Poland. When your roots are messed up like that, you have to cling to some traditions of your ancestors just to know what's what and where you are in the scheme of things. In my study of this hurried departure, I saw again how it goes to show quite clearly that bread is always involved in revolutions and uprisings, but when I first read these words 'bread of distress', I was confused, assuming it to mean matzoh is not very nice and is distressing to eat and intended to make you feel bad in memory of slavery and subjugation and having to pass up on bagels for a while. I had to check with Jude who explained how the taste issue is not really the point, though not before collapsing in a heap of mirth and derision and pounding all over the house to inform every single Weiss of the stupid thought I had. Thanks, Jude.

Jude. How many pairs, what pair are you on?

And therewith the tears fell in his eyen. And then he said, 'Gawain, Gawain, ye have set me in great sorrow, for I have great doubt that my fellowship shall never meet here more again.'

Harriet is right. I am always reading this book, my book with death in the title, *Morte*, French death with an e on the end, death in the feminine form, yet for a king, and no resurrection, though who knows? It is said Arthur was led away in a ship wherein were three queens, one of them being that famous Queen of the Waste Lands. *Where are you headed?* Concentrate. *15 heures 37 minutes.* Soeur Rosa is no help. She is strolling up and down the aisles in a threatening manner, discursing on Art & Catechism, passing close to my desk and moving away again, so that I think about the redshift of sound which is measured in frequencies and comes in waves, same as light, and I think about radios and tuning, how the volume goes up and down, in and out, and gives me a headache and a crazed feeling like Soeur Rosa is doing now. Concentrate. Read your book.

I love this, the way the king and Guenevere and all the knights and ladies are always having emotions, and making speeches about emotions, and planning quests and rescue operations and making speeches about these, so it is a wonder they get anything done at all. I see Jude and Zach, and my dad gives Jude a bear hug. Mum turns away, she does a spot of urgent pruning and disappears into the house with Yaakov's arm around her. They are having emotions, Gus is having emotions, all of us are, but nobody says it, Don't go.

'Ah, Launcelot,' said the king, 'the great love that I have had unto you all the days of my life maketh me to say such doleful

words; for never Christian king had never so many worthy men at his table as I have had this day at the Round Table, and that is my great sorrow.'

Soeur Rosa is saying, You cannot paint absence, it is impossible to paint absence, and maybe she has that woodcut in mind, the one by Mr Albrecht Dürer that made me famous, of Jesus rising in a puff of smoke like a rocket to the Moon, leaving behind a lot of frantic disciples and two neat footprints on a mount, in which case, she definitely has a point. That is quite a bad painting. Woodcut. No. Wait. I have seen it, absence. In a painting. Where? I can't think. My head hurts. Brainpan. Don't wash it. Let it soak.

Then the queen departed into her chamber and held her that no man should perceive her great sorrows.

Soeur Rosa looks so much like Mussolini, I swear she is related, a niece perhaps, a great niece who became a nun and Bride of Christ, fleeing her homeland for the New World in disguise. *Wot ye what I am?* Yes, Sister. I know you. And I wot also that there are enemies everywhere.

Absence. Yes, you can paint it.

Branwell Brontë paints a portrait of his three living sworn sisters, and himself among them. Then he scratches himself out of the painting, leaving only a ghostly shape. He is so very there, and he is absent.

'No, Sister,' I say, standing quite suddenly. Whoa! Silver fish again. 'Yes, I mean. Yes, you can paint it.'

'Mademoiselle Weiss? Well, why don't you take the class for the last few minutes?' says Soeur Rosa, offering me her chair with a showy sweep of the arm.

'No thank you, Sister,' I reply, dropping to my seat because everything has gone black and my heart is thumping in a strange manner, loud and fast, quiet and slow. Arrhythmia. Dad has it, he told me. It's OK, it is just heredity. *Arrhythmia* might be the name of a ship! All aboard – oh! That's it! Harriet's painting. Mummy there, and absent! *Shiver me timbers.* And the – two pictures in one, whatsitcalled? Buy one, get one free! Diptych! The Diptych. *Don't say manger or the Little Lord thing!*

'Mademoiselle Weiss? We're waiting.'

'It's Gus. My brother. There, in the – I mean, last Saturday – Gus and Mum, singing. Never mind, excuse me! I was daydreaming. Holmes, he always says that – never mind. Actually, I don't feel very well – Gus, you see, his heart stopped and – anyway, he's fine now. But the painting – it doesn't matter. Honestly. Sorry.'

'This is your mother?' says Soeur Rosa, tapping the print by the Unknown Umbrian. 'And Jesus is your brother?'

'No! Well, yes –'

Gales of laughter in the classroom. Is Marie-Laure laughing? I look round for her. I can't see properly. I have to go home, I must go home. 'Sister, I feel . . . um, Harriet and I are expecting . . . I mean, our father is coming in a minute –'

'Your Father is coming?'

'Yes. It's nearly time!'

'Really. And would your Father be coming for us too, or just *your* people, Mademoiselle Weiss?'

More hilarity.

Your people. *You people.* I know you, Sister, I do. Amalek. Snake, snake, go away.

Soeur Rosa raises an arm quite slowly and points to the door, so I gather my things, my face burning, and I stand in a flurry which is when the floor tilts wildly, ahoy there! Hold your course! and I stumble, glancing at Soeur Rosa in alarm, because she is the only grown-up in the room and is supposed to look after me, these are the rules. Just before I faint, crashing against Karina's desk on my way to the floor, I do have a vision, in a field of flashing silver, a black-and-white picture of pressing detail and awful gravity that is a huddle of speechless strangers on a train platform, and a man in an officer's uniform, impeccable, raising one decorated arm, pointing left, pointing right, this way slavery, that way a quick march in a straight line for the shortest distance between two points. Safe return, doubtful.

All kings are soldiers, but not all soldiers are kings.

Jude, do you believe in God, do you?

I believe I was a stranger in a strange land.

You could be that again, it could happen again.

Yes.

God is a dying star.

The last time I tell my story that evening, Harriet acts out all the parts and she is very good. She plays Soeur Rosa, a performance with an air of Mussolini about it, and then she is all the laughing girls, and then she does me in a faint whereupon Gus remarks, *Elle tomba doucement comme tombe un arbre*, and we all pause thoughtfully, as is befitting, and Harriet goes on with the show, playing Watchdog Nun, and then Dad who came for me with a mighty hand and an outstretched arm, and last of all Harriet plays herself, hauling her satchel as well as mine out of the convent gates, because I am still wobbly on my feet due to persecution, temporary aberration and near brain damage.

'I am a slave,' declares Harriet, 'a slave in the land of Egypt.'

'Bravo!' says Gus. 'Bravo!'

'Very moving,' says Mum, rewrapping my head bandage in the neatest folds and applying some special ointment to my hands and knees, and the relief is amazing, the fiery red scratches and bumps fading almost before my very eyes, a sight that sends my sister into raptures.

'Mother Mary, Jesus and Joseph and Heavens to Betsy,' she says, pawing me all over in a rapturous manner. 'Hallelujah! Halle-LUJAH!'

'Amen, Harriet,' I say.

At suppertime, my dad tells me I do not have to go to the convent next year, we'll find some new place between then and college, though Harriet argues the case for liberation altogether, enumerating the benefits of a life of piracy and high-sea adventures, and Ben finishes making that paper crown for Gus, proclaiming him Serene Highness in Absentia of Jude, Absentia which is not a snowbound country, or even a ship, or a house, but a state of things, and Gus wears the crown without protest and in all humility, all evening, tipping it back in a rakish fashion before doing his specially ordained assistant-chef task of passing out bagels and chopped liver and coleslaw and pickles, big pickles for Dad and Ben, and wee cornichons for himself and us girls. Mum gives me passing glances of empathy and medical know-how while Yaakov swears that latkes are just the thing for head wounds, then Ben rattles through a list of tortures and punishments famously inflicted on saints and visionaries in medieval times as I cut open a sesame seed bagel and remember what Jude told me the night of Jeremy's funeral, how bagels are symbolic of eternity and are meant to ward off evil and that is why they are served at funeral parties in honour of the guest not coming, served *in absentia*, and suddenly I call out for Jude, I call his name out loud, Jude!

And therewith the tears fell in my eyen.

'Sorry!' I say. 'Sorry.'

'It's all right,' says Frances. 'It's been a long day.'

'God bless our dear dogs!' I cry, slightly hysterical, searching all the faces at my table. 'Feed my dear dogs!'

'Jem,' says Dad. 'Hey there,' he says, reaching out for me.

And I cry for a time, Sabbath crier, town crier, I cry for the real peril I see, for departures and accidents and terrible train rides, and piles of shoes with no owners, and for bread of distress, for failing eyesight, arrhythmia and romantic respiratory disorders, for inflammations of the skin and this clamour in my ears, the sound of a story with death in the title, sorry, Harriet, crying until I close my eyes and will that sound to ring instead like bells in winter, bells on a sleigh coming closer, ever closer, and Jude is driving, cold bottles of something fine clinking merrily at his feet, for drinking at night, in the snow, my time of day.

'Mac,' he says. 'Have you ever been in love?'

Yes. Yes, I have.

And I close my eyes to keep the vision in.

A Study in Scarlet.

How could this happen?

Play the Why game, demand the reason.

If you have an obsession with numbers and rules, and you are mourning an immediate relative, b?, d. much too soon, then you will find plenty of regulations in the first twelve months to keep you happy and free from society where people are walking to and fro in that determined manner, and getting on with life, unlike the perplexed and mournful who may well be overcome by a strange horror of the laws of motion and gravity, and an overly sensitive dependence on initial conditions, a sensitivity amounting to another obsession, one to do with the deduction and analysis of pattern formation, which is chaos itself, that everyday magic balancing act between the forces of stability and instability a person is expected to master in this dangerous world. Show no cracks! If you have this kind of obsession, you might remind yourself in dark times how those laws of chaos apply to the heart, and chaos might well = health, it depends how you look at it. The other thing to do in such times, is observe some basic rules and numbers. Here are some basic rules and numbers to observe.

7, 3, 11, 12 and 4. 2,400. 1.5, 2.5. OK.

7. *Shivah*. This part is a breeze and a lot like being a kid on holiday, because you can be a wee bit slapdash with your ablutions and haul on the same old clothes every blessed day and go around barefoot, which brings Babar to mind, Babar *l'éléphant* before the pressing responsibilities of kingship befell him, and before he met the posh cotton top in Paris who introduced him to the finer things, such as bespoke tailoring and daily PE and morning *croissants au beurre* and *chocolat* in a bowl, fine things not widely seen in the happy jungle he left behind, Bingo-bango-bongo, I don't want to leave the jungle! Congo, Zaire, Absentia, *shivah*. 7. This part is a breeze, furthermore, because you can eat whenever the fancy strikes, and pass up on plates if you are so inclined, and most delightful of all, it is more or less recommended that you live on bagels the whole time, bagels with appropriate side dishes of symbolic boiled eggs, which is to say, that for 7 days, you are kindly excused from niceties in general, but remember not to look in the mirror, do not look in the mirror! Mirror of your imperfection.

3, 11. Kaddish. I have perused this prayer you are supposed to recite 3 times daily for 11 months of the first year and it's a puzzle. I read it in English and not in Aramaic because I cannot read Aramaic. The prayer makes no single reference to death and is more akin to a prize-giving speech to the Lord for Lifetime Achievement in Everything, meaning, of course, Eternal Lifetime Achievement in Everything because He is the beginning and the end. He is also the one true judge and not immune to high praises and flattery, but time is a bit of a problem for Him, not His own time, which is eternal, but ours, which is not. We only have so much of it for pleading on behalf of casualties of our acquaintance, and then there are the sheer numbers of plaintiffs, which is why it is a good idea to worry Him 3 times daily with your soft murmuring, so He might remember to raise up the beloved dead person, level by level, all the way to Eden where the weather is clement, fine enough, even, for garden parties under skies coloured della Robbia blue.

11. The prayer is recited on behalf of the immediate relative for 11 months only so as not to be mistaken for a petition read out on behalf of a felon, such as Bill Sikes, for instance, a felon who has to wait a full 12 months before the one true judgement on him is passed, and I hate to say it, but for Bill, the prospects are not good. Bill's

felony was a *crime passionnel*, meaning, murder of a beloved, and for which there is a let-out clause, though I believe this applies only in France and to French people who are prone to excesses of temperament and displays of emotion and get very confused when it comes to blood and sex matters. As do Italian nuns, which is no doubt why they use this word Passion for the demise of Jesus by crucifixion, they call it Passion and a crime to boot, a murder committed by Jews and Judaism, according to nuns, though Jesus was nailed up by ROMAN soldiers and condemned by a ROMAN governor now celebrated as a saint in Ethiopia, which might be down to the fact there are a lot of Italian people in Ethiopia ever since that rash invasion in 1935 by Benito Amilcare Andrea Mussolini, who may be an immediate relative of Soeur Rosa. Nevertheless, Bill Sikes is not French or Italian and he committed his *crime passionnel* as an Englishman in London, where, all in all, a walking stick not used for walking but for doing in the beloved is considered a murder weapon, no two ways about it. Bill's prospects are not good.

11. Because God is the one true judge, etc., He must attend to each petition personally, and with deadlines looming daily, there is simply no time for bail and appeals in cases of outright felony, not with all the more pressing issues, such as pesky cases of suicide and so on, where judgement does not come easy. What-shall-I-do, what-shall-I-do, what-shall-I-do? wonders God. How could this happen?

12. After 12 months the mourner is expected to scrub up a little and shake a leg, and go forth into the great world in nicely polished shoes, ready to carry on regular conversations and even give in to musical moments if he feels a song coming on, no holds barred. He may not be inclined towards the great world, still favouring darkened rooms, but that is when musical moments are helpful. *Baby, it's cold outside! I simply must go!* According to the Talmud, this 12-month marker denotes a change because, allowing for varying weather systems and geological conditions at the different compass points and hemispheres, after 12 months it is safe to say the dead beloved is a physical ruin and the soul has stopped rising and falling, rising and falling in a state of confusion and longing for its old home the body, which is all very poignant, as poignant as any farewell scene in a favourite black-and-white film. Finally, the soul simply must go, it rises, it has no choice. *Don't you see my house has collapsed?*

4. Aside from the first 7 days, when a candle burns for 168 hours, and before the anniversary, you have 4 official opportunities within the 12 months, and for all 12-month periods thereafter, to light up a 24-hour memorial candle and watch the light flicker on the ceiling, assuming a ghostly shape, short change for the body it once was, this shape of a soul rising and falling, rising and falling, finding its feet, so to speak, flickering in the visible spectrum of gold to red. Absence is a sensation. In my opinion, it is a good idea to place the candle in a window just to hedge your bets in case of mistaken identity and the possibility that body in the oblong box is not the beloved, who is merely lost, stolen or strayed, and on the way back. A lit window is a helpful landmark, a lighthouse thing, especially if the immediate relative is in a very far-off place and equipped with only a *telescopio* for navigation purposes, hopefully something like the 100-inch reflecting telescope George Ellery Hale built in 1918 with its light gathering power 16,000 times the human eye, or an ability, that is, to spot a candle 2,400 miles away, or an emergency light on a sinking ship, a light with a persistent flicker.

Shackleton watches the *Endurance* disappear, falling quickly through the ice in a dive of terrible grace. 'She's gone, boys,' he says. And later he notes in the logbook, 'At 5 p.m. she went down. I cannot write about it.'

2.5, 1.5. Before bed, I set the table for breakfast, just the way Jude learned in mining camp, setting long tables for dusty men with bristling chins, beards of isolation. I set the table for two. I am waiting and hoping for one, and I aim for patience because I know a hero is always on the move, it is what Frances was trying to tell me in my extreme youth when she planted those sexpot cherubs all over the joint. It was a clue and I missed it.

In the building plans for the Tabernacle in the pages of Exodus, there is a design motif for the lid of the Ark involving golden cherubim with wings, and they sit right on top of the Ark which is 2.5 cubits long and 1.5 cubits wide, and high. The cherubim are guarding the two tablets of testimony, in its famous second printing, handmade on a mount. They guard from both ends of the empty space where God might perch, except He is always on the move and the winged cherubim are symbolic, therefore, they are symbolic of mobility, same as the angel of the Lord, you might say, the descending angel with the countenance like lightning and the snow-white raiment who sits upon the sepulchre, according to Matthew, and spooks the keepers of the sepulchre so they shiver and shake and become as dead men. Fear not, he says in that angel manner, before passing on the message regarding the whereabouts of the Lord, how He is not where expected, He is not in the sepulchre and has risen, etc., and this is why I say the angel of the Lord is a symbol of mobility, same as cherubim, though they themselves are not much given to mobility. Angels do very little travelling, it seems to me, they do a lot of sitting. They sit atop sepulchres and arks in a symbolic fashion.

She left so many clues, the open desire for space travel, a camera in her hands trained on a seemingly bland patch of sky, a postcard of St Catherine who exchanged her perfectly good heart for someone else's, and one called *Faith*, depicting two cherubim either side of a woman draped in elegant folds and holding a chalice with a boiled egg aloft, the egg that is symbolic of Resurrection, and the cherubim either side are like statuary, heavenly escorts coloured earthy gold and winged for mobility and special ops in angel work, and for those Highest Honours they share with six-winged seraphim in the angel firmament. Highest Honours, VC, Victoria Cross, she left that also, highest British decoration for bravery in presence of the enemy, forged from the metal of Russian guns seized in the Crimean War, a bronze cross on a scarlet ribbon won by her father and tenderly wrapped in tissue paper, for you, Jem, because you are so interested in war, you are so taken with valour. Be prepared!

I read in some ancient commentaries written by scholars in beards of isolation, scribes of unwavering purpose, about a custom wherein, if a newcomer strolls in on a congregation and is surprised by the sight of types rending garments and looking a bit desperate, the leader of the prayers comes to the rescue, calling out, Gentlemen! Demand the reason! thereby voicing a question the newcomer is too shy to ask and prompting him to utter some safe and hopeless blessing in the spirit of things, and covering for the mourner, who is too desperate to explain the awful trouble he is in for which he is wholly unprepared, or the special attentions he may now require yet cannot ask for, at least not with any particular grace and clarity, because he is moving inwards into the Worlds of Thought and must create a system or be enslaved.

Cantor: Gentlemen, demand the reason!

Newcomer: Blessed be the judge of truth!

Mourner: Everybody fuck off! Stay, go, I don't care! *Excuse my rudeness! You broke the thread of my thoughts; but perhaps it is as well. A Study in Scarlet, 1887.* Let me not be mad. Redshift, red dress. Frances folds the red dress away very neatly that first Christmas Jude is not there and then she wears it one last time, but she leaves the shoes. Mummy, you left your shoes, you wore them to death.

> James James
> Morrison Morrison
> Weatherby George Dupree
> Took great
> Care of his Mother,
> Though he was only three.
> James James
> Said to his Mother,
> 'Mother,' he said, said he;
> 'You must never go down to the end of the town,
> if you don't go down with me.'

A Study in Scarlet, Chapter II, The Science of Deduction.

Holmes: Yes; I have a turn for both observation and for deduction . . . I have a trade of my own. I suppose I am the only one in the world. I'm a consulting detective, if you can understand what that is. Here in London we have lots of Government detectives and lots of private ones. When these fellows are at fault, they come to me, and I manage to put them on the right scent . . . There is a strong family resemblance about misdeeds, and if you have all the details of a thousand at your finger ends, it is odd if you can't unravel the thousand and first.

Watson: But do you mean to say that without leaving your room you can unravel some knot which other men can make nothing of, although they have seen every detail for themselves?

Holmes: Quite so. I have a kind of intuition that way. Now and again a case turns up which is a little more complex. Then I have to bustle about and see things with my own eyes.

—You are very agitated today. Do you want to tell me what's going on?

—It is quite a three-pipe problem, and I beg that you won't speak to me for fifty minutes. *The Red-Headed League,* 1891.

—Ahhh.

—Life is a great chain!

—Would you like to explain that?

—I have no data yet! It is a capital mistake to theorise before one has data. *A Scandal in Bohemia,* 1891.

I want to explain, I do, but everything is hard and I cannot, not aloud in words, not now, not with any grace and clarity, I am turning inwards, ever inwards, Baby, it's cold inside! I ought to have a dog and a sporting activity, I know it, and were I not a girl, my beard would be long and sweep the crumbs from books. Let me not be mad! *What country, friend, is this?* Mine. This is my country. Absentia is the name of my country.

Holmes: So all life is a great chain, the nature of which is known whenever we are shown a single link of it.

Merlin leaves the Round Table for the forest and his sister builds a house for him with seventy windows and doors so they can devote themselves to observation of the stars, and to prophecy. William Herschel and his sister leave Holland for England and she forsakes musicianship to aid him in astronomy, keeping vigil in freezing fields where one night Caroline has a tiny accident, falling in snow, cutting her leg. *Elle tomba doucement.* Everything's OK, she says. It's not serious. Frances is a musical prodigy and I never see her touch the piano keys. Sacrifice. Aged eleven or so, she wins Highest Honours for some études of Chopin who died of a romantic disease and for whom a street is named in Lublin in honour of his Polish side. Frances never touches the keys again, but she hears it all in her head when she builds her house filled with light and straight lines and tall windows. William Herschel writes, 'I have looked further into space than ever human being did before me.' Pride is not a problem for him. He is also an expert in mirror-making, his telescopes are very fine. Telescope, spectroscope. Fraunhofer is an expert in glass, in optics, he makes prisms and counts over five hundred lines in the spectrum of sunlight, what does it mean? He will never quite know, he dies too soon of a romantic disease. Very close to the stars.

Tuberculosis, blindness. Galileo goes blind. He says there is ice on the Moon. Everyone laughs, ha ha ha, but four hundred years later NASA announces there is ice on the Moon, 100 million tonnes of it. Ha! Forty-four years earlier than NASA, though, Tintin chases after his dear dog on the very first Moon walk of all time, chasing Milou who has disappeared in a crevasse. Tintin slides down a slope of ice. *De la glace!* He has rescue in mind and his discovery of ice on the Moon is not uppermost. *Milou! Te voilà!* Shackleton slides down a rock face with Crean and Worsley because their shoes are worn and there is no time to lose. He has rescue in mind. Frances leaves her shoes together very neatly where the ice ends, and the floes and frozen waters begin. No shoes in or on water, those are the rules. She tucks a silver cross with a moonstone at the heart of it into the left shoe, left is propitious. *Provide neither gold, nor silver in your pockets, nor scrip for your journey, neither shoes.* Matthew. Rule of St Francis. *And those who are forced by necessity may wear shoes.* Francis goes barefoot. Francis has an eye disease, he is a visionary, and hears a voice in a painting of the Crucifixion. *Don't you see my house has collapsed? Go and fix it!* Yessir. Francis is the mirror of perfection. Hubble Space Telescope. A tiny accident in the workshop causes spherical aberration in what was to be the most perfect mirror in the world. How could this happen? Let's go fix this thing! Seven astronauts distinguish themselves in flight and mid-air DIY in a shuttle named *Endeavour*. James Cook achieves special distinction in the art of navigation and astronomy in his own *Endeavour*, observing the transit of Venus and charting New Zealand and the east coast of Australia. Good work, guys! Edwin Hubble watches the Universe expanding in every direction, the centre everywhere and nowhere, the end is the earliest light, it has not had time to reach us. Hubble makes a study of redshift with Milton Humason, ex-mule driver. Speed, they deduce, increases with distance. Far gets farther, so quickly. Hubble makes Humason do the donkey work. Milton sits up late in the freezing observatory because at night, in winter, skies are clearest.

Fantasy increases with distance! Hubble lies about his war record. And he was an amateur boxer, just an amateur, like me. Munich, 1933. The German Boxing Association excludes all Jewish boxers. Arno Penzias, Jewish refugee, radio astronomer, b. Munich, April 1933. His family flees by ship. At the Bell Telephone Laboratories in New Jersey, 1965, Arno hears a soft murmuring sound, greater than Jansky's hiss, and he knows what it is, the echo of the Big Bang, sound of the beginning of unrecorded time, everything has a sound. Frances is b.? She has no name, there are no records. Never mind. An old soldier is coming for her. He will sign with an X.

Victoria Cross, Distinguished Flying Cross, Iron Cross. Karl Schwarzschild, b. Frankfurt, 1873, soldier, astronomer, pioneer in photography and black-hole theory. He contracts pemphigus on the Eastern Front, a fatal skin disease, no hallelujahs. He is awarded the Iron Cross, one of the 100,000 German Jewish soldiers to serve, the 78,000 at the front, the 30,000 decorated, and the 12,000 to die for a country that from 1933 will worry all such names away from war memorials. What country, friend, is this?

Otto Dix is an old soldier. Dresden, 1933. Dix is dismissed from the Art Academy for the doomy *War Triptych* he paints, an echo of Grünewald's *Altarpiece*, with a Crucifixion in the middle but no view of redemption. He fought on the Somme, at the front. *Lice, rats, barbed wire, fleas, shells, bombs, underground caves, corpses, blood, liquor, mice, cats, gas, artillery, filth, bullets, mortars, fire, steel: that is what war is! It is all the work of the Devil!* The right panel is a night scene of terrible devastation featuring a war-torn soldier with a fallen comrade-in-arms, a man with a bloody head wound, a lost cause for whom St Jude, as everyone knows, is patron saint. The survivor is also a lost cause and he asks a question, his survival is a question. How far is this my fault? How could this happen? *Crime passionnel.* War and prejudice. Arrhythmia, pemphigus, tuberculosis, asthma, tinnitus, romantic diseases in the rhythm of things, chaos applying to breath and heartbeat, to the feel and sound of things. Everyone close to me dies, and I hear it all, I hear them all, an emanation of sound and light. I remember everything and everything has a sound, even the unrecorded. Play!

This is my three-pipe problem, Mrs Rosenfeld, but I cannot speak it aloud, some devotions are private, and all I tell you is this.

—Eight hundred thousand pairs of empty shoes in Chopin Street!

—What?

—July 1943! Russian troops enter Lublin, near Majdanek, into the warehouse there, filled with pens and clothes, haberdashery. And toys, all the toys, and 800,000 pairs of empty shoes, all the people who will never walk to and fro in them again! My fault, it's all my fault! Because of Gus, you see, how I blinked, and how everything changed, the conditions – all things are sensitive to initial conditions, it doesn't take much! That is how it all happens, always, someone has to pay, something has to give. It's my fault!

—Your mother's death too?

—I don't want you to say that word about her, I have asked you not to.

—Yes.

—I will find her. Him. Her. There will be such a reunion in Paradise! What larks! *For everything exists & not one sigh nor smile nor tear, one hair nor particle of dust, not one can pass away.* Blake! She left footmarks. *Our Mother Jesus, our beloved mother! Weiss on ice.* Did I tell you? In the snow, in a straight line. A straight line is the shortest distance between two points, but not always! It is not true of navigation, which is an art. It is not true, because you have to allow for winds and currents, and it is not true of light, of course, light that comes in waves, you see, like sound, water, ice. She left marks, footmarks.

—What do you think about the footmarks?

The Sign of Four, 1890.

Watson: What is your theory, then, as to those footmarks?
Holmes: My dear Watson, try a little analysis yourself!

Trembling I sit night and day. I rest not from my great task:
To open the Eternal Worlds, to open the immortal Eyes
Of Man inwards into the Worlds of Thought,
Into Eternity.

Three years after Jude's great expedition, when Gus had grown into his ears and paws and attained stateliness in the manner of Pax! as well as a pair of Kojak boots to call his own, there was a convocation of Weisses held in an atmosphere of deep deliberation and eyebrow-raising worthy of sages. The result is a decision of the collective allowing Gus to bash off on his very first solo weekend adventure, to his friend Luc's farm in the Townships, Luc whose big brother Bruno rides a kart and whose mother comes from Deauville in Normandy, and will dish up *crêpes Normandes* and *gigot d'agneau aux haricots blancs* to her houseful of men and most appreciative guest, our own Gustavus, who recites the menu to us daily over the telephone in an excited voice, although we do not insist he call. Travel is important. His excitement is infectious.

Gus also tells us how he tinkers successfully with Bruno's kart engine, no surprise to us, what with his special skills and instinct for the mechanics of speed and velocity well beyond his years. He does not have the opportunity to tell us how Bruno gave him a go on the kart, rewarding him for his ingenuity, Gus raising a tempest of happy clouds of dust and petrol the next morning until his lungs collapse for joy and shock, death coming so very quickly because Luc and Bruno are not apprised of rule # 9 and Gustavus Weiss has reached *status asthmaticus*.

Sixty to 65 per cent of childhood asthma cases worsen. Established asthmatics may experience attacks following exposure to sudden changes in temperature or humidity, or both, and to exertion, and to emotional stress. A person experiencing a prolonged attack that is resistant to drugs is said to be in *status asthmaticus*. A kind of rapture. I hope so. I pray so. Gus's excitement is infectious.

There are some sudden changes a person will never recover from, sudden change that sears the brain, heart-stopping, blood-draining, forever-estranging loss, such as one beginning with the collapse of Gus and ending in blessed footmarks on ice, an eternal cycle of horror I did not foresee, because there are some things for which there is no readiness.

Frances? Where are you headed?

Oh. Just driftin'.

Whoa, the Moon. So white. Like ice, luminous. Frances will not need a torch, no, she has the light of the world, she is the light of the world, and at night, in winter, skies are clearest. Black, white, red. She wears the red dress. Oh my dear dogs! She holds a hand up to her eyes. Five-finger exercise! Play! Five dogs, four, her nearest so very far, her universe now a place of receding horizons. She will not be a casualty in this house. No imperfection. Yaakov. My beginning and my end. Feed my dogs. It's cold outside, I simply must go. Farther than any ship can carry me.

Then the queen departed and held her that no man should perceive her great sorrows.

Where the ice ends and the floes and freezing waters begin, Frances removes her shoes and places them together very neatly, the cross with the moonstone at the heart of it tucked into one shoe, the left, because Yaakov, she knows, is a southpaw, and left is propitious, and she has great expectations of him, of all of them, God bless her dear dogs. *Great Expectations* might be the name of a ship! A house, a ship! Frances, mirror of perfection, effecting a dive of terrible grace.

Elle tomba doucement comme tombe un arbre.

Dot says, Fluffy, you swim like a fish!

Gus says, *Ma fleur est éphémère.*

Jem says, Lo, I will be with you alway, even unto the end of the world. That's what you told me, I heard you, although I was only eight days old, a soft murmuring sound like the beginning of time. I remember everything.

Queen of the Waste Lands: When heard ye tidings of your mother?
    Sir Perceval: Truly, I heard none of her, but I dream of her much in my sleep; and therefore I wot not whether she be dead or alive.

I am quite cheered by astronomy, and how star death is so spectacular, especially the death throes that are a pulsar, say, spinning like a dervish and releasing enough energy to illuminate an entire nebula, showering radiation in two powerful beams that can be read by the distant observer as a signal from a lighthouse. This is a star's Last Stand, one of epic proportions and not at all depressing, especially when you know a pulsar may have started out in life as two, a pair of stars so inseparable, they became one, indistinguishable in effect, spectacular, a *son et lumière* show, and akin to genetic duplication, meaning, of course, *the existence of two copies in one; the process by which it arises.*

There are some things a watcher of the skies should know about night vision, how the eye is made up of rods and cones, and cones are sensitive to colour and concentrated at the heart of the retina, whereas rods are off-centre, and twenty times more numerous, sensitive to low light, able to make out shades of grey and outlines and silhouettes even in near pitch black. There is a technique for the amateur observer engaged in the true observation of the very faint and distant, and that is to avert the eye a little so light falls on the rods which are so very light-sensitive, though as you glance back and away at the faint and distant object you may have a false impression of that object blinking on and off, pulsing.

And lo, the Lord passed by. There was a great and mighty wind . . . but the Lord was not in the wind . . . not in the earthquake . . . not in the fire. And after the fire, a soft murmuring sound.

I keep vigil all the same, in low-lit rooms, a torch with a red lens always to hand for observation purposes and the consultation of books, and wandering to and fro without injury, a red lens because rods are least sensitive to red light and I need to preserve my adaptation to darkness. I have great expectations of night vision.

Red.

I set the table for two, every night, and on Fridays, at eighteen minutes before sunset, why not, I light up. Yes. If she does not come – they, she – I will find her, I will go to and fro in the earth, I will walk up and down in it, in the Eternal Worlds if I have to, anywhere, whither she goest, even unto the end of the world, or the end of the Universe, which is not *there*, as starmen say, but *then*, a time, a place, and I've got it all, visual purple, look-back time, great expectations, cowboy-toughness, and she is everywhere, they are everywhere, my whole world is a woman and a boy with a centuries-old name, having a strange sound of snowy countries, a realm, some true region not yet discovered and ranged with mountains deemed impassable and of epic beauty. And until I get there, I must wander for ever.

I have this new vision now and it always comes the same way, with a rushing sound in my ears, the shimmy of bells, and with a fiery, scratchy sensation in my hands, and an irregularity of the heart. I close my eyes to keep the vision in, my true regions of reminiscence, and I see a person standing at a window looking in, a person with great composure and a graceful demeanour, and the air of someone forever on the move.

—Don't just stand there, I say. You'll catch your death of cold.
—Are you all well?
—All well, Boss.
—Feed my lambs. My dogs. My Dear Dogs.
—What?
—Don't you know me?
—I know your voice.
—My name is Frances.

Me, I turn away and weep.

Ah, Frances. Ah, Frances. Baby, look what you did.

My mother built a house, I tell you, and the street of the city was pure gold, as it were transparent glass.